Amanda is a two-time Scribe Award winner, a two-time Tin Duck Award winner, an Aurealis and Ditmar Awards finalist, and author of several novels and short stories. She is also a screenwriter.

Her original fiction includes the sci-fi crime thriller The Subjugate, which is being developed for TV. Her media tie-in fiction includes that written for Marvel (X-Men), Black Library (Warhammer 40k), and Z-Man Games (Pandemic).

Also by Amanda Bridgeman

Aurora Series
#1 Aurora: Darwin
#2 Aurora: Pegasus
#3 Aurora: Meridian
#4 Aurora: Centralis
#5 Aurora: Eden
#6 Aurora: Decima
#7 Aurora: Aurizun
#8 Aurora: Atlas

Salvation Series
#1 The Subjugate
#2 The Sensation

The Time of the Stripes

Marvel: School of X
Sound of Light

Pandemic:
Patient Zero

Short Stories & Novellas:
'Paragon of Faith' – Warhammer 40K:
Paragon of Faith And Other Stories Anthology
'Reconsecration' – Warhammer 40K:
The Emperor's Finest Anthology
'Rogue T.R.A.I.N.' – SNAFU Punk'd Anthology
'Resistance' – SNAFU Comms Anthology
'Eye of the Storm' – Marvel: School of X Anthology

Aurora: Decima

Amanda Bridgeman

Copyright

First published in 2016
This edition published in 2025 by Amanda Bridgeman
Copyright © Amanda Bridgeman

The moral right of the author has been asserted.

A CIP record for this book is available at the National Library of Australia

Aurora: Decima (Aurora 6)
EPUB format: 9780648216230
Print format: 9780995425903

Edited by Stephanie Smith
Cover design by Red Tally Studios

We acquire the strength we have overcome.

~Ralph Waldo Emerson

Prologue

Dr. Valerie Pullman leaned over the shoulder of data analyst Tim Loynd.

"You're sure?" she asked, eyes fixed on the signal reading.

"Yes. It was a separate signal. Completely distinct from the others," he replied, tapping away at the screen before him. He brought up the sound wave data of the original signal and overlayed it on the new data. Together they studied the comparison graph of audio readings.

Valerie straightened up and folded her arms across her chest, her brow furrowed. "It was just the one signal?"

"Yes, just one. But as Admiral Arken states, it's far too early for the UNF *Barbican* to have picked it up. It means at least one Zeta ship is a lot closer to Earth than all the others."

"How close?"

"Using the others as a comparison, and the *Barbican*'s location, the delivery speed indicates it's very close."

Valerie turned her eyes to Tim, her protégé. She'd worked with him for two years and trusted him totally. "How long would we have?"

"I don't know." He shrugged and looked back at the screen. "It's disappeared again. It was only brief. We don't have much to go on, but if my calculations are right, then... maybe ten years to Earth? Fifteen?"

Valerie looked at him as fear shot down her spine. "Ten years?"

He shrugged again. "I'm guessing here. But it was a direct reply to the last comms the *Barbican* sent out. Based on the original sources we've been communicating with they should not have received a response this early. A closer source has picked up this signal and replied to them."

Valerie raised her hand to her silver hair and ran her fingers through it, massaging her scalp. It was an unconscious motion, something she did when she was deep in thought.

"It's the same *type* of signal, though," Tim said. "At least we're not dealing with another race of beings. It's the same kind, just closer."

"Maybe they've sent a group ahead somehow," she mused, trying to ignore the flutter inside her chest. The flutter of anxiety. Uncertainty. "We have hyperflight, why wouldn't they?"

"Or maybe they're a completely different group? Same race, different tribe."

"Perhaps," Valerie said. "The most important thing we need to work out, is how soon they could be here. *If* they're coming here, that is."

"Sure. But how? The signal is gone."

"Keep the frequency open. We monitor this as we have the others. Twenty-four hours a day. Constant. This new signal takes priority over the others. Ensure the *Barbican* continues to keep us informed."

Tim nodded. "At least it was only the one signal, right? The original sources are up to the hundreds now."

"Yes," Valerie said, "so let's hope this closer source *is* just one ship."

Tim stared at her hesitantly, curly hair framing his face, along with his glasses that reflected the screen's dancing lights. "You really think they might come early?"

"I don't know, but we can't take the risk. I'll report this to Colonel Marchant."

With that she turned and began to make her way to her office. As head of the UNF facility in the Murchison, she made the day-to-day decisions here, but in the grand scheme of the Zeta watch, she was but one of a panel of experts who fed information to the UNF. The Zeta Archelois Executive Panel, known as ZAEP, met regularly to discuss new discoveries and agree on a way forward. Valerie, being head of the UNF facility responsible for contact with the alien signals, had so far, been the most important panelist. The UNF listened to her and she liked that. To have her work respected was one thing, but it also secured better funding for her facility.

As she entered her office, ready to transmit to Marchant, she felt a little concerned. What did this new Zeta signal mean? What if they were no longer heading to Earth in the great numbers the UNF expected? What if they were sending just this one envoy? If the threat receded, so too might her funding and her level of power in Centralis. What would that mean for her facility and the fifty rotational staff she managed?

But what if the Zetas were still coming as planned? What if they had sent forth ships that would arrive earlier than planned? The UNF was not expecting the visitation for another 23 years. What if she told the members of ZAEP that the threat had receded, and then thousands of ships suddenly filled their skies? She was responsible for their warning system. She was the most critical factor in Earth's defense against the Zetas.

Whatever the outcome, threat or no threat, she had to proceed with caution.

PART ONE

1

A New Path

Dr. Marcus Scavesci walked along the corridor eagerly. He seemed to have found a renewed vigor for his work, as though matching that of the star patient in his care. As he walked, he listened to his footsteps, a soft patter against the polished stone floor, the sound comforting in the otherwise lonely silence.

Very few people had access to the sub-levels of Command. And fewer still had access to the wing in which he now strode. This was a special wing that currently contained only one inhabitant: Professor Raymond Sharley. The UNF's most prized detainee.

He saw the glass walls up ahead to his right and felt a smile slide across his face. He wondered in what state he would find his patient today. It was less than eight weeks ago that he'd found Sharley at death's door, lying in a pool of blood from torn wrists. The scene had been horrific. The professor, distraught over what he thought was the loss of Sergeant Carrie Welles to his man Drazen, had ripped open his wrists with his teeth and smeared a bloody message across the walls. The message was simple. Scavesci knew the reasoning behind it. Professor Sharley wanted the last word, wanted the control to remain his, even in death.

Scavesci remembered finding the professor, remembered the utter dismay that had overcome him. There was his prized patient, bloodied and lying on the floor beneath his scrawled words, moments from death. In an instant, Scavesci had been on his knees, sliding in the blood, reaching desperately for the professor's wrists to hold the blood in. He would not let his patient die, he could not let *this* patient die. Sharley was the most important man to the UNF, and that in turn made Scavesci, the man's psychologist, a professional of important standing within the UNF.

He had screamed for help, but of course, down in the bowels of Command no-one else was close by. Having no other choice, he dragged the professor by the wrists to the panic button by the door, slamming his own forehead against the button repeatedly, keeping his grip on Sharley's wrists. And as he puffed and panted and waited for help to arrive, he sat there and stared at the words smeared across the walls in all its red, meaty, glory:

If I can't have you, no-one will...

On the other wall he'd written: *Carrie Welles.*

There was another mark. Later, through studying photographs, he realized it was the letter "H". The professor tried to write Harris's name, too, but had run out of time and succumbed to blood loss.

Still, that seemed a lifetime ago. The professor had been saved, and upon recovering and hearing the news that Drazen had failed to kill Carrie Welles, Sharley had become more alive than ever. It was like he had been born again as a brand new man. A brand new Jumbo.

Dr. Scavesci began to slow as he approached the professor's cell. He liked to try and sneak up on him every now and then, to capture a sense of Sharley when unaware of the spectator. It was a hard thing to do given the professor's Jumbo senses, even with the unbreakable glass wall between them. It was the vents. Scavesci had learned that he only had a few seconds before Sharley would detect his scent. But, for those few seconds a glimpse of the professor in an unguarded moment was a treasure. The truth was, Sharley absolutely fascinated him. And as Dr. Scavesci laid eyes on him this day, the professor fascinated him once more.

In the middle of the cell Sharley was lying on the floor on his back. The professor exhaled and sat up, and that was as long as it took for him to sense Scavesci. Holding his body rigid, arms behind his head, the professor paused and those dark beady eyes shone in the doctor's direction.

With the glass on two-way vision, Scavesci reached out and switched on the room's comms. "Good morning, professor."

Sharley eyed him, the glint of silent evil so present Scavesci had to fight a smile. *Fascinating...* The professor was deranged and the UNF needed Scavesci to control him; to try and heal him; to find a way through the darkened, tangled forest of Sharley's mind – so the UNF could harness it once again.

"Good morning, doctor," Sharley smiled, then continued with his sit-ups. Scavesci eyed the professor's body. He'd been putting on weight, which was good to see. Right before his suicide attempt the professor had been thin and gaunt, and just plain filthy. He had refused to bathe and would let no-one near him. His teeth had yellowed, his hair had been slicked with grease, the stench from him had been foul. Back then, he bordered on animal.

But Scavesci had cracked the professor. He saw the life spark in his eyes upon hearing Welles had survived. He'd noted the professor's decline before the attack, when Welles refused to see him. Scavesci now knew that to keep Sharley alive he needed to feed him bits of Welles and Harris and McKinley, to sustain his will to live. To feed his need for control and revenge.

So, every day Scavesci spoke to him of the *Aurora* crew. Told him whatever he could, letting the professor think he was in control again. He pretended to be Sharley's puppet, and every day the professor came back to life, piece by piece. He began to eat again, to bathe, and when he was strong enough, he began to exercise. So much so that he was approaching good health, and the UNF were very happy. They wanted him alive and functioning and Scavesci was responsible for delivering them that.

Sharley finished his sit-ups then stood, arms by his sides, eyes fixed sharply on his visitor.

"Did you pass on my letters?" he asked.

"Not yet, I'm afraid—"

"Why not?" Sharley cut him off, but his voice was even, unemotional.

"I've not seen her yet."

"She is supposed to bring the twins into Command for Dr. Morgave to examine, is she not?"

"Yes, but I missed her the last time she was here."

"What about your own sessions with the twins?"

"It wasn't appropriate to pass them on then."

"Why not?"

"Because Welles is very strict on my allotted time with them. As soon as the hour is up the Sentinels whisk them away. For that hour, my focus is on the twins and nothing else."

Sharley turned and walked away, arms folded, one hand to his chin, as though deliberating on Scavesci's failure.

"She will be in again soon," Scavesci said to appease him. "I'll try then."

"I don't want her to read the letters here. Not in a place like this." He continued to pace. "She must receive them at home. They're personal. She must read them in a personal space. Not here."

"If I give them to her here, I can watch her. Make sure she reads them. If we send them to her home, she may throw them out."

"Then you must go to her home and give them to her personally."

"I still think here at Command, in a controlled environment, is better."

"No," Sharley shook his head. "Here she will feel safe. Inside these walls she will feel safe. I must reach out beyond these walls. Here she can ignore me, but if I reach out, force my way into her home, and therefore into her mind, then she can never get rid of me."

Scavesci watched his patient closely. Sharley stopped pacing and turned his dark stare toward him.

"She must learn that I will never let her go. No matter what. I created the program. I created her, therefore I own her. I own all of them. And they must obey me or they will be punished."

Scavesci continued to study the professor, unable to hide the doubtful look upon his face.

"Just as *you* must obey me," Sharley said, dark eyes glinting with derangement.

"Excuse me?" Scavesci crinkled his forehead.

"I'm no fool, doctor," he answered, moving right up to the glass wall and standing just centimeters from Scavesci. "The more alive I am, the more alive you are. You thrive on my survival. I've seen it. Your eyes do not lie. My hunger for Welles, feeds your hunger for success. So, feed me what I need and reap the rewards."

Scavesci placed his hands in his pockets, his ego prickling a little at Sharley's observation.

"Go, now." Sharley waved him off in a bored fashion, stepping away as he turned his back.

Scavesci continued to stare, refusing to move. Sharley stood there silently, back turned, staring at the wall upon which he'd once scrawled his bloody ode to Carrie Welles. But then he turned his head slightly, Jumbo-like, and his dark eyes focused a hard, threatening gaze on the doctor.

Scavesci contemplated his patient for a moment, then silently turned and left as bidden.

Sergeant Carrie Welles stood in the kitchen of her home, known as the Fortress, and stared over the counter at the twins in their high chairs. Brody grinned at her with his dark-brown eyes and hair, every bit Doc's son. She smiled back at him, then shifted her eyes to Freya, who was patting her hand on the tray in front of her. Her daughter seemed to be studying the sound, fascinated. Although Carrie and Brody had the heightened eyesight, they did not share Freya's sense of hearing or smell.

"Hey?" she called to them and Freya looked up. "You hungry?" She pulled out their favorite yoghurt and placed it on the counter. Freya squealed with delight and Brody grinned wider.

"*Miss Welles?*" The AIS's calm British voice sounded overhead.

It had taken her some weeks to get used to talking to Archie, the Fortress's Artificial Intelligence System, but given he was all she had to talk to aside from her father and her Sentinels, his company had been growing on her.

"Yes, Archie," she answered.

"*You have three new mail items,*" Archie advised. "*Would you like me to open them?*" Not only was his company growing on her, but she'd gone so far as to trust him with the inbox of her personal portal.

"Who are they from, Archie?" she asked, moving over to the twins.

"*The first email is from Ellen and David Walker. The second is from Fort Centralis Postal Services. The third is from Dr. Marcus Scavesci.*"

Carrie scooped some yoghurt into Brody's mouth, then gently scraped the spillover onto the spoon. Brody grasped for the spoon and she gave it to him.

"*Would you like me to open them?*" Archie asked again.

"That's okay, Archie," she said, picking up a second spoon for Freya. "I'll read them later."

"*Yes, Miss Welles.*"

She knew roughly what each mail would be about. Ellen and David, Doc's parents, wanted to arrange another visit to see the twins, the FC Postal Service were announcing the delivery of some new toys she'd ordered, and Scavesci was trying to arrange another counseling session on the recent Drazen attack that took place in Eden. That, and all the other attacks. She'd lost count of how many there had been now.

Carrie scooped some yoghurt into Freya's mouth, studying her left wrist as she did. Drazen had snapped it like a twig, and she still wore a support glove, but it was due to be removed soon. She wiggled her fingers and flexed her hand, then eyed the scar that now trailed up her left arm. She recalled the large hunting knife that had pinned her to the wooden floor of the Eden resort's villa. Then she thought of her dislocated shoulder and rolled it around. Then she thought of her injured ribs and jaw, the two teeth missing from the back left corner of her mouth...

Freya gurgled and Carrie's mind came back to her children. The reason for Drazen's attack: Sharley had sent him to claim them all. One way or the other.

Her children stared at her, their vibrant Alpha eyes curious, wondering why their mother had suddenly become so solemn. Carrie forced a smile and kissed Brody on the top of his head, fighting the images of his father dying in her arms. Then she kissed Freya on the top of hers, fighting the memories of McKinley struggling with Drazen; the awful thudding sounds of Alpha and Jumbo fighting to the death; the spike wound in McKinley's side... Thankfully, he'd survived that battle – with a little help from herself and Harris, of course. Regardless, he'd held his ground well and had, perhaps, been winning until Drazen decided to fight dirty with that spike.

She sat back in her chair and took in her children again. There they were, fourteen months old, with no idea what their future held. No idea that when they hit a mere twenty-five, they would be asked to fight a battle to save Earth from a deadly alien attack. She didn't want to believe it was true, but she'd seen it for herself through sharing certain dreams with her captain, Saul Harris. Her Guardian; her Connected. In the last shared dream, they had all been standing before a massive army. War was coming. She knew it.

Just as it had been Carrie's fate to become the first female Alpha soldier, and to bear the first Alpha children, it would be her children's fate to stand beside the *Aurora* team and face the terror when it hit. Younger, no doubt stronger, her children would be the ones to stand on the front line if it was called for.

Carrie had spent time over the past eight weeks reflecting on her own role in that future. She'd always wanted to be a soldier, like her father, and had never planned on being a mother. But now she saw how the two were entwined; how the two had become one. This was her destiny; to be a soldier-mother, to prepare her children to fight and prevent the end of the world.

"Miss Welles, I detect that the mood has dropped," Archie said.

Carrie eyed the roof. "Seriously, Archie, how do you do that?"

"This house is filled with many sensors, Miss Welles. It is my job to read them, analyze them, and ensure that things are as they should be and that you are safe. When you are still and quiet during the day this raises a flag on my system. You should only be still and quiet when you sleep. You often sit still and quiet, Miss Welles. Are you all right?"

"I'm fine, Archie. I just like to reflect sometimes," she said, taking the spoon off Brody and scooping more yoghurt for him to messily smear into his own mouth. She paused and looked up at the ceiling. "You promise me you're not sending any of these reports to Command?" She'd asked him this a few times, and she expected him to deny it, as always, but she couldn't help the paranoia. Archie was, after all, hooked into every facet of the house and, yes, she'd granted him access to her portal... although she suspected he would access it regardless. He knew just about everything there was to know about her, and she wasn't sure how she felt about that. But after Eden she'd been too tired and injured to care.

"No, Miss Welles," Archie told her. *"I will only alert Command of your well-being if I believe you or the children are in danger. Otherwise I am your personal AI security feature. My loyalty is to you, first and foremost."*

"Even over Command?"

"Yes, Miss Welles. Even over Command."

Carrie wondered whether that would be true if it came to the crunch. No technology could ever be failsafe, could it? Still, Archie was not only someone to talk to, but he was useful in myriad ways. She'd found he could assist with just about anything she requested. If she wanted the children's baths to start running, Archie could do it while she was still making her way up the stairs. If she wanted a coffee first thing in the morning, Archie would set it going, ready for when she got out of bed. When she ran out of grocery items, she'd simply tell Archie and he'd keep a list, and arrange delivery. He would set the right room temperatures for her, find the TV channels, give her weather reports, send messages to her head Sentinel, Roy, located in the booth by the Fortress's entry gate. What she found most useful was if she ever wanted to know anything about *anything*, she'd simply ask Archie. And if he didn't already have the answer stored somewhere in his databank, then he'd find it for her.

"Miss Welles, I have detected a car pulling up out front," Archie announced. *"Sentinel Roy is at the gate."*

"Thank you, Archie," she said. He always reported such movements to her. "Do you know who the visitor is?"

"Accessing cameras, Miss Welles. One moment, please... I have a facial match. It is Lieutenant James McKinley."

Carrie paused a brief moment, then smiled softly. She'd had Archie tracking Space Dock arrivals for news of the UNF *Aurora* and he'd advised earlier that the ship had landed. So she'd been expecting him, but had allowed a couple of hours for the crew to lockdown the ship and gain quarantine clearance.

Her father had suddenly disappeared into town about an hour ago, no doubt vacating the house for their reunion. She had said very little to her father about her relationship with McKinley, but she didn't have to. He just knew.

She hadn't seen McKinley in almost seven weeks, although they had spoken on occasion via their portals. Once Carrie, her father and the twins had been settled into the Fortress, the *Aurora* had taken off on a training run. She didn't know where they'd gone and McKinley, following protocol, didn't tell her. Harris had a team of new Alpha soldiers whose first test had been fighting Drazen's Jumbos in Eden. They'd won that test, though it hadn't been an easy fight. She could tell that it had rattled Harris, so she could just imagine the training the captain had been putting them through.

She felt a little nervous at the thought of seeing McKinley again. Aware of the privacy levels on their UNF portals, their messages had been platonic. He'd enquired about the twins, and she'd enquired about the team. Fairly innocuous stuff.

They had been together barely a few days before Drazen's attack. Then they'd both been recovering, then he'd been called away on the *Aurora*. Aside from inviting him to live in the Fortress with her and the twins, they'd not really had time to discuss anything else. But McKinley knew he wasn't just invited to stay at the Fortress because he was Freya's father.

She took a cloth and wiped the yoghurt from each child's mouth, then ran her hand through her long brown hair, checking her reflection in a window. She heard Roy communicating with Archie and advising him that McKinley was making his way up to the house. She was tempted to move to the large windows and watch him, but she didn't. She sat at the table calmly, waiting.

"First Lieutenant James McKinley," she heard him say into the authentication panel at the front door, his deep tones soothing to her. He was one of three men who had been trusted with access to the Fortress's security, the other two being her father and Harris.

"Welcome, Lieutenant McKinley," Archie greeted him.

She heard the door unlocking with its buzzing sound that she felt was more akin to a prison cell than a home, then heard the door open. She turned to see his tall Alpha form enter the room wearing a bulky weather jacket, and a six week growth of dark-blond beard.

"Lieutenant," she said, giving him a soft smile.

"Sergeant," he said, his vibrant blue Alpha eyes piercing hers like they always did. He dropped his kit bag to the floor and headed straight to Freya, who was squealing with delight. Her keen senses always recognized her father. McKinley picked her up, kissed her cheek and cuddled her, then he ran his hand over Brody's hair. "Hey, champ," he said.

Finally, McKinley moved his eyes to Carrie again and a moment of silence passed.

"Would you like me to prepare your room, Lieutenant McKinley."

McKinley's eyes searched the ceiling as though looking for a speaker, but didn't respond. He looked at Carrie, curious. Last time they'd spoken of rooms, they'd decided he was going to sleep in hers. Although, for secrecy's sake, he did select a room of his own to keep up appearances.

"He means the temperature," Carrie told him, then tilted her head slightly and said, "Maybe later, Archie."

"Yes, Miss Welles."

McKinley glanced up and around. "That's kinda weird."

She smiled. "You get used to it after a while."

"So, how you doing?" He motioned to her body, eyeing the support glove on her wrist.

"Better," and she waved her gloved hand in the air. "You?"

He glanced down at his side. "Good as new."

"Harris didn't work you too hard, then?"

"Nah. He kept me on the sidelines until Gregson gave the okay."

She nodded, and he looked back at Freya. Carrie could feel the weeks of separation between them; the memories of their affair clashing with all the platonic keeping-up-appearances they'd done since. But here he was, in the flesh, away from the UNF's prying eyes. At least she hoped it was away from prying eyes. There was still the Archie factor to consider.

"I didn't realize it was snowing out," she said, motioning to McKinley's bulky weather jacket. Through the large windows of her living room, she could clearly see bright blue skies and sunshine outside.

His mouth curled in humor as he put Freya back down, much to his daughter's displeasure, then peeled off the jacket. She eyed his torso and arms as he did. "We've been down in Antarctica."

"Yeah?"

He nodded, taking a seat at the table, and picking up the demanding Freya again. "Harris is all about extremes these days. Last time we trained in the desert. This time it was the ice."

Carrie shrugged. "Well, I guess if you can kick ass in extreme conditions, then you'll really kick ass anywhere, right?"

He nodded in agreement. "There're no excuses anymore," he agreed. "The team are all Alphas now and we know what's coming for us."

Carrie thought about the earlier invasion that Harris dreamed would occur when the twins were around 10 years old, a whole 15 years earlier than the UNF were expecting. She still wasn't exactly sure what the *Aurora* team were going to be able to do about that, but she guessed they had around eight years to figure it out.

"How did Hunter's conversion go?" she asked, referring to the *Aurora*'s pilot, and the last of the team to undergo the transition.

"Good. He's Jumbo strong. I mean, *Alpha* strong." They exchanged smiles at the slip. Before, when Professor Sharley was in control, they were called Jumbos, but the UNF wished to dissociate the professor from the program, hence, moving forward they would now be called Alphas.

"I bet," she said, imagining Hunter's new Alpha physique. "Guess that means I won't be able to beat him now, huh?"

McKinley grinned. "We'll see. Speaking of training, you done any?"

"Some," she told him. "As best I could with this damn wrist, anyway."

"Lucky it wasn't your shooting hand."

Carrie nodded. "Oh, yeah."

Freya grabbed two handfuls of McKinley's new beard and pulled, making him wince.

"You look like you could use a drink, lieutenant," she chuckled, standing and collecting the yoghurt containers off the table, thinking they could both do with taking the edge off.

McKinley's blue eyes twinkled back at hers. "Thought you'd never ask."

They were on their second drink and starting to relax by the time Carrie's father returned to the Fortress. They ate dinner together as her father tried to extract information from McKinley on the plans the UNF were making.

"I don't know a hell of a lot more," McKinley shrugged. "We've been training these past weeks, but apparently there's going to be another briefing tomorrow. Harris wants us to check in with Marchant."

"I hope the *Barbican* knows what it's doing," her father said. He was an Original. He'd been at the forefront of the UNF when the first signal was detected. Of course, now it was many. Although he was no longer in the UNF, Carrie had updated him on everything. She'd told him about the signals originating from the Zeta Archelois system, and the theories the UNF had regarding the Zetas being responsible for fertilizing all life on Earth, and their follow-up visit during the time of Homo heidelbergensis; how the Zetas enslaved the heidelbergensis humans before something drove them away. *A revolt? An illness?* The only thing she hadn't shared with him was news of the early invasion. She couldn't do so without breaking Harris's trust and the captain wasn't ready for anyone else to know about his gift of foresight. Outside of McKinley, that is.

"I'm sure it does," McKinley told her father. "Admiral Arken has a good reputation."

"Yeah, he's a good man," her father said.

"You know him?" McKinley asked.

"I've met him a few times. He wasn't admiral back then, but he was coming up the ranks."

Carrie couldn't help but stare at her twins while they talked, wondering again just what her 25-year-old children would do when the big war occurred. That is, if they made it through the first attack which Harris predicted would occur when they were about ten years old.

The tenth year war…

McKinley noticed her eyeing the twins and glanced at them too. "Well, we'll know more tomorrow."

"Yeah." Her father sighed, then rose from the table. "Well, I'm beat. I'll leave you to it."

"Archie?" Carrie called. "It's time for the children's bath."

"*I will run the water now, Miss Welles,*" he replied.

McKinley stared at Carrie. "Are you kidding me?"

"The Fortress does have some perks," she smiled.

She and McKinley bathed the twins and put them to bed, then returned to the kitchen and began to clear away the dishes. They did this in silence, albeit a heavy one. There was a huge elephant in the room. Them. Their past. The time they spent in Eden. The Alpha sex. The secrets shared. *Everything.*

Carrie studied him as he stood with a glass of bourbon in one hand, scratching his bearded jaw with the other. She smiled.

"What?" he asked, noticing.

"The beard," she said.

"Yeah, well," McKinley replied, running his hand over it, "Antarctica's fuckin' cold."

Carrie chuckled, studying him some more. "It suits you," she said, then peered a little closer. "Do I see ginger strands in there?"

McKinley nodded. "That's the Viking, I'm told."

"Viking? I thought McKinley was a Scottish name? Or Irish, or something?"

"It does have Scottish origins through my father's line. But my mother comes from Viking ancestry apparently. She swears that's where I get it from. My father never got the red in his beard."

"Viking, huh?" Carrie said as she reached up and brushed her fingers over the hints of ginger in his beard.

McKinley's blue eyes flamed back into hers.

"It's kinda funny that I named your daughter Freya then," Carrie said, eyeing his blond hair. "After the Norse goddess."

McKinley took her hand from his beard and studied the glove she wore. He squeezed her wrist gently, as though testing whether the break was healed.

"The glove comes off soon," she told him.

He nodded and their eyes fixed upon each other's. Another moment passed while he still held her wrist. A moment, she noticed, that saw the temperature in the room increase, along with the rise and fall of their Alpha chests.

"So," she said softly, leaning back against the kitchen counter as he released her wrist, "how do we go about this?"

"Go about what?" he asked, sipping his drink, eyes still fixed on hers, challenging her like he did.

Carrie could feel her Alpha eyes flaring back at his. "Dealing with the elephant in the room," she said bravely. "Us." The truth was, she'd thought of him every day while he'd been gone. Thought about him, what he was doing, their time in Eden.

McKinley seemed to think for a moment, placing his drink down on the kitchen counter and running his hand over his beard again. "Well... the way I see it, there's only one way to go about it."

"And that is?" she asked.

He stepped closer, slid his hand over her hip, and leaned his face down into hers. "We dive right in the deep end."

She smiled as he kissed her. She kissed him back, sliding her hands up over his arms. It took a few moments, but the awkwardness from weeks apart soon dissolved as she remembered what it felt like to have his naked body pressed against hers. And she wanted it again.

She pushed him backward, then took his hand and led him to her bedroom. They closed the door and began to undress. As soon as his UNF shirt was off, she ran her hands down his torso, paying delicate attention to the scar on his left side from Drazen's spike wound. The scar was pink, almost healed. He removed her shirt and did the same, tracing his fingers down the long scar on her left arm... Drazen again. Then he nestled his face into her neck, the new beard tickling her. They moved back toward the bed and fell on it, shedding more clothing as they went; the Alphas within flared, eager to get started. She kissed him long and deep, tongue teasing his, as he lifted her further back onto the bed then lay his naked weight upon her. Her limbs encircled him, pulling him closer, the heat rising between them in synch with their appetite.

And then suddenly music began to play...

Carrie pulled her mouth away from his and listened. The music was slow, maybe a little jazzy. McKinley listened briefly, then switched his attention to her breasts.

"Archie?" she said. "What the hell is that?"

"*It's program number 69, Miss Welles,*" he responded.

"What?" she asked, brow furrowing in confusion, but it quickly melted away as she focused on what McKinley's tongue was doing.

"*I have a number of preprogrammed functions. Under certain conditions they will automatically deploy, Miss Welles. You have just triggered program 69.*"

"What?" she asked again, trying to listen and to understand what he was saying, while also trying to focus on where McKinley's hands were now and how they made her breathe hard.

"*Your body heat signature has crossed over with Lieutenant McKinley's,*" Archie told her. "*Your heartbeats are accelerated, your body temperatures have risen, your breathing rate increased. This indicates you are engaging in sexual intercourse—*"

"What? Archie, no!" Carrie said quickly, mortified that her AIS may have spoken loud enough for her father to hear in his room down the end of the hall.

McKinley paused and looked at her, then up at the ceiling. "Are you kidding me? This thing is spying on us?"

"*I can change the music if you like? Perhaps some rock 'n' roll? I know you like that, Miss Welles.*"

"Archie, no!" Carrie said again, covering her face with her hand. "Look, when my heat signature crosses over with McKinley's you just... go away. Okay?"

"*But, Miss Welles, it is my job to observe and protect you.*"

"I'm fine, Archie. Just focus on the kids."

"*I must watch you all equally—*"

"Archie!" McKinley growled softly, throwing a piercing glare up at the ceiling. "I got her covered," he said, then looked down at his naked body pressed against hers, "Literally..." His voice trailed off as he finally entered her and Carrie closed her eyes, exhaling loudly.

"Miss Welles?"

"Archie, I'm fine. Please go," she managed, as McKinley's body slowly rocked hers.

"Yes, Miss Welles."

"And Archie?" she breathed, threading her fingers tightly through McKinley's hair.

"Yes, Miss Welles?"

"Delete program 69. Permanently."

"Yes, Miss Welles."

Captain Saul Harris stared at the frame-screen magnetically attached to the freezer door of the fridge in his Centralis apartment. Right now, the small screen was showing that childhood picture of him and his sister, Holly, with their grandmother Sibbie and great-grandmother Etta. He stood there, staring and staring into the eyes of his ancestors. The picture almost felt lifelike, the way they stared back at him. It made the hairs on his neck stand on end. Part of him felt glad that he'd finally accepted the gift he'd inherited from them, but part of him felt ashamed for having denied it for so long.

He turned away, took some toast and black coffee to the small table he had in his minimalist apartment. All the while the image of Sibbie and Etta's eyes followed him in his mind. He sat there eating and thinking about the training he'd done with his Alpha team through the ice of Antarctica. He'd worked them hard. Well, as hard as he'd could given some of the injuries they were still recovering from after the battle in Eden. His own Alpha muscles still felt tight from the strain he'd put them through, but after the fight in Eden he knew they had to step up their game. The *Aurora* crew were good, and they could certainly take on any human enemies, but they'd just barely won against Drazen's Jumbo fighters. If they ever faced a Jumbo opponent again, he wanted to ensure that his team won clearly... not marginally. They had to be indestructible and they had to ensure any soldiers who followed were of the same standard.

His mind moved to ponder the meeting with Colonel Marchant scheduled for this morning. He was itching to learn more about the alien signals, but something was bugging him. He realized it was the same thing that had bugged him the whole time he was down in Antarctica, leading his team on long runs, making them haul heavy chunks of ice up hills, enacting war games in the snow. It was the thought of Welles that bugged him... it was the fact that she wasn't with them.

Welles was an Alpha soldier, she was his "connected", and she was the mother of the First Gens who would be on the front line when the big war hit. She was very much a part of this mission to prepare Earth's defense. Technically, she was on maternity leave, and although he'd included her in Marchant's recent briefings, it wasn't enough. He needed her to be a full-time member of the *Aurora* crew again; he needed to train her and get her back to peak fitness. And, truth be told, he felt as though it was the right thing to keep the twins close to the *Aurora* crew as well. Not necessarily for their protection. He was confident in the Fortress's security, confident Sharley would never get out of Command. He wanted the twins close to the *Aurora* because the more they learned now, the better soldiers they would be when the time came: although he cringed a little at this thought. This was what he'd argued against Marchant doing when discussing the UNF's idea to create their own First Gen soldiers via artificial wombs. But still, the things the twins could learn subconsciously... What could it hurt? Harris knew that he, Welles, and McKinley, would instill in them the most important quality any soldier could ever possess: a sense of right and wrong.

Regardless, first he had to figure out how to get them down to the *Aurora* more often.

First Lieutenant Lincoln Gold of the UNF *Carcharias* watched as Captain Rovine approached.

"We'll be a few hours," Rovine said. "You told the men I'm locking this ship down at 2200 and if they're not back, then they're sleeping elsewhere, didn't you?"

Gold gave a single nod. "Yes, sir. They're very grateful to have new surroundings to look at. They'll comply." Even if their new locale was only

Station Navarone, which had limited bars, at least they were finally back in space and away from Fort Centralis, he thought.

Second Lieutenant Andy Ryker stepped forward then, and Gold motioned to him.

"Lieutenant Ryker will accompany you on your visit to Colonel Hensford."

"Oh," Rovine said. "And why not you?"

"Well, sir—" Gold began but Ryker cut him off.

"Captain, I'm on a health kick. No drinking. If I go to that station on leave for a few hours, I guarantee you I'll break it. Rubber arms, you see?" Ryker's Aussie accent sounded quite comical as he shook his arms about and pulled a drunkard's face. "So, I volunteered to escort you."

Rovine's eyes returned to Gold. They were a little scornful, as though he were being derelict in his duty.

"I hope that's alright, sir. Besides, I really need to pay a visit to Sergeant Maggie Rochester. I think she may have bought a voodoo doll in my name." Gold smiled. "I need to convince her to remove the pins, sir."

Rovine waved his hand in a motion that indicated that he didn't want to hear any more. "Whatever. Let's go, Ryker."

"Sir!" Ryker nodded and followed Rovine out the door, but not before throwing Gold a glance and shooting him a wink.

Gold watched the door close and exhaled loudly.

"We clear?" he heard C:Drive's voice behind him. Gold turned and gave him a nod.

"We need to move fast," he said. "I need as much time as possible to search through his portal. Understand?"

"On it," C:Drive said, then hurried off to the comms room.

Only C:Drive and Ryker knew what Gold was up to. The rest of the team had headed out onto the station, blissfully unaware, for a few hours R & R. But Ryker and C:Drive had stayed back. Gold needed C:Drive to hack Rovine's portal, and he needed Ryker to keep the captain busy. He trusted Ryker, and in turn Ryker trusted him, so he hadn't questioned Gold too much about it. Ryker knew he would have a good reason for doing this, and that he would keep his promise to spill the beans if he found something. Now Gold just hoped he did find something and that this hadn't all been for nothing. Risking their careers, that is.

He had almost changed his mind when he'd found out that the *Carcharias* was finally heading back into space and leaving the *Aurora*'s shadow. He'd started to tell himself that maybe whatever happened down in Eden with the *Aurora* team had been the end of it. But images of the bodies had haunted him, especially that of Sergeant Packham's at the bottom of that Balinese ravine. And when he'd last checked, Corporal Colt, formerly of the *Aurora,* was still listed as missing on the FRS. Then there was the image of the bruised and bloodied *Aurora* team, sitting on the villa porch in Eden like wounded caged beasts. That one probably haunted him the most; that one wouldn't let him go. He'd seen soldiers on the other side of a bloody battle before, but this was something else. Something about it didn't seem right, didn't seem normal.

And so he'd decided. Even if the mission of being the *Aurora*'s shadow-ship was over, he still had to know. He had to know what the *Aurora* had been chasing and running from all this time. He had to know why some of their soldiers had died. He had to know why Corporal Colt was missing, presumed dead. He had to know why Sergeant Welles had been allocated Sentinels and why she was constantly under threat and the target of the events in Eden.

Maybe then he could close out this mission in his mind.

Maybe.

Professor Jenkin LeFroy watched from the cell door as the Jumbo Sabrina Colt struggled against the digital cuffs that locked her wrists to the sides of the cot.

"Let me *fucking* go, or I will *fucking* kill you!" she spat viciously, the Jumbo anger boiling on her dark skin. Her muscular arms tensed and bulged and she shook the whole cot with such force he thought it might tip over.

"You need to calm down," he said holding out his hand.

"Fuck you! What did you do to me?" she yelled, still trying in vain to break the digital cuffs that restrained her.

"You know what I did to you," he said evenly.

"What did you do?" Her brown eyes burned fire.

"I made you a Jumbo," he said.

"I'm not talking about that! I know you made me a Jumbo, you fuck! I'm talking about what you did to me when you drugged me the last time!"

"They'll be back soon. You need to calm down."

"It's been weeks! They're not coming back! You need to release me!"

"I can't release you."

"Why not?"

"Because. Because they'll—"

"THEY'RE NOT COMING BACK!" she yelled, veins bulging in her Jumbo neck.

LeFroy looked at the door to the lair they were being kept in. It was true. It had been weeks and Drazen's mob hadn't returned. He had been starting to think that they would never show again and part of him was happy. If he could break this chain around his ankle, he would be free.

However, the packages still came. Once a week, food parcels and other supplies flew down an old kitchen chute, banging against the door as they landed. And their waste was being emptied. LeFroy would put garbage bags in the second chute, and when he next looked, they were gone. Someone knew they were in here. Someone was keeping them alive. That someone must work for Drazen. And that thought sent a spike of fear through him. What if Drazen was still out there? If he escaped, Drazen might track him down. He had to wait. He just had to.

Besides, he'd gone too far now. Scared of what might happen if he didn't do as ordered, if Drazen did eventually return and found no progress. Lefroy had been following Sharley's instructions. He had turned Colt into a Jumbo, and then he'd taken the next step Sharley had wanted. And she knew he had. That was why she was ready to kill him. And, boy, if he released her from those digital cuffs, she would do just that: kill him. He was a scientist. She was a soldier, and a Jumbo one at that. He couldn't let her go. If need be, he'd make her stay like that her entire pregnancy.

"What did you do to me?" she said, tiring now. Her eyes were scrunched closed, shaking her head, and it sounded as though she were on the verge of crying. "What did you do to me?"

"I did what Sharley ordered," he said softly.

She paused and her eyes opened, her chest still rising and falling as she caught her breath. She stared at him with a furrow in her brow, a look that said, *'How could you?'*

"I did it for both our sakes," he told her. "If you want to live, this is the only way."

She shook her head again. "What did you do…"

"You know what I did," he said, taking hold of one of the cell bars. "Trust me, they won't hurt you while you're carrying them."

Colt looked at him again. "*Them?* How many did you implant?"

He shrugged. "We don't have the facilities here to be exact and this isn't my specialty. You'll carry however many that take."

"Who?" she said through gritted teeth. "Whose are they?"

"The fathers?"

"Fathers?" she asked. "There's more than one?"

"They left me a variety of samples depending on the host. Why do you want to know?"

"WHO?" she yelled.

He analyzed the anger boiling within her; a second wind of violence ready to surface.

"I'll tell you once they're born."

She screamed at him, tugging at her cuffs, and he turned away from her. He wasn't sure if she knew the fathers or how she might feel about them, but either way he could not let her kill whatever she was carrying. They must be born.

And if they were born healthy, maybe, just maybe, they might buy his freedom.

Glenashe Arken, admiral of the UNF *Barbican*, stared at the image of his wife and daughter on the screen. He pressed play and began to rewatch the transmission he'd had with them almost three months ago now, before the ship moved past the point of instant communication.

Bec had held up a painting she had done in school the previous day, of a sunny afternoon at the beach. Shaded in pastel hues, it was a memory of their last holiday together before he left on his current mission. Although it had felt like only weeks or months to him, in Earth time he had actually been gone over a year, and his daughter had grown so much. His heart had felt heavy with guilt as he looked at her, but eventually his resolve hardened: she was the very reason he was on this mission.

"It's beautiful, honey," he'd said. "You certainly didn't inherit your artistic skill from me."

"Or me!" Elaine, his wife laughed. God, he missed that laugh. Her smile. The softness of her skin. The smell of her hair fresh from a shower.

"I'll send it through to you, dad," Bec told him, then turned to the scanner sitting on the desk beside her and fed it through. He'd smiled at her.

"I'm sorry I won't be there for your birthday, honey," he said as his wife's smile disappeared. The truth was, he didn't know how many birthdays he was going to miss. But, handed a mission as critical as this, sacrifices had to be made.

"That's okay, dad," his daughter had smiled sadly. "Mom says you wouldn't do it if you didn't have to."

He felt pain inside his chest upon hearing her words. He darted his eyes to Elaine's and saw her wipe away a tear. He looked back at his fair-haired, pale-skinned, skinny-armed daughter. At only nine years old she was used to him going away for long stints. He'd done it all her life. Although this would, by far, be the longest. At best, she would be in her late teens by the time he returned; at worst, she could be middle-aged. But he would return. He'd promised himself that when he'd left them. He *would* return to them. One way or the other.

A box popped up in the corner of the transmission screen telling him his time was almost up.

"Oh," Elaine had said. "Gosh, it goes so fast."

He smiled at her. "I know."

"Well... stay safe," his wife had said softly. He remembered staring calmly and confidently down the camera, trying to instill the same into them. It was important they didn't worry. He turned his eyes back to his daughter on the screen.

"Thanks for the painting, Bec," he'd told her. "I'll hang it in my office when it comes through."

She'd grinned at him and he'd looked back at his wife.

"Same time next month?"

She nodded, her eyes glistening. "It's starting to get longer and longer between transmissions."

"Yeah," he said. "We're a ways out now."

"Soon you'll hit the terminator," she said quietly.

He gave a firm nod. "We will. But that only ends the video transmissions. We'll still have data comms, albeit increasingly delayed. Just not the instant visual or audio anymore."

She nodded.

He decided it was best to change the topic. "I saw a shooting star the other day, watched it through the observation window on the flight deck. We caught it on film. I'll send it to you," he told them both. "I made a wish on it, so you keep it safe for me, alright? Until I get home."

They'd both nodded silently and his wife had hugged his daughter close.

He raised his hand to his mouth and blew them a kiss as the final seconds counted down. They reciprocated, then the screen went black.

Arken exhaled audibly as he pressed stop on the playback, and ran his hand over his mouth, brushing down his taupe-colored mustache. He tried not to view the transmissions as being difficult. He made a point to view them as positive, because modern tech had enabled him, this far out in space, to remain in contact with Earth. And barely hours from that transmission, Bec's artwork had come streaming out of the special printer in his office, so it almost felt like he was still on Earth. That's what he told himself, anyway. It was no different from being on the other side of the globe from them. Space was just another locale.

Albeit a dangerous one.

By now, Command would've received the *Barbican*'s comms on the early interception of the Zeta signal. He wondered what would they think? Would they panic, knowing that it would be weeks before the *Barbican* received their reply? Arken had done his best to ensure that Command knew that they were still alive and all was well. Every single day, they sent reports to Earth to reinforce their confidence, to ensure they did not fear their biggest warship had been destroyed.

He lifted his cup of coffee and drained the remnants, then rose from his chair. He was currently off-duty, but after watching that transmission again he wanted to go and check the flight deck to keep his mind centered on why he and his crew were doing this. They were on a reconnaissance mission to try and find the source of the stray signals being picked up by the Australian UNF post. A potential future threat? The chance to make first contact with another species?

An alert alarm suddenly sounded from the comms panel by the door. High-pitched and urgent, it gave him a fright. He moved over to the panel and answered it.

"Admiral Arken."

"*Sir,*" he heard the voice of Senior Comms-Tech Garth Walon say, "*Sir, we need you on the flight deck stat.*"

"On my way," Arken answered. He didn't bother asking what it was about. If they needed him, then they needed him. He would find out when he got there.

It took him two minutes and fifty-seven seconds, at a swift pace, to reach the flight deck from his quarters. He entered and the team of 25 officers present looked at him anxiously.

"Report!" he said.

"Sir," Walon said, "we've just picked up our target, or should I say *targets*. There're three individual targets, sir."

"Targets?" Arken asked.

"Yes, sir," Chief Flight Officer Sasha Ulgari reported in her Russian accent. "We've got three targets registering on our radar, sir."

Arken paused a moment. "We can see them? They're that close?"

"Yes, sir," she answered and brought the radar image up on the large screen set into the table in front of him. He stared down at the red blinking blobs, counting them.

"I'll be damned," he said quietly.

Rina Pulloy, the navigation officer, was unable to hide her concern. "Sir, how did they get here so fast? We weren't supposed to cross paths with them this soon."

"There are no definites here," Arken told her. "Maybe these aren't the ones Command has been communicating with. Maybe these are the ones we picked up earlier." He studied the screen in front of him. "How long until they reach us?"

"I estimate 36 hours, sir," Ulgari told him, "if we stay on course."

"And if we stop?" he asked.

Ulgari glanced at him, then turned back to her screen, her hands darting around the console, reading figures. "If we stop, I estimate it will be 72 hours."

Arken nodded, eyeing the screen and rubbing his jaw.

"Stop the ship," he said.

"Sir?" Ulgari said.

"They may see our approach as threatening. So, let's stop, raise shields and lower guns."

"Lower guns?!" Pulloy exclaimed, eyes popping white against her short black bob.

"We don't want them to view us as a threat," Arken said firmly. "We need to proceed with caution. It's not our mission to start a war, people. It's our mission to make contact."

The team on the flight deck stared at him.

"Slow the ship. Raise the shields. Lower the weapons," he repeated firmly, eyeing them. Then he looked back down to the image in front of him of the three red blobs on approach. "Let's see how they react to that."

2

Going Deep

Carrie awoke slowly to realize she was alone in her bed. She stretched out and squinted her eyes at the clock. It was late. She sat up, her body feeling the effects of her night with McKinley. They'd barely slept. Even when they did finally drift off, all it took was for one of them to roll over and brush against the other's body, and lo and behold the Alphas within would stir again. She'd actually lost count of how many times it was... *talk about diving in the deep end*, she thought sleepily.

After the very last time, she'd looked at him through the darkness, barely able to keep her Alpha eyes open, and murmured: "You ever had this much sex before?" He'd given her an equally tired look and, with a hint of a smile, said quietly: "Can't say that I have..." And that was the last thing she remembered before sleep had finally claimed her.

She made her way out to the kitchen area, where the twins were in their highchairs already. McKinley was standing, swiping a finger over one of Archie's console panes, which were located throughout the house.

He glanced at her. "Morning,"

"Morning," Carrie said, running her fingers through her hair. She glanced back down the hallway and saw McKinley's bedroom door open. They'd forgotten to close it last night and pretend he was in there. "Archie, where's my father?" she asked.

"He went into town early, Miss Welles."

A cheeky smile curled the corner of McKinley's mouth. "So… enjoy your sleep-in?"

Carrie folded her arms and gave him a challenging look. "Yes, I did, thank you. But I didn't need it."

"Sure you didn't," he grinned.

She raised her gloved hand and flipped him the bird. "Laugh it up, McKinley. You're sleeping in your own room tonight."

He chuckled. "Yeah, we both know that's a lie."

"I feel like I've run ten marathons," she told him, yawning.

"Miss Welles, there are some isotonics in the fridge. You need to replenish your fluids after all your activity last night."

"Archie!" Carrie admonished.

McKinley glanced up at the ceiling. "That is really starting to bug me," he muttered.

"You, too, should have some isotonics, lieutenant. I detect your fluid levels are even lower than Miss Welles. You lost quite a lot last night."

McKinley gave Carrie a disturbed look. "How does it know that?"

"Archie knows everything," she said, then looked up at the ceiling. "Archie, moving forward, when it comes to my sex life, you don't comment at all. Understand?"

"Yes, Miss Welles. I was just looking out for your well-being."

"I understand, Archie. But you're overstepping the mark. Who I sleep or how much fluid we lose is none of your business, nor is it the UNF's. You keep my… *interaction* with Lieutenant McKinley a secret. Do you understand? No-one is to know."

McKinley darted his eyes back to her, curiously. She caught his eyes narrowing slightly and felt a slight flush of guilt wash over her, but she quickly shed it. Doc had only been dead for coming up to nine months now. It was too soon for anyone to know that she'd moved on with McKinley. Too soon for the *Aurora* team to know, and definitely too soon for Captain Harris, Doc's best friend, to know. Although, she suspected that Harris may have already dreamed it. If he had, then he only knew it would happen sometime in the future. He didn't need to know that she and McKinley were happening right now.

"What are you doing?" She changed the subject, motioning to Archie's console pane that McKinley had been prodding.

He looked back at the pane and began scrolling through screens. "Checking out what other program surprises Archie has in store for us."

"Good luck," she said, moving to the fridge and reaching for the isotonics, taking Archie's advice after all. She handed one to McKinley. "He won't even tell *me* the tricks he has up his sleeve. Apparently, it's for my own protection. Whatever you find won't be important." She sipped the drink. "I've already tried," she smiled. "I've had a few weeks to kill."

Just then the melodic chime of an incoming call sounded.

"Miss Welles, Captain Harris is calling."

Carrie and McKinley exchanged a glance before she moved to one of the phone consoles, built into the walls of the Fortress, lifted the handset and tapped the "answer" button.

"Captain," she answered. "Hi."

"Welles," Harris's deep voice sounded. *"How you doing?"*

"I'm good, sir. And you?"

"Fighting fit, sergeant. Are you up for another briefing this morning?"

"Yes, sir." She exchanged another look with McKinley.

"Good," Harris said, *"we're overdue. I'll see you and McKinley in 45 minutes."*

"Yes, sir," she said firmly, then hung up.

McKinley looked at her questioningly.

"Harris wants me to attend the briefing," she told him. "I'd better get ready. We'll leave in thirty minutes."

"You don't want us to arrive separately?" he asked, and she sensed a small barb hidden in his words. His fingers still played over the pane, like he didn't care, but she could tell that he was interested in her answer.

"No." She shook her head. "Harris knows you come to see Freya. We're good."

He eyed her for a moment, then turned back to Archie's console.

Gold watched as Captain Rovine took his plate of breakfast and headed back toward his office. His mind went with the captain, no longer listening to the men around him telling tales of what they'd done the night before. Gold was agitated, having found nothing in Rovine's portal. He'd searched and searched, but had run out of time in the end. They were going to have to attempt a second try. And that increased the risk. With every hack, they increased their chances of being caught. But he had to find something. He *would* find something. He just knew it.

Glances from C:Drive and Ryker caught his attention and made him snap out of his reverie. He was being too serious, too introverted, and it was drawing attention. He forced his face to crack one of his award-winning smiles and turned to listen to their pilot, Reece, tell a story of a sassy private who'd put him sharply in his place.

Harris watched as Colonel Marchant entered the briefing boardroom and Harris, Welles and McKinley stood. Marchant gave them a quick nod to sit.

"How was Antarctica?" he asked Harris.

"Cold and brutal," he answered plainly. "But good, sir. Very good."

Marchant nodded, then looked at both Welles and McKinley. "And how are the recoveries going?"

"I'm all good, sir," McKinley answered.

"As am I, sir," Welles responded.

"You still got a glove on?" Marchant motioned to her wrist.

"Hopefully, Dr. Morgave will remove it today."

"Good. Captain Harris tells me he'd like you back in training."

Welles glanced at him, then back at the colonel. "I'd very much like that too, sir."

Marchant looked at Harris. "I take it you've seen the Universal Press report filed by Miranda Finch on what happened in Eden?"

Harris gave a nod. He had. Finch definitely had her sights set on him and didn't look like letting go any time soon. He tried to play it down though. "The footage was hazy."

"Three tourists in surrounding villas caught the fighting on their PDPs, captain. Granted, some of the vision was questionable, but that footage of Steinberg killing the one ID'd as Hazus Marinov was pretty clear."

"It was self-defense," Harris said.

"Yes, it was, but what the rest of the population saw was a bunch of UNF soldiers on holiday getting involved in a massive brawl that ended in the deaths of six men. We've had a hell of a time talking that down."

Harris shrugged. "I'm sorry, sir, but what could we do? We were under attack."

"I know," Marchant said. "Regardless, there will be no more group gatherings in public. Do you understand? We cannot risk something like this again. One soldier in a fight we can talk our way out of, but not a whole team! Not on Earth in a country that is not at war, and certainly not fighting to the death!"

Harris stared firmly at the colonel. "I understand, sir." And he did. He didn't want to see that happen again either. The colonel was right, it was too damn risky. The world was not ready to know about the impending invasion. If they found out about the Alpha soldiers, they would want to know why the UNF was creating them. And if they found that out? There would be absolute chaos.

"Have you had any problems with the return of Packham's body to her family?" Harris asked.

"No," Marchant said. "The autopsy confirms what the police report said. That they were set upon by as yet unknown thieves. They've accepted the story. Jacques's family were a little more pushy, thanks to Finch doing a report on that too, but they've quietened down." Marchant sighed. "On that note, I've approved the replacements you've requested to fill the gaps in your team."

"Thank you," Harris said as Marchant referred to his PDP.

"Staff Sergeant Eki Tikaani and Sergeant Bon Frazer for your new co-pilot," he said. "Tikaani's a big woman for an Inuit. Six foot."

"Yes, sir. And as an Alpha I have no doubt that she'll bust some heads."

"I bet," Marchant said. "Frazer's young. He has a few warnings on his record?"

"Yes, sir, for risky flying. But he hasn't crashed yet. I may just need that risky flying one day. Until then, Hunter will balance him out. He'll train Frazer to keep that edge but also to know when to use it and when to stow it. Hunter loves his ship. He won't let Frazer crash it."

Marchant gave a nod. "They'll be briefed and ready for when you next head out."

"Colonel," Welles spoke up. "I take it there's been no word on Corporal Colt?"

"No. Unfortunately, other than locating her vehicle which was clean, we've found no trace of her."

"I heard you called off the search, sir," she said, brow furrowed with concern. "But if her body hasn't been found, doesn't that mean she could still be alive out there somewhere?"

"Not necessarily. It means that we can't find the body. Drazen may have buried her, or thrown her in a ditch out of town. It could take months, years, until someone discovers it."

"But—"

Marchant held up his hand to stop her. "Her face will remain on the FRS, but we cannot expend more resources in searching for her. We just can't, sergeant. The likelihood of her being alive is slim."

"They didn't kill Packham, sir. She jumped."

"We *believe* she jumped, because her only other choice was to go with Drazen and his goons. Who knows what would've happened if she let them get their hands on her. I think we still would've found a body, sergeant. Just one a whole lot more wrecked than the one we found."

"But Drazen gave me a choice," she countered. "He said come with me or die. Packham obviously chose death. She probably saw them kill her partner, Jacques, and she wasn't that close to her family. Colt... Colt loved her family more than anything. She would've chosen life, I know it."

"I think we should move on," Harris said firmly, closing down the discussion. He exchanged a glance with Welles. He didn't want her torturing herself with thoughts of Colt being alive out there somewhere. The truth was, those thoughts already tortured him daily: the thought of her dead, the thought of her alive. He didn't want Welles thinking about what she, too, could've become. She was a survivor and she was free. That needed to be her focus.

Marchant gave a nod, then moved his fingers across the glass panel in the face of the boardroom table to bring up a star map on the three screens along the wall opposite to where they sat.

"Alright, I have some news to share," the colonel said, looking back at them. "It would seem the *Barbican* has made contact. We don't know if they are the same ones we've been communicating with, or another, closer source. The analysts have been studying the comms, trying to figure that out."

"Closer source?" Harris asked. "When did the *Barbican* make contact?"

"Word came in a few days ago. The *Barbican* confirmed their location at that time and they were still only a fraction of their way toward the Zeta Archelois system. As you know, due to the lack of satellites out that far, our transmission response time slows down once ships are past the Belt, and it gets slower the further the distance. We estimate, based on their current location at that time, the message was sent approximately six weeks ago. And the time lag will only get worse."

"So, they could be dead right now and we wouldn't know," Harris said, thinking aloud as he stared at the star map.

Marchant fixed him with a stare. "Possibly, but we don't believe that to be the case. They simply reported that they'd picked up the response earlier than planned. And the agreed protocol was that they would send us a communication every single day to confirm their status. Unfortunately, a day out there isn't a day back here."

"What was their reaction going to be to the earlier reception of the signal?"

"They were proceeding onward."

"So, they could be dead right now," Harris repeated bluntly.

"What makes you so sure that they're dead?" Marchant asked.

Harris shrugged, his stomach tightening. "They got the response to the signal earlier than planned. That means the Zetas are closer than we think." In his peripheral vision, he noted both Welles and McKinley shoot him a glance.

"Or they've communicated with a closer ship," Marchant countered. "It was one signal. Not many."

"Either way, whether it's a different source or the original source, the Zeta signal was closer than we expected," Harris said firmly.

Marchant studied him again, and he felt McKinley and Welles tense as they sat alongside. They knew Harris had dreamed of an early attack. They knew he was right. Now they just had to convince Marchant of that, without divulging *how* Harris knew it and without Marchant thinking him crazy and locking him up alongside Professor Sharley.

"You're worried they're going to attack us sooner than we think," Marchant said, studying him.

Harris considered his words carefully. "I think it's wise to be prepared for any outcome. If that signal response is early, that means they're closer than we think. If they're closer than we think, that means they could be here earlier than we've planned for. And if they attack us earlier, we could be annihilated. We need to be ready."

"I agree," Marchant said, eyes narrowed as they took him in. "That's why we're monitoring the situation. Regardless, I think we need to be smart about our decisions. Knee-jerk reactions won't help anybody. There was panic when we first picked up the signal all those years ago. People died," he said, referring to Colonel Strasser and Welles's mother. "We need to make the right decisions, calmly and rationally."

"Agreed," Harris said. "In order to make these decisions we need to examine all the information and all our options. How soon can we take a look at one of those ships you found?"

Marchant looked at his watch. "I can make a call and get you to the one near Roswell by this afternoon."

"Good," Harris nodded, "let's do that."

Miranda Finch, reporter for Universal Press, smiled, brushing her long dark hair back off her shoulder.

"Captain Morrell," she said in greeting. "How are you?"

"I'm well," he said, but didn't smile. She watched her reflection in his mirrored sunglasses. They seemed to suit his graying crew cut.

"So, to what do I owe this pleasure?" she asked. She'd been sitting in Coco Joe's cafe writing up her latest story when the Earth Duty captain had approached her.

"I haven't seen you in a while," he said.

"I've been away on assignment."

"I know," he said, placing both hands on his hips. "You've been in New Zealand covering the Eden incident. And you were also in Bali, tracing the last movements of the *Aurora*'s former pilot who was found dead at the bottom of a ravine."

Miranda smiled. "It's good to see you watching the right news station. You've been doing your homework, captain."

He seemed to humor her with a smile, but she sensed it didn't meet his eyes. "Did you find what you were looking for?"

Miranda shrugged. "You saw the news reports."

"I saw only what you could publish without being sued for defamation. What else did you find out?"

"Captain?" Miranda's smile dropped a little.

"You've been hunting for information on Captain Harris and those Blue-boys. I'm just wondering if there was anything you wanted to share?"

She paused a moment, eyeing him. She studied his jaw, the scar on the side of his neck, his broad shoulders. She didn't like his intimidating stance.

"Whatever I uncovered, I showed in the news report," she said.

Morrell laughed as he swung a chair over beside hers and sat down. He leaned in toward her and pulled his sunglasses down. "Now, Miranda, I thought we had a deal."

"A deal?" Her smile slid away entirely.

"Yeah. You told me if I had anything on Harris and those Blue-boys to come to you. And you agreed to do the same."

"So?"

"So," he leaned closer, "you got something and you're not sharing."

"Neither are you," she countered.

"I got nothing," he said firmly.

"Well, the deal was about sharing. If you have nothing to offer, then neither do I."

Morrell gave a humorless chuckle, then gave her a hard stare. "I think you'd better tell me what you know, Miss Finch."

"I told you, everything you saw in that news rep—"

"Bullshit!" he cut her off.

Miranda stared at him, her heart beginning to race a little. She'd been in tight spots before and was confident she could handle this, although Morrell did worry her a little. But what she'd heard in New Zealand and Bali worried her more.

"Why are you trying so hard to get dirt on Captain Harris?" she asked.

"Why are you?" he threw back.

"I'm not chasing dirt on Harris. I'm chasing the truth."

Morrell laughed. "Bullshit! You want a story, pure and simple. Don't make out like you're doing this for the greater good."

"I'm doing my job."

"Yeah? And I'm doing mine."

"It's funny, you know," Miranda said, analyzing him, "because most soldiers band together, *especially* against the press. It's not often you see one side trying to take the other down."

"I'm not trying to take anyone down," he said, voice tight. "I'm trying to find out if there's something I should know."

"If there's something you should know, I'm sure your superiors would tell you."

Morrell leaned in closer, millimeters from her face. "Don't you tell me how the military works, Miranda. I think I have a better understanding of it than you do. In fact, I would counsel you against sticking your nose in if you can't handle what you find."

"But I haven't found anything," she said, holding her ground.

Morrell grinned, as he leaned away from her. "You have and you're not sharing, Miss Finch. That is not a wise move."

"Are you threatening me?"

Morrell's grin slid away and he stared at her for a moment, before standing up. He leaned down and rested his hands either side of her on the arms of her chair, trapping her within. He got in her face again.

"You sleazed your way up to me for information and you promised to play fair," he said quietly. "I don't like it when people lie to me or use me, Miss Finch. So, you have a good hard think about what you learned down in New Zealand and whether or not you want to share it with me. Understand?"

Miranda stared back at the image of herself reflected in Morrell's sunglasses: tense and frightened. The captain gave a smile and stood again.

"Have a nice day, Miss Finch. I'll be seeing you around."

Miranda watched as Morrell left the cafe. She glanced around at the other patrons to see if anyone had noticed their interaction. They seemed oblivious. She took a moment to collect herself, then began packing up her things, wanting to get back to the safety of her apartment as soon as she could.

Carrie stepped out of the patrol vehicle and eyed their surroundings. They'd taken a Z-flyer to the Roswell airfield, then driven directly to this site between the Lincoln National Forest and the Carlsbad Caverns in New Mexico. There was nothing particularly engaging about the spot in which they'd stopped. The forest was close and the Sierra Blanca range could be seen further on, but otherwise they stood on the edge of an open, deserted plain. The sandy ground around them was covered in low shrubs and clumps of grass.

"Are we waiting for someone?" Harris asked, as if reading her mind.

"Here they come," Marchant said, eyeing the distance. They all turned and saw another PV headed their way.

The PV eventually came to a stop beside them and two men got out.

"Colonel Marchant." The taller and thinner of the two men, British according to his accent, extended a hand. Marchant shook it, then turned to them.

"This is our lead archaeologist, Professor Matthew Ross," he said, then introduced Harris, McKinley and her. The other man who had arrived with Ross remained silent, standing by the car. Carrie figured he was Ross's driver.

"Shall we head to the site?" A boyish smile crossed Ross's middle-aged face, as he headed back to the PV. They followed him and climbed aboard.

"I thought you said it was near Roswell," Carrie commented to Marchant when they finally reached their destination and exited the PV.

The colonel shrugged. "Well, it is near Roswell. Kind of. Not everyone outside of the US has heard of Carlsbad, but if you say Roswell, they generally know where it is."

Harris closed the PV door and placed a pair of dark sunglasses on his face. "So are you telling me the Roswell hoax isn't a hoax? That it's related somehow?"

Marchant smiled. "The crash of the weather balloon was real, but it happened north of Roswell near Corona. Although it wasn't merely a weather balloon; they were analyzing various readings in the area, like chemicals and compounds in the air, to see if they could pick up anything unusual that might lead them to other underground areas."

"Does the Zeta site link to the Carlsbad Caverns?" McKinley asked.

"No," Ross, the archaeologist, answered him, "but they're right next door to them." He smiled. "This way."

The archaeologist and his driver – the latter armed, Carrie realized – led them along a rugged path into the thick cover of trees forming the edge of the forest. She noted the driver stayed with Ross, noted his closely-shaved hair and fit physique, and figured that he was actually Ross's personal security. The lead archaeologist for the Zeta sites was obviously very important to the UNF.

They continued along the track for a while until they came across a wall of large beige-colored boulders, about four times her height. There was a crack in the middle of the boulder wall, maybe a meter across. Ross disappeared within, motioning them to follow, while the driver waited outside. Carrie, Harris, McKinley and Marchant stepped inside the crack and followed Ross down a narrow snaking path that led through the middle of the boulder. About 15 meters in, a section of the large boulder wall to their left suddenly slid back, startling her.

Ross turned around and smiled, his grin nearly poking the corners of his mouth past the cheeks on his thin face. He looked like a kid entering a toy shop. She supposed to someone in his profession this would feel a bit like that.

"Security keep watch on this area from the inside," he explained. "That's the only way this door will open. Should anyone else pass through here, it's just a big rock."

Carrie eyed the archaeologist, the thinning brown hair and laugh lines around his moss-green eyes, then gave a stilted smile back. She threw a glance over her shoulder at Harris and McKinley, before entering.

It was dark at first, but it only took a split second for her Alpha eyes to adjust and see clearly. She noticed Harris, whose sunglasses were now perched on his head, put his hand out against the wall to guide himself. His human eyes taking longer to adjust. She glanced at McKinley. Thankfully, his eyes weren't glowing due to the special Alpha contact lenses Marchant had supplied to them both as the Z-flyer had come into land. The contacts were covered in a film that blocked the too obvious cat's-eye glow that sometimes occurred.

"We wait until the door is closed before these entry lights come on," Ross explained. "In case any hikers notice the abnormal light in the wilderness."

Marchant and the driver were the last in and the door closed behind them. They stood in total darkness for a moment before the lights came on and illuminated a long tunnel, lined intermittently with halogen globes.

"It's a bit of walk to the nest," Ross said.

"Nest?" Carrie asked.

Ross grinned at her again. "That's our little nickname for it. We call them Zeta nests. Burrowed into the ground as they are. Clever aliens."

Carrie really didn't like the words "aliens" and "nest" being used together. Not at all.

"We wanted the entry points as far away as we could manage, so as not to draw attention, you see," Ross said as he began walking down the corridor. "There is one other entry point that's easier to access for our equipment, but we try not to use it if we can. If it's just visitors on foot, then we use this one, as it's nice and hidden."

Carrie eyed the endless corridor. It was solid rock; the floor sandy; the air musty.

"Did we make the tunnels, or did they?" she asked.

"Oh no, we made them," Ross said. "This ship, best we can estimate, was wedged in this rock some 700,000 years ago. We've examined sections of the outside and we've concluded that they burrowed down here. It wasn't a crash. There are scratches and scrapes and dents, but we believe if it crashed then it would be in a lot worse condition. It is entirely intact, so we believe the ship's technology enabled it to cut through the rock and wedge itself down here on purpose."

Carrie noted the sloping floor. She decided another thing she didn't like were the words "down here" used in reference to "aliens" and "nest".

"Why do you think they burrowed down here?" she asked with a little trepidation.

"We're not sure, exactly, but we do have some theories," he said, as a corner appeared, leading them down a steeper path. The halogen lights still lined the corridor, but her Alpha eyes saw the amount of shadow and light. It was pretty dim up ahead. "Firstly," Ross continued as though he were leading a museum tour, "it's possible that they are a species not accustomed to our bright sun. From what the UNF scientists have told us, the Zeta Archelois system has a sun, but it is only about half the strength of our sun."

"So they're like vampires then?" McKinley asked dryly.

Ross gave a hearty chuckle. "No, we don't believe so, lieutenant. The iconography we've uncovered shows no images of drinking blood. They may have simply burrowed down because they prefer the dark and the cool. Or, a second theory posits that they're smart and burrowed down for their own protection. They were obviously an intelligent species to have this kind of ship, so they would've realized it would be best to hide themselves on a strange planet until they could confirm that no life-forms here posed a threat."

"How did they get in and out?" Harris asked from behind Carrie.

"There is another path, since closed off by rockfalls, that we believed they used. It was how we first made the discovery. An archaeologist was scouting the surrounds of the Carlsbad Caverns and stumbled across the opening and called it in to the authorities. Thankfully, he didn't try to enter the ship without sufficient back-up. When it was in place we gave him the honor of going through first, as he had been the one to make the discovery. He became the first of the five people we lost trying to gain access. The original path had clearly been made with some kind of advanced technology as the walls had a clean, smooth cut. It looked safe, but we know now that it was set with traps. That's the reason for the rockfalls. We realized we had to find another way in. Our *own* way in. It's interesting, though. The path the aliens cut through the rock is high and narrow, which seems to have suited their physiques."

"Tall and narrow?" Harris asked the archaeologist.

"Yes." Ross glanced around, grinning happily. "The iconography in the mothership indicates they were of similar appearance to us, in that they have two arms and two legs, but the most prominent images indicate that, some at least, were much taller and much slimmer, and very pale."

"Mothership?" Carrie asked.

"Yes, the ship found in Egypt is much larger than this one. We believe that it was the first ship to arrive. Then other ships, smaller ships, were sent out across the other landmasses. Whether to begin some kind of roll-out of population or for their own study purposes, we're not yet sure. However, whatever their aim, they failed."

"Why did they fail?" Harris asked.

Ross stopped and looked around at them. "We're not sure exactly, but based on the artwork in the mothership, we believe they began to fall ill. One can only assume a bacteria or virus found naturally on Earth did not agree with them. We think they realized they were unprepared for our planet, so when they left, they took some Homo heidelbergensis with them, no doubt for study purposes."

"Which means," Harris said flatly, "they've probably found a way to overcome their weaknesses."

"Yes." Ross's eyes lit up. "Survival of the fittest!" He looked around at another turn in the sloping corridor, then back to them again. "We're almost there."

Harris noticed their movement along the dim corridor began to slow. He also noticed the surface of the rock walls began to shimmer with some kind of pearlescent dark-gray material.

"Is this from the ship?" he asked the archaeologist.

"Yes," Ross replied, studying the surface. "It's some kind of residue, or dust, that came from the ship when we cut it to access the inside. We can't liken it to anything on Earth. It's beautiful, isn't it?"

Harris raised his hand to touch it, but decided against it.

"Is it safe to humans?" he asked.

"Yes," Ross smiled. "Its base component is a metal not of our world. So, it's not biological. We've been assured there is no danger to humans."

"We're trying to replicate the material the ships are made of," Marchant added from behind Harris. "If it can cut through rock with barely a scratch, we think it'd make some great armor, maybe even use it on our own ships."

Harris glanced at the colonel. "Indeed," he said, looking back at the wall. "And if they've been studying the HH humans, finding our weaknesses and fixing theirs, then we can study their ships, find their weaknesses and correct ours."

"Exactly," Marchant said firmly.

"How did you get it open if it was strong enough to cut through this rock and get down here?" Harris asked.

"With great effort," Marchant told him. "It took several concentrated streams of laser to do it. The equivalent concentration of what the *Aurora* would fire from its onboard weapons at close range."

"Jesus," Harris said.

"Okay," Ross said, eyes virtually glowing with excitement, "are you ready?"

Harris gave a nod and Ross turned to another wall and waved to a camera in the corner of the roof.

"We've used the material we cut away to make our own door," Ross told him with pride. A large black door hissed and ejected forward slightly, then split in two, yawning open to provide a gap large enough for them to pass through. "Welcome to the Zeta-1 Nest!" he said, dipping his head slightly as he entered.

Harris followed Welles and the archaeologist into the ship. Ross moved well forward, but Welles stopped over the threshold, eyes wide in astonishment as she scanned the surroundings. Harris moved to stand to her left and did the same, while McKinley moved in and stood on her right. Before them was a round chamber, the pearl-gray walls of which were predominantly smooth and featureless. The only thing of note was a 30 centimeter lip that jutted out about halfway down the wall and curved around the room. Harris moved over to where it started just inside the door and noticed that it was at lower chest height, but figured that, given what Ross had said about the Zeta's physiques, it was probably only at their waist height. He looked at Ross.

"Can we touch it?"

"Yes, go ahead!" He motioned for Harris to do so.

Harris placed his hands on the jutting lip, which seemed to be covered in a soft squishy skin-like material that matched the walls. Where he touched it, the surface glowed a faint blue. He quickly removed his hands.

"What is that?" he asked.

Ross moved toward him. "Their technology. This, we believe, is one of their flight decks. There are three in these smaller triangular-shaped ships, and six in the larger hexagonally-shaped Egyptian ship. We believe in order to burrow down, the ships must work into a very fast spin, which creates a movement similar to that of a drill. We've been unable to ascertain how anything actually works as yet, but a popular theory is that all of this is thought generated."

"Thought generated?" Harris asked, as Welles moved up beside him and traced her fingers along the pearl-gray surface, a shimmer of blue light, paler than Harris's, following her movement.

"Yes," Ross nodded. "We think perhaps their ships are heavily engineered to interface with their biology. Hence our inability to work things out."

"How is this thing still powered after all these years?" McKinley asked, hands on hips, his brow furrowed.

Ross shrugged. "We believe the ships are designed to conserve their power when not used. So, they're in hibernation."

"Hibernation?" Welles asked looking at Ross. "You think this ship is alive?"

Ross nodded. "Yes. We do."

Welles quickly removed her hand from the panel. "So, we just woke it up?"

Ross smiled. "Yes and no." He moved up beside her. "We believe the ships to be a machine structurally, but to have biological interfaces to make it operate. We also believe that our DNA must be similar to that of the Zetas in order to get this reaction." He swiped his fingers over the lip and the light-blue glow shimmered. "It recognizes enough of our make-up to react, but we are obviously different enough that we can't get any further inside."

"So how do you get around that?" Harris quirked an eyebrow.

Ross exhaled heavily. "We can't. We'd need a live Zeta specimen."

"But that, in itself, would be very dangerous," Marchant said. "If we could get our hands on a live specimen, that is. If we connected a Zeta to one of these ships it's possible it could instruct the ship to kill us all. We'd be dead before we knew what hit us."

"Quite," Ross nodded.

Harris watched as Welles traced her fingers along the lip again, watching the blue glow follow her fingers.

"Mechanical hardware, biological software," she said, thinking aloud. "And thought-technology to make it work..." She glanced back at Harris and, as she did, he felt a strange sensation shoot down his spine.

He looked back at Ross. "So, this thought-technology..." he said, motioning to the lip.

"Subliminal Neural Association," Ross interrupted. "We call the process SNA, and we refer to the console," he motioned to the lip jutting out and the walls above it, "all of this, as the axon terminal."

"The axon terminal?"

"Yes, an axon is involved in the neuronal process of sending a signal, a message, away from a cell body toward target cells or neurons. An axon terminal is the very end part of an axon making a synaptic contact with another cell: the point where neurotransmitters are released. In short, it's all neurological terminology. The Zeta pilot connects itself to the console, which we're suggesting acts as the axon terminal, and hence the transmitter which connects the Zeta's mind to the ship."

"Right," Harris said glancing around the room. "So, SNA is how they fly the ship."

"Yes," Ross answered.

"And the only way we can figure out how this ship works, and who the Zetas are, is to try and connect a human to the ship?"

"In theory," Ross shrugged, "but as I said, the ship won't let us in, because we're only a partial match to Zeta DNA. Right now, we're a foreign body that the ship won't let inside."

"Wait, what about the skulls you found?" Welles asked Marchant. "In that first briefing, when you told us about the connection with the HH, you mentioned skulls that weren't quite human. We have their DNA, don't we?"

Ross smiled at her as if he was a teacher proud of his student. "We do. Unfortunately, we need a live specimen, not just the DNA."

"We've got people looking into it," Marchant told them, "and we're currently recruiting new talent into the mix to help us out. Ship engineers, designers, and the like. We'll figure out these ships one way or the other."

Harris stared at him. "And the DNA?"

Marchant stared back. "We're looking into that too."

"In what way?" Harris asked.

"Exploring our options," Marchant said with finality, shutting down the line of questioning.

Harris darted his eyes to Ross and decided not to pursue it.

"So, what else is on this ship?" McKinley asked, hands on hips, looking ahead to where another doorway stood.

"It's much the same, but come, I'll show you," Ross said, then made his way toward it.

Carrie was glad to see sunshine and breathe fresh air again. They'd spent two hours down that hole inspecting the ship. It was consistently plain, covered in smooth surfaces that glowed a faint blue when touched. As Matthew Ross had said, there appeared to be three flight decks, one positioned at the nose of the ship, and one either side of its triangular-shaped body. It was hard to say how many Zetas the ship would carry. There wasn't much inside except those smooth walls, floor and ceilings, with the occasional lip jutting out: a console which would no doubt extend and retract items from the walls as needed. So, all in all, other than learning that the ships were meshed mechanics and biology, not much else had been learned.

Carrie looked behind her to see Harris and McKinley appear from the crack in the rock wall. They both pulled their sunglasses on, eyes squinting against the sun. They climbed into the PV, and having left Ross inside the ship, they made their way back to the airport, each silent as they mulled over what they'd seen. As they approached the Z-flyer, parked to the side of the airport buildings, Brody and Freya came running out to her. They trotted up on their little chubby legs, arms held high to be picked up. Carrie smiled and scooped up Brody, while McKinley came alongside and scooped up Freya.

"Were they alright?" Carrie asked Roy.

"Yes, Miss Welles," he said, "although they were starting to get restless."

"They've certainly got a lot of energy, hey?" her new Sentinel, Sampson Warra, said.

Carrie smiled at him. "They sure do."

Sampson had arrived to replace Shane barely a few days after her return from Eden. She'd even helped Roy make the selection, no longer willing to just sit back and let people make decisions for her. The man they selected was Australian, of Aboriginal heritage, and had grown up in Western Australia not far from the UNF facility that had been communicating with the signals.

Sampson was relatively new to this line of work, but she didn't have a choice in that. That was the way they did things on Sentinel Duty. The juniors had to learn from the seniors, and with Shane gone, they needed a new junior in the team. This was a strategic selection in a way. Although Roy was also from the area, he hadn't been back in some years. Sampson Warra, however, was fresh from home, and Carrie knew that local knowledge might come in handy. After all, in her shared dreams with Harris of the early invasion, that is where they'd been. In Australia, near the gnarled tree, not far from the UNF facility. Although Roy was unaware of the connection Carrie had with Harris, or of the early invasion Harris had dreamed of, he knew about the UNFASP and the impending invasion expected in another 23 years.

When Roy had first introduced Sampson, Carrie remembered thinking he looked younger than expected. Certainly younger than Shane. And leaner.

"Sergeant Carrie Welles, this is Sampson Warra, your new Sentinel."

"Sampson," she'd said with a nod, and extended her hand.

Sampson had shaken her hand as a big smile cracked his face, flashing a row of teeth. "Nice to meet you, Miss Welles."

She smiled. "So, how long have you been a Sentinel?"

"About three months now," he smiled proudly.

Carrie's face had frozen a little. She'd known he was in his first year of service, but hadn't quite realized he was *that* fresh. She darted her eyes to Roy.

"He's fit, he's fast, and he knows our target area well," Roy told her.

"Yeah," Sampson said, tilting his head to the side as he studied her. "Roy told me you're interested to know about Gero and Greenough. Why's that?"

"Er…" Her eyes had flashed to Roy again, "that's a topic for another day, I think, Sampson."

"Okay," he shrugged. "No worries, Miss Welles."

Carrie had smiled at him, at the familiarity of having yet another Australian accent around. "Welcome, Sampson. I look forward to working with you."

"Working *with* me?" he seemed amused. "Don't *I* work for you?"

"No, Sampson. Here, we work together."

Sampson turned his young face to Roy in question. Roy gave a small smile, then motioned toward the door. "Come on," he said. "It's time to start work."

Carrie, sitting in the Z-flyer, watched as Sampson flashed his trademark bright grin at Freya, making her grin back at him. She realized his youth might just come in handy with the children. That only made her think of Novak, her Sentinel injured in the Eden attack. She missed him. He had always been so good with the children.

She kissed Brody's cheek and looked back at Roy. "Is Novak still on track to return tomorrow?"

"Yes, Miss Welles," Roy said, and she could tell he also looked forward to the Slovenian Sentinel's return.

"Good," she nodded. Enough time had passed and she wanted her new Sentinel team to integrate as soon as possible.

Before Carrie knew it, they were climbing out of the Z-flyer, back at the Space Dock of Fort Centralis.

"Ah, that Space Dock Spice!" Harris said, taking a deep breath and looking around.

Carrie smiled. "You taking off for the mainland? Or you want to head back to the Fortress for some dinner?"

Harris looked back at her. "Sounds good. I told Taya I'd be in first thing in the morning. I wasn't sure how long today would take."

Carrie pulled out her PDP. "I'll let Archie know we're heading back."

"You can call your AIS?" Harris asked, arching his eyebrow curiously.

"Yep. He'll order us dinner and let my father know."

McKinley grunted, shaking his head, and Harris glanced at him.

Carrie smiled. "McKinley's taking a little while to warm to Archie," she said. "He takes some getting used to."

"Archie?" Harris asked, "Why's that?"

"Don't ask," McKinley said with finality, heading toward the dock's exit with Freya on his hip.

Harris stood at the floor to ceiling window in the Fortress's living room and stared out at the Space Docks as darkness descended and lights began to twinkle.

"Quite a sight, huh?" Welles said, handing him a scotch.

"Thank you," he said, taking it, then glanced back out the window. "It sure is."

They moved into the kitchen area and took a seat at the table, where McKinley and Colonel Welles were positioned with a scotch of their own.

"Biological technology, huh?" Welles's father shook his head. "Doesn't that sound like an oxymoron."

Harris shrugged. "It sounds like the future to me." He sipped his drink, looking back at the colonel. "Think about it. The UNF here on Earth has started bioengineering their soldiers. We think these Zetas are many hundreds of thousands of years in advance of us. What the Zetas are doing now, is what we'll be doing in the future. We're effectively them, just a little behind the times."

"Except we've spent all these years evolving on this planet, which sounds much different to theirs," Welles said. "So, we're the same, but not."

Colonel Welles shook his head. "I just hope the UNF can get their shit together in time. But, hey, we got about 23 to 24 years, right?"

Harris saw Welles shoot him a glance. He met her stare firmly. He knew she wanted to tell her father about the early attack, but Harris wasn't ready to let anyone else in on that just yet. Welles and McKinley knew about his gift, and that was enough for now.

"So, the ship near Roswell," Welles said, turning to her father, "was the first one the military, which evolved into the UNF, knew about. Then, years later, we picked up the first signal."

Her father shrugged. "They'd managed to debunk the Roswell incident as an urban legend decades before I joined the UNF. Even after I did, after I was there during the whole signal fiasco, they still never revealed to me anything about those ships. As a colonel, I was of high enough rank to help make a decision about the signals, but they still weren't sharing news of the ships found."

"That doesn't make sense," Welles said. "They expected you to make a decision about preparing for a war, but they didn't give you all the information you needed to make that decision."

Her father stared back at her. "Welcome to the military and politics, Ree," he said, then took a sip of his drink. "The ones who knew about the ships were the ones keen to go to war, obviously. The ones who stopped at nothing to get their way." A moment of silence passed, Harris noted, that was no doubt filled with thoughts of Welles's mother. "Had I known about the ships," the colonel continued, "had I known they'd already been here before, who knows what my decision might've been." The colonel looked at his daughter. "Your mother might still be alive."

"Dad," Welles said, reaching her hand out across the table automatically, to clasp his, "you didn't know."

Her father squeezed her hand, then pulled it away, glancing at Harris and McKinley.

"Besides," Welles said firmly, "you found the fucker who ordered the hit and you killed him." She raised her glass to toast him, as a heavy silence fell over the table.

The colonel darted his eyes to Harris and McKinley. Harris detected a nervousness shoot through the man at the revelation Welles had just divulged. Harris tried to hide his shock, though he noticed it flash across McKinley's face. Harris thought about Welles's statement for a moment, then held his glass up to toast the colonel as well.

"Sounds like a job well done, colonel," Harris said, wanting the man to know his secret was safe. "If someone murdered my wife, I would do the same thing."

"And me," McKinley said, raising his glass, before quickly adding with a smirk, "if I ever get married, that is."

Harris threw him a grin as the four of them connected their glasses and took a drink. The colonel looked at his daughter and pointed to the roof, referring to Archie.

Welles wiped her mouth and nodded. "Hey, Archie?"

"*Yes, Miss Welles.*"

"Erase the last part of our conversation, please. And delete it from your back-up also."

"*Miss Welles?*"

"I know you record things, Archie, in case you need to use it as evidence later. I understand why, but your loyalty is to me, yes?"

"*Yes, Miss Welles.*"

"Then please delete the last part of that conversation."

"*Yes, Miss Welles. Erasing records now.*"

"Good."

"Thanks," the colonel said quietly to his daughter.

"No problem," Welles smiled. "I'll do anything for my family."

"As will I."

3

He Said, She Said

Carrie jolted awake from her dream. She'd been running with Harris and the twins while the fireballs hit the Earth. Then suddenly they'd been on that Zeta flight deck, tracing their fingers along the lip, watching the faint blue glow follow their movement. Sharley had appeared next, standing on the Zeta flight deck with them. Carrie immediately went into attack mode and tackled him to the ground. When Harris finally pulled her back, they both looked down to see Sharley's bloodied corpse lying beneath her. Harris had been startled at first, but when he looked at her, she told him she wasn't going to be a victim anymore. Harris had smiled, held out his hand and she'd slapped it. The touch of their skin sent that electric jolt through them, and she'd suddenly awoken.

"What?" McKinley stirred beside her.

"Nothing," she said, nestling her head into the pillow. She lay curled on her side, McKinley behind her, his arm over her waist. She slid her hand over his and pulled it closer. His naked warmth, soothing. They'd disappeared into their own bedrooms last night, keeping up the façade, but as soon as Carrie heard her father go to bed, she snuck into McKinley's room and he'd welcomed her. They hadn't quite replicated their marathon from the previous evening, however.

"Yeah, I know about your dreams now, so I don't believe that," he murmured sleepily.

"This was a good one," she said softly. "I told Harris I'm done with being a victim… and I killed Sharley."

"Yeah?"

She nodded. "I don't know how. I just jumped on him and then he was dead."

"If only it were that easy."

She sighed. "Yeah."

The silence sat for a moment before she rolled onto her back and turned her face to his. He traced his fingers down the scar beside her left eye.

"Logan's scar," she whispered, "from the Darwin mission."

McKinley watched her.

She rolled back onto her left side, brushing her hair away from her right shoulder. "Chet's scar from the Pegasus mission," she said. McKinley traced his fingers over the scar running down her shoulder blade. The one she'd received in the Hell Town Dungeon; the one he'd witnessed; the one he'd traded his senses for, to stop her pain.

She pulled her hair right up off her neck and showed him the scar cutting across the snowflake tattoo that sat there. "Quint, I imagine," she said, "where he cut out my TD on Meridian."

Again McKinley's fingers traced over it. Then she rolled onto her back once more and looked down at her caesarean scar, much longer than a normal caesar scar would be. It almost ran from hip to hip. "The damage done when they stole my twins here in Centralis."

McKinley traced his fingers across the scar. She met his eyes. "Where they pulled the twins from me," she whispered.

He continued to watch her as she rolled onto her right side and faced him, raising her left arm to display her latest scar, the vertical one along her left humerus.

"Drazen's souvenir from Eden," she said with finality. Again, McKinley traced his fingers down the scar. She reached out and traced her fingers over the scar on his side, also from Drazen.

He looked down at it, then back up at her. "You win," he said softly.

"Every Aurora mission has scarred me, but I'm done with them now," she said.

McKinley ran the backs of his fingers across her cheek.

"I'm not going to be a victim anymore." Carrie said, then broke into smile, as she pushed him onto his back and slid her naked body on top of his. "It's my turn to be on top for a while."

McKinley chuckled, but it was cut short as she planted her mouth on his.

Harris slid his hand over Taya's slightly protruding abdomen.

"I felt the first flutter a few weeks back."

He smiled and kissed her.

"My next appointment is tomorrow," she said. "We can find out the sex if we want. What do you think?"

Harris shrugged, remembering one of his dreams of his Overseers – Sibbie, Etta, his mother – where he held a little girl in his arms. "I don't know. What do you think?"

"Well," she shrugged, "surprises are good. But it's also good to plan things out."

"So," he asked, "which way do you want to go?"

Taya thought for a moment. "I think I want to know."

Harris smiled. "Then let's find out," he said, curious about whether his dream had been correct.

Tyson came bounding through the front door then.

"Hey!" Harris called to his son. "Where you been?"

"At the courts," Ty said, grinning, voice that little bit deeper. "Where else?"

"Oh, yeah." Harris arched an eyebrow. "And how's Candy?"

Ty's grin grew. "She's good."

"You're not going to ask how your father is?" Taya asked him. "He just got back from several weeks away."

Ty shrugged. "He hasn't asked me how I've been."

"I just did," Harris said.

"No, you asked about Candy."

"Same thing," Harris said, smiling.

Ty shrugged, eyes darting to his father's still relatively new physique. "How're your ribs since Eden?"

"Good," Harris said casually. "Everything's fine."

"Is it?" Ty grunted. "It looked like a bloodbath. It was all over the news. Steinberg looked like a freaking monster."

"Ty," Taya said.

"What?" Ty shrugged. "He had blood running down his face, squeezing that guy in a bear hug. Everyone's still talks about it at school."

"They were bad people, Ty," Harris said.

"So, where were you?" he asked. "While your team were getting pummeled. You weren't on the footage."

"I was helping someone else in another area," Harris said, staring at his son, trying to gauge where the attitude was coming from, trying not to let the Alpha within rear up.

Ty shrugged. "Just as well I guess. It's bad enough the reporter mentioned you by name. It'd be worse if you were in that footage, too. I'm sick of people asking me about it."

"Are you staying for dinner?" Taya said curtly, changing the topic.

Ty shook his head. "Nah, I'm out with the boys tonight."

"But it's a school night?" Harris questioned.

"We're just going to the movies. Chill, captain."

Harris watched his son take off upstairs, his face firm, his eyes matching.

"Just let it go," Taya said quietly.

"What the hell is wrong with him?"

"He's a teenager, Saul. He has a problem with everything."

"He never used to."

"Yeah, well, he's sixteen and an up-and-coming basketball star with a cute little cheerleader girlfriend. He thinks he's a big shot who knows it all."

"He knows shit about life."

Taya caught Harris's eyes with an agreeable but non-encouraging look.

"You think the pregnancy is affecting him? Making him act out."

"I don't know. He doesn't mention it. Possibly. There's been a lot of change around here the past year or so, I guess. You and me back together, this baby on the way, your sudden increase in physique, seeing your team all over the news."

"Does he give you this attitude when I'm not around?"

"Sometimes."

"And you let him get away with it?"

"No, I don't, Saul. But there's only so much I can say or do."

"Sounds like he needs a little one-on-one with the old man," Harris said, gazing up the empty stairs.

"He does," Taya said firmly. Harris looked at her and she sighed heavily. "There're cracks in the pavement, Saul. You need to fill the gaps before they get any wider."

Harris said nothing, but turned his gaze back up the empty stairs.

Carrie waited for her returning Sentinel, Novak Skoda, to arrive. As Roy escorted him through the door, a smile slid across his face.

"Miss Welles." He gave her a formal bow. He was looking a little thinner, a little paler, but a lot better than when she'd last seen him – bleeding heavily across his gut from Drazen's hunting knife.

Carrie didn't care about formalities, she rushed up and hugged him. "I'm so glad to see you back, Novak."

"Thank you, Miss Welles," he said, humbled by her show of affection. He pulled back from her. "And thank *you* for the assistance you provided my family. The care packages were welcomed."

"It's the least I could do, Novak," she smiled. "You nearly died for me and the kids."

Novak glanced around. "And where are they? The children?"

"They're sleeping," she said, "but when they wake they're going to be so glad to see you, I know it." She reached out and touched his shoulder. "Thank you for returning to us."

"Thank you for having me back, Miss Welles." He gave another humble bow.

"I don't trust anyone else, Novak."

Her Slovenian Sentinel smiled back at her before Roy led him out the door again.

Corporal Sabrina Colt stared at the man holding her captive. He'd just moved to a small chute, having heard a loud bang. The man opened it and a box fell on the floor at his feet. The man tried to look up the chute, as though hoping to see whoever had sent the item down, but Colt saw his shoulders slump as he closed it.

"Could you see?" she demanded.

He shook his head.

"What's in the box this time?"

The man bent down, squatting like a child, and began to remove its brown paper wrapping and string. He opened the box's lid and Colt spied bread, meat, cheese, and other foodstuffs.

"Maybe they don't know the others haven't come back," she whispered, thinking aloud. She looked at the man. "We have to get word to them. They can get us out!"

The man didn't move as he eyed the goods eagerly, but she saw he was torn. She looked at the digital cuff around his ankle, which was attached by a long chain to the wall in the cell in which he slept. Despite what he'd done to her, he was also a prisoner here. She had to use that to get close to him. She had to befriend him and convince him to get them out of here.

Then, once they were free, she would kill him for what he'd done.

She closed her eyes, feeling the Jumbo surge within her. She had to control it. Any more outbursts like she'd had before and he would probably drug her again. She knew what he'd done the first time he'd knocked her out. She didn't want to believe it was true, but deep down she knew it was. She'd seen the test result he'd shown her. She'd felt the surge of sickness in her belly.

But she couldn't think about that now; she was alive and she needed to stay alive. Despite how angry she was that he'd made her a Jumbo, she knew she could use that extra strength to get her out of here. Once she'd managed that, she could terminate what was growing inside her. But, until then, she could use her pregnancy. She was sure he wouldn't hurt her while she was pregnant, just as she was sure she could hurt him.

"Someone is sending us food," she tried again, forcing the Jumbo down, trying to sound like a soft human woman and not the soldier she was. "Someone knows we're here. They can help us."

"Whoever is doing it, works for Drazen," the man said, still squatting. He looked up at her. "You think they're going to help us?"

"Drazen isn't coming back," she said tightly.

"You don't know that."

"I do! You said they went after Packham and Welles. They would've been surrounded by the *Aurora* team. They had at least three Jumbos among them including Welles."

"Drazen had six!"

"It doesn't matter, man." She shook her head. "They're not back. That means the *Aurora* team won."

"No!"

"Yes!"

"No, you didn't see them. They were big. They were terrifying—"

"Have you seen McKinley in action?" Colt asked. "He's a Jumbo, he's big. He'd be hard to beat, and he was training up Evenssen."

"Drazen had six," he repeated.

"Jumbo or not, the *Aurora* team had Steinberg, and the captain, and Brown..." her voice cracked with emotion.

"They couldn't win."

"THEY HAVEN'T COME BACK!" she shouted, unable to control the Jumbo. Her muscles tightened as her wrists tried yet again to break the cuffs pinning her to the sides of her cot. "And they're not going to come back. They lost! When will you get that through your thick head?"

He stood up, an angry look upon his face. "It's too late."

"What's too late?"

He walked up to the bars of her cell. "I've gone too far to turn back now."

"What?" Her face scrunched in confusion.

"I made you a Jumbo and now you're pregnant." His face held a look of regret and sorrow. "There's nothing I can do to change that. We have to go through with it."

"No, we don't!" she pleaded trying to sit up. "If you help me, I won't tell anyone. I promise. Just let me go! Let me get rid of them!"

"I can't," he said, barely whispering, eyes on the ground. "I don't know who he has watching this place, but they are. Someone is bringing us food."

Colt fought hard as the tears tried to battle their way past her anger. "We can make it out. I can protect you. Just let me go!"

"No," he said firmly, "we can't. It's too late. We have to see it through to the end."

Carrie entered the *Aurora*'s mess hall with the twins in tow, while the Sentinels remained in the ship's corridor.

"How you doing, Welles?" Brown asked, as the team stepped toward her.

"I'm good, Brownie," she smiled, eyeing the subtle pink scar on his cheek. A souvenir from the fight in Eden. "You?"

"All good," he nodded, bending down to pick up Brody, while McKinley lifted Freya.

"Welles," Hunter stepped forward giving her a nod.

She eyed the *Aurora* pilot's new Alpha physique. "Impressive."

Hunter looked down at his larger arms, folded across his larger chest. He nodded to himself. "Still getting used to it."

She studied him a moment, sensing the Alpha within clouding his normally sunny disposition a little. She could feel the increase in his strength just by looking at him. "Yeah, it takes a little time."

"I fuckin' love it!" Murphy said, grinning.

Steinberg glanced at Murphy, a smile curling the corner of his mouth. Carrie eyed the new scar running partway down the center of the German's forehead. Another souvenir from the Eden fight. She turned to look at Brown's cheek again.

"Looks like Eden left a few of us with scars," she said, and saw their eyes fall to the scar down her left arm.

"Not all of us," Evenssen said with that hint of a Swedish accent. He lifted his fingers to wiggle his nose: "Though my nose isn't quite as straight as it used to be," he smiled. "It would've been worse if it hadn't been for Yughi, though."

Yughiarto gave Evenssen a quick nod in appreciation, his Alpha stature giving the placid Japanese comms-tech a much more intense look.

Gregson stepped forward, hands on hips as he eyed the team. "Yeah, they came out of it with a few scratches. We were lucky it wasn't worse."

"Thank you," Carrie said to the medic, "for saving my Sentinel, Novak."

Gregson gave her a gentle smile that contrasted with his own Alpha physique. "To tell the truth, it was close."

"Well, we got those fuckers!" Murphy said defiantly. "That's what counts. We made it out."

Carrie looked at him. "Not everyone did," she said, and a silence fell over them. "My Sentinel, Shane, and Packham…"

"Word is she took her own life," Hunter said, brow furrowed with emotion. Carrie couldn't tell if it was anger or sadness, or both. "You think that's true?"

Carrie stared at him, then nodded. This was something she'd thought about a lot over the past weeks since the Eden incident. "Packham was always adamant Sharley would never get his hands on her, that she would never have 'his' children. If they backed her into a corner, if Jacques was already dead… yeah, I think she made a choice."

"And Colt?" Brown asked, not turning his face to look at her, as though he were afraid of the answer.

"They haven't found her yet," Carrie said quietly.

"What were her thoughts about Sharley getting his hands on her?" Gregson asked, and the room looked at her for the answer.

Carrie thought for a moment. She'd also had a lot of time to think about this too, and these thoughts killed her the most. The scene of her discussion with Colt in the Centralis Command hospital, after her stolen twins had been returned, flashed inside her mind. "Colt once told me that she didn't want to die, and that she didn't want to be a coward either. If they gave her a choice, I think she would choose life."

"What does that mean?" Brown said, a little Alpha anger rising in his voice. "That she's alive out there somewhere," he gestured in an outward direction, "being held prisoner?"

Carrie felt her eyes suddenly sting and a lump grow in her throat, the guilt smacking her. That she was here and Colt was not.

"I don't know," she said, and for a moment it felt strange, as if the others had disappeared and only she and Brown stood there, staring at each other. "How's Keisha taking it?" she asked, referring to Colt's cousin who Brown had been dating.

"Wouldn't know," Brown said, his voice deep and at first sounding emotionless, but as the words hung in the air she sensed a bitterness lingering.

She wondered what that meant, whether they had broken up, but she didn't pursue it, as an awkwardness suddenly settled over the room.

Murphy gave a friendly slap to Brown's shoulder. "Fuck her, man," he said quietly, then moved over to the mess hall tables and the team began to follow suit.

Carrie locked eyes with McKinley, but she quickly looked away, not wanting to draw attention to the two of them.

*

Carrie felt odd sitting in the *Aurora*'s mess hall with the crew as though she were about to take off on a mission with them. It felt even weirder to watch the twins walking around and exploring the room as though it was natural for them to be there. Everyone was in their uniform, even Carrie herself. This was a formal situation, and yet the twins were waddling around.

The *Aurora* team had had their physical conversions and were about to commence their senses soon. She thought it somewhat poetic that they'd undergone their physical transformations, then almost immediately had their first test in using those new bodies, those new reflexes, that new strength. Once they had their senses done, they would need to test them, too, although hopefully in a more planned way.

While the sense surgeries took place, Harris had told her, the team would be based in Fort Centralis, which would provide Carrie the opportunity to be a part-time soldier. She could spend her days with the crew and nights back at the Fortress. This made her happy. She was being given an opportunity that allowed her the best of both worlds: getting to be a soldier *and* a mother. She wanted to do both, needed to do both, and had been uncomfortable with having to choose one or the other in the past.

Something about Eden had changed her. Of all the suffering and pain she'd been through, Eden seemed to have affected her more than anything else. Drazen's attack had been the closest she'd come to death. Admittedly, she'd come close when the twins had been stolen on Centralis, but, in part at least, that was caused by her own actions. Eden was the closest someone else had brought her to death. And after almost losing her life, after losing Doc, she knew more than anything that she wanted to live. She wanted to see her twins right, she wanted to be there when the Zetas hit. She wanted to stand beside Harris and McKinley and do what needed to be done.

Besides, the *Aurora* team had become her family; her closest friends now. Her old friends had fallen by the wayside these past couple of years. She'd stopped returning their calls and emails. How could she go back to playing the ordinary soldier in front of them after all she'd been through? Since the Darwin mission she'd become another person, one that couldn't talk about everyday stuff any more. Her world had become filled with bioengineered soldiers, Alpha babies, an alien invasion, and a violent psychopath who was obsessed with her. Normal people wouldn't understand, but the *Aurora* team did. They were 'her people' now.

Harris entered the mess hall, two new crew members in tow, and everyone stood to show their respect for him. The captain gave them a nod and they sat again. She was still getting used to his Alpha physique and presence, and how they boosted his air of command – which had been pretty solid to begin with. She eyed the human man and woman standing next to him.

"*Aurora* crew," Harris called, "meet your new team members. Staff Sergeant Eki Tikaani," he said, pointing to the woman, who was around Brown's height, with styled, short brown hair and muscular arms, "and Sergeant Bon Frazer, your new co-pilot!" He pointed to the man with burnt-orange colored hair, who looked to be mid-twenties, of average height. Harris set about introducing the *Aurora* team, one by one, announcing Carrie as a non-permanent member of the team. Brody walked up to Harris, and she saw the new soldiers eyeing the twins, confused by their presence.

Harris looked down at his godson, a smile curling his mouth, then turned to the new recruits. "This is Brody, and that's Freya," he introduced them. "The ones you were told about in your briefing. You'll be seeing them around from time to time."

"Yes, sir," they answered, eyeing the twins curiously.

"Take a seat," Harris ordered.

The woman – Carrie recalled Marchant saying she was of Inuit descent – took a seat near Steinberg. The co-pilot, Frazer, relatively trim in build compared to Tikaani, sat near Brown.

"Alright!" Harris claimed their attention. "Welcome back. Our two new recruits have been briefed on our mission and they've also been briefed on our past missions. So, as of this point, we move forward as though they have been with us the whole time. Understand?"

"Yes, sir," the team replied.

"Now, how we're going to move forward is this," Harris said firmly, meeting eyes with each and every one of them. "We will begin the first sense transformation of the team. Starting with the sense of smell. While this occurs we integrate Tikaani and Frazer into our routines and activities. Then they will undergo the body transformation. Then, as a whole, we will move forward with the next two senses."

"Sir?" Tikaani raised her hand.

"What is it?" Harris asked.

"I'm ready to go now, sir." She shrugged her bulky shoulders. "Why wait?"

"The team needs to get to know you as a human first," Harris said bluntly. "They need to know the basic you before they get to know the Alpha you."

Tikaani seemed to mull over his response, then nodded an acceptance.

"Alright. We will go in order of our making, but as captain I'll go before you Evenssen," he said, then looked over to the *Aurora*'s pilot. "And now that you're an Alpha, First Sergeant Hunter, you will be last."

Carrie eyed Hunter's strong Alpha face as he gave a nod back to his captain.

"Good," Harris said. "While we go through the change, one by one, the rest of you will get to training. McKinley, you know what to do."

McKinley stood and looked around at the crew, pointing to the mess hall doorway. "You heard the man. Get your asses to the training facility before I kick each of you there myself!"

The team's faces curled into grins, and Murphy chuckled, but they all stood and obeyed their First Lieutenant.

Admiral Glenashe Arken of the UNF *Barbican* stood, eyes fixed to the screen. The icons indicating the three Zeta ships had just disappeared from the radar. He clenched and unclenched his jaw repeatedly. They'd been at this cat and mouse game for days now.

When they'd initially slowed the ship and raised the shield, they'd spent three days just sitting there, motionless, while the Zetas slowed and remained stationary also, mirroring them. The *Barbican* had been trying to communicate with the foreign ships, but had received no response. After those three days, Arken powered the ship back up and began to move parallel to the Zetas. He was loath to approach them head on. If the *Barbican* continued on their original course it could be seen as an aggressive move on their part, and he was mindful not to start a conflict.

Perhaps the Zetas had a colony out here, somewhere close by? Perhaps these three ships were scouts or guards? He didn't know. Therefore, he'd decided they were going to continue onward, but alter their course so as not to pose a threat. Although technically they were inching closer to the Zeta ships, they just weren't heading directly for them.

For close to 24 hours they had been cruising parallel to the Zetas, inching closer, and the Zetas had mirrored them. At first the crew were intrigued by their behavior, but as the hours turned into days, it soon began to grate and the anxiety and frustration set in. This game of cat and mouse wasn't changing. And although the Zetas had communicated with them previously, since they had appeared on the *Barbican*'s radar they had not released one single signal. They simply mirrored the Barbican's actions.

And now, just like that, the Zetas had disappeared from the *Barbican*'s radar altogether. They were out there somewhere, but the *Barbican* was now blind to their movements.

Arken stared out of the observation window into the endless black of space, feeling the muscles down his back tighten and his palms begin to sweat. *What the hell are they playing at?*

What worried him most, now, was the lack of a response from Command on the interception of the signal earlier than planned, let alone the news that Zeta ships had appeared on their radar. That news would no doubt still be weeks away from reaching them.

He exhaled measuredly and worked to steady his resolve.

The Zetas haven't attacked us. That's a good thing. Maybe they don't wish us harm? Unless they're luring us into a trap...

Either way, he had no choice. They had to continue and discover who these ships belonged to.

Carrie, covered in sweat, faced off against Tikaani again. The woman was big and strong. In fact, if it wasn't for the moderate swell of her breasts,

Carrie thought, with those arms she could be mistaken for a man. Despite her muscled physique, her short dark hair accentuated the pretty, mischievous eyes that nestled atop her smooth, rounded cheekbones.

"So, where are you from?" Carrie asked.

"Trying to distract me with conversation?" she said, hunching her shoulders like a boxer.

Carrie smiled. "Is it working?"

"Nope," Tikaani said, lunging for her, but Carrie darted out of the way.

"Ooh, you like a little butterfly, girl!" Tikaani said. "Flittering and fluttering."

Carrie eyed her over. "And you're like a wall of concrete."

"Damn straight. Don't let me catch you. I'll drop you on your ass."

Carrie darted her eyes to McKinley who stood, arms folded, watching them, his face passive as he assessed the new recruit.

"Harris told you I'm an Alpha, right?" Carrie asked.

"Don't care," Tikaani said, shrugging. "If I catch you, your ass is going down."

Carrie laughed. "Yeah, but you gotta catch me first!"

"Hooo, I can't wait until I'm an Alpha!" Tikaani said, lunging again, faking left, moving right. Carrie knew what she was trying to do, trying to trick and trap, but she wouldn't fall for it. She felt the air rush past her as Tikaani swiped. There was power behind those arms.

"You never told me where you were from?" Carrie asked as she ducked and weaved from Tikaani's grasp.

"Alaska. You?"

"Australia. Can't you tell from the accent?"

Tikaani shrugged again. "Thought you were English or something."

"Yeah. Everyone does."

"Evenssen," McKinley called. "Get on Tikaani."

Tikaani gave McKinley a disappointed look. "But I was having fun here?"

"She's smaller, but too fast for you," he said bluntly. "Try someone closer to your size. Start with Evenssen, and if you can't catch him, I'll throw in Gregson."

"That's cool," Tikaani said. "Bring him on then."

Carrie stepped back, eyeing McKinley, then turned to watch Murphy and the new guy, Frazer, wrestling on the mats.

Murphy grunted and with a forceful thrust, flipped Frazer onto his back. Frazer looked up at him and Murphy held his arms out in question.

"Typical Scot, lying on his back!" Murphy said.

"Typical Irish, shooting off his mouth!" Frazer shot back.

"So, what'd they call you in school? Red?" Murphy grinned, motioning to his burnt-orange hair.

"Chucky, actually," Frazer said, getting to his feet.

"Chucky?" Murphy questioned.

"Yeah, as in Bon *Charles* Frazer."

"Chucky." Murphy laughed.

"How long you been flying for?" Hunter questioned, standing on the sidelines with his tattooed Alpha arms crossed, assessing his new co-pilot.

"Long enough," Frazer said, then grinned. "I haven't crashed yet."

Hunter stared back with a passive face.

"Don't go threatening his big brown bird, now," McKinley warned with a smile.

"His bird?" Frazer said. "This ship ain't no bird!"

Hunter stepped forward, about to say something, but McKinley, reflexes sharp, stepped in and cut him off.

"Frazer," McKinley said, "I should warn you that Hunter is a brand new Alpha and he loves his ship. He's also your boss on the flight deck. Probably best not to upset him. You wouldn't want to get off on the wrong foot."

Murphy chuckled in amusement.

"What ships have you flown?" Yughi questioned him.

Frazer glanced at him, then began listing ships. Carrie lost count after about number seven.

"A Blitzkrieg?" Hunter asked, sounding doubtful.

"What's a Blitzkrieg?" Murphy asked.

"It's the Ferrari of pleasure-cruising spaceships," Steinberg answered.

"A rich boy's toy," Hunter answered. "You a little rich boy?"

Frazer eyed him up and down. "Takes one to know one."

"I'm not rich," Hunter said.

"You used to be," Frazer pointed to him. "I can tell."

"You don't have to be rich to know expensive flyers." Yughi shrugged. "I've seen one before at an air show on the mainland."

"You into ships?" Frazer asked him.

"I'm a comms-tech. It's my job to check out the latest gadgets."

"It's not a gadget," Frazer said, a condescending look on his face. "It's a supreme piece of engineering."

Yughi smiled. "I guess it depends what toys you're into."

"When did you get your hands on a Blitzkrieg?" Hunter asked, amused. "There're only a handful in existence."

Frazer paused before answering. "A couple of years back. I knew a guy who had one."

"You knew a guy?" Hunter smiled, still doubtful.

Again Frazer paused, then held out his arms and shrugged. "Alright, maybe it was my uncle."

"So, you *are* a rich kid." Hunter's smile turned into a grin.

"No," Frazer said, staring at him, "I just have a rich uncle."

"Yughi!" McKinley said, then pointed to Frazer. "Enough talk. I want you two on the mats."

Yughi gave a slight bow, then stepped forward, and Frazer lined him up.

Gold walked the streets of Fort Centralis, wondering why Rovine had brought them here again. The team had a night off, so they were splitting up into groups and heading off to the various bars and clubs. He'd wanted to hang around the ship and see if Rovine was going to leave, but he knew he wouldn't. Not tonight. He knew how Rovine operated and could tell the captain was well ensconced in his office and wasn't going to leave it.

He sighed as he walked along beside his second lieutenant, Andy Ryker.

"That's a loud sigh, boss," Ryker said. "Cheer up. We got a night off."

"Yeah," Gold said, pushing his hands into his jeans pockets.

"Look, maybe there's nothing to find in that portal," Ryker said, shrugging. "Things seem back to normal, right? Maybe you should drop it."

"Maybe," Gold said, exchanging a look with him.

Ryker broke into a smile. "You're determined, I'll give you that." He looked past Gold, then smacked him in the chest. "This one looks good!" Ryker walked off into a bar on their right and Gold followed. "Make yourself comfortable," Ryker said. "I'll buy you a drink."

Gold smiled and watched as Ryker weaved his way to the bar, which was positioned against the back wall of the venue. Dimly lit and roughly square-shaped, the building was the last in a row of commercial tenancies in a larger complex. It opened up on two sides, one facing the street and the other facing a side alley, with tables and chairs spilling out onto the sidewalk. Inside the bar, against the left wall, a band played on a small stage and a female singer with purple hair was belting out a synth-rock tune.

Someone suddenly knocked into him as they rushed past into the venue, and he saw it was the reporter from Universal Press, Miranda Finch. She hadn't seen him, though. Her eyes were scouting the bar for someone, an angry look on her face. Her eyes caught what they were looking for, and she made a beeline to the alley side of the bar. Gold darted his eyes to the other side of the bar where Ryker was ordering drinks. He looked back at Finch and realized she was headed to where Captain Morrell sat with some of his crew, dressed in civilians, off duty.

Finch barreled up to him, pointed a finger in his face and started yelling. Gold couldn't hear over the music but saw well enough. Morrell swatted her pointed finger away, but as Finch continued, an angry scowl overtook his face. The Earth Duty captain abruptly stood, grabbed Finch's arm and pulled her out into the alley, much to the amusement of his crew. Gold darted his eyes to the two doormen, but they seemed to have missed the incident. Or they were ignoring it, he couldn't tell. He decided to follow Morrell and Finch into the alley to make sure things didn't get out of hand. As he stepped outside, he saw Morrell drag Finch around the corner into a recessed area behind the building.

"You're a goddamn liar!" Miranda Finch yelled. "Get your hands off me!"

Morrell pointed a finger in her face, his other arm still gripping hers tightly. "You'd better watch your tongue, Finch, or I'll—"

"Everything alright here?" Gold called chirpily as he approached them, flashing his award-winning smile.

Morrell and Finch glared at him.

"You got your goons on standby?" Finch accused Morrell.

"Goon?" Gold said. "I'm not his goon."

"Fuck off!" Morrell spat at Gold. "This ain't your business."

"Yes, it is," Gold said calmly. "You're causing a scene."

"So?" Morrell said.

"So, you're a man who wears the uniform and you're dragging a woman out of a crowded bar."

"I'm not in uniform!"

"Yes, you are," Gold told him. "It's always on." He tapped his temple. "Let her go."

"There you go, telling me about the fuckin' uniform again." Morrell let Finch's arm go and turned to Gold. He looked ready for a fight. Miranda seemed to breathe with relief as she raised her hand to rub the arm Morrell had been holding.

"Get the fuck out of here before I kick your ass back to your pretty little spaceship." Morrell gestured toward the Space Dock.

"I think you should calm down, captain."

"Fuck you!" Morrell stepped toward him. "*Lieutenant!*" he said, reminding Gold of his lower rank.

"Stop it!" Miranda called. She stepped between them. "It's fine," she told Gold. "I'm alright."

"Do that again and you won't be!" Morrell warned her with a hard stare. He turned to Gold, looked him up and down, then gave him a hard shoulder as he passed. Gold held his ground and took it. He watched Morrell return to the bar, then looked back at Miranda. She was breathing heavily and looked agitated. Scared.

"You alright?" he asked, reaching a hand to her shoulder.

She flinched away from him.

"Hey," Gold held his hands up in surrender. "I'm not Morrell."

She stared at Gold for a moment as though trying to gauge his sincerity.

"What happened?" Gold asked gently. "What'd he do?" He motioned to where Morrell had disappeared into the bar. "You looked pretty angry in there."

Miranda glanced around suspiciously. She looked back at Gold. "Not here."

Gold's brow furrowed in confusion, concern. He checked the area too. "What's going on? You in trouble?"

"Get me back to my apartment," she said quietly. "Please."

Gold studied her. Finch was scared. The usually confident reporter was scared.

"Alright," he nodded, then held his arm out to usher her forward.

He quickly slipped into the bar to tell Ryker he was leaving. Ryker was about to complain, until Gold motioned subtly to Finch waiting for him outside. Ryker suddenly broke into a smile, happy to bid him farewell.

They drove back to Miranda's apartment in her sleek black bubble car, barely big enough for the two of them. Gold drove. Miranda had fumbled with the keys and he noticed her hands shaking, so he took them from her.

She lived in the civilian zone on the south-eastern edge of the island, near the ocean. It was a nice apartment from the outside, but when they got inside he saw the reason why she was so shaken up. She'd been broken into, her place trashed. He looked around at the mess. Everything had been opened and tipped out. Even her underwear drawer. Whoever had done this, had also stabbed a knife into the kitchen bench and left it there, threatening.

"Shit," Gold said, looking at it.

Miranda looked uncomfortable and went to remove the knife, but Gold stopped her, catching her wrist. "Don't," he said. "Prints."

Miranda lowered her hand.

"Why do you think it was Morrell?" Gold asked her.

She hesitated, as though suddenly wondering whether she wanted to tell him.

"Relationship turn sour?" Gold asked.

"No!" she said adamantly. "You think I'd sleep with that asshole?"

Gold looked at her and shrugged, unable to stop the skeptical look that spread across his face. He recalled how friendly she'd been with him when they'd had drinks together before.

"Look, I *flirt*," Miranda said, looking offended, "but I don't sleep around."

"Alright." He held his hand up in surrender. "But why him? Why do you think this was him?"

"He wanted information and I wouldn't give it to him. It had to be him."

"What information?"

She eyed him again, unsure.

"Miranda, someone trashed your apartment," he said motioning to all that lay before him. "This isn't a joke. What the hell have you got yourself into?"

"I don't know," she said, walking over to her couch and slumping down.

Gold followed and sat opposite her on a single chair. They stared at each other for a moment, both waiting for the other to speak.

She ran her fingers though her hair, exhaling loudly. "I don't have anything concrete. I just have bits and pieces. Morrell wanted to know, but I didn't like his attitude. So, I told him nothing."

"Told him nothing about what?" Gold said, leaning forward, elbows on knees, hands clasped in front.

She glanced around her apartment, then met his eyes. "Captain Harris and the *Aurora*."

Gold felt his body still. "What about them?"

"He wanted to know what I found out in New Zealand."

"And?"

"You should know. You were there."

Gold stared at her, but said nothing.

"I accessed the local dock logs. I saw that the UNF *Carcharias* arrived shortly after the Eden incident."

Gold nodded to himself. "And?"

Miranda shrugged. "You tell me."

"Why does Morrell want to know?"

"I don't know. He hasn't said much. When I first spoke to him, the day you ran into us at Coco Joe's, I asked him in general conversation what he knew about the *Aurora.* He suddenly became interested and when I asked why, he said they were fish out of water and that things were starting to stink in FC." Miranda eyed him. "He said the same of you and the *Carcharias.*"

Gold nodded. "So? What happened in New Zealand? What does Morrell think you know?"

"Like I said, you tell me. You were there."

"*After* the incident," he said firmly. "Not before. Not during. *After.*"

"But you were still there. You were still called there, despite a contingent of UNF Earth Duty troops being present in the area. *Everyone* noticed," she told him. "After the incident, the local troops were shut out. Even the doctors. They wanted to know why this off-duty group of SD soldiers were given such control over the situation. Why this *captain*, this *mere* Captain Harris, was given control of what happened. Why you and the *Carcharias* went down there and were allowed to take over."

Gold stared back at her. He couldn't think of anything to say.

"So?" she asked finally. "Why is that? What did you see there, lieutenant?"

He gave her a soft smile. "You going to run another story?"

"No," she said unexpectedly, "not yet."

"Not yet?"

"I don't know," she said, looking at the trashed apartment. Her eyes returned to Gold's. "Something is going on here. Something big. I want to make sure I have all the information to hand before I do another story."

"But you already did one," Gold said, unable to hide the accusation in his voice. "I saw the news report with that PDP footage of Staff Sergeant Steinberg fighting that big guy."

"That footage was going to be aired whether I bought it or someone else did. That was a given."

"But you drew the line? Where?"

"Like I said, I spoke to the resort staff, I spoke to the local command hospital. I've spoken to people here in Fort Centralis. For his rank, Saul Harris is given a lot of leeway by FC Command. Why is that?"

Gold shrugged. "What makes you think he's given leeway?"

Miranda tilted her head slightly, analyzing him as if to gauge whether he was playing dumb. "His team rarely enter Command via the Tube. They enter through Quarantine. And even then, they bypass the security measures. Harris and his first lieutenant, they have access to secured areas. Sergeant Welles goes with them. And her children visit Command regularly. They are given access and privileges other soldiers don't have."

Again, Gold stared at her, but didn't say anything. He remembered bumping into Harris and his lieutenant at the same secured elevator that Rovine had disappeared into.

"They get more privileges than you, lieutenant," she said. "And yet wherever they are, you're following them."

Gold sat back in the chair, placing an elbow on the armrest and rubbing his jaw.

"So, what do you know, lieutenant?" Miranda asked. "I've shown you mine. Now show me yours."

"All I know is what you've just told me."

"I don't believe that."

He shrugged and looked her in the eye. "It's the truth."

"Do you know why Sergeant Welles has been given Sentinel protection?"

"No," Gold said, "I haven't had much to do with her."

"Her partner, the father of her children, was killed in an attack on her apartment."

Gold nodded. "First Lieutenant Walker."

"Yes. She's since moved. And after Eden, she received medical treatment. She was wounded badly in another, second, attack scene there, but it was kept from the press. I'm keeping that ace up my sleeve for now."

"Whoever they were chasing... as far as I'm aware, it's all over. There's no story to follow, Miranda."

She stared back. "I'm right though, yes? Something is going on here? Something big, in the background."

Gold motioned to her upturned apartment. "Yeah, I'd say there's something going on. And I'd say it's something you should be careful about pursuing."

"It's a little late for that warning, lieutenant."

"Lincoln," he said. "It's Lincoln."

"Lincoln." She gave him a nod. "Anyway, they wouldn't have found anything. I'm not that stupid. I keep my information secure."

Gold studied her. "I know you, Miranda. I know you well enough. You're always chasing a story. Why didn't you tell Morrell what you found out? Use it to exchange information?"

She thought for a moment, struggling with something in her mind. "I don't trust him," she eventually said. "There's something about him." Then added, "He scares me."

Gold's face softened. "Yeah, he scares me a little too." He gave her a gentle smile. She smiled back. "I think Captain Harris is a good man, though," he said. "I trust him."

Miranda stared at him.

"I don't know why," Gold shrugged, "but I do." He stood from his seat and looked down at her. "I don't know what's going on, but I think he's a good man. So, whatever story you're chasing... don't destroy him if you don't have to."

Miranda's face looked a little worn, childlike. "I know," she said quietly. "I get that feeling too. That's why I didn't tell Morrell anything."

Gold nodded, then looked around her apartment again. "You gonna call it into the MPs?"

"Yeah," she said.

"You should probably stay at a hotel tonight, too."

"Yeah," she nodded, glancing around.

"I'll wait while you call," Gold said, "and make sure you get to the hotel alright." He held his hand out to her. She hesitated, then took it and stood.

"Thank you," she said quietly. "I mean it. Thank you."
"No problem," he said.

4

Depth Of Vision

Harris awoke feeling as though his nose had been stung by a thousand bees. It felt swollen, but when he looked in the mirror it didn't look too bad, despite the wads of padding that were stuffed up there.

"I got a funny taste in my mouth," he said to Dr. Morgave, "and my throat's dry."

Morgave studied his patient through his black-rimmed glasses, then handed him a cylinder of water. Harris took a sip and swallowed, while another funny taste filled his mouth. He tried to pull a face, but then gasped as his nose hurt. He raised his hand and wiped it, collecting a small dribble of blood on his skin, despite the wads.

"Why does it taste funny? The blood?"

"Yes, captain," Dr. Elle Forcaster answered. She was the sensory expert they'd brought in to replace the original surgeon, who was now dead by suicide. Apparently, Forcaster had a history of consulting for the UNF, so she had the necessary security clearance to join the UNFASP medical team. She was attractive, with brown eyes and straight shoulder-length brown hair. Harris pegged her to be in her thirties, but it was hard to tell these days with cosmetic surgery so widely accepted.

"Keep in mind the receptor cells in your nose have been impregnated and enhanced with the virus," she told him. "Your nose and throat are closely connected. You will smell what you taste and you will taste what you smell."

"Really?" Harris asked, not sure he liked the idea of that.

"Yes," she smiled, her teeth looking like something out of a dentist's catalog. "Just like with your body, whatever you had before has been magnified. I'd suggest the funny taste could also be related to the padding we have inserted into your nostrils. They're scent free, but your nose will still identify a strange smell. And then there's the water you just drank. Your senses will be picking up all sorts of information from that."

"I can't wait until I'm near a garbage can or toilet," Harris said flatly.

Forcaster smiled again. "Thank your lucky stars I didn't wear perfume today, captain. *Then* you'd really know it."

He eyed her. "Well, thank you for that."

A knock at the door stole their attention. McKinley entered and he exchanged a look with Forcaster. The lieutenant had not yet met her.

"Dr. Forcaster, this is First Lieutenant McKinley."

"Lieutenant," she said, smiling. She held her hand out. McKinley obliged and shook it. "I've been looking forward to meeting you," she said.

"Yeah?" McKinley said.

"Yes, of course. Professor Sharley's number one prototype! You're the one I've modelled all the surgeries on."

McKinley glanced at Harris, then looked back at Forcaster and nodded.

"I've been going through your UNF Alpha file and I've studied the notes Professor Martin put together. It's nice to finally meet you in the flesh."

McKinley nodded again, uncomfortable with the focus being on him, then shifted his gaze back to Harris. "How you doing?"

"Good, I think. Right now I'm just tasting blood and cotton."

"Yeah," McKinley nodded. "It starts with the taste. Once your nose calms, the swelling goes down, and the drugs wear off, the smell takes over."

"But the taste remains?" Harris arched his eyebrow.

McKinley nodded. "They pretty much become one and the same in the end. The smell is the strongest feature, but the taste is there underlying it all."

Harris's face betrayed his lack of enthusiasm.

McKinley grinned at him. "You get used to it, sir. You'll have good days and bad days. Or should I say good smells and bad smells, but I'm not sure

I could live without it now. It's hard to explain, but scent is… information. It identifies people in ways you can't imagine. There're so many layers to it."

"Mm-hmm," Harris said flatly.

"That is so fascinating," Dr. Forcaster said, staring at McKinley. "Lieutenant, I would really love the opportunity to pick your brains." She looked at Harris. "Would that be alright, captain? Do you mind if I steal your lieutenant for a couple of hours one day?"

"Sure, if he's okay with it."

She looked at McKinley. "I'll buy you coffee, lieutenant," she smiled. "It won't hurt, I promise."

McKinley scratched his bearded jaw. "Yeah, alright. Not right now, though. I'm here to take the captain back to the ship."

Carrie sat on the couch in the Fortress's living room, rubbing her tired neck as she stared at the Space Dock.

"*It's getting late, Miss Welles,*" Archie said.

"Yeah," she said, "but I think I'm onto something here."

"*With which aspect of your research, Miss Welles?*" Archie asked. "*The Greenough location, the reports on mind control, or the link with Colonel Jesse who took Lieutenant McKinley out of juvenile detention?*"

"All of the above, Archie."

"*Well, it is late, you don't have to solve it tonight, Miss Welles.*"

She sighed. "No, I guess not." She dropped her hand from her neck. She had a burning desire to ask her father some questions, but he was long asleep. Archie was right, she needed rest if she was to be fresh for Harris's training in the morning.

"Alright, Archie, you win. I'm going to bed."

"*I think that is wise, Miss Welles,*"

"I need to switch my mind off, though. How about a little TV?"

"*It is on and waiting in your bedroom, Miss Welles. Which show would you like to watch?*"

"I don't know, Archie. What's on?"

"There's a British reality-com, a medical show, the news, a chat show, a police drama from the 2020s, a documentary about—"

"How about the news, Archie," she interrupted, not wanting a recital of every program on every channel.

"Yes, Miss Welles."

Carrie stood from the couch, working her neck and shoulders to relax the muscles, and stepped toward the window. She saw the dock lights, sparkling against the black of night, and glanced skyward, thinking about the Zetas, their ships, their thought-technology. She sighed and turned away, walking past the kitchen to the steps that led to her bedroom. As she moved, Archie turned the lights out behind her.

She entered her room and slumped down on the end of her bed to watch the Moon President, Mason Gillet, giving a press conference about plans for a second military base. It was to be located between the colonies of Meridian and the resort of Elysium, although slightly closer to Elysium. Naturally the people based in Elysium were trying to fight plans for the second base, stating that it would ruin the tranquility the resort offered.

Carrie sighed and shook her head. *If only they knew why...*

She studied President Gillet as he told the assembled reporters that the new base was necessary for man's progress in space. He state the military provided key support in preparing new locations for colonization, and in order to progress they needed more facilities to house the military, whose numbers were increasing in concert with the growth of space population. Elegant, handsome and assured, the President handled the questions from the press with confidence, managing to exude concern and care for the Moon's population while maintaining a strong front that this would happen, that it wasn't negotiable.

Carrie suddenly wondered if the President knew about the signals. Now the UNF was charging ahead with their plans for defense, would they have needed the agreement of the space leaders to do so? Apart from the Moon's President Gillet, there were also the heads of the space stations, known as 'Ministers'. Up until now, the two Mars colonies had been run by the UNF, but according to another news report the UNF was calling for elections to be held, stating that it was time for the Mars colonies to be led by a President of the people. Carrie wondered what had sparked the decision to finally hand over the running of Mars.

"Back to matters on Earth..." the female newscaster announced, launching into a story about the last oil reserve on Earth, now dubbed 'Noah's Well'. Carrie felt a sense of déjà vu. She recalled seeing a news story on this when she'd been waiting for the Darwin debrief hearing, and she'd seen a few reports on it since. Although the courts had ruled the reserve to be under Australian jurisdiction, it would seem multiple objections had been submitted arguing against the ruling, which could mean years of legal debate. Carrie studied the map that came onscreen, showing the size of the oil reserve, its location off the coast of Western Australia, and the boundary line for international waters which cut off about a third of the reserve from Australian territory. Several countries based in the Indian Ocean in those international waters were staking a claim on that oil.

Carrie sighed, her eyes wandering away from the location of the oil reserve to the coast of Western Australia, perched close to the disputed area. Her eyes traced down the coastline, reading some of the labels on the map: Exmouth, Ningaloo Reef, Shark Bay, Geraldton, Perth. The map disappeared from the screen and the newscaster came back on, but Carrie zoned out. She lay back on her bed, that map of the Western Australian coastline sticking in her mind.

She was trying to relax and remove herself from thoughts of the Zetas, but those two news stories had just yanked her back in again.

Gold smiled confidently and gave a nod as Captain Rovine left the ship for a meeting at Command. As the door slid shut, he turned and headed back to the mess hall to speak to his team.

"Ryker!" he called, and Andy looked up.

"Yo!"

"I think it's time the team moved their butts a little, don't you?

"Yes, I do!" Ryker said, understanding the call to action. He began rounding up the troops and ushering them to the door to head for the ship's gym.

"C:Drive," Gold said, pulling him aside.

"Yeah?" Sergeant Stevens said, fixing his bright blue eyes and wide ears on him.

"That portal problem I've been having…" Gold said, as the team disappeared through the door into the corridor, leaving the two alone. Gold eyed the empty doorway, then turned back to C:Drive. "We've got about an hour to give it another try."

C:Drive nodded. "Yes, sir!" he said then jogged out of the room.

Gold followed, feeling his muscles tighten. He was close, he knew it. He thought of Miranda's trashed apartment, wondering what Captain Morrell had been hoping to find.

If it had been Morrell.

Whatever it was and whoever it was, Gold was determined to beat them to it.

Carrie left the twins in the *Aurora*'s mess hall with Sampson and Novak while she hit the training facility. When she entered, she saw the team on the gym equipment, and approached McKinley.

"You got a moment?" she asked, then lowered her voice a little. "In private."

He eyed her, then stood from the weight rack he'd been working on and they began to move away from the team.

"What is it?" he asked.

"Not here. Weapons Store," she answered. He eyed her cautiously, but followed. He swiped his pass, and they entered, then she hit the button to slide the door closed.

"Trying to get me alone, sergeant?" he said as a smile curled his mouth.

She flashed one back. "Dream on."

He chuckled. "I bet you dreamt about me." He stepped forward sliding his hand over her waist, but she raised her hand to his chest and pushed him back.

"Cameras," she said.

His eyes flickered to the corner of the room, then back to her. "They get erased every 72 hours if nothing out of the ordinary happens." He moved to kiss her, but she stopped him again.

"And if something happens?"

He stared down at her with his piercing eyes.

"What was the full name of your Colonel Jesse?" she asked.

"What?" he said, taking a step back.

"Colonel Jesse," she said. "The one you told me about in the bar that time. The one that took you out of juvey. The one that got you to sign up for the army. Was it Colonel Robert Jesse?"

McKinley studied her. "Why?"

"Because I came across his name while doing some research. Colonel Robert Jesse, my father tells me, was one of very few Earth Duty soldiers included in the briefings on that first signal. He was at the UNF Space Duty Leaders' Forum in Poland where my father was supposed to give that protest speech... Until they killed my mother and threatened me, that is. The majority of those at the briefing who knew about the signal were Space Duty soldiers, but there were representatives from Earth Duty present and Colonel Robert Jesse was one of them."

"So, what does that mean?" His brow furrowed.

"Depends," she shrugged. "Was that your Colonel Jesse?"

McKinley nodded.

Carrie's face softened. "It means he knew about the signal when he recruited you."

"But what does that mean?"

"He knew about the signal and he was at that meeting in Poland, which means he knew the suggested response was UNFASP."

"What, you think... all that time, he knew?"

She gave him a sympathetic look. "I've done the timings. My mother was killed about a year before he took you out of juvey and convinced you to enter the army. He knew about the signal. UNFASP was off the table at that time, but he must've figured it was only a matter of time before it was thrown back on. He knew the UNF was going to need soldiers."

"Not for years, though."

"No. But he knew, back then, that at some point they were going to have to start working on the program again. He was going around and recruiting as many people as he could. He found you, he liked you, and he got you fast-tracked into the army."

McKinley slowly paced, staring at the ground as his mind churned.

"I spoke to my father this morning," Carrie told him. "He said Jesse was one of those that voted yes to the program. He wanted it put into play."

"That doesn't mean..." McKinley's voice had faded, his eyes searching the room.

"My father said that even after the program had been put on hold, the UNF had begun ramping up their recruitment drives. I researched it. There was a spike in recruitment afterward. The intake doubled. Colonel Jesse knew about the signal and the proposed program and it was his job to recruit."

McKinley stopped pacing and looked at her. Carrie stepped closer to him.

"I think you were picked for this program way before I ever was. Sharley chose me, but he only came into this a few years back. Jesse handpicked you years ago."

"Nah." McKinley shook his head and frowned. "He was just getting me out of juvey and into the army."

Carrie's shoulders softened as she watched him examining the two bands around his right wrist: the silver one and the leather woven one. The bands he'd received on that trip to Myanmar with Colonel Jesse. The moment, he'd said, that had turned his life around, that had changed his life forever. How right he'd been.

"It can't be..." he said quietly.

"I thought you'd want to know. No more secrets, right?" she said.

He nodded, then glanced over at the door, before returning his eyes to hers. "Almost."

"Almost?" she asked.

"We're still hiding behind closed doors."

She exhaled softly. "It's too soon."

He stared at her.

"He's only been dead coming up to nine months now," she said. "The team needs time—"

"The team? Or you?" he challenged.

She couldn't answer him.

"It's funny, Welles," he said. "You don't seem to have a problem inviting me into your bed every night, but come daylight you steer clear of me. What's that about?"

"I don't steer clear of you."

He continued to stare at her, his eyes a little accusing.

"The team aren't ready—"

He gave a short, sharp laugh. "Nope, not buying it."

She studied him, wondering if he was grabbing hold of this issue to distract him from the last one.

"Just a little longer," she said softly.

He stared back but didn't respond. Instead he walked past her and left the store.

Harris made his way through the corridors of Command to Colonel Marchant's office. It was an odd experience to walk past people and smell a seemingly infinite rainbow of scents: a coalescence of body odor, breath, perfume, aftershave, oil, sweat, coffee, cigarettes, gum, hairspray, gel and cosmetics, mixing with smells coming from the building like disinfectant, window cleaner, polish, dust, glue... hell, even the metal of the elevators had a scent. In truth, it was making him feel nauseated.

Marchant's aide, smelling of things Harris couldn't quite discern, ushered him through to the colonel. He noted a waft of coffee, perhaps some aftershave, and something food-based that, again, he couldn't quite pick. Harris made a note to visit people before meals in the future. At least, until his stomach could handle it.

"How's the nose?" Marchant asked. "Looks a little swollen."

"It's getting there. Slowly," Harris said, unable to hide his displeasure.

"They say it takes a while to lock down the scents," Marchant said sympathetically. "It's a good thing you did it first to give yourself time to work on it."

"That's not why I chose the nose first," Harris told him.

"Oh, yeah?" Marchant asked curiously.

"We were trialing this new sensory expert of yours. If she was going to screw up, I decided I could live without my sense of smell, but I could not live without my eyes or my ears."

"Fair point. But she passed?"

"It would seem so."

"Good. Who's under the knife today?"

"She's doing Murphy and Brown today. Gregson's decided to go last again, so he's on hand to help with the others."

"So, the noses will be done by the end of the week."

"Yes, sir," Harris nodded.

"What next?"

"Next, I'd like a visit to the mothership. And I'd also like to take a trip to Station Navarone."

"And why's that?"

"I saw President Gillet's press conference on the Moon's second military base. He's working in conjunction with senior officers on Station Navarone. As Navarone is currently our biggest military base in space, I think it's time we start spending a little more time there. Yes?"

"Agreed," Marchant said. "They're also handling the plans for our new superstation and our roll-out to increase fortification of existing sites."

"Who's leading it?"

"General Berger is the official senior officer overseeing it all, but Colonel Hensford of Station Navarone is handling the day-to-day running of things."

"I'd like to meet with Hensford," Harris said.

"I'll arrange it."

"Thank you. If you could arrange the tour of the mothership, let me know when we can head out there."

"Will do. It may take a few days to liaise with the Egyptian authorities."

Harris eyed his superior. "Tell me, colonel, who else besides President Gillet knows about the signals?"

Marchant stared at him.

"He wouldn't just agree to a second military base without wanting to know the reasons behind it," Harris said. "How long has he known? If he was pals with Professor Martin, he knew."

"He's known for a while," Marchant conceded. "We needed someone we could trust presiding over the Moon, someone to help steer our space colonies in the right, and safest, direction."

Harris nodded, his memory flashing back to his brief meeting with Gillet when he'd been searching for the AWOL Welles on the Moon. "I see you've also announced elections for Mars?"

"Yes. The UNF has other matters to attend. It's time we handed Mars over to another trusted source to take care of the administration."

"And which candidate are you going to back in that race?"

Marchant studied him for a moment, as though contemplating whether to tell him, finally saying, "Apparently Charles Mortimer has expressed a strong interest."

"Mortimer?" Harris said quickly. "The owner of the All-Station franchise?"

"Yes," Marchant said simply, then shrugged. "He has a head for business and he has a lot of influential allies, including President Gillet. He also has a lot invested in our human settlement in space, given the spread of his All-Station chain. Should he succeed, we think he'll be compliant with the UNF in order to protect his assets."

A puppet on the UNF's string, Harris thought as he sat back in his chair. A whiff of his own scent suddenly spiked in his nose, perhaps in reaction to the Alpha rising slightly within. "And Regan Lotz?" he asked. "The owner of the Space Mart franchise. The one whose company leased out that lair Sharley used on Meridian to hide Welles. How does he fit into things?"

"He doesn't," Marchant said simply. "Although I've heard through the grapevine that he plans to challenge Mortimer for Mars President."

Harris stared at Marchant, his mind ticking over.

"Lotz has established his franchise across the space stations and on the Moon," Marchant told him, "and he's trying to establish the business on Mars. It's an obvious step for him to take. Mortimer still has the larger stake of space business in total, but Lotz has been creeping up on him."

"And if Lotz wins the presidential race?"

"He won't," Marchant said confidently.

"He won't?" Harris arched an eyebrow. "You're going to rig it so Mortimer wins?"

"The UNF can't rig anything, Harris. We will show our support to all candidates. But we ourselves have voting power too, don't forget."

"What does that mean?"

"It means that Finn Harkowitz has also signaled his intention to run. Finn, the son of ex-soldier Gentry Harkowitz, the man who founded the first successful space station."

"And if Lotz or Mortimer pips him at the post?"

"Then we welcome whoever it is and tell them what they need to know. If the UNF can't get our preferred candidate in place, then we'll work with whatever we got."

Harris clenched his jaw a little. "How many people know about the signals? I want to know just how far it goes."

Marchant shrugged. "Within the UNF, it's selected colonels and above, plus you and your team."

"And Captain Rovine," Harris said.

"And Captain Rovine of UNF *Carcharias*."

"And outside the UNF?"

"President Gillet and some of those who've worked on UNFASP. And some of those who've begun on AWAFP, our Advanced Weapons and Fleet Program."

"Which could be hundreds."

"Working on the programs, yes. But very few know the real reason why we're deploying them."

"And aside from President Gillet, any Earth leaders?"

"Very few. Only those where the ships have been found. The rest are ignorant. Not even the ministers of the various space stations know yet."

"So, why Gillet?"

"Because the Moon was our first settlement of a landmass in space. It was always referred to as Earth-2 by the UNF, and it was always going to be a stronghold, a support for Earth. We need a strong military force there that can scramble to defend our space stations when needed. Scrambling help from Earth, as you know, would take too long."

"What's Mars, then? Earth-3?"

"Yes. It has the potential to be Earth's back-up for life support. While the Moon acts as an orbiting stronghold, Mars will eventually be a place of mass colonization. We've given the go-ahead to commence terraforming it as soon as possible. Just in case. The domes won't be sufficient in the long term. Especially if those Zetas hit. We need to make it livable and sustainable in the long term."

Harris nodded, realizing he still had a lot to get his head around. His mind had been so focused on Sharley and his Jumbos that he'd been blind to the bigger picture. He needed to tour the military space stations as soon as possible; he needed to meet with Colonel Hensford and President Gillet; he needed to inspect the Zeta mothership; and he needed to get his team to their full Alpha capacity.

"Any word from the *Barbican*?"

Marchant hesitated. "Not for a little while."

"That normal?"

"They're a long way out in space, Harris."

"You didn't answer my question."

"We're expecting contact from them soon."

Harris eyed the colonel for a moment, aware of a scent spike from the man. He wondered what it meant. Fear? Panic? Stress? He stood from his chair, a little frustrated that it would take some work to interpret the heightened sense abilities.

"Let me know when you've arranged the visits, sir."

Miranda Finch walked down a corridor of offices at Universal Press HQ, a cylinder of spiced coffee in her hand, on her way to meet with Bob Franklin, the editor-in-chief. She sipped her coffee, the hints of cinnamon tickling her tastebuds as she savored the flavor before swallowing. She didn't get much sleep last night but was feeling a lot better after a tough session of taip-ga, the mutant exercise program bred from tai chi, pilates and yoga.

She approached Bob's assistant Kendra Suto, aka the Fox. She'd gained the nickname for a variety of reasons: she was attractive and took care of herself, the 57 year old out-styling most 20 year olds, but mainly she was very intelligent and cunning. Some said most of Bob's success came from his gatekeeper, Kendra.

"Kendra," Miranda greeted her.

"Miranda," she smiled back. The two women weren't friends by any stretch, but they did respect the other's success. "Take a seat. He'll be with you shortly."

Miranda took a seat on a plush lean-back chair and pulled out her PDP. She started searching through her emails and saw one from the insurance company relating to her break-in. She'd filed a report with the MPs, but as there had been no prints or DNA left at the scene and no witnesses, no arrests had been made. The MP she'd spoken to at the time of filing hadn't seemed that interested in it. He told her that as she was a reporter it was probably bound to happen sooner or later. In other words, that's what she should expect for poking around.

Knowing this, she had done her best to avoid Captain Morrell since. Although she had to admit, despite her dislike and fear of Morrell, she never thought he would stoop that low. She thought he was smarter than that, given he was the lead Earth Duty soldier on FC.

She heard a little *ding* sound and looked up at Kendra who smiled and motioned to Bob's door.

"He'll see you now, Miranda."

Miranda made her way to Bob's door, taking a sip of her coffee.

Entering, she saw Bob at his desk, surrounded by monitors and studying the one that displayed the stock market.

"Made your millions today yet, Bob?" she asked.

Bald, pudgy and mustached, Bob looked up at her. "Not yet," he said flatly.

"Well, it's only 11 a.m.," Miranda said. "The day is young."

"This is true." Bob turned his focus to her. "How's things? I heard about the break-in."

Miranda stared at him, figuring he must've heard through his extensive grapevine. Besides, Centralis wasn't exactly a big place.

"Alright," she shrugged. "I'm fine, really."

"Yeah? So, what was it about? I hear nothing was stolen, but they tossed your place pretty good?"

She nodded. "I guess someone doesn't like the questions I'm asking."

"Where are we at with the follow-up story on the Eden incident? I was expecting that last week."

"It's not something that has a deadline, Bob. It will take as long as it takes."

"But are you any closer to knowing what it was about? UNF soldiers don't engage in a rumble like that. It was freaking brutal. That big guy, Steinberg? He used to be a Sentinel for some top UNF brass. The link's gotta be with him, right?"

"I don't know," she said, thinking it unlikely. "Maybe if it was just him fighting, but they were all in it. It was definitely a targeted attack, but probably not him specifically. Pretty much the whole team was treated by medics after it was over, and two of the team wound up in the hospital. If there was a target, I'd say it was them because they were most badly damaged."

"Them?"

"Sergeant Carrie Welles suffered the worst injuries. Her fight happened away from the scene caught on those PDPs. She was in a different battle alongside First Lieutenant McKinley and Captain Harris."

"Yes," Bob's eyes narrowed in curiosity, "and what else have we found out about our intriguing captain?"

"I'm still working on it."

"But there's something, there has to be. Centralis Command giving him authorization to take control of things down there in New Zealand? I mean…"

"I agree. It's very unorthodox to give a captain such pull. It seemed very black ops to me. No-one outside of the *Aurora* or the *Carcharias* was privy to much detail."

"And how are investigations going with the *Carcharias*?"

"I'm in touch with Lieutenant Gold. He hasn't given me anything yet, but I think he will in time. Once the trust is built."

"Good. Keep working on it."

"I will," she said, smiling.

"Go make an appointment with Kendra to see me again in a week or so with an update." He motioned for her to leave and turned back to the stocks.

"Sure thing." She rose from her chair and headed for the door. As she reached it, she stopped, however. "Bob?" she said, something niggling her.

"Yeah." He looked over.

"What happens if I uncover something big?"

"What do you mean?" he asked. "If you uncover something big, that means we sell it and make a lot of money."

"But what if I uncover something big that pisses off the UNF if we release it?"

Bob stared at her, not quite comprehending the problem. She saw the dollar signs in his eyes.

"Am I going to be used as the fall guy?" Miranda asked cautiously. "I mean, I know how these things go, right? You get my scoop and I'll be asked to take the heat, while you stuff my pockets and chop me from the team."

"Miranda…" Bob said, trying to find the right words. "Look, if it came to that, you'd be handsomely rewarded for your trouble."

Miranda stared back at him.

"And," Bob added, "you'd also be known as the reporter who broke a big story. That's a nice piece to add to your CV, don't you think? Maybe net you an award or two."

Miranda nodded at him, picturing herself receiving an award for her brilliant exposé.

"But first," Bob said, a firm look in his eyes, "you gotta bring me that story."

Miranda gave another nod, then left the room with her spiced coffee in hand.

Harris looked at Hunter for confirmation, and his pilot gave him the thumbs up.

"Permission to disembark at your leisure," Hunter called.

His new co-pilot, Frazer, grinned. This was the first space flight he'd done with the *Aurora*, and things had gone well. Then again, the day and a half trip to Station Navarone wasn't exactly a difficult one.

"This ain't a leisure trip," Harris said flatly, reminding them they were on business.

McKinley stood from the chair beside him. They exchanged a glance as Harris moved past him toward the flight deck stairs and the team followed.

It had been a while since Harris had been to Station Navarone. Given it was the largest military station in space and housed thousands of soldiers, he hadn't really had a need to attend. The *Aurora* had always been a mobile unit, cruising around to wherever they were required to be. The 'space knights in shining armor' types, helping out those in need and capturing those on the run.

They walked along the docking chute that extended from the ship to the main concourse of the station. The station itself was basically rectangular in shape, consisting of many levels, the top and bottom levels jutting out further than the rest as a protective measure; they became a lip, or shelf, shielding the layers in between. Basically, it looked like a giant sandwich, albeit one surrounded by a whole lot of guns and other defensive weaponry.

"Where to first, sir?" Brown asked, as they poured out the station end of the chute, which had been scanning and clearing them as they walked. Had they been carrying unauthorized weapons or any biological warfare agents, the end of the chute would have sealed, keeping them inside. The chute technology was the next generation of the Tube technology in place at Command on Centralis. Given Harris and his team were now Alphas, the scanning should've been of concern to him, but thankfully Colonel Marchant had cleared them a path. Colonel Hensford, after all, was privy to UNFASP.

"McKinley, Gregson and I are going to check in with Colonel Hensford, who runs this place," Harris said. "While we're doing that, I want the rest of you to take a walk around and become familiar with the station if you're not already. No doubt we'll be spending some time here in days to come."

Carrie looked up from the screen in front of her. It showed an image of the strange curved and gnarled tree, running almost parallel with the ground, that she and Harris had been dreaming of.

"Yes, Archie?" she said.

"A visitor has arrived. They are speaking with your Sentinel, Sampson."

"Do you know who it is?"

After a brief pause, Archie responded. *"According to the UNF database, it is Dr. Ricardo Scavesci."*

"Scavesci?" Carrie asked, feeling a strange sensation wash over her. "What's he doing here?"

"He wishes to see you. He has something for you."

"He the shrink?" her father asked, sipping a cup of tea at the opposite side of the dining table.

She nodded. "He doesn't normally make house calls though."

"Sentinel Sampson would like to know if you wish to see him. Should he let the doctor proceed?"

Carrie nodded. "Yeah. Send him up." At the very least, she was curious.

"You want me to disappear?" her father asked.

"No, it's fine," she said, closing her wafer-thin perspex datatop.

"Welcome, Dr. Scavesci," Archie greeted him. They heard the buzzing clank of the front door unlocking, and Carrie saw the portly Scavesci enter. Dressed as he always was in dark trousers and a white button-up shirt, his UNF security ID was pinned to the pocket of the shirt. He adjusted the square glasses sitting on his face as he saw her.

"Sergeant Welles," he smiled in greeting, the gray bristles of his beard moving upward.

"Dr. Scavesci," she said. "This is a surprise."

"I hadn't seen you in a while and I was going past so I thought I'd pop in," he said. "You've been so busy on the *Aurora* lately, but I hear they've gone to Station Navarone. And you stayed behind."

"Yeah." Carrie studied him. The Fortress wasn't really on the way to or from anything. Although it *was* close to Command. "The twins haven't been cleared for space travel yet, so we stayed here."

Scavesci nodded and looked over at her father.

"Colonel Welles, Dr. Scavesci," Carrie introduced them.

Scavesci stepped forward and shook the hand of her father, who had stood to meet him.

"Colonel," Scavesci said. "It's always an honor to meet an Original."

Her father gave a brief nod in acknowledgment.

"We only have one left in service now," Scavesci added.

"Yeah, Major General Ventnor," her father said.

"Indeed. You've kept in touch, I take it?"

Her father considered his response. "We're more acquaintances than friends."

"I see," Scavesci said, then glanced around. "You look like you've settled in, Sergeant Welles."

"Yes," Carrie said, glancing around too. "It's alright."

"And the children?" he asked. "Where are they?"

"Taking a nap."

"Oh, that's a shame. I would so like to see them."

"It took me a long time to get them down to sleep, I'm not waking them up for anybody. I don't know how much longer they'll take these naps, so I want to enjoy it while I can."

"They are growing up fast."

"Yes, they are," she said.

A moment of silence passed where no conversation was exchanged. Carrie looked at her father, then back at Scavesci, fighting herself to offer him coffee. She didn't want him to stay longer than needed, but she didn't want to be rude either. Technically, Scavesci hadn't done anything wrong that she knew of, other than treat her nemesis Sharley and keep him alive, that is.

"Would you like some coffee?" she asked, dragging the words a little.

"Well, thank you," he smiled, "but, unfortunately I can't stay."

"That's a shame," Carrie lied.

"I did, however, want a quick *private* word," Scavesci said, darting his eyes to Carrie's father. "If I may?"

Carrie nodded to her father.

"I'll go check on the Sentinels, then," the colonel said.

They watched her father leave, then Scavesci stepped closer to her. He pulled an envelope out of his pocket and held it out to her.

"What's this?" she asked.

"Open it."

Carrie narrowed her eyes at him, then took the envelope. She saw her name handwritten on the front, then flipped it over and opened it. A letter was inside, and as she unfolded the pages, she saw it was roughly written with a child's crayon.

"It's important you read it," Scavesci said. "He wants you read it."

"He?" Carrie asked, flipping through the pages to see who had signed it off.

Sharley.

She glared at Scavesci. "Are you kidding me?"

"Why don't you just come and see him?"

"Are you kidding me?" she asked again, her eyebrows leaping to the top of her forehead, feeling the Alpha within awaken.

"You won't come to see him. He has no choice, but to resort to these letters."

Carrie's eyes skipped over some of the words in the letter, then she looked back up at Scavesci. "Have you read this? You condone this?" She held the letter out.

"I don't condone the contents of the letter, but I do condone the process of him writing that letter and getting his emotions out."

"Are you *kidding* me?" she asked again, her voice rising in volume.

"He needs a release, sergeant. He is full of Jumbo rage and obsession, and a whole raft of psychological issues. If we let him bottle that up, it will build and build until he explodes. I'm trying to treat him. This," he pointed to the letter, "is poison, but it is also therapy. He needs to get it out. Right now, if you won't go to see him, this is the only release he has."

"So, let him write then. Why do I have to see these?"

"Because he needs to know that you're listening to him. He needs to know that you're paying attention. Ignoring him will only make matters worse. The more you ignore him, the more he wants to kill you."

"Oh, so this is *my* fault?" Carrie clenched her fists, scrunching the letter within as she felt her inner Alpha rear up.

"I'm not saying that," Scavesci held up his hand in a placating manner. "I'm just saying that you're not helping the situation. He's very troubled—"

"So, this is about him and what he needs! What about me? What about my children? What about what *we* need?!" Carrie's face flushed warm with her raised voice, the Alpha anger breaking the surface.

"I assure you—" Scavesci began, but he was cut off by Archie's voice.

"I believe that is enough, Dr. Scavesci. It is time for you to leave."

Scavesci looked up to the roof, eyes darting around. "Excuse me?"

"You are upsetting Sergeant Welles and that is not acceptable. Please leave."

"I beg your pardon?" Scavesci started to argue.

"You have three seconds," Archie warned, and began a countdown.

"I'm just trying to talk to you," Scavesci held his hands out in a calming manner.

Movement through the window over Scavesci's shoulder caught Carrie's eye. Roy and Sampson were racing up to the house with her father in pursuit. Archie must have warned them.

"Miss Welles?" Roy and Sampson burst through the door, guns in hand, and walked toward them. The Sentinels moved to stand either side of Scavesci.

"Please escort Dr. Scavesci from the premises," Archie told them. *"He is not to return until Miss Welles permits it."*

Her Sentinels moved up to Scavesci and grabbed his arms.

"Alright, alright!" Scavesci said, holding his arms up in surrender. "Just *please* think about another visit. Help me to help you!" he called out, as Roy and Sampson escorted him from the building.

"What the hell was that about?" her father asked, darting glances between her and Scavesci being led away.

"Nothing," she said.

"Your AIS doesn't seem to think so."

"*If you would like,*" Archie said, "*please place that letter in this waste receptacle.*" A small portion of the wall by the kitchen bench suddenly opened and a compartment slid forward. Carrie walked over and examined it. "*Anything deposited in there will be incinerated, Miss Welles. That might be the best place for that letter.*"

Carrie looked up at the roof. "You read it? How?"

"*This house has many sensors and scanners, Miss Welles. As you flipped the pages I scanned and deciphered the scrawl. Those words are not from a sane man.*"

"Let me look at that." Her father reached for the letter with a scowl on his face.

Carrie swiftly held the letter out of reach. "No."

Her father stared at her, as both he and Archie silently waited.

"Just... just leave me alone. Everyone!" Carrie said, stalking toward her bedroom, letter in hand.

5

Questions And Answers

Harris and his two lieutenants sat in the waiting room of Hensford's office. The area was relatively small and bare: metal flooring and walls, with long windows punched in to view the walkway outside. He stared at the UNF Space Duty logo on the wall opposite him, inhaling the scents of the room and trying to analyze those of his two lieutenants beside him. He concentrated hard on separating and identifying each one. And he could. *Just.* Above the smell of the Space Duty uniforms and natural body scents, Harris could detect what he identified as the slight scent of rubber gloves, of sterile disinfectant. That, he knew, was Gregson. Every day the medic had to clean the *Aurora*'s hospital and keep it sterile. Harris could smell the gloves he'd worn earlier that day, the disinfectant he'd used, and even the soap he'd washed his hands with after.

McKinley carried the scent of metal. Harris knew he'd worked out in the gym earlier, and he could smell the powder and the metal still on his hands from the weights he lifted. And the smell of the guns; McKinley and Murphy had done some work in the weapons store, and Harris could identify the gun metal on him. He smiled to himself. Scent really was information. But he knew both McKinley and Gregson, knew what they did for a living. Who knew whether he could be so accurate on strangers.

"Captain Harris?" Hensford's aide called from behind his desk. "Please go through. He'll see you now."

Harris gave a nod and stood, following the pointing arm to a doorway on his left. He walked through to see the colonel, his back turned, standing before another long window and staring out of it. There seemed to be an open, empty space beyond, as the colonel looked down at a lower level of the station.

"Colonel Hensford," Harris said, as McKinley and Gregson moved to stand either side of him.

Hensford turned around and took them in for a moment. He was balding, but his face had few wrinkles, and as he looked back at Harris, he smiled broadly. Hensford walked over and held out his hand.

"Gentlemen," the colonel said, shaking Harris's hand, "you are a sight for sore eyes." He moved to shake hands with Gregson, then McKinley, as he gave a laugh. "I gotta say you're giving me a boner!"

McKinley dropped the colonel's hand.

Hensford laughed again. "Don't worry, soldier, I don't want to fuck you. But I have to say," he said, moving back to give them a once-over, resting his hands on his hips, "I'm fucking glad to see you. Alphas… *Goddamn Alphas. Finally*!"

Harris exchanged a glance with his two men.

"I've been waiting a long time for the UNF to get their shit together and get this moving. Finally they've done it." He shook his head in awe, eyes shining with excitement. "*Damn*, you look strong. Are they all your size?"

Harris glanced at his two soldiers again, then looked back at Hensford. "Pretty much."

"Good. Because we might have war coming and there'll be fighting to be done."

"Yeah," Harris said cautiously, his inner Alpha feeding a little off the colonel's excitement, "but we Alphas are only good if those things come out of their ships and fight us hand to hand. If they have hands, that is. We're no good if they blow our ships up before we get that chance."

"No," Hensford agreed. "That's why we're building the superstation, fortifying the fuck out of everything we have, and improving our fleet. The ships of today will be scrap metal come crunch time. Like I say, we've started working on all of that. Ships, guns, you name it."

Harris nodded. "So I'm told. That's what this visit is about today. You're going to show us what you got planned."

"Damn straight." Hensford motioned toward a series of chairs placed before his desk. "Take a seat and let's get to it."

Harris and his men moved to sit down as Hensford communicated with his aide out front, ordering some coffee. The colonel paused mid-order, however, and looked back at the three of them. "Do you like coffee?" he asked. "Or do you take something different now?"

Harris exchanged another glance with his men, before looking back at the Colonel again. "No, coffee is fine. We're still humans, sir. Everything else about us is the same."

Hensford studied them, then gave a nod. "Of course."

Lieutenant Lincoln Gold was on his third attempt to search Captain Rovine's portal. C:Drive and Ryker were starting to doubt him. Maybe they were starting to worry about getting caught. The more they did this, the riskier it was. Gold had already thought about the consequences though. If they were caught, he would take the fall and say that he forced the others to do it. Whether it would stick was another matter.

He looked at his watch. He figured he had about another 30 minutes before he had to get out. So far in his searches, he'd just literally taken a look around, opening various folders and drives, but he hadn't stumbled across anything of interest. Now he was at the point where he was going to have to search keywords. This meant C:Drive would have more work to do in clearing up after he exited.

But what to search? One word immediately came to mind. *Aurora*. He typed it in, then waited a moment. Suddenly the screen beeped as items began appearing on the screen. There were various logs from their time on Mars, Meridian, Centralis and Eden – all of which would, of course, refer to the *Aurora*, given the *Carcharias* had acted as their shadow-ship. He noticed two other folders appear alongside the series of logs, however. The folders appeared as shortcuts to drives he had not yet seen in this portal. One folder was titled UNFASP, the other ALPHA-1-AURORA.

He tapped the screen to open the second of the two folders, curious as to what Alpha-1 meant. Another beep sounded, and a box appeared asking for a seven key password.

"Shit," Gold muttered. He then tried to open the UNFASP file, and the same thing happened. He studied the screen as a strange feeling washed over him. His heart was racing a little, his hand shaking slightly. He knew he'd found what he was looking for. Now he just had to get inside.

His hand darted out to the intercom. "C:Drive!" he called. "Come find me. Now."

Colonel Jeffrey Welles sat in the cafe, sunglasses on, enjoying the warmth of the sunshine. He sipped a coffee, checked his watch, then scanned his surrounds again. He saw Aiden Ventnor approaching. Dressed in civilians and sunglasses, his hair had grayed rapidly with the passing of time.

"Jeff," he said as he reached his table.

"Aiden," he replied.

Ventnor signaled a waiter and took a seat beside him. Colonel Welles smiled at the fact that neither had wanted to sit with their back facing the park. Both had opted to sit with their backs to the hedge behind them. *Old, paranoid habits die hard*, he thought.

"Here's the thing," Ventnor said, looking at him. "I don't see you for years and years, then suddenly you're becoming a regular, popping into my office to inquire about your daughter's unit, then inviting me out for a coffee."

"Just catching up with an old acquaintance," Colonel Welles said lightly.

"Yeah," Ventnor smiled, "that's not your style, Jeff. You don't do shit for the sake of it. You were always lean and precise with your time."

Colonel Welles shrugged. "I'm a grandfather now. I've had to learn how to slow down."

The waiter arrived and took Ventnor's order, then swiftly left.

"I don't picture you playing the grandfather," Ventnor said.

Colonel Welles gave a laugh. "Well, neither did I. But you know how I am with family." He dropped his smile. "I feel very strongly about them."

Ventnor stared back a moment, then gave a nod. "Yes. I know you do." He glanced out at the park before them, at people walking dogs, running, playing with children. "Greene was a fool to think he would get away with it."

Colonel Welles stared at Ventnor but didn't respond. They knew. They all knew he'd sought his revenge on Greene for ordering the hit on his wife. They just didn't have the proof to nail him for it. Ventnor was right when he said that Welles was lean and precise. Greene was a coward, paying someone else to do his dirty work. As soon as Colonel Welles had found out who had ordered the hit, he personally sought Greene out and killed him, brushing off his sharpshooter skills and nailing the man with one to the head. Although he'd wanted to do it more personally than that, face to face, he was smart enough to seek his revenge in a way that made it difficult to find the killer.

Colonel Michaels, who had supported both Welles and Strasser in their bid to slow down the program, had pushed to put the program on hold due to the deaths. Colonels' Linecutte and Ventnor had been neutral parties who'd agreed things had gone too far, and supported Michaels' motion. Colonel Harbourg, who had been on Greene's side in pushing forward with the program, had no choice but to agree. It was clear he wasn't happy about it, but his hands were tied.

The waiter returned with Ventnor's drink.

"You ever see Clint around?" Welles asked Ventnor, referring to Colonel Harbourg, one of the four Originals who remained alive, along with the two of them and Michaels. The latter, Welles had heard, was working as a private security contractor now.

"Harbourg's around," Ventnor said, sipping his drink.

"So, you see him?"

"No. He's somewhat of a recluse, I'm told."

"A recluse?"

Ventnor studied him from behind his sunglasses. "Why the interest?"

"I'm making conversation, just catching up with a fellow Original."

"No, you're not," Ventnor said. "You invited me here to shake me down for information. Cut to the chase."

Welles shrugged, glancing out at the park. "I'm just wondering if there's anything going on that I should know about? It seems anything relating to the UNF tends to relate to my daughter in a roundabout way these days. As

I said before, I have a keen interest in looking out for my daughter, and now my grandchildren."

"Well, as a current member of the UNF, you realize that I can't tell you a hell of a lot, Jeff."

"Well, let's call it a favor then."

"A favor?"

"Yeah," Colonel Welles looked at him. "I know you claimed you were neutral, Aiden, but I know Greene got in your ear. I know at the next vote he'd persuaded you to vote yes. Then my wife got killed, then Greene got killed. That's the only reason you agreed with Michaels to shelve the project for a while. Otherwise, you were going to vote yes."

"What's my vote got to do with it?" Ventnor's face hardened a little. "That vote wasn't about you, Jeff. It was about the potential fate of the Earth. I, too, have family here I'd like to see protected."

"I know," he replied, "but you lied to my face, and you fueled Greene's ambition. You know it." He looked out at the park for a moment. "You and Liz used to come to our house for dinner, for god's sake," he said quietly.

Ventnor's face fell. "If I'd known he was going to hit Sue, I would've stopped him. I never would have agreed to that!"

"But you see where I'm coming from. You owe me something. And you're going to give it to me. To appease your guilt over my dead wife."

"Give you what?" Ventnor's brow furrowed angrily.

"Information."

"What information?"

"I don't know yet. But when I do, you'll give it to me. Or if something comes up that you think I should know, you will tell me."

Ventnor stared at him.

Colonel Welles decided to elaborate. "For instance, Dr. Scavesci came by the Fortress the other day with some sicko letter from Professor Sharley. I want to know what he's playing at, and what that means for my daughter and her children. If he's conspiring with that nutjob to hurt them... well, you know what I'll do," he said. "I want you to watch them... Scavesci and Sharley and anyone else who might be a risk, and I want information. Anything that helps keep my daughter and her children safe... for Sue's sake."

Ventnor stared back at him.

"Understand?" Colonel Welles said, as he stood. He shot back the rest of his coffee and threw some money down on the table. "Coffee's on me." Then he turned and walked away.

Carrie woke with a sheen of sweat across her forehead. She sat up. It was early morning and she was in bed. She stared at the wall opposite her, thinking about her dream. It had been of Colt. She was hiding in the shadows, both terrified and terrifying. It left Carrie with a sick feeling in her gut and a sense of dread hanging over her shoulders. The sick was guilt. Guilt that Carrie was alright and Colt was not. The dread was for the fear that as they had not yet found Colt's body, that she could still be alive. But if she was, she had to be a prisoner somewhere. Colt would not disappear from her family like that. If she was still alive, then she was being kept somewhere. And that thought alone made Carrie want to tear the place apart to try and find her. But where did she start? The UNF had searched and found nothing, and there had been no hits for her face on the FRS.

"Another bad dream, Miss Welles? Your heartbeat is slightly accelerated, your body heat has increased, you're sweating, and there is a strong mix of pheromones in the air."

"Archie, stop studying me," she said. "You freak me out when you do that."

"It's my job to do that, Miss Welles. Your health is directly aligned with your safety. It is a security measure."

Carrie sighed, still staring at the wall ahead. Her eyes fixed on the slight grooves in the walls running along both vertically and horizontally for various lengths. When she'd first moved in she had thought it was just a decorative pattern in the walls of the building, but after seeing that compartment pop out yesterday – the incinerator for the letter – she was starting to think otherwise. Did these grooves indicate secrets of the Fortress she did not yet know?

She got out of bed and moved over to the wall, tracing her fingers along the lines, pressing here and there to see if she could get anything to move.

"Miss Welles?" Archie asked. *"Are you looking for something?"*

She glanced up at the ceiling. "Yes," she said. "Your secrets."

"No-one can uncover my secrets, Miss Welles. Not even you. That is part of my security. They are only revealed when necessary. Some are less classified than others, but there is no need to show you until they are required."

"It unnerves me that you can do any number of things that I don't know about, Archie. How do I know you're not going to melt down and trap me in here?"

"Impossible, Miss Welles. Remember I am designed to protect you, not harm you. Even if there was a chance of my systems malfunctioning, I have the ability to shut myself down."

"But what if you can't shut yourself down in time?"

"Then the other AISs will step in and take control."

"The other AISs?"

"Yes. There are five AISs currently in existence. There is myself, of course, dedicated to you. Then there is Benedict, who serves Colonel Marchant, Wilfred who serves General Berger, Josiah who serves Lieutenant General Wilton, and Eugene who serves Major General Ventnor. We are the five prototypes deployed."

"'Prototypes' sounds like something still being refined, Archie."

"No, Miss Welles. Wilfred was the first, and one by one we have been rolled out. I was the last, so any minor issues that were raised have been fixed, I assure you. We are considered so successful that they have begun work on programming more AISs to join our ranks."

"So how do they shut you down if you lose control? Did they build in a back door? I don't like the idea of other AISs tapping into you either?"

"We AISs have what's called a support network. We are linked to each other, although for the most part, these links stay dormant. We are required to send status reports regularly to confirm that we are working as we should, but other than that we do not communicate with each other unless necessary."

"Why would you communicate with each other?"

"If one malfunctions, one of us will attempt repair or shut down the other if required. An AISs delegate, such as yourself, may also request that we communicate if necessary."

"Have any of the other AISs tried to communicate with you?"

"Not as yet, no."

"And have any needed to be shut down or repaired so far?"

"Not as yet, no."

Carrie stared at the wall, her fingers still resting in one of the grooves.

"Miss Welles, please believe me when I say that your safety is paramount. I am here to help you. I mean you and the children no harm. This house and my Artificial Intelligence System is the most superior offering of protection there is."

Carrie nodded to herself, looking away from the wall and back to her bed. She felt a sudden pang of remorse and guilt for Doc, wondering if she'd moved into the Fortress sooner whether he would still be alive today. There would've been no way that Chet and Logan could've broken in. Her apartment in the civilian sector had been an easy target.

But that thought made her chest tighten even more. Because if Doc had still been alive today, then where would that have left McKinley?

Harris, sitting in a room with McKinley, Evenssen and Brown, buttoned up his shirt as Dr. Morgave moved away to record his results. The team, having just landed back in Centralis from Station Navarone, were getting their regular check-up to see how they were handling their relatively new Alpha status. Harris's results were good, which meant he could turn to getting the next sense done.

He smelled Forcaster's perfume before she entered the room.

"Afternoon, gentlemen," she said. "How are the noses doing?"

"Good," Harris said, "although your perfume is rather strong."

"How far away could you smell me?"

"Right down the corridor," McKinley said.

Harris smiled in admiration. "I only got you by the door."

"It'll improve with time once it's fully healed and you learn to use it properly and differentiate the scents." She turned to McKinley, watching as Morgave placed white discs across his torso and studied his heartbeat.

"Sounds like a strong heart to me," Forcaster said.

"Yes," Morgave agreed.

"Has it been traveling well over a period of time?" she asked, stepping forward to check the results over Morgave's shoulder.

"Yes, it's remained steady. There's been no indication of weakening or the general physiology degrading in any way. He's strong and he's staying strong."

"I can see that," she smiled, motioning to McKinley's torso. "It's impressive, lieutenant." McKinley glanced at her, then darted his eyes to Harris and the others who smiled. Forcaster moved over to Harris then and checked his results.

"Captain," she smiled, "you're doing well also."

"That's the plan, right?" he said.

"It certainly is." She placed his e-file down, then moved to Evenssen. "Have you gentlemen been having any headaches as a result of the stronger sense of smell?"

"A little," Harris answered for them, "but McKinley told us that was to be expected."

"Yes," she said to Harris, then glanced around to McKinley again. "Speaking of which, you promised me a coffee last time we spoke, lieutenant. I want to pick your brain. Do you have time today before you leave?"

McKinley looked at his watch. "Maybe next time."

"I won't keep you too long, I promise," she said. "I suspect it may take a few coffees to pick all that knowledge from you."

Brown chuckled, and Forcaster looked at him. "Something funny?" she asked.

"Yeah," Brown said, "McKinley being full of knowledge."

McKinley grinned at Brown and flipped him the bird.

"Now, now, gentlemen," Forcaster said with a flirty smile, "I promise to pick all your brains eventually. There's no need to be jealous."

Harris exchanged a smile with Evenssen before he slid off the table and reached down to grab his bag. "I don't know about you guys, but I got a pregnant wife to see."

"What?" Morgave pivoted around, as did Forcaster, alarmed looks on their faces. His men stared at him, shocked. All except McKinley, that is.

Harris shrugged at them. He guessed now was as good a time to let the cat out of the bag as any. "Don't panic." He held his hand up to Morgave. "It happened before I became an Alpha. It's human."

"No shit?" Brown looked at him.

"No shit," Harris said.

"Congrats, Captain." Evenssen smiled warmly.

"Thank you."

"My man!" Brown held his hand up and Harris received the clap of congratulations.

"Nice one, cap," McKinley said with a glint in his eye as if he already knew.

Harris gave him a nod. "Anyway, if you're done, Dr. Morgave, I'd like to get home to my wife."

"Yes," Morgave nodded, "you're free to go."

"Speaking of kids, I'll come with you," McKinley said, getting to his feet.

"Captain!" Forcaster stopped Harris. "We'll have to record the details of this child you understand?"

"Yeah, I figured you might," he said, then hiked his bag over his shoulder and left with McKinley in tow.

Dr. Scavesci sat opposite Sharley at the small table in his cell. He glanced at the long glass corridor wall to make eye contact with the two guards outside. They both stood by the doorway, ready.

"Did you give her the letter?" Sharley asked, eyes bright with excitement.

"Yes, I did."

"And? Don't keep me in suspense."

"She scanned it, but we didn't get to chat much."

"What do you mean? Why?"

"Archie kicked me out."

"And who is Archie?" Sharley asked.

Scavesci paused. He probably shouldn't have mentioned him. "Her new guard."

"Oh, Sentinel Roy is no longer with her?"

"Yes. He's still there as well."

"Why did this Archie kick you out?"

"Because Carrie had become upset at your letter."

A smile slid across Sharley's face. "Good. It's about time she felt some of my pain. You said she scanned it. Do you think she read it properly?"

"I have no idea. But I left it with her, so..." He shrugged.

"Good."

"I also mentioned that she should come to see you."

"And?" His eyes lit up again.

"I'm not sure she will."

Sharley's smile slid away. He turned his face to stare at the floor. Scavesci watched him carefully. The professor's face was still, but he could see the calculation in his eyes.

"What if," Sharley turned back to him, "you bring me the children instead?"

Scavesci moved uncomfortably. "Well, I don't think—"

"They're my children."

"No, professor. We've discussed this. They are not your children."

"They *are* my children. And we have indeed discussed this, doctor. They may have Walker and McKinley's DNA, but it's I," he pointed to his chest, "who impregnated her. I brought them to life."

"Professor," he said as Sharley stood and began to pace. "Professor, if you want to get technical about things, it was actually Bradford Chet who impregnated her. Wasn't he the one to perform the insemination?"

Sharley stopped pacing and looked at him. "At my order."

"But, *physically*, he was the one to do it."

Sharley moved slowly over to him, then leaned down. Scavesci darted his eyes to the guards. "At. *My*. Order." Sharley said emphatically.

Scavesci held up his hand. "Alright. Okay."

"So, you must bring them to me. Every father must have visitation rights."

"That's not going to be easy to arrange."

"I don't care."

"Professor, the children rarely leave her side, and certainly not the Sentinels' side."

"I don't care."

"If she won't come and see you, do you really think she'll let the children come?"

Sharley turned his dark eyes back to him, "I. Don't. Care," he enunciated, then suddenly broke into a big beaming smile. "I appreciate your efforts, Dr. Scavesci, I really do. I mean, look at me?" He held his arms out to display his body. "Look how well I am doing! And that is all thanks to you."

"Well, thank you, professor. I am very pleased with how well you're doing." Physically, Sharley had never looked healthier, he'd been gaining weight and muscle, but Scavesci was unconvinced about the health of his mind.

"How much longer do I need to stay in here?" Sharley said, sitting opposite him and clasping his hands together on the table.

"For the time being."

"I would so love a window to look outside."

"I'm sure you would, professor, but unfortunately we can't move you just yet."

"Why not?"

"Because you need a secure, safe, environment."

"But Command is so large."

"I understand, but currently this is the most suitable facility for you."

"Will you ask General Berger for me?"

Scavesci stared at his patient, trying to find an answer to give him.

"I've been good. You said so. All I ask for is a window. So much time has passed in here. I've missed winters, summers. I may be Jumbo, but I am still human, doctor. At least give me yard time under escort. Just think how the fresh air and sunshine would heal me."

Scavesci held his hand up. "I'll ask," he said. "All I can do is ask."

"Thank you, doctor. And in the meantime you'll bring me the children, yes?"

Scavesci studied his patient for a moment, then slowly stood, glancing at the guards, who were ready to open the door for him.

"I'll see what I can do," he said as he left.

Harris stood in the kitchen of his house in Detroit, arms wrapped around Taya.

"Yeah?" he asked her.

Taya nodded and smiled, looking up at him. "It's confirmed. We got a little girl on the way."

Harris smiled. His great-grandma, grandma and mother – his Overseers – had been right. Or maybe he had. He was the one who had dreamed of holding a baby girl in his arms. His little girl who would inherit the family gift. He had mixed feelings about it. He didn't want his daughter to have to carry this burden of the knowledge the gift could bring, but at the same time, he knew how it might just save her life, or that of someone else. And knowing what he did about the future, his daughter might just need a little foresight on her side.

"So?" Taya said. "You've got nothing to say?"

He smiled. "There is nothing to say. Except I'm happy."

"Yeah?"

"Yeah. That, and I'm going start polishing my weapons for when she starts dating."

Taya laughed, moving away from him. "You didn't for Ty, so you won't for her either." She stopped and looked back at him. "Well, maybe one weapon. Just in case."

Harris grinned. "Speaking of Ty, am I going to get to see him this visit? I'm starting to forget what he looks like."

"Yeah," Taya smiled, "that's what he says about you."

"I've been out earning money to put clothes on his back and food on his table."

Taya held up her hand to stop him. "Really, you two can sort this out."

"Sort what out?"

"This," she said. "This distance that's growing between you two. It's only going to get worse as he gets older, Saul. Two damn males vying for dominance."

Harris huffed in protest. "I work away, what can I do about that? I come back and he's out with his friends."

"Just try and make time."

"I will if he will."

"No, Saul. *You* make time for him. *You* be there for him, and he'll want to spend time with you."

"You make this sound like it's my fault."

"No," she shook her head, "but you're the adult. Ty thinks he's an adult, but he's not. So you're the one who needs to take the higher ground and set the right example."

Harris stared at his wife. Her posture softened and she wrapped her arms around his waist, her small pregnant belly pressing into him. "Time makes you a stranger, Saul," she said softly. "And this?" She pulled back and studied his new physique. "Makes you stranger still." She looked up into his eyes then. "Close the gap now. That's all I'm saying." She leaned closer, hugging him tight. He lowered his face and kissed the top of her head.

"I'll do what I can."

*

Harris sat in the stands, alone. It was halftime and Ty had left to go chat with friends. Harris could see them on the far side of the basketball court. He knew one or two were Ty's school friends, but the rest were unfamiliar. Some of them were dressed in Pistons' gear, but the rest were dressed like any other kid their age – all trying to look tough.

Harris waited the entire halftime for Ty to leave his friends and return. He had to focus hard on keeping his Alpha anger in check. Here he was trying to spend time with his son, but, first chance he could, Ty left him. They'd barely spoken through the first half. Harris had tried to make conversation, but Ty was so focused on the game he simply grunted or gave one word answers.

Harris was trying to be patient. *Very* patient.

By the time the game was over, however, Harris had managed to settle his anger. They stood from their seats.

"Let's go get a bite, huh?" Harris said.

"Nah, I'm cool," Ty said. "I'm meeting up with the guys."

Harris saw him motioning to the crew he'd been chatting with at halftime.

"This is my last night of leave, Ty," Harris said, arching his eyebrow.

"That's a'right," his son said. "I'll catch you next time."

"No."

"What?"

"I said, no." Harris looked at him firmly. "It's game night and we always go out for a bite afterward."

"Well, I can't tonight." Ty shrugged. "I got plans."

"Ty, you're always making comments about how you never see me. I'm trying to spend time with you here."

"I'll have dinner with you next time," Ty said. "What's the big deal?"

"The deal is that I'm trying to spend time with you. *Son.*"

"Well..." Ty looked around awkwardly, "I'm with the guys tonight."

"You came out tonight to watch a game with your old man, not them."

"So? We watched it. It's over."

"No, now we're going to have a meal."

"Says who?"

Harris looked around at the other spectators leaving the stands who were darting them glances.

"Move your ass, we're going," he said, then turned to follow the crowd. After a few steps he looked back to see that Ty hadn't moved. He turned back to him.

"I told you no," Ty said as he approached, his brow slightly furrowed, his mouth pouting slightly like a child. "I'm going out with the guys tonight."

"Ty."

"No!" he said stubbornly. "You can't just come back into town and demand that we drop everything for you."

"I'm not asking you to drop everything. I'm asking you to have dinner with your father."

"And I will. Next time." Ty moved to walk past him, but Harris caught his arm.

"What the hell is wrong with you?"

"What the hell is wrong with you?" Ty shouted, yanking his arm away. "I have a life too, you know. You can't just come back whenever you like and expect me to do what you want. I'm not one of your damn soldiers! The whole world doesn't revolve around you, you know."

"I have restricted leave. I don't have a choice on the timing, Ty."

"Well, that's too bad then! Coz I got plans." With that Ty turned and stormed off.

Harris stood still as a statue, staring after him, trying very, *very* hard to control the Alpha within.

LeFroy paused at the sound and his head turned to view the entry to the lair. He saw the door handle turning. He darted his eyes back to Colt, who grasped the bars of her cell, eyes wide with what he could only assume was fear. Was Drazen finally returning?

The door creaked open slightly. LeFroy waited for someone to enter, but they didn't.

"D—Drazen?" he asked.

The door creaked open some more before a man finally appeared. It wasn't Drazen. This man looked to be in his early 60s, slightly overweight and wore a blue baseball cap.

"You're not Drazen," LeFroy said.

"No. I'm not," the man said, his face devoid of emotion. "I'd like to know where he is, though." The man entered the room followed by two enormous acquaintances, perhaps bodyguards. Or perhaps friends of Drazen. They looked like they would fit right in with the men that Drazen had been with when he left.

"Who are you?" LeFroy asked.

"Who are you?" the man threw back, coming to a stop as he spied Colt in the next cell. "And who the fuck is she?" He looked at LeFroy and noticed the chain running from his ankle back into the second cell. "What the fuck is going on here?"

"You know Drazen," LeFroy asked. "Do you work for him?"

The man stared at him for a moment, then burst out laughing, along with his two burly companions as they exchanged glances.

"You got it the wrong way around," the man said. "Drazen works for me."

"You're the one who's been dropping the food down the chute?"

The man's eyes scanned the room and paused when he saw the chute's closed door. "No, but the woman who has, led us to you."

"You don't know where Drazen is?"

The man's eyes caught on the three pictures of female soldiers on the wall. He moved over to get a good look at them, then glanced at the calendar and the big red cross.

"Who are they?" He motioned to the pictures, darting another glance at Colt. "That you?" He pointed to her picture on the wall. She didn't answer.

"They're Drazen's targets," LeFroy said. "Or perhaps they're your targets, if Drazen works for you."

"Whatever he was doing here, he wasn't working for me," the man said, then looked hard at the two prisoners. LeFroy was surprised that Colt hadn't uttered a word as yet, but he could see her mind turning over, trying to work out if this man was friend or foe. The truth was, LeFroy was wondering the same thing.

"You didn't order the hit?" LeFroy asked.

"On them?" The man hiked his thumb toward the women on the wall.

LeFroy nodded.

"Why'd he want them dead?" the man asked.

LeFroy wasn't sure what to say. Would he get in trouble with Drazen if he talked?

The man glanced at one of his companions, a tall, beefy redhead, who pulled out a knife and stepped toward LeFroy.

"I don't like asking questions twice," the man said.

"He was following Sharley's orders," LeFroy said, glancing at the knife in the redhead's hand. "Y—you don't work with Sharley?"

"Sharley?"

"Professor Raymond Sharley. He used to work for the UNF."

"The UNF?" The man's gaze paused on LeFroy's face.

LeFroy nodded. "But Drazen worked for you, too?"

The man looked at Colt. "So, Drazen caught this one, and he's now out catching the other two?"

"I—I think so," LeFroy said.

"You think so?"

"He's been gone for some time. I expected them back a while ago."

"Them?" The man's eyes were grimly focused on LeFroy like circles of gray metal.

"Drazen and his companions."

"How many 'companions' did he have?"

"Five."

The man pulled a PDP out of his jacket pocket and stepped toward him. "This them?" LeFroy studied the pictures the man showed him. He nodded. It was the Monsignor, Meat, Hexus and Hazus, and Bakur.

Suddenly Colt thrust an arm through the bars. "You have to get me out of here!" she yelled, startling them. "They kidnapped me! They've held me prisoner for months. Let me out! Let me out now!"

The man moved up to her cell. "Why does Sharley want you?"

"Because he's fucking crazy that's why!" She grabbed at the man, but the redhead stepped forward and knocked her hand down.

"Don't!" LeFroy said. "Don't hurt her! She's pregnant."

"GET ME OUT OF HERE!" Colt screamed.

The man held his finger up to his mouth, indicating for her to be quiet. Colt's frenzied eyes stared at him like he was crazy.

"Is she some kind of sex slave?" the man asked LeFroy.

"No, she's just a vessel for what she's carrying."

"And what is she carrying?"

LeFroy suddenly knew that *now* he'd said too much.

"I asked you a question," the man said.

"Will you let us go if I tell you?"

The man glanced at his second companion. A Hispanic man with two prosthetic fingers and a gold grille in his mouth. He stepped forward and suddenly LeFroy was kneeling on the ground gasping for air, a swift punch to the gut having put him there.

"I asked you a question," the man said again.

LeFroy looked up to see the gold grille just centimeters from his face. "She... she's been impregnated with Jumbo children."

"What?" the man said, a deep furrow of confusion across his face.

The Hispanic man grabbed LeFroy's hair and yanked his head back.

"She's part of an experiment," he wheezed. "UNFASP. But it's off the books."

"UNFASP?" the man said stepping closer. "Did you just say UNFASP?"

LeFroy nodded. The man walked up to Colt and studied her carefully, running his eyes up and down her physique.

"What's your name?" he asked her.

"Fuck you!" Colt spat. "You let me out of here and I'll tell you."

The man turned to LeFroy. "What's her name?"

Colt widened her eyes in threat at LeFroy not to say anything, but the boot of the Hispanic man convinced him otherwise.

"Corporal Sabrina Colt," he groaned, holding his gut again.

The man turned and moved back to the pictures on the wall. "And who are they?"

Pain piercing through him, LeFroy caught his breath. "Sergeant Sarah Packham and Sergeant Carrie Welles."

"Welles? *Carrie Welles*?"

LeFroy nodded. "You know her?"

The man didn't answer. He scanned the lair again as his jaw hardened. "Someone tapped into my fighters," he muttered, his clenched jaw turning into a sardonic grin. "Son of a bitch," he shook his head. "They tapped into my fighters."

The man turned and headed for the exit.

"Wait," Colt yelled. "You can't leave us!"

The man paused and held his finger up to his mouth again. "Keep screaming like that and I'll have Savoy tear out your voice box. Understand?" he told her, motioning to the redhead and his knife.

"Are you going to leave us here?" LeFroy knew he sounded pathetic, but he didn't care.

The man looked at him. "For now. But do as you're told, and you'll stay alive and unharmed."

He headed for the door and his two companions began to follow.

"Wait!" LeFroy called. "Wh—who are you?"

The man stopped and glanced back at them both.

"You can call me the Greenback."

6

New Faces, Old Secrets

Major General Aiden Ventnor strolled with his pooch Mindy along the path that curved around the Centralis coastline, looking for any indications that a storm might be building. It was relatively windy and he was wondering whether the weather shield might be deployed over the island today.

Mindy paused to sniff some shrubs, forcing Ventnor to stop. He looked out over the choppy sea and inhaled deep breaths of salty air, then glanced at his watch and realized it was nearing 6 a.m. He needed to get moving, but saw Mindy was now busy adding some of her own scent to the shrub. He sighed, then suddenly noticed a man standing further up the slight incline to the road, looking down at him. It wasn't a casual glance. The man was blatantly staring at him.

Ventnor squinted his eyes to try and get a better view of who it was. Then suddenly he realized he knew who it was.

"Holy shit," he whispered. "Clint Harbourg."

*

Ventnor eyed Clint Harbourg up close. He'd put on a little weight since he'd last seen him and his face had a slight pink flush to it. He'd been enjoying retirement, by the looks of it, indulging in plenty of food and booze.

"Clint," he greeted him.

Harbourg gave a nod, a well-worn blue baseball cap shading his eyes.

"It's been a while," Ventnor said, keeping a grip on the leash as Mindy tried to explore. "To what do I owe this pleasure?"

"Business," Harbourg said, his eyes steely. He was obviously pissed about something.

"What business could you possibly have with me?"

Harbourg gave a bitter laugh. "Someone stole my fighters."

"Excuse me?" Ventnor said, tugging Mindy's leash.

"Let's cut the bullshit," Harbourg said. "You know what I do for a living now. You all do. And you let me do it because you know I could possibly provide a back-up plan for the UNF. I know that. I'm not stupid. But I *am* a businessman. And if you think you can steal some of my best fighters, get them killed, and not reimburse me for them... well, we've got ourselves a problem."

"What are you talking about?"

"You know exactly what I'm talking about!"

"No, Clint. I don't."

"The Eden incident. It was all over the news. They were *my* fighters. And they were fighting someone else's battle."

Ventnor stared at Harbourg. When he'd read the report of the men who had attacked the *Aurora* team, he'd had his suspicions. He didn't know exactly what Harbourg did now, but he knew it was something to which the UNF turned a blind eye. Something to do with an underground fighting ring, something about Harbourg training brutal fighters.

"Why would your men be fighting someone else's battle?" Ventnor asked.

"Because someone poached them."

"Well, it wasn't me."

"No, it was Professor Sharley. Heard of him? He bought one of my fighters in the past, Mattieus Logan. And he'd paid a fee to 'loan' my guy Drazen. I wasn't letting that one go for good. But it seems he paid Drazen a whole lot more to lure some of my other fighters away for a private job. So, I want to know why? Who were they targeting in Eden?"

Ventnor sighed. "You know I can't tell you."

Harbourg stared at him. "How the hell did Jeff's daughter get involved?"

"How did you know she was involved?" Her name and the second fight scene had been kept from the press.

"Apparently she was one of the targets."

"And how do you know that?" Ventnor pushed, knowing the *Aurora* files were locked on a Level 4.

"I just do."

Ventnor tugged Mindy back again. "Well, I *just* can't tell you."

Harbourg took a couple of steps forward to stop right in front of him. He'd always had a menacing presence about him and now, years later, he still had it.

"I want my money. You tell General Berger that." He moved to walk away but stopped. "In fact, you tell General Berger that I want *in*."

"In on what?"

"UNFASP."

Ventnor stared back at him, wondering how the hell he knew all this.

"It's back on the table, isn't it?" Harbourg asked. "*Finally*."

Ventnor didn't answer him.

Harbourg nodded to himself. "I rewatched the Eden footage. My fighters were a lot stronger than when they left me; and it goes without saying that so were the soldiers they fought. The UNF has moved forward with the program." He shrugged, glancing around. "If you need guinea pigs to use in the experiments, I have a good stock of fighters the UNF could use. For a price."

"I don't know what you're talking about," Ventnor repeated.

Harbourg laughed. "Yeah, you do. I'm an Original just like you, Aiden. I was there at the start. You can't hide this from me. The UNF has the program in motion, and by the looks of it, it's gaining speed." Harbourg's face suddenly fell. "Are those things going to hit us earlier than we thought? Has there been an update?"

"I don't know what you're talking about," Ventnor repeated, his face a mask.

Harbourg gave him a hard, cold stare. "You always were a fence-sitter, Aiden. Isn't it about time you chose a side?"

"I have," Ventnor told him. "I chose the UNF's side."

"Majority rules!" Harbourg laughed again and shook his head. "Well, it's about time those cowards did the right thing for the people of Earth." He looked at their surrounds, then gave a big sigh. "Well, I gotta go now, Aiden. You be sure to tell General Berger what I said. I want reimbursement for my lost fighters and I want in on UNFASP." He shrugged. "They were obviously going to cut me in eventually, so they might as well do it now."

"You can tell Berger yourself."

"No," Harbourg shook his head. "The general doesn't want to be seen with me."

"Neither do I."

Harbourg laughed again. "You sure you don't want to earn some extra money, Aiden? I got a good fighter in the next bout. Great odds."

Ventnor called to Mindy, tightening her leash, then turned and began to walk away.

"One more thing!" Harbourg called.

Ventnor turned his head.

"How the hell did Jeff's daughter get caught up in this? Don't tell me he swapped sides?"

Ventor didn't answer.

"You make sure he knows I had *nothing* to do with the attack in Eden, you hear?" Harbourg pointed at him. "Last thing I want is to end up in his sniper's sight like Greene did."

Pulling on Mindy's leash again, Ventnor turned and walked away.

Gold stared at C:Drive. "Fourth time is a charm! I ever tell you that was my number when I played football?"

"Number four?"

"Yeah," Gold said, "and that's why I know you can do this C:Drive. Fourth try, let's get in."

"What the hell you think UNFASP stands for?" the sergeant asked. His blue eyes and sticking-out ears had earned him the nickname Dumbo in school, but Gold made a point of making it C:Drive on the ship to accentuate where the sergeant's talents lay.

"It's UNF something," Gold said. "And that's all we're going to know until you get me in there, C:Drive."

"Alright, let me get to it. How long you think we got this time?"

Gold checked his watch. "I'd say we've got 50 minutes." C:Drive had tried to break the code last time, but they'd run out of time, and it had been days before Rovine left the ship again and they'd been given another chance. Either way, Gold would be patient. Now he knew which folders to crack, he would keep on it. He'd been itching to have another try since they'd failed last time. The three key words circled his mind constantly: *Aurora*, Alpha, UNFASP.

He began to pace the comms room while C:Drive worked, thinking about those three words as he absentmindedly swung his arm as though throwing a forward pass. He reflected on the things he had witnessed in the Hell Town dungeon on Mars, of his time roaming the streets of Meridian, the search of the locked-down Fort Centralis for Corporal Colt and two babies, and the things he saw in Bali and Eden. Especially Eden. The image of the *Aurora* team sitting on the porch of that villa – bloodied, bruised, sweating, like wounded animals, ready to keep on fighting if need be. Then he recalled the image of the wounded Harris approaching him, glancing at the bodies on the ground, almost as intrigued as Gold himself. The look Harris had given him, like he wanted to say more, but couldn't.

"Whoa!" C:Drive exclaimed. "I got it! I got it!"

Gold spun around, surprised that he had cracked it so quickly this time. He scooted up as C:Drive opened the folder, but Gold quickly reached forward and placed his hands over the screen.

"C:Drive, if you don't read it, they can't punish you," he said. "Let me look first. That way I'm the only one putting my neck on the line."

"What do you mean?" he said. "I hacked the captain's portal and I cracked the file. You think they're going to believe that you did this?"

"It doesn't matter. I can claim I ordered you, forced you to crack it. They can question you, but it won't take them long to figure out you didn't read what's in here."

C:Drive stared at him, eyes searching his as he thought things over.

Gold stared back. "Just let me read it and see if it's worth risking your career for. Let me do this for you and Andy, please. I promise I'll tell you if it's worth it," Gold assured him.

"Alright," C:Drive nodded then stood, glancing at the screen. "I'll go keep watch with Andy."

"Thank you," Gold said, and watched him depart. As soon as he was alone, he dropped his hands from the screen and sat in the chair C:Drive had vacated. There was a whole spread of documents in the Alpha-1-Aurora folder. Each crew member of the *Aurora* seemed to have at least one document named after them, and there were several other documents on the team in general. He checked the dates on each and selected the most recent one: Alpha-1-Aurora-Olfaction.

The document opened and Gold scanned it quickly. It was a report on a series of surgeries the *Aurora* team had undergone on their noses. A lot of it was medical jargon, but he saw a few words that triggered his curiosity, along with his heartbeat that seemed to be echoing loudly in his ears: *Alpha virus, UNFASP, experiment, success, biologically engineered weaponry...*

"Biological weaponry," Gold whispered, picturing the *Aurora* crew sitting on that porch in Eden again.

His eyes trailed over the document, falling on that 'UNFASP' word again. He read the sentences around it. The olfactory surgery looked to be part of a series of sense surgeries these things called Alphas were going to undertake. These Alphas were products of UNFASP. He looked at the title of the folder again: "Alpha-1-Aurora". This meant the *Aurora* team were these things called Alphas. But exactly what that meant, he didn't know.

He ran his hand over his mouth, stroking his jaw a moment, before stretching out his hand and hitting the intercom.

"C:Drive! Report back to the comms room."

A minute or so passed before C:Drive came jogging in, "Sir?"

"I need you to crack that UNFASP file."

"You read the other one already? You found something?"

"Not yet," Gold lied, "but I think I need to start with the UNFASP folder first."

Carrie slowly awoke and stretched out, her skin sliding along the warmth of McKinley who lay beside her.

"Morning," she whispered, looking over at him.

He was propped up on the pillows, Sharley's letter in hand.

Carrie sighed. "It was a mistake showing you that, wasn't it?"

He looked at her, then back at the letter. "This isn't curing him. It's making him more delusional. And *dangerous*."

Carrie reached for the letter, but McKinley whisked it away.

"Hey," she said, sitting up, rubbing her eyes.

"I'm going to have a fucking word with the good doctor."

"No!" Carrie said.

"Then Harris needs to," he said. "This has to stop!"

"It will," she said, "as soon as I incinerate it."

"Until he sends you another."

Carrie stared into McKinley's fiery blue Alpha eyes. She couldn't argue that point.

"Archie," McKinley said, eyes darting up and around a little awkwardly.

"Yes, Lieutenant McKinley."

"If Scavesci or anyone else tries to deliver another letter like this, you stop them, alright. What you did, kicking him out. That's good. Do that every time. But faster. Understand?"

"Yes, lieutenant. If Sergeant Welles agrees."

McKinley looked at her. "I thought he takes instruction from me?"

"Only if I'm unable to give instruction," she smiled. "Now," she said, snatching the letter out of his hands, screwing it into a ball and throwing it on the ground, "let's turn your mind to other things."

"Other things?" McKinley said, checking his watch. "We're gonna be late. Harris will kick our butt."

"We've got a few minutes," she said, sliding her body onto his.

He groaned loudly as he looked at her naked body on his, then glanced at his watch. "Yeah, okay, I think we can fit that in." Then he took hold of her and flipped her over onto her back. "But this time," he smiled down at her, "I'm on top."

Lincoln Gold closed down the files and stood, a little shaky, from the comms console. He stared at the floor, unseeing, his mind frozen, trying to get his thoughts to break through the ice wall of shock. The UNF were experimenting on their soldiers. The *Aurora* team were already part of the experiment. The *Carcharias* was on a small list to join them.

And Captain Rovine knew.

He closed his eyes, feeling the sweat building on his forehead. He tried to force his mind to think, but all he could see were the anatomical drawings in that file of larger, stronger bodies, of animal senses with increased abilities. And then there was all the mechanical stuff; what looked to be the next phase of the program. After they'd merged the enhanced humans with the animal senses, next, they would merge them with robotics.

Humans + animals + machines = Alphas.

And the *Carcharias* soldiers were lined up to be next.

And Rovine knew. *Goddamn Rovine knew...* He was going to offer them up like guinea pigs.

He exhaled heavily and leaned forward on the desk to gain his breath. What the hell was he going to tell the guys? He needed space to think. If he saw the guys like this, they would know something was very wrong and they would panic. He needed to be calm and confident, so that they wouldn't do anything stupid. But he wasn't sure how long it would take him to get into that state of calmness.

He quickly closed the portal down, and checked the desk to ensure that Rovine would be none the wiser. He eyed the doorway, approaching it slowly. Feeling a sheen of sweat building over his body, he very carefully peered around the doorway to check the corridor both sides. It was clear. *Good*, he thought. Because right now, he had to leave the ship - as fast as possible.

Moving with more purpose than he'd had in some time, he quickly and quietly disappeared from the ship.

Carrie tried not to think of how fine they had cut it that morning. They didn't have time for a shower and had to scoff breakfast on the way. She figured it didn't matter, though, because the training was making her hot and sweaty and in need of a shower anyway.

"Come on, little butterfly," the newly Alpha Eki Tikaani waved her forward. The woman was a small mountain of muscle now. Carrie noted the new tattoo she must've gotten on her leave.

"I like your tattoo," she said, motioning to the 1940s style pinup girl, clad in some scanty underwear, that rose up her left upper arm. "You into pinups, retro stuff?"

Eki looked down at her tattoo. "This is my girl, Paulita."

"Your girl?" Murphy asked from the sidelines.

"Yeah," Eki smiled. "My girl."

Murphy stared at Eki and Eki stared back.

"As in, your girlfriend?" Murphy asked.

"What? You thought I liked boys? Pfft!" She waved her hand at him dismissively. "Hell, no! I got no time for little tails. I like curves and crevices, baby." She winked at Murphy.

Murphy beamed a grin, which turned into a laugh. "I like you Tikaani. You're my kinda gal."

"I ain't gonna sleep with you," Eki said, smiling at him.

"Don't want ya to. But next time we're near a strip bar, I know I've got a partner in crime!"

Eki smiled wider. "I'm down with that, little Irishman."

"Little?" Murphy's smile faded as he crossed his arms.

"Come and prove otherwise, little Irishman," Eki challenged, making kissy noises at him.

"Ooh…" Murphy's grin returned. "Game on, snow woman!"

Eki laughed and Carrie stepped back to let the two face off. She turned to see Hunter come to a halt beside her.

"I like her," Carrie said, still amused.

"Yeah," Hunter smiled. "I think she's fitting in just fine."

"And how's Chucky doing?" she asked. "Do you trust your baby to the co-pilot yet?"

"He's alright," Hunter said, nose twitching. "He seems to know what he's doing. But I'm not ready to take my eyes off him just yet."

Carrie smiled. "I understand. Your ship is your baby."

He was looking at her curiously, his nose twitching again.

"Still getting used to it, huh?" She motioned to his nose.

"Ah, yeah," he said, with a little sparkle to his eyes, "something like that."

He moved away, as Carrie stared after him, wondering what the look was about.

She wondered whether maybe she stank after the training. Normally it wouldn't matter, but now they had the extra sense, things would be different.

She paused as another thought suddenly occurred to her. *Oh, shit!* What if he could smell McKinley on her? She'd been fighting Eki all morning, but she and Frazer hadn't had the olfactory surgery as yet. The others had. And they had probably spent enough time with McKinley to know his particular scent by now.

She quickly glanced around and noticed some of the team – namely, Hunter and Steinberg – darting glances at both her and McKinley. McKinley, she noted, stood to the side, away from the guys, seemingly fixated on Yughi and Evenssen fighting, but she didn't really buy it. Then she glanced nervously at Harris, but he didn't look at either of them.

Harris sat in his office, finalizing the plans to visit the Zeta mothership in Egypt. He was keen to see the iconography Ross had spoken about, and wanted to take his new sense of smell on an excursion, exploring a different environment to test it further.

And, boy, were these senses taking time to get used to. He wondered whether the sense of smell had been the right choice to get done first. It had been a lot to get his head around, all this new information flooding his brain. But he was processing it, and he was progressing. And today, he felt, had been the first time that his upgraded sense of smell gave him information he would not have otherwise known. At least, information he would've been quite happy *not* to have known.

Although he had previously sensed something, maybe even dreamed of it, the evidence today had confirmed it. Harris had slowly been getting used to his team's scents, had been working at identifying individuals by it. Welles often smelled like the twins, of babies. And today, he could clearly smell Welles on McKinley. And not just her natural body odor; he'd smelled sex. On both of them. Welles on McKinley, and McKinley on Welles. They were sleeping together. And he knew he wasn't the only one who picked that up.

Harris sighed heavily, recalling the unmade bed he'd seen in their shared villa in Eden, the sheets pulled back on both sides. This wasn't really a surprise, but that didn't mean the confirmation came easy either. Doc had been dead almost ten months now and he knew at some point she'd move on. That wasn't the problem. The problem was that she'd moved on with McKinley. He was part of the *Aurora* team, which meant things had the chance of getting messy if it turned sour.

Goddamnit, Welles, he thought. *And goddamnit, McKinley!*

But would it turn sour, he wondered. Both of them had been in his dream, the one depicting the eve of the big war. They were both there and from what he could tell they seemed amicable at least. Not only that, he'd dreamt their son was there as well. That's why Harris couldn't interfere with what was going on. Whatever it was, it was going to have to run its course. But he couldn't have them turning up to training like that, distracting the other Alphas.

A knock at the door caught his attention. He stood and made his way over to it. The door slid back and McKinley stood there.

"You asked to see me?" he said.

"First Lieutenant," he said formally, "if either you or Welles turn up to training in that state again, I will send you home. Do you understand?"

McKinley stared back at him. "Sir?"

"I know you could smell it, too," Harris said, as an awkward look crossed McKinley's face. "We have a team of potentially aggressive Alphas with enhanced olfaction. Trying to train them in hand-to-hand combat, and get them to focus, when all they smell is you, and Welles, and sex, is a little hard. So, do us all a favor and shower next time!"

"Sir—"

Harris held up his hand to stop him, "McKinley, I don't give a shit what you do. It's none of my business. But you leave your personal life at home. Understand?"

McKinley stared at Harris, trying to read him.

"*Do you understand*?" Harris asked, emphasizing each word.

"Yes, sir."

"Good," Harris said, then hit the button to close the door and cut himself off from McKinley.

Gold stared down into his eighth drink. No, maybe it was his tenth. He didn't know anymore. He did know that the shot glass he held was a little wobbly. Or maybe he was. He knocked back the drink and placed the glass on the bar.

"Another, please."

"You sure about that?" the barman asked. "I could call you an air-taxi instead."

"Another, please," he said.

"Won't your unit be expecting you?"

Gold looked the barman in the eye, trying to look as sober as he could. "Another, please."

"How about a water?" a woman's voice said.

He turned to see a gorgeous redhead in Space Duty uniform. She smiled. "Or the air-taxi is a good idea, too."

"Have we met?" Gold furrowed his brow, trying to recall her face.

"Yes," she said, smile still in place as Gold stared at her still trying to figure it out. "You don't remember ramming into me at Command and making me drop what I was carrying?"

"Oh!" Gold finally twigged. When he'd been following Rovine to that subterranean elevator, he'd seen this woman every day, then used her to get a look inside the elevator. "I gave you your pen back!"

"Yes, you did." Her blue eyes shone with humor.

"God, you're beautiful," his uninhibited brain thought aloud.

She blushed a little. "And you're drunk, lieutenant."

"I'm okay," he said, brushing it off. "Would you like a drink?"

The barman brought a water over and the redhead took it and placed it in front of him.

"I might rain check that one. But here, you have this." She indicated the water. "Then head back to your ship, soldier." She looked to the barman. "Call him an air-taxi once he's drunk that water."

"Sure thing," the barman nodded.

"I'll see you later, lieutenant."

"Wait?" he called out. She turned around. He gazed at the red hair pulled up in a bun, the bright blue eyes, the svelte body tucked nicely into her Space Duty uniform. "What's your name?"

"First Lieutenant Andrea Skordan."

Gold raised his hand in a salute: "Lieutenant." He gave one of his award-winning smiles, although given the way she laughed it might've been a little lopsided. She turned and walked away. Gold looked back at the barman. "I think I just fell in love."

The barman smiled at him and pointed to the water. "Drink that and make the good lieutenant happy then."

Gold picked up the water and studied it. "Nah," he said putting it back down and tapping his empty glass of tequila. "Another one of them, please."

Harris strode down the corridor toward the mess hall.

"Sir?" McKinley's voice sounded.

Harris turned around.

"I need a word," McKinley said, following him down the corridor.

"I'm on my way to dinner," Harris said, continuing on.

"I don't care," McKinley said. "You can't just close the door on me like that. Not after what we talked about."

"I can't? Pretty sure I can, lieutenant."

"Would you just hear me out?" McKinley said, stopping and placing his hands on hips. "*Saul.*"

Harris stopped and stared at him.

"Or is Doc the only one who was allowed to call you that?" McKinley challenged.

Harris sighed, glancing around the corridor to ensure they were alone. "What?"

McKinley moved toward him. "I need to know this isn't going to cause a problem between me and you."

"What?"

"Me and Welles."

Harris stared at him. "Why would it cause a problem?"

"Doc?" McKinley suggested. "You were good friends."

"Doc's dead, McKinley. Welles can do what she likes."

"Can she?"

"Yes. She can. Is that all you needed to know?"

"I need to know we're good, here. We can't go out in the field if you've got a problem with me."

"Like I told you earlier, I don't care what you do. Just don't bring it on my ship."

McKinley stared at him, not convinced.

"What?" Harris said. "You want my blessing or something?"

"No," McKinley said, then looked uncomfortable. "I don't know. Maybe."

"Since when did you give a shit what people thought of you?"

"I don't."

"So?"

"So… you're my captain. I need to know this won't be a problem."

Harris studied his lieutenant, surprised by this line of conversation.

"I respect you, sir," McKinley continued. "And you've always respected me. I need to know that won't change."

"Why would it?"

McKinley shrugged. "Like I said. You were close to Doc. You're godfather to his son."

"McKinley, you are my first lieutenant, my right-hand man in the field. That hasn't changed." Harris stared firmly at him. "Like I said, I got no problem. I just don't want you bringing that shit on the ship. I need everyone's mind on the war coming our way. Understand?"

McKinley searched his face, then gave a nod. "Alright."

"Good. Now let's eat. I'm hungry."

"Sir?" McKinley called, stopping him again. "Would you mind if I took an hour to see to something? Off the ship."

Harris stared at him.

McKinley held up his hand. "Just this once."

Harris stared at him, plain-faced. "One hour."

Miranda Finch leaned on the bar and examined Gold. He was drunk. Very drunk.

"You know this guy?" the barman asked.

"Sure do," she said.

"There's an air-taxi rank outside," the barman said. "Please convince him to use it, or I'm going to have to ask security to convince him."

"He doesn't look like he's causing any harm," Miranda said.

"No, but he's going to fall asleep any minute, and he's not sleeping on my bar."

"Good point," she said, studying Gold's drooped shoulders. She wasn't sure he'd noticed her. He was just staring at his glass, lost in thought.

"Hey," she said, gently shaking his shoulder.

He looked up.

"Big night?" she asked, then glanced at her watch. "Day, more like."

"Miranda Finch," he slurred.

"The one and only," she smiled.

She pulled up a stool beside him.

"So, what's her name?" Miranda asked, motioning to the barman to get her a drink.

"Her name?" Gold asked.

"Something's driven you to drink."

He turned his bleary eyes back to his glass. "I don't want to talk about it."

"Sounds serious," she said, as the barman placed her usual on the bar. She took a sip, eyeing Gold cautiously. In all the times she'd crossed paths with him, she'd never seen him like this. "You sure you don't want to talk about it?"

He wobbled a little in his chair. "Positive."

"You sure about that?" she asked. "Because right now you're on your way to becoming a big mess, lieutenant."

"Says who?"

"Well, it's only dusk and you're very drunk. And you're still in uniform, which means you're either on duty, or you didn't change when you got off. That there is a penalty, lieutenant."

Gold glanced down at his uniform. "Shit," he muttered.

"Forgot, huh?"

He didn't answer.

"Guess that means you'll be in a whole lot of trouble with your captain."

Again he didn't answer. He placed his head in his hands briefly, then glanced around at the other patrons.

"Tell you what," she said, "how about we get you out of sight for a while. You walk out to the air-taxi rank with me and we go back to my place for some coffee and food to sober you up. When you can walk without falling over, you go back to your ship."

"I'm not going back. I can't," he said.

"You're not going back?" she asked, startled.

He glanced at her, realizing what he'd said. "Not yet."

Miranda faced the bar casually. "Alright, Lincoln. What's going on?"

"Nothing."

"Your eyes and the tone of your voice tell me something different."

"I'm drunk. My eyes tell you I'm drunk."

"Come on, let's get out of here." She tapped him on the shoulder.

"No." He looked at her, still wobbling. "Why?"

"Because you helped me once, now I'm trying to help you."

"You're trying to help me?"

"Yes. To keep your job. Let me get you out of here and sober you up."

"You wanna get me out of here so you can get my story."

Miranda stared at him. "I thought you were just drunk."

He stared into his glass.

"Look," Miranda said, "whatever's going on, you're not going to find the answer there."

"No, but it's making me forget things I don't want to know."

"Is it? I'd say it's doing the opposite."

"Look, I don't need your help, alright." He looked at her. "Just go."

"That's what I told you the last time we met, but you didn't take no for an answer."

"So?"

"So, I guess I'm not taking one now." She folded her arms.

He gave a laugh and looked away.

"Look, you don't want to listen to me, fine. But if you don't, those security guards will call the MPs. Do you want that?"

"Why are you here?" he asked.

"I came for a drink, found you here."

"Yeah?"

"Yes," she said firmly. "I'm a reporter, Gold, but I'm not always on the clock you know."

He laughed. "Yes, you are. Found out anything else about the good Captain Harris?"

She analyzed his words. "That almost sounded bitter. You've had a falling out?"

Gold glared at her, then looked away. He ran his hand over his face as though trying to sober himself up.

"Look, lieutenant—"

"Just..." He stood up abruptly, knocking his chair back and wobbling a little. "Just leave me alone, alright. Stay away from me."

He went to walk away, but she grabbed his arm.

"Lincoln!"

He shrugged her hand off. "No, you're right. Drinking won't solve my problems," he said. "I need to face them head on."

And with that, Lincoln Gold strode drunkenly out of the bar and into the street.

7

Crunch Time

Major General Aiden Ventnor sat beside Colonel Marchant in General Berger's office.

"I think this is a problem. A big one," Ventnor said.

"Why?" General Berger asked, his presence as formidable as ever.

"Because we have an ex-Original, one who's involved in illegal activities with human killing machines, making demands and threats of us."

"Threats?" Berger queried.

"It's blackmail!" Ventnor said.

"How can he blackmail us for something that Professor Sharley did?" Marchant asked.

"Think about it," Ventnor said. "How did Sharley find out about what Harbourg was doing? How else did Drazen and Mattieus Logan come to be in Sharley's employ? Did Sharley just happen to stumble across Harbourg's fighting ring? I don't think so. He found out from us, somehow."

"He can't blackmail us when he's doing something illegal," Marchant said.

"Something that the UNF knows about, apparently, but turns a blind eye to," Ventnor said, unable to hide the accusation in his voice.

Marchant held up his hand. "Hey, I didn't know about it."

Ventnor turned his eyes to Berger. The general stared back, unapologetic.

"Don't act the saint, Ventnor," Berger said. "You knew he was up to something too. None of us did anything about it, because we figured it couldn't hurt."

"Placing bets on illegal fighters?" Marchant asked.

"No," Berger said bluntly. "Having a Plan B."

Marchant glanced between the other two. "What do you mean, Plan B? Using Harbourg's fighters as Alphas?"

"It was an option," Berger said. "Harbourg felt very strongly about the program and he was pissed off when it got shut down. When he retired from service, he began gathering tough guys and training them up. He soon learned he could make some money from it by fighting them on the side. A few of us knew. I went to check out the odd bout. I couldn't help but agree that they'd make vicious Alphas. He started setting up groups in Europe and Asia, and it soon became an international network." The general shrugged. "My guess is that Sharley found out about the ring from one of the inmates in Hell Town. That's where he was when he first hired Logan, after all. Then he got the job on Darwin Station. Sharley's a man who likes to research. He would've found a link between Harbourg's fighters and the UNF. He obviously liked the idea of using these fighters as Alphas, so he kept using them."

"But still," Marchant said. "Undisciplined street fighters as Alphas?"

Berger shrugged, unconcerned. "If the UNF wasn't going to give Harbourg options against the Zetas, then he was going to make some himself."

"Back in those days, they didn't know much about the Zetas," Marchant said. "How could he know what we'd be up against?"

"He still had a lot of friends in the UNF."

Marchant's eyes drifted to Ventnor.

"Don't look at me!" he said. "I hadn't seen Harbourg for years."

"Who then?" Marchant asked, then looked at Berger. "Aside from yourself, sir."

Ventnor glanced at Marchant and thought him brave to challenge the general like that.

"My guess," Berger said, flatly, "is Linecutte. He only died a few years back. He was an Original. He knew enough."

"He was neutral, though," Ventnor commented. "Like myself."

"Neutral, back then, just meant that he hadn't made his mind up either way. Years had passed. Information to hand had grown. Minds can change. Besides, you may have started out neutral, but word had it you were tipping into the affirmative, Ventnor. Greene managed to convince you, so what's to say Harbourg hadn't convinced Linecutte?"

"Don't associate me with Greene," Ventnor said in a low voice.

Berger stared at him. "Relax. Jeff Welles isn't here."

"I wouldn't care if he was here!" Ventnor said. "I've said it once, and I will say it until I'm blue in the face, I was not aware of any plan to kill Colonel Strasser or Sue Welles! And had I known I certainly would *not* have condoned it!"

"Even if the fate of the world depended on it?" Berger asked him.

Ventnor stared at him, baffled.

"A handful of lives is a small cost to save many," Berger explained. "This is the UNF, Aiden. We live by those rules if we have to. Ever heard the terms 'casualty of war' or 'collateral damage'?"

Ventnor threw up his hand to stop him. "Don't lecture me about the UNF, general. I've been in its service for a long time."

"We're off point, gentlemen," Marchant said. "What are we going to do about Harbourg?"

"Someone needs to speak to him," Berger said, "and reiterate that we didn't know what Sharley was up to. We let him know that we'll keep turning a blind eye to his activities, if he turns a blind eye to Sharley and what happened down in Eden."

"Harbourg is a hard man," Ventnor said, "he won't bow or break."

"He will if the UNF helps fund his activities," Berger said bluntly.

Ventnor and Marchant shared a surprised glance then looked back at the general.

"You're not serious?" Ventnor said.

Berger stared coldly at him, but didn't answer.

"We have the program running legitimately," Ventnor said. "We don't need his street scum."

"How do you know?" Berger asked him.

"Because," Ventnor said, "the results speak for themselves. The *Aurora* team... their reports tell us we're doing things the right way."

"They do," the general agreed, "but as with any war, you need a back-up plan or two. If our soldiers get wiped out, we're going to need to send Harbourg's in."

Marchant held up his hand. "Harbourg probably won't be around when the Zetas hit. Who's going to run his ring, then? How do you ensure their compliance in the years to come?"

"If Harbourg's not around, then his daughter will run it," Berger said bluntly.

"Excuse me?" Marchant said.

"She can't be more than, what, 29, 30?" Ventnor said. "You think those street fighters will listen to her?"

Berger smiled. "Trust me, she's a chip off her old man's block."

"How do you know this?" Ventnor asked.

Berger stared at him like he was stupid. "Do you really think I'd just turn my back on Harbourg and leave him to it? I've had him watched. I know exactly what he's doing."

"Still," Marchant said, "who knows how the ring will be operating in another twenty-odd years?"

Berger turned his eyes to Marchant. "We need to be prepared. Comms from the *Barbican* have finally been received. They've made contact earlier than planned for."

"Yes, we know this," Ventnor said, "they received the signal earlier than expected."

"No," Berger said, "I mean they've made *contact*. As in, they've registered them on their radar."

"What?" Marchant said, straightening. "They're that close to the *Barbican*."

"How many were there?" Ventnor asked.

"Three ships came up on their radar."

"So, what happened?" Marchant asked.

"We don't know. We're waiting for the next comms to arrive." Berger turned his gaze to Ventnor. "Regardless, that's why I want Harbourg's men as Plan B."

The room was silent for a moment.

"So, who's going to deliver this message to him then?" Marchant asked.

Silence sat among them again as their minds turned over.

"I might know someone," Ventnor offered. "Someone who's outside of the UNF, but who is privy to UNFASP and what's going on."

"Who?" Berger asked.

Ventnor glanced at Marchant, then looked back at Berger. "Colonel Welles."

"Welles?" Marchant asked, his eyebrows climbing to the top of his forehead.

Ventnor nodded. "He pretty much knows everything, and you know how territorial he is with his family. He'll want to make sure no more of Harbourg's men come for his daughter. If Jeff goes to see him, it will ensure that we're left out of it, and it will keep Welles happy; give him a sense of control, make him feel like he's being useful. Besides, let's face it, he's a good match for Harbourg." Ventnor gave a little smile. "I think Welles is the only man to have ever scared Clint."

Berger considered the notion for a moment, then gave a small nod. "Alright. See to it."

Carrie watched McKinley walk through the door of the Fortress.

"Hey," she said, checking her watch. "Harris let you off the ship?"

"Yeah," he said. "I asked for some time."

"What's up?"

"Your father here?"

"No, he was catching up with a friend. What's going on?"

McKinley rested against the kitchen bench. "They know."

"Who knows what?"

"The team. Some of 'em anyway."

"Know what?" she asked, although she had a feeling she already knew.

"About us."

Carrie stared at him.

"We fucked up," he said, then shrugged. "It's not so easy now they've got the sense of smell."

"What exactly do they know?"

"Your scent was all over me. Mine was all over you. They're not stupid."

"Did someone say something?"

"Yeah," he said. "Harris."

"Harris?!" She folded her arms.

"Yeah." He studied her. "He told me if either of us turn up smelling like that again in front of the team, he'd kick us out."

"Smelling like what?"

"Sex."

Carrie baulked. "Excuse me?"

"It's different for you," McKinley said. "You don't have the Alpha nose. I do. We should've showered."

She felt a slight anger flush her cheeks. "Why didn't you say something before we turned up like that?"

He locked eyes with her but didn't say anything.

She felt her shoulders slump a little and nodded to herself. "You wanted them to find out."

He shrugged.

"Why?" she asked.

"Why not?"

"It's too soon!"

"*It's too soon*. You keep saying that. You sound like a stuck record."

"It's too soon."

"Is it ever going to change?" he said. "What, are you embarrassed or something?"

"No!"

"Are you scared?"

She frowned. "No, I..."

"We've got a kid together, Welles," he said. "Doc's been dead coming up to a year. What's the problem?"

"Why are you so keen to air our business? You! Mr. Mystery Man suddenly wants the world to know his business."

"I don't want the world to know my business," he said, "but I'm sick of hiding. That's not what I do, Welles. I live my life the way I want to, and fuck everyone else and what they think. *That's* where I'm coming from!"

"You couldn't talk to me about this first, though?"

"I've tried to."

"So, you just outed us like that?"

"Yeah, just like you did when you outed me as Freya's father to the Colonel. You think I didn't want a heads up about that?"

She felt a flash of guilt wash over her and exhaled angrily. "I just wanted to wait a little longer!"

"Why?"

She stared, finding that she couldn't give him an answer.

"Why?" he demanded, the Alpha within rising up through his flaming blue eyes. "What are you so afraid of?"

She turned away, trying to think.

"You asked me to move in here! *You* climbed on me that first night we slept together, Welles. *You* started this! So, what's the problem? Are you embarrassed to be seen with me?"

"Don't be stupid."

"Then what?!" He raised his voice. "You change your mind?"

"Fuck you!" She shook her head. "You know I haven't."

"Then what?" He held his arms out, stepping toward her. "WHAT?"

"It's Doc!" she blurted.

He dropped his arms and stared at her.

"I still feel guilt for Doc," she said helplessly. "And if I feel it, the team will too." She looked into his eyes. "I don't want them to think any less of either of us for moving on so soon."

"Fuck the team and what they think," he said, clenching his jaw as he turned to leave.

"Wait!" she grabbed his arm.

"No, Welles," he said, ripping his arm away. "And fuck you too for making me the stand-in!"

And then he left.

Gold entered Captain Rovine's office.

"Where the hell have you been?" Rovine spat. "I don't remember you requesting permission to leave the ship?"

Gold walked as straight as he could over to the chair and flopped down.

"Jesus," Rovine said, recoiling. "I can smell the alcohol from here."

Gold laughed and shook his head. "Fuck you, sir. You're the reason I'm drunk."

Rovine's eyebrows jumped to the top of his forehead. "Excuse me?"

"You heard," Gold said. "When were you gonna tell me?"

"Tell you what?"

Gold stared at him, trying hard to see him through the booze, to read his face, his lies.

"What the hell is this about, lieutenant?" Rovine spat. "You are *this* far away from getting thrown off my ship."

"*Your* ship," Gold said, a smile sliding across his face. "*Your* ship? This is my ship, sir. I'm the one who leads those men. Not you. You sit here behind your desk like a coward, while we do the work."

"What the hell has gotten into you?"

"What's gotten into me? What's gotten into *you*? When did you turn on us?"

Rovine stared at him, an angry furrow in his brow, but he didn't answer.

"Huh? When did you decide to offer us up like lab rats?"

"What the hell are you talking about?"

"UNFASP!" Gold raised his voice.

Rovine's brow smoothed out and he slowly leaned back in his chair. He reached out and hit the button to close his office door. "What do you know about UNFASP?"

"What do *you* know about it, sir?" Gold threw back.

Rovine didn't answer, just stared coldly at Gold.

"You put us forward for the experiment." Gold's face crinkled with emotion. "Were you ever gonna tell us? Give us an option?"

"There are no options in the military," Rovine said, voice emotionless. "Just orders. And you do what I order you to."

"Fuck you, sir," Gold said again, shaking his head with disappointment, despising his captain. "This," he gestured at nothing in particular, "experiment, isn't normal, sir. You can't just throw men into that."

"I can do what I like," Rovine said bluntly. "Did you not pledge allegiance to the uniform when you signed up, Lincoln?"

"Of course I did."

"Then you pledged to do as told, when told. For your country, for Earth, and for our settlements in space."

"Yes, I pledged to do that, but I never agreed to be part of some Frankenstein experiment! Why didn't you talk to me about this?"

Rovine's eyes narrowed. "I see I made an error of judgment with you."

"What error?"

"You're weak. Too much emotion. And soldiers with emotion, they die. But soldiers who can operate regardless of emotion, well, *they're* the ones who should be in positions of leadership, guiding the others. You will just get them killed."

"I would do anything for them!" he hissed, tensing his body.

"Clearly," Rovine said sarcastically, motioning to him. "You're a drunk, emotional fool, Gold."

"You *lied* to us. This whole time, following the *Aurora* around, you lied. You lied about what you had planned for us, about what they were, about everything!"

"Well, now you know," Rovine said, standing. "What a pity you'll be taking that classified knowledge with you back to the Army, after your demotion."

"What?" Gold said standing, too. "This isn't over."

"I'm afraid it is, soldier." Rovine walked around his desk and began heading toward the door, but Gold stopped him.

"I want answers!"

"Get your hands off me!" Rovine hissed.

"Not until you tell me everything you know."

"What I know?" Rovine said. "What I know is this. You will pack your bags immediately and get off my ship. You will be charged with theft—"

"Of what?"

"Information. Did you hack my portal? No, you're not smart enough to do that. It must've been Sergeant Stevens. Looks like I'll be demoting several soldiers then."

"No," Gold said grabbing Rovine's shirt and slamming him back against the wall. "You leave them out of it!"

Rovine threw a punch at Gold, but it was weak and just clipped his chin. Gold swung back, however, and didn't miss. He hit hard, with all that emotion Rovine had just derided him for. He stepped back, shaking his fist, and watched his captain fall to the floor, unconscious and bleeding.

"Fuck," he slurred.

Carrie stood at the living room windows, looking out over Centralis Space Docks. Against the dark of night, the terminal lights sparkled, and the various ships' lights flashed to their own beat within plumes of smoke and fire from those taking off and landing.

"Miss Welles."

"What," she said quietly, not in the mood to talk to her AIS.

"If you talk to him, explain yourself further, I'm sure he will come to understand."

Carrie eyed the ceiling. "You're a counselor now?"

"I know that I am still relatively new in my observations of you both, but I am a fast learner."

"Hmph," she grunted skeptically, looking back into the night.

"You are both fiery and stubborn, which will inevitably cause problems in your relationship, but the similarities can also work for you. You both have pride, you both are fiercely loyal. You are both used to doing things on your own. It will take work to learn to live together and to learn when to give and when to take. But your pairing is a very strong match. The loyalty and the fire will see you through the hard times."

"You predict hard times, huh?" she said, humoring him.

"I am privy to UNFASP, Miss Welles, and the reason behind it. I have no doubt there will be hard times ahead."

Carrie continued to stare out the window and sighed. "Hard times..."

"We are somewhat alike, Miss Welles. We are both prototypes that, if successful, will be rolled out on a wider scale. Earth needs each of us to do our best and play our part. I believe you and McKinley will have a stronger chance of doing your part, if you stand by each other's sides."

Carrie's eyes scanned the night sky. The dark depths of space so close, but so far beyond reach. She wondered where the Zetas were, whether they had begun their final journey toward Earth as yet. Knowing the *Barbican* had picked up the signals earlier than planned, she wondered whether or not they had yet crossed paths with them.

"Just like you and the twins, Lieutenant McKinley is also critical to Earth's future. He is the first official Alpha, and he has fathered the first female Alpha child. 000001A-01, the premier First Gen female: Freya Grace McKinley." Archie was quiet for a moment. *"I believe he cares deeply for you, Miss Welles."*

Carrie glanced up at the ceiling again. "And how can you know that, Archie? Is there some key biorhythm that tells you that?"

"Based on my total analysis of his character and his biophysics, yes. He cares for your well-being and that of the twins. And, yes, Miss Welles, his pheromones do spike when you're around. I believe I can trust him, and that he would do anything to keep you all safe. I think he has character worthy of my respect."

Carrie stood still, reflective, as she looked blindly at the Space Dock.

"And I haven't respected him…" she eventually said in a quiet voice.

"Based on your character and your biophysics, Miss Welles, it is clear to me the feeling is mutual. I believe you are still dealing with the loss of Brody's father, but a loss such as this can take years to recover from. I am an AIS and I do not have the emotions that humans do, but I do know that failing to commit to Lieutenant McKinley may be to your detriment in the long run."

Carrie continued to stare into the night.

"If your heart wants to sing, Miss Welles, let it. Do not fear you will be judged by others. Sing to your heart's content, for it is your ears alone that matter."

Carrie stood there, tears threatening to fall from her Alpha eyes. She pictured Doc in the window's reflection on her left and McKinley on the right. She stared and stared at the image of Doc, watching as it slowly faded from her mind. Then, as a tear rolled down her cheek, she turned her eyes from the ghost, to the living.

Harris looked up at a knock on his office door. He pressed the button and the door slid back. Evenssen stood there.

"What is it?" he asked the corporal.

"Er, sir, Lieutenant Gold from the *Carcharias* is at the ship's entrance. He wants to see you. He's, er…"

"What?"

"Drunk, sir. He stinks of booze."

Harris stared at Evenssen a moment, wondering why Gold would show up unexpectedly like this, not to mention drunk. "Bring him through."

He closed down the document he was working on – updating his diary account of the team's progress, particularly his discovery of the potential power of the new sense of smell. Although he'd left names out of the entry, it probably wouldn't take a genius to figure it out looking back.

Gold walked straight into his office without being invited. Harris had expected him to wait at the door first, being a visitor to the ship. The disheveled lieutenant came to a stop in front of the desk, a waft of alcohol fumes preceding him, then turned around and gave Evenssen a you-can-disappear look. The Alpha Evenssen didn't move, looking to Harris for his order. Harris took a moment for his new olfactory senses to adjust to the brewery stench emanating from Gold, then gave a nod for Evenssen to leave. Harris closed the door behind him. He figured whatever made Gold turn up in such a state might need a little privacy.

He looked back at Gold, his unsteady stance, his hard-set jaw and dark, brooding eyes.

"Drinking on duty, lieutenant?" Harris arched an eyebrow, scanning Gold's uniform, noting the shirt untucked and stained.

Gold stared him hard in the eyes – as hard as a drunk man could – then slowly his eyes lowered to examine Harris's shoulders, arms and chest.

"I knew there was something different about you," Gold said quietly.

Harris sat still, not sure what was going on.

"Did you know?" Gold asked, looking back up to Harris's eyes.

"Did I know what?"

"That I was pegged to become one of you?"

Harris didn't respond. *What was Gold on about? Did he know? How could he know?*

Gold's brow furrowed. "You tried to warn me." He nodded to himself. "You tried to warn me about Rovine… you wanted to tell me. But you couldn't, could you?"

Harris's eyes were fixed on Gold. "Tell you what?"

Gold began to pace back and forth in front of his desk.

"Tell you what?" Harris asked again.

"This whole time…" Gold said, shaking his head.

"Tell. You. What?" Harris said more firmly.

Gold stopped pacing and turned to stare at Harris again. "About this!" he said, motioning to Harris as the case in point. "About you! Your team. What you are now. What we're supposed to become!"

Harris leaned back slowly in his chair. He watched as Gold began to pace again, running his hand through his hair. As he did, he saw the knuckles on Gold's right hand were bruised.

"You been in a fight?" Harris asked.

Gold looked at him, then at his knuckles, before hiding them in the palm of his other hand as a tortured look came over his face.

"Jesus, what have I done..." he muttered, squeezing his eyes shut briefly.

"I don't know," Harris said carefully. "What *have* you done?"

Gold continued to pace. "What the hell am I going to tell the guys?"

"What guys?"

"The team! I promised I would tell them. I told them if they needed to know, I would tell them. I... I can't *not* tell them this. This is their life we're talking about. They need to know. They *should* know! Goddamn *lies*!"

"Know about what?" Harris asked again, eyes fixed on him.

Gold continued to pace, looking more frantic, and still a whole lot drunk.

"What should they know about?" Harris asked firmly.

"*Goddamn* UNFASP!" Gold burst out, stepping toward his desk. "And aliens! What the fuck is that about? UNFASP is in response to alien signals? Are you kidding me?"

"Who the fuck you been talking to?" Harris asked quickly.

Gold kept pacing, running his hand through his hair.

"Where did you hear that?"

"What do I do?" Gold said to himself.

Harris stood up. "What are you talking about?" Gold kept pacing. "Lieutenant!" Harris barked. Gold stopped pacing and looked at him. "What. The. Fuck. Are you talking about?"

"I know," Gold said, nodding to himself. "I know everything. About it all. About UNFASP, the Alphas... and I know we're on the list. That's why we've been following you all this time. They want to make us like you. They're going to experiment on us and turn us into Alphas, into bioengineered... *freaks*!" Gold broke off to focus on Harris' physique again.

"Who told you this?" Harris asked. "Rovine?"

Gold laughed bitterly. "That coward didn't tell me anything."

"So, where did you hear this?" Harris asked, careful not to admit to anything.

"I hacked his portal," Gold said with bitterness. "I knew he was up to something, lying to us. I asked. I tried to ask, but he brushed me aside, again and again. So, I found out for myself."

"You hacked Captain Rovine's portal?" Harris asked, aghast, knowing what a shitstorm of trouble Gold would be in if he had.

"What was I supposed to do?" Gold held his hands out in question. "How many missing people and dead bodies have to pile up before someone did something about it?"

"We *were* doing something about it."

"My team could've been next!"

"You weren't in danger."

"Says who?" Gold said, the angry crease returning to his brow. "Wherever you went, we followed. It was only a matter of time before we got caught in the crossfire. I was looking out for my team!"

Harris sighed and briefly lowered his head into his hands, before looking back at Gold. "Does Rovine know you hacked his portal?"

Gold glanced away guiltily.

Harris sighed again. "Who else knows?"

"No-one," Gold said sullenly, staring at the floor.

"Just Rovine?"

Gold nodded.

"What did he say when he found out?"

Gold shook his head, scorn washing over it. "He doesn't care what I think. He manages the farm, I control the herd. That's what he's always said to me. He doesn't care about them, the team. He barely knows who they are or where they come from."

The intercom on his desk beeped. Harris glanced at it but took no action.

"So, what's Rovine going to do now he knows you hacked his portal?" he asked.

Gold shrugged, refusing to meet his eyes.

"How much do you know?" Harris asked, then looked him over. "A lot, I guess, looking at the state of you." He felt a pang of sympathy for Gold, receiving that information in one hit. At least he and the *Aurora* team had learned in small doses over the past two years or so. Gold had learned everything in one afternoon. No wonder the bastard was drunk.

Gold suddenly dropped down into a squatting position, squeezing his eyes shut and throwing both arms over his head. "Oh god, what have I done?"

Harris quickly stepped around the desk toward him, wondering if the lieutenant was going to vomit on his floor. Instead, he just seemed to squat there, silent and still, head lowered toward the floor.

Harris's intercom beeped again. He sighed and walked back over to it, keeping his eyes on Gold as he did.

"What is it?" he answered it.

"Sir," Frazer said, *"we've got MPs at our door. They want Lieutenant Gold."*

Harris looked from the intercom to Gold.

"What the hell did you do?" he asked.

Gold stood again, wobbling a little, looking around the room helplessly.

"*What* did you do, lieutenant?" Harris asked again.

"He deserved it," Gold said quietly.

Harris stepped up to him, his Alpha stature like a storm cloud casting a shadow over the drunken form of Gold. "What the hell did you do?"

Gold looked down at his bruised fist.

"Who?" Harris asked.

Gold's bloodshot eyes looked up to meet his. "Rovine."

Harris took a moment, inhaling deeply, before he exhaled a *"Jesus..."*

Gold stared at him, waiting to see what Harris was going to do. Whatever it was, Gold looked as though he wasn't going to fight it.

"How bad?" Harris asked.

"One punch," Gold said, then shrugged. "It was enough. He was out cold."

"Sir?" Frazer's voice sounded again. *"They're getting antsy. If we don't bring him out, they're coming in."*

Harris walked to the intercom. "Alright. Tell them to chill. He's coming out." He looked at Gold. The lieutenant was staring fixedly at his feet.

"You can't run from 'em," he said.

Gold nodded, then held his fists out as though Harris were going to throw digital cuffs on him.

Harris eyed the extended arms, then pushed them down. Gold looked up at him.

"We deal with the battery, hacking and drinking charges first. *Then* we deal with what UNFASP means. Got it?"

"We?"

Harris gave a soft nod. "We."

"You're going to help me?" Gold asked, his brow furrowed in confusion.

"Yeah," Harris said, brow raised. "That's why you came here, isn't it?"

"I don't know," Gold said, sounding dazed. "I just wanted answers."

Harris nodded. "And you knew I'd give them to you."

Gold's face softened, repentant.

"First we deal with whatever Rovine is going to throw at you," Harris said. "For now, you push UNFASP and the rest of that shit aside. Keep it to yourself. Then, once we make it through, I'll tell you what you want to know. Understand?"

Gold nodded, brow furrowing with conflicting emotions.

Harris looked over at the door and held his hand out, ushering him forward.

Gold exhaled loudly, sending another whiff of alcohol Harris's way. Then he turned, ran his hand through his hair, opened the door and walked into the corridor. Harris followed, glancing at McKinley, Steinberg and Murphy who'd gathered beside Evenssen in the corridor outside his office. Perhaps curious about the commotion, or perhaps Evenssen had fetched them for back-up, Harris wasn't sure.

"I'll be back," he told McKinley. "Might be a while."

McKinley gave a nod and watched as Harris left the ship, escorting Gold.

*

Harris stood in the observation room, looking through the window at Gold sitting alone, digitally cuffed to the table in the center of the small room. Harris heard a noise and turned around to see Marchant enter.

"What the hell's going on?"

Harris turned to view Gold again. "We have to bring the *Carcharias* online a little earlier than expected."

"Why?"

The door opened again and Captain Rovine entered. Harris studied his swollen black eye. Gold had whacked him good. Real good.

"What happened to you?" Marchant asked the captain.

Rovine walked up to the window of the observation room seething with anger. "I want him destroyed," he demanded.

"Your lieutenant did that to you?" Marchant asked.

"I want him removed from my ship," Rovine hissed.

"Now, hold on a minute," Harris said.

Rovine turned his enraged stare to Harris. "What business is this of yours?"

"Oh, it's my business," Harris said, then pointed through the window at Gold. "Your lieutenant turned up to *my* ship drunk with MPs on his tail."

"Why?" Marchant asked.

"Because he knew something was going on and wanted answers," Harris told him.

"He hacked my portal!" Rovine spat.

Marchant glanced between them. "What are you telling me? He knows about the Zetas?"

Rovine turned back to glare at Gold through the one-way glass. "I want him *ruined*."

"He knows the basics, but not much detail, I think," Harris told Marchant. "That's why he's so drunk."

"Jesus Christ!" Marchant muttered. "Who else knows?"

"No-one, he tells me."

"He didn't hack my system alone," Rovine said with narrowed eyes. "The MPs have been instructed to collect my comms-tech." His eyes narrowed even further. "It wouldn't surprise me if Ryker was in on it as well."

"So, what are you going to do?" Harris asked him. "Have your whole crew arrested?"

Rovine turned to him, eyes still narrowed. "Why did he go running to you?"

Harris stood his ground, nonchalant. "I guess he wanted a captain he could trust."

Rovine turned his full attention to Harris.

"The kind that stands *beside* his soldiers," Harris continued. "Not the kind that hides behind his desk, too afraid to come out of his ship."

Rovine took a step toward him, so Harris turned his Alpha body to face him. Rovine didn't step any further, but a look of loathing crossed his face.

"You think you can say what you want because you're an Alpha now?" Rovine asked.

Harris thought for a moment, then shrugged. "Pretty much. We are, after all, both Space Duty captains," Harris added. "We're of equal rank."

"I've been in service a lot longer than you," Rovine said, eyes narrowed again.

"Yes, you have," Harris nodded, "but look how quickly I caught up."

"Alright, enough," Marchant said.

"I want him charged!" Rovine spat, pointing back into the interrogation room.

"I want him released," Harris countered.

"Released?" Rovine said, exasperated. "He assaulted his commanding officer, he hacked my portal and he was drunk and disorderly in uniform!"

Harris held his hand up to Rovine. "Yes, he was, and yes, he did. I'm not denying that. But I do think the circumstances need to be taken into account."

"The circumstances are irrelevant," Rovine said. "What he did was inexcusable!"

"What are you getting at, Harris?" Marchant asked him.

"He's the first lieutenant of the *Carcharias*. They are pegged to join the *Aurora*'s ranks. He knows about UNFASP and Zeta signals. What will kicking him off the ship do now?"

"He's not coming back on my ship!" Rovine snarled.

Harris sighed and turned to Marchant. "Can we speak in private, colonel?"

Marchant nodded and motioned for Rovine to leave the room. The captain did so, resentfully.

"Rovine won't let him back on the ship," Marchant said as soon as they were alone.

"I know, and I don't blame him. But if he kicks off Gold, the comms-tech and the other guy, Ryker, how much of a team will he have left?"

"He'll fill the holes. Just like you did."

"From what I've seen, Gold is a good soldier," Harris said.

"There are many good soldiers out there."

"I mean he's a *good* soldier. The kind worth keeping."

"So we put him elsewhere."

"He's been pegged for the program. He knows too much now."

Marchant gave Harris a flat stare. "We can make sure he doesn't open his mouth, Harris."

Harris held up his hand. "You won't need to do that, sir. Once I explain things, he'll come around. I know it."

"Why are you defending him?"

Harris exhaled and looked through the window at Gold. "Because I trust him." He looked back at Marchant. "And I don't trust Rovine."

"You think he's lying?"

"No." Harris shook his head. "I think Gold clocked him alright. It's true. All of it."

"So?"

"So, Rovine's a coward," Harris said bluntly. "When the *Aurora* team signed onto this program and I became an Alpha, you put me in charge. As of that moment, I became the senior officer over all Alpha soldiers."

"Yes," Marchant said, wondering what he was getting at.

"Well, I'm telling you, colonel, that I wouldn't hesitate to fight alongside Gold, but I would Rovine. The man is a coward, whose team does not respect him. They do respect Gold." Harris pointed through the window.

"What are you saying here?"

"I'm saying that I do not wish to fight alongside Rovine. I do have a say in who comes into this program, yes?"

"But what are you saying? We remove the *Carcharias* from the program?"

"No, I'm saying we remove Rovine."

Marchant stared at him, but didn't respond.

Harris folded his arms across his chest. "I know it's early days. We don't need to convert the *Carcharias* just yet, but we do need to convince Gold to take this on. We need his buy-in. If he agrees to take this on, his team will agree too, because they trust his judgment. That way we haven't lost the *Carcharias*. They are a good team, and they will make a solid, trustworthy Alpha team that will complement the *Aurora* nicely."

A look of comprehension crossed Marchant's face. "You want Gold to captain the *Carcharias*."

Harris looked back at Gold in study. He could see the concern for the *Carcharias*' team in Gold's eyes; the concern for their future and whose hands held that future.

"Yes," he said. "We remove Rovine and make Gold captain."

"The man assaulted—"

"I know what he did," Harris cut him off. "And in exchange for dropping the charges, we buy his silence. We give him a reprieve and give him a chance to make the right decision. We give him what he wants. The truth.

And in return, we get a good, solid Alpha team at our disposal who haven't been thrown into the program, but have *chosen* to be there. I know full well what it's like to have had the truth kept from you, to have been thrown into this program without a choice, but I also know what it's like to have been given the final choice to undergo the transition. To have been given the full facts, and to have been able to make that decision for myself. I am a better Alpha for it. And so, too, will he be."

Marchant sighed heavily. "I get what you're saying, Harris. But Rovine is tight with Lieutenant General Wilton. It's not going to be easy to remove him. What about *his* knowledge?"

"He's not a Space Duty captain. He doesn't leave the ship, he doesn't go out in the field with his men. He'd be better served working here at Command. You can put his knowledge to good use here, out of the immediate line of fire."

Marchant turned back to the glass and stared in at Gold.

"Don't look at him the way he is now," Harris said, mirroring Marchant. "He just found out about the world of shit coming our way, and his proposed involvement in the resolution. I'd be drunk too."

Marchant looked at Harris, then at Gold, and sighed heavily.

"Captain Gold of the UNF *Carcharias*, huh?" Marchant said.

"It feels right, sir." He turned to face Marchant. "And I've learned to trust my gut."

8

The Path Is Set

Colonel Jeffrey Welles glanced at the leafy surroundings as he approached Aiden Ventnor. The man was sitting at an outside table at the park's cafe. The same place they had met last time. He grabbed the chair opposite Ventnor, pulling it up alongside him so they both sat with their backs against the tall hedge where no-one could approach from behind.

"An invitation from Aiden Ventnor. This is intriguing."

"You said I owe you something," Ventnor said, looking out across the parklands. "So I'm giving it to you."

"Yeah? And what's that?"

"I know who owned the men who attacked the *Aurora* team down in Eden."

Welles stared at Ventnor, but didn't respond. Ventnor turned to look at him.

"He didn't send them, he didn't know anything about the attack before it happened, but he knows about UNFASP and we think he could be of use to us."

"What's this got to do with me?"

"He can keep an ear out for any more attempts on your daughter."

Jeff Welles stared hard at Ventnor. "You telling me this because you think I'm going to track him down and kill him for you?"

"No. Like I said, the UNF wants to keep him on side. But—"

"Here it comes," Welles said, smiling grimly.

"He's trying to blackmail the UNF for cash. He knows Sharley took his men and he knows that Sharley used to work for the UNF. Therefore he claims the UNF need to reimburse him for his lost men."

"So?"

"So, the UNF will not be blackmailed. And yet, we want to keep him on side."

"Why?"

"Because he's running an underground fighting ring, he's training men in hand-to-hand combat. The UNF see this as a pool to tap into, if required, to fight the Zetas."

"To make them Alphas?" Welles asked flatly.

"Yes," Ventnor said bluntly.

"Why are you telling me this?" he asked. "What's your angle? You want me to tell my daughter and her team?"

"No. You are to keep this from them. We want you to go and see this man and let him know the UNF's stance on things."

Welles studied him for a moment. "Why me? I don't work for the UNF anymore."

"Neither does he."

Welles couldn't help his look of surprise. "He's ex-UNF?"

"Yes," Ventnor said, looking back at him, "and you know him quite well."

"Who?"

Ventnor stared at him for a moment as the silence dragged out. "Clint Harbourg."

"Harbourg?!" His face hardened. "And you don't want me to kill him?"

"You won't kill him, Jeff. I know you. You hate him, because you knew he was on Greene's side of things with the vote, but you don't kill innocent men. Harbourg had no knowledge of Greene's plans to kill your wife or Colonel Strasser."

"So, why the fuck do you want me to go and see him? I don't work for the UNF anymore, Aiden. What exactly do you think I can say to him? What weight do you think my words will have?"

"Plenty. He's ex-UNF, so are you. You both have knowledge of UNFASP, although I dare say you know a lot more than he does. The UNF can't be seen to be dealing with him, but you can. You have ties to the UNF, in that your daughter and grandchildren are a part of UNFASP. Harbourg has no ties anymore. You have the edge on him as someone privy to the inner goings-on of the UNF. Harbourg will listen to you. He respects you and fears you, Jeff. He knows what you did to Greene and what you can do to those who cross you."

"There's no proof I did anything to Greene."

Ventnor stared at him but didn't respond.

Welles shook his head and stared out into the park. "And what exactly is the UNF going to do for me for doing their dirty work?"

"We continue to keep you privy to all things UNFASP, and you get an inside look at what Harbourg's doing as Plan B. Information is power, Jeff, and it will help you sleep at night knowing that you're aware of everything you need to be to keep your daughter and grandchildren safe. You can't put a price on that access given you don't work for the UNF anymore."

Welles gave a laugh. "You know as well as I do, Aiden, that you never leave the UNF. Once it has its hooks into you, you're a lifer. Whether you like it or not."

"So, we have a deal then?"

Welles sat and stared, his mind ticking over. "What exactly would you like me to tell him?"

Miranda Finch froze as she watched Captain Morrell approach her. She quickly glanced around at the other patrons of Coco Joe's, then relaxed a little. Plenty of witnesses if anything happened.

Morrell placed his sunglasses on his head and took a seat opposite her. She noted he was in his Earth Duty uniform.

"Taking a break, captain?" she asked.

"Just a quick one," he said.

"Well," she asked, "what do you want?"

"The favor you owe me."

"I don't owe you a favor."

Morrell held his hand up to her. "I don't have time to argue the point, Finch. Just shut up and listen."

She sat back in her chair and crossed her arms, giving him an unimpressed look.

"Our friend Lieutenant Gold of the UNF *Carcharias* was taken away in cuffs last night from the Space Docks. Know anything about that?"

"Really?" she said, furrowing her brow as she leaned forward to rest her forearms on the table. "Where did you hear this?"

"I didn't. I saw it. My unit patrols Command and the Space Dock area. MPs took him away. They picked him up from the *Aurora*."

"The *Aurora*?"

He nodded.

"They had him arrested?"

"Don't know. Orders came over the comms to detain Gold if we came across him. The MPs tracked him down to the *Aurora*. I'm not sure if they called it in or they were hiding him."

Miranda stared at Morrell's face, her mind turning over the information.

"Interesting, isn't it?" Morrell smiled.

Her focus came back to his eyes. "So, what do you think I can do for you? This is the first time I've heard about it."

He shrugged. "You're a reporter, the Centralis liaison. It's your job to cover the UNF. Go do your job, speak to their PR, find out what happened."

"You think they're going release a statement about his arrest? Soldiers get arrested every day for drunk and disorderly—"

"How do you know he was drunk?"

Miranda paused, darting her eyes away. "I, er, I ran into him last night at a bar."

"Yeah?" Morrell leaned forward. "What did he have to say?"

"Go away, pretty much," she said bluntly. "So, I did."

"Squeaky-clean Gold, all drunk and disorderly. The plot thickens."

"How do you know he's squeaky-clean?"

Morrell looked at her, smiling. "You're not the only one with friends around here, Finch. Gold's clean with a good record. I wonder what pushed him over the edge?"

Miranda shrugged. "You tell me."

Morrell stood and placed his sunglasses on. "I've just given you information, Finch. I expect some return. Go do your job and dig up what went on."

He turned and left the cafe. Miranda watched until he disappeared, then stood and headed for Command.

Harris entered the interrogation room. It was mid-morning. They'd given Gold time to sleep off the alcohol, shower and eat, and now he sat at the table, uncuffed this time, with Marchant already seated opposite him.

Gold gave Harris a look that seemed to be a combination of curiosity, shame and concern. Last night they hadn't told him anything. Marchant wanted Gold to stew first, to think about the assault on Rovine. But Marchant had laid out the basics to him this morning.

"Captain," Marchant greeted Harris.

Harris gave Gold a nod. "How's the head this morning, lieutenant?"

Gold looked abashed. "Punishing, sir."

Harris nodded. "For every action, there is a reaction."

"Yes, sir."

"I was just telling Gold," Marchant said, "how the UNF is prepared to not lay charges on him, but there would be a cost for this. His silence."

Harris took a seat beside Marchant, facing Gold. "And how do you feel about that, lieutenant?"

Gold glanced between the two of them. "Honestly? A little torn."

"And why's that?" Marchant asked.

Gold seemed to struggle with something. "Because I told my men that I would never lie to them. Withholding the truth can be the same as a lie."

Silence sat in the room for a while.

"And what if you were allowed to tell your men?" Harris arched his eyebrow.

Gold studied him. "Tell them what, though? I still don't know all the details."

"And if we gave them to you?" Marchant asked.

"I guess it would depend on what you tell me," Gold said. "I know it's my job to take orders, but I won't commit to anything, certainly can't commit my men to anything, until I know what I'm dealing with. What I saw in those files…"

Harris exchanged a look with Marchant, as if reiterating that Gold was the right man for the job.

"Fine," Marchant said, rising from his seat. "I think you two have some things to talk about."

Gold watched Marchant leave the room, then turned his eyes back to Harris.

"*You're* going to tell me?"

"Yes," Harris said. "I am officially in command of all Alpha soldiers."

Gold seemed to pause, shocked by what Harris had said so openly. His eyes traveled over Harris's physique again.

"You're already one of them?" he said, needing it to be officially confirmed.

Harris nodded. "But I'm not yet complete. I've been through the body transformation and recently had my olfactory sense done, but I still have my eyes and ears to do."

Again, Gold stared at him. "So wh—what exactly are you? What's UNFASP and what the hell are these alien signals about?"

Harris looked back at him with sympathy. "I think we'd better start from the beginning, don't you?"

Gold nodded. "Yeah, I think that's a good idea."

Carrie entered the *Aurora*'s training facility, leaving the twins and the Sentinels in the mess hall. Yughi was over on the mats running through meditation exercises with some of the team. A few of them glanced over at her. Something about Hunter's glance suggested a spark of curiosity, but she quickly swept it away. She knew this would be hard for her to deal with if some of the team knew about her and McKinley.

McKinley had glanced at her as she entered, but quickly focused back on Steinberg and Brown on the two weight racks. She made her way over to them, coming to a stand beside Brown's rack.

McKinley glanced at his watch, then at her.

"Sorry I'm a little late," she said. "Alpha twins are hard to wrangle in the morning on my own."

"Where was your father?" he asked.

"He took off for the mainland. Said he had something to do."

McKinley didn't respond but kept watching Steinberg as he brought the weight up and down. Carrie glanced around and saw that Harris was missing. In a way she was glad, given her conversation with McKinley last night.

"No Harris?" she asked.

"He's at Command," McKinley said, stepping forward to help Steinberg with his weight. He then turned and walked off over to the mats. Carrie watched him. He was avoiding her, or ignoring her. She sighed, then headed over to the treadmill and started to run. All the while her eyes could see McKinley on the mats, reflected in the mirror in front of her.

After a while he called the rest of the team to the mats to face off against each other. He paired her with Frazer this time. Although he was a new Alpha and strong, he still wasn't fast enough to catch her.

"She's beating you, boy!" Tikaani teased him from where she stood beside them, facing off against Gregson.

"No, she's not!" Frazer protested.

"You just can't catch me," Carrie smiled.

"Hope you're better with ships!" Tikaani chuckled.

"Fuck you, snow woman. Are you even a woman?"

"I don't know," Tikaani shrugged, "you might have me beat there, girlie!"

Gregson's mouth curled into a smile. "Alright Tikaani. How about you turn that attention back to me."

"Whatever you say, doctor!" she said casually, then lunged at him, but Gregson was too swift and darted to the side.

Just then Evenssen entered with a woman dressed in a Space Duty officer's uniform, consisting of blouse and skirt. She was attractive, with brown hair to her shoulders, red lipstick and bright eyes. The team slowed to stop and looked at her.

"Oh, please don't stop on my account!" she said holding up her hand.

McKinley moved over to her. "Dr. Forcaster. What brings you here?"

"Please, it's Elle. I came to watch you train, if that's alright?" she said. "More research."

McKinley glanced around at the team, then back at her. "Sure. Knock yourself out."

"Thank you, lieutenant," she smiled.

Carrie watched as the woman moved to stand beside McKinley and study the fighting pairs. She pulled out her PDP and jotted down some notes with an e-pen. When they came to the end of their session, McKinley sent the team back over to the gym equipment. Carrie went to follow the others, but the woman stopped her.

"Sergeant Welles?" she said.

"Yeah," Carrie said.

"I'm Dr. Forcaster," she said holding out her hand. "I'm in charge of the sense surgeries."

"How're you going," Carrie said, shaking her hand.

"Well, thank you. And you?"

"I'm good."

"And the children?"

Carrie darted her eyes to McKinley. "They're fine."

"I would love to have a session with them, if I may?" she said then held up her hand. "Providing Dr. Morgave doesn't mind me joining him for their next consult."

Carrie shrugged. "If Dr. Morgave is okay with it, then I am too."

"Excellent. Have you thought about getting the extra senses?"

Again Carrie darted a glance at McKinley. "Yeah, I guess at some point I will. When my son's ready to, I'll go through it with him."

"Well, whenever you're ready, I'm ready to take that next step with you."

"Thanks," Carrie said.

Forcaster smiled at her, then turned to McKinley. "Now, lieutenant, you promised me a coffee and we've not had it yet. What are the chances of me stealing you away for an hour or so today?"

"Ah…" McKinley scratched his jaw, glancing over to the team.

"Surely the team can train on their own for a little while?" Forcaster smiled.

"The captain's over at command. I'm in charge of the ship until he comes back," McKinley said.

"Lieutenant, I'm starting to think you're avoiding me." Her smile grew a little wider and, Carrie noted, flirtier.

McKinley darted his eyes to Carrie's, then looked back at Forcaster.

"I promise we'll go when the captain returns," he said.

"Are you telling me these soldiers can't cope for one hour without supervision," she said. "If that's the case then I'd say Earth is in a whole lot of trouble, lieutenant."

McKinley studied her for a moment, then darted his eyes to Carrie again. "Alright, give me a second." He moved past them and headed over to the rest of the team.

"Excellent," Forcaster smiled, then looked at Carrie. "I'm utterly fascinated by you Alphas. There's so much to explore, and so many places we can go with the program."

"Yeah," Carrie nodded, noticing her staring at McKinley.

"I'd like to pick your brains too one day," she said.

"Sure."

McKinley came back. "Alright, you got me for an hour."

"Wonderful, lieutenant," she smiled, then waved her hand like a game show hostess toward the door.

McKinley glanced briefly at Carrie, then began to leave, Forcaster moving to walk by his side. She said something that Carrie didn't hear, then laughed, touching McKinley's arm as she did.

Carrie watched them walk out the door, as her inner Alpha flared.

Harris looked at his watch, then at Gold, who sat elbows on the table, hands clasped in front of his mouth. He looked exhausted. Between the hangover and all the information Harris had just shared with him, Harris wasn't sure the lieutenant could take much more right now.

"I have to get back to my ship," Harris said, "and you have to get back to yours. You've already been gone long enough."

"Is Rovine there?"

"For the time being."

"So, they'll know I knocked him out."

"Yeah."

"What do I say about that?"

"You say it was a personal issue, one that you don't wish to discuss."

"Some of them... two of them, know I was looking for something. They'll know. They'll guess that's why I hit him."

"So you go back there and you tell them the truth. But if you do that, you lock them into UNFASP."

Gold nodded.

"So, what's it going to be?"

"I don't get time to think about this?"

"No," Harris said bluntly. "You've had time since you read the information on Rovine's portal. I have just given you the background and filled in some details. Either way, you assaulted your CO and answers need to be given to your team. That, I guess, is your punishment."

Gold lowered his hands to the table.

"You want to face the Zetas as a human?" Harris asked.

Gold stared at him silently.

"You want to sit back and do nothing about their attack?"

"*Potential* attack," Gold said. "You have no definites here."

Harris thought of the dreams he'd been having. "Oh, they will attack, Gold. Of that I am sure."

"Being an Alpha will only do good if they come out of their ships," Gold said. "Even then we don't know what weaponry they'll have. Who's to say taking on the virus will do any good?"

"Who's to say it won't?" Harris shrugged.

Gold ran his hand over his face.

"Do you trust me?" Harris asked.

Gold studied him.

"Do you trust me?" Harris asked again carefully.

Gold relented and gave a nod.

"Do you think I would do this, would take on the virus, would ask my team to take on the virus, if I thought it wasn't necessary?" Harris asked him. "Do you think I would risk my wife and children?"

Gold sighed. "No."

Harris sat back in his chair. "I like you Gold," he said. "I think you'll make a good captain. And I think you'll make a solid Alpha. One that I can trust."

Gold nodded to himself, staring down at his bruised hand.

"This is an incredible honor, you know," Harris said. "To be appointed the second official Alpha unit in history."

Again Gold nodded, his mind ticking over.

Harris stared at him, waiting for Gold to say something.

"I need an answer," Harris said softly. "What's it going to be? Will you join me? Will you help me prepare for this attack?"

Gold clenched his jaw briefly, then fixed his eyes decisively on Harris's.

"Yes, sir," he said.

"You're sure?"

Gold nodded. "Yes, sir," he said firmly. "If it had been under Rovine, then no... but if you put me in charge of the *Carcharias*, so I can lead my men the right way, be in charge of their fate, then yes."

"You think they'll follow you into this?" Harris queried him.

"Did yours?" Gold asked him.

Harris nodded.

"Then so too will mine," Gold said confidently.

Harris analyzed him for a moment, before a smile broke out on his face. He stood and held his hand out for Gold to shake. Gold stood on the other side of the table and clasped his hand with Harris's.

"Welcome to UNFASP, Alpha-Two Captain Gold," Harris said.

The new captain nodded. "Thank you, Alpha-One Captain Harris."

They dropped hands, but Harris continued to smile.

"We'll call Rovine in and let him know of his transfer."

Gold nodded.

"Don't worry," Harris said. "You'll have some time to get used to the idea before we do anything physically. You tell your men, then give them a short leave stint before they give you their answer. That's what I did with mine."

"Yes, sir."

"Alright." Harris gave a nod and turned for the door, but Gold stopped him.

"Thank you."

Harris looked back at him.

"For everything," Gold said. "Thank you for everything you've done for me."

Harris looked at him. "Just remember what your captain did to you. How he treated you. And don't ever do that to your men. Or me."

"I won't," Gold said firmly, giving Harris a look to match.

"Good."

First Lieutenant James McKinley rose from the cafe table, along with Dr. Forcaster.

"Thank you for your time, James. It's been fascinating to hear your perspective. I have so many more questions to ask, though. We must do this again."

He eyed her attractive red-lipsticked smile and gave a nod. "Yeah, sure."

"If you have any questions at any time," she said, pulling out her PDP, "please call me." She reached forward and pressed her PDP against his, which was still clipped onto the front of his belt. He looked down at the two PDPs pressed together, then back at her. "I mean it," she said, meeting his eyes. "My door's always open. Here, or at home."

She flashed him a sultry glance that sent his Alpha spiking, then she took her PDP back and placed it in her bag.

"Well, I should let you get back to your ship."

"Yeah," he said, checking at his watch.

"Thanks again," she smiled, placing her hand on his shoulder. "I appreciate it. And remember, call me. Anytime."

She turned and began to walk off. He looked down at his PDP, unclipped it from his belt and saw her contact details on the screen: her phone number and office address... and her personal details: home phone number and home address. He looked up to watch her walking away and saw her glance over her shoulder, throwing him another sexy smile.

"*Fuuuuck...*" He exhaled heavily and ran his hand over his beard.

He made his way back to the ship, trying to shake those red lips and sultry eyes from his mind. As he walked into the training facility, his eyes immediately fell on Welles. She was on the mats fighting Yughi. He paused and watched them. She was fast and a good match for her opponent's skillful moves. He watched her pull a great maneuver, getting in behind Yughi and tripping him backward onto the mat. Panting, she looked up and saw him watching her. She was sweating, strands of her long brown hair had come loose, and he couldn't help but picture her lying naked beneath him, looking up at him with those same vibrant green Alpha eyes, just as she did now.

He turned away from her toward Steinberg and Brown. He tried to focus his attention on them sparring, but found it hard with Forcaster's red-lipsticked smile popping into his mind, the touch of her hand on his shoulder, and her personal details burning through the PDP clipped to his belt. The old him would've grabbed a bottle of bourbon, called Forcaster's number and taken her up on the offer, no hesitation. So, what had changed?

He glanced at Welles again and saw she'd moved on to the shooting range. He watched her line up and take a shot, then saw the result on the screen. It was a perfect one. He turned away again.

Of all things, he thought of Freya then. He pictured not living at the Fortress with her; raising her, protecting her. He imagined not living with Welles. He thought of Brody; of not looking out for him in Doc's stead; of letting him grow up without a father. He thought of the Zeta invasion coming their way.

But just because he didn't live with them anymore, didn't mean he couldn't still raise them, right? He thought of Forcaster again, and just knew if he used her number, Welles would shut the door on him for good. He pictured Doc's face again, disappointed in him. Hell, he even pictured the Colonel's face. And Harris's... He'd just made a big point about being with Welles, now he was thinking of walking away? Was he running? This is what he did, wasn't it? Run away to Vegas, get blind drunk and forget his troubles. Only, it never got rid of his problems forever. They always followed him.

He glanced back at Welles again on the shooting range. If he walked away, would she move on with someone else? He tried to picture her with another guy; their arms around her, in her bed, but quickly erased the thought as he felt his Alpha suddenly spike. He didn't want to see that. And he didn't want someone else raising Freya and Brody in his stead.

And that's what had changed in his life. It wasn't just about him anymore. He couldn't just take off to the nearest bar and forget the world for a while. He had to think about his daughter, and her brother, and their mother. He had ties now. He had family. Something he'd never really had before. Was he going to piss that away?

As tempting as it was, somehow a one-night stand with Forcaster didn't quite stack up. Not in comparison with what he would lose if he went through with it.

At least, it wouldn't stack up until he was sure that he and Welles were over.

He breathed in deeply and exhaled heavily in frustration as he made his way over to the weight rack. He loaded it up as much as he thought his body could take, then he slid underneath the bar and took hold. He was going to push his body to its limits until he forced his mind to clear.

Colonel Jeffrey Welles approached the two large men guarding the wooden arched door of the bar called Hell's Gate – an old church in a previous life – owned by Clint Harbourg, aka the Greenback. Colonel Welles shook his head, wondering if Harbourg had given himself the moniker 'the Greenback' or whether he'd been given it by others. It wouldn't surprise him if Harbourg had given it to himself. The man always had an ego and liked money.

The two doormen stared at him, refusing to move aside. Colonel Welles looked at them curiously.

"What?" he asked. "Is there a secret password to get in here for a drink?"

"This is a members' only club," the one on the left said, a white guy whose nose was spread wide across his face, probably from one too many fights.

"Well," the colonel said, "I know the owner. I think he'd like to see me."

"Is he expecting you?" the one on the right asked, his black hair so oiled it shone in the dim light.

"No, he's not expecting me," Colonel Welles said. "But I think he'll want to speak to me."

"Yeah?" flat-nose guy said.

"Yeah. Go tell him an old acquaintance is here to see him. Go tell him the Pitbull is here," he said, referencing a name Harbourg often used to describe him.

"The Pitbull?" Flat-nose guy smiled condescendingly as he eyed him up and down.

Colonel Welles stared back with a plain face.

"The owner," flat-nose guy said, "don't like to be disturbed. If I go to him and disturb him and he gets angry because you're wasting his time, that means he's gonna get angry at me. So, tell me, why should I go disturb him?"

"Because I said so."

"Because you said so?" He looked at oil-slicked hair guy and they shared a laugh.

"What drugs you on, old man?" oil-slick guy said.

Colonel Welles stared back at him. "Go get him. Trust me, he's gonna want to see me."

They laughed again.

Welles hardened his face. "You keep me waiting much longer, I'll be sure to let the Greenback know just how fucking disappointed I am with his service."

Something about him mentioning the Greenback caught their attention. Or perhaps it was the hardness in his voice. Their laughter and smiles faded away. Flat-nose guy looked at oil-slick and motioned for him to go inside. Oil-slick disappeared within and Welles waited patiently, staring at the guard who remained.

Eventually, oil-slick came back and nodded to flat-nose. "Send him through."

"Yeah?" flat-nose seemed surprised. He looked at Welles again, eyeing him over, then moved to let him pass.

Welles did so, giving him his best hardened colonel stare as he did.

As he stepped inside, he noted how dim the bar was, with candles dotted around and a few spotlights on the walls. He scanned his surroundings, eyeing the other patrons carefully. Aiden Ventnor had told him what this place was, told him to be careful. Welles wasn't stupid. He wasn't about to start a brawl in a fighters' bar, but at the same time he knew it was important to show he wasn't afraid. It was just like he was back on duty and facing a platoon of soldiers. That's how you earned their respect: be smart, be sharp, and show no fear.

"You the Pitbull?" a woman's voice said behind him. She moved to stand by his side, her perfume invading his senses. She must've been waiting by the door for him. Although she wore a floor-length dress, it was entirely see-through, showing the black underwear she wore and the array of tattoos covering her late twenty-something body. He gave a nod.

"That's an interesting name?" She smiled, her lipstick so dark that in this light it looked black.

"Isn't it."

"Come this way," she said, all smiles and flirty lashes. She walked toward the back of the old church, passing tables and chairs to the left and a long bar down the right-hand side. He glanced up at the colorful stained glass windows puncturing each wall, lit from outside. They appeared to depict what he imagined were some of the Greenback's fighters in action.

"So how'd you get the name Pitbull?" the woman asked, glancing over her shoulder at him. Her eyes were like poisoned darts through a veil of straight blond hair.

"Let's just say I'm like a dog with a bone. When I got something in my teeth, I ain't letting go."

She laughed, throwing her head back. "I see."

They approached the far end of the bar, where an altar still remained. The woman pulled back a velvet rope and ushered him forward. Through the dim light and incense haze he saw Harbourg sitting on a red velvet couch against the far wall. He was alone.

"Go on," the woman said, dark lips bared in a smile, "don't be shy."

Welles eyed her briefly, then moved up the three steps toward the red velvet couches where Harbourg sat waiting. He glanced back at the woman and saw she was leaving again, pulling across a red sheer curtain to give them some privacy. He scanned the room one last time, then sat beside Harbourg with his back to the wall.

Harbourg, scotch in hand, looked at him over the glass as he took a sip.

"You not going to offer me a drink?" Welles asked him. "For old times' sake?"

"She'll bring one in a moment. I know what you drink." he said. " So, *Pitbull*, what brings you here?"

"You tell me, *Greenback*," Welles replied.

Harbourg analyzed him. "General Berger sent you?"

"No," Welles responded.

"Ventnor, then?"

Welles nodded.

Harbourg smiled. "Maybe he did, but make no mistake, all roads lead back to General Berger."

"No doubt. So tell me, how does Berger know where to find you?"

Harbourg smiled again. "Everybody has a weakness, Pitbull. Gambling is his."

"Not the kind of man you want in charge of countless soldiers. A gambler."

Harbourg laughed. "Gambling, like war, is a risk. You need the balls to make the call. You'll win some and lose some. That's how it goes."

"War is about strategy, not gambling," Welles said. "Money can be earned again. Lives can't. Once they're gone, they're gone."

Harbourg shrugged, uncaring.

Just then the woman returned and placed a bottle of top shelf scotch and a spare glass down. "Anything else?" she asked Harbourg. He shook his head and she left again. Welles watched her return the tray to the bar, then move to stand by the velvet rope again.

"She your security?" Welles asked. "Interesting choice."

"Don't even think about it. She's my daughter."

Welles glanced at him. "That's Roxy?!" He looked back to the woman. "She's... changed."

Harbourg laughed loudly. "It's been a while, Jeff. She's all grown up. And let me tell you, she's as hard as they come."

Welles studied the woman, the way she stood scanning the room, her face hard. No smiles or laughter to be seen.

"I can imagine, if she grew up around these guys," Welles said, motioning through the sheer curtains to the patrons of the bar. "You trained her?"

"Yeah," Harbourg said, smiling with pride. "She's daddy's little killer. She can handle herself. But she doesn't need to. My fighters know what happens if they touch her uninvited."

Welles raised his eyebrows, then poured himself a drink.

"So," Harbourg said, "as you say, Ventnor sent you."

Welles sipped his drink, then placed it down. "I'm to deliver a message."

Harbourg's focus sharpened. "Oh yeah?"

"They like what you're doing, and they want you to keep on doing it." Welles said plainly.

Harbourg laughed again. "Well, I'm so glad I have the UNF seal of approval to run my own goddamn business!" he said sarcastically.

Welles looked at him. "They want you to be Plan B."

Harbourg stared at him, but didn't respond.

"That's why you started this, isn't it?" Welles waved his hand around. "You were pissed the UNF put the program on hold, so you decided to do something about it yourself."

Harbourg's eyes narrowed. "Someone had to do something. Someone had to have the balls to fight."

Welles stared back at him. "But fight what?" he said. "Back then, we didn't know shit."

"Yes, we did. Something out there was communicating with us, and whatever it was, was getting closer."

"Yes. Something was getting closer," Welles said, "but we had no proof it was a threat to us. But creating an advanced army could've been."

"Why are you back working for the UNF after all these years? *You*, who hated them more than anything."

Welles looked back over to Roxy. "I have a daughter too, Clint."

"So?"

"She's been dragged into UNFASP." Welles looked back at him. "Which means I've been dragged back in too."

"She part of the program? An enhanced soldier?" Harbourg asked, his eyes fixed to the bottom of his glass as he knocked back the contents.

"What makes you say that?" Welles narrowed his eyes.

"You said she's been dragged in."

"Doesn't mean she's an enhanced soldier."

Harbourg chuckled. "I guess that would be kind of weird for you, wouldn't it? What with you having been so against it and all." He poured himself another drink. "Or is it just that your daughter is smarter than you? That she can see the truth for what it is. That she had the balls to do what her old man couldn't?"

Welles's face hardened as he stared back at Harbourg. "Careful, Clint."

Harbourg stared back, his face dropping slightly.

"You know my weakness, but I know yours." Welles motioned to Roxy.

"Roxy can take care of herself."

"So can Carrie."

Harbourg conceded with a nod and held his hand up in a peaceful gesture.

Welles sighed and loosened his shoulders a little. "We got something in common, you know?"

"Yeah, what's that?"

"We both think we're out of the UNF, but we aren't." Welles looked down at the glass in his hands. "What happened all those years ago hooked us in for life. Whether we wanted it or not. Knowledge, information... You can't unlearn things, you can't forget. *We* can't forget, and neither will the UNF."

Harbourg said nothing, but his attention to Welles didn't waiver.

"We got shit coming our way that we need to deal with," Welles said. "And we've got two choices. We work with the UNF and give ourselves a chance at survival, or we tell them to go fuck themselves, go it alone and potentially die."

Harbourg sat forward. "What's changed?"

"What do you mean?"

"You're now backing the UNFASP army. Why?"

Welles stared at him, thinking about how to answer that.

"Why are you back?" Harbourg asked. "*You*, of all people. Something's changed. Why the urgency? Why has the UNF started transforming people?"

Welles felt a strange sensation overcome him. "How do you know they're transforming people?"

Harbourg paused. "I saw the news. Those men in Eden, my fighters? They were enhanced, I know it."

"You couldn't tell that from the news—"

"I could. They were infected with the virus. So, what's changed with the aliens? Why is the UNF suddenly moving forward?"

"You think I could tell you if I knew?"

"Yes, if you wanted to." The silence sat between them for a moment. "Why have you changed your mind, really? Does the UNF have something over you?"

"Yes, they do," Welles said bluntly. "My daughter. I told you. Therefore, they got me too."

Harbourg just stared, analyzing him, waiting for more.

"I stand by my actions of the past, and I stand by my actions now. Because *now*," Welles said emphatically, "is the time to act."

"What have you seen?"

"What do you know?" Welles threw back at him. "You know more than you're letting on. How do you know the UNF has begun transitioning people? How do you know there's a virus? There's no way you could know that. And don't tell me you saw it on the news. That's bullshit. What have *you* seen that you're not telling me?"

Harbourg relaxed a little, sipping his drink. He shrugged nonchalantly.

"Are there more out there?" Welles asked him. "Any more of your fighters being transitioned somewhere?"

"You tell me. Someone connected to the UNF is the one stealing them."

"He's in custody now."

"He is?"

Welles didn't respond.

"So why are you here?" Harbourg asked. "Really?"

It was Welles's turn to shrug. "They can't be seen with you. So, I'm here. The message is simple. Keep doing what you're doing, and don't be surprised if one day they suddenly show up and want to do a deal."

"For my men?"

Welles nodded.

"The UNF want my gladiators to be Plan B..." Harbourg mused quietly, staring at the patrons of his bar.

"The UNF has an empire of soldiers at hand," Welles said, "but if shit turns bad, they're going to want the *gladiators* you've got hidden around the world as reinforcements."

Harbourg turned his eyes back to Welles. "So, it's bad then? What's coming for us is bad?"

Welles threw back his drink, then stood. "It might be. It might well be. So, we need to be prepared." He turned to leave, but Harbourg stopped him.

"What happens now?"

Welles looked at him with something approaching resignation. "Just keep doing what you're doing." He went to walk away, but stopped and turned back, feeling the need to address the niggling feeling within. "If you come across anyone else messing around with transitioning people, experimenting with them, you'll let me know, right? This has to be controlled through the UNF. There can be nothing off the grid."

"Whatever you say." Harbourg raised his glass in salute.

"That wasn't a straight answer."

"A straight answer costs a straight answer and you gave me shit."

"If you're transitioning people somehow..." Welles warned him.

"And how could I do that? I'd need a stock of the virus, wouldn't I?"

Welles stared at him a moment but decided not to argue the point. Not here in Harbourg's den of what he called 'gladiators'. He turned and walked to the rope, Roxy unhooking it to let him pass. "Roxy," he acknowledged. "I didn't recognize you. Last time I saw you, you came up to my knee."

Roxy smiled. "Things change."

Welles nodded, glancing back at Harbourg, aka the Greenback. "Yes, they do indeed."

Harris watched as Rovine glared at Marchant.

"You're going to let him walk?"

"No," Marchant said. "The charges will remain pending for now, until he proves he's worthy of them being cleared."

"You can't be serious?"

"Captain Rovine," Marchant said, "we are moving forward with this program and there is much to be done. The *Carcharias* has already been selected to take part in the initial trial of UNFASP. That selection was made according to a thorough examination of the team profiles. Part of that profile included how the team worked together. And Gold is critical to that. He's the glue that keeps them working as well as they do. We can't remove him from that team."

"You're going to let him back on my ship?" Rovine gritted his jaw so hard, it pulled the skin on his face tight, making his swollen black eye bulge even more.

"No," Marchant said, "because it's no longer your ship."

"Excuse me?!" Rovine straightened in shock.

"Like I said, we need to move forward on this program. There are things to be done to progress it, and we feel the time is right to promote you."

Rovine went to say something but stopped. His expression showed confusion now, as if finding it hard to parse Marchant's words.

"We will soon have two units online in the Alpha program. That means we need to start building up our strategists and leaders, who have UNFASP knowledge, here at Command. We've decided the time is right to promote you and bring you into a new role here at Command."

"You're taking the ship off me?"

"No, we're promoting you."

"But you're giving the ship to Gold? You're effectively rewarding him."

"Is it a reward?" Harris asked, arching his eyebrow at Rovine. "You get to stay here at Command, get to stay human. Gold *must* become an Alpha and fight those Zetas when they hit. I'd say you probably got the better end of the deal."

"He needs to be thrown out of the Space Division!"

"Well," Harris said, "he's agreed to become captain of the Alpha-2 unit, so I can't let that happen. I need him. I want him to fight beside me. And as the leader of Alpha units, I'm afraid it's my decision."

"This is absurd!" Rovine spat.

"You don't want your promotion?" Harris asked. Then added, "To safety."

Rovine gritted his teeth and flicked his eyes to Marchant. "Lieutenant General Wilton will be hearing of this!"

"Lieutenant General Wilton has already heard about it," Marchant told him. "It's done, Rovine. Just accept your win. You are getting a promotion that, quite frankly, you haven't earned. You are getting moved to Command. You will have increased power and financial gain in your new role. Accept the offer and let's move on."

Rovine glared at the both of them, then stormed out of the room in rage.

Marchant and Harris stared at the door that closed behind him.

"In this new role of his," Harris asked Marchant, "what power does he have exactly? He can't touch my Alpha units, can he?"

"His is one of strategy. Don't worry, you're still in charge of the Alpha units. He'll have his say in what strategy you take, but I know that if you don't agree you'll stand your ground. Regardless, you will have to work with him at some point. Keep that in mind."

"Just so long as he keeps what happened with Gold out of it, because if that shit influences his strategies, he'd better know I will break him in half if he jeopardizes my soldiers."

A smile slid across Marchant's face. "That's why I put you in charge of the Alphas, Harris. Sometimes the ones at the top forget what it's like to be the one on the ground. Someone's got to look out for them. And you're the man for the job."

"Yes, I am, colonel."

9

Mothership

Carrie stepped off the Z-flyer into a warm Egyptian wind. The flight hadn't been long from Centralis, but it felt strange to go from an island of ocean breezes, to an elevated landmass of dry desert.

She placed her mirrored sunglasses on and glanced back at McKinley as her feet touched the dusty tarmac. They had barely spoken since their argument. It didn't help things that he was currently based on the *Aurora* and she wasn't. She'd tried to contact him via his portal, but received no response. She pictured the attractive Forcaster in her mind and wondered how the coffee between them went. He'd seemed even more distant since then. Again, she felt her inner Alpha stir territorially.

McKinley briefly glanced her way as he placed his own sunglasses on. She wondered whether he detected a spike in her pheromones or something, somewhat paranoid now she knew how much her body might give away to Alphas with the olfactory sense.

Escorted by the lead archaeologist, Matthew Ross, again, they piled into a small carrier and set off to the location of the mothership, east of the Valley of the Kings.

Sharing a back seat with Harris and McKinley, she looked out the window at the creamy beige-colored rocky landscape. Despite it being on the verge of winter, her Alpha eyes could still see the heat rising up off the ground in near-invisible waves. She took her cylinder of water and sipped it, noticing the sweat building upon her skin. Ross thought it better they acclimatize to the heat, so he turned off the air conditioning in the vehicle.

"We've been working closely with the Egyptian government to keep this place a secret," Ross told them. "Thankfully, there're enough distractions for tourists in other areas. All those ancient temples and pyramids. Not too many people are keen on heading further into the desert, despite some oases being close by. They've had one or two accidental trespassers over the years, but they quickly move on when they see the Egyptian guards." Ross glanced around at them. "That's part of the deal with the government, you see. Only their people are allowed to guard it."

"But they've been sharing any of their finds, yes?" Harris asked.

"Yes. It's their relic, their site, but they don't pretend to know what to do if the Zetas return to Earth so they're cooperating with the UNF. They've been giving us full access to the ship, they just make sure we know it's theirs."

Carrie began to unbutton the UNF shirt she had on over her singlet, realizing she clearly hadn't thought things through when wearing both on this trip.

"I wouldn't if I were you," Ross told her, motioning to her shirt. "You'll need to cover up, if anything." He smiled. "It will be considered disrespectful otherwise."

Carrie paused her unbuttoning, staring at Ross as he passed her a cream-colored shawl. "I have to layer up? Really?"

"I'm afraid so."

"We'll all sweat together, Welles," Harris said.

She looked at the captain, wondering how his nose was coping with the sweat and body odor it must be detecting, but decided against asking him about it. She still felt awkward about the discussion he'd had with McKinley. She glanced at the lieutenant again, but his eyes were looking outward, scanning the distance.

The journey in the small vehicle was long and hot. They listened to Ross as he related how the ship came to be discovered many years before the UNF became aware of its existence. Technically, historically, it was the first to be found, but since the UNF only became aware of its existence after the smaller ship near the Carlsbad Caverns had been discovered, to the UNF it was the second.

As they approached the location, Carrie noted how well hidden it was. The area was quite mountainous and although the UNF had beaten a path as close as they could, the last part had to be undertaken on foot.

They walked through a narrow ravine, which at this time of day was, thankfully, cast deep in shadow, and eventually they came across the relic's guards. Although they didn't realize they were guards at first. Dressed like Egyptian farmers, they soon revealed their hidden weapons, exposing their true role. There were ten of them spread out along the ravine, on approach to the entrance, and Carrie noticed others higher up the cliffs, nestled on small outcrops.

The entrance itself was very low-key, just a natural fissure in the side of the mountain. No-one would probably ever discover it, she thought, although if anyone saw the gathering of men in the area, it would draw interest.

One of the guards pulled out an ID device and held it up to Ross, although the look in his eye confirmed that he recognized the archaeologist. Ross placed his palm on the screen, then held it up to his eye to scan his retina.

"Each of you do the scans," Ross told them, then passed the device to Harris. "They are expecting us, but it's a requirement for entry."

They each completed the scans, then the guard lazily motioned them through; perhaps he was bored, or perhaps this duty was below him.

Similar to the last ship, a long, dark narrow path took them where they needed to go. McKinley and Carrie could see just fine, of course, but both Harris and Ross needed the aid of the dim artificial lighting. Soon enough they noticed the walls changing color, taking on that pearly sheen; it was almost beautiful, Carrie thought, the way it glowed and shimmered in the dim light.

More guards awaited them outside the entrance to the buried ship.

Ross motioned them forward with a wave, and stepped aboard. Carrie followed, then Harris, then McKinley. As Carrie stepped aboard, she immediately noticed the size of it. A long corridor stretched out before them.

"This ship must've left some hole when it burrowed down?" she said.

"You would think so," Ross said. "However, the tunneling system of this ship enables it to remove the rock in front, then sweep it around to the back, so it covers its tracks. But the rocky covering remains loose. We think the ships are designed to hide in the ground, but then rise again if needed."

"So, there could be hundreds more buried around Earth?" she asked.

Ross shook his head. "Not likely. Even though the material these ships are made out of isn't found on this Earth, our scanning systems are advanced enough to detect similar rock displacement patterns. So far, we haven't located any, other than the six ships already found, but we continue to scan just in case."

"Do you think there's a risk that when the Zetas return they could somehow bring these ships to life again with their thought-technology?"

Ross threw her a serious look. "It's quite possible, sergeant. We will need to be prepared for the fact that these ships could become their reinforcements, if activated."

Carrie glanced worriedly at Harris and McKinley.

"That's why we're trying to ensure we locate them all first," Ross said, then motioned for them to turn into another corridor.

They followed him along a series of turns, down curved corridors – like being inside ridged pipes – gradually making their way into the belly of the ship. Carrie noted that the pearlescent residue had all but disappeared, and now the walls looked normal, like a metal covered in that soft, dark-gray skin.

Ross finally stepped into a large, rounded room. Carrie and the others followed him and they stood looking around at the walls.

"What's this room?" Harris asked.

"We're not sure exactly, but we think it might be the equivalent of a ceremonial hall or something." Ross moved to point out the images depicted along the walls. "These images seem to tell the story of their time here on Earth, as well as painting a picture of the Zetas themselves."

Carrie, Harris and McKinley spread out, stepping closer to examine the images. The images were of the same material as the walls, as though they were part of them and not printed onto them. On the wall in front of Carrie were images of tall, human-like creatures. They were bald with slightly flat, elongated heads, and long necks, and wore flowing garments that curled around their feet.

"These are the Zetas?" Carrie asked.

"We believe so, yes," Ross answered. "That's one of them, at least."

"One of them?" Carrie asked.

"We've identified five different Zetas. This one we call the Priestess." He pointed to the tall, bald one depicted in front of Carrie. "She seems quite revered in this mothership." Ross moved to another section of wall, close to where Harris stood. "This one," he said, pointing to a stockier figure covered in flowing hair, "we call the Alma Mater. She's always depicted with either a pregnant belly or breast-feeding." He moved to another section. "This one we call the Zisis. Basically, the name is an amalgamation of Zeta crossed with Isis." He pointed to a form with long arms spread wide, like wings, and a small pot belly.

He moved over to where McKinley stood. "Here we have Amphibia." He pointed to a creature with a thick neck and broad shoulders, its head slightly lowered, and bulging black eyes staring straight ahead. "And," he moved to another, "this one we call Salacia." It was tall with gray skin and muscular limbs.

"They all look human," she said, "but not."

"Yes," Ross said, moving back to the first, the Priestess. "There are five Zetas featured in these images. Can you make the connection with our Earth?"

Carrie, McKinley and Harris glanced around the walls but didn't offer comment.

A large smile spread across Ross's face. "Remember, you're looking at the makers of the majority of life on our planet."

Silence filled the room as the three of them stared at Ross.

He pointed to the first one again. "The Priestess, the way she stands, resembles a snake, don't you think? The way her robe curls around her feet like a tail." He moved to the second. "The mother, covered in hair and nurturing her young, just like a mammal would do." He moved to the third. "Zisis. Look at those wings!" Then he moved to the fourth. "Amphibia, with her hairless skin and bulging eyes. Very frog-like, wouldn't you say?" Then he raced to the fifth. "And Salacia, named after Neptune's queen. The strong limbs, depicted near water."

"The animal kingdom." Harris's voice punctured the silence.

"Yes!" Ross's eyes grew wide. "These five Zetas are essentially human, but they are each fused with one of the main classifications of the animal kingdom. The Priestess is the mother of reptiles, the Alma Mater is the mother of mammals, Zisis is the mother of birds, Amphibia is the mother of amphibians, and Salacia is the mother of fish."

"So where does that leave the other animals?" Carrie queried. "The ones without backbones."

Ross grinned. "This is what we're just discovering! The invertebrates evolved on Earth naturally. The vertebrates came here, long ago, from the Zetas."

"So, humans are not natural to this planet?" she said.

"No, we are not," Ross said, "but we've been here long enough to have evolved and adapted to it."

"Holy shit," she muttered. "Earth isn't our true home."

"You mustn't think like that," Ross told her. "We've been here for many, many generations now. This *is* our home. We were born here. We, humans, have evolved from the apes just like we've always been led to believe. What we didn't know was that the Zetas were the ones to put the animals here in the first place."

"So, somehow," Harris said, "genetic material from these Zetas made its way to Earth and started vertebrate life."

"Yes. Whether it was an experiment to expand into the galaxy or whether it was by accident we don't know. But it does seem strange that material from all five Zeta types developed here on Earth. I'm thinking that this wasn't accidental. It was intentional."

"We humans, effectively, evolved from the Alma Mater," Carrie said.

"Yes. She's our 'mother'."

Carrie moved closer to stare at this creature being posited as her original creator. Voluptuous, with full, curved breasts, rounded belly and a face that seemed to resemble several barnyard animals in one. She thought of her own mother, then, and swiftly wiped the Alma Mater from her mind. *My mother is dead.*

"And these must be the Homo heidelbergensis?" Harris said, drawing their attention to another section of the wall that depicted a row of warrior-looking humans with long, matted hair and lean, but muscular bodies.

"Yes," Ross moved to stand beside him, "that's them." Then he pointed to a different section. "This image depicts the HH being marched into one of the ships."

They gathered around and studied the picture. Carrie counted twelve HH in the line, naked but for a loincloth. Her eyes moved to one of the

Priestesses who stood watching the group move onto the ship. She counted five of the Priestesses standing about, regal and androgynous.

Carrie turned and moved back to view the other Zeta forms: the Alma Mater, Zisis, Amphibia and Salacia. She looked back at Ross.

"Is it just me, or has anyone else noticed that the Zetas are all women? I don't see any males here."

The archaeologist's face lit up. "Wonderful! I was waiting for one of you to notice."

"They're *all* women?" she asked again.

"Yes."

"What does that mean?" Harris asked arching his eyebrow at them.

"It means," Ross's smile grew wider, "we're dealing with a female-dominant race."

"The Zetas are all chicks?" McKinley said. "How do they breed?"

"Well, until we find a live specimen to study, we're going on guesswork. But, given what we've found so far, we don't think they're a single sex being that fertilizes their own eggs." Ross pointed to the image of the HH being marched onto the ship. "That could be why they took the HH. They needed them."

"They're all male," Carrie said, coming to stand by the image again.

"Yes. Breeding stock." Ross crossed his arms.

"Breeding stock?" Harris arched his eyebrow. "You think this is all about finding breeding stock? Not land or territory or dominance—"

"Oh, it is about dominance," Ross interrupted. "But this isn't about land or territory, this is about survival. For whatever reason, there are no images of male Zetas here on this ship. That means one of two things. They are virtually extinct on the Zeta home planet, or they are not worthy enough to be depicted among the five Zeta queens."

"But... breeding," McKinley said flatly, disbelievingly. "You think that's why they're coming here?"

"Well, they're responding to us sending their signals back to them, mirrored comms if you like, but yes," Ross nodded, "I do. It's the most logical explanation. The Zetas depicted here are female. The HH they are marching onto the ship are male. There's not one female prisoner among them."

"How do you think they overpowered the HH?" Harris asked.

"Well, they had technology at their disposal for one. You forget the HH were extremely primitive; they had not yet developed any intelligence of note. These Zetas came with their technology, their intelligence and their superiority. From the outset, they would've treated the HH as inferior and beaten them into submission at every turn." Ross seemed to think for a moment. "I suggest it would've been a similar experience to that of many of the early human settlement colonizations that took place here on Earth. I say it could be similar, but the reality is that the Zeta invasion would've been extreme, given there must have been a huge disparity in skills and technology."

"So, the Zetas are colonizers and we're so-called savages?" Harris said staring at Ross.

"It's the closest analogy we have," Ross said. "It's similar, but different. But I'm guessing it must be inherent somewhere in our genes, this seeking dominance over another. And I have no doubt that that is what the Zetas plan to do… We have communicated with them, and so they are coming back to reap the crops they planted all those years ago. Coming back to claim us. And while they're here they might just top up their pool of breeding stock."

Breeding stock… Carrie stared at Ross, then moved her eyes to the image on the wall of the HH being marched into the ship, then turned her gaze to Harris and McKinley, then back to Matthew Ross.

Then she burst out laughing.

The three men stared back at her with puzzled faces.

"I'm sorry." She held her hand up, struggling to keep the laughter at bay.

"Something funny?" Ross asked, uncertainly.

Carrie looked at him, then at the picture again. "Yeah."

"Care to explain?" Harris asked, eyebrow arched again.

Carrie looked around the room then back at them. "This whole thing, for me, started with the Darwin. The mission I was sent on, along with two other women, to be forced into a breeding program with the Jumbos. A mission I was sent on by my male superiors. And now look at this." She indicated the walls. "This is what we're going to be fighting against. A female-dominant race that wants to use you boys as breeding stock. Do you not see the irony?" She exploded in laughter again as the three men stared back at her. Ross, in particular, seemed not quite sure what to make of her.

"The tables have turned," she said, trying to control the grin on her face.

"Just remember, Welles," Harris said, "that we," he motioned between himself and McKinley, "helped stop you from being forced into that breeding program on the Darwin."

Carrie's laughter died down and her face settled into a serious look. "I know, sir." She glanced around the walls again, then looked back to him. "And that is why I'll do what I can to protect you from these Zeta bitches when they come to claim you." She turned her eyes to McKinley, and they exchanged a brief look before he turned away again.

"Um, Jumbos?" Ross asked hesitantly. "Darwin?"

"You didn't hear that," Harris said firmly with a look to match.

"Right," Ross said, clearing his throat. "Well then, shall I take you through to the next room?"

Harris gave Ross a nod. "Lead the way."

The *Carcharias'* new captain, Lincoln Gold, sat in the interrogation room staring at the contract in front of him. He'd read it back to front and clarified anything he needed to with the UNF legal counsel they'd sent him. He should've been surprised when she walked into the room, but he realized that after all the secrets he'd learned nothing should surprise him anymore.

He looked up at Lieutenant Andrea Skordan – the bright blue eyes, the vibrant red hair pulled tight into a bun – and wondered whether she'd run into him at the bar that night he was drunk by chance or whether she was keeping an eye on him. Whether she knew what the UNF had in store for him.

"Do you have any other questions, captain?" she asked.

Gold shook his head, glancing at the document in front of him. "Not about the contract," he said, then looked back up and met her eyes.

She stared back, and he thought he saw a certain sparkle of recognition, of suspicion; that maybe she knew what other questions he would like to ask of her.

"Very well," she said, gathering her things. "If you do think of anything you need clarified, contact Command and they'll get word to me."

Gold watched her stand.

"Congratulations, captain," she said. "Welcome to the Advanced Soldier Program."

With that she left the room. Marchant entered and sat in her place. Gold stared at him.

"So, what next, sir?" Gold asked.

"Now we wait until Captain Harris returns from Egypt."

"Egypt?"

"He'll explain that when he returns."

"What about the ship? The guys will want to know what's happening to me."

"Rovine has advised them that he has received a promotion, and that you, in turn have received a promotion also."

"They know I hit him," Gold said. "One of the guys would've found him."

"They do," Marchant nodded. "They've been given a few days leave, until Harris returns and we can release you."

Gold nodded, then motioned to the closed door. "How long has Skordan been part of the program?"

"She's fairly new. She has a sharp legal mind and specializes in UNF law. She'll be an asset to the program."

Gold nodded again. "So why are you keeping me here until Harris returns? Why can't I go back to the ship if it's empty?"

"We wanted to give you a few days to get your head around this. And while you're doing that, we want to keep you away from potential..." Marchant seemed to be thinking of the right word to use, "problems. Keep you out of harm's way."

"Problems? Harm's way?"

"You hear of a reporter by the name of Miranda Finch?" Marchant stared at him as though trying to read his reactions.

"Yeah."

"She tried to post your bail."

"She did?" he asked surprised.

"When we denied her request, she left a message for you to call her if you needed anything."

Gold stared at Marchant, not sure what to say.

"You sleeping with her?" Marchant asked bluntly.

Gold gave a short sharp laugh and shook his head. "No, sir."

"You sure about that?"

"Quite positive, sir."

"Well, she's a reporter who's been picking around the edges of UNFASP. If we're not careful, she'll uncover something that could cause us a lot of problems. We can't have that. The rest of the population does not need to know about the Zetas yet. Let them live their lives in the bliss of ignorance for a few more years."

Gold nodded in agreement. He realized just how much his own life had turned upside down the past day or so since learning the truth. Ignorance really was bliss.

"You stay away from her," Marchant said firmly. "Understood?"

Gold nodded, his mind turning over. "Yes, sir."

"Good, I'll have the guards escort you back to your room. Harris will return soon. We move forward then."

"Sir," Gold called. "One thing?"

Marchant stopped and turned around.

"Did the UNF toss her apartment?"

"Excuse me?" Marchant asked.

"Someone tossed Finch's apartment looking for something. Was that us?"

"No, first I've heard of it. What were they looking for?"

"I don't know, but it happened after her reports on the Eden incident."

Marchant nodded, mind ticking over. "Well, it wasn't ordered by the UNF. That's not quite our style when it comes to dealing with reporters."

Gold nodded, believing him, and Marchant left the room.

Harris looked around one of the supposed flight decks of the Zeta mothership. There were no controls as such, just the smooth walls with that curved lip jutting out. The room was large, about 10 meters by 15 meters. This, according to Ross, had been labelled Flight Deck 1, the first of six on this ship.

Harris watched Welles as she walked along the wall, dragging her fingers across the lip's smoothness and watching the faint blue light follow them. McKinley didn't touch anything. Instead, he stood with arms folded and seemed to scan the walls, fixing his Alpha senses as though trying to uncover something not yet revealed.

"Why do you call this the mothership?" Harris asked Ross. "It's larger than the one in New Mexico, but to my mind, it doesn't evoke a ship the size of what a mothership should be."

"No," Ross agreed. "We call it the mothership, because, yes, it is larger than the others we've found, but mainly because of the images depicted in that other room. This ship is the one that gave us most of the information we have been able to gather on the Zetas. This ship showed us they are a female-dominant species that we think is in search of breeding stock. That's why the term mothership is used."

"Is there any evidence they bred with the HH while they were here?" Welles asked him.

"This," Ross's eyes lit up again, "is something that has become our most important research. The DNA that was pulled from the skulls we unearthed, sequenced, and found to not quite match that of a typical human skull, has been studied thoroughly. We've identified certain Zeta markers which we've then compared to our database of human DNA samples to see if there are any matches. We've identified a few cases of human DNA that possess these special Zeta markings."

"What does that mean?" Harris asked.

"It means there are humans on Earth today who have Zeta DNA within them."

"Of course we do," Harris said. "You said they're our makers, so that fits."

"No," Ross shook his head. "We were originally created by the Zetas. Our basic human DNA came from them, but there are certain Zeta-specific markers that have been reintroduced to the human species since, making them more abundant in some humans. Don't get me wrong, we predict the instances will be very rare, but it does exist in some humans, which indicates they could well be a direct descendant of a Zeta and HH pairing."

Harris stared back at Ross blankly.

"Over time," Ross elaborated, "some genetic traits have been bred out of the human race. Just like a dog breeder can breed aggressiveness or certain illnesses out of their dogs, so too time has watered down Zeta specific traits in humans. Initially, with our evolution from the ape into our modern form, then with exclusive human to human breeding. *But*, based on our database of human DNA, we've found occasional occurrences of these Zeta markings that are much stronger than in others. These Zeta markings found in the human DNA samples match those found in the unearthed Zeta skulls, which date back to the time of the HH. We believe the prevalence of these Zeta markings in certain human DNA are a direct result of recent Zeta-human pairings. Or should I say, Zeta-HH pairings."

"What are you saying?" Harris asked. "There are half-breed Zetas walking around here today?"

"Well, I wouldn't call them half-breeds, captain. We have had several hundred thousand years of watering down that has taken place. But, we believe there does exist a clear lineage of Zeta-HH pairings to some humans today. Humans who had their Zeta DNA topped up during the Zetas last visit to Earth, which has made their Zeta markings more prevalent than in others. Based on our DNA samples on file, it's extremely rare, but the proof is there."

"So, they bred with some of the HH back then." Welles nodded in finality. "I wonder which Zetas?"

"Until we get our hands on samples from each of the five Zetas, we won't know."

The thought of Zeta-HH pairings actually disturbed Harris a lot. He quickly wiped it from his mind, fixing his attention on Welles and McKinley instead. They stood on opposite sides of the room, Welles trying to interact with the ship, and McKinley avoiding it.

Harris turned back to Ross. "The Zeta ships we've found so far… is there any pattern to their locations, their positioning?"

"Not that we can discover. They appear to be randomly placed. Although some seem to be located near mountains or natural underground cavities. The only one that doesn't fit this profile is the one in Australia."

"Is there anything different about that ship then?"

"No," Ross said, "it's no different to the one you saw in New Mexico."

"I'd like to see a map of all locations, just the same," Harris said.

"Of course, captain, come this way." Harris moved after Ross, throwing a look at Welles and McKinley to follow.

As Harris stepped out into the rounded corridor that felt like a metal artery, he glanced over his shoulder. Welles and McKinley were at the doorway, having reached it at the same time. The two looked at each other and Welles's face softened, but McKinley's remained emotionless as he moved through the doorway first.

Harris realized something was up between them. No doubt it had everything to do with his discussion with McKinley the other day, but he didn't want to deal with that problem now. He followed Ross as the archaeologist left the ship and headed toward an open cavity in the rock where a small control center had been set-up. Three Egyptians manned the consoles there. Ross explained that two of them worked for security, and the other was a local scientist who ran regular tests on the rock surrounding the ship to detect any changes.

Harris viewed the map of the ship's locations while Ross began speaking with the local scientist about the latest readings from the site. Harris tuned them out, though. It was Ross's job to disseminate any useful information that Harris, as part of the UNF, could use in combat against the Zetas. So, he'd let Ross sift through the jargon and trusted he would pass on any nuggets he found.

*

When they were done for the day, they made their way back through the heat to where the UNF hangar lay, to await their scheduled departure. Harris almost wished to be back in that spaceship in the cool of underground. It gave him a thought.

He turned and looked at Ross. "You think they can't handle the heat maybe?" he asked, eyebrow arched. "That's why they bury themselves underground."

"That's one theory. Underground they are protected from the elements, but they are also disguised from their enemies. With few entrances onto the ship, they can kill anything that moves toward it."

Harris nodded and Ross chuckled, pointing to Welles fanning herself with the shawl he'd given her. McKinley stood a ways off, wiping his brow.

"I don't think your soldiers care much for the heat either," Ross said. "It is unusually warm for this time of year. I'll fetch some water." With that Ross moved off into the terminal building.

Harris wiped his brow and stole a glance at Welles and McKinley again. They'd barely said a word to each other today. McKinley was clearly avoiding her. Harris sighed. This is exactly what he didn't want to happen;

to have their relationship get in the way of their job. And right now it was. They needed to communicate with each other, they needed to contribute to his plans and strategies.

He felt a pang of loss for Doc shoot through him. His sounding board, his co-strategist. He'd only entered his dreams that once since passing away; to say goodbye. Right now, more than ever, he could do with Doc, and his mind, here by his side.

He scanned his eyes around the dusty oven of a tarmac, then looked back over at Welles and McKinley, and sighed. He didn't have Doc anymore, he had these two: Welles and McKinley. They needed to step up and deliver him support in Doc's absence.

He watched as Welles headed toward the bathroom. As she disappeared inside, he moved over to McKinley.

"So," he said to his lieutenant, "your thoughts?"

"On the mothership?" McKinley asked him.

Harris nodded.

McKinley shrugged. "I don't know. It's a bunch of pictures."

"But they tell a story," he said.

"Or they're just pretty pictures."

"Think of them like a satellite image. A moment captured in time."

McKinley studied him. "You believe the theory?"

Harris shrugged. "Well, there's not much else to go on. I'd say it's the best bet we have."

McKinley chuckled. "Slaves for breeding? Really?"

"Yeah, I know, but I'm still not taking the chance. I've already got another kid on the way. I sure as hell ain't breeding with no fish or bird woman."

McKinley laughed.

Harris laughed with him. "First time I've seen you crack a smile for days, lieutenant."

McKinley's smile died down, and his face returned to normal.

"Everything alright with you and Welles?" he asked casually.

McKinley glanced at him, then looked away. "Fine."

"McKinley," Harris said flatly, "we had a conversation the other day. I gave you leave from the ship to see her, now you're not talking. Don't take me for a fool."

McKinley shrugged, scanning the camel-colored rocky mountains in the distance.

"You told her I knew. So, what, she's stopped things?" Harris asked.

"Nope," McKinley said, "I did."

"You ended things?" Harris's eyebrows climbed to the top of his forehead.

"Not *ended*..." McKinley hesitated, searching for the right words. "It's just on pause."

"Why?"

McKinley looked at him, then shook his head as though it were nothing.

"What?" Harris said bluntly, challenging him. "It was just the thrill of the chase? You wanted her, you got her into bed, now you're bored with her?"

McKinley threw him an offended look. "No."

"Good," Harris said firmly. "Because if you want to get laid, go find it some place else. Don't fuck with Welles like that."

"I'm not," McKinley's brow furrowed angrily.

Harris analyzed him for a moment, then nodded. "I know, McKinley, I just wanted to hear you say it." Harris rested his hands on his hips. "Look, I'm not a blind man. I know you care about her. You have a child together. You've been through hell together. And..." it was Harris's turn to search for the right words. "I know this thing hasn't just happened since Doc's been gone."

"We never—" McKinley began defensively, but Harris held his hand up to stop him.

"I know nothing *happened* while Doc was alive. Not consciously, anyway. But thinking back over everything that's happened since the Darwin mission, I know something happened, subconsciously, in here," and he pointed to his temple, then to his chest, "and in here." Harris sighed and glanced about the empty, dusty tarmac, at the two of them standing in the heat, mirrored sunglasses on. "This shit isn't easy, McKinley. Women, love, any of that shit. There's no easy answer or clear path to take."

"Sir, it's fine," McKinley said, "don't worry about it. It's not your problem."

"Oh, but it is," he said. "This, you two not talking, avoiding each other. It is. The three of us are in this future war together, McKinley. I need you and Welles to step up and help me. So this shit? Sort it out."

McKinley exhaled and placed his hands on his hips. "It won't be a problem, sir. When I'm in the field, my mind is fixed on the job. You don't have to worry about that."

"I know," Harris said, "but there's a lot of work to do off the field, too. When we're in the field, you keep talking to me like that, like a soldier. But when we're out of the field, I need you to talk to me like a living breathing human. The kind that will do anything to sort out Earth's problems and try to save his family from this invasion."

McKinley looked back at him and Harris detected another furrow in his brow. Harris stepped toward him.

"You bailed me up on the ship to ensure that this thing between you and Welles wasn't going to be a problem between us. Why? Because she meant something to you. And I knew, McKinley, from the look in your eye, that no matter whether I had a problem or not, you weren't going to let her go. Tell me I'm wrong."

McKinley looked away to the mountains.

"What's changed?" Harris asked. "You've been fighting for her all this time, putting your life on the line to save hers, so don't give me this 'I don't care' bullshit. 'Cause I don't buy it."

"It doesn't matter what I think," McKinley objected. "It's *her*."

Harris studied him, not sure what he meant. McKinley seemed to struggle with what he wanted to say.

"She won't let Doc go," the lieutenant eventually said. "And I can't live in his shadow any longer."

"So, you're just going to walk away? Give up?"

McKinley shrugged. "What else is there to do? She won't let his memory go, she's too scared of what people will think of us. I'm not living like that."

"So, you're just going to walk away. Give up?" Harris repeated, staring at him.

McKinley stared back. "Do you know how hard it is to live with the *glorious* Doc present everywhere I turn? The saint? I can't live up to that!"

Harris stared at him suddenly understanding the problem. "Do you remember the conversation we had in that Command hospital cafeteria after the twins were returned? The one where you didn't think you were good enough to be Freya's father and I told you, you were? Remember that? Are you telling me we need to have that same conversation again about Welles now, and whether you're good enough to be with her?"

"I'll never be Doc," McKinley said, eyes on the mountains in the distance.

"No, you won't," Harris said matter-of-factly, "because you're *you*. And Welles seems to have fallen for *you*. I told you, I'm not a blind man, McKinley. I see her, and I've seen the way she looks at you. Now, you can snap up that woman, or you can be a fucking idiot and walk away, that's up to you."

McKinley looked at him, listening to what he was saying.

"If there's one thing I know, McKinley, it's that love, a relationship, isn't just one fight. It's not a matter of winning her hand and that's it. You fight every *single* day together. Taya and I learned that the hard way. On and off. Off and on. That was my fault. I thought it was too hard, so I walked away. But it's meant to be hard. To a certain extent, anyway. That's how you know which one is worth it. The one, that no matter how hard the fight is, you find yourself not wanting to let go of. Still finding yourself *wanting* to fight for them." He glanced around and saw Welles emerging from the bathroom, then looked back at McKinley. "If you want to be with her, then you fight for her. Either way, sort this shit out, because I don't want to see it in my presence again."

With that, Harris turned and walked away.

Miranda Finch held her PDP close to her ear.

"I'm not lying, Morrell," she said. "They won't let me near Gold. I have no idea what's going on."

Morrell was silent.

"You're part of the UNF," she said, "why don't you try and find out?"

"It's none of my business," he said gruffly.

"Oh, but it's mine?"

"You're a reporter. They expect you to be nosy. I'm a soldier. We mind our own business."

"I guess we're both out of luck then," she said and hung up the PDP.

She rose from her office desk, moved over to the window and looked out at the Centralis Command Centre.

"What the hell is going on, Gold," she whispered to herself. "What the hell is going on?"

10

Affirmation

Corporal Sabrina Colt sat upright at the sound of the door opening. The same man as last time entered the lair, the one they were to call the Greenback. LeFroy moved toward him, but stopped short at the sight of his two bodyguards.

"Will you let us go now?" LeFroy asked in a pathetic voice.

"No," the Greenback said bluntly. He came to a stop in the middle of the room and placed his hands on his hips, studying the two prisoners.

"Have you heard from Drazen?" LeFroy asked.

"He's dead," the Greenback said. "They're all dead."

"W—what?" LeFroy said.

Colt nodded to herself. "The *Aurora* team stopped them," she whispered, feeling the sting of tears in her eyes.

"It would seem Drazen's band of merry Jumbos weren't quite the match for a unit of enhanced soldiers."

"The soldiers were Jumbos?" LeFroy asked.

The Greenback nodded.

"Were there any casualties on the *Aurora* side?" Colt asked.

"From what I gathered from the news, some were hospitalized. One Sentinel died."

Colt felt herself slump as she thought of the *Aurora* team. Of Welles, Harris, Brown...

"So, what happens now?" LeFroy asked. "Why won't you let us go?"

The Greenback turned his eyes to LeFroy, stepping closer to him.

"The UNF, through Sharley, used some of my fighters without permission. They think I'm some kind of bank they can tap into and make withdrawals from. Except they're not so keen on paying back what they loaned. So, I'll take payment another way." He turned his eyes to Colt, then moved to stand in front of her cell. He studied her a moment. "I want what you're carrying."

Colt's spine straightened with a spike of fear. She didn't want this pregnancy, but it made her uncomfortable to have someone lay claim to what grew inside her body.

The Greenback turned back to LeFroy. "How many is she carrying?"

"We don't know."

"How far along is she?"

"She's just under three months."

The Greenback nodded. "Alright, I'll come back in six months to collect."

Colt audibly gasped.

"They could arrive earlier," LeFroy said. "It's not a normal pregnancy. I'm certainly not equipped to handle—"

"I'll send someone here daily to check on her," the Greenback said.

"I can't offer her any assistance," LeFroy continued. "You don't need me anymore."

Colt's face was taken over by a terrifying Jumbo look which she fired directly at LeFroy. The weasel did this to her and now he was going to run. As she stared at him, she promised herself again that she would make him pay for what he did to her.

The Greenback laughed. "I don't think she's a fan of yours."

"That's why you have to release me," LeFroy said in a small voice.

The Greenback moved over to his cell and stared in at him. "You know, I think I'm on her side here."

"Drazen brought me here by force!" LeFroy objected. "I'm just as much a hostage as she is."

"Then you'll see this through together," the Greenback told him. "You make sure she stays healthy and safe, and delivers whatever she's carrying. You do that, then I'll let you go."

"You expect me to live down here for another six months," Colt spat. "In these conditions?"

"No," the Greenback said, glancing around. "I'll make things a little more homely, bring you a TV, books, better food, better bed." He looked at her. "I'll do that for you, and you grow me some good little enhanced humans in return. Deal?"

Colt stared hard, the Jumbo look piercing through him.

The Greenback laughed. "I'll take that as a yes." He stepped closer. "Just remember," he said, lowering his voice, "if you do anything to kill what's inside you, I'll kill you. That's the deal. You deliver them good, I'll set you free." Then he looked at LeFroy. "I'll set you both free. So, you both better make sure she delivers healthy."

As the Greenback departed, Colt turned her glare back to LeFroy, who was staring at her, troubled and frightened. They were in this together. LeFroy wouldn't let her destroy the children, because his life depended on it. She was trapped. Locked in this cell with no way out. They weren't going to give her any other choice.

She dropped her eyes to her abdomen as a sense of hopelessness washed over her. She really had no choice. She was going to have to carry these Jumbos babies - whoever they belonged to.

Carrie was pleased to finally arrive home after a long day. She couldn't wait for a shower to wash the Egyptian sweat and dust off. She opened the carrier door and looked up at the Fortress, its lights stark against the black of night. Her eyes met her Sentinel Novak's at the entrance and they exchanged a nod. She couldn't wait to hug her twins, who she'd left in her father's care, and strangely enough she looked forward to chatting with Archie about all she had learned. However, right now, she was most curious about McKinley's presence in the carrier with her. Once they'd landed at the Space Dock, she'd made her way to the carrier that would take her home and was surprised to see McKinley had followed her. He should've gone back to the ship with Harris. She gave him a quizzical look as he climbed into the carrier after her. He'd simply said: "Told Harris I'd see you home."

Sitting in the carrier outside the Fortress, she looked at him. "Well, I'm home... You wanna come inside and see Freya?"

He nodded silently, then followed her exit from the vehicle.

They made their way inside to a warm welcome from Archie.

"Sergeant Welles, Lieutenant McKinley. Welcome home."

"Hi, Archie," she said. "Is everyone okay?"

"The twins are sleeping soundly, as is your father. I believe they wore him out today."

Carrie laughed. "Yeah, Alpha twins do that." She made her way to their room to check on them, McKinley following silently behind. She kissed their sleeping faces and caressed their hair, promising herself she would give them extra cuddles tomorrow.

She looked up from Brody's cot to where McKinley was hunched over Freya's. She watched him through the darkness, feeling her heart crush in on itself at the sight. She hated this distance between them. Hated the thought that what they had could end, because she was afraid to let go of her past, because she was avoiding facing the future.

He straightened up and turned to look at her, his blue Alpha eyes glowing slightly from the light in the hallway. They left the twins sleeping and made their way back to the kitchen.

"Do you have time for a drink?" she asked him.

He glanced at his watch, seemed to mull something over.

"I'd like it if you could stay," she said, to reassure him.

"Would you? Or is that the Alpha talking?" he asked, acknowledging he could sense her Alpha stirring. *Damn pheromones.*

She stared back at him but didn't respond, sensing his Alpha stirring, too.

"You want *me* to stay? Or you just want my Alpha in your bed?" His words were blunt and they cut her, but she sensed they cut him just as much.

"Both," she cut back.

"Both?"

"I want this to end."

It was his turn to stare at her and not respond.

"Not *us*," she clarified, "just this fight we're having. I want it to end."

"So end it."

"Tell me how."

McKinley shook his head. "I can't tell you how, Welles. This is yours. If you want *me* here, then I'll be here. If you just want my Alpha in your bed, no strings?" He shrugged. "I can do that too. But just know, 'no strings' means no monogamy."

"I'm not really a 'no strings' kind of girl."

He shrugged again. "Then I guess you got a choice to make."

"I already told you, I want both," she said firmly. "I want *you* and I want your Alpha." As she said that she noticed her chest swell and her heart start beating double time, the Alpha within clearly rearing its head now. McKinley's too, was now clear and present, reacting to hers.

"Do you? Really?" he asked.

"How many ways do I need to say it?"

"I'm not much of one for words, Welles," he said. "That was Doc. He was the man of words, always saying the right thing, knowing how to handle them."

"And you?"

McKinley threw his arms wide. "I'm a man of action. That's what I do. So, if you want to get to the heart of me, don't tell me, show me."

"Show you? How?"

"Stop hiding," he said bluntly. He was reeking of the old McKinley, the one who didn't mince words, but there was a certain familiarity with this. She knew his bluntness was born of an emotion he didn't know how to deal with.

She stepped toward him. "You want me to stop hiding? You want us to come out of the closet? Then let's do that."

"Yeah?" he questioned, folding his arms. "Just like that? What changed your mind? The other day, you wanted to run a mile from that."

"What do you want from me?" she asked. "I'm giving you what you want and it's still not good enough. It sounds like *you're* looking for an excuse to end things. Are *you* trying to cut and run?"

"No," he shook his head.

"Then what? You're going to have to use words to tell me."

"Coming out of the closet is one thing. But the bigger problem here is…"

"What?"

He looked at her and clenched his jaw. "Doc."

She furrowed her brow. "What about him?"

He stared at her a little longer, then shook his head. "I'm sick of living in his shadow."

"What do you mean?"

"I'm sick of being the stand-in. I've taken his place on the *Aurora*, I've taken his place with you, I'm raising his son. I have taken his place in everything and everywhere I look, he's there. Some memory, some relic. I can't escape it."

"You haven't taken his place with me. You're too different for that to happen."

"What's that supposed to mean?"

"Stop thinking of yourself as second best!" she couldn't help but raise her voice.

"Tell me how I'm supposed to do that with the shadow of Saint Doc everywhere I turn?" he demanded, raising his voice in turn.

"Don't say it like that. Don't talk about him like that."

"This is what I mean!" His hands motioned to her in exasperation. "How can I compete with the ghost of a man who was fucking perfect?"

"He wasn't perfect."

McKinley raised his eyebrows skeptically.

"Look, I'm not going to lie to you," Carrie said. "You know I loved Dan with all my heart. Those kids were born because of him—"

"Yeah, I know, and I was the asshole who told you to get rid of them." McKinley lowered his eyes to the floor.

"Hey, if Dan hadn't been there *I* would've gotten rid of them. I thought the same way you did at the start."

"But because of *him*, they were born. Then he raised my daughter when I couldn't. He was the savior and I was the asshole."

"Would you *fucking* listen to me?" she hissed.

He shot her a piercing look, but relaxed against the kitchen bench, folding his arms.

"I'm not going to lie to you," she said gently. "Every time I look at Brody I see Doc, and I think of him."

"Understood," McKinley said with a sharp nod, then moved to leave, but she stopped him.

"Goddamnit! Let me finish!" she said, squeezing his arm so tight he winced and looked down at it. "You might be about the action, but I am about the words, so let me talk!"

His blue eyes blazed back into hers.

"Every time I see Brody, I'm gonna think of Doc. But every time I see Freya I think of *you*... I don't know how that's possible, to have felt the same intensity for the both of you, but it is."

McKinley shook his head, glancing around the room. "Harris told me if I wanted you, I should fight for you, but I can't compete with a dead man. I'm not him, I'll never be him, I'll always be second best. Doc will always win."

"Don't say that." She let his arm go and stepped back. "Doc's dead, McKinley. He hasn't won anything. *You* did. *You* won. Because you're alive and you're the one who gets to have me. He doesn't."

"You need to let him go," McKinley said. "There's no room for three of us in this."

Carrie stared at him, searching his face. "I thought I had," she said quietly. "I honestly thought I had."

"If you want me," he said, "you need to let him go. I'm not saying you have to forget him. I'm just saying you gotta let him go. Stop acting like he's still here and you're fucking cheating on him."

A tear appeared from somewhere and rolled down her cheek. "I know. I will."

"I'm not hiding anymore," he said, as his eyes pierced into hers, although the intensity had lessened. "So, you're either with me, or you're not."

They stared at each other and Carrie felt a lump swell in her throat. She reached out and grabbed a handful of his shirt in her fist, anything to stop him walking out the door, anything to hold onto him.

"I'm with you," she whispered. "Until the end."

His eyes remained fixed, analyzing her.

"And will *you* be with *me* until the end?" she countered.

"Why wouldn't I?"

She shrugged. "You have options. Dr. Forcaster, for instance."

McKinley stared at her in silence.

"Yeah, I noticed," she said, then looked him up and down. "She wants you... for what you are." Then she stepped close to him. "But I love you, for *who* you are... So, I guess I'm not the only one who has a choice to make."

He studied her a moment, curiously. "There's no choice to make. I'm in this as long as you are."

She nodded. "So, tell me."

"Tell you what?"

She took another step toward him, her body just touching his. Her human nose could smell his scent, her body felt the heat radiating from his. "You're the man of action, I get that. But I need to hear the words."

"What words?"

"You know which ones."

"*Those* ones?" he said.

She nodded.

He shrugged. "I haven't heard them from you yet."

She smiled. "I literally just told you."

"Guess I want to hear it again, then."

"It's always a competition with you."

A smiled curled his mouth. "I have my pride."

"And I have mine. So, say it."

"You first."

"Alright," she said. "I always did have more courage than you."

A short, sharp laugh escaped him. She studied him: his blond hair, those blue eyes, the broad shoulders.

"I love you," she said simply, then added, "you stubborn asshole."

His grin grew wider.

She shook her head and chuckled. "If someone had told me on my first day on the *Aurora*, that we would end up like this? Together? That I would go on to have your child? I would've laughed in their face. You were an asshole, you know?"

"And you were a princess."

"No," she smiled. "I was your match. And you'd never been matched before. Not by a woman, anyway."

McKinley continued to grin, a mischievous look in his eyes. "And you think there's a choice between you and Forcaster? I think you just answered that riddle yourself. No way she can match you on the range or the mats."

"So, you concede I'm your match," she grinned. "Your equal."

"Well, I wouldn't go as far as to say equal," he said, looking her up and down.

She gave a swift, but soft, Alpha punch to his gut and he chuckled.

"I'm still waiting to hear it," she said.

McKinley looked her up and down again, then suddenly grabbed her, lifted her up and spun her around to sit up on the kitchen bench.

"Like I said, Welles, I'm a man of action. How about I show you." He leaned in to kiss her, but her fingers stopped his mouth from touching hers.

"I want to hear the words," she said.

Those blue eyes blazed into hers. "They're just words."

She studied him a moment. "You've never said them to anyone before, have you?" she whispered.

A strange look briefly swept across his face that was boyish, soft, and vulnerable. She slid her fingers down his mouth and over his bearded chin, then she leaned forward and kissed him. It was soft at first but filled with copious emotion. And then it grew, as his mouth claimed hers with more vigor. He pressed his body against hers and she tightened her legs around his hips, threading her fingers through his hair. They kissed warmly and passionately until she pulled her mouth away, resting her forehead against his.

"I still want to hear the words," she whispered.

He groaned quietly, closing his eyes briefly.

"Yes," she smiled, squeezing his body tighter against hers.

He groaned again and quietly exhaled. "I... love you... you stubborn princess."

Carrie broke into a laugh as McKinley lifted her off the kitchen bench and walked her to her bedroom. They swiftly stripped and set their Alphas free, mouths tasting, hands caressing, naked skin sliding over the other's. As McKinley kissed her stomach and made his way up her torso to her neck, she heard him inhale her scent and moan, "God, you smell good." She thought nothing of it until she heard him mutter it again quietly: "You smell so damn good." And suddenly she knew what that meant.

She groaned, half in ecstasy at his wandering mouth and hands, and half because she thought he was going to stop. If she smelled good, didn't that mean she was fertile?

But he didn't stop.

Carrie's thoughts suddenly washed away as he entered her, making the two of them exhale heavily with delight. There really was something to be said for reconciliation sex. She opened her mouth to his, tongues connecting like the rest o them, and they lost themselves to their Alphas.

As they came to their end, heartbeats thumping against the other's chest, she heard him inhaling her scent once more. And through the post-orgasmic glow, it slowly dawned on her once more. She smelled good. She was fertile. They hadn't stopped.

Her eyes flashed open, and as she looked at the ceiling, she couldn't help wondering if this was the moment their son would be conceived. The son she'd dreamed of, standing along the battlement before the big war...

McKinley never mentioned how good she smelled again. He'd known, yet he'd continued to have sex with her. He knew the potential consequences and it didn't stop him. And she realized why. They had agreed not to hide anymore. They were together and they weren't going to care who knew. He was claiming her, subconsciously at least, in the most primal way: filling her with his seed, impregnating her, claiming her body for their child.

And she let him.

Because she was claiming him, too, wanting a piece of him inside her, wanting their child to grow within. Just like Freya had, but different. This time they were together.

They lay side by side afterward in silence, stared at each other through the darkness, offered soft caresses, until eventually he stirred.

"I have to get back to the ship," he said, rubbing his face.

She nodded sleepily. "Better shower this time."

He flashed her a smirk, then disappeared into the bathroom. He eventually returned showered and dressed. She dressed too and walked him to the front door.

Her father surprised them. He was in the kitchen, leaning into the fridge.

"Oh. Hi," he said, straightening and giving McKinley a nod. He looked at Carrie. "I was thirsty." He looked back at McKinley. "You heading back to the ship?"

"Yeah," McKinley responded. "I'll see you later."

McKinley turned for the door, but Carrie stopped him, grabbing his shirt front and pulling him toward her. She planted a kiss on his mouth, long and deep, running her hand down his cheek as she did. When she pulled her mouth away, she saw McKinley's eyes dart over to her father, then back to her.

"No more hiding, right?" she said softly.

He nodded and looked at her father again.

"I'll see you around, James," her father said casually.

"Colonel," McKinley said.

"I guess you'd better start calling me, Jeff, huh?" her father said, motioning to Carrie and making her smile.

McKinley smiled too. "Jeff," he said. He looked back at Carrie, eyes twinkling, then turned and left.

Harris stared across his desk at Colonel Marchant.

"How was Egypt?" the colonel asked.

"Interesting," Harris said. "You heard the theory about the Zetas being a female-dominant race?"

"Yeah, it's interesting alright."

"Any news from the *Barbican*?"

Marchant paused for a moment. "Actually, yes, we have."

"And?"

"They made contact with three ships. On the radar."

"They what?" Harris said sitting forward. "So soon?"

"Wait up," Marchant said, raising his hand. "They did. But the ships have since disappeared."

"The *Barbican* has only been gone two and a half years. Does that mean we could have Zetas on our doorstep in two and a half years?"

"No, Harris. They disappeared so the *Barbican* continued onward."

"How long has it been since their last transmission?"

"Not long. We don't expect their next one for a while yet."

"Jesus," Harris said.

"Admiral Arken thinks it may have been a different group of ships. There were only three of them. The ones we've been communicating with are in the hundreds."

"It unnerves me that they made contact so close to Earth," Harris said.

"It unnerves me too," Marchant said.

"Is that why you allowed the *Carcharias* in so easily?" Harris arched his eyebrow. "I was expecting a harder fight than I got."

Marchant held his hand up again. "We need to proceed with caution. But given the update from the *Barbican*, and Gold's situation, then, yes, we didn't see what harm it could do."

"So, I can get more units?"

"No, I said we need to proceed with caution. We'll wait and see what the next comms from the *Barbican* say. Until then, we stay calm. We can't go rolling this program out on a whim, Harris. The wider population will find out, then we'll have a real problem on our hands. We'll have mass panic to deal with."

Harris sighed heavily and ran his hand along his jaw. "The *Barbican* is out there somewhere with no immediate comms at their disposal. Our priority is to protect Earth. We need coverage here."

"We do, but you need to remember that the signals we've been communicating with are still estimated to be decades away."

"The three ships the *Barbican* crossed paths with could still do damage, sir. We need to protect ourselves. What if the *Barbican* never returns? What if we never hear from them again?"

Marchant gave him a hard look. "Then it's like I once said. It'll be up to you and your Alpha army."

"But I don't have an army yet."

"You have the *Aurora* and you'll soon have the *Carcharias*."

"Two ships, two units."

"The rest of the UNF's fleet will assist you. You don't need to be an Alpha to fight in the skies."

"The *Barbican* made contact with some Zetas just two and a half years out, sir. That means those ships could be here in two and a half years. What happens if they get reinforcements and come a whole lot sooner than we expect?"

"You sound so sure that it will," Marchant quizzed him.

"I think it would be foolish to think that we have time on our side. What if we don't? What if they use their superior technology and suddenly appear on our doorstep tomorrow?"

"Impossible. We'd track them. We do have satellites on the UNF zone border, Harris."

"Maybe," Harris shrugged, "maybe not. How did the *Barbican* lose the signal of those three ships? Maybe they can't be tracked with our technology? We need to make sure we have coverage when they hit."

"*If* they hit. Remember we don't know for sure they will. In that regard, I always applauded Colonel Welles's caution. They could be friendly."

Harris's recurring dream, the one he shared with Welles, flashed through his mind: the fireballs hitting Earth when the twins were still children.

"But what if they aren't and they do hit us?" Harris asked. "And what if they hit us earlier than expected? How do we explain that to the people? That we knew, and we did nothing? If they hit us early we'll fail. We'll be annihilated. We'll become slaves."

"We won't let that happen," Marchant told him. "That's why we're preparing now."

"How many years before the UNF plan to roll this out?"

Marchant shrugged. "I don't know. It will be done in waves. I'd say we'd have a strong position in fifteen years or so."

Harris stared at Marchant. If his dream was right, the first invasion would occur in around eight or nine years. The UNF's plan would be too late. He tried hard to recall how many Zeta ships he'd seen in his dream. How many units would he need?

"We need to have a good contingent ready in eight years," he said.

"Eight years?" Marchant asked. "Why eight years?"

Harris shrugged. "Seems like a good number to me."

"If we roll-out too many units too soon, we risk detection. You know this. And the worst thing that could happen to us if it did, would be watching Earth disintegrate in fear and panic, well before any threat came our way," Marchant sat forward in his chair. "If the population falls apart, so too will we. And if that happens, we'll all make easy pickings for the Zetas. Right now, stability is our friend."

"I understand," Harris nodded, "and I agree. You're right, we do need to keep this classified for now. People need to carry on as normal and live their lives. But... if they do hit us early, we need a chance, colonel. The *Aurora* and the *Carcharias* alone won't be able to cut it if they hit Earth and come out of their ships. We need more back-up on standby."

Marchant sighed as though tired of this argument. "What numbers are you talking?"

Harris shrugged. "Well, the six ships Sharley selected is a start, but I'll need a lot more."

"You want to go with that madman's recommendations?"

Harris thought for a moment, then nodded. "Yes, I do."

Marchant looked at him thoughtfully.

"We'll also need some units on the ground, some Earth Duty units," Harris told him, "because if we lose the battle up there," he pointed to the sky, "then the guys on the ground become the second wave."

Marchant nodded. "We've got some units in mind. At least, Sharley did. He outlined them in a separate document."

Harris arched his eyebrow. "Anyone good?"

Marchant sat back in his chair. "Remember when we talked about the Threat Assessments, and I told you that no-one had been over a 6.5."

"Yeah."

"Well, that 6.5 is still in service."

"They are?"

Marchant nodded. "He'll be too old when the invasion occurs though. It's a shame."

"Will he be too old in, say, eight years time?"

Marchant's eyes narrowed in curiosity. "He'll be borderline. What's with this eight year fixation of yours?"

"Who is he?" Harris ignored the question. "Do I know him?"

Marchant nodded. "You've met, albeit briefly I think."

Harris stared at him, waiting for an answer.

"Captain Edwin Morrell, Earth Duty, Unit 505."

"Morrell?" Harris asked, surprised. "He's the 6.5."

Marchant nodded. "The only one to date."

"That's why you've had him working close to Command."

"We've been keeping an eye on him."

"Well, there you go." Harris nodded to himself, picturing Morrell in his mind, wondering whether he could work with him. "I'd like to see the profiles of the ED units."

"So soon?"

"I told you when I agreed to become the Alpha leader, colonel, that there could be no more secrets. You tell me everything you know, you share everything with me. That's the only way this is going to work."

Marchant's face remained passive, but his eyes were firm. "Just remember your place, Harris. Making demands of me is one thing, but don't try that shit with Berger."

Harris held his hands up in surrender. "But, in order to lead, I need to see."

"I'll have them sent to your portal."

"While we're at it, in my discussions with Gold and what he saw in those files, he told me there was another wave to the UNFASP program that we had not yet discussed, colonel."

"Which is?"

"Robotics. Infusing robotics into Alphas. When were you going to tell me about that? It wasn't in our contracts."

"That element is still being refined. There was nothing to tell you, because it hadn't been finalized or approved."

Harris stared at him.

"Harris, when Sharley put this program together, he started with the idea of the perfect soldier, then he worked his way back from there. His idea of the perfect soldier, which I'm inclined to agree with, was a culmination of the base human element, maximized and enhanced to physical perfection, coupled with sharp animal senses, and finished off with sophisticated tech and robotics fused with the body: in-built body armor and intelligence systems. This culmination would mean an incredibly smart, strong, and somewhat indestructible soldier. One that would be very hard to beat, alien or not."

"So, when were you going to tell me about this?"

"When the tech and robotic design had been completed. So far it has not been."

Harris exhaled loudly and sat back in his seat. "For all of Sharley's batshit craziness, he got something right. He put together a tight program."

"That he did. You see why we wanted to keep him alive all this time."

"He still asking for Welles?" Harris asked.

"Every single day," Marchant said. "And you. And McKinley, too."

"I guess some things never change."

"No, they don't. In that regard, Professor Sharley is 100 percent reliable."

"And that's what bothers me. Just like this program he pulled together, his fixation on Welles is precise. There's no shifting it, no breaking it. It will only end when one of them dies."

"Well, I guess we need to make sure it's the right one, then."

Harris nodded. "Yeah. We do."

Lincoln Gold accepted the cylinder of coffee, glad to have been released from Command. While Rovine was elsewhere, he'd informed the team of his promotion to ship's captain, and briefed them on UNFASP. He'd then sent them on leave to think over their answers. They'd naturally been shocked, but they also understood the classification of what they'd been told, as well as the honor they were being given. He was sure they'd come back to him with a 'yes'.

He tapped his PDP on the pay-pole, then turned to leave. As he did, he noticed Andrea Skordan walk in. He couldn't miss her with those bright blue eyes, bright red hair, and bright red lipstick. She was curvaceous and feminine, but left him in no doubt that she could probably kick his ass if she wanted to. He smiled at the thought as she approached the café's counter.

"Are you following me, Lieutenant Skordan?"

She smiled. "Don't flatter yourself, Captain Gold."

"Well, I don't know, you keep frequenting the same places I do. First the bar, now here?"

"You remember the bar?" She raised her eyebrows.

Gold blushed slightly. "Just. I was pretty drunk."

"This is Coco Joe's," she said. "Everyone on the island comes here for coffee."

Gold chuckled. "Fair point. So, Marchant tells me you're a valuable asset?"

"I am," she said confidently, then turned to the counter to place her order.

Gold held out his PDP. "Allow me," he said tapping it against the pay-pole.

"I can pay for my own coffee, you know."

"I'm sure you can," he said. "I just wanted to say thanks."

"For?"

He shrugged. "Telling me to leave the bar that night, going over the contract with me. I don't know."

"Well, then, thank you," she said to him, collecting her coffee.

"Where are you headed?"

"Back to Command. Why?"

"Can I walk you?"

She shrugged an 'okay', they stepped out into the sunshine, and began meandering back toward the glass pyramid structure that was the Command building.

"So," Gold said, "how long have you known about UNFASP?"

She threw him a cautionary glance. "Is that wise, to talk in the open like this?"

"I'd ask you back to my house, but you may get the wrong idea," he grinned.

She smiled, her red lips parting to flash white teeth.

"So?" he prompted her.

"Not too long," she told him. "A few months before you did. As soon as they decided to sign up the *Aurora* team, they needed an official UNFASP legal team, so the roles were created and me and my boss stepped into them."

He nodded. "You knew that night in the bar that I was on the list, didn't you?"

Her blue eyes glanced back at him briefly, before eyeing the road ahead again. "I did."

He studied her. "That's why you tried to get me to leave the bar. Didn't want me to ruin my chances of being part of UNFASP?"

"They need soldiers who don't draw attention."

"Wow... I don't know whether to thank you or not. Some might think that signing up for UNFASP is a curse."

"You obviously don't," she said, "or you wouldn't have done it."

"How could I say no to leading the Alpha-2 team? Besides... it was hard to say no to you. Is that part of their plan to get soldiers to sign up? Have you go over the contract with them?" He smiled. "Make it hard to resist?"

She flashed him a look through her lashes, fighting a smile. "Do you regret your decision?"

"No," he said, shaking his head. "Besides, I'm still human for the moment. I got a little while before they turn me." He pulled a face and held out his hands out all crooked like he was Frankenstein or something.

Skordan laughed. It was soft, feminine, musical. "Don't be like that. You've seen the *Aurora* team. They're pretty much normal."

"They're huge."

"That too."

They approached the entrance to Command.

"Well, thank you for the walk, captain," she said. "And the coffee."

"Thank *you*." He gave her a slight bow.

She smiled, then turned for the entrance.

"Hey, Skordan?" he called.

She looked around at him.

"What time do you get off?" he asked her, deciding to shoot his shot.

"Late. Why?"

"I'm on leave," he smiled. "Fancy a drink?"

"Do you think that's wise?"

"Yeah, I do," he said, before his smile dissipated. "It's nice having someone I can talk to about this stuff."

Her face softened. She glanced at the Command entrance, then back at him. "1900, captain. Here. Don't be late, or you'll be talking to yourself."

He raised his hand and gave her a salute. "Yes, ma'am."

General Berger stared across his desk at Professor Derek Martin, sitting in the guest chair.

"Is what I said clear?" he asked Martin.

"Yes. Yes, sir, it is," he said adjusting his glasses. "Can I, er, ask... why me?"

"After the events on Darwin, and after you failed to report your suspicions of Dr. Jarvis and the twins were consequently stolen here in Centralis, you wanted a chance at redemption, a chance to get back in favor with the UNF. This is it."

"But no-one outside of yourself in the UNF is aware of what I'll be doing?"

"That is correct," Berger said bluntly. "For the moment no-one can know. But should we succeed? I believe we'll be hailed as heroes."

"Yes, of course, but how am I to go about this?"

"You will be released from Command and you will set up a laboratory here in Centralis and you will commence your work. You will report to me weekly, and you will not leave the island. Do you understand?"

"Yes, sir. But am I to have any assistance?"

"No, you're on your own. If we see success, I'll give you help. But first you need to prove success."

Martin nodded, his mind thinking things over.

"Is there a problem?" Berger asked him.

"No. No, I... it's just not my forte."

"Can you do it or not?" Berger asked bluntly.

"Yes," Martin held up a hand to pause him. "Yes, general. Leave it with me."

"Good," Berger said. "I'll expect the first report in a week. Don't fail me."

"Yes, sir," Martin said as he stood.

"And Martin?"

"Yes?"

"If you breathe a word of this to anyone..." Berger didn't finish his sentence. He didn't need to. The look he gave Martin said everything it needed to, and the slightly terrified look Martin flashed back spoke volumes.

"I'll get right on it, sir," Martin said, and left the room. "Thank you for releasing me."

Lincoln Gold walked Andrea Skordan to her front door. They'd had a drink, a nice meal, another drink, then they walked back to her apartment, talking all the while.

"Well," she said, pulling out the security pass for her door, "I hope you enjoyed our talk tonight?"

"I did," he smiled, studying those beautiful blue eyes of hers.

"I'm glad I could help," she smiled back, and in the glow of the apartment's external lights, Gold soaked up the sight of her.

"I'm very grateful," he said.

She turned and walked up to her door and swiped her pass. The door opened with a beep and she turned back to him.

"Well, goodnight, Lieutenant Skordan," he said.

"We're off duty, Captain. You can call me Andrea."

"Andrea," he said with a slight bow. "You can call me Lincoln."

"Well, thank you, Lincoln." A sexy, confident smile spread across her lips. "I had a good time."

"Maybe we should do this again sometime?" he said, sliding his hands in the pockets of his jeans.

"Maybe we should," she replied, and the two of them stared at each other for a moment, before Andrea laughed. "I don't sleep with people on the first date, Lincoln."

"Good," he volleyed. "Neither do I."

"Really?" she teased.

He nodded. "But I have been known to kiss them."

"Really..."

"Where do you stand on that?"

She analyzed him a moment. "I stand over here."

"Over there?"

She nodded.

"So, I should move over there, then?" he said.

"Well, that's up to you."

He thought for a moment, then took his hands out of his pockets and stepped closer to her. She was almost his height in her heels. "How's this?"

Her blue eyes stared into his. "Not bad."

"How about this?" He slowly leaned in to kiss her. Her mouth was soft and welcoming. He slowly pulled away again, but she slid her hands over his cheeks and pulled him back toward her. She kissed him passionately and he reciprocated. Then she kicked the door fully open, pulled him into her apartment by his shirt and closed the door.

"Whoa!" he said, eyeing the closed door behind him. "I thought you said you didn't sleep with people on the first date?"

She shrugged. "I guess rules are meant to be broken. Besides, you don't have long left as a human." She kissed him hard, then pulled back, her blue eyes staring into his. "I assume that's okay with you?"

He pursed his lips and pretended to think about it for a moment. "I can make an exception for you." Then he broke into a smile and slid his arms around her waist.

She gave a musical laugh and pulled him toward her bedroom.

PART TWO

11

Positive Intrigue

Carrie awoke from the dream again. They were becoming more frequent. More frantic. She was in that field, the horizon ablaze with the setting sun that burned an electric orange right along the coast as far as she could see. At first she admired it, standing there with Harris and the twins, but soon it became night... and those lights appeared in the sky... the thudding impacts into the Earth, the running, the screaming, the desperation...

She sat upright and realized it was early morning. She was alone in bed. McKinley was back on the ship, but she expected him home on leave soon. She lay back down and stared at the ceiling.

"Archie," she said sleepily. "Are the kids up yet?"

"Yes, Miss Welles. I've put on an educational TV program in their room, but it would seem they are more interested in their toys."

Carrie smiled. "Attention spans aren't so good at their age."

"Yes. I have researched this."

Carrie sat up again, throwing her legs over the side of the bed, pausing as a sick feeling pooled in her gut. She threw her sheets back and ran into her en suite bathroom, coming to a stop on her knees in front of the toilet. She waited to see if the sick feeling was going to emerge in a more physical way, but it didn't. It just sat in her belly like a balloon full of milky water.

"Miss Welles," Archie asked, *"are you ill?"*

Carrie focused on her gut, looking down at it, then she lowered her eyes further to her womb.

"Miss Welles, would you like me to call Dr. Morgave?"

"No," she said, swallowing, "I'm fine." She stood and moved over to the basin and washed her face. She knew exactly what the problem was.

"Miss Welles, you're sweating. You're pale."

"You can tell changes in my skin color?"

"Yes, Miss Welles. I've been fitted with state-of-the-art cameras with high definition color and sound. Your skin is paler than normal, you are sweating, and you were about to vomit, were you not?"

Carrie looked into the mirror at her reflection, unsure whether she should tell Archie or not.

"Would you like me to take a blood test and scan for viruses?"

"You can do that?"

"Yes, Miss Welles. I am here for your protection. Should you fall ill I need to assist you where I can."

"H—how can you do that?"

"I'll take a small sample and compare it to samples I have in my database. There are hundreds of common illnesses in my database, and should I not be able to identify the cause, I would arrange an appointment with Dr. Morgave."

She thought about this for a moment. If her instinct was right, she wouldn't be able to hide this from Command for long.

"What if I knew what it was, Archie?"

"You know what is making you feel unwell?"

"Yes."

Archie was silent for a moment.

"Are you pregnant, Miss Welles?"

Carrie's mouth fell open. "What makes you say that? You can't know that?"

"Miss Welles, I know everything about you, and the twins, and even your father and McKinley. It is my job to analyze and study you to know you better."

"So?"

"So I am aware of your menstrual cycle, Miss Welles. You're late."

Her eyes nearly popped. "Archie! I've told you before, this freaks me out! This whole you knowing me better than I know myself thing. Stop it!"

"*I'm sorry, Miss Welles, but you asked.*"

"Why did you play along if you knew?"

"*I was trying not to pry as you keep scolding me. Alas, the truth is out, but we must be certain. Would you like me to give you a pregnancy test to confirm?*"

Carrie put her hands on her hips. "And how exactly would you do that?"

"*I can either test your hormones via a blood test, or I can sample your urine.*"

"Jesus."

"*Which will it be?*" Archie asked. "*Or would you prefer I arrange for you to meet with Dr. Morgave?*"

"Wait a minute," she said. She wasn't quite ready to bring Command into this just yet. She remembered how obtrusive they were last time. She didn't even know for sure that she was yet. She glanced around the bathroom at the light brown stone facade, then gave in.

"Which is easiest?"

"*The urine test is easier, but I think the blood test would be more beneficial.*"

"Show me how you do it," she ordered.

"*Yes, Miss Welles,*" he said, then a quiet noise sounded beside the bathroom cabinet. A section of the stone wall slid back and a gray metal drawer slid forth. It came to a stop, extending about two feet from the wall. A small metal arm rose up from within and, with a hissing noise, a fine needle extended from the end.

"*I have precise positioning, Miss Welles. I will take the required sample, then run it through my database to test for the right hormone levels.*"

"I see," she said studying the needle. "And the pee test?"

"*Pee? Oh, you mean urine.*" With that, the toilet seat lifted of its own accord and she peered inside. Suddenly another thin arm rose from the extended drawer, holding a small empty vial. "*Simply urinate into this vial, then return to its place.*"

Her eyes darted between the needle and the empty vial, before she plucked the vial from Archie's arm.

"I'm going to take the pee option, Archie."

"*I thought you would, Miss Welles.*"

She looked up at the ceiling, picturing Archie smiling. If an AIS could, that is.

Carrie, sitting on the closed lid of the toilet, felt strange, both nervous and calm at the same time. Nervous, because she was indeed pregnant again. Calm, because she had dreamed of her son, so this wasn't a surprise.

"What would you like me to do now, Miss Welles?"

"Nothing."

"Miss Welles, you're pregnant. Dr. Morgave and his associates will need to examine you—"

"All in good time, Archie."

"All in good time?"

She looked up at the ceiling. "First, I need to tell McKinley."

"Of course."

"I just want some time to enjoy it, you know?" she said. "Before Command get involved and I become an experiment again."

"Why would you be an experiment, Miss Welles? They will need to watch you closely, yes, but surely there will be less excitement this time. After all, you've already delivered the twins."

"I'm carrying an Alpha child," she said. "Trust me they'll want to study him."

"Him?" Archie asked. *"You're certain it's a boy?"*

Carrie nodded to herself, picturing her dream. "Yes."

"They will need to add him to their register. You may be disciplined for conceiving a child outside of Command orders."

"Screw Command's orders," she muttered.

"It's clearly stated in the contract both you and Lieutenant McKinley signed. Would you like me to read the relevant section?"

"No. Trust me, Archie, they'll pretend to be angry at us, but inside they'll be salivating because I'm giving them another First Gen Alpha to study."

Archie was silent for a moment. *"So, what would you like to do now?"*

She glanced around the room, her eyes falling on the panel where the drawer had emerged from. She pictured the needle again in her mind as she looked down at her hands. Turning her wrist over, she studied the barcode tattoo that Sharley had branded her with. Then she thought of McKinley's, now covered with the phoenix tattoo. She pictured his other hand, the one with the two bands; the silver one, and the one woven of leather.

"Miss Welles?"

Carrie stood up, resolute. "What do we do, Archie? We prepare to tell McKinley."

"*And how will you do that?*"

"I'll tell you when I get back."

She smiled and left the room.

Dr. Scavesci stared across the table at Professor Sharley.

"I have good news for you. Would you like to hear it?"

Sharley eyed him coldly. "I assume you didn't come here to keep it from me."

Scavesci smiled. "A second team is being brought online in the UNFASP program."

Sharley perked up a little. "Who?"

"The *Carcharias*. There was an altercation between Captain Rovine and his first lieutenant, and now Rovine has been promoted to Command to work in strategy and the first lieutenant has taken control of the ship. He's agreed to join the program."

"Why the rush?" Sharley asked, eyes fixed on his. "They haven't finished converting the *Aurora* team yet."

"I believe there will be a small window before they convert the *Carcharias*. They will aim to finish the *Aurora* team first, but the *Carcharias* is certainly lined up to be next."

"But why the rush? We have years, don't we? It wasn't my intention to bring another online so soon."

"Two units can't hurt, and they widen the study of the program."

"Yes," Sharley said, eyes glazing over in thought, "as long as they keep things controlled."

"Still, it is good news," Scavesci said. "It means they're taking it seriously and there should be no more delays. I thought you'd want to know."

"The UNF are the ones who delayed things," Sharley said, his voice a little acidic. "If they'd just let me be, I'd know everything I need to know about the original prototypes by now."

"Perhaps."

"No, doctor. There's no 'perhaps' about it. That's why the UNF won't let the *Aurora* team see me. They're trying to keep me away from my own program."

"The UNF isn't stopping them from seeing you."

"They wouldn't pass my letters on!"

Scavesci patted the air softly, signaling for Sharley to calm. "No, but *I* did. I passed them on for you."

"And yet, I've not seen her," Sharley accused.

"I can't force her to come."

"I want to see the children."

"I know you do, but it's not easy—"

"Stop giving me your excuses!" Sharley spat, then stood from his chair and leaned over the table, "and start delivering me results."

Scavesci stared firmly back at the Jumbo in front of him. "If you want me to help you, then you need to stop with the threats."

Sharley's hard Jumbo face suddenly softened into a warm smile. He shrugged innocently, pulling back. "But it's the only thing you respond to," he said lightly. "I read people, doctor. Just like you do. And that's how you best respond. I'm sorry."

Scavesci stood from his chair and stared back at his patient. "So, far this has been a one-sided relationship. If you want me to keep helping you, then you need to start helping me."

"And how would I do that?"

"Start showing some improvement. Start controlling these violent outbursts."

"But I'm a Jumbo," he said, his voice suddenly low. "It's what I'm designed to do."

"I don't care."

Sharley studied him, as though trying to gauge the truthfulness of his statement. Scavesci stared back, doing well to hide any fear he felt.

"Alright," Sharley said, "I'll behave like a good boy… if you bring me the twins. I just want to look at them."

Scavesci didn't respond. Instead, he headed for the door and left.

Carrie watched as McKinley dumped his bag on the floor. Freya moved up to him, arms in the air, and Brody followed.

"Daddy," Freya squealed, as he swooped and collected her then Brody, hauling them both up to sit one on each hip.

"Daddy!" Freya squealed again, clamping her hands on his face, one over his mouth and one over his ear. He pulled his face away from her grasp, looking at Brody.

"Hey, champ," he said.

"Daddy!" Brody squeaked, mimicking Freya.

McKinley's eyes flickered to Carrie's to check her reaction. She stood from the kitchen table and walked over to him. She lifted her hand and caressed Brody's hair.

"He's right," she smiled, looking at McKinley. "You're his dad now."

"Daddy!" Freya called again, smacking her little hand on his chest. He smiled and kissed his daughter on the cheek. Then he looked back at Brody, and kissed his, too.

Miranda Finch was doing another drive-by. This had seemingly become a hobby of hers now, between working on other stories: driving around Centralis trying to catch of glimpse of Lincoln Gold. It was as though he'd gone into hiding or something. Perhaps he was busy, given his recent promotion to captain. But that's what she didn't understand. First he gets arrested, then he becomes captain. And the old *Carcharias* captain had been promoted to a position in Command. It reeked of story.

That aside, she was genuinely interested in what had happened, because she actually liked Gold. He was loyal to his uniform and she respected that, but he also seemed a decent person underneath. When her apartment had been ransacked a couple of months back, he'd helped her out when he didn't need to. Whatever was going on was more than just a story to her, she actually wanted to make sure he was alright. She'd been trying her hardest to cross paths with him, but so far she'd failed. He was holed up on his ship and she couldn't access the Space Docks.

She'd managed to cross paths with Morrell a few more times, though. They would each ask the other what they knew, but neither had much to say. Then the last couple of times she'd seen Morrell, he'd looked right through her, as if he didn't know her, but she realized he only did that when she approached him in front of his team. He clearly did not want to be seen talking with a reporter and she was fine with that. If Morrell stayed away from her, that was a good thing. She still wasn't sure who was behind her break-in, and the local MPs had lost interest in the case.

Suddenly, after days of driving around, she finally caught sight of Gold. He was walking along the road to Command with another soldier. She quickly pulled the car over and watched them. The soldier he was with was in Space Duty uniform. She was attractive, with bright red hair, and as Miranda watched, she noticed a little flirtation exchange between them: laughter, smiles, and warm looks. Finally, the woman walked into Command. Gold seemed to wait a few moments, then followed her inside, as though not wanting to be seen entering together. *Is this where he'd disappeared to? With some woman?*

By the time Miranda got out of her car and walked into Command, he was gone. But he could only be in a meeting somewhere, so she decided to wait. Eventually, he walked out into the grand reception area with another officer. Miranda watched them speak for a moment, then the officer made his way back to the elevator. Gold turned and began to head for the exit. Miranda met him there.

"Lieutenant Gold," she smiled, stepping into his path, causing him to pull up short. "Oh, sorry, I believe it's *Captain* Gold now."

Gold glanced around to the elevator, then looked back at her.

"Miranda."

"Long time no see," she said, folding her arms. "I was starting to get worried."

"Yeah, I've been pretty busy."

"I know. Last time I saw you, you were very drunk. Then I heard you got arrested. Then I heard you got promoted. You *have* been busy."

Gold stared at her a moment, before beaming a broad smile. "There's no story, if that's what you're asking."

Miranda studied him. He seemed to be the cool, calm and collected Gold from before. Her features softened.

"I'm not here for a story. I just wanted to know that you're okay... I owe you one."

His eyes analyzed hers. "Well, thank you. I'm fine."

"Do you have time for a coffee?"

He glanced at his watch. "I'm sorry, no. I don't."

"Will you ever have time for a coffee?" she asked directly.

He stared at her.

"I'm putting two and two together here," she continued. "You didn't return my messages when I came to help you after your arrest. You haven't returned them since. I'm getting the impression that suddenly you can't be seen with me. Is that it? Is your new position at risk if you do?"

"I have new responsibilities now and less time. That's all."

"So, you're helming the *Carcharias*. Are you still the *Aurora*'s shadow-ship?"

"I can't divulge UNF missions to you, Miranda, you know that."

She nodded, analyzing him for a moment. She knew she wasn't going to get anything out of him, so she stepped out of his path. "Well, good luck, Captain Gold. I wish you all the best in your new role. I'm sorry to keep you."

"Thank you, Miranda. I wish you all the best in yours, too." With that he moved on, making his way to the Space Dock. She watched him until he was out of view. All the while her mind ticked over. First Harris and the *Aurora* drawing her attention, now the *Carcharias*. Where once Gold had been as curious as her, suddenly he was throwing a wall between them and avoiding her. Something had happened that had pushed his loyalty to the UNF to the forefront. Gold, like Harris, was tight-lipped and unreachable.

It only made her think of Morrell. He was on the inside of the UNF. Was he her only hope of getting answers? She didn't like the idea of forming an alliance with him, but if he was a means to an end? She exhaled loudly, relenting, and nodded to herself. There was no other way around it. She had to enter the lion's den. She made her way back to her car. It was time to find Morrell.

Carrie and McKinley ate dinner with her father, put the children to bed, then came out to the lounge at her father's request. She was a little anxious for the night to end, wanting to be alone with McKinley to tell him her news, but her father seemed insistent, apparently having some news of his own.

Carrie and McKinley sat on the couch and her father sat in one of the single lounge chairs, the large windows overlooking the Space Dock providing a scenic backdrop behind him.

"So, what is it?" Carrie asked him. "What do you want to talk about?"

"I've found out some information. The kind the UNF has requested I don't divulge to anyone. I've been waiting to see if you knew, but you haven't mentioned it, so I've been waiting for James to return to see if he knew."

"Knew what?" he asked.

"About the Greenback."

Carrie glanced at McKinley and his face was blank. He shook his head.

"He's the guy Drazen and his Jumbos worked for," her father revealed.

"I thought they worked for Sharley," she said.

"They did. Sharley, it turns out, stole them from the Greenback."

"So, who is he?" Carrie asked.

Her father seemed to pause a moment, as though wondering whether to tell her, but he relented. "Clint Harbourg."

"The Original?" Carrie was taken aback, her face puzzled.

Her father nodded. "He knows about the old signal, like I did. I haven't told him about the new signals, but he's not a stupid man. He knows his fighters were borrowed without his permission, and he knows they were turned into Jumbos. Now the UNF wants to keep him on side, in case we need his fighters at some point."

"You met with him?" Carrie asked.

"At the UNF's request."

"At their request?"

He shrugged. "It would seem I am of use to them. They're using me as the conduit between them and him. They can't be seen to be condoning what he's doing."

"They're going to roll-out the program on these fighters?" McKinley asked.

"No. Not yet. But one day they might. They're Plan B. I've been fighting with myself as to whether I should tell you, given Ventnor's warnings, but I thought you should know."

"But he has nothing to do with the Jumbos sent to Eden to attack us?" Carrie asked.

"Apparently not. But his interest has been sparked. He wants in. And from what I can tell he's got a few fighters at his disposal. He has an international network of them."

"You went alone to meet him? What were you thinking?" Carrie scolded him.

He held his hand up. "Ree, I may not be an Alpha like you, but I was a soldier for a long time. I know how to handle myself."

"Does Harris know?" McKinley asked.

"Not that I'm aware of. Look," he said, sitting forward in his seat, "obviously I'm not supposed to be telling you this. Just keep it under your hat for now, but be mindful of what's going on in the background."

"We have to tell Harris, you know that," Carrie said.

"I know. Just make sure he sits on it."

"There's no risk to us, though, right?" Carrie asked. "From these fighters?"

"No," he said, "Harbourg's interest lies in what's coming for us, and how he can screw the UNF for money for providing his assistance."

McKinley sighed and relaxed back into the couch. "Well, they were strong fighters. Providing their loyalty aligns, they could be useful if needed."

Carrie looked at him. "I don't like it. If they're doing this behind our back, then what else are they doing? Harris is supposed to be in charge of the Alphas, and he doesn't know about this."

"Yeah," McKinley said, leaning forward again, "but he will soon."

"What is it, Ree?" her father asked, studying her troubled face.

"I know they're doing this in order to survive the Zetas, I get that. But why hide it?"

Her father shrugged. "They've got to have a Plan B."

"Yeah?" Carrie said, feeling the Alpha within rear up slightly. "I thought the First Gens were their Plan B."

"The twins?" Her father's brow furrowed.

"And any others they manage to create."

"You don't think…" McKinley looked at her. "The pod cases?"

"Who knows," Carrie shrugged. "It was a genuine plan of theirs."

"Pod cases?" her father asked.

"The UNF was looking into creating First Gens themselves, without the need for a mother, using artificial wombs."

"You're kidding."

Carrie shook her head. "They want strong disposable soldiers without any ties."

Her father stared at her, dumbstruck. Then he shook his head and exhaled loudly as he sat back in his chair.

"They're planning on having us, the Alpha soldiers," Carrie said, "and the First Gens, and these fighters of the Greenback. How many more plans might they have out there that we don't know about?"

"Three waves," her father mused aloud. "The enhanced soldiers, the First Gen creations, and the renegades if all else fails."

"And Harris is going to have to try and control all of 'em," McKinley said.

Carrie nodded. "We all will."

Her father sighed loudly, the years showing on his face.

"What?" Carrie asked.

"I just got a lot more worried about our future than I was before," he said tiredly. "Making it through the war is one thing," he said as he stood, "just so long as people remember that, even if we win, we're still going to have to deal with what's left. Be it Alphas, First Gens or renegades. This was my argument all along. If we don't control things from the start, we won't have control of it at the end, either. We may win the war against the Zetas, but we'll have an Earth torn up by civil war if we lose control of the different, aggressive factions that are left."

The silence sat between them as Carrie and McKinley stared at her father.

He sighed again. "I'm going to bed." With that, he left the room.

Carrie stared out the window at the Space Dock; the lights sparkling against the dark sky.

"I'll tell Harris when I'm back on the ship," McKinley said.

Carrie nodded. "He needs to know all the players if he's going to win this game."

McKinley agreed silently, then stood. "Speaking of bed," he said looking tired himself.

In her bedroom he went straight for the shower. She watched him undress, wondering how he would take her news. Just because he'd been caught up in the moment didn't mean he wanted to be a father again.

He came out after a while, a towel wrapped around his waist, and she crossed paths with him as she went in to shower. She was buying time, she knew it, but there was a part of her that also liked keeping the secret. Carrying her child silently, no-one the wiser. But she knew it couldn't stay that way.

When she came out, adorned in a robe with long sleeves, McKinley was sitting on the bed, still wrapped in his towel and flicking through the TV channels. She saw a news piece running about the last oil reserve on Earth, Noah's Well, and the latest court challenges.

"Will they ever sort that out?" Carrie asked, climbing onto the bed and laying beside him.

"Who knows," he said, quickly losing interest in it as he rolled onto his side and began to undo her robe. She grabbed his hand and stopped him.

"You kept something from me."

He paused. "What?"

A smile slid across her face. "Your birthday."

"How did you find out?"

"Archie is a fountain of knowledge."

McKinley's eyes flicked up to the ceiling. "He know my jock size, too?"

Carrie chuckled. "Probably. Why didn't you tell me?"

"My birthday has never meant much to me, Welles."

Carrie's face fell. "Well, we need to change that."

"It's just a day."

"It's the day you were born. I hope you don't apply that opinion to our kids' birthdays."

He shrugged. "They're different. They're kids."

The lights were dim in the room, casting them in a soft glow. She looked into his eyes. "Well, I guess you'd better unwrap your present then."

A smile curled the corner of his mouth and he pulled at the tie around her waist, loosening her robe. He slid it down over her shoulders, then threw it off to the side. He leaned forward and kissed her, and she took hold of his jaw and moved him back. "Don't you want to see your present?"

"I thought you were my present?"

"Kind of," she smiled, then rolled over and pulled her hair forward to show him her new tattoos.

"Whoa," he said quietly, his fingers sliding over the back of her neck.

"I finally got the snowflake retouched and I added Brody Daniel to it," she said. Brody's name had been added in slightly curly text that curved around the bottom of the snowflake tattoo, the scar across it barely visible now.

She felt McKinley's fingers slide down her back to the base of her spine.

"And I got one for Freya too," she said, picturing the Arizona Sun blanketflower she'd had tattooed, with Freya Grace written in the same text, curved along the top.

McKinley was silent for a moment,

She glanced over her shoulder at him. "It's an Arizona Sun—"

"Blanketflower. I know."

"Do you like it?" she asked. She loved them, the snowflake and the flower: one at the top of her spine, one at the base of it.

"Yeah," he eventually said, "I do."

"Good," she said, rolling back over, "because that's not your present. This is," and she held her right hand up, turning her inner wrist to him. He took her wrist and studied the tattoo she'd had done there. It was in the shape of a band, with foreign writing across it.

"White warrior," she said softly, as his eyes went to hers.

She took his wrist and studied the silver band around it, holding it beside hers. The writing was identical. She'd had his band tattooed around her wrist.

"Guess you're stuck on me forever now."

His eyes flicked between her wrist and her eyes.

"Do you like it?"

He nodded silently, holding her wrist and tracing his thumb across it. Then he suddenly reached out and kissed her. She'd been about to tell him of the other gift, but it would seem he couldn't be swayed from his current line of thinking.

She didn't tell him so much in the end, her body did the talking for her. Lying there after sex, she suddenly felt that sick feeling in her stomach and had to run for the toilet. She didn't actually throw up, she just knelt there until she felt better.

McKinley came and stood in the doorway looking at her.

"I have one more surprise for you," she said, pulling herself up to sit on the now-closed lid, "but it's one you won't get to see for another eight months or so."

They stared at each other in silence for a while, McKinley's brain processing what she had told him.

"I'm pregnant," she said, just to be clear.

Still he was silent.

She slid her hand across her womb.

"I didn't think you could have any more?" he finally said.

"They said it was unlikely I would carry another child to term, due to the damage I received when the twins were taken."

"So?"

"So, they're wrong."

"But, if Dr. Morgave said—"

"He's wrong."

"Welles—"

"I've dreamed of him," she cut him off. "Our son. He's there at the end with us, with Brody and Freya... He'll be born."

McKinley stared at her.

"Harris has had the same dream. He's seen Jesse, too, I'm sure of it."

"Jesse?"

She smiled. "That was his name in the dream. After your Colonel Jesse, I guess."

"The colonel who handpicked me for this years ago? The one who sealed my fate." McKinley almost sounded bitter.

"I know," she said sympathetically, "but if you think about it now, knowing what's coming or not knowing what's coming, what would you choose? I know you. You'd choose knowing. Besides, that Jesse, in a roundabout way, brought you to me."

McKinley sighed and ran his hand over his face. "That aside... is it dangerous?"

"No." She stood and moved to him. "I will survive this pregnancy and so will he."

McKinley's eyes fell to her womb. She took his hand and slid it over her skin.

"We made this one," she said quietly. "Not Sharley, not Command. Us. He's all ours."

McKinley kept staring at her womb, silent.

"Surprise," she added, with a grin, trying to lighten the moment.

He looked at her, but still said nothing.

"No more hiding, right?" she whispered.

"Not with this, there won't be." He finally offered words. "I knew you smelled different when I came back."

She stared at him silently, waiting for more.

"You and Harris dreamed this?" he asked.

She nodded.

"And you didn't say anything?" he half-accused.

"And what would you have said if I told you? You would've freaked out."

"Probably," he said, running his hand through his hair.

"Are you freaking out now?"

He glanced down at her womb again, then shook his head.

Carrie studied him. "I mean, last leave, you said I smelled good. We both knew it was a risk."

He nodded. "What's done is done, right?"

"You're good? You don't want me to get rid of him?"

His Alpha eyes sharpened on hers. "No. I don't."

"Good," she said, then leaned forward and slipped her hands around his waist, pressing her naked body against his. "He's ours and we're keeping him."

Harris kissed Taya on the cheek and ran his hand over her protruding belly. She was seven months pregnant now. As his hand came to a rest his felt his daughter kick and smiled.

Taya watched him with a smile of her own. Nestled on the couch, they were warm and snug as winter approached outside.

"Has Ty been helping you out around here?" Harris asked.

"A little. He's not home that much between school and basketball."

"How are his grades?"

"They were slipping a little, but I set him up with a tutor. I told him if he wants to play college ball, he's got to get into college. He can't rely on that scholarship for everything."

"Good," he said.

Taya yawned.

"Why don't you go to bed," Harris said. "I'll clear things away out here."

Taya smiled tiredly. "I wish you were home more often."

"Yeah," he said, kissing her lips, "me too."

Taya headed upstairs while Harris moved to the kitchen to clear things away. He noticed a photo on the fridge that Taya must have recently put there. It was a photo of them in the hospital when Ty was born. Over sixteen years ago. Almost seventeen. *Man, how time flies...*

And now he was about to do it all again.

He liked that. It felt like a second chance, to do things differently. To do things right that he got wrong the first time. He knew the biggest thing he'd gotten wrong with Ty, was time or lack of it, and now, with what he had coming, things were bound to be just as time restricting, if not worse. He had to find a way to beat it this time.

He replayed that dream in his mind, the one standing on the battlements before the big war, when his daughter came and stood by his side. She told him it would start soon. And he realized the reason she knew that was because of the family gift. Which one, he wasn't sure yet, but his gut hinted that she might be like his grandmother Sibbie, a dreamer of the future. Just like he did, but she'd be stronger, because that would be her only gift. Where he divided his strength between the two, she could pool her strength into one.

He cleared away the things in the kitchen and just as he was about to head upstairs to bed, Ty came home with a few of his friends.

"Hey," Harris said, recognizing them from the last basketball match he'd been to with Ty where they'd had a fight.

"Captain," Ty said.

Harris was going to correct him and tell him it was "Dad", but decided against it in front of his friends.

"Captain," Ty's friends nodded as they went into the kitchen and began to raid the fridge.

"I just tidied up in here," Harris said. "Make sure you clean up after yourselves."

"Yeah, yeah," Ty said, pulling things out of the fridge, while one of his friends opened the cupboards and pulled out a frying pan. They knew their way around. They obviously did this regularly.

He moved up the stairs and into the bedroom, wanting to question Taya about it, but he found her fast asleep. So, he curled up beside her, sliding his hand over her belly, and lay quietly until he fell asleep too, dreaming strange dreams of Taya laying beside their baby girl.

Carrie enjoyed the past month's leave that McKinley had had. For a whole month, no-one but them and Archie knew she was pregnant. And she loved every second of it. But that was about to end. Today, McKinley was going back to the ship. Today, he was going to tell Harris their news. She had suggested they do it together, but McKinley insisted that he'd tell Harris. So they'd agreed that he'd tell Harris and she'd tell her father.

As McKinley packed his bag to leave, she stood in the bathroom and washed her face. She was feeling sick again. McKinley watched her through the doorway as she hunched over the basin, willing her stomach to settle. The twins were with them; Brody played with a toy at her feet, Freya badgered McKinley to pick her up. He did so, swinging her around onto his hip, then he moved to lean on the doorway and look in at her.

"You alright?" he asked.

"Yeah, I'm good," she smiled at him in the mirror. "I feel sick, but I haven't actually vomited yet. That's a good sign."

He glanced at Freya on his hip, then looked back at Carrie again.

"What?" she asked.

He didn't answer, just stared at her.

"What?" she said again.

"Marry me," he said bluntly.

Carrie paused, then slowly turned around to look at him. "What?"

"You heard," he said, then repeated himself just in case she hadn't. "Marry me."

Carrie stared at him. "Why?"

He motioned to her abdomen. "You're having my kid."

"I've already had one of your kids."

He glanced at Freya, then looked back at Carrie. "That was different. You were with Doc then."

Brody tugged at her robe, wanting to be picked up like Freya. She bent down and lifted him up to her hip.

"Why didn't you ever marry Doc?" McKinley asked. "He ever talk of marriage? Strikes me as the kind who would."

"No," she said quietly, "it never came up. I guess with everything else going on..."

"Well, I am," he said, with McKinley directness.

She nodded and smiled. "I never took you for being old-fashioned."

"It's not old-fashioned," he said. "You've had one of my kids, now you're having another. We're together. Makes sense, doesn't it?"

A sudden thought occurred to her... his comment before, asking whether Doc had ever proposed. She knew now why he wanted this. This was the one thing he could have of her that Doc never did. Marriage. She was never Doc's wife, but she could be his.

"Yes," she blurted out.

He straightened a little, maybe in surprise. "Yes?"

She smiled. "Well, it wasn't the most romantic proposal in history, but... that's you. Direct and blunt. So, yes. That's my direct and blunt response back. I'll marry you."

McKinley nodded softly to himself.

"What, did you think I would fight it? If you wanted the answer to be no, you shouldn't have asked."

"I wouldn't have asked if I wanted a no."

They stared at each other for a moment, soaking up the situation and what had just transpired, a child on each of their hips as though joining in the conversation.

Carrie stepped toward McKinley and placed her hand on his chest. "We're in this together until the end," she said, "so let's do this right," then raised herself up and they kissed. The touch of Brody's hands on both their cheeks made them stop. Carrie pulled away as Freya mimicked her brother, hands on their cheeks and the twins giggled.

She looked back at McKinley, and grinned. "Together."

Miranda Finch knocked on Morrell's door. It was the first time she'd been to his apartment. She figured he would be a 'stayer', one of those soldiers who lived in Centralis even when they were on leave. While lots of soldiers preferred to leave the island and return to their normal lives, others couldn't find comfort in the so-called real world and chose to stay close to base. Morrell was one them: a stayer, a lifer. She guessed she understood, though. He was middle-aged, single, with no children. What exactly did he have, other than soldiering? Fort Centralis had everything he needed.

He eventually opened the door and surprise registered briefly on his face. Then his eyes hardened into a skeptical look, adding to the harshness of his features, his gray crew cut and square jaw.

"What do you want?" he said gruffly.

"To talk."

"About?"

"You want to discuss it out here?" She looked up and down the corridor outside his apartment.

He stared at her, then closed the door in her face. She stood there for a few moments, confused, before he opened it again and motioned her inside. He didn't bother asking how she found out where he lived. She was a reporter. Of course she'd find out.

Morrell, surprisingly, had a neat apartment: cream walls and simple furniture that looked like it was made of real wood. She saw he was in the middle of cooking breakfast; two plates were laid out on the kitchen counter.

"Oh," she said, "I hope I'm not interrupting something?" She eyed the door to the hallway wondering where his guest was hiding.

"What do you want?" he demanded, before she had more time to study his apartment.

She turned to him and suddenly wondered whether it was a good idea to have come here. That solid square jaw matched nicely with his blunt shoulders and muscular arms.

"Gold's a closed book," she said, folding her arms, partly as a defense.

Morrell stared at her.

"He's been made captain of the *Carcharias*. Did you know that?"

"I heard," he said.

"So, he's arrested, then promoted. It doesn't make sense."

Morrell remained silent.

"Ah, so you're going to close up, too," she said. "You found what you're looking for and now, just like Gold, you close up?"

"Gold found something?"

"Yeah," Miranda said, "a promotion."

Morrell shrugged. "Well, it don't make sense to get a promotion then stir up trouble for the UNF, does it?"

"What's your story then?"

He gave her a patronizing look. "Since when have you been interested in my story?"

"Since you approached me for information." She paused a moment, contemplating whether to say the next bit, but she decided to go ahead. "And then, when you didn't get any, you raided my apartment."

"We've discussed this already."

"And you never gave me an answer."

"Because Gold came along before I could give you my answer."

"You're denying it?"

"Yes. I am." He stared firmly back at her, then a slight smile curled his mouth. "You think raiding apartments is my style? Really? You're a reporter, Finch. You probably have a few enemies out there."

"What about your men?"

"My men wouldn't do it either."

"How do you know?"

"Because they don't do anything unless I order them to."

"Someone raided my apartment not long after one of our early discussions in Coco Joe's, where you were less than civil. My apartment was trashed and whoever did it left a knife sticking out of the kitchen bench in warning."

"Someone knifed your bench and you think it was me?" he laughed. "I told you, that's not my style, Finch. If I got a problem with someone, I deal with it face to face." He motioned to the door. "Get out of here, reporter. Go blackmail someone else."

"Are you telling me you didn't raid my apartment?" she demanded, dropping her arms.

"Yes! That's what I'm telling you." He stepped toward her. "And I really don't like being accused of things I haven't done."

"So, who did then? It wasn't long after the Eden incident. Who else would've done it?"

Morrell shrugged. "How the hell would I know?"

"Someone else wanted information on Eden," she said quietly, her eyes drifting off into space as her mind turned over.

"What about Gold?" he said. "Wasn't he digging around for information?"

"No," she shook her head. "He's not like that. That's not his style either."

"Who says?"

"Gold wouldn't rifle through my underwear drawers and knife the kitchen bench."

Morrell paused a moment. "Oh, but I would?"

Miranda winced her eyes shut. "Look, I'm sorry. You didn't do it. I believe you."

Morrell stared at her with his hard eyes.

"Why the hell have you been pretending not to know me?" she asked. "What the hell is going on? You're all acting funny and nothing is making sense and everyone is hiding something."

"I'm not hiding anything."

"Aren't you?"

"No, I'm not."

"Well, Gold is now. He saw things in Eden and it made him curious. Something happened with that arrest, now all of a sudden he is tight-lipped. It's not just the promotion. He knows something."

"Yeah, but what?"

"I don't know, but it has something to do with the *Aurora*. I'd bet my life on it."

"The *Aurora*?"

"First Mars, then the Moon, then the Centralis lockdown, then Eden."

Morrell's eyes shone with curiosity as they stared at her.

"Everywhere I turn, there's a closed door," Miranda huffed with frustration. "My leads have dried up. You need to look into this. You're on the inside."

"Oh, yeah? And what makes you think if I find something I'll want to share it with you."

She shrugged. "Because your curiosity is just as fierce as mine. And, if anything, this affects you more than me. Something is going down in the UNF and you want to know what it is... and I want to know if this goes beyond the UNF to something civilians ought to know."

"And what makes you think I'd betray my uniform to you?"

"I guess it depends on how much you like being kept in the dark by those Blue-boys, doesn't it?"

With that she turned and headed for the door.
"Finch!" Morrell called after her. She stopped and looked back at him.
"Don't ever come to my apartment uninvited again."
"Suits me," she said, and closed the door after her.

12

History Repeats

Harris dumped his bag in his quarters, then made his way to his office. He felt conflicted about leaving Taya. After his month's leave, it was only a matter of weeks now before their daughter was born. Before his life changed again. So many major changes had come his way this past couple of years, it was hard to keep up.

It felt a little odd that Ty's independence was growing by the day, and he would soon leave home, while his daughter was just coming into his life. It seemed to mirror his life with the UNF. The life he once had as a normal human; the father he was to Ty during that time. Now he was an Alpha, commencing a new phase of life with the UNF. Now he would be an Alpha father to a gifted daughter, working their way toward a potential war. And he knew in his bones that his relationship with her would be different. Their shared gift would form a bond that neither Taya nor Ty could understand. He was adamant that he would raise her to accept her gift, and he would raise her to be strong in the face of that war. He'd raised Ty to be normal; he'd raised Ty to think that he would live a long life that would never ever see carnage or war or terror. Had Harris failed him?

As he entered his office he detected the fresh coffee in the machine. His nose flared and his mouth watered. He turned the machine on, wondered what it would be like with his new hearing, the next sense. In a matter of days, he would hear just about everything.

He moved to his desk and caught sight of Smith's urn on his bookshelf. He traced his fingers down the side of it, then shifted them over to the old-fashioned photo frame containing the photo of himself and Doc. He thought of Carter and Louis and Bulk and Packham. His heart felt heavy at the latter image: Packham. Where the others had died in the line of duty, had been killed at the hands of their enemies, Packham had killed herself. And that only led his mind to wonder about Colt. Was she still alive? Had she been killed by Drazen? Or had she, too, ended things herself to avoid that fate?

And that's what troubled him the most, because something lay there in the pit of his stomach, a little pocket of hope. Something that refused to believe Colt was dead. With the rest of his soldiers he felt it... that they were truly dead. He knew it for certain, of course, but his thoughts of them were cold, empty, untouchable. But Colt, she remained warm. Whole. She had to be alive, he was sure of it.

"Where the hell are you, Colt?" he whispered.

"Sir?" McKinley's voice sounded from the doorway.

Harris looked at him, then glanced at his watch. "You're early?" He arched his eyebrow.

"Yeah," McKinley said, entering and dropping his bag on the floor. "We need to talk."

Harris turned to face him. "About?"

"The future."

Harris took a seat at his desk and watched McKinley move to stand on the other side. He glanced at Harris's bookcase, spying the photo of Doc.

"Were you... were you talking to Doc?" he asked awkwardly.

"I can't talk to the dead while I'm awake," Harris said plainly. At least, he didn't think he could.

"But you can when you dream?"

"Sometimes."

"Have you spoken with Doc?"

"Once," he nodded, looking down at his desk in thought. "The night I finally told Welles about my gift and the connection."

"What did he say?"

Harris shrugged. "Not much. That he was happy I told her."

McKinley nodded.

"But I haven't dreamed of my dead soldiers of late. Hopefully, that's a good thing. They're not trying to warn me of anything. So, what did you want to talk about?"

The lieutenant studied him, as though thinking through one last time what he would or wouldn't say.

"Welles is pregnant," he blurted. "It's mine."

Harris paused as his mind processed the information.

"We're going to have it," McKinley told him.

Harris continued to stare at him, working on getting his mouth to move. He eventually nodded, running his hand across his jaw, as though shaking off the numbness. "I thought she couldn't have any more kids?"

"It may be risky carrying them, but falling pregnant is fine apparently."

Harris nodded. "How far along?"

"It's early days. She's under two months."

McKinley sat down in a guest chair, as though a weight had been lifted off his shoulders. "I just wanted to tell you first before it became common knowledge."

"I guess you two made up then?"

A sheepish look crossed McKinley's face, before a smile curled the corner of his mouth. "I asked her to marry me. She said yes."

Again Harris paused. He never thought he'd hear the words "getting married" come out of McKinley's mouth. He sat back in his chair and studied his lieutenant. "You marrying her because she's pregnant? Or because you love her?"

McKinley looked back at him thoughtfully. "Both."

"You love her?" Harris asked again. "Why?"

"Why?"

"Tell me why you think you love her?" Harris challenged.

McKinley stared at him, then shrugged. "I just do."

"Give me more than that."

McKinley stared at him a moment, his mind turning over. "Alright... I can't stop thinking about her. When I'm not with her, I want to be with her. When I'm with her, I can't keep my hands off her."

"That's the Alpha talking," Harris said. "Give me something else."

McKinley thought again for a moment. "She knows me like no-one else does. She calls me on my shit and she's usually right. I listen to her like I haven't listened to anyone else. She... I don't know. She's just everything.

I can't imagine my life without her... I even took her to meet my mother. No-one's ever met my mother."

"Yeah?" Harris raised his eyebrows.

McKinley nodded. "Yeah. So, does that convince you?"

Harris nodded gently back. "She's my Connected, McKinley. And you're my First Lieutenant. I need both of you when the war comes. I just wanted to make sure no-one's making any hasty Alpha judgements here."

"We're not. Archie seems to think we may run into a problem with Command," McKinley said, "given the contracts we signed. Unauthorized breeding and all that."

Harris sighed heavily. "Yeah, they'll have something to say, no doubt."

"They'll be all over her again."

Harris nodded. "It could be dangerous for her, you know. The pregnancy. Given what happened last time with the twins."

McKinley shrugged. "She's convinced he'll be fine."

"He?" Harris looked at him quizzically.

"Yeah." McKinley studied his captain's face carefully. "She says she's dreamed of him. Our son. She says he's there at the end. Have you? Dreamed of him?"

Harris recalled the dream he'd had in Eden, the one where he stood on the lookout with his adult daughter, and Brody and Freya and Welles. And he remembered the other soldier who'd walked out to join them. McKinley's son.

He nodded slowly. "Yeah. I guess I have."

McKinley's eyes pierced into his. "So, you knew this was coming?"

"Fates can change."

"But you saw my son way before I... before we..." McKinley gave a quiet, yet astonished, laugh and shook his head. "Holy shit."

Harris watched him.

"Anything else I should know?" McKinley asked.

Harris gave a smile. "No."

McKinley nodded, eyeing Harris again. "So, we're good?"

"We had this conversation already, McKinley."

McKinley glanced down at his hands. "She wanted to tell you herself, but I wanted you to hear it from me."

"Well, thank you."

"We can keep it quiet for as long as you want, but she'll have to stop training. It won't take long for people to figure it out."

"No," he agreed. "I think it's best you get Dr. Morgave on it as soon as possible. Make sure everything's okay."

McKinley nodded, looking relieved.

"It'll be a shame to sideline her training again," Harris said, "but I guess that's the price to pay to bring your boy into this world."

Again McKinley nodded.

Harris sighed. "Well, I guess congratulations are in order, lieutenant."

"Yeah," McKinley said, looking a little stunned, before he grinned. "Who would've thought, huh?"

Harris smiled. "If any woman was going to be able to handle you, it's her."

McKinley continued to grin. "And me, her."

"Yeah, you're two peas in a pod."

McKinley's smile faded and his face fell serious. "As Welles keeps saying, we're in this together. Until the end."

"Yeah," Harris agreed, "until the end."

They sat in silence, before McKinley finally stood. He moved to the door, but Harris stopped him.

"James," he said.

McKinley turned around to him.

"I only have one request of you."

"Yeah?"

"I know you'll take care of Welles, and Freya's your daughter... just promise me you'll take care of Brody, too. Promise me you'll take care of Doc's son."

"Of course," McKinley said firmly. "I know what it's like to grow up without a father and I don't want that for him... He may not bear the name McKinley, but he'll be just as much my son as the one Welles is carrying now. I won't let him down."

Harris nodded at his lieutenant, content. "I know you won't."

With that, McKinley turned and left the room.

Corporal Sabrina Colt looked at her exposed swelling belly, then quickly pulled down her shirt to cover it again. She was far beyond the point of getting rid of them now. It was too late to do anything without putting her own life in danger. And she certainly wasn't going to get any help from LeFroy.

She eyed the nurse they'd been sending to check on her as the woman packed away her things. She was old, probably pulled out of retirement for some good cash. Colt thought of taking her hostage, using her to gain her own freedom, but the Greenback was too smart for that. He'd been sending muscle with the nurse every day and they'd been cuffing her to the bed, minimizing her movement.

The nurse closed her bag and turned to look at Colt, narrow lined face and faded green eyes appraising her.

"You should be happy," she told Colt. "Your boys are healthy."

Colt's eyes burned a hole of scorn through the woman. Scorn for the fact that a woman could take part in this, watch another be caged and forced to go through a pregnancy she didn't want.

"They're big, though," the nurse added. "I'll keep monitoring you, but you'll probably need a Caesarean to deliver them."

Just like Welles, Colt thought, picturing the faces of Brody and Freya in her mind. Welles... Colt envied her right now. Although Welles had had a pregnancy forced upon her, she had ultimately made the decision to have the children. She'd been given the luxury of choice. Colt had not. Welles was lucky. She'd been given the choice, and the paternity of her children was known, was two men she had been amicable with. The paternity of Colt's children, however...

When she'd heard the nurse carelessly mention the fathers' names one day, Colt had frozen in fear. The nurse had carried on, unaware of the awful news she'd just delivered. Colt, horrified, had snatched the e-clip from the woman's hands and read the information, sought out the names just to be sure. And there they were. She'd heard right. The *Aurora*'s enemies, the men from her nightmares, were alive inside her.

The nurse left the cell, and exited the building with the muscle in tow. LeFroy moved over to the cell door and stared at her.

"They're healthy. That's good news," he said as though trying to look on the bright side of things.

"I need to get out of here," she said quietly.

LeFroy watched her in silence for a moment. "And where do you think you will go? How far do you think the Greenback will let you get?"

Colt stared at the man, her eyes pleading. "If we work together, we can both get out of here."

"And go where?"

"To the UNF! To the *Aurora*!"

"That's if we make it that far. We don't even know where we are."

"Will you stop being a coward!"

He looked at her, offended. "I'm trying to stay alive."

"So, let's get out of here!"

"And what if we fail? If we try to escape, they will *kill* us."

"And what do you think they'll do when they're done with us?"

LeFroy was quiet for a moment. "They may let us go."

"Do you really think he'll do that? We know too much, we've seen too much. We're a danger to him."

LeFroy shrugged. "Then I'd suggest they'll give you a small break, then impregnate you again, and they'll need me to watch you."

"Oh, no. No, no!" Colt shouted, shaking her head. "They will have to kill me first. I am not carrying more, I swear to God!"

"Why do you hate them so?" LeFroy asked. "I understand your hate for the people keeping you here, but I don't understand your hate for the children."

Colt tugged on her cuffs, willing them to break. "Let me out!"

"Why did you snatch the e-clip off the nurse?" he asked. "You knew the fathers, didn't you?"

"Let. Me. *Out!*" she hissed in an animalistic growl.

"No, not while you threaten me like that."

"I'm not threatening you!"

"You are," he said, "with your eyes. I see the hate burning within them."

Her voice seemed to drop several octaves as she glared at him murderously. "There's not much to love around here."

"There is," he said, gripping the bars between them and pressing his face close as though to make a point. "The children. Regardless of who their fathers are, they're your children. You need to take care of them, and yourself."

"Shut up!" she snarled. "Stop trying to get inside my head. You're just trying to ensure their survival."

"Maybe," he shrugged. "I told you, my life is connected to theirs."

"Get away from me. Don't even look at me. Or I swear to God I will *kill* you!"

"You're only stressing the babies by acting like this, you know."

"Fuck you! You'd better hope I don't get out of here, because I promise you if I do, I will beat the living *shit* out of you!"

"I don't doubt that," LeFroy said, "and that's why I won't ever let you out."

With that he moved back into his cell, turned on his TV and ignored her.

Colt bowed her head and squeezed her eyes shut, trying with all her might not to burst out crying, not to let him see her as weak. But it was a struggle. She was at the end of her rope. She wasn't sure how much more she could take.

She'd been trapped here for months now. Her entire pregnancy. Although things had been a lot more comfortable, even homely, since the Greenback had taken over, she was still a prisoner. She still had not been out of this lair for months, had not seen the outside world for months. At least, not in person. She found herself grateful for the TVs he had brought them. That was her only proof that life carried on outside her prison, her only inspiration to hold on. Knowing that if she held on she could one day be back outside, amongst all that life.

Thoughts flooded into her mind of her parents: her mother's embracing arms, her father's proud smile. She thought of her twin sister and her brother. Then she thought of Malik, her dead brother. And she thought of what her parents must be going through right now with her disappearance. She couldn't let them lose another child. She couldn't. She had to survive. She had to make it out alive.

Even if that meant seeing these children born safe. She had to survive. As soon as they were out of her and as soon as she was able, she could escape and she would run for her life.

And she promised herself that she would kill anyone who got in her way.

Harris stepped into his office to take the call on his PDP. He knew why she was calling.

"Welles," he answered.

"Sir," she said. He detected a little nervousness. "I, er, believe you met with McKinley this morning."

"I did. I hear congratulations are in order," he said, wanting to make it easy for her.

"Thank you. So, everything's okay?"

"Why wouldn't it be? You're both happy, so long as it stays that way, I'm happy too."

"Thank you, sir. I know it must be a bit of a shock—"

"Not really," he said. "You forget, I dream the future. Besides, my gut's known there was something between you two for a while."

"Of course," she said and he could hear her smile. "Well, I guess I just want you to know that I will always love Doc, but—"

"He's gone," Harris cut her off again. "And it's time to move on. I get it Welles. Just answer me one question."

"Sure."

"Do you love him? McKinley? Or are things just convenient? You're both Alphas, you got Freya. I'm throwing no shade here. I get it. I'm just asking."

There was a pause over the phone. "Of course I do." She sounded offended. "You think I'm using him for convenience?"

"No," Harris softened his voice. "I was just asking because I know McKinley's in deep for you. We got a war coming. You're my Connected and he's my first lieutenant. I just wanted to know where y'all stand. I asked him the same question."

"Well," she said softly. "I love him, sir. That's why I'm having his kid. It's why I'm marrying him. He's drives me crazy sometimes, but... I love him and I'll be by his side until the end."

"Then I'm happy for you Welles," Harris said, then hesitated a moment before adding. "And I think Doc would be, too."

"Thank you," she whispered, heavy with emotion. "I think he would be, too."

*

Harris watched as the team paired off on the mats and began to train.

"Sir?" Eki Tikaani threw her hands out in question. "Where's that little Welles? She's my partner."

Harris threw a glance at McKinley.

"She won't be training with us for a while," McKinley answered for him. "She'll still come watch but she won't actually physically train."

"Why not?" Tikaani asked, as the team looked to him for an answer.

McKinley eyed them all. "Because she's pregnant."

"Pregnant?" Gregson's eyes flew wide. "Whose is it?"

McKinley stared at him. "Mine."

"Yours?" Brown's face furrowed.

McKinley turned his eyes to the sergeant. "Yeah. Mine."

Silence filled the training facility until Frazer broke it.

"What?" the Scot asked, sounding a little confused, folding his arms. "She had another one implanted? Why would she do that? Are they paying her or something?"

Silence remained as the team glanced at Frazer. Murphy chuckled and threw his arm around Frazer's shoulders and said. "I don't think this one was made in a lab, Chucky."

Frazer looked at Murphy for a moment, before his face revealed he understood. "Ah! *Yours*," and he nodded at McKinley.

Tikaani laughed. "Didn't your papa ever tell you about the birds and the bees, Chucky?" She looked at McKinley. "Nice going, stud!"

McKinley's face lightened a little with amusement. "We're also getting married."

"Married?!" Hunter laughed and clapped his hands.

"Wow," Yughi said, scratching his head. "You and Welles, huh."

Hunter nudged Yughi's shoulder playfully. "Like you didn't know." He stepped forward and held his hand out to McKinley. "Congrats, bro," he said with a smile. McKinley gripped hands with him, before Hunter pulled him in for a hug and slap on the back. Evenssen followed suit, smiling.

Steinberg stepped forward with a sly grin. "I wondered how long it would take you two to come out of the closet."

"You knew?" Gregson asked.

Steinberg grinned, pointing to his eyes. "I noticed."

"Noticed what?" McKinley said defensively.

"Everything," Steinberg said, his grin broadening. "The way you two look at each other. You spend every free moment together. You're very protective of he—"

"Yeah, alright," McKinley smiled, until his eyes caught on Brown's face. The sergeant was unmoving, his brow still furrowed.

"Alright!" Harris called for their attention. "How about we get back to some training, huh?" he said, clapping his hands. And with that they turned and faced off against their partners.

Carrie stared at Dr. Morgave.

"Really?" He sounded surprised.

"What are you surprised about?" she asked. "That I'm pregnant again or that it's to McKinley?"

Morgave shrugged as he gave her question some serious thought. "Both, I guess." He glanced at the results showing on the screen, then back to her. "You were a reluctant mother the first time around."

"Yeah," she conceded, "but I wouldn't give them up for the world now."

"Yes," he smiled, his face showing lines of age creeping in, despite his jet-black hair. His smile faded a little. "I'll be honest, I'm a little concerned. Your uterus took some damage last time. It could be unstable. I'll need to monitor you carefully."

"Yeah, I figured you would."

"I'll need to inform Colonel Marchant." Morgave threw her a careful glance. "You're supposed to apply for children first."

"Yeah, well, that policy might need some work," Carrie told him. "Accidents happen."

"Apparently," he smiled.

"Anyway, I'm sure the UNF will be delighted to have another pregnancy and child to study."

"I'm sure they will."

A knock on the door caught their attention. It slid back and Dr. Scavesci stood there.

"Sergeant Welles!" he smiled, then turned to Dr. Morgave. "I do apologize for interrupting your appointment."

Morgave gave a steely smile. "A closed door generally means, do not disturb."

"I was informed that Sergeant Welles was here," Scavesci continued as though he missed the barb. Or ignored it. "I wanted to catch her before she left."

"Let me guess," Carrie said, "you want me to pay Sharley a visit."

"You know me so well!" he smiled, coming to stand by the desk and steepling his fingers together over his rotund belly.

"Yes, I do," she said, "and I told you before I don't want to see him."

Scavesci held up his hand. "What if you just came and stood outside the glass of his room. You don't have to converse with him. Just let him pick up your scent."

"Excuse me?" she said, throwing Morgave a glance.

"It will please him no end, if he knows you've paid him a visit."

Carrie shook her head and folded her arms, sitting back in her chair.

Scavesci looked to Morgave as though seeking support. "Doctor, surely—" Scavesci's voice cut off. Carrie glanced at him and saw his eyes were fixed to Morgave's monitor. Morgave quickly closed it down as he also noticed, darting Carrie an apologetic look.

"You're pregnant?" Scavesci turned to her, eyeing her up and down.

Carrie didn't answer, just stared back.

"And who, may I ask, is the father?"

Again she didn't answer.

Scavesci looked at Morgave, whose shoulders slumped in resignation. He looked at Carrie. "He'll find out eventually."

"The father?" Scavesci pressed.

"Lieutenant McKinley," Morgave said.

"Really?" Scavesci smiled, his gray bristly beard twitching. "Congratulations, sergeant. I didn't realize that Colonel Marchant had approved for you to have another."

His comment was met with silence from both Carrie and Morgave.

"Oh, I see," Scavesci said, nodding to himself. "Well, what's done is done." He patted her on the shoulder. "We'll take good care of you, sergeant. You've nothing to fear." He looked at Morgave. "I do apologize for interrupting." Then he glanced at Carrie. "If you change your mind and would like to see the professor, please pop by my office."

"Doctor?" Carrie stopped him as he turned for the door. Scavesci looked back at her. "You keep this from Sharley," she told him in a low, threatening voice. "Understand? He doesn't need to know."

"Of course," Scavesci left with a slight smile on his face.

Carrie looked back at Morgave and sighed, her shoulders slumping. "And so it begins."

Harris sat down in his chair and looked across his desk at Brown, who he'd invited to his office.

"I just wanted to talk with you about McKinley's announcement. I saw your reaction."

Brown frowned. "He hasn't been dead that long."

"Brown," Harris said simply.

Brown shrugged. "What?"

"Doc's dead."

"I know. I notice it every night he's not bunking up beside me in our room."

Harris nodded and sighed. "Yeah, and I do too... miss him sitting right there where you are now, talking about whatever we got going on. But we can't do that anymore, hold onto the past. I had to move on. And so do you."

Brown's face furrowed further.

"Welles and McKinley are adults," Harris explained. "It ain't our damn business what they're doing. Besides, are you really surprised? Don't tell me you didn't already guess something was going on between them."

"You think it's okay?"

Harris shrugged. "Ain't my business."

"But you think it's okay? Them moving on while his grave's barely cold. How long has it been going on for?"

"McKinley is Freya's father. He's always going to be a part of their lives."

"So?"

"Brown, look," Harris said, sitting back in his chair, "they got a long history. They're both Alphas, they've both been through a lot, they got a kid together. It's a natural path, I guess."

"So? Don't mean it's right. He promised Doc as he was dying that he would look out for them. That didn't mean he was supposed to move *in* on them!"

Harris sat forward. "How many women out there do you think would understand what McKinley is? Understand everything that comes with that." Harris paused briefly, remembering Colt's cousin Keisha and how she dumped Brown after the events in Eden. "Not many is my guess," he said gently. "As you well know... Welles understands what he is, and she knows how to handle him. Now, how many men out there do you think would understand what Welles is and what her kids are? How many men do you think would understand the Sentinels and the Fortress and the invasion we got coming our way. Very few, Brown. Very few normal men could handle any one of those things let alone all of it. McKinley knows, he understands. He can handle Welles, and he is going to raise Brody like his own son. *That's* what I care about. Welles and McKinley can do what they want, but what I care about is that boy. Doc's boy. *My* godson. And I gotta say, outside of myself, there's no-one else I'd trust the life of Brody to more than McKinley."

Brown threw him an offended look. Harris held up his hand in apology. "Or you."

"I'd die for that boy," Brown said adamantly.

"As would I," Harris agreed, relaxing a little.

Brown sat quietly thinking over their discussion. Harris sensed the Welles and McKinley issue wasn't the sole reason for his mood. It was just the easiest target.

"Have you heard from Keisha?" Harris asked.

Brown scoffed and waved him off. "Waste of time, that was."

"How is she coping with Colt's... disappearance?"

Brown shrugged. "Don't know. She hasn't spoken to me since Eden. I've tried to call her and her family, offer my condolences, but they won't take my call. I don't know what Keisha said, but... I think they blame me, us, for it."

"Even Colt's family?"

"Nah, they've been good."

"You've seen them?"

Brown nodded. "I've been dropping by every leave."

"That's good of you, Brown. To do that."

He shrugged. "I liked Colt. She didn't deserve this."

"No, she didn't."

"You think she's dead?" Brown asked.

Harris stared at him. "I don't know."

"Why hasn't her body shown?" Brown asked. "They didn't bother trying to hide Packham's, so why would they hide hers. Wouldn't they leave it as a message for us?"

"Unless someone's taunting us?"

"Nah." Brown shook his head. "The only time people go off the radar is when someone's got them underground somewhere. Just like they did with Welles. Twice. I think she's still alive, sir."

Harris sighed.

"You do, too," Brown said, almost accusingly. "I can tell. You think she's still alive."

Harris didn't answer, but simply looked at him.

"So, what the hell are we going to do about it?" Brown asked.

Harris held his arms out wide in question. "What *can* we do? She's off the radar. How are we supposed to find one person, who could be anywhere across the entire UNF Space Zone?"

"There's gotta be a way!" Brown growled, flashing the Alpha within.

"Brown—"

"You think she's alive, and yet you just sit there! When Welles was missing, we searched for her. We searched and searched and searched. Even when it looked hopeless."

"The UNF has been doing that, Brown. They're still doing that. I'd remind you that Colt has been put on the FRS just like Welles was. And there came a time when we were put back on normal duties when Welles was missing on Meridian. We just had to carry on until we got a sign to move." He sat forward again, giving Brown a firm look. "And I assure you, as soon as I get a sign that Colt is alive, I will move like the wind."

They held each other's Alpha stare until Harris eased back in his chair.

"I know you're still getting used to the Alpha within, Brown, but you need to control it. It's hard, I know. Especially when you're passionate about something, but control is fundamental. That's where the power of the Alpha lies – knowing when to hold back and knowing when to launch it. Understand?"

Brown exhaled long and controlled, then nodded.

"Now, I expect your relationship with McKinley to remain solid, alright?" Harris said. "He's with Welles, they're having a kid, that's it. End of story."

Harris watched as Brown looked down to his lap.

"Brown," he said gently. "I think if Doc could, he'd approve. McKinley loves her," he continued. "Genuinely. Never thought I'd see McKinley fall in love with anyone, but it's happened. He'll take care of her, he'll take care of the kids, and I think that's what Doc would want."

Brown nodded, finally looking up to meet his eyes.

"And I promise," Harris said, "if Colt is still alive… if she gives me a sign, I will run for her, just like I did for Welles. You have my word."

Colonel Marchant watched as General Berger and Lieutenant General Wilton reviewed Dr. Morgave's report. Doctor Scavesci was also present at the General's request.

"We were under the impression that she would not be able to bear another child." Wilton's unimpressed face looked up at him.

"Dr. Morgave advises that it's a risk. Her uterus received substantial damage in the previous attack."

"What's the likelihood of survival?" Berger asked.

"Of Welles?" Marchant asked.

"No, the child."

"Well, right now, all Dr. Morgave will commit to is that we'll have to monitor her carefully, and if required, take the necessary measures."

"Which are?" Wilton asked.

"If things look unstable she'll be confined to bed rest. If things look bleak, we'll have to remove the child early, seal it in a pod and hope it survives."

Berger nodded, "Alright. Now what do we do about them breaking their contract?"

Marchant stared at them both, thinking. "I guess this is a little different. They're both Alphas and they've had Alpha children before, so it's nothing new."

"You're suggesting we let the first Alphas who bred of their own accord to get away with it?" Wilton asked. "What kind of message do you think that sends to the rest of our soldiers? That the contracts they sign with the UNF are worth nothing."

"He's right," Berger agreed. "We can't let them think that uncontrolled breeding will be tolerated. It'll start with this, then spread to breeding with humans, which could well result in someone's death."

"And then there're the clauses on all the other behavioral matters," Wilton added. "The drinking, the fighting. Where will it stop?"

Marchant sighed heavily. "I understand what you're saying, and I agree. But I also think we need to tread carefully here. Right now, we only have one Alpha unit, and both Welles and McKinley have served the UNF honorably. Because of Welles, we have a lot of data on the First Gen program. And McKinley is Harris's right-hand man. If we punish them—"

"We cannot let horny Alphas do as they please," Wilton said acidly.

"My understanding is," Marchant said, "from what Morgave has told me, they're a couple. This isn't the result of some casual Alpha sex. Apparently, they're to be married."

Berger and Wilton stared at him, while Scavesci did too with a slight smile.

"Nevertheless, we cannot be seen to let them get away with this," Berger eventually said. "They've broken their contracts."

Marchant stared at him, biting back his thoughts.

"You disagree?" Berger asked.

"Yes, I do. I understand your point, but we've finally made good progress on this program because we now have their full buy-in. This wasn't a foolish one-night stand with a human. If we punish them, they may turn their backs on us again, and where will that leave the program?"

"Discipline of our Alpha soldiers is fundamental," Wilton said.

"Yes, it is," Marchant agreed. "So, let's note this in their files. If they play up in the future, we can use it against them then. But for now, we let this slide as a favor."

"A favor?" Berger asked incredulously. "We need to be careful about how much power and leverage we give the *Aurora* team, colonel. This is *our* program. They are working for us."

"I agree," Wilton said. "How many times have we already changed the rules to suit them? And the *Carcharias*," he added acidly.

Marchant nodded, understanding now where Wilton was coming from. Wilton, who was friends with Rovine. "We do need to be careful," Marchant said, appeasing them. "But do you not think we owe them for all they've done for the UNF, and for all that the UNF has put them through?"

"We cannot repay every soldier for the hell they have been through," Wilton said.

"They could've died on the Darwin," Marchant said. "Some of the *Aurora* team did die. And the UNF sent them there, into a trap, without warning."

"We didn't know Sharley was planning that massacre," Wilton said.

"Not you, perhaps, but others did. Welles had those twins, and in doing so, gave us valuable information. She's not fighting us on this new pregnancy. She knows we're going to study her and she is allowing it, because she believes in what we're doing now and why we're doing it. McKinley, too. He held back in the beginning, made things difficult for us, but he's seen the light. He, like Harris, like the rest of the *Aurora* crew, believe in this fight. They are with us and will do what it takes. We are just gaining speed on this program. I think that if you come down harshly on them, they will pull back again."

Silence sat in the room for a moment.

"I'm inclined to agree," Doctor Scavesci said to Marchant, then turned to the General. "If Welles lets us study her child unhindered, the data would be worth more than anything."

"We already have data on the twins," Wilton snipped.

"Yes, the twins that Sharley created in a lab and implanted her with," Scavesci said. "This new child was created in the wild, so to speak. This one is all natural. We can compare its results to the manufactured children and use that to guide us on Alpha mating rules in the future. I think it's terribly important we keep Welles on side. We overlook their breaking of the contract in return for unfettered access to the child."

Marchant nodded. "Right now, we need their cooperation. Right now, another Welles pregnancy won't hurt things. But if we punish them, that will."

"What do you suggest we do?" Wilton asked tersely. "We still can't let them flaunt the contract they've signed."

"We lie," Berger said bluntly, his mind spinning behind calculating eyes. "The official word will be that we approached them and asked Welles to give us another child. We'll get them to sign contracts to that effect. They will be an exception to the rule, only because of these contracts. And we let the other soldiers know that."

"You're talking about their crew members," Wilton said. "They train with these people. What makes you think they don't already know about the two of them? What makes you think they'll buy this story?"

"This story won't be for the *Aurora* team," Marchant said, running with Berger's idea. "This story is for any others that come along. For the *Carcharias*, for all of them."

Again silence sat in the room, as both Berger and Wilton regarded him.

General Berger glanced at Wilton, then looked back at Marchant. "Agreed. Have Skordan draw up the contracts, stating that this child was requested by the UNF. They'll receive a strike on their records, but due to their compliance allowing the UNF access to study the child, their punishment will remain on hold." Berger stood. "But if they step another foot out of line…" He pointed threateningly at Marchant.

"Understood," Marchant nodded.

Harris stood in the interrogation room and watched as Lieutenant Skordan explained the new contract that Welles and McKinley were being asked to sign.

"Why do I feel like I'm signing over my child to the UNF every time I sign one of these things," Welles said.

"The child is yours," Skordan assured her. "However, for the sake of the, er, ruse, for want of a better word, it does state that you've agreed to have this child for the purpose of UNF study. It's worded in a way to make it appear you signed the contract first, then fell pregnant. We will backdate the signing of the document."

"So, there's absolutely nothing in here that enables the UNF to think they can lay claim to my child?"

"No. Just the right to study the child, in all ways, from DNA to life development. You are having this child at the request of the UNF, but child belongs to you."

Welles gave McKinley a nervous glance, and he gave her a wary glance back.

"Is this meeting being recorded?" Welles asked Skordan.

"Yes," she answered.

"Good," Welles said. "I'll sign this document, but if anyone tries to lay claim to my child or lay a hand on them in any way that I disagree with, the UNF won't be able to hold back the Alpha within me. Is that understood?"

Skordan studied Welles, before breaking into a smile. "Would you like me to add that in writing?"

Welles stared back at Skordan, unsure how to take her.

"Yes," McKinley answered for her, staring at Skordan, "and make sure you put down double from me."

Dr. Scavesci smiled across the table at Professor Sharley.

"You have something to share," Sharley said, smiling back. "I can tell."

"Yes, I do." Scavesci's grin grew wider. "I think you'll enjoy hearing this one."

"Yes?" Sharley said quietly, leaning forward slightly.

Scavesci saw the eagerness in his eyes and he thought once more of how much his client had come back to life these past months. No longer was he thin and frail. No longer was he dirty and unkempt. Sharley looked normal. Almost. Except for that dark gleam in his eyes.

"Is Welles coming to visit me?" Sharley asked.

Scavesci shook his head. "No, and I suspect that she won't for some time."

"Why?" Sharley asked, tilting his head. "What's changed?"

Scavesci thought things over one last time. He knew he'd been asked not to, but he simply couldn't hold back this information from the patient. Not when the revelation could unlock the door to his mind.

Scavesci took a breath, preparing himself to gauge the professor's reaction.

"She is with child again."

Sharley's eyes widened slightly. "Whose?"

"Whose child?"

Sharley nodded, his eyes pinning Scavesci to the spot.

"Lieutenant McKinley's," Scavesci said smoothly. "They are to be married."

Sharley stared at him a moment before a smile grew across his face. "I knew it!" he whispered.

"What did you know?" Scavesci asked. It was time to begin their session.

Sharley's smile couldn't get any wider. "That they wouldn't be able to keep their hands off each other."

"Yes?"

"It was only a matter of time," Sharley said, his eyes glazing over as his mind raced away. "And now she bears his child."

"But she's already borne his child. Freya. What's so special about this one?"

Sharley's gaze returned to him. "This one proves I'm right. This one proves they were a good match. This one is born of pure Alpha passion."

"This one excites you," Scavesci commented.

"I want to get my hands on it. I want to study it."

"More than the others?"

"No, alongside the others. They are all special. They are all unique. But this new one proves I'm right. This new one is the future, created by my own hand."

Scavesci couldn't help but furrow his brow in confusion. "I'm sorry? How do you think you've created this one? The others I understand, in a roundabout way. They were created and implanted at your behest, but this one was created purely by them."

Sharley's eyes flashed darker. "And who do you think created Welles and McKinley? *I* did. I created them, and they've created this child. Therefore, this one belongs to me too." Sharley stood and began to pace slowly, rhythmically, deep in thought. "I told McKinley she would bear our child, but he didn't believe me. How far along is she?" Sharley stopped and looked back at Scavesci for an answer.

"It's very early days. You know her uterus received damage last time, so there's no guarantee she'll deliver the child alive."

Sharley gave a laugh, although it had a jagged edge to it. "Come on, doctor. Have you not learned anything about Welles yet? You can't kill her. She's a survivor."

"Perhaps she is, but what about the child?"

"McKinley's a survivor. She's a survivor. Their children are survivors. She's a protective momma bear, and she will ensure they live. I bet my life on it."

Scavesci watched, fascinated at seeing the delusions being woven before him, by this man who believed he really was in control of all these people, like he was a god who could control someone's life and death.

"I must see the children," Sharley said. "You must bring them to me."

"Professor, I've told you—"

"No," Sharley shook his head confidently. "I've had enough of your excuses, doctor. You're letting the team down."

Scavesci stared at him. Sharley placed his hands on the table and leaned over it toward him. "Things have turned," he said quietly as though conveying something very important. "The *Aurora* team are all Alphas. The program is moving ahead. The twins are growing, this new child is coming. A new day is dawning, doctor, and we must keep up. They need us. We must do our part."

"Our part? Who needs us?"

"The world, doctor. The world needs us to save them from the invasion. Bring me the children. Let me study them. Let me see what needs to be done." Sharley began to pace again.

Scavesci wasn't sure how to respond, but finally said, "You really think the children are going to save us?"

Sharley stopped pacing and looked back at him. "Of course," he said. "That's what I created them to do."

13

New Gens And First Gens

Carrie sipped a tea, watching as Ellen Walker played with the twins. David Walker was at a conference in Chicago, so Ellen had used the time to visit her grandchildren. Of course, only Brody was genetically so. She felt a twinge of guilt as Doc's mother kissed and cuddled Freya.

"Oh, boy," Ellen said, groping her way up onto the couch. "I'm getting too old for the hands and knees stuff!"

Carrie smiled. She liked Ellen a lot. She didn't want to lie to her anymore. She had to tell her.

"Ellen," she said quietly.

She didn't hear, though, as she was laughing at Brody drawing on his sister. Carrie smiled, didn't want to ruin this moment, but she couldn't carry on this way. Before long, her secret would be out anyway. People knew at a high level within the UNF, and the *Aurora* team now knew. McKinley had told them while she'd visited Dr Morgave, but the next day she'd attended the *Aurora* training, wanting to show her face and move forward. She was relieved to see how happy and congratulatory they were. Hunter had joked about her finally making a man out of McKinley, which made everyone laugh. While the team trained, she'd stood on the sidelines watching with McKinley, and he'd slid his hand over her abdomen. They'd exchanged a glance – his testing the waters, and hers confirming they weren't going to hide anymore. She'd smiled at him and slid her hand over his. The team had seen and smiled to themselves, but nothing more was said.

Now, she had to tell Doc's family before any more time passed.

"Ellen," she said firmly.

"Yeah, honey?" She turned to her.

"I'm pregnant."

Ellen paused a moment. "Oh."

"It's James McKinley's. We're… he and I… we're together now. He asked me to marry him and I said yes."

Ellen stared for a moment longer, processing all the information, before she broke into a soft smile. "Oh, honey, I'm happy for you."

"You are?"

Ellen nodded. "I wondered when the two of you were going to make things official."

Carrie stared at her, unable to speak.

Ellen smiled warmly. "Honey, he's been living with you for some time. Even the best of friends don't do that. Especially single heterosexual ones of the opposite sex."

"Freya's his," she blurted.

"Sorry?" Ellen leaned closer, like she hadn't heard.

"Freya. She's McKinley's daughter. Brody is Dan's. It's hard to explain." She sighed heavily, heartbeat racing with nerves. "Dan was supposed to explain it to you, but he never got the chance."

Ellen stared at her. Her expression wasn't accusing, wasn't hurt, wasn't really anything. Maybe, at a stretch, a little melancholic. Ellen looked at Freya.

"I never could figure out who she looked like," she said, then smiled sadly. "It makes sense. Blond hair, blue eyes."

"She's still your granddaughter though," Carrie said quickly. "She's Brody's twin. Dan was going to raise her as his own."

A tear rolled down Ellen's face. She wiped it away. "How did it happen?"

"How did what happen?" Carrie asked wondering if she wanted detail on Doc's death.

"The twins."

"I... can't really go into it, Ellen. It was an experiment. It's classified." Carrie didn't have the heart to tell her the experiment was forced upon her. Didn't want Ellen to think that, at first, the children had not been wanted.

"I wondered," she said quietly, "about their eyes."

Carrie felt panic shoot through her. *Their eyes?*

Ellen saw her shock and looked back at the children. "I snuck into their room one night, just wanted to check on them. Brody opened his eyes and I saw... they were so unusual. I wanted to ask, but Dan never said anything and I knew you two must've known his eyes were different."

"They're okay," Carrie rushed to reassure her, remembering Ellen used to be a GP. "It was part of the experiment, but they're fine. Their eyesight is actually enhanced. It's a blessing... like mine."

Ellen stared at her a moment, studying her eyes. She glanced at the twins. "Are they in danger?"

Carrie shook her head. "Not anymore." She had no guarantees of that, but for now it was the truth.

Ellen smiled ruefully and gave a soft chuckle as she looked at her granddaughter. "I always thought McKinley had a way with Freya." She turned and looked back at Carrie. "I'm glad for you, Carrie. Honestly. I'm glad you found happiness again."

Carrie's eyes suddenly stung and her throat tightened.

Ellen moved closer and hugged her, sniffing her own tears back. "We never expected you to stay single forever, honey. James is a good man. I can see he's been looking out for you and, well, if Freya is his daughter..." she shrugged, "it makes even more sense."

"Thank you," she whispered to Ellen. "I mean it. Thank you."

Ellen sighed. "Well, seeing how it's confession time." She stood and moved over to her handbag and fished something out. "I had an ulterior motive for coming to see you." She sat down beside Carrie and opened her hand to reveal something wrapped in a piece of cloth. Ellen folded the cloth back and Carrie saw Doc's Blue Nova medal, awarded to him posthumously at his UNF Release Service.

Carrie looked back at Ellen.

"I know after his death you didn't want it," Ellen said, "but I really want the kids to have it." She glanced over at them, then back at Carrie again. "At least, Brody. His son."

Carrie looked over at Brody, playing with some building blocks; his brown eyes, his chubby cheeks. Carrie placed her hand over Ellen's.

"Thank you," she said. "I'll pass it on when he's older. When he can appreciate what it means."

Ellen placed her other hand over Carrie's and together they held the Blue Nova tightly.

Freya walked over to Ellen, then, and handed her a doll. "Nanna!" she said. Ellen took it, brushing Freya's hair off her face, smiling.

"My mother is dead," Carrie told her. "McKinley's mother is… My kids need a grandmother. I'd like you to be that for all of them."

Ellen looked at Carrie, then back at Freya. "Honey, I'm not going anywhere. I've been this little girl's grandmother for too long to back away now."

Tears ejected from Carrie's eyes and rolled down her cheeks. Tears of happiness, of relief, now her secret had been unburdened. She watched as Ellen Walker moved to the floor again to play with the children. Carrie suddenly pictured the photo that Ellen had sent her of Doc beaming a smile on the ski slopes. It made her smile too. But then it faded as she thought of the Zetas and what was coming their way. She focused on Doc's mother again.

"Ellen?" Carrie said, glancing down into her cup.

Doc's mother looked back at her.

"There's going to come a time when I will call you and tell you to take your family into the basement, and you'll have to stay there until you hear it's safe to come out again."

Confusion swept across Ellen's face. "Honey?"

Carrie's pleading eyes looked into Ellen's. "I can't tell you anything else right now. You just have to promise me that when I call you, you'll do as I say."

The confusion on Ellen's face slowly dissolved into concern. "Carrie, you're scaring me. What's going on?"

"I can't tell you anything else. I'm sorry. You just have to trust me."

Ellen glanced at the children, then looked back at her.

"For Dan," Carrie said. "You have to promise me you'll do it for Dan."

"Honey—"

"Promise me!" she said firmly.

Ellen stared at Carrie, worried and studying her, but she relented with a nod. "Okay, honey. I promise."

Admiral Arken sat on the flight deck, trying to decide what to do. It had been days now since the Zeta ships disappeared from the radar. Well, days out here in space; back home on Earth, weeks had now passed. Months, even.

"When are we expecting the next package from Command?" he asked Senior Comms-Tech Garth Walon.

"Two weeks, admiral," he replied.

The silence sat as Arken contemplated his choices. Since losing contact with the Zeta ships, they had continued onward, but were largely in the same general position, still light years away from the Zeta Archelois system, and also light years away from Earth. He'd been hoping the Zetas were playing with them, hoping they would show up again on their radar, but they hadn't.

Arken exhaled measuredly. "Provide Command with the same report. We continue onward and give them our latest coordinates."

He noticed several of the other officers present turn around and look at him.

"We need to find them again," he said firmly. "We need to get closer to them. We need to get eyes on their ships. Any information we can pass back to Earth could be critical. Right now, all we know is that they're curious and they like playing games. The Zetas have gone shy on us, so it's up to us to make the next move. So, we continue toward the Zeta Archelois system until we see them again."

"What if they went home for reinforcements?" Navigation Officer Rina Pulloy said, her straight black hair and dark eyes hinting at her Asian heritage.

"Then I guess we'll meet more of them," he replied confidently.

"We'd be seriously outnumbered," she said.

"We would," he agreed, "but the ships that came up on our radar were just a fraction of the size of the *Barbican*. There may be many, but they were much smaller. The *Barbican* is a hell of a ship, Rina. She's a beast. If anything, we probably scared them away."

"To get reinforcements," she repeated.

"Maybe," he said calmly. "Whether they're friendly or not, our job is to feed intel back to Command, and that's what we're going to do. Besides, the recent sightings may well be different targets to the ones we've been communicating with. Our mission is to find the ones we've been communicating with."

He looked over to his Russian Chief Flight Officer Sasha Ulgari. She stared back at him with her short, spiked hair and pierced face, awaiting his order.

"Continue with our course, keep the weapons and shields on standby."

Carrie looked at McKinley and smiled. They were standing in front of the large windows overlooking the Space Dock, dressed in their Space Duty uniforms, as a celebrant, also in uniform, married them. It wasn't a traditional wedding but that's what Carrie liked about it. She wasn't the kind of girl who wanted the dress or the cake, and she sure as hell knew that wasn't the kind of guy McKinley was either.

Short, sharp, to the point. They exchanged rings in front of her father, Harris, Hunter, the twins, and her Sentinels. Even that was a larger crowd than they'd planned on. The rings were simple gold bands that had once belonged to his parents.

"You don't think it's bad luck?" McKinley had asked when he showed them to her after a visit to his mother. "Grace thinks it is. Bad luck."

"No," Carrie had told him, examining one of the rings. "Your father loved her, yes?"

McKinley nodded.

"And your mother has never let him go," Carrie said. "How is that bad luck? That's a connection for eternity. That's good luck."

"Let's hope," he'd said.

She'd had the ring resized and now it slid onto her finger, a perfect fit.

"Locked in," she said, looking into McKinley's ocean blue eyes.

"Not until you sign on the dotted line," the celebrant smiled.

Carrie smiled back. "It's all about the paperwork these days. You need a legal department for everything." McKinley and Harris smiled.

After the rings had been exchanged and the right words said, the celebrant announced, "You are now wed, Mr and Mrs McKinley."

Carrie cleared her throat loudly and threw the celebrant a look that said, think again. He bowed slightly in apology. "I'm sorry. Mr McKinley and Mrs Welles-McKinley."

When she'd first told McKinley of her name plans, she'd teased it out a little.

"I'm keeping my name," she'd told him bluntly.

He'd just nodded. "Figured you would."

"But I'm also taking yours," she'd said, as a smile grew across her face.

He'd looked back at her, unsure of whether she was being serious.

"Carrie Welles-McKinley has a nice sound to it, don't you think?"

"It's a mouthful," he'd said bluntly.

She'd crossed her arms over her chest and given him an Alpha stare.

A smile crept across his face in response. "But you do like to be difficult, so it's very you."

The celebrant now motioned toward them. "Well, now's the time," he smiled. "You may kiss!"

McKinley gave the celebrant a nonchalant look, like he didn't need someone to tell him when he could kiss his wife.

They leaned forward to seal their fate, but the touch of little hands taking hold of their legs stopped them. They glanced down to see Freya and Brody pushing between them as they moved toward the window. They laughed at their children, then looked back at each other.

"Let's get this over with," McKinley said, motioning to Harris and Hunter. "They gotta get back to the ship."

"You're such a romantic," Carrie managed before his mouth was on hers. She held his kiss for a few seconds as she closed her eyes, relishing the feeling of kissing her husband.

McKinley, her husband. Who would've thought?

Hunter clapped and laughed, as Freya squealed with delight. McKinley pulled back and they darted a glance at their spectators to see they were looking past them, out the window. They turned to see a large ship taking flight, a fireball at its tail.

"That was awesome!" Hunter said. "Just as you kissed, that ship took off in the background. Couldn't have planned it any better!"

As Hunter moved over to slap hands with McKinley, Carrie realized it was the first time they'd kissed in front of any of the *Aurora* team. And here it was on their wedding day.

"Congratulations, Miss Welles! Congratulations Lieutenant McKinley!" Archie called out. Carrie smiled up at the roof.

"I'm happy for you, Welles," Hunter said, stepping forward and hugging her. "It's about time."

"About time?" she asked, as they separated again.

Hunter grinned. "I'll let you in on a secret, Welles. There was no villa shortage in Eden. Lei and I put you two together for a reason."

"You did?" she asked. She glanced at McKinley to see if he knew about this, but he looked just as curious as her.

Hunter's grin grew wider. "Saw it coming a mile away. I take all the credit for this union, you know."

Carrie thought about telling him that she and McKinley had been together before that, but she let it slide. Instead she smiled, shaking her head, then hugged her father.

"Congratulations," Harris said as he, too, hugged her. The touch of their cheeks sent a zap through them, though, and they quickly pulled away, exchanging a look.

Carrie turned and moved to her twins, cuddling them in her arms.

"You're now legit, kids," she joked.

Harris looked at his watch. "We gotta go," he said to McKinley. "You've got a couple of hours, then you get back. Understand?"

"Yeah," he said, then grinned. "That ought to be enough time to consummate the marriage."

"I'm gonna pretend I didn't hear that," Harris said, as Hunter chuckled.

"I definitely didn't hear that," her father said.

Carrie laughed and watched them leave.

Colt exhaled as she raised herself up.

"Why are you doing that?" LeFroy asked her. "I mean, I commend the fact that you're trying to stay healthy with exercise, but why do you push so hard? Are you trying to harm the children?"

Colt's eyes moved to LeFroy's. She wiped her sweaty brow, then lowered into another squat.

"If you're trying to hurt the children, I'll be forced to tell the Greenback's nurse."

"I'm not trying to hurt them," she said, glancing down at her protruding belly, then glowering back at LeFroy. "I'm making sure that after the birth I'm still strong enough to kill you all."

LeFroy studied her, a look of worry in his eyes. "And what if I tell the Greenback that?"

"I'll just have to kill you before you can," she said, moving into another squat.

"You're alive," he said, "and so am I. Do you *not* see that? We both had to pay a price for survival."

She glanced at him, uninterested, then continued with her squats.

"If I didn't obey them, they would have killed me!" he said, pleading.

"You didn't have to impregnate me," she said. "If you hadn't, we could both be free right now. But you did, and then you told the Greenback about my situation and you signed our lives away to be kept down here."

"The Greenback probably would've killed us anyway."

"I guess we'll never know," she said flatly.

She lowered into another squat, eyeing the three photographs still stuck to the wall. The Greenback had confirmed that the *Aurora* team had beaten Drazen's Jumbos, but she wondered whether Welles and Packham were alright. Were they safe or had they been caught and kept in another facility? She wondered whether the *Aurora* team were still looking for her, or whether they'd written her off as dead. Should she have stayed on the ship? Would she be in this mess now if she had?

No matter how hard she tried to distance herself, somehow the *Aurora* kept pulling her back. And for the first time, she wished she'd stayed with them. Here she was, alone, a pregnant Jumbo. How could she go back into the world like this? How could she face her family? This monstrosity she'd become.

She stared at the photo of Welles, and felt soothed, felt a connection. If she ever made it out of here, no matter what happened, she knew there might be one place she could go. One place she could seek shelter: the *Aurora*.

Harris squeezed Taya's hand and kissed her sweating temple, as she groaned in pain.

"Almost there!" the doctor told her. "One more big push ought to do it."

Harris glanced down at her bulging belly. "You're doing good, Tay," he whispered. "You're doing good."

With a loud groaning scream she pushed through clenched teeth.

"There we go!" the doctor announced. "We have a girl!" He swooped Harris's daughter onto the table to check her vitals. Harris heard her loud screeching cry and smiled back at Taya, who had tears rolling down her face. Harris kissed her lips.

"Our little girl's finally here."

*

"You dreamed we were having a girl, didn't you?" Taya asked sleepily, wrapped up in her hospital bed, as she looked over at him.

Harris walked up and down the room holding his tiny daughter in his Alpha arms, rocking her to sleep. He smiled at her, then looked down at his little girl again. "Yeah. I did."

Harris, with his new Alpha hearing, heard footsteps approaching. He looked at the door before a knock sounded.

"Is it safe to come in now?" Ty said dryly.

Harris beamed a grin and moved over to him. "Sure is! Tyson, meet your little sister, Sarai."

"Sarai?" Ty asked, as Harris placed her in her brother's arms.

"You like it?" Harris asked.

"Yeah. It's nice."

"You're officially a big brother now," Harris said, giving him a friendly slap on his broadening shoulders.

Ty smiled down at Sarai, as he moved over to Taya's bed. He leaned down and kissed her forehead. "Good job, mom."

Taya laughed. "Yeah, we did good there," she said, eyeing Sarai with pride. Then she raised her hand and brushed Tyson's cheek. "Just like we did with you, baby."

"Oh, you scored big with me," Ty said. "That goes without saying."

Taya chuckled.

Amused, Harris said, "Yeah, we still need to work on that ego, though, huh?"

Ty grinned. "You can't hide the magic, captain!" He looked down at Sarai again, kissed her forehead, then handed her back to Harris. "I gotta go."

"Go?" Harris asked, taking Sarai. "Where?"

"Where else? Basketball."

"You don't want to maybe miss it just this once and spend time with your new sister?"

"You guys got it covered," Ty said, moving over to kiss Taya again. "I'll see her tomorrow."

"It's fine, let him go," Taya said quietly, as her son left the room. "I'm tired anyway."

Harris exhaled his disappointment.

"Bring me my little girl," Taya said. He moved to her and went to pass Sarai, but Taya stopped him. "No, you hold her. I can't think of anything more beautiful than the sight I'm seeing now. You standing there holding our baby girl."

"I disagree," he said. "The most beautiful thing right now is you and this beautiful little gift you have given us." He suddenly felt his throat tighten and his eyes sting with tears, but he didn't try to fight it. He looked at Taya with wet eyes as she lifted her hand and caressed his cheek.

"I love you," he whispered.

Taya smiled, lowering her hand to run her finger down Sarai's cheek. "I love you, too," she whispered back.

Miranda Finch stared across the desk at her boss, Bob Franklin.

"What do you mean there's no story?" he asked. "You've been on this for months."

"I know," she said casually, "but all my leads have gone cold."

"There's got to be something," he said, nostrils flaring and eyebrows wrinkling with annoyance.

"I'm telling you all my leads have gone cold. It seems to be business as usual. The *Aurora* team train and have meetings at Command. The *Carcharias* seem to be doing the same."

"What about your Earth Duty contact?"

"He's gone cold on me, too."

"What, so the Green-guys suddenly have solidarity with the Blue-boys?"

"I wouldn't go that far, but apparently loyalty to the UNF is paramount."

"So, what do you propose we do?"

"We put the story on ice. If something else happens, I'll bring it out and dust it off. Until then…" She shrugged, as his brow furrowed with anger. "Hey, look, if you want me to keep burning through money with no results, I'm happy to do that."

"But what are you proposing to do instead?

"They're about to commence construction on the new superstation. The official launch party is coming up in a month. Thought I'd do some prep work on that and then turn to the Mars elections."

"Is Charles Mortimer still the frontrunner for President?"

"Sure is, but Regan Lotz is nipping at his heels. I wouldn't discount Finn Harkowitz either. He's an outside chance, but you never know. He has military ties."

Bob studied her thoughtfully. "Alright, work on those two events, but keep the *Aurora* story alive. There's gotta be something there."

"Sure thing," she said, standing up. She gave Bob a wave goodbye, then left his office. The truth was, she would never let go of the *Aurora* story. However, she knew from experience that sometimes, when something wasn't working, she had to take a step back from it. And, more importantly, she had to let everyone else see that she was taking a step back from it. Because when people thought the coast was clear, that was when a new lead would present itself. So, she would wait patiently for the right opportunity to appear, and when it did, she would pounce.

Carrie watched as Morgave slid the sensor glove over her uterus.

"Do you want to know the sex?" Morgave asked her, eyes fixed to the corresponding monitor.

She smiled. "Let me guess ... it's a boy?"

Morgave paused and looked at her. "How did you know?"

"I dreamed it."

"You dreamed it?" Morgave chuckled. "That sounds to me to be a lucky guess."

Carrie kept her smile in place.

"Where are the children today?" he asked.

"They were overdue to have their session with Dr. Scavesci. He's observing them while they play with their toys to see if being an Alpha makes them any different to human children."

Morgave nodded, curious.

"I left two Sentinels with them," she added.

"I have no doubt," he said.

"So," Carrie said, "we have one boy this time."

"Yes," Morgave removed the glove and wiped the gel off her belly. "Everything looks fine at the moment. I've taken a set of measurements and we'll compare them with the next scan to see how his growth is doing."

Carrie sat up. "Is there anything Command has told you that I should know about?"

"Command?"

"I don't know. Is there any scheming behind my back?"

"Well, if there was scheming, I wouldn't be able to tell you, would I?"

She gave him a deadpan look, to which he smiled.

"They've said nothing that you're not already aware of. I watch your pregnancy closely and report to them regularly. They'll be interested to know there's another boy on the way. Next they'll be asking about the senses and whether he's inherited them."

"Freya did."

"Yes, but we're not sure how much engineering Sharley did before he implanted them in you. This one is purely up to nature and the laws of inheritance."

"He'll be like Freya. I can feel it."

"Did you dream that, too?"

Carrie smiled broadly. "Maybe."

Dr. Scavesci walked down the corridor, holding the hands of the twins. He knew he didn't have much time before Welles came looking for them. He had convinced the Sentinels to let them leave the toy room under the pretense that Scavesci wanted to examine their reactions in new surroundings. Two of Welles's Sentinels now followed close behind them, but they had agreed to the excursion.

The twins held his hands and walked along, their eyes wide, curious as to where they were being taken. Brody looked straight ahead or at the walls they passed or glanced back to the Sentinels, while Freya kept glancing down to their reflections on the polished marble floor and listened to the sound of their footsteps, repeating the word Scavesci had taught her: "Floor!"

As they approached Sharley's glass cell, Scavesci's heartbeat shot up a notch. He was excited to see Sharley's reaction, but also nervous to see the Sentinel's reaction. Roy, from what he'd seen, was very loyal to Welles. The other Sentinel, Novak, was very protective of the children.

The cell was now right there. Scavesci held the twins back, just out of sight.

"Well, what do we have here?" Scavesci asked the twins, as he flicked the switches to ensure the glass was on two-way vision and the sound was on. "Hmm? Brody and Freya, what's in here?"

Holding the hand of each child, he stepped into sight of the cell and saw Sharley standing close to the glass. His eyes were wide and fixed, his eyes darting back and forth between the children. Scavesci moved right up to the glass with the children and stopped in front of him.

"What are you doing?" the Sentinel Roy asked firmly, when he realized who was behind the glass wall.

Sharley bent down to his knees, right in front of the glass, barely 30 centimeters from the children, who looked at him, curious.

"My children..." Sharley whispered, placing his fingers on the glass as though caressing their cheeks.

"I said, what the hell are you doing?!" Roy moved up and placed himself between Sharley and the children, facing Scavesci. "Sergeant Welles did *not* approve this!"

"No harm is coming to the children," Scavesci told them calmly. "I'm just assessing their reactions to Sharley, and Sharley's to them."

"She doesn't want him near them!" Roy told him firmly.

"He's just looking at them, no harm can come of that."

"My boy, you've grown," Sharley said to Brody, peering around Roy's legs. "So much like your father." The Sentinel turned around to face Sharley as Novak pulled Brody into his arms. "And my Freya, you are beautiful. A perfect specimen."

"Enough!" Roy barked, swooping Freya up.

"What harm is it doing?" Scavesci protested, trying to stop them. "He's just looking."

"You son of a *bitch*!" Welles's voice rang out from down the corridor. Scavesci turned to see her racing Alpha quick toward them. He glanced back at Sharley to see him smiling and waving his fingers at Brody in Novak's arms. Brody saw his mother and cooed, pointing in at Sharley, but the Sentinel Novak quickly turned him away.

"They're okay!" Roy called out, placating her.

"Who brought them here?" she barked on approach, slowing to a brisk walk.

"We didn't know he was leading us here," Roy said, holding his hand up to her.

Before Scavesci could gather his thoughts, Welles charged up to him and snapped a right hook at his face. He felt a crack of pain across his jaw and went tumbling to the floor.

"I didn't give you permission to bring them here!" she yelled, standing over him.

"Miss Welles!" Roy barked, his hand to Freya's face, to block her view of the violence.

"You son of a bitch!" Welles yelled at Scavesci, leaning over him, her face furious.

He held his jaw with one hand, using the other for protection in case another blow came his way. "He can't touch them! He just wanted to see them!"

"FUCK YOU!" Welles screamed, landing a kick to his gut. Sentinel Roy got between them and moved her back, the stunned child still in his arms.

Loud laughter rung out and ceased their commotion. They turned to look at Sharley.

"Pregnancy hormones, my dear Carrie?" he said, grinning.

Welles looked back at Scavesci. "You told him?! You fucking told him!" Before she could lunge again, Novak joined Roy in holding her back, one hand on Welles's shoulders, one holding a twin.

"I'm so pleased, Carrie," Sharley said, catching her attention again. The angry Alpha woman glared back at him, panting. Sharley pointed to her belly, still grinning. "You're building my army. Just like I always wanted you too."

"Fuck you!" she hissed, breaking free of her Sentinel's hold and moving right up against the glass as though ready to face off and fight.

"When will you admit that I'm right, Carrie?" Sharley said calmly. "I've always been right about everything. I knew you'd bear more children to McKinley. I *knew* it."

"Take a good look, Sharley," she hissed, her fists clenched, "because this is the last time you will *ever* see my kids again."

The sound of running footsteps came from down the corridor and Scavesci, still on the floor, looked up to see UNF guards headed toward them.

"Let's go," Roy ordered.

Welles stayed, glaring at Sharley. "One day soon, I am going to kill you. I promise. I will take pleasure covering myself in your blood, Sharley. I will make you feel more pain than you've *ever* given me!" Scavesci, on the floor, noted she was repeating similar threats to those that Sharley had once made to her.

"Enough!" Roy barked again, tugging her arm back from the glass.

The Alpha woman moved this time, allowing herself to be guided by the Sentinel. She reached up and took Freya from him and held her tightly, throwing one arm out to caress Brody's cheek as they moved off down the corridor.

The guards came to a stop and helped Scavesci off the floor.

"Are you alright, sir?"

Scavesci looked back at Sharley and saw a huge grin beaming on the man's face. "Thank you, doctor," Professor Sharley said. "You did very well."

Scavesci, not sharing the professor's enthusiasm, looked at the guard as he caressed the side of his face. "I think I have a broken jaw."

Harris stared at Welles who stood on the opposite side of his desk. "You broke his fucking jaw."

"He stole my kids and took them to Sharley!" she flared.

"The Sentinels were with them and Sharley was locked in his glass cage."

"That doesn't matter. I don't want my children *anywhere* near him. The fact that he's even laid his eyes on them makes me feel sick!"

"Welles," he said, holding his hand up, the Alpha within her very present, "you need to calm down."

"Calm down! He was *this* close to my kids. That's too damn close! You heard the things he's said to me in the past. I don't want his fixation to pass on to them."

"He's always had a fixation on your kids, Welles."

"Well, that's why I want him to stay away!"

"What the hell's going on?" McKinley said, barging into the office. "I can hear you yelling down the corridor."

"Scavesci!" Welles spat. "He took the twins to Sharley."

"He what?" McKinley's voice fell about four octaves as his body straightened. "Where the fuck were the Sentinels?"

"Everybody calm down!" Harris said firmly, his own Alpha rising up in reaction to Welles and McKinley's.

"What the fuck happened?" McKinley asked Welles.

"I left the twins with the Sentinels and Scavesci. He spun some bullshit story about taking the twins for a walk to analyze their reactions to things. He took them straight to Sharley!"

"What the fuck did Roy do about it?" McKinley asked.

"He was in the process of removing the twins," Harris jumped in to explain, "when Welles burst onto the scene and broke Scavesci's jaw."

McKinley glanced from Harris to Welles. "You broke his jaw?"

Welles nodded, chest still rising and falling with Alpha emotions.

McKinley put his hands on his hips. "Good."

Harris sighed. "I understand your anger—."

"Do you?" Welles said. "Because it sounds like I'm on trial here."

"You assaulted Scavesci," Harris said. "You, an *Alpha,* broke a human's jaw! Might I remind you we're a test case for the UNF. It's our job to convince them that we are *not* a threat to the human population."

"I would've broken his jaw whether I was Alpha or not," she said firmly, crossing her arms.

"Might I also remind you," Harris said, "that you're pregnant, Welles. Scrapping in your condition's not a good idea."

She threw her arms wide. "Then people shouldn't mess with my kids!"

"Enough!" Harris yelled. "I've now gotta spend my time calming down Marchant and Command and making sure you don't get charged with assault. You need to watch yourself," he said, pointing to her. "They've already given you a strike for the pregnancy. You want an assault charge thrown into the mix? What I have said in the past still stands, Welles. Don't ever give them an excuse to hold something over you. *Ever.* Do you hear me? Show some *goddamn* discipline!"

She exhaled loudly and he sensed her Alpha receding a little. "I'm sorry, sir," she said more calmly, "but it's not just that Sharley saw the twins, it's because Scavesci told him I'm carrying McKinley's kid."

"He did?" McKinley asked.

Carrie nodded at him, then looked back at Harris. "It's what Sharley always wanted. If he was obsessed before..."

"This'll make him worse," McKinley finished her sentence.

"I get that, Welles," Harris said, "and I'll be having a word to Marchant about that psych, but you can't be breaking anyone's jaw like that. Understand?"

She nodded. "Yes, sir." She seemed to bite her tongue a moment before she added, "But just to be clear, sir, if *anyone* takes my kids anywhere near Sharley again, I *will* kill them."

"And if she fails, I'll finish the job," McKinley added, giving Harris a solid stare.

Harris sighed and sat back in his chair. "You two need to calm the fuck down. You've been Alphas longer than anyone else. You're the ones everyone else looks to. I need you to control it. I need you to harness that shit and lead the others. Are we clear?"

"We understand," McKinley said, "but the UNF, Scavesci, Sharley, whoever, needs to understand that if they mess with one of us, they're going to face both of us."

"Yeah, yeah," Harris gave them a studied look, "you're a match made in heaven."

McKinley shrugged and grinned. "Or hell. One of the two."

Welles glanced at the lieutenant as a matching grin slid across her face.

Harris shook his head and chuckled. "If that boy has half your feistiness, those Zetas better start running."

"Amen," McKinley said.

"Speaking of kids, when do we get to see photos of Sarai?" Welles asked.

A grin slid across Harris's face then. He stood and pulled out his PDP, bringing up an image to show them.

"Oh, she's beautiful, sir."

"Yeah, she is," Harris eyed the image.

"We'll have to start a crèche soon, huh?" Carrie smiled. "What with Lei and Hunter having their second boy, Zane, too."

"There'll be no crèche here," Harris said putting the PDP away. "Now, both of you get out of my sight! I gotta go."

General Christoph Berger stood looking out his office window at the ocean in the distance, trying to absorb the peace and tranquility it gave, although he took in only a little of it. He had decisions to make that weren't for the faint of heart, and he needed his mind sharp to do so. But that was his job, making the decisions that no-one else wanted to make. Or could make.

"Sir," Professor Derek Martin's voice sounded behind him, "you asked to see me?"

"Yes, I did," he answered, still staring out the window, wanting to absorb more of that tranquility. The silence sat behind him, until he eventually turned around to lay eyes upon his guest.

Professor Martin stood before him looking somewhat anxious.

"Report," Berger said simply.

Martin sighed. "There has been no progress, sir."

"Why?"

"Because you've given me little in the way of resources or time."

"I can't give you any more resources. I explained this. No-one knows this project is underway. Not even Lieutenant General Wilton."

"Well, I'm doing the best I can," Martin said, unable to hide his frustration.

"You need to do better."

Martin stared back at him. "How long is the UNF going to hold me over a barrel?"

Berger stared back at him but didn't answer.

"I fucked up on the Darwin. I get that. I let Sharley take the program offline. That was my fault, I know. I should've raised the alarm earlier, but you can't hold me responsible for everything that has occurred since."

"Can't we? Your failure to act led to the series of events that followed."

Martin exhaled and placed his hands on his hips. "What do you expect me to do?"

"I expect you to succeed."

"Then give me resources!" Martin said.

Again, Berger didn't respond, just stared back at him.

"And if I don't succeed, what will you do with me then?"

"That's up to you. If you succeed, we don't need to have the conversation."

"Look," Martin said, raising one hand to accentuate his words, "my skills have always lain in managing scientific projects. That is what I do best. Undertaking the actual science itself has always been done by someone more skilled than I."

"Like Professor Sharley," Berger said.

It was Martin's turn to stare at him and not respond.

"That's why the program on Darwin was a success, right?" Berger asked. "Because of what *Sharley* did up there with his group of scientists and lab techs. That success had nothing to do with you."

"I helped put the program together, General. I helped select Sharley. You know this. That was me using my skillset."

"But you assured us that we needed your help with Sergeant Welles's first pregnancy. That you were the expert. Are you telling me you lied to us?"

"No. That was a simple process of recording her results and reporting on her progress. I had the background knowledge that wouldn't affect your classification of the project, and I knew Sharley. I *was* of use and you did need me."

"But you're telling me that you can't complete this new project?"

"No, I…" Martin's voice drifted off. "I just need more resources, and time, and—"

"And I need results!" Berger snapped.

"What happens if I can't give them to you?"

"Then you are of no use to me."

"Will the UNF finally release me, let me go, if I admit defeat?"

"You know too much, professor," Berger said simply.

"You know that I have kept my word and not spoken to a soul outside of the program. You can trust me, General. In fact, you must trust me or you wouldn't have handed me this new project in the first place. I do recall you once telling me that I would never work for the UNF again. Did you not?"

"I did. This was your second chance, and it seems to me that you have blown it."

"General—"

"You're no longer on the program," he said bluntly.

Martin stared at him in disbelief.

"People's lives are at stake, professor. It's the UNF's job to save them. It's *my* job to save them. And I will do whatever I have to, to make that happen. So if you can't help me, I will find someone who will."

The silence sat for a moment, before Martin broke it. "What does this mean for me?"

Berger thought for a moment. It was true, from the intel he'd received on Martin, the man had been true to his word. It appeared he knew how to keep his mouth shut.

"You're free to go," Berger said after consideration, "but don't think for a moment that we won't have you followed, or bugged, or flag you in every possible way. You're free to leave Command, but you will never be free *of* Command. Ever. Do you understand what I'm saying to you?"

Martin considered his words for a moment, before giving a nod. "Yes, sir."

"Dismissed," Berger said.

Martin turned and walked slowly toward the door. When he reached it, he stopped and looked back at the general.

"Who will you get to replace me?" he asked.

Berger didn't answer. He just gave Martin a direct, which Martin registered. He chose to continue with his exit.

As the door closed Berger took a deep breath in, and out, and turned back to the window. He had run out of options. Undertaking this project on the side, without UNF consent, was a massive risk, but should it prove successful, he had no doubt that it would be welcomed. If he could create an army of disposable First Gens to face the Zetas, the world's human soldiers would be saved, and he would be hailed a hero. He had to succeed.

And time was running out.

As it was, even if he got the program up and running this year, come the invasion he would still be sending soldiers barely 21 years old out to fight. But they were better than nothing. As long as they could shoot and fight, he didn't care.

He looked out on the ocean in the distance, at the blue-gray sky overhead. He breathed in again as though standing on that beach and smelling the ocean breeze.

And he felt surprisingly calm and resolute.

This had to be done. There was no other way.

Turning back to his desk, he picked up his PDP and made a call.

"*Yes, General?*" Dr. Scavesci answered.

Berger took one last moment to think things through before he spoke. "I would like to see Professor Sharley. Bring him to my office."

14

Sons And Superstations

Harris looked through the glass windows at the last two *Carcharias* crew to be transformed. He blinked his eyes to clear his new Alpha vision, still getting used to it. When he could focus clearly, he realized that he could see every bead of sweat on their recovering bodies. He shook his head, amazed at the detail he could now take in.

He heard footsteps approaching from behind. He studied the sound, inhaled the scent, wanting to learn it, then turned face and saw Gold walking toward him. The first to be transformed and now recovered, the *Carcharias* captain came to a stop beside him. Gold had handled his transition relatively well, from what Harris had seen when he'd checked in on him. The captain had had time to mentally prepare for it and it seemed to have aided the transformation process. Harris studied his new Alpha stature. Tall, broad, and not quite as relaxed and carefree as the Gold he once knew, the man looked strong, although the old Gold was still there underneath. His gut could feel it.

Harris held his hand out to the other captain.

"Good to see you back on your feet, Alpha-Two captain."

Gold looked back at him and held out a muscular forearm. "Thank you, Alpha-One. It's good to finally be here."

They shook as Harris studied him. "No regrets? You sure?"

Gold nodded and stared through the window at his men. "This is an honor."

"It is," Harris said, "but it comes with a price. Sacrifices have to be made."

Gold looked at him and Harris contemplated whether or not to say anything further.

"How does Lieutenant Skordan feel about you becoming an Alpha?" He said quietly as he arched his eyebrow.

Gold appeared a little taken aback at first but he quickly hid it.

"I came to check on you while you transformed," Harris said. "I found her standing right here, watching you." He offered Gold a gentle smile. "She seemed concerned. It was toward the end, you were out of it by then."

"She was probably just checking on my progress for the legal department."

Harris smiled. "I've never seen a lawyer so concerned before."

They exchanged a look before Gold seemed to relent, looking back in at his men. "She's the one who signed me up to the contract. She knew what I was going to become."

Harris looked at the *Carcharias* crew as well. "Still, it's not going to be easy, you being Alpha, her being human."

"We'll figure it out."

"You will," Harris agreed. "You're a capable soldier and decent human being. Still…"

Gold looked at him, wanting Harris to get to the point.

"Just be careful," Harris told him. "You know how Command feel about Alphas and humans. They take it seriously."

"She'll be safe with me," he said firmly. "Andrea and I have talked about it, captain."

"I've sure you have but Command aren't stupid," Harris continued. "If they don't know about you two yet, they soon will. We're their only Alphas, Gold. You can expect they'll be giving us their undivided attention."

"You're saying I should tell them."

"It's up to you. But it might limit the fallout if you go to them first."

"It's only a new thing," Gold said.

Harris shrugged. "Like I said, it's up to you."

Gold exhaled, and a flash of the Alpha crossed his face. "Reporting who we're sleeping with…"

Harris gave a sympathetic smile. "It was in the contract when you signed up for this honor, captain. You think the rest of us haven't had to do that? But rest assured, it won't be a problem. I'm Alpha, my wife isn't."

Gold stared through the window, hands on his hips, jaw clenching and unclenching, as his mind ticked over.

"Make the choice," Harris said. "Officially report the pairing to Command, or end it. Either way, Command will find out. I suggest you volunteer." Harris eyed him again for a moment, then gave him a friendly slap on the shoulder. "I'm afraid getting the chance to be a hero has its drawbacks."

And with that he left Gold alone, staring at his recovering team.

Corporal Sabrina Colt didn't know how to feel.

She'd gone into labor early, there in her cell with LeFroy watching on and no way to call anyone for help. Despite how much she loathed LeFroy, she was grateful for his presence. It meant she didn't have to go through it alone. He did what he could to help, rummaging through the lair for painkillers and towels and hot water. They knew the nurse would be by later that day, but what was done was done. Colt had given birth, quickly, painfully, and her two sons now lay on the bed before her.

"I think they're going to be alright," LeFroy said, giving her a smile. "Their breathing and heartbeats appear to be stable and regular. You did well to give birth naturally."

Colt didn't think so. She eyed the heavily stained sheets. She'd lost a fair bit of blood in the process and now felt weak; her tired eyes were unable to shoot LeFroy any Jumbo venom. She swayed a little. She was exhausted, sweaty, pained. But despite her longing for sleep, she couldn't. She couldn't stop staring at the two wriggling newborn babies in front of her.

Her babies. *Her* children.

Whether she liked it or not.

Her boys, who she'd been carrying for the last eight or so months.

She eyed LeFroy, then looked at her babies again. Despite the exhaustion she couldn't drop her guard. She suddenly feared that LeFroy or the nurse might try and take them from her. What kind of life would these babies have with the Greenback? What would he put them through? What would he use them for?

"Do you want to name them?" LeFroy asked.

She reached out a heavy arm and touched the first one's cheek, then the other, as they lay swaddled close together. They seemed so small, yet big. Bigger than she remembered her sister's kids being at birth. That was the Jumbo in them, she guessed.

Their skin was a much lighter shade of brown than her own, hinting at their white fathers. She closed her eyes and hung her head. That one thought broke her, sending the tears down her cheeks like waterfalls. She hated their fathers. She didn't want to love their sons, but she struggled trying to stop herself. She'd carried them for eight months. For eight months they grew and kicked and fluttered and writhed inside her. Inside *her*. At first, she detested them because all she could think of was their fathers. But as time passed, the memories had faded. They were *hers*. Not theirs. She grew them, and now she'd given birth to them. These two little boys were hers. And she couldn't help the urge to protect them, like any mother would. So fragile, so vulnerable.

"Names?" LeFroy prodded her.

She flicked him a glance, wiped her face, then lifted the two boys to her chest, holding them close and rocking them.

She thought of her dead brother then, how they would never get to meet their uncle, and again the tears slid down her cheeks. "Malik," she whispered.

"Malik?"

She nodded. "My brother."

"You want to name one after your brother?"

"He was a good man," Colt whispered, peeking at her sons' faces. "This one, he's Malik." He motioned to the one on the left.

"And the other?"

She glanced at the one on her right and studied him. "Casim... after my father."

LeFroy watched her carefully.

Colt hugged her boys close to her chest and began to rock them again. "They were good men... they were good men. That's what these boys are going to be too... Good men."

Colt's eyes grew heavy, as her body grew tired and weak. She didn't know how long she sat on her bloodied bed, rocking her sons, before the nurse came. But suddenly there was a commotion in the room. She knew it, but she was too tired to care. As the nurse paced the room shouting down her phone, Colt rested back against the wall and kept holding her babies to her chest with what little strength she had left.

Carrie sat upright in her bed, sweating, panting.

"Miss Welles. Are you alright? Is the baby alright?"

She slid her hand over the slight protrusion of her womb.

"Yeah," she said.

"Did you have a bad dream?"

She nodded.

"What happened this time?" Archie asked.

"Everything," she said, swallowing. "The invasion. Explosions. Running... and Colt. I dreamed of Colt. She asked me if I'd heard the news."

Archie was silent.

"Archie?"

"I know what you're going to ask, Miss Welles."

"Please check it. One more time."

Archie was silent a moment. *"I have checked it countless times for you, Miss Welles."*

"One more time, Archie," she said, not taking no for an answer.

"One more time, Miss Welles." Archie went silent as he scanned police records for any bodies matching Colt's description.

Carrie lay back down and wiped the sweat off her brow.

"There are no matches."

Carrie nodded to herself. "That's because she's still alive. I know it."

Colt lay down on the bed as the nurse checked her drip. The woman turned to the Greenback.

"They really should go to a hospital," she told him. "The stitches will hold, but she lost blood and she's weak."

The Greenback shook his head. "No."

"I don't want their deaths on my head," the woman said.

The Greenback looked at her. "You said they were fine."

"Yes, from what I can tell. But to be safe, to ensure Sabrina or the boys don't get an infection, they should be monitored in a safe, sterile environment."

"They've got you."

"You told me they'd have a hospital when the time came."

"Listen," he said taking a step toward her, "do we have a problem here?"

The nurse stared at him.

"Hospitals will ask too many questions," he said.

The nurse held her hands in the air, exasperated. "Look, I just don't want you pointing the finger at me if anything happens."

"I won't," he said, looking back at Colt and the two boys swaddled beside her. "They're enhanced. They're supposed to be tougher than normal humans." He reached out and pulled the blanket back a little from Casim's face. "They were made to be strong and survive."

"They still die," Colt said in a low voice. The Greenback moved his eyes to hers. "I've seen Jumbos die. They're not invincible."

"And yet here you are," he said. He turned to the nurse. "You stay here for the next 48 hours. Give me updates every four."

The nurse nodded, and the Greenback headed for the door.

"What happens now?" LeFroy called after him from his cell.

Their jailer paused and looked back. "You await further instructions." Then he turned and left.

Colt looked at her two newborn sons and placed her arm protectively across them. Then she closed her eyes and fell into a deep sleep.

Harris, dressed in his official uniform, glanced around the packed Command Ceremonial Hall. The *Aurora* and *Carcharias* teams had been invited to attend the launch of the new superstation build. Tonight, Command would unveil the final design to the media and announce the winning contractor to be tasked with its construction. It was UNF PR in overdrive, and Harris couldn't help thinking that the *Aurora* and *Carcharias* teams had been requested to attend to strengthen the "look and feel" of the future the UNF was promising. After all, putting your two Alpha teams on display seemed a little risky to Harris. He wondered just how many in this room knew what they really were.

The *Aurora* team, Welles included, stood along the back wall, to the right of the entrance doorway. The *Carcharias* were positioned to the left. A decorative show of UNF Space Duty soldiers to represent those who would one day fill the new superstation.

As the rest of the room mingled, Harris, Gold, and their teams remained in position. He recognized some of those present: Marchant, Berger, Wilton, Dr. Morgave, Dr. Scavesci, Dr Forcaster, and Lieutenant Skordan. A few other guests arrived who attracted Harris's curiosity, namely the three Mars presidential candidates: Charles Mortimer, Regan Lotz and Finn Harkowitz. Then the whole room seemed to pause as President Gillet arrived; a rock star entrance complete with heavy security. Gillet appeared to the be the star of this event, the political heavyweight of space colonization.

Harris then noticed another face he recognized: Rovine. Now a colonel, the ex-*Carcharias* captain was here in his official capacity. The man's eyes caught his and held his glance, emotionless, before turning and spying Gold. The look on Rovine's face hardened and his jaw clenched, but he soon moved further into the crowd.

Harris had noticed the *Carcharias* team were somewhat oblivious to those in the room, not fully understanding who all the players were, and they certainly hadn't seen Rovine. They seemed more interested in shooting glances to the *Aurora* team, scrutinizing their fellow Alphas, looking to them for their lead. He arranged to have the teams officially meet after the function was over. They'd crossed paths before on Meridian and here in Centralis, but if they were going to work together in the future, then he wanted them to get to know each other real well, but he'd intentionally given them several weeks of recovery time to get used to their new Alpha bodies first. Now it was time to mix them, and allow the *Aurora* team to provide support for the newly Alpha, and no doubt antsy team.

With his senses now complete, Harris tried hard to direct his hearing to single out conversations, but it was hard with so much talking going on. Added to that was the movement of the guests his eyes were fixing on, and the flourishing of scents like aftershave and perfume, beer and wine, and hors d'oeuvres. It was sensory overkill.

After a short time, Colonel Marchant, dressed in his finest, approached. "Come and join us, captain," he said, ushering Harris forward. "It's not a good look to have the UNFASP leader lined up along the wall like a common soldier. These people need to get to know you. They need to respect you. That's the only way you'll get things done in the future."

"But most of these people don't know what UNFASP is." Harris cocked an eyebrow at him.

"No, not yet. But one day they will. We want them to remember you."

Harris moved with him to where Finn Harkowitz stood alone. He had been chatting with Lieutenant General Wilton, but seeing them approach, Wilton moved to another group.

"Finn Harkowitz, this is Captain Saul Harris of the UNF *Aurora*," Marchant introduced him. "Captain Harris, this is Mars presidential candidate Finn Harkowitz, son of Gentry Harkowitz, who founded the first successful civilian space station."

"Inca 2 Station, right?" Harris asked as he shook Finn's hand.

"Yes, indeed," Finn smiled, creating traces of wrinkles around his eyes. It was hard to gauge his age, given his dark-blond hair, but he gave the appearance of having money: the cut of his suit, the styled hair, the tan from countless tennis lessons.

"Your father brought hope back to the people after the failure of Inca 1. You should be proud," Harris said.

"I am," Harkowitz agreed, his accent British. "He was a good man who believed in our future in space. It's always been my aim to carry on his legacy. That's why I'm running for Mars president. The UNF has done a great job establishing the two colonies and the prison there, but now it's time to take it to the next level. Given time, I think it will eclipse the Moon as the ultimate space destination." He smiled and leaned in. "But don't tell Gillet I said that."

Harris laughed politely.

Just then Regan Lotz approached their group. He shook hands with Marchant and then Harkowitz, then turned to Harris.

"I don't believe we've met," Lotz said, with an American accent, and they went through the introductions again. Lotz shook his hand then turned to Marchant.

"Have you heard the latest with the African Consortium?"

"No?" Marchant said.

"They've filed another appeal for Noah."

"Another one!" Marchant said, then shook his head. "How many years can that go on for?"

"Noah's Well?" Harris queried.

"The last oil reserve on Earth, my friend," Lotz said. "I guess it's worth fighting for."

"As long as the fighting stays in the courtroom and doesn't spill outside," Marchant said.

"Indeed," Harkowitz agreed. "The last thing we need is another foolish war. If we're going to pour money into something it should be out there." He pointed to the sky, then turned to the banner across the stage. "And into that superstation."

"Agreed," Marchant said.

Harris agreed also but knew the superstation was estimated to take 15 years to complete. Which would be about seven years too late for the first invasion he'd dreamed of.

"Colonel?" General Berger called, waving Marchant over to the group in which he stood, which included Mortimer and Gillet.

"Excuse me, gentlemen," Marchant said to Lotz and Harkowitz, then turned to Harris. "Captain, come with me."

Harris gave the two a nod in farewell, then followed Marchant over to the other group, where introductions were made.

"Captain," Gillet smiled. "It's nice to see you again."

"And you, President Gillet," he answered.

"How long has it been," he asked in his French accent, "since we met in Galilei?"

Harris thought for a moment. "It's got to be almost three years."

"Three years!" Gillet shook his head. "How time flies."

The UNF events manager approached, whispered in Berger's ear, and stole him away, heading toward the stage.

Harris looked at Gillet. "How's your campaign for the second military base on the Moon doing?"

"Successful!" Gillet smiled. "We have commenced design."

"That's good news," Harris told him.

"Isn't it," he replied. "You will have to come and tour our facilities again, captain. Three years is a long time between drinks."

"Indeed it is. And I plan to, very soon."

"Excellent." Gillet's eyes darted over Harris's shoulder. "Excuse me, if you will. I must speak with some others now."

Gillet moved off as Mortimer placed his empty wine glass on a passing waiter's tray.

"I'm looking forward to seeing the design of the superstation, colonel," Mortimer said to Marchant.

"I think you'll be satisfied."

"I hope so. But what would satisfy me even more are the deeds allowing the placement of a series of All Stations on the orbital paths to the superstation's location," Mortimer said, smiling.

Marchant laughed. "Well, you never know, Charles. Let's build the station first, then we'll see about that. Besides, you might be too busy being Mars president to worry about the space station race anymore."

Mortimer laughed. "I may need someone else to run them, yes, but I don't plan on giving them up. Space is our future," he grinned. "Make no mistake about that."

Marchant laughed, but it was cut short as General Berger called everyone's attention to the stage.

Carrie stood against the back wall with the rest of the *Aurora* team. She wasn't quite sure why the top brass of the UNF wanted them here. *Wasn't UNFASP still a big secret? Why have their first Alpha units on display?* Unless they were being shown off to those in the room who *did* know what they were.

She watched the crowd as General Berger gave his welcome speech, then handed over to Colonel Hensford of Station Navarone, who was heading up the design team for the superstation. The information given to the crowd was merely an overview. A flashy one, for sure, but Carrie noted no real detail was revealed in the presentation, other than its name: Atlas

Station. Hensford showed artist impressions of what Atlas Station would look like, which Carrie decided was something like a large turtle shell, flat along the bottom and curved along the top. It was dark-gray in color, would be armed to the teeth in weaponry, and it would house 10,000 soldiers and military contractors.

The camera flashlights going off caught her attention and she saw members of the press present. She recognized one in particular, a woman of East Asian descent, who had filed the reports on the Eden incident. Carrie made a mental note to stay well clear of her.

When the grand speeches were over, the crowd gradually broke up into groups and Harris came over to order them to be at ease, encouraging them to circulate. Carrie gravitated to stand by McKinley, and Captain Gold of the *Carcharias* came up and shook his hand.

"Lieutenant," he said.

"Captain," McKinley returned. "Congratulations on the promotion."

"Thank you. This is First Lieutenant Andy Ryker." Gold introduced the soldier by his side.

"G'day," Ryker said, shaking McKinley's hand.

"Australian," Carrie smiled.

"Yeah, we're everywhere," he smiled, nodding at her.

"Sergeant Welles? We haven't met properly," Gold said, holding his hand out to Carrie. She shook it.

"I know we crossed paths on Mars," she said, "but my head was a little hazy after the Hell Town Dungeon."

"Yeah," he said, his expression serious. "You didn't look too good in Eden either."

"No," she said, dropping her smile briefly, then resurrecting it to say lightly, "But those days are in the past now."

Gold studied her, then his eyes seemed to catch on someone in the crowd behind her. Carrie turned to see a man of colonel rank giving Gold a rather unfriendly stare. She looked back at Gold and saw his face harden a little.

"A friend of yours?"

"No," Gold said, returning his eyes to hers. "Just an ex-captain of mine."

"So," McKinley said, moving the conversation along, keeping his voice low, "how are things now the team has been phased in?"

"So far, so good," Gold said. "I can't believe they wanted us here tonight."

"It's a show of force to those in the room who know," Carrie said, eyeing the crowd.

"I've noticed there's no security here tonight," McKinley said. "Looks like it's us."

"I guess they don't need any with two Alpha units here," Gold said.

"I think Harris is going to arrange for you guys to come train with us soon," McKinley said.

"Yeah, I think that's a good idea. We've suddenly got energy to burn."

"Come on, I'll introduce you to the rest of the team," McKinley said, and they moved over to where Murphy and Evenssen stood.

Carrie scanned the room and saw Dr Forcaster approach.

"Sergeant Welles," she smiled, although Carrie sensed an awkwardness to it. "I hear congratulations are in order." Forcaster glanced at her abdomen as she came to a stop in front of her. "I had no idea you and Lieutenant McKinley were… I thought you were just co-parenting."

"It started out that way," Carrie smiled back, unconsciously sliding her left hand over her abdomen.

"Well, I'm happy for you," she smiled, glancing at Carrie's wedding ring. "It'll be great for the UNF to have another First Gen to study."

"Yeah," Carrie's smile faded a little.

"I must go speak with the *Carcharias* crew." Forcaster touched her shoulder and moved over to the teams. Carrie watched her, feeling a little irked by her comment. The child she carried wasn't just something for the UNF to study. It was so much more than that.

Carrie glanced back to the crowd to see Harris making his way toward her.

"Everything alright?" he asked, obviously noticing the furrow in her brow.

"Yes, sir."

"I see you're acquainting yourself with the *Carcharias* team. Good."

"Yeah," Carrie said, "they seem alright."

"Captain!" The reporter Carrie had seen earlier approached, smiling. "Long time no see."

"Ms Finch." Harris gave a hesitant but polite nod.

"I told you it was Miranda," she said.

Harris motioned to Carrie. "This is Sergeant Carrie Welles."

Miranda held out her hand. "Sergeant. Nice to meet you. I'm glad to hear you're alright. I believe you were injured in the Eden attack?"

"I'm fine," she smiled, exchanging a glance with Harris.

"That was quite some attack," Miranda said, then scanned the crowd. "And I see the star of the show is here. That giant Steinberg."

"Miranda," Harris said, with a slight warning note in his voice. She turned back to him. "Don't go trying to interview my soldiers," he said. "They are on duty. You know you have to contact the press department for quotes."

"Of course," she smiled. "Well, if I can't talk about that, can we talk about Atlas Station? It's also interesting that both the *Aurora* and *Carcharias* teams were selected to be here tonight. No comment to that?"

"No," Harris said.

A silence sat for a moment as Miranda stared at Harris, and he back at her. Carrie glanced between the two of them, uncomfortable, before Miranda cleared her throat.

"Well," Miranda said, looking back at Carrie, "it was nice to meet you, sergeant. I'm glad you've recovered from the attack." The reporter looked back at Harris. "I'll see you around, captain." And with that she moved off into the crowd.

As soon as she was out of earshot Carrie turned to Harris. "Did I miss something? Something happen between you two?"

"No," Harris said firmly, then he too moved off into the crowd.

She watched him, then glanced around at the faces in the crowd again. And as she stood there, eyeing the room, she couldn't help but feel as though a significant moment was taking place. The future was getting closer. She could feel it in her swelling belly, and she could feel it swelling in the atmosphere around her. Atlas Station had been launched, there were now two units inducted into UNFASP, and the Advanced Weapon and Fleet Program was underway.

This, here, was a moment in history, she thought. This gathering of key players in the future of human space settlement. One day, as they did with her father, people would look back and say she was one of a special few - standing here at the start of it all.

She suddenly realized that she was about to achieve what she'd set out to do, to leave her mark. Just like her father was a respected Original, she was the first female Alpha soldier, member of the first Alpha unit, mother of the first-born First Gens. It had been a long tortuous road to get to this point, but she'd done her time and she'd earned her stripes so to speak. She had become a part of history.

But now it was time to fix her sights on the future. She had to grip this opportunity, her position, with both hands... and not fail. She had to succeed and leave a lasting impression for the generations to come.

Miranda Finch opened her apartment door to see Captain Morrell standing outside.

"Morning," he smiled.

"Morning," she said suspiciously.

"Not going to invite me in?"

"I didn't invite you here."

"Yeah, but I figured I owed you one."

Miranda considered the advisability of letting him in. He seemed to read her mind, holding his palms up.

"Just want to talk," he said, then lowered his hands. "And I told you, breaking into someone's place and leaving knife threats isn't my style."

She opened her door and let him in. He walked into her open living room and kitchen and stood beside the breakfast bar.

"So? Why did you come here?" she asked, crossing her arms.

"I just wanted to know how the Atlas Station launch was the other night? I see you got an invitation."

"And you didn't."

"Nah, that was Blue-boy business. Us Green-guys were locked outside patrolling the streets." His eyes fixed on hers. "So?"

"So it was a PR event for the UNF. You think I'm going to get anything off the record there?"

"You must've come across something?"

She shook her head. "The superstation looks... *super*, and everyone seems to support it. President Gillet was there and the Mars presidential candidates. It was a show of strength and money. They even had the *Aurora* and *Carcharias* teams lined up along the back of the room as though they were security or something."

"The *Aurora* and the *Carcharias*, huh?" he asked.

"Yeah."

"Well, aren't they Command's favorite sons."

"It looks that way. Colonel Marchant was introducing Captain Harris to all the VIPs."

Morrell nodded as his mind seemed to tick over. "I guess Gold found whatever he was looking for then. All of a sudden he's Harris's best friend."

"It would seem that way. Although I never sensed hostility between them before. Only with you."

Morrell waved her off. "That's just a Blue-boy, Green-guy, thing. It's what we do. Challenge each other to prove who's best. It's what the UNFer Bowl is all about."

"So the Green-guys here in Centralis don't resent the favor the Blue-boys seem to get?"

Morrell locked eyes with her but didn't respond.

"Anyway, that's all I can tell you," Miranda said. "The *Aurora* and *Carcharias* teams are in good stead with those at Command, and they seem suitably recovered from the Eden attack. In fact, they looked fighting fit. Gold's been working out, he's beefed up a little. He seemed quite focused. Must be taking his new role seriously."

Morrell nodded, then glanced around. "So how'd they get in?"

"What?"

"When your apartment was raided. How did they get in?"

"Broke a window in the bathroom."

"They climbed up the outside?"

She nodded.

"They really wanted something, huh." He glanced around again then looked back at her. "I tell you what, Finch. You feed me whatever information you come across, and I'll try and track down who did this."

"The MPs were informed. They were *supposed* to be on it, but their interest went cold fast."

"Break-ins aren't high on their list of priorities."

"I know. Especially when it's a snooping reporter." She narrowed her eyes. "Why do you want to help me?"

"I told you. Information."

"Why do you care so much about the *Aurora* and the *Carcharias*?"

He stepped toward her. "Look, Centralis is my patch. I'm in charge of the Earth Duty units securing this place. If we're in the process of being ousted, or if something's happening on my turf, then I want to know about it."

She nodded, reassessing him. "Alright. You find who broke in and I'll feed you information."

He held out his hand. She looked down at his thick arm and large hand, then shook it.

"I'll send someone around to advise you," he said. "The security on this place is shit." Then he walked to the door and let himself out.

Professor Sharley, with an escort and digital cuffs around his wrists and ankles, was ushered into General Berger's office and placed in the chair opposite his desk. Berger stood looking out his window at the beach beyond. The general looked calm and focused as he finally turned around.

"So, professor. Your thoughts?"

Sharley gave a small smile, working to keep his satisfaction in check. Satisfaction that the tables were turning, that a new day was dawning for him. Professor Martin had failed and Berger had no choice but to look to *him* for results.

"I have read Professor Martin's..." he cleared his throat, "attempt at initiating this program."

"And?"

"It had some merit, but I believe we can improve upon it. Vastly."

"And how is that?"

"I believe we can use similar technology to that of Phase Four of the Jumbo program. Oh, apologies, general." Sharley raised his cuffed hands. "The Alpha program."

"That technology has not been finalized as yet. It's still in progress."

"Yes, but if you allow me to take part, I can help speed it up."

Berger stared at him. "What do you think you can do that our experts can't?"

"You tell me, general? You invited me to take part in this, er, what would you call it? Phase *Five* program?"

The general continued to stare at him with hard eyes, and Sharley knew the man would not easily submit to him. No, the general was sitting very firmly at the top of the UNF tree. Sharley could tell that he'd fought hard to get there and he would not let it go easily. Especially to someone like Sharley; someone the general saw as quite below him.

"I believe it can it be done, general," Sharley told him. "And it will be done."

"How?"

Sharley pointed to the thin perspex screen on the side of Berger's desk. "It's all there in my report, general. I've thought long and hard about this, well before your offer to assist. The pod cases should be developed based on our medical pod-bed technology, and they will work in a similar way for this program. These cases will keep the organic bodies sealed within alive. They will supply nutrients to our organic wombs and filter wastes away."

"But you claim we need organic wombs, that we can't make them artificially?"

"We could, general," Sharley said, shrugging lightly, "but I believe the best results would be gained from real, organic, tissue."

Berger, for the first time, took his eyes off Sharley and reviewed the screen.

"To begin with," Sharley continued, "we can test using normal human wombs and embryos if you'd like, but the results would be faster if we access an Alpha womb and Alpha embryo cells from the outset."

Berger returned his eyes to Sharley. "Start working on the pod case technology. Once you get them up and running, we'll look at the organics."

"I'll need both, general. They must be developed in unison. What we're talking about here is an integrated mechanism for growing the UNF's First Gen army. The pod case technology must function, must integrate, with the organics. They must be one and the same. Just like I'd planned for Phase Four of the Jumbo program."

"Alpha program," Berger corrected him.

"Alpha program." Sharley gave a nod of apology. "Our Alpha soldiers are to be fully integrated with the robotics and technology as one cohesive, magnificent product. A soldier that is wholly man, and animal, and machine. One and the same."

"I'll send you human cells to work with," Berger said after some thought.

"I need Alpha cells, general."

"We don't have the right Alpha cells yet," the general said, then paused in hesitation. The first slight moment of weakness Sharley had ever seen from the man. It was only brief, but it was there. The human flickering within the soldier. "But in a few months, we will," Berger said.

Sharley stared keenly at the general. A tingling sensation flushed over him, warming him with pure excitement. "Welles?" he asked carefully.

Berger did not respond in words, but the hard stare he gave Sharley told him what he needed to know: that Berger would do what he had to... not for Sharley, but for everyone else on Earth. He would give Sharley, Carrie's cells.

Sharley kept his face even and calm. "I'll start on the pod cases, general, and I look forward to receiving the Alpha organics when they become available."

PART THREE

15

Into The Time Slip

Colt paced her cell, rocking Malik as she did. Casim lay on her bed, stirring, crying a little.

"Would you like me to pick him up?" LeFroy asked, motioning to Casim.

"No," Colt said in a low, threatening voice.

"You can't rock both of them."

She threw LeFroy a murderous stare, then lifted Casim up as well. She began stalking up and down again, rocking her boys and staring at LeFroy.

"I'm just trying to help," he said, slumping back on his bed. "I have to listen to them too, you know."

"Should've thought of that before you did what you did."

"Must we go through this again?"

Colt just threw him another glare. They had discussed this until she was blue in the face. Right now she was tired, and hungry, and Jumbo, and she had two crying Jumbo babies to boot. She continued to pace. It may have been the effect of her tiredness, of her recovery from the birth, but she was starting to lose hope of ever getting out of here.

She'd searched for a way out, but the Greenback hadn't taken any chances. Every time he or the nurse came to visit, there were two security with them. And with LeFroy added into the mix, she was vastly outnumbered. She'd tried on occasion to turn LeFroy her way, but the man was a coward and she despised him. After a while, her Jumbo pregnancy had drained her too much and she'd stopped looking for a way out and only sought rest.

And now, after the birth, she was still getting on her feet. At first it had been recovering from the birth and all the stitches she'd received, then it was getting her head around all that had happened: the fact that she'd actually given birth and had these babies to care for, the lack of sleep, fighting the helplessness, fighting the emotions unleashed inside when she thought of who their fathers were.

But whether she liked it or not, she couldn't fight the fact that she was indeed the mother of these two babies, and that these two helpless babies needed her. Some instinct deep within would not let her leave these boys to LeFroy or the Greenback. Somewhere along the way, she didn't quite know when, whether it was before the birth or after, she had decided to protect them from these people.

So right now she couldn't deal with escape. She would let herself adjust to the birth and adjust to being a mother. She couldn't make a move until she was sure of what she was doing, until she was strong enough to protect them. Until she was sure they could all make it out alive.

Miranda Finch answered the ring of her PDP.

"Yeah?" she said, stretching out on the couch of her apartment.

"It's Morrell," the gruff voice said down the phone.

Miranda sat up a little straighter. "Yeah?"

"I spoke to the MPs about your break-in. We went through the security footage and at best we picked up three potential suspects lingering around your apartment at the time of the break-in. It's not a great angle, so the footage isn't the clearest. None of them match any suspects on file and they left no fingerprints or DNA. That's why the MPs haven't done anything."

"And here I was thinking they were just being unhelpful to a reporter," she said sarcastically. "You got more out of them than I did."

Morrell ignored her comment. *"Best they can do is put the three faces up on the FRS, but like I said, the images aren't that good."*

"Mystery men," she said, thinking aloud.

"Looks like it. Did my guy come around?"

"Yeah, he's recommended a few changes. I told him to go ahead."

"Good. I've done my part, Finch. Now you do yours."

She paused for a moment, thinking about his gruffness. He wasn't a particularly likable man, but it would seem he was a man of his word.

"I will," she told him.

"If anything comes up with the suspects, I'll let you know. If anything comes up on your end, you let me know."

"Deal," she said. "Morrell, before you go?"

"Yeah."

"I... I just want to say thank you."

Silence poured down the phone.

"I appreciate you looking into the break-in and sending your guy around," she told him. "I feel safer now. So, thank you."

"I pay my debts," he said without inflection. Then he hung up.

Miranda looked at the PDP, shook her head and laughed.

Carrie waited calmly as Morgave examined her swollen belly. She saw the look of concern across his face.

"I feel fine," she jumped in to say.

"Your uterus is struggling."

"I know, but we're so close now. We'll be fine."

"The boy is on track to be 14 pounds."

"Fourteen pounds?!" she said.

"Yes. He's a big Alpha child, and your uterus was badly torn previously. It is stretched to its limit and I fear it will split again if we're not careful. If it splits, you risk both your life and his."

"He will be born," she said firmly, Alpha jaw tightening.

"Why, because you dreamed it?" Morgave looked at her with troubled eyes. "Dreams are just dreams, sergeant."

"He will be fine."

"The slight bleeding has continued," Morgave said. "Have you been resting like I told you?"

"Yes."

"Yes?"

"Yes. But I do have two-year-old Alpha twins as well."

"You need to promise me that you will do nothing but lie in bed, or I will take this child out of you now."

She went to object, but stopped at the concerned look on Morgave's face.

"I'm serious, sergeant. Your uterus is weak and your son is large."

"I'm not quite eight months yet. Just a little longer."

"Promise me you'll do nothing, but rest in bed. I can have extra helpers sent to the Fortress for the twins, if you need."

She looked down at her exposed swollen belly and ran her hand over it. The boy – she'd resigned herself to calling him Jesse, just like in her dream – seemed to move inside her at her touch.

"Alright," she nodded. "You give him a little longer inside me, and I'll lie in bed until it's time."

"Good. I don't suppose I can convince you to take that bed rest here at Command?"

She gave him a look that spoke volumes.

"I am a medical professional, you know," he defensively. "I do know what I'm talking about."

"I know," she said, shoulders softening. She reached out and put her hand on his shoulder. "I appreciate all that you've done for us."

He smiled and lines bracketed his eyes. "Does this mean I finally have your trust?"

She hesitated but smiled back. "Yeah. We're all still here, thanks to you. I guess that means you're okay."

Morgave laughed, then looked at her belly again. "We'll make sure this one is born safely, too." He looked up into her eyes. "But you do need to rest, and I'll be passing my orders onto Captain Harris, Lieutenant McKinley, and your father, to ensure they're kept."

"Yes, sir."

Harris, sitting at the kitchen table with Colonel Welles and McKinley in the Fortress, watched as Welles waddled in.

"Hey," she said, her hands stretched around below her belly, as though helping to hold it up.

"Sit down, Ree." Her father stood.

"I'm just going to go check on the twins."

"Sit down," her father said firmly.

"Archie passed on Dr. Morgave's orders," Harris told her. The AIS had done so just moments before she'd arrived. Morgave had made sure to stress the importance of bed rest.

"Already?"

McKinley pulled out the chair beside him. "Sit."

"Actually, I'm supposed to lie down in bed," she said as she moved over to him and punched his arm, "because your *goddamn* son is going to be a 14 pounder!"

McKinley rubbed his arm. "How is that my fault?"

"Well, look at you!" She motioned to his frame. "He didn't get his size from me."

"Hey," McKinley said defensively, "Grace told me I was barely a seven-pound baby. It's not me, it's the Alpha. And you're one, too," he pointed at her.

"He did *not* get it from me!"

"Er, honey?" her father said.

Harris watched as Welles threw an annoyed glance to her father.

"I was a ten pound baby," the colonel told her. "*You* were nine pounds. It's a Welles thing. We have big babies."

McKinley gave her a smug, satisfied look.

"What?!" she said in disgust. "How can I have been a bigger baby than him?" She looked at McKinley, then at Harris and her father as they all stared at her, trying not to show their amusement.

"It's official, then," McKinley said dryly. "You're the bigger baby." A grin broke out across his face before he erupted into laughter.

She punched his arm again, and he cowered away, still laughing, as Harris and her father openly grinned.

"Screw you all!" she muttered, turning to leave the room.

"I'll accept your apology later," McKinley said arrogantly.

She flipped him the bird and disappeared.

Harris, unable to hide his amusement, looked at McKinley. "Pregnancy hormones, huh?"

"*Alpha* pregnancy hormones," he said flatly.

Colonel Welles gave a throaty laugh and patted McKinley on the shoulder. "You're a brave man, James. You're a brave, brave, man."

Dr. Angus Morgave walked down the corridor toward the labs, eager to speed up the results of Welles's blood test. Given how large the child was, he wanted to ensure things were at least in line with the twins' gestation records.

As he entered the lab, he stopped short, seeing Professor Sharley there with two guards and Scavesci standing close by.

"What's going on?" Morgave asked.

Scavesci turned around, as Sharley looked up from a screen he'd been reading.

"Dr. Morgave," Scavesci said, surprised. "You're not meant to be down here."

"Neither are you," Morgave returned.

"We have the lab booked," Scavesci said. "I'm sorry, you'll have to come back."

"Booked? Doing what? Why is he here?" Morgave motioned to Professor Sharley who had turned back to his work.

"It's part of his rehabilitation. We're allowing him to do some work."

"What work?"

Scavesci stared at him, but did not respond.

"I don't like this," Morgave said, eyeing Sharley, "him being here in the lab."

"It's not for you to like or not," Scavesci told him. "The general has given his approval. We're letting the professor be of use, checking some figures, that's all. It's good for his emotional and mental state."

"Why must I leave then?"

"Because this doesn't concern you."

Morgave stared at Scavesci, then over at Sharley.

"You may come back in an hour," Scavesci told him.

Morgave's brow crinkled in annoyance at Scavesci's smugness, but he turned to leave.

"Doctor Morgave?"

He turned back around.

"You must speak of this to no-one. General's orders. If you don't believe me, feel free to ask him yourself."

"Oh, I will," he said firmly. He gave them both one last stare, then left.

Carrie lay on her bed, on her side, staring at the wall and running her hand over her belly. The truth was, she could feel it. She could feel that Jesse was much stronger than the womb that held him. It felt so stretched around him like a wafer-thin second skin.

"Just hold on," she whispered to him. "You need to stay in there just a little bit longer."

She heard the door open and McKinley entered. He crawled on the bed and lay down behind her.

"Here for your apology?" she asked.

He laughed quietly, resting his arm over her waist and laying his hand flat on her swollen belly. Whenever he could, his hands were on her. Other than that one time she'd forced him to, McKinley never got to feel Freya inside her, so he was making up for lost time with this pregnancy.

His hand spread wide and warm over her exposed skin, as though holding Jesse in place.

"Morgave says it's serious," he said quietly.

She nodded. "I know."

"Then stop being stubborn and taking stupid risks."

"I won't," she said, then looked over her shoulder at him. "This is the last. My womb won't hold any more kids after this. I'm done."

McKinley nodded. "Three's enough."

She looked at the wall again. "Morgave's talking about removing the womb altogether. He says I'll have no end of problems if they leave it in."

"Whatever it takes," McKinley said quietly as his hand grasped more tightly on her belly and his son within.

"Whatever it takes?"

"To keep you both here," he explained.

She rolled over carefully, with effort, to face him, her belly pressing into his.

"We're in this until the end, right?" he said, his warm blue pools pouring into hers.

She nodded.

"So, we keep each other here until then," he said. "Just like in the Hell Town dungeon. You keep me alive, and I'll keep you alive."

Carrie nodded and lifted her hand to caress his bearded cheek.

His blue eyes twinkled back at hers as a grin crossed his mouth. "Now about that apology…" Carrie chuckled as he kissed her.

Admiral Arken stared at the picture his daughter had sent him approximately one Earth year ago now. They were well past the terminator and comms were something that took months to come and even then only arrived as packets of data. Streams of text. They were well and truly in the vast vacuum of space now.

And the crew felt it. They had of course, expected it, trained for it, but not even he had really been prepared for it. The long silence due to no human contact from Earth, the apprehension as to where they were headed, the endless, virtually empty space that surrounded them. The solitude, the nothingness, the unknown.

But every day he reminded his crew why they were doing this. Every day he would bring up an image of Earth on the screens, promising they would return there one day. But first they had to ensure there would be something to return to. They had made and lost contact with the Zetas, and they had to follow things through to ensure these aliens did not turn hostile.

And so, they continued toward Zeta Archelois… with no word from Earth, and still no contact from the Zetas.

Carrie looked down at the newborn son in her arms. Jesse Ethan McKinley had been born by caesarean section, without fuss, alive and well.

"The biggest First Gen on record," Morgave said, smiling at her over the cotton screen across her waist. Carrie smiled at her son. He'd made it to 13lbs before they'd had to remove him.

McKinley, sitting beside her on a stool, ran his fingers down his son's cheek.

"Jesse Ethan," she smiled at him. Ethan, after McKinley's late father.

McKinley's Alpha eyes sparkled in the theater lights. He gave a smile and squeezed his hand around hers.

"We're going to have to move onto the next part now," Morgave said, giving the somber news.

"It's no good?" Carrie asked.

Morgave shook his head. "It needs to come out."

Carrie nodded. "Take it," she said, looking back at her son. "I have everything I need from it."

Morgave gave a brief nod, then looked at McKinley. "You'll need to leave for this part," he said. "Sergeant Welles will be sent to sleep for the procedure."

McKinley looked back at Carrie and Jesse. She squeezed his hand.

"The Sentinels have the twins, you go with Jesse. I'll be fine."

McKinley kissed her temple, his beard brushing her skin, then followed the nurse who took Jesse from her arms.

"This will be over before too long," Morgave told her as a nurse made an adjustment to the drip in her hand.

Carrie exhaled slowly. She was at peace with this. She had Brody and Freya, and now Jesse was here. She had brought three First Gens into existence. She'd played her part in the breeding process. Now it was time to get her body back on track and become the soldier. And removing this womb was the start of that.

Dr. Angus Morgave watched as the unconscious Welles was wheeled out of the operating theater on her way to recovery. He glanced around at the nurses who swiftly set about cleaning and making the environment sterile again after the caesarean birth. The obstetrician, Mike Carver, was already outside washing-up, done for the day. Morgave, however, liked to ensure that everything was in order before he left.

He was relieved that the birth had gone according to plan, and he was proud. There were now three First Gen children in the world and he had safely overseen their births. They, and their mother, were alive because of him.

He looked down at the container in front of him, at Welles's removed uterus, and the accompanying placenta and umbilical cord. The uterus had been the only casualty of these births, but it was through no fault of his own. Welles had been incredibly lucky to have carried that third child, although it had meant many weeks of bed rest. But that used uterus now sat in pieces in the container; it had been in no condition to stay inside her.

The doors to the theater banged open and he looked up to see a man he didn't recognize, donned in full theater garb and holding two silver cylindrical containers.

"Can I help you?" Morgave asked, furrowing his brow. "You're not authorized to be in here."

The man came to a stop in front of him. "General Berger sent me."

"Yes?"

The man eyed the nurses. "Please leave us for a moment," he told them. They glanced at Morgave and he gave his approval for them to do as the man said. As soon as they'd left the room, the man spoke again.

"The general's been informed that you had to remove the uterus from Sergeant Welles. Is this correct?"

"Yes."

"General Berger has asked that I run some tests on it before disposal."

"What tests?" Morgave asked. "It's my responsibility to undertake any testing and disposal. She's my patient."

"General Berger has tasked me with this. If you check your portal, there will be direct orders from him outlining this."

"Who are you?"

"Dr. Brenam." The man spied the kidney dish. "Is that it? I'll need the placenta too."

"What tests?" Morgave insisted.

"Please check your portal for your orders. As to my orders, they're classified."

Morgave stared at him, then glanced back at Welles's womb. "Give me a moment to wash up, then I'll check my portal. You will do nothing until I have."

The doctor gave him a nod, then stood patiently in the theater while Morgave washed up and grabbed his PDP. He checked his portal, and sure enough, General Berger had requested that Welles's uterus and placenta be handed over to this man. Morgave looked through the window of the prep area, into the theater where the man stood with his containers. A sudden thought struck ice through him. Berger had ordered this, Berger had okayed Sharley to be working in the labs again. *What were they up to?* When he'd questioned General Berger about Sharley working in the labs, he'd been told in no uncertain terms to mind his own business and had been threatened with being stood down as the official doctor of Welles and the twins. So, he'd done as he was told and kept his mouth shut. And now this.

He walked back into the theater and looked at the man through narrowed eyes. "Go ahead," he said. "You can take it, but I'll be having a word to General Berger. This is highly unorthodox."

The man took the uterus, placenta and umbilical cord, and placed them in the sealed silver containers he'd brought with him. "You may discuss this with General Berger, but no-one else. Not even the patient."

"But it's her uterus?"

"Not anymore. It's in this container." He held up the silver cylinder. "And it's now the classified property of the UNF," the man said firmly. He gave Morgave a nod, then turned and left the room.

Morgave watched him leave as an incredibly uneasy feeling settled within. Caught between patient loyalty and Berger's threats to his career, he was unsure what to do. *Perhaps they really were going to destroy it. Perhaps Berger was just making sure that happened.* He thought of Sharley in the lab again, but quickly brushed it aside. *That was just his rehabilitation*, he told himself. *Sharley was being rehabilitated and Dr Brenam was just destroying all evidence of Welles's womb. Yes. That was it. There's no connection. There is nothing to worry about.*

He moved for the exit, forcing down that uneasy feeling within, and convincing himself that he felt reassured.

Harris sat up in his bed, in his quarters, panting and sweating. He'd just had another one of his strange dreams. It was a jumbled dream. He'd been running with Welles and the twins in that field and the lights had been in the sky, heading toward the Earth. Then he was suddenly back on the flight deck on one of the Zeta ships and it had been waking up beneath his fingertips, shining a bright blue. Then he'd been trapped in that wreck and he saw Welles running toward him, her green Alpha eyes piercing through the night. Then he'd been standing in a white room screaming in absolute agony, in absolute Alpha rage.

The screams had awoken him, and he'd flinched upon seeing his Overseers standing at the foot of his bed: Sibbie, Etta and his mother.

"The pieces are falling into place," Sibbie said, as though comforting him.

"What pieces?" he asked, still panting.

"All the players," Etta nodded in agreement.

"What players?"

"All the players in this war," his mother said.

And as if a leaf on a breeze, as one all three vanished.

PART FOUR

16

The Marching Of Time

Harris stared into the mirror, examining his features; the deepening lines across his forehead, the gray beginning to glisten through his hair. He still felt Alpha strong, but he guessed that, despite its strength, the virus couldn't actually stop human ageing. Although perhaps it slowed things down a little. Today was his 48th birthday, but he felt like he was barely 40.

Six years had now passed since the Darwin mission. Brody and Freya were now four and a half years old, which meant in just five years the early invasion could occur. If he had predicted it right. After all, it had been years now in Earth-time, and the *Barbican* had not made any further contact with the Zetas. And the comms facility in Australia, although still occasionally registering the many signals from farther away, had picked up nothing either. *So, what did that mean?* He had absolutely no idea. But still the dreams had come, of seeing the lights in the sky, of the twins being around 10 years old, of his Overseers staring at him like they did.

"Daddy!" Sarai called loudly at his side.

He looked down at the chubby face of his three-year-old daughter, who held up a sheet of paper to him.

"What's this?" he said, taking it from her as Taya appeared in the bathroom doorway.

"Happy birthday, daddy," Sarai said, grinning.

"Oh, you made me a present!" he gasped, over-exaggerating for his daughter's sake. "What is it?" He turned the picture over, and saw an array of straggly lines and circles across the page in a rainbow of colors.

"Spaceship!" she squealed, pointing to the shapes toward the top of the page.

"A spaceship! Honey, that's beautiful." He leaned down and kissed her forehead, then picked her up. He looked at Taya while she smiled at them both.

"Are you hungry, Mr. Harris?" she asked.

"Am I ever!" he said, tickling Sarai and making her giggle as he carried her down the stairs to the breakfast table.

Sarai, not content with sitting in her chair, climbed onto his lap. She was growing by the day, but she was still his baby girl.

Taya smiled at them briefly, then seemed to fall into sadness. "One baby is just starting out, and one baby is leaving me."

Harris gave her a soft smile. "Ty will be calling on us for a few years yet, Tay."

"My baby boy will soon be halfway through college. I can't believe it!"

"Yeah, well he'd better focus a little more on his studies, or he won't be at college for much longer."

"Focus on his studies?" Taya asked sarcastically. "He's the star of his college basketball team, Saul. He's intelligent enough to get through college, but that won't be his career and you know it."

Harris kissed the top of Sarai's head. "Yeah, I know. Our son, the basketball star."

"I'm proud of him, Saul."

"Yeah, I am too," he said, feeling a little wracked with guilt. In some ways he felt like he barely knew his son because of all the time he'd spent away as Ty grew up. And now, Tyson seemed even further away, living in LA and splitting his time between college and games. Already Harris had had to miss two of Ty's college breaks, running exercises with Carcharias team, undertaking regular visits to all the UNF space stations and planetary bases, reviewing updates on the Advanced Weaponry and Fleet Program. He couldn't pause those things.

He wrapped his arms around Sarai and cuddled her to him. He didn't want to make the same mistakes with her. Although as time moved closer to the Zeta's arrival, he wasn't sure how he could do anything different. The uniform needed him more than ever.

He looked over to the picture that Sarai had drawn him, which now lay on the kitchen table. He viewed the scrawlings that were meant to be the spaceship, then looked into her pretty brown eyes staring up at him. He hadn't figured out which gift she had inherited yet. He had avoided talking about it with her so far, not wanting to place that burden on one so young. But then he thought of his mother, and what she had done to him by not telling him the truth when she should have.

He kissed her forehead and cuddled her again. *Soon*, he thought. He would start talking about it to her soon.

Carrie exhaled as she pressed up from the floor. Brody and Freya laughed, making her smile. She glanced around at Jesse who sat on her back, giggling also.

"Look at mum!" Freya said, pointing to her.

Carrie looked up at who her daughter was speaking to, and saw McKinley leaning on the doorway, arms folded.

"That the best you can do, soldier?"

She grinned wider as he stepped forward to Brody and Freya.

"Sit on her back," he told them. "Pile her up!"

Brody and Freya giggled and moved to ride her like a horse. Carrie grinned and clenched her teeth. Two four and a half year olds and one two and half year old on her back. She could do this in her sleep. She exhaled loudly and pushed herself up, feeling the burn in her strong Alpha arms. The kids laughed and she heard a clicking sound. McKinley had taken a photo on his PDP.

Carrie lowered herself again and laid her arms out flat on the ground.

"Oh, you've beaten me!" she lied, as the kids kept laughing and jumping up and down on her back.

"Hey, Frey, you hear that?" McKinley asked her. "Know what time it is?"

"Ooh!" Freya leapt up and went running over to the large windows in the living room and Jesse trotted behind her. Brody sat on the floor beside Carrie and they looked at each other.

"When am I going to hear stuff like they do?" he asked, scratching his knee.

Carrie moved to sit up and ran her hand over his hair. "I can't hear the stuff that they do, either."

"Is it because I had a different dad?" he asked, grabbing a toy truck and rolling it back and forth along the ground.

Carrie glanced up at McKinley, then looked back at her son. She slid closer to him and brought him into a cuddle.

"You take after me," she said, kissing his head. "I only have the Alpha eyes, too. But when you're ready, when you're older, you can get the other senses if you want. We can both do it together."

Brody nodded, eyes still focused on the truck he rolled back and forth.

"C'mon," McKinley said, holding his hand out to help Brody up, "let's go watch the midday ship."

Brody took McKinley's hand and stood, and the three of them moved to the windows to watch the midday ship takeoff. It was a K-Class Hanser, the largest model of ship that departed the Space Docks, and every two days one left bound for Mars. The midday ship was responsible for taking supplies and the crew, who were on rotation, for the construction of Atlas Station which was well underway. Piece by piece they built it on Mars, and then shipped the modules to the site in space, to be added to the main structure.

"Look!" Jesse squeaked, placing his hands flat against the window and pressing his nose against it.

Carrie studied his little blond head, darker than what Freya's had been at that age. Where Freya definitely had her father's looks; she was going to be tall and blond and had McKinley's same ocean-blue eyes, Jesse so far appeared to be a mix of both grandfathers. He had Carrie's father's blue-gray eyes, and the darker blond hair of McKinley's father. She moved her eyes to Brody, who continued to be the spitting image of Doc.

She felt her PDP buzz as McKinley tapped his against hers. She pulled it off her belt and saw that he'd transferred the picture he had taken. She smiled at the image. There she was in the midst of a fully extended push-up with her three children on her back: Freya at the front, Jesse in the middle, and Brody at the back, holding onto each other and laughing wildly.

"It's a great picture," she smiled.

McKinley glanced at his watch. "We gotta go soon."

"Yeah," she said, putting the PDP away. She clapped her hands in an attempt to get her children's attention. "Alright, let's go pack our things for Command!"

Miranda Finch picked up the remote and changed the visibility of her hotel window. The dark tint vanished and she looked out at the hazy orange air of windblown dust.

"Goddamn Mars," she muttered.

She'd been based here for the past 18 months, ever since the construction of Atlas Station had begun to ramp up and the focus had moved from construction on Mars to the actual build in space.

"Come back to bed," she heard his voice say sleepily.

She looked around at her lover of the past 12 months. Regan Lotz, the loser of the Mars presidential election. Still, there wasn't that much choice of partners on this planet. Given her job of reporting on the progress of Atlas Station and the Mars presidential election, she'd kept running into Regan who had set up an office here in Colony Brahe, working hard to expand his Space Mart franchise. She had gotten to know him and it turned out he was good company. She was lonely, and he treated her well enough. And she had to admit his suite here in Brahe was much nicer than her room at the White Sands Hotel in Colony Elon.

She crawled back into bed and snuggled up behind him, wrapping her arm around his waist. He moved his arm to lay atop hers and they threaded fingers.

"I'll take you to Sercio's later," he said, referencing the best restaurant on Mars.

"That'd be nice," she whispered.

Just as she started to relax again, her PDP began to ring. She pulled away from Regan and picked it up, then paused when she saw who the caller was. Captain Morrell.

"Hello," she said, throwing the sheets back and sitting up.

"Finch, it's Captain Morrell, Earth Duty."

"Morrell. It's been a while," she said, standing and moving to the window. They'd kept in touch over the past few years and she'd fed him what information she could, but there had been nothing scandalous. The *Aurora* and *Carcharias* teams had been back on normal duty, although they both returned to Command every three months to meet. About what, she still didn't know. Regardless, there had been no out of the ordinary events, so she'd had no need to touch base with the Earth Duty captain.

"*It* has *been a while,*" he agreed. "*Do you remember that break-in you had me look into a few years back?*"

"Er, yeah," she said, running her fingers through her hair and eyeing the orange haze outside the Colony Brahe domes. It had been some time ago and as there had been no other incidents, she'd virtually forgotten about it. "After the Eden event?"

"*Yeah. It appears one of the suspects we had on the FRS just raised his head. Got busted at an underground fighting event in Miami.*"

"No shit! You're sure it's him?"

"*The security footage wasn't that great if you remember, but from best we can tell, the face matches. And believe it or not, he was busted wearing the same jacket he wore on that footage. It must be an old favorite of his.*"

"No shit," she said again, incredulous. "Who is he?"

"*A Miami local by the name of Darrel Gomez. Know him?*"

"No," she said, "nor do I know anything about any underground fighting events."

"*What do you want us to do?*" Morrell asked. "*You haven't had any other troubles far as I can tell, so it might've been a one-off break and enter. You want us to pursue it or drop it?*"

Miranda sighed and looked out the window again. It had been years and nothing else had followed. Maybe it *had* just been a one-off event, but something niggled her about it. The break-in occurred not long after her reports aired on the Eden incident. The Eden incident... which involved a Space Duty unit brawling with some unidentified men. A bloody brawl that had resulted in several deaths. Then someone had broken into her apartment and had been searching for something. Had someone seen her reports and been looking for more information on what happened down there? *A bloody brawl...* Her mind tossed around those words. This suspect had been busted at an underground fighting ring. Had members of this fighting ring been the ones to have brawled with the *Aurora* team in Eden?

Could these events be connected? Could the Eden incident, her apartment break-in, and this fighting ring be connected?

"Pursue it," she said firmly.

"*Yeah?*"

"Yeah. That break-in had to do with my reports on Eden. Someone was after something. I want to know what this guy's connection is."

"*You're sure?*"

"Do you still want me to supply you with information?" she asked, knowing full well her position here on Mars, including being with Regan Lotz, was a valuable one.

"*Yes, I do.*"

"Then find him and shake him down. I want to know what he knows. Don't you?"

Silence sat on the line for a moment before Morrell answered. "*Alright. I'll get an ED brother on the mainland to track him down.*"

"Good."

"*Let you know when I got more.*"

"Thanks." Miranda hung up the phone.

"Who was that?" Regan asked, now sitting up in bed and rubbing his eyes.

"No-one," she said, making her way back to bed.

"You said 'shake him down'. What's going on?"

"Nothing you need to worry about," she smiled, sliding on top of him.

Just as she was about to kiss him, his PDP beeped.

"Hold that thought," he said, grabbing his PDP and reading the message. "Fuck. The bastard's done it again."

"Who?"

"Charles Mortimer. Just announced another six All-Stations."

"Where?"

"Between here, Pegasus and Atlas Station," he said heavily. "I'm never going to beat that bastard, am I?"

She shrugged. "He lost the election, too."

"I don't care about the election. That was just PR. Everyone knew Finn Harkowitz had it nailed, riding on the coattails of his hero father. I'm talking about business."

"Charles Mortimer is only winning because he's older than you. He's had years of a head start at building the equity he needs."

"Not just a head start with age," Regan said, "the man was born into money. I wasn't. I had to work hard for everything I have."

"You did," she said, kissing him gently on the lips. And it was true. It was what attracted her to him. He didn't come from money, he'd worked damned hard for what he had, and she respected that. "You're made of stronger stock, so just hang in there. At some point, he'll fail and he won't know how to cope with it. That's when you lunge and take it all, because you know how. You know how to fight and to survive."

Regan eyed her carefully. "Underneath your sweet exterior lies the heart of a viper, doesn't it?"

Miranda smiled winsomely. "Maybe."

Regan gave a quiet laugh as he ran his fingers through her hair. "You're my secret weapon, you know that?" he said. "Don't tell anyone."

Her smile grew wider. "I won't."

General Berger, sitting at his desk, closed down the file he'd been reading, ensuring the security measures were in place to keep it invisible on the UNF's systems. He turned in his chair and looked out upon the ocean in the distance. And he felt strange. Calm and content, yet nervous and hesitant.

Professor Sharley was making great progress. With each report, with each success, Berger had slowly but surely granted him more help and more funds. And he'd been forced to unveil the results to Lieutenant General Wilton, who in turn had brought in Colonel Rovine, formerly of the UNF *Carcharias* to handle the day-to-day management of the program, similar to Colonel Marchant's management of UNFASP. Wilton had, of course, been angered that Berger had commenced this program without his consent, but only at first. Wilton couldn't deny the security this program offered them if required. They had agreed, however, to keep this from Colonel Marchant for the time being. He was deemed a risk. He had worked with Harris for too long and too closely now for his loyalties not to be suspect. He would be told in time. Just not yet. Not while there was a chance of anyone trying to stop them.

And so, with the aid of Wilton and Rovine, they'd been forced to take their program outside of the UNF, outside of Command's facilities, away from prying eyes.

They had secured a facility close by and hired a team for Sharley to work with in bringing this dream to life. Berger had Dr. Scavesci keep a close eye on the professor, who, so far, had not been allowed to leave Command and had had to rely on video links to work with his team at the facility. However, Scavesci was convinced that Sharley had come back to full health, that this was as close to sane that the professor had ever been.

Berger was wary, knowing what could happen if Sharley was let loose and then destabilized again, so for now he was keeping the man on a very short leash. But he could not deny Sharley's accomplishments to date. Sharley, with the aid of his scientific team, had successfully grown healthy replicas of Welles's womb. And, more importantly, he'd also successfully created a healthy embryonic clone of her son, Jesse. Codenamed "JEM" after the boy's initials, the clone was now on ice, ready to be rolled out at his order.

All that remained was the final critical step of integrating the high-tech pod case with the organic Welles wombs. And once this final doorway had been breached, they could begin growing their First Gen Army.

Their JEM Army.

Their *real* "Plan B".

Colt watched the nurse and her security guard leave the lair. She looked at Malik and Casim as they pulled their new toys out of the bag.

"What have you got there?" she asked.

Casim held up a box with toy figurines in it. She took it off him and eyed the ugly warriors within. She sighed and opened the box as Casim banged on her legs, eager to play with them. She handed them down, then looked at the toy gun Malik held. Every gift the Greenback sent had to do with battles and wars and fighting. Her boys were a few months off three years old now, and these toys and this cell were all they'd known. Control and violence. She'd tried hard to overcompensate for that with love and kindness.

Colt looked at their toys and wanted to cry, but she couldn't. It was more like she knew the right thing to do would be to cry, but she just didn't have it in her. It had been too long. Too long wishing for a way to escape, of trying and failing. Of losing confidence. Of resignation and reluctant acceptance.

It only took one failed escape to make her change her mind. She'd tried taking the nurse hostage, but somehow the security had overpowered and beaten her. Badly. Very badly. All the while her boys had watched on, scared. Knocked unconscious, she had awoken in a broken, bruised and bloody heap. The Greenback told her that if she tried again, he would kill her. And if he did, her sons would be orphans, left solely to the devices of these people. And she couldn't allow that to happen. So, she slowly, begrudgingly, accepted her fate. She'd lost hope that rescue would come. It had been too long now. Everyone thought she was dead. Maybe she was. At least the old Sabrina Colt was. This woman here was just a Jumbo mother with no identity. Nothing more.

Besides, it had been so long that she wasn't sure how she would cope on the outside. A Jumbo mom with her Jumbo kids. The only outside world she knew was the one she saw on the TV; on the news, on the movies; on the ever more degrading reality shows they made these days.

For a brief moment, her parents' faces flickered in her mind, but she quickly erased them. She was dead to them now. She had to be. The daughter they knew, the happy-go-lucky Sabrina, was dead. And this woman sitting here, this beaten-down Jumbo, was someone else. A wounded woman who did nothing but pace this small space, or sit around bored, or watch TV, or read books. Tame as tame could be... unless someone messed with her young, then the Jumbo inside her would awaken. *That* Jumbo was the only part of her left alive, she thought. Except for the part of her that lived for her boys. But maybe that part was the Jumbo too.

She was pulled from her thoughts by the sound of the entry door's handle being rattled. She fixed her eyes on it. So, did LeFroy who sat up slowly, curious. The door handle rattled again. Then silence.

Bits of wood suddenly spat out and the handle disintegrated into chunks, falling onto the floor. Colt swiftly stood, grabbing both boys and pulled them back behind her. Eyes wide and shoulders squared, she faced the door.

A man appeared, slowly, carefully, gun in front. She hadn't seen him before. He was of medium height with a decent build, wearing jeans and a dark jacket.

"Who are you?" she blurted, stepping forward, as LeFroy moved backward in his cell.

"Who the hell are you?" he asked, gun aimed. "Why the fuck are you in cages?" He glanced around the room, eyed the medical supplies, the toys. He froze when he noticed the two boys peering out from behind Colt's legs.

"Jesus Christ," the guy said. "How long have you been here?"

Colt froze, too scared to speak. *Was this real? This guy didn't work for the Greenback?*

"Answer me!" he said more firmly, like an order.

Like a soldier…

"Answer me! How long have you been here?"

"We've been here a long time," LeFroy said huskily, in shock.

Colt stepped toward the cell door and grasped the bars. "A—are you a soldier?" she asked, her body beginning to shiver with shock.

He gave her a quick nod, gun still aimed, eyes still darting around the room. "Captain Fayden, Earth Duty."

"Where are we?" Colt's voice seemed much like LeFroy's now, husky with shock and emotion.

"Where are you?" Fayden asked, brow furrowing. "You don't know?"

Colt shook her head as her eyes began to sting with tears. She didn't want to believe this might be a rescue. She didn't want to get her hopes up. She couldn't go through the disappointment if it wasn't.

"Miami," he said. "You're underneath an old Chinese laundry."

"Wha—?" Colt slowly sunk to her knees, overwhelmed by what was happening. This whole time, she'd been right here, barely hours from her parents' home in Orlando.

"Get up!" the man ordered. "Tell me who you are, and what you're doing here."

Colt looked at the man and felt a sudden surge of desperation. She stood again and began spewing forth words as soon as they formed, begging, pleading with him to release her.

"They've kept me hostage here! They made me have these kids! He made me have these kids!" She pointed to LeFroy, who held his hands up in defense and began shaking his head. "You have to get me out of here! They'll be back soon! You have to get me out of here *now!*"

"Calm down!" the man said. "Just calm down!"

Colt kept rattling on, as tears began to stream down her face. "Don't let me die here! Don't let my boys die here!"

The man moved toward her, holding one hand out peacefully and tucking his gun in the back of his jeans with the other. "Just calm down! I need you stay calm, understand!"

Colt nodded, her face wet.

"Where are the keys to your cell?" he asked.

"Over there!" LeFroy pointed, eyes wide, apparently in just as much hope as Colt. "In the drawer!"

Fayden went to the drawer and found them, then moved back to Colt's cell. He held his hand out again. "I need you to stand back. Stand back!"

Colt nodded, her whole body visibly shaking like it was undergoing its own personal earthquake. She scuttled back, grabbing her boys as though the cell door might explode.

Fayden unlocked the door, then slowly opened it. He kept his hands out, part peacefully and part defensively, while slowly reaching one back to rest on his gun.

"Just stay calm," he said evenly. "I'm here to help you. I'm not going to hurt you or your boys, alright?"

Colt gasped at the sight of the open door. At freedom. She stepped toward it slowly, feeling as though invisible lines of spiderweb clung to her and tried to pull her backward. But she moved on, step by step, keeping the boys close by her side. With each step she took forward, Fayden took one step back. She made the door and stepped outside. Eyes still wide, she gasped.

She glanced around the outside of the cell, eyes darting here and there, then looked back at the man, Fayden. "I—is this real?" she whispered. "Is this really real?" She reached toward him. "Are you really here? Are we really free?"

His face flashed sympathy as he let her pat his forearm. "It's real. I'm here."

"What about me?" LeFroy squeaked from his cell, arms reaching through the bars.

Fayden turned and moved toward his cell with the keys.

"No!" Colt called.

Fayden glanced over his shoulder at her, but placed the key in the lock.

"NO!" Colt yelled, running up and throwing her weight on the door. "He doesn't deserve to live!"

"What the hell?" Fayden said, pushing her back. "Just calm down."

"No, *he* did this to me!" Colt shook her head as angry tears streamed down.

"No, no, no." LeFroy shook his head in denial, begging Fayden. "Let me out!"

"You're a liar!" she yelled, lunging at the cell door.

Fayden grabbed her by the shoulders and moved her back. "Just calm down. Help will be here soon. I'll call them in a second. Just let me release him, too."

Help? she thought. *What help?*

She didn't trust anyone. She was a Jumbo, so were her kids. No-one was touching her or her kids. No-one would ever touch any of them again.

"Alright?" Fayden said, holding his hands out, asking for calm.

Inside, her body was frozen. She looked into his eyes and nodded. She didn't know what to do. She'd given up on ever getting out of here, now all of a sudden freedom had been sprung on her. What did she do? She hadn't thought this far ahead. Not for a long time.

She looked around at her sons. They were crying, equally terrified by what was happening. They'd known nothing else, but that cell and this small lair.

What the hell was she going to do with her Jumbo kids? What would this "help" do when they learned they were Jumbos? What if they sided with the Greenback?

She spun back around to Fayden as he unlocked the cell and slowly opened the door. His eyes were fixed carefully on LeFroy's movements. Colt saw the gun tucked down the back of his jeans, and without thinking, Jumbo-swift, she lashed out and snatched it.

Fayden spun around. "Hey, no! No!" he held his hands out to her. "I'm trying to help you! I'm trying to help you!"

Colt held the gun in her shaking hand. It had been a long time since she'd done this. It felt heavy, but it also felt comfortable. Safe. She held it at the two men and they both raised their hands.

"Just let me help you!" Fayden said calmly. "I'm only trying to help you."

"I know," Colt said flatly. "Move." She turned her eyes to LeFroy.

"I had no choice!" LeFroy pleaded with her. "You know it. I had no choice."

She stared at him, feeling strangely hesitant. LeFroy had been her only company these past years. She might've gone insane if she hadn't had him to talk to and fill the long silences of her incarceration. But then she reminded herself that she had been here all these years *because* of him.

"You did," she said, her voice dropping several octaves as the Jumbo within rose up and took over. "You had a choice."

"Don't do it!" Fayden said carefully. "I don't know what he did to you, but don't do it. Drop the gun!"

"Move," she said again.

"You're free," Fayden told her. "You don't have to do this, you're free."

Colt nodded, as more tears rolled down her face. "I do… I do. If he lives he'll run back to them. He kept me here all these years. He could've set me free but he didn't."

"Mama?" Casim's voice sounded from behind her.

Colt paused a moment. Forgetting that her children were there.

"Turn around and face the door, baby," Colt said, her mind still numb. "You too, Malik. See that door behind you, you turn and look at that."

"Please!" LeFroy begged.

"Don't do it," Fayden said, eyes fixed desperately on hers.

"Move," she said again to the stranger.

Fayden glanced at LeFroy.

"I don't want to kill you," she told Fayden. "Don't make me kill you."

Fayden eyed her for a moment in consideration, obviously analyzing whether he should try and take her down. He glanced between the two of them, then at the children, then finally slumped his arms and shoulders and reluctantly stepped aside. "I don't know what the hell happened here."

"No!" LeFroy squeaked.

"You facing the door Casim and Malik?" she said, her voice still low, her mind numb with Jumbo hate.

"Yeah," Casim answered.

"Good," Colt said. "You're going to hear a very loud bang…"

"Please, no," LeFroy cried.

"… and when you do, you don't turn around. You hear me?" Colt said firmly. "Do you understand?"

"Yeah," their small voices answered.

She looked hard at LeFroy, as the sweat built around her hand on the gun. She had to forget the past few years. She had to remember the start, and everything he did to her to save his own skin. Now she was saving hers. Making sure he could never hurt her again.

"Go," she told Fayden in a low voice.

"I can get you help," he said gently.

"I'll take care of myself." She turned the gun on him. "Go."

Fayden stared at her, at the gun, breathing hard.

"Last chance," Colt told him. "You stay, you die too."

He held his hand up peacefully to her. She watched him, kept the gun on him until he passed and headed up the stairs.

Then she turned her eyes back to LeFroy.

"Your eyes still on the door, boys?" she asked, as LeFroy sunk to his knees crying and pleading for his life.

"Yeah," her children answered.

"Good," she said. Then she took aim and fired.

Miranda Finch pulled her MaRz over to the side of the road.

"Yeah?" she said, answering her PDP.

"*Your story just got bigger*," said Morrell's voice.

"Morrell? What is it?"

"*I had an ED brother on the mainland trail the suspect after he was released. Off the books. He watched him for a few days and saw him escorting a woman every day to this old, unused Chinese laundry. He figured something illegal was going on, so he decided to take a look and found something very interesting in the basement.*"

"What?" she asked, clutching the PDP tight.

"*He found two cells with people locked in them. One woman, one man, and two kids as well.*"

"Shit!"

"*That's not the best of it. The woman's description matches a soldier on the FRS who's been listed as missing for a few years now. A soldier, formerly of the UNF Aurora.*"

Miranda's mouth fell ajar.

"He had to call it in," Morrell continued, *"so it's now official. But he sent me photos of the room. On the wall were pictures of three women. The black woman, who escaped—"*

"Escaped?"

"Long story, but she took off with the kids. The two other women on the wall were also soldiers of the UNF Aurora. One of which is now dead. One of which is currently serving."

"Sergeant Welles," she whispered.

"Bingo. You met her?"

"Briefly. A few years ago at Atlas Station launch. Anyway, you say Colt escaped with the children?"

"You know her name?"

"As you say, she's been on the FRS. I've done my research on the *Aurora*, Morrell. She was the soldier who went missing briefly with the children when Centralis was locked down a few years back."

"Yeah. Well, she escaped, but she killed the other hostage before she did. She let my guy go. That is off the record, by the way."

"Why did she kill the other hostage?"

"I don't know. My source said she seemed to blame the guy for her being in there. Shot him clean through the head. There were lots of medical supplies down there. I don't know what the fuck they were doing to them."

"Does Captain Harris know yet? About Colt escaping?"

"He's being informed as we speak."

"Jesus Christ," she said, shaking her head and looking out at the roadway and the dome walls in the distance. "That is some serious shit."

"Yeah. I guess no matter how far the Aurora goes, this shit just seems to follow them, huh?"

Miranda clutched her PDP, watching some UNF Space Duty soldiers pass by on the road. "Yeah, but did they cause the shit? Or did they just get sucked into it?"

"Sympathetic to the old captain, eh?" she heard Morrell smiling down the phone.

"I haven't had much to do with him, but from what I have, he seemed honorable." She cringed a little inside as she recalled the night she had hit on Harris in that bar in Centralis, and how he'd turned her down rather bluntly. "Gold, too," she said, moving her thoughts along. "They just don't strike me as the type to be purposely mixed up in something bad. Something illegal. Not willingly, anyway."

"*Well, looks can be deceiving,*" Morrell said. "*First rule of survival, Finch. Trust no-one.*"

"I've been trusting you," she said.

He didn't respond to that, instead saying, "My work here is done," and ending the call.

Harris stared at Welles. She looked back at him silently for a moment.

"S—she's alive?" she asked, the shock evident in her voice, as she reached for a seat.

He nodded. "We think so."

"You think so?"

"The room they found, there were three pictures on the wall. Colt, Packham and you. We think it was the home base that Drazen had been using."

"But we killed him… and she's been trapped there ever since." Welles looked as though she'd been gut-punched, severely winded. "How has she survived?"

"People were taking care of her. A nurse visited daily from what we can tell."

Welles lowered her head into her hand and closed her eyes. "This whole time she was alive and we left her there."

"We didn't know," he told her softly, feeling equally winded. "She was off the grid. We couldn't have known."

"So was I, in Hell Town, on Meridian. But you kept searching and you found me."

Harris leaned closer to her. "Because you were my Connected. I felt something with you, I dreamed it. With Colt I had nothing to go on, because she is not my connected." He leaned back again. "Also, in Hell Town you had a TD, and you got yourself to a room where it would transmit. In Meridian, you talked Baker into escape. You effectively saved yourself."

"Because of you!" she said. "You had Meridian locked down, the streets were thick with soldiers. Why didn't we do that for her?"

"Because we didn't know where she was! She vanished off the face of the Earth. With you, we tracked you to Meridian because Baker attacked Lee. If he hadn't…" Harris clenched his jaw. "We might never have found you."

Tears shone in her eyes. "I gave up on her," she said, swallowing hard. "I should've kept searching… I should've—"

"There was nothing you could've done. Nothing any of us could've done. What we need to focus on now, is that she is alive. She is alive and she is out there somewhere on the run."

"On the run?"

He nodded. "It looks like she killed LeFroy. He was a prisoner too. We don't know why, but she killed him."

"Who was he?"

"We met Professor LeFroy on Station Columbus. He was a connection of Professor Martin's that had input on the early stages of UNFASP. Sharley must've had Drazen capture him. He was one of very few on the outside who knew about UNFASP. LeFroy had been listed as missing for some time. Looks like they were using him to… do to Colt what they did to you in Meridian. What Sharley planned to do to all three of you in Drazen's mission. Except Packham killed herself before they got the chance. And you were with the *Aurora* team." Harris shrugged. "That's what the attack in Eden was all about."

"I was safe, and Colt…" Her words drifted off again and she closed her eyes.

Harris reached out and squeezed her shoulder, careful to touch only clothing to avoid the spark and vibration of their connection. "She's alive, Welles."

She nodded and wiped her eyes. "I knew in my heart she was. I kept asking Archie to check the police reports."

"There's something else," Harris said.

She fixed her glistening eyes on him.

"Apparently there were two young boys with her."

Welles stared at him a moment, her mind ticking over. "How young?"

Harris hesitated, then sighed heavily. "Young enough to have been born in there."

Welles's face flushed pale. "Oh, Jesus…" She glanced helplessly around the room. "Whose? Whose are they? LeFroy's? That why she killed him?"

"I don't know," he said. "They're still going through the lair."

Welles looked down into her lap, shaking her head.

"She's alive," Harris said firmly, squeezing her shoulder again. "She's alive and she's on the run with two small boys. We'll find her."

Welles reached up and gripped the arm holding her shoulder. It was skin on skin, and they felt the static zap and subsequent buzzing sensation. He eyed her hand and felt the grip tighten.

"Do you think she'll try and find us?"

"I don't know," he said, feeling the sensation travel up his arm. "She's had almost four years down there. She's going to be a whole load of messed up."

"If they find her, you need to call me!" Welles said desperately.

Harris stared at her.

"She'll be scared, but she knows me. She'll trust me."

"Maybe," he said, "but she's been gone a long time, Welles."

"She's one of us. She's an Alpha now. We have to protect her and her boys."

"I will," he said firmly. "If she comes to us, I will."

"She will," Welles nodded, releasing his arm. "I know it."

Harris stood. "I'll be in touch."

Carrie paced along the kitchen.

"Archie?"

"*I know what you're going to ask, Miss Welles. I've already scanned.*"

"And?"

"*There's been no sighting of her.*"

Carrie ran her hands down her face.

"*As soon as she registers, I will let you know,*" Archie told her.

She felt something bump into her leg and looked down to see Brody wrap his arms around her legs.

"What's wrong?" he asked.

Carrie looked down into his brown eyes, then loosened his arms and squatted in front of him. "An old friend is in trouble," she said. "I need to help her."

"What did she do?"

Carrie ran her hand down his cheek. "She just tried to survive, honey."

He looked at her, but she could tell his four-and-a-half-year-old mind didn't quite understand. She smiled at him. "Do you remember me telling you about your godmother, Sabrina?"

He nodded.

"Well, hopefully, you'll get to meet her real soon."

"Yeah?"

"Yeah," she nodded and pulled him into a hug. She kissed his head and stared out the windows at the Space Dock.

Make your way back to us, Colt, she whispered in her mind. *Come find me and I'll help you. I promise.*

Colt tried to ignore the tiredness clawing at her, and the pains in her stomach as it screamed for food. But these physical ailments were nothing compared to the emotional ones she was battling. She had been free for barely 24 hours, and she still didn't quite know how to handle it. And her boys? They definitely didn't know how to handle it.

Holed up in a deserted building, she'd had to fend off other homeless people, quickly marking her territory and asserting her claim. The Jumbo within was good for something, at least.

But she feared for her boys and what this freedom was doing to them. They'd been absolutely terrified as she'd dragged them down the streets in the open air, the sunshine battering down on them, the people, the smells, the sounds. Malik had barely said a word since, and Casim had clung to her endlessly. Not only was it being out of that cell, that room, that had startled her boys, but it was having seen, or rather, heard the things that she'd done to protect them.

Leaning back against a wall, she sat on the floor between them and pulled them in close.

"I did it all for you," she whispered, kissing each of their heads. "We're free now. We're free."

"I'm hungry," Casim whined in a small voice, rubbing his face into her, tired.

"I know," she said. "I am too." She wasn't quite sure how to deal with that problem. In order to seek food, she had to take them with her. She had no money, no nothing. And no doubt her face would now be on the FRS, thanks to that soldier. If it wasn't already on there, that is. But how long had it been? Would they have kept her face up on the FRS for all these years?

It didn't matter. It would be there now. As soon as she stepped near a security camera, she would be ID'd. She had to change her look, her clothes, hide her face, if she was to get around unnoticed.

She felt a tug on her rough, fuzzy braids and looked down to see Malik had latched onto them.

A sudden thought struck her. She removed her arm from around Casim and dug her hand into her pocket and pulled out the small knife she'd stolen from the homeless guy who had lived in this room before she'd taken it from him. She flicked it open and stared at the blade. Casim raised his hand to it, but she swiftly whisked it away.

"No! That's dangerous!" she told him.

His pale blue eyes stared back at her.

She stood and moved over to search the windows until she found a spot where she could see her reflection. She paused in shock at first, unable to remember the last time she'd looked at herself. The reflection she saw looked nothing like she remembered. Once the shock had subsided, she grabbed hold of a handful of braids, she began to cut through them with the knife.

When she'd finished, her hair was a short, choppy mess. She definitely looked nothing like the Colt of old. Well, maybe the old Colt was there in the eyes. *Just.* But the rest of her was gone. She stared down at the pile of long braids on the floor, seeing the cell, the lair, her prison. And how she was now free of them.

"Why did you cut your hair, mama?" Casim asked her.

She turned to face her boys. Casim sat upright looking at her, and Malik lay on his side, sucking his thumb.

"We need food," she told them. Again she wondered how she would do that with two small boys by her side. She watched as Casim rubbed his tired face and the realization swept across her that they needed more than food. They needed shelter, security and sleep. They needed support. She needed support. She'd barely slept the previous night, too scared to lower her guard, afraid that Fayden might find her. *Who had he been working for?* He mentioned Earth Duty, but he wore no uniform.

And what about the Greenback? What would happen if *he* found them? Although it might be a few days until he realized she was gone. The nurse had only just left before Fayden had arrived. She wasn't due back for days.

Colt stared at her boys resting on the dirty floor in the abandoned room. Suddenly overwhelmed with loss and loneliness, she slumped to the ground, her hands to her forehead. Without warning the tears began to roll down her cheeks, followed by a flash of Jumbo anger. She wasn't sure how long she could keep this up. On her own, she might be alright, but with her two boys... they were too young. She couldn't do it.

A bang caught her attention and she looked up. Malik had kicked his foot against the wall.

"I'm hungry!" he cried with tears rolling down his face.

"I know," Colt said, trying to calm him.

And the helplessness grew even heavier upon her shoulders.

What was she going to do? She was a murdering Jumbo on the run with two Jumbo kids. They wouldn't just let her go. Any of them. They would hunt her down no matter what. Her mind continued in circles. She was weak and tormented from being trapped for years in that lair. She was an angry, unstable Jumbo, with fragile Jumbo babies. She was tired, she was hungry, she couldn't do this alone.

She needed somewhere to go. Somewhere she could let her guard down. Somewhere she would feel safe. She needed people who would help her. People who would understand her situation. Understand what it was to be Jumbo and have Jumbo kids.

Welles...

But Colt had been gone a long time. Was Welles even still alive? Where would she find her? Still living in her Centralis apartment? Could she make it there undetected?

An image flickered in her mind, then. It was of the *Aurora*, waiting at the Space Dock. If she couldn't find Welles, then maybe she could find Captain Harris and Brown. They would help her, wouldn't they?

Tears began to flow down her cheeks like a waterfall. She couldn't hold back the sobbing. She was too tired, now. Too weak. She had to let it out.

She couldn't do this alone. She needed help. She had to risk it.

And they would help her, wouldn't they?

All she needed was the strength to get there.

17

Reunited National Forces

Carrie looked up to the ceiling.

"What is it, Archie?"

"A ferry has just docked at the Sea Port. I've registered a black woman with two small children disembarking."

"How old are the children? Are they black too?"

"I cannot tell. They are wearing party masks. The Wolverine and the Hulk, I believe."

"Can you show me the footage?" she said desperately, moving over to the monitor on the wall beside her kitchen.

It came to life and footage began to scroll. It was hard to tell for sure if it was Colt, but it could be. She looked about the same height but was bulkier. The bulkiness could've been the jacket she wore, but Carrie didn't doubt that Colt was a Jumbo now. She wore a floppy hat, and her hair looked to be cut into a red, shiny bob. *A wig?* The boys were small. Carrie pegged them to be close to Jesse's age. Maybe slightly older.

"Do you think it's them, Miss Welles?"

"I don't know," she said, "but I guess we'll find out soon enough. Report this to Harris. Tell him to send the team down to the Sea Docks and see if they can find her. I'll wait here and see if she comes to me."

"How will she know where to find you?"

"Shit. Good point," she said, running a hand over her face. "Last she knew I was still in my old apartment. Tell Harris that I'm heading over there in case she comes looking for me."

"You'll need protection, Miss Welles."

"He's right," her father chimed in from the doorway where he'd been listening.

Carrie shook her head. "No, you stay here with kids," she told her father. "I'll do this alone."

"Alone?" Archie queried.

"This is Colt we're talking about. She's not going to hurt me."

"Colt, who's probably an Alpha and has been kept prisoner for well over three years," her father added. "Who knows where her mind or loyalty lies now."

"This is Colt," Carrie said again firmly. "We're friends."

"You can't take the chance with an Alpha, your father is right."

"She may be an Alpha, Archie, but so am I," Carrie said. "And I've had *years* of training that she hasn't. Years of training with McKinley. If she attacks me, I'll be safe."

"I think you should reconsider."

"Just tell Harris that if he can't find her, to make his way to the apartment and wait for my signal."

"What will the signal be?"

"He'll know," Carrie said, heading for her room to collect her gun, muttering along the way, "He'll feel it."

Harris stood outside the wall of the Sea Dock and watched as Murphy and Yughi approached.

"She's definitely not here," Murphy told him.

"The local footage?" Harris asked.

"It lost her outside the wall," Yughi said. "Somewhere between getting off the ferry and walking through the customs channels, she just disappeared."

"If it was her," Murphy shrugged.

"It was her," Harris said.

"You sure?" Brown asked moved up beside him. "Why would she be hiding like this?"

"Because she killed someone," Harris said bluntly. "And she's an Alpha now. She's smart enough to know how dangerous a position that is to be in."

"Is there anything we can get a scent off?" McKinley asked quietly.

Harris looked at him, then shrugged. "She left nothing behind, and the ferry's about to leave with a new load of people heading out."

"Maybe one of us should go to the *Aurora*?" Brown asked, visibly coursing with Alpha energy. "Maybe she's coming to find us?"

"How would she get through the checkpoints?" Harris arched his eyebrow.

"Three o'clock," Steinberg said urgently, eyes fixed in that direction.

Harris turned and saw Captain Morrell and his team on approach.

"Just what we need," he muttered under his breath.

Morrell came to a stop in front of him with his first lieutenant, Grenner, by his side. Harris eyed them carefully. He hadn't seen much of them over the past few years, but since learning that Morrell was the only 6.5 ranked human within the UNF, and that his team were on the list of Earth Duty units to convert, Harris had a new-found interest in them. Morrell and Grenner were both of a good size for humans. Harris could just imagine the power they would have as Alphas.

"I hear you're searching for somebody?" Morrell asked.

"That's correct."

"You always seem to be losing them here on Centralis?" Morrell smiled.

Harris shrugged. "We just like to give you something to do, I guess."

"Yeah, I noticed that. Where do you think she went?"

"You've been briefed?"

"It was our Earth Duty brother who found her in that basement," Morrell said matter-of-factly.

"And how did he know where to look for her?" Harris wanted to know.

"Following a lead."

"What lead?"

"That's Earth Duty business."

"Well, given it relates to this circumstance, it's now *my* business," Harris said firmly, giving Morrell a strong Alpha look.

Morrell eyed him a moment in consideration. "The lead was a suspect in a break and enter here in Centralis."

"Where'd he break into?"

Morrell didn't answer him.

"Where?" Harris asked again. "Maybe we should be looking there for answers."

"A reporter's apartment. It was three or four years ago."

"Who?" Harris asked, but the tingle down his spine already told him.

"Miranda Finch, Universal Press," Morrell said, then added, "I believe you're acquainted."

"What's she got to do with this?" Harris frowned.

Morrell motioned Harris away from the others. Harris followed him several meters until Morrell stopped and turned to face him.

"This guy broke into her apartment looking for something. She seems to think it has something to do with what happened down in Eden and her reports on it. Don't want to shed any light on that now, do you?"

Harris stared at him. "No. I don't."

"Well," Morrell shrugged, glancing around the area, "this same guy knew where your soldier was. He was taking a retired nurse to her every day." He looked back at Harris. "Whatever was going on in that basement is somehow related to the break-in. Someone linked to that basement wanted information on the Eden incident. And we, on Earth Duty, would like to know why."

"*You* specifically, on Earth Duty? Or Earth Duty as a whole would like to know?" Harris asked sarcastically.

Morrell's face hardened and he stepped closer to Harris. Harris, a good half-head taller, stared back at him. "You caused Centralis to be locked down. Then whatever you did in Eden, got the reporter's apartment ransacked and her life threatened. Now, you're here again looking for this missing soldier. The same one that went missing last time, along with a couple of babies. Are you going to lockdown Centralis again?"

"If I have to," Harris said simply.

"Then *I* want to know why!" Morrell hissed.

"If and when you need to know, captain, you'll be told."

"No," Morrell shook his head, "you Blue-boys are infiltrating our turf enough. If you want our help, you tell us why!"

Harris stared at him, mind ticking over. "You want to know what's going on?"

"Yes!"

"And you're prepared to handle the fallout from what I might tell you?"

Morrell paused, brow furrowing. "Yeah. I am."

"Do you swear allegiance to that uniform you're wearing?"

Morrell glanced down at his shirt, then back up to Harris. "I have done for years."

"And do you swear allegiance to the UNF as a whole. Blue-boys included?"

Morrell took a step back from him. "What the fuck is this about?"

"You really want to know?" Harris said, stepping forward and placing his face close to Morrell's.

Morrell's eyes fired back into his. "Yes!"

Harris stared at him for a moment, considering his options. "Then meet me at Command when this is over and I will tell you. But just know, once you walk down that road, you can't turn back. Understand?"

Morrell stared at him, chewing over his words, but unable to hide his keenness to know. It was oozing from him.

"You're right, Morrell." Harris gave a brief nod. "It is time, because I need your help. And I believe you're going to want to give it to me."

Morrell stood there looking a little surprised, as if he was expecting to have to fight harder for it. At the same time, he looked wary, as though questioning what he had just stepped into.

"Take the east side," Harris ordered him. "You spot the woman, you call us in. Do *not* approach her. We'll take the west and we'll call you if we need assistance. Understand?"

Morrell stood still and silent.

"Do you understand, captain?" Harris said firmly.

Morrell glanced at the two teams standing in the distance watching them: one blue, one green. He looked at Harris. "Yeah, I understand, captain. And I will see you at Command when this is over."

"Good," Harris said clearly, then turned and headed back to his team.

Carrie lingered in the foyer of her old apartment building. If Colt was going to come looking anywhere, it would be here. She wouldn't be able to access the Space Dock to get to the ship, and she would be frightened. Just like Carrie had been when she fled Sharley's lair on Meridian and made her way back to the *Aurora*. The only difference was that Carrie had prosthetics to hide her identity. Colt did not.

She really hoped Colt would come to her. If she didn't, then she hoped the *Aurora* crew found her. She had no idea what Colt had been through, but Carrie knew that she would need safe hands. And the *Aurora* could provide that. They would protect her, bring her back where she belonged.

But would Colt consider the *Aurora* to be where she belonged? She had questioned her position in the past and now she had been missing for well over three years. That was a long time. God knows what trauma she had had experienced. Well, Carrie could guess half of it. The two children Colt had been seen with were proof of that. Carrie wondered who they belonged to, wondered why Colt had come back to Centralis. Was it to seek shelter with the *Aurora* team? Or had they warped her mind? Was Colt coming back to finish what Drazen couldn't? Was Carrie expecting a friend but would instead find an enemy?

She paced endlessly as her father's and Archie's concerns flashed through her mind. She rolled her neck and shoulders loosening them, clenched and flexed her fists. She didn't know why, but she was antsy. The Alpha within was alert and ready. Ready to deal with whatever Colt threw her way.

Harris walked toward Murphy and Tikaani. "Report!"

"Morrell's unit saw her, but she got away," Murphy said.

"She's a fast one," Tikaani nodded. "Even with the kids."

"Where was she headed?"

"North," Murphy said.

"Toward Welles's old apartment." Harris nodded, then clicked his comms unit on. "Everybody head to the meeting point, but stay back, you hear? We don't want to spook her again. Just surround the apartment, but stay out of sight, and wait for my signal. Welles?"

"Yeah," her voice said through Harris's earpiece.

"Looks like Colt's headed your way."

"Good! I'm ready for her."

"Let's move out!" Harris said to Murphy and Tikaani.

Carrie looked out the glass windows of the lobby. It was dark now and the streetlights bathed the roads in circles of white. As she scanned the street outside, she wondered whether Colt had undergone the sense surgeries. Would she be able to see as good as Carrie could in this dark? Did Colt have the advantage of smell and sound that Carrie didn't?

As she looked down the east side of the street, she suddenly caught movement in her periphery to the west. She paused. Keeping her face east, she scanned the west with her Alpha eyes wondering if it was just the *Aurora* team moving position.

It wasn't.

A lone figure peered around the corner of a wall.

The hair was different, short and choppy, but the face, the eyes... they were Colt's. Carrie's heart lifted while her spine also tightened. She moved slowly to the doors and stepped outside as they slid open, keeping her face east, away from Colt. She watched Colt in her periphery, though. The former *Aurora* soldier seemed to look behind her at something, then peered around the wall again. Carrie loosened her shoulders, relaxed her face, wanting to appear as unthreatening as possible. Then, still looking east, she raised her arm in Colt's direction and waved her forward.

Colt seemed to pause in confusion, turning her head to see who Carrie had motioned too. Finally, Carrie turned her face to Colt's, smiled softly and waved her forward again. Colt's eyes went wide and she visibly gasped. She stood fixed a moment, staring at Carrie, who raised both arms now, smiling hopefully, and gently motioned her forward.

Colt's suspicious and angry face suddenly darted around her surrounds again as though looking for a trap. Then, in the blink of a panicked eye, she spun around and ran away.

"Shit!" Carrie muttered, dropping her smile and racing after her.

"What's going on?" Harris's voice said in her earpiece.

"She's running. I got her," Carrie said, sprinting down the street Alpha fast.

"*You need back-up?*" McKinley asked.

"No, I got it," she panted. "Tell everyone to back off."

As Carrie turned the corner of the wall, she couldn't see Colt anywhere. She figured Colt must've cut down one of the side streets. Carrie raced for the first intersection then stood there, fixing her eyes to the ground and checking each street in her periphery. She saw movement, a dark shape ducking around another corner down the street to her left. Carrie snapped a quick turn and raced after it, starting to wish she had the extra senses right about now.

She raced to the corner she'd seen the figure at, and saw it was an alleyway with a dead-end. As her eyes scanned the darkness, it looked empty. Again Carrie stood still and focused her eyes on one spot waiting to pick up any movement.

And she did.

Beneath the large dumpster, toward the end of the alley on the left-hand side. There was a small gap between the dumpster and the ground, and she saw movement there. Someone was hiding behind it.

She walked calmly into the alleyway, eyes fixed to the dumpster, while scanning the surrounds, making sure Colt was alone. The alleyway was empty but for the dumpster, some old furniture that didn't fit in it, and the shadow that lingered behind it.

"*Welles?*" Harris's voice sounded in her ear. She ignored it. She crept forward, step by step, until she finally stopped about five meters from the dumpster.

"Colt?"

No-one came out from behind the dumpster. No-one moved.

"Colt?" she said again. "It's me. Carrie. Carrie Welles."

Silence. No movement.

"Colt? We've been looking for you. You've been gone a long time."

Still silence. Still no movement.

"You don't have to hide. I know what happened. I know what they did to you... you're safe with me. I won't let anyone hurt you. I promise."

Slight movement. Still silence.

"Colt," she said softly, "you can trust me."

More movement. Carrie stood watching it in silence.

"Are you alone?" Colt's voice sounded deep and husky. Whether from the running or perhaps emotion, Carrie didn't know, but she felt relief wash through her. It really was Colt.

"Yeah," she said, her own voice a little husky with emotion. "It's just us here."

"Soldiers were chasing me. Where are they?" Colt asked.

"They're staying back."

"But they're here. They got me surrounded."

"I won't let them hurt you."

"But you'll let them arrest me? Put me back in a cell? You try put me in a cell again, I'll fuckin kill you!"

"I won't let them do that!" Carrie said fiercely. "You're an Alpha now. Harris will protect you."

"An Alpha? What the hell is an Alpha? They made me a Jumbo!"

"We're not Jumbos, anymore. That's in the past. We're Alphas now. It's a whole new world. There's a lot you need to catch up on."

Colt laughed bitterly. "Yeah, there's a lot you need to catch up on, too."

"Why don't you come out and tell me then?"

"No."

"Maybe I'll come to you then?"

"NO!"

Carrie paused at the viciousness in her voice.

"Why not?" she asked gently but received no response. "Colt?"

"No-one's touching them… no-one's touching my boys. They're all I got."

"Of course not," Carrie said. "No-one will touch them. I will defend them as I will you."

Colt laughed bitterly again. "No, you won't."

"Colt, you can trust me."

"I don't know why I came here. I don't know why I came here," Colt started chanting quietly.

Carrie took a step forward. "Colt. If you don't come out, they will come in."

"They? Oh… you mean the soldiers. You set me up, didn't you? You knew I'd come for you and you put them on standby."

"No, Colt. I *hoped* you would come and find me, because I wanted to see you again."

"Why have the soldiers on standby, then?" she accused. Carrie heard the Alpha within close to the surface; could feel it from where she stood.

"You're wanted for questioning, Colt. They were always going to be tasked with finding you. You can't think they'll just forget about you. They need to know what happened. But if you cooperate, I promise that Harris and I will look after you."

Colt suddenly stepped out from behind the dumpster. She'd lost the jacket and wore only a singlet and jeans now. Carrie eyed her over. Colt had always had a strong physique, and now, as an Alpha, it looked infinitely so. Maybe not soldier-toned, but the strength was there. Colt's face was slightly lowered, her shoulders hunched, her fists clenched. Her eyes looked troubled and wild, just like her choppy hair.

"I missed you, Sabrina," Carrie told her, a tear stinging her eye.

"Did you?" Colt said, her eyes darkening. "How long was it before you stopped looking? Before you assumed I was dead."

"We never stopped looking."

"Oh, yeah?"

"Yeah. The UNF kept your face up on the FRS for over three years. I wouldn't let them take it down. I had Archie scan the police reports regularly for someone resembling your description. I never gave up hope."

Colt's eyes narrowed. "Bullshit."

"It's true."

Colt suddenly looked over Carrie's shoulder and tensed further. Carrie looked around and saw Harris step into the alleyway.

"I got it!" Carrie called to him.

"Welcome back, soldier," he said calmly to Colt.

"You're a Jumbo!" Colt said suspiciously, eyeing Harris up and down.

"A lot's happened since we last saw you," he told her.

Colt's stare looked over Carrie's other shoulder now. Carrie turned her head slightly and saw Brown step into the alleyway.

"Your family's been worried, Colt," Brown told her. Carrie saw his eyes pooling with emotion that his inner Alpha was trying to beat back.

"Don't you talk to me 'bout my family!" Colt hissed. "What do you know?" Then she suddenly gave a nasty smile. "Oh, I forgot. How's my cousin doing?"

"Haven't seen her in years," Brown said. "Not since you've been gone."

"Then how do you know what my family thinks?"

Brown stared at her, his eyes saddened, seemingly searching for the Colt of old. "Because I visited them every leave."

The Alpha quickly melted from Colt's face as she stared back at Brown. The silence sat for a moment, before she spoke again, eyes falling to the ground. "H—how are they?"

"They gonna be glad to see you, I tell you that now."

"Did you tell them?" Colt blurted. "Did you tell them I'm back?"

"Not yet," Brown said. "Had to see it was you first."

"Don't!" she blurted again, pointing a finger at him. "Don't you tell them!"

"Colt—" Carrie began.

Colt started stepping backward. "No, no, no, they can't know."

"Colt—" Carrie stepped forward, but Colt stopped her again.

"Don't! Don't you take another fuckin' step or I'll kill you!"

"Colt," Harris said in his commanding voice. "We're here to help you. We are *not* going to hurt you."

"Touch me and you die!" she hissed, pacing agitatedly. "This was a mistake. This was a mistake…"

Carrie stepped forward again. "Sabrina, it's me, Carrie. Your *friend*. You will be safe with me. I will *not* let anyone hurt you."

Colt lashed out and picked up a rickety old chair that sat upturned on the ground, smashing it against the wall.

"Come closer and I will cut you!" she said, eyes wide and desperate, holding out a broken chair leg.

"Welles," Harris called in warning.

"You, too!" Colt yelled in Brown's direction, as he also stepped forward.

Carrie held her hands up to Harris and Brown. "Stay back!" She looked at Colt again and held her hand out. "I know that someone hurt you. I can't begin to imagine—"

"No, you can't! No you fucking can't! I was stuck in that cell for years! For *years*! You have *no* idea!"

"I know," Carrie said, taking another step closer to her, one hand out in a calming manner. Colt didn't like it, though. She swiped the piece of broken chair at Carrie, but her reflexes were sharp. She pulled back and it missed her.

"Fuck you!" Colt yelled.

"I know," Carrie said calmly approaching her. "I know what it's like. They kept me in Meridian, and in the Hell Town dungeon. I *know* what it's like."

"No, you don't," Colt said, shaking her head as the tears began to pour down her face, "you don't."

Carrie felt her own eyes stinging with tears again. "I know some of it."

Colt kept shaking her head. "No, you don't. Your babies are different. Their fathers…" Her voice drifted off into sobs as she lowered the piece of broken chair to her side and looked around the alley hopelessly.

Carrie was just a few feet from her now, heart heavy, but racing too. "Let me help you," she said, arms out peacefully. "Let me help your babies—"

"NO!" Colt swung the leg of wood again, then lunged. Carrie ducked the wood, but couldn't avoid Colt's Alpha body barreling into hers. She hit the deck with a whump, but quickly latched onto Colt and swung her over, struggling to hold Colt's fists back. She saw Harris and Brown jogging toward them, as McKinley and the others stepped into the alleyway.

"No!" Carrie yelled at them through gritted teeth as she struggled with Colt. "Stay back! I got this!"

Her moment's distraction enabled Colt to throw her back over, but Carrie quickly reversed their positions again. Colt grasped her throat, but Carrie quickly elbowed her arm to remove it. Colt yelled in pain and grew more Alpha vicious. Carrie struggled against Colt's strength, swiftly wrapping one arm around both of Colt's pulling them out of the way, then firmly pressing her other forearm against Colt's throat.

"Calm down," Carrie said through gritted teeth.

"Fuck you!" Colt yelled, trying to buck her off. Carrie curled her feet around Colt's lower legs and pressed her thighs in tight, trying to restrict her movement. Colt continued to struggle, and Carrie had to use all the Alpha power she had to contain her, every single muscle straining to contain the angry untamed Alpha beneath her.

"Let me go!" Colt struggled to yell with Carrie's forearm pressed against her throat.

"No," Carrie said firmly. "I'll never let you go again."

Colt's wide and frenzied eyes glared into hers.

"You're safe," Carrie said calmly, staring back into her eyes, as her body continued to squeeze every muscle against Colt to restrict her movement.

"I won't let anyone hurt you. You understand me? I've got you, Colt. It's me. Carrie... I'm your friend!"

Colt growled in anguish and frustration, and Carrie leaned forward and pressed her forehead against Colt's gently. "I'm your friend," she said softly.

Colt's fight began to wane, as more tears pooled in her eyes and slid down the sides of her face. Carrie, still gripping her, began to rock her slightly, side to side, in a calming, soothing manner. "I got you, Sabrina," she whispered. "You're safe. I won't let them hurt you again."

Colt began to sob heavily, as though floodgates had opened inside her. Carrie removed the arm from her throat, then slowly, cautiously, slid off her. She pulled Colt's weakened, crying frame to sitting, then brought her forward into a firm hug, wrapping her arms around her.

"It's alright," she said, holding her, rocking her. "It's gonna be alright." She looked up and saw the *Aurora* team gathered at the mouth of the alleyway, the slight shimmer of their Alpha eyes in the dark as they watched on.

"Mama?" a small voice croaked from somewhere, and Carrie realized it had come from inside the dumpster.

Colt gasped as everyone looked for the voice. She pushed Carrie away and moved over to where the lid had begun to rise. Colt pushed it back down.

"Mama?" the voice said again, sounding more scared.

"Mama?" a second voice cried.

"Colt?" Carrie stepped forward. "What are you doing? Let them out."

"Don't hurt them," Colt said, her body visibly shaking. "Don't you hurt them. It's not their fault."

"What's not their fault?" Carrie asked.

Colt looked at Carrie, eyes wide in shock or terror, she wasn't sure. Colt looked at the team, then back at the dumpster lid.

"Who their fathers are," Colt said flatly. She turned back to the dumpster and opened the lid, then reached in and pulled out a little boy and placed him on the ground. She reached back for the second, as the first instantly clung to his mother's leg, and looked at Carrie with his scared face.

"Hey," Carrie said gently, squatting down and holding her hand out to the boy. He looked to be around Jesse's age, maybe a little older. His skin was a lighter shade of brown than his mother's and he had tight frizzy curls and pale-blue eyes. "What's your name?"

The boy didn't answer, but Colt did, placing the second boy down. "That's Casim, and this is Malik," she said, motioning to the second boy who had buried his face into Colt's legs. Colt's hands clung to each of her boys as she looked back at Carrie warily.

"It's not their fault," Colt said again.

"Who are their fathers?" Carrie asked.

Colt didn't answer, but the second boy, Malik, turned his face to look at Carrie and the instant she saw his eyes she knew. Emerald green in color with strange gold flecks, they sent a shiver down her spine. She had to stop herself from gasping. She looked back at Casim, and his pale-blue eyes suddenly registered with her too.

Carrie slowly stood back up, staring at Colt, as she spoke their names.

"Chet and Logan."

Harris walked into the hospital room, deep in the bowels of Command. He saw Colt and her boys asleep in pods. It had taken some coaxing, but Colt eventually let Dr. Morgave examine them all. They were in relatively good health, physically. Whoever had kept them prisoner had fed them well, and it appeared they had managed to exercise. But they had a long road of emotional recovery ahead. After nearly four years in that basement, reintegration into society would take some time.

The two boys had naturally been distraught, having never seen this many people before, or this much open space. Their brains were overloaded. They shook, they cried and yelled and screamed. And all the while Colt held them and rocked them. In the end, Morgave recommended sedation. They were all too wired to sleep, and it was what their bodies needed most of all. Harris gave the okay, and with Welles's assistance, they sedated all three. Colt had resisted at first, but Welles somehow managed to calm her, promising that she wouldn't leave their sides.

Harris looked at Welles now, standing over the pods of the sleeping boys. He moved to stand beside her.

"I know what you're thinking," he said.

"Yeah, what's that?"

"Colt's right, they're not Chet and Logan. We can't think of them like that."

"I know," she said softly, looking down at Malik. "They have their father's eyes, though. Especially Malik."

"It's just DNA," Harris said. "That's all it is."

Welles looked at him. "Sharley can never know about them. Scavesci can never know. Or he must be sworn to secrecy. We think Sharley is crazy about my kids, but can you imagine what he would do if he knew Chet and Logan's boys existed?"

"Yeah. It'll be hard keeping this from Scavesci, though. He's the Alpha psych. I'll speak to Marchant and see if we can get the fathers' details erased."

Welles's face hardened. "I meant what I said. If Sharley touches my kids I will kill him. The same goes for Colt's kids." She turned to face him. "These boys have a chance to be something their fathers weren't. If Sharley touches them I will fucking kill him."

Harris looked back her as his mind flashed over the dream he'd once had, of Welles and Sharley fighting to the death in that sealed room. He nodded. "I know you will."

Welles looked over at Colt's sleeping frame. "She's going to take a lot of healing."

Harris sighed. "I know. I'm going to need you to stick close to her for the next while. Ease her mind when she needs it, and be her leash when she needs it."

Welles nodded and smiled. "It's the least I can do."

"When she wakes up in the morning, we interview her and try and figure out who the hell kept her there."

Welles nodded in agreement.

Harris looked at his watch. "I gotta go," he exhaled. "I'm meeting with Marchant to debrief him on this and pave the way for our third Alpha unit."

"Oh, yeah?" she said. "Finally. And who is it?"

"Captain Morrell's Earth Duty squad."

"We're branching into Earth Duty?"

Harris nodded. "We're going to need soldiers on land as well as in the sky. It's what the UNF is all about, what the Pegasus insignia means. Land and sky," he said. "Land and sky."

Carrie peered around the door to Colt's room. She was awake, sitting up in her pod with both boys snuggled close either side of her. Carrie knocked gently on the door and Colt looked at her, startled by the sound.

"You said you wouldn't leave," Colt said with an accusing tone.

"Sorry, I just had to meet someone down the hall and collect something. I was hoping to be back before you woke." She stepped into the room and approached the bed slowly. Malik and Casim watched her carefully, glancing at their mother, holding her tight.

"Hey," Carrie smiled at the boys. "Good morning."

They didn't respond, but continued to glance between Carrie and their mother.

Colt looked at her boys and squeezed them closer to her. "This is Sergeant Carrie Welles. She's okay. Say hello."

Carrie gave them another gentle smile. "Hi."

Casim stared back, maybe a little less scared, but Malik pressed his face into Colt's side.

"They're still getting used to all these new faces," Colt said, "and all the new surroundings." She looked around the room. "Hell, so am I. I think I've developed agoraphobia or something."

Carrie stood beside the pod. She lifted her hand and ran it gently over Malik's hair, as Colt watched carefully, the protective Alpha mother on guard. "You don't have to be afraid," Carrie told the boy. "I'm going to look out for you, just like your momma does."

Colt's eyes shone with tears as she watched Carrie caress Malik's head.

"I know this must be hard," Colt said.

"No," Carrie shook her head, "don't you worry about that. You're right, it's not their fault." She looked from Malik to Casim, whose eyes watched her intently. "This isn't Chet and Logan. These are just two innocent boys caught in the crossfire." She smiled at Colt. "This is Malik, and Casim, *Colt*," She emphasized their surname.

"Thank you," Colt whispered as a tear rolled down her cheek.

"I meant what I said yesterday," Carrie told her. "Me, Harris, the team, we've got your back. You're one of us. You're an Alpha, and we look after our own."

Colt nodded, sniffing.

The silence sat for a moment before Colt broke it.

"What happens now?" she asked.

"If you're up to it, they want to ask you questions about your captors and what happened the day you escaped."

Colt nodded, turning her face away.

"And then, in a few days, if you can handle it, Captain Harris will update you on the *Aurora* team, and the things you'll need to know."

Again she nodded. "The whole team are Jumbos now, huh? I saw the captain, and Brown. They're... *big* now."

"Yeah. They're big. They're strong. And we're going to need them."

"For what?"

Carrie studied her, then the boys. "Let's just get through the questioning on your captors first. When you're ready we'll tell you the rest. But you'll need to know. It will affect you and your boys."

"Because they're Jumbos?"

"No," Carrie said. "Your boys aren't Jumbos. Their fathers were. You, and your boys, will be Alphas."

"What's the difference?"

Carrie reached out and brushed the backs of her fingers down Casim's cheek. "A lot. Alphas fight for good. They do the right thing. They're heroes."

Colt looked at each of her boys, her face softening as she hugged them to her again.

Carrie smiled. "You know how I said I had to collect some things?"

"Yeah."

"Well, I think it's time I bring them in." She turned her face to the door. "Roy?"

Her Sentinel Roy entered holding Jesse, while Brody and Freya walked in beside him. Carrie took Jesse and swung him around onto her left hip, then ushered Brody and Freya forward.

Colt's mouth fell open. "That's not... how big are they!"

Carrie smiled. "Brody, Freya, this is Sabrina Colt and her boys Casim and Malik. Brody," she knelt down beside him, "this is your godmother."

Brody smiled at her, holding a toy truck in his hand, rolling its wheels over his free hand.

"And who is that?" Colt asked, looking at Jesse.

"This," Carrie said standing up again, "is my son, Jesse." She looked back at Colt. "Jesse McKinley."

"McKinley?"

Carrie nodded, smiling. "I'm now known as Carrie Welles-McKinley."

Colt's jaw fell open. "No shit?"

Carrie laughed. "No shit."

Colt nodded as she studied both Carrie and Jesse. "Guess you moved past that whole fighting and arguing thing then?"

Carrie laughed again. "Not really. We still fight every day. Although most of it is in training these days."

Colt nodded, her face falling. "You fought good. Against me. You're a lot stronger than you used to be."

"Not as strong as you."

"You beat me," Colt shrugged.

"Only because your Alpha energy isn't controlled. But train with us, with McKinley, for a while and you'll be hard to beat. Combine your strength with skill and agility," she smiled, "and you'll make a hell of an Alpha soldier."

"Can we play with the toys now, mum?" Freya asked, pointing to the bag she carried.

"Yeah, honey. Go say hello," she said. Brody and Freya moved forward. Freya leaned on the bed, smiling at Casim and Colt as she began pulling toys out of the bag. Brody stood in front of Malik, who peered out from his mother's side.

"You want to play with my truck?" he asked Malik, holding it up and placing it on the bed in front of him.

Carrie and Colt exchanged a glance as they watched the children. Malik, still frightened, looked on as Brody rolled the truck back and forth along the pod-bed in front of him. Carrie had told her kids before they came in that Malik and Casim would be shy and scared, so they had to be gentle and kind with them. As she stood there, Jesse on her hip, she watched as Brody and Freya played with Colt's boys: kindly, gently, just like their mother had asked.

Colt's eyes filled with tears and Carrie's, too, stung as she watched them. It was a beautiful sight.

In that moment, Carrie saw true innocence. Their fathers had killed each other, but that didn't mean they had to. Things had changed and the past had to be left behind. The future was approaching swiftly, and if they were going to make it through, they needed to unite.

And this scene, before her, gave her true hope for their survival.

*

Carrie hung up her PDP, feeling strange inside. Shocked.

"What is it?" her father asked.

"An update on Colt."

"And?"

"They got a description of the guy who was in charge. Apparently, he called himself The Greenback," she said staring at her father.

"What?" he blurted, eyes fixed on hers.

"Clint Harbourg. He was the one keeping her prisoner all this time?"

Her father stared at her, before lowering his head into his hands. "Jesus," he said.

"He never said anything to you? Hinted—"

"No. No, I didn't know." Her father sat down at the kitchen table, as though to catch his breath. "I wondered where he got some of his intel from, but... I never thought..."

"No."

"I went to see that man. I sat in his bar and drank with him! And all this time he knew she was down there. He was the one keeping her there."

"Why would he do that? Didn't he claim not to know anything about what Drazen was up to in Eden?"

Her father nodded. "Yeah. But Clint was pissed at the UNF when he found out that Sharley had stolen his fighters. He told them he wanted in on the action, but the UNF kept him at arm's length. I guess Colt and her children meant he had some Alphas of his own."

"*Fucking* asshole!" Carrie seethed.

"Oh, yeah! So, what are the UNF doing about it?"

"They're sending MPs to arrest him."

"They are?"

She nodded. "I guess they've decided to shelve their Plan B. The trust is broken."

Her father looked away from her.

"What?" she asked.

"Tell the MPs to hold off. I'm going there," he said with a determined look upon his face.

"Why?"

"Because I want to see his face as they take him away."

"Then I'm coming. The Sentinels and Archie will watch the kids," Carrie said as she moved to grab her jacket.

*

Carrie nodded to the UNF guards and followed her father through the large wooden doors of Hell's Gate. She saw a bar on the right-hand side along the wall, tables to the left, filled with terrifying patrons. Fighters, who eyed everyone walking through the door with hate. The MPs were stationed in an area at the back of the room behind velvet ropes, cuffing Harbourg.

They moved toward him, passing the stained glass windows on both sides of the building, which had images depicting fighters in the midst of brutal bouts. Carrie's eyes fell on one of the windows behind the bar, featuring a man with a blue cross tattooed on his forehead. She paused briefly on seeing it. It was the man she'd killed in Eden. Her eyes quickly scanned the others until she saw another she recognized. One that sent a shiver down her spine. Drazen. She pictured him leaning over her, the hunting knife in his hand, but quickly recalled the memory of his death and used it to erase the former. In fact, as she walked along, she felt a confidence swell within her. She had outmaneuvered and helped kill two of the Greenback's prized fighters. Maybe not only with her bare hands, but with her gun. She had won. She had beaten them.

As Carrie neared Harbourg, she saw he'd aged much like her father had. Gray dominated his hair, little pillows of fat sat underneath the eyes, his body shorter, more stooped than she recalled it to be, and his belly fuller with excess. She wasn't sure whether her memories of him were really hers, though, or whether they had been built from the photographs she'd seen of the Originals around Command. Images of the heroes who had helped pave the way for man's future in space.

Harbourg's eyes caught on her father's and they hardened.

"Come to see the show, huh?" Harbourg accused.

"I always thought you were a sadistic prick, Clint," her father said, "but I never thought you were this sick. Keeping that woman and her kids prisoners? You disgust me."

Harbourg laughed. "Fuck you, Jeff. I did nothing to her. I kept her fed and sheltered, that's what I did."

"You kept her locked in a cage!" Carrie hissed.

Harbourg turned his eyes to her. "And who's this?"

"Yes," a blond woman said, stepping forward from the side, dressed in a sheer black dress, "who *is* this."

"Ah, Carrie! I almost didn't recognize you," Harbourg chuckled. "You're all grown up."

"Carrie Welles?" the blond woman asked.

"And who are you?" Carrie asked bluntly.

The woman smiled with a touch of menace, as she sized Carrie up. "Roxy Harbourg. At your service."

"Roxy?" Carrie's face screwed up.

"It's been a long time between playdates in the sandpit, Carrie."

Carrie stared at her for a moment, then looked back at Harbourg as they began marching him toward the door. He halted in front of her father, however.

"If the UNF think they can lock me up to keep me quiet, they can think again!" he hissed. "They need me. So, they have two choices. Cut me in, or kill me and silence me for good! But killing Originals is a tricky business, isn't it, Jeff?"

Carrie's father stared back at Harbourg with cold, hard eyes. "I'll be sure to pass the message on."

The two MPs holding Harbourg pushed him forward to keep him moving, but Harbourg tugged away from them.

"They embarrass me in my own place!" Harbourg hissed back at her father.

"Don't worry, dad," Roxy called, "I'll take care of this place for you." She watched them remove her father from the premises, then turned her sharp eyes and that menacing smile back to Carrie and her father. "Get out. You're no longer welcome here."

Carrie and her father glanced at each other, then happily left.

Sharley stared at General Berger sitting before him and smiled.

"We've had success, General."

"Yes, tell me."

"We have successfully melded the organic womb to the technology of the pod case. We have tested it with a JEM embryo. It is now at three months gestation."

"Just one?"

"Of course, general. You had not approved the roll-out as yet."

"And you're sure the Jesse DNA is viable source material?"

"I have no doubts on this. He is born of McKinley and Welles. An army of him will do great things, General. Trust me."

The general seemed to ponder the matter.

"Do I have permission to roll-out the JEM army?" Sharley asked.

The general stared at him as though thinking things through one last time. "Yes. Go ahead."

"Here in Command?"

"No. In the facility we've provided your team."

"Still hiding, general?"

"Yes."

"May I make a request?"

"What's that?"

"A visit to the facility. I have earned it, yes?"

The General stared at him but did not answer.

"I have worked tirelessly for you these past years. I have brought this program to fruition."

"The program will be deemed a success when I see an army of JEMs before me. Until then it is merely in progress."

Sharley's smile stayed pasted across his face, on the surface only. Had it not been for his shackles, he would've lunged at the general and slit his throat then and there. *In progress... how dare he say it is merely in progress?* Sharley had been the one who oversaw the cloning of Welles's womb, the cloning of Jesse, and the successful integration of organics and robotics – the precursor for Phase Four of the Alpha program – and Berger devalues its success like it was nothing. This was exactly why Sharley had taken the

Jumbo program away from the UNF in the first place. They didn't appreciate the science, the achievement. They just stood there with their hands out wanting more. and wanting to take the credit for his hard work, no less. They didn't deserve to survive the Zeta invasion.

Berger seemed to have second thoughts about his comment. Perhaps he saw something in Sharley's eyes. "I appreciate how far we've come, professor," he said, "but we still have a long way to go."

Sharley was too offended and too above this fool in intellect to bother responding.

"I can't let you leave this Command facility," Berger told him, "but as a reward I will shift you to a new room. One with sunlight. I believe you've been asking Dr. Scavesci for one for some time now for a new room?"

"Yes," he managed to say calmly, his mood brightening somewhat.

"Very well," Berger said. "I'll see that it happens."

"Thank you, general," Sharley said, forcing a smile, then turned and let his guards usher him from Berger's office. All the while he fantasized about the many ways in which he could kill the general as soon as he got the chance.

Admiral Arken stared fixedly down at the table screen. There, flashing before him, was a single red blip.

"The signature is more dense than the others we recorded," Comms-Tech Garth Walon said. "This indicates it's a bigger ship,"

"Still smaller than the *Barbican* though," Arken said.

"Yes, still considerably smaller, but we don't know what weapons they have."

"Raise shields," Arken ordered.

"Shields raised," Chief pilot Sasha Ulgari answered in her Russian accent. "Continue course?"

"Yes," he said, "but slow it down."

"Roger that," she said, hands darting around the flight deck console.

Within seconds he felt the slight reduction in speed as he continued to stare at the screen before him, eyes fixed on the red blip.

"Where have you been all this time?" he whispered, then looked up through the forward observation window. "What do you want from us?"

18

ALPHA-ONE, -TWO, -THREE

Miranda Finch cancelled the PDP call. Morrell hadn't answered. In fact, he hadn't answered any of her calls since the suspect in her apartment burglary had shown up. She doubted he was *that* busy that he couldn't take any of her calls. Which meant he was avoiding her. Why? Was he done with their agreement? Or had his ED brother stumbled across something that had now sealed his lips too? Just like with Gold.

"Well, isn't this interesting," she said to herself, as she gazed out the window of Regan's apartment in Colony Brahe. "A link between the Eden incident and my apartment break-in is established, the *Aurora*'s long-lost soldier suddenly turns up, then Morrell goes cold." She shook her head and narrowed her eyes. "All roads lead back to the *Aurora*. Time and time again."

She folded her arms and tapped her foot as her mind ticked over. The orange haze outside was thinning, but was still thick enough to make her feel claustrophobic. She needed a change of scenery, she thought. She needed some fresh air, some clarity.

And within minutes she'd made her decision.

She packed her bags and left Regan a note of goodbye.

It was time she headed back to Earth.

Harris woke up in a pool of sweat, thrashing about trying to douse the flames that engulfed his body. It took him a moment to realize he was in his quarters on the ship, and that he'd been dreaming. Relieved that Taya wasn't beside him, he lay back, panting and catching his breath.

The image of his dream remained, however. He saw the fireballs hitting Earth, burrowing into the ground; saw himself jostling about in the cabin of a PV, McKinley seated beside him; saw battlefield carnage, and broken pieces of flaming ship scattered across a field; saw himself standing on that Zeta flight deck with Welles trying to connect with it...

The dreams were much clearer now. Perhaps, in part, because he was more attuned to his gift, more attuned to listening, but mainly, he felt, because the day was drawing nearer. The early invasion the UNF did not yet know about was coming.

He sat up, threw his sheets back and placed his feet on the floor. He had three units at present: the *Aurora*, the *Carcharias*, and Morrell's team. Just three. He figured, based on the ages of Brody and Freya, that he had about five years. Just five years to prepare the UNF for this invasion without any evidence on his side. He sighed and ran his hand down his face.

One step at a time, Harris, he told himself. Get your first three units streamlined, then think about the fourth and the fifth and the sixth.

After the Colt situation had been settled, he had briefed Morrell as planned. Marchant was hesitant at first, but Harris managed to convince him that three teams would give the scientists and medical professionals a little more data, not to mention being a test of Harris's leadership skills. The *Carcharias* team had always been compliant, thanks to his relationship with Gold, but Morrell was different. Harris wasn't sure he had the man's true allegiance yet, but given his status as the most dangerous human in the entire UNF, Harris wanted him on his side.

They'd had no further news from the *Barbican*. According to the last update they'd received, the *Barbican* continued onward with no new sign of the Zetas. And the further they moved away, the longer it would take to receive any news saying otherwise.

And the longer it would take the *Barbican* to return should they be needed.

When he'd briefed Morrell, the man had sat plain-faced, listening carefully. He gave little away, but Harris saw a slight flicker of surprise in his eyes at the news of the Zetas. After that flicker, he also saw a resolve settle across the man's face, a hardness. The look in his eyes said, "Game on!" And in that moment, Harris knew that Morrell was on board. Although he did ask him to confirm it in words.

"So, there it is," Harris had said. "Will you join our fight? Will you become the leader of the Alpha-Three unit?"

Morrell nodded silently at first, before uttering just one word: "Yes."

"You understand that I am in command of the Alpha units? You agree to accept my command, obey my orders."

Morrell stared at him. "Yes," he said, "I do."

Harris nodded back, studying him. "Do you have any questions of me?"

"Yes," Morrell said, "when do we start?"

"That keen?"

"Yes. In fact, I'm a little pissed you didn't bring me in on this sooner. Why the delay? Every second counts. We should be out there fortifying the fuck out of everything and getting our soldiers ready."

Harris held his hand up to stop Morrell going further. "Trust me, getting to this point has been a long time coming. The *Aurora* team has been through a lot and we've got the scars to prove it. But we're here now, and it *is* happening. But a word of caution… I see the eagerness in your eyes and you need to restrain that shit. We've still got a long way to go and the UNF wants to take baby steps to ensure we do this right. So, I need you to keep your head and listen to my command. Do you understand?"

Morrell gave him a hard look, then nodded.

"And your men… if this all goes well, I'm going to need someone to lead the Earth Duty units. I'd like that to be you. Gold will lead the Space Duty units. The *Aurora*, well, we're a special case. We'll be flying somewhere in the middle of y'all. But I need you to lead the Earth Duty troops and keep them in line, and I need you to work with Gold and the Space Duty troops. I know you and Gold haven't exactly been the best of friends, but I need you to drop this Green versus Blue shit. If we are going to survive the Zetas, we're going to need each other."

Morrell looked serious, then broke into a smile. "Don't you worry about me and the little Blue-boy. We'll get along just fine."

"Yeah?" Harris arched his eyebrow.

"Look, I like to play around with him and his little bluebells, but so long as he doesn't disrespect me or my guys, and he does his part in this war, I'll work with him just fine."

Harris stared at him, letting the Alpha within sit just below the surface of his skin and stare back at Morrell.

"United we stand," Morrell said, registering the look. "And united we'll fall... but I'll do my best to stop that from happening. And so long as Gold does too, we ain't got a problem."

"Good," Harris said, and Morrell flinched as he abruptly stood up, Alpha shoulders sprawled and looked down at the Earth Duty captain. The seconds passed before he held out his hand for Morrell to shake. "Welcome to UNFASP."

Morrell stood and shook his hand. "Glad to be aboard."

Harris thought back on those memories, and recalled the conversions of Morrell's team, then he sighed and pulled himself out of bed.

Today would be the first day that all three of his Alpha units would be in the same room together.

Carrie knocked on the door to the housing unit Colt and her boys were now living in. Once a site for storage sheds, the area had been cleared and 20 compact prefab houses had been erected. And fenced off. This had now become the first accommodation facility for Alpha soldiers. And Colt and her boys were the first occupants.

The door opened a crack and Colt peered through at Carrie. She paused, then opened the door wider and let her in. Carrie smiled as she stepped inside, eyeing Malik and Casim sitting on a small couch watching TV.

"Hey," Carrie said gently to them, not wanting to scare, mindful that they were still getting used to her.

"So, what brings you to the neighborhood?" Colt asked. She placed the knife she'd been holding on the table, then put her hands on her hips.

Carrie eyed the knife then smiled at Colt, still getting used to her stronger frame, and the Alpha fierceness to her face.

"I just wanted to check that you'd settled in alright."

"Yeah, we're in," she said, then pulled the curtain back and glanced outside, "but it's a little strange being the only ones in the neighborhood."

"Well, it's probably for the best," Carrie said. "Ease you into being around other people and all that."

Colt stared at her. "I hear they gave you a mansion?"

Carrie glanced at Malik and Casim, whose eyes were still fixed upon her. "It's a little bigger than here, yes, but I wouldn't call it a mansion. They call it the Fortress. I guess I was lucky they had one going when we needed it. After the events in Eden," she locked eyes with Colt, "they didn't give me a choice."

Colt nodded, then motioned for her to take a seat.

"Is everyone treating you alright?" Carrie asked. "Dr. Morgave's been coming to see you, I believe."

"Yeah," Colt said sitting down as well.

"You can trust him," Carrie said.

"Can I? I seem to remember you not trusting anyone with your kids."

"That's true. But I made a mistake with Morgave. He saved my life, he saved the lives of the twins. I owe him."

Colt looked down at the kitchen table where they were seated, tapped her fingers on the surface. Carrie looked around. Other than the furnishings provided by Command, there were no personal touches anywhere. When Colt had arrived, she had done so with only the clothes on her back. Command had since furnished her with uniforms and supplied the boys with basics, but that's all they had.

"Are you sure you don't want me to fetch your things?" Carrie asked quietly.

Colt shot her a fierce glance. Carrie had asked this question before but had hoped Sabrina would change her mind.

"I told you," Colt said, "Sabrina is dead."

"She doesn't have to be."

"She's dead! Let my family move on. They think I'm dead, it's best that way."

"Colt—"

"I can't show up like this! A goddamn Jumbo—"

"An Alpha," Carrie corrected her.

"—with two damn Jumbo kids!"

"Colt—"

"Let my family grieve! Tell them you found my body."

"No," Carrie said, "I won't lie to them. And Brown doesn't want to lie either. You're alive! Let them have their daughter back! Let them know they have grandchildren!"

"I said no!" Colt banged her fist on the table, making the boys jump with fright.

Carrie sighed, then held up her hand. "Alright. Okay."

"Is that all you came here for?" Colt asked, brown eyes piercing hers.

Carrie met her stare but kept her face soft. "I came to see you," she said. "I came to see Sabrina. My friend."

"Well, she don't live here anymore."

Carrie watched as Colt looked over at her boys. Carrie didn't know what else to say, but knew she couldn't push it. Colt had been held prisoner a long time and it was going to take a lot for her to feel normal again, for her to trust again. Carrie just had to be patient and wait. But she knew, in time, Sabrina would come back. Carrie would make sure of it.

A knock at the door stole their attention. Colt eyed the door, glanced at Carrie. "What is this?" she asked, snatching up the knife. "Visiting day!"

She walked over and opened the door to reveal Brown standing there in all his bulk.

"What do you want?" Colt asked.

"Well, hello to you, too. You gonna let me in, or make me stand here."

"I don't know yet," she said, showing him the knife.

Brown looked at the knife, then stared at her. Colt grunted, threw the door open and walked toward Carrie again. "Come on in! Join the freaking club!"

Brown stepped inside, giving Carrie a nod. "Welles."

"Brownie."

"How you doin', boys?" Brown asked Colt's sons, but they didn't respond. They just stared at him.

"They're still not used to seeing black men in the flesh," Colt told him. "Just on TV. They've only known white men their whole life."

"Well, it's a good thing we're changing that then, huh?" he said, looking back at Colt.

Carrie stood and patted Brown on the arm as she passed, heading for the door. "I'll leave you to it," she said. "Try and talk some sense into her, would you?"

"I'll try," he said, "but I ain't Superman."

Carrie smiled. "I'll see you at the big training meet later."

"Yeah," he said, nodding. "Our Alpha brethren are growing in number."

As Carrie moved to close the door behind her, she threw one last glance inside. Colt stood there with one hand on the back of a chair and one hand on her hip, while Brown just stood in the middle of the room staring at her. And despite the tension on Colt's face and in her Alpha body, Carrie still felt a sense of hope. Hope that Brown, with his connection to her family, might be the one to get through to her.

Harris entered the training facility and saw his three Alpha units standing in groups: the *Aurora* team to his left, the *Carcharias* team in the middle, then Unit 505 to the right. Two groups dressed in their Space Duty gray and electric-blue, one group dressed in their Earth Duty green and gold.

He came to a stop, placed his hands on his hips and studied them. Each team had gathered behind their leaders; McKinley, Gold, and Morrell. They were all a picture of Alpha strength, but the *Aurora* and *Carcharias* teams had that slight edge. The senses. They stood staring at Harris, but he could tell their senses were on alert, feeding their brains with information on their surroundings, and on their comrades.

Harris took another couple of steps forward.

"Welcome," he said, "my first three Alpha units. The beginning of our future." He took another few steps forward until he was just a couple of meters in front of the *Carcharias* team. "We got a hell of a mission to prepare for in the coming years. But before this blows wide, we start small. We train our three groups, we perfect our skills, we learn to manage our temperaments. Why? Because it's going to be up to our three teams to lead all others into war should it occur. The *Aurora* team, the Alpha-One team, will help me lead all of you. The *Carcharias* team, the Alpha-Two team, will lead the Space Duty troops. The Unit 505 team, the Alpha-Three team, will lead the Earth Duty troops. We three teams will be the very core of UNFASP. So, we need a damn good handle on our ourselves, as individuals and together, before we can even think of controlling other Alpha teams. Understand?"

"Yes, sir!"

"Alright, I want you to start training in your current teams. After a while, once everyone has settled, we'll mix it up. Begin."

The teams began to move in different directions. The *Aurora* team headed over to the weights, Unit 505 to the mats, while the *Carcharias* moved over to the rock climb. Harris caught McKinley's eye and motioned him over.

He'd made a point of leaving McKinley to kick things off with the teams, as a way of letting Gold and Morrell know McKinley's new place in the *Aurora* team – as Captain McKinley. Now there were three Alpha teams in place, Colonel Marchant had told Harris he needed to step back from the day-to-day running of the ship, and focus on leading all three Alpha teams. He was still stationed on the *Aurora*, that hadn't changed, but he was now known as Major Harris. And that, in turn, led to McKinley being given the opportunity to step up also. And as far as the *Aurora* team was concerned, that had been seen as good news.

"So, *Captain*," Hunter said as he approached McKinley after the announcement had been made. "You realize you can't boss me around now, right? I mean I'm second in command."

McKinley laughed. "Oh, just you wait!"

"Hey, I'm First Lieutenant!" Hunter said, referring to the promotion he'd received in turn. Although Gregson was next in line for that position, when Harris had spoken with him about it, Gregson had been frank.

"You know what, sir?" he'd said. "I don't want it. And to tell the truth, I don't deserve it."

Harris had stared at him, waiting for him to elaborate.

Gregson had shrugged. "I'm the medic. It's my job to help save lives, not lead them. If I'm saving lives, I don't have time to lead. And I don't want to stop doing what I'm doing. I like being the medic."

Harris had eventually smiled at him. "I appreciate your frankness."

"I think you and I know that Hunter is the right choice. He's a natural leader and he works well with McKinley. He's the man for the job. Not me."

Harris had already come to that conclusion, but he needed to know that Gregson would be okay with things if Hunter leapfrogged him.

"How'd things go with the introductions?" Harris asked as McKinley reached him.

"Alright," McKinley answered. "Gold's crew were good, of course. Morrell's were a little frosty, but I put that down to them being new Alphas still getting used things."

"Well, like I said, if we're going to lead all the others, it's critical that we three can work together. You don't have to be friends, but you do have to respect each other. Remember what our endgame is: destroying the threat to our survival. Understand?"

"Crystal clear, sir."

"And *you* need to remember when I'm not around this shit devolves to you. You're the new captain aboard the *Aurora*, which means you're second in command of all the Alpha units. If I die, you step up. Don't forget that."

McKinley seemed to pause a moment, as though he hadn't thought that far ahead, but then he nodded in acceptance. "Yes, sir."

"Alright, get back to it. Go lead our team."

*

Harris watched carefully as the three teams began to mix, each soldier finding someone not on their team to face off against. He saw Morrell approach Steinberg and Harris smiled to himself. Morrell, the man highest on the UNF Threat Assessment watch list, was picking the biggest man in the room to face off against. He had balls, Harris had to give him that.

He looked around at the other pairings. McKinley faced off against Ryker from the *Carcharias*, and Gold took on a sergeant from Unit 505 by the name of Sanjit Kumar. Meanwhile, Welles motioned to Grenner who stood near her. A slight smile flickered across Grenner's face, then he glanced around to see that everyone else had paired off.

"It's okay," Welles said, "I don't bite."

Grenner scratched his jaw, shook his dreadlocks, then stepped toward her, his face showing no humor now.

Harris smirked, then turned his eyes to watch Morrell and Steinberg. Already they were locked in a wrestling pose, straining and grunting, trying to put each other on the mats. Beside them McKinley and Ryker were ducking and dodging, faking and darting. He scanned over the paired teams and could easily see the stages of their development. The *Aurora* team were clearly the most adept, having been trained Alphas the longest. The *Carcharias* were next most adept, being comfortable in their Alpha

368

bodies; then there was Unit 505, new Alphas full of angry energy who didn't know how to control it yet.

He heard a loud whump and a vibration shook the floor beneath his feet. He looked over to see Welles on her back and Grenner standing over her.

"Sorry 'bout that," Grenner said, his voice showing no hint of remorse, as Welles visibly gasped, winded.

Harris's Alpha eyes saw McKinley turn toward them, but he quickly stepped in front, shouldering him back and shooting him a glare. McKinley threw Harris an angry look, but saw Harris moving over to where Welles lay.

"Is there a problem here?" Harris asked, noticing that everyone else had stopped and was watching them.

"Nope," Grenner said, shaking his head and stepping side to side, oozing Alpha energy.

"I'm fine," Welles panted, pulling herself up.

"Gregson?" he called and the medic stepped forward, as Welles leaned her hands on her knees, catching her breath. "Take Welles for a walk."

"I'm fine!" she insisted, straightening up.

"Take a walk," he ordered her.

"I'm fine," she repeated, lining up against Grenner again.

"I said, take a walk," he glared at her.

She scowled but obeyed, heading for the exit with Gregson in tow.

Harris looked around at the troops. "What you stopping for?"

They all turned back to their partners and lined up again.

Grenner gave a laugh under his breath. "No place for a woman to be fighting 'ere."

"What was that, sweetie?" Tikaani held her hand up to her ear. Harris motioned for her to carry on, then looked back at Grenner, laughing and shaking his head as he did. Harris's laugh was a lie, of course. He held out his hands in question. "Looks like you need a partner?"

Grenner eyed him, then nodded. "Yeah, okay."

Harris rolled his neck and shoulders, shook his arms out, then faced off against him. "You ready?"

"Always," he said. Before he could finish the word, Harris barreled into him hard. He slammed Grenner backward onto the floor and placed his boot on the man's throat. The movement had been so swift, Grenner didn't know what hit him, but once the shock had subsided his anger flared.

Harris pushed his boot more firmly into the man's throat. He was choking. The training facility fell quiet. All eyes were on him, in awe.

Morrell was the first to move, albeit slowly. He came to a stop beside Harris and looked down at his soldier.

"You're choking him," he said, casually.

"Am I?" Harris stared plainly at Morrell.

The Earth Duty captain nodded. Harris eased his foot up a little. Not enough for Grenner to do anything, but enough to let a little air in.

"We are a team," Harris said to the room. He didn't need to raise his voice; it carried just fine in the silence around him. "We will train together and we will fight each other, but make no mistake, we *are* a team." He looked around with a hard Alpha stare. "This is *my* team. All of you? *My* team," he pointed to himself. "And if you fuck with someone on my team?" He pushed harder on Grenner's throat and the man gargled again. He let the silence sit among them for a moment, with only Grenner's gargling to break it. Harris didn't need to finish the sentence. Staring at each one of them, he finally said, "Do you understand me?"

He saw a lot of nods, but heard only a few "Yes, sirs". He raised his hand to his ear, like Tikaani had done earlier. "I'm sorry?"

"Yes, sir!" they said more resolutely. He eased off Grenner's throat and looked down at him as he coughed and spluttered and glared back at him.

"Do you understand me, Lieutenant Grenner?" he asked.

Grenner flashed his eyes to Morrell.

"No," Harris shook his head, "*I* was asking the question."

Grenner looked away but nodded. Harris glanced at Morrell.

"Do your soldiers not make eye contact when they answer your question, Captain Morrell?"

Morrell stood silent a moment, staring down at Grenner and keeping a good handle on his own Alpha, which Harris felt was sitting just below the surface. "No," he said, "they look me in the eye real good."

"Is that so?" Harris leaned down closer to Grenner. It was risky, but the man would be an absolute fool to strike him. "You better look me in the eye then, Lieutenant Grenner."

Grenner coughed some more, rubbing his throat which was patterned like the bottom of Harris's boot, but he looked Harris in the eye.

"Yes, sir," he said with a husky voice.

Harris stared at him a little longer, then stood back up. "I'm glad we got that cleared up then." With that he turned and moved away, everyone's eyes still fixed on him, as he slowly, calmly, let his Alpha slide back down inside. "Get back to training," he said, then calmly stood off to the side, observing them.

He watched as Morrell stood in place, staring down at Grenner. The lieutenant held his hand out for his captain to help him up, but Morrell just stared at it.

"Don't embarrass me again," he said, then walked back toward Steinberg.

Admiral Arken stood on the *Barbican*'s flight deck and eyed his crew.

"Still no comms from the Zetas?" he asked Senior Comms-Tech Garth Walon.

"Negative, sir," he replied. "They won't respond to us."

Arken nodded. He wasn't surprised by the lack of response, the Zetas clearly liking to play games, but he *had* been surprised when their numbers had grown.

And how they had grown.

The new ships didn't approach the first Zeta ship slowly as though they were merely catching up. They'd just appeared: first it was one blip, then two, then three, then five, and before he knew it, well over 40 blips were blinking on the radar. Over 40 Zeta ships, so close they appeared on the radar. How many more could be out there that hadn't shown themselves?

"What about Command?" he asked.

"Nothing, sir."

Arken nodded again. That also wasn't a surprise. They were very far from Earth and it would take months for Command to receive word that the *Barbican* now faced over 40 Zeta ships.

But what troubled him most was this: the *Barbican* was only a fifth of the way to the Zeta Archelois system. These Zetas were too close to Earth for his comfort.

"Alright," he addressed the entire flight deck, "for now we stay put and observe. I want our scientists studying every facet of these ships, gathering every piece of data we can. I want reports every three hours, and I want data packets sent back to Command every six. Understand?"

"Yes, sir," they replied.

"Good," he said, moving for the admiral's table. When he reached it, he stopped and made sure to lock eyes with each and every one of them in return. "It's been over five years since we left Earth, people. I know it doesn't feel that long out here, but it's the truth. It's been a long journey, but this is where our mission truly starts. From here on is where we make a difference. From here on, the fate of Earth, our colonies and stations, rests with us. So let's do this right. Focus your attention and your discipline, and let's find out everything we can about the Zetas and their ships, and let Earth know what's coming for them."

"Yes, sir!" his team called out firmly.

Arken smiled, his eyes filling with pride, as he watched the *Barbican*'s flight deck suddenly become a hive of activity.

Carrie frowned at Gregson. "I'm fine! Why the hell did he send me away like that?"

Gregson looked at her as he leaned against the pod-bed opposite the one she sat on and folded his arms. "It doesn't matter why."

"Yes, it does! He embarrassed me in front of the other teams. He made me look weak!"

Gregson didn't say anything this time, he just looked at her.

"Look," she held her hand up, "I know it's not easy winning hand-to-hand combat against the male Alphas, but if I don't train, what does he expect me to do against the Zetas?"

Harris walked into the hospital room.

Carrie turned to him. "You can't do that to me!"

Harris motioned for Gregson to leave. He did.

"I'm fine!" she said.

"I know you are."

"So why did you send me away?"

"Because I had a point to make."

"Which was?"

"That I am the lead Alpha, and if anyone fucks with my team, I will fuck with them. And they *really* don't want to be fucked by me."

"So you look strong while I look weak."

Harris shrugged. "I'm sorry, Welles, but right now, as leader, my positioning with the crew is more important. I had to establish my position, my dominance, early. I didn't think I'd have to do it this early, but that's just the way it is. I should thank Grenner for that."

Carrie stared at him. She understood what he said, but it meant she had twice the work to do now.

Harris's voice softened a little. "It was always going to be tricky, having only a couple of female Alphas amongst the rest of us."

"Oh, bullshit! The *Aurora* team have coped just fine with me and Tikaani around, and Colt and Packham before that."

"Because the *Aurora* team know you. And they know McKinley. And they know *me*. Fucking with you wouldn't cross their mind. These other guys, they don't know you and they don't know your standing with McKinley. And they still don't, because *I* stepped in." Harris shrugged. "McKinley can prove himself next time. It'll be important that he establishes his position too."

"I thought we were in this to save the world," Carrie said. "When did this become a dick-swinging contest?"

Harris stared at her for a moment. "This is how we save the world, Welles. Through control, and discipline, and loyalty. They need to fear me just as much as they fear those Zetas. So, yes, I'm going to have to swing my dick from time to time. I make no apologies for that." He turned and walked back to the door. "Take the rest of the session off."

Admiral Arken stood, hands leaning on the table in front him, as the whole flight deck listened to the Zeta comms filling the speakers: humming, buzzing, clicks.

"Do I send the signal back?" Garth asked.

Arken shook his head, eyes narrowed in thought. "I don't think it's directed at us."

"What makes you say that?" Rina asked.

"Because we've been trying to communicate with them for a while now with no response. Why would they speak up now? I think they're communicating with the rest of the ships in their fleet."

Sure enough, one of the Zeta ships began to move forward. It was one of five that contained a denser heat signature than the rest.

"We got movement!" Ulgari called out in confirmation.

"Yes," Arken said, eyes fixed to the screen before him, "we do."

Carrie stared at her datatop as Archie filtered files through from Command. Although, technically, he'd hacked the files he was showing her, she figured it was okay because she was 'working' on the Zeta problem for the UNF. And she was doing it as a means of distraction, to channel her bubbling frustration from what had happened at training earlier that day. She was still pissed about that.

She stared at the photos of the unearthed Zeta skulls and wondered which type of Zeta they were. The skulls did look human-like. Mostly. Maybe a little elongated. Rubbing the back of her neck, she stood and moved over to the windows of the living room and stared out. She was currently alone. McKinley was on the ship, her father was out, and the children were in bed asleep. She liked it. It gave her time to think. She wasn't sure what she could uncover with this research that the experts hadn't already figured out, but she wanted to do something. After what happened at training, she felt the need to prove herself useful. It was the least she could do as only a part-time member of the *Aurora* crew.

She pictured the face of the Alma Mater, the mother of mammals, in her mind. Then she thought of the others: the Priestess, Amphibia, Zisis and Salacia. The Zeta queens. These alien women with their thought-controlled ships. Where were their men? Where were their children? Were they confined to their home planet? Had they become an infertile species? Were they dying out?

"Archie?" she said.

"*Yes, Miss Welles?*"

"Can you bring up the iconography again?"

"*Yes, Miss Welles.*"

She moved back to the datatop and studied the imagery from the Egyptian mothership again. She paused on the picture of the HH being marched onto the Zeta ship. She studied the row of male slaves, saw the Priestess standing by watching. "Does Command have any other images on file of Zetas marching the HH males onto their ships?" she asked.

"No, Miss Welles. Just that one."

"Just that one..." she repeated. "Have you noticed it's only the Priestess in that image, Archie?"

"You are correct, Miss Welles."

"So, where are the others? Did they take slaves too or only this one?"

"I cannot answer that, Miss Welles."

She sighed and stood, gravitating back to the window overlooking the Space Dock. "All women..." she mused aloud. "Only the Priestess pictured with the HH slaves. Zeta DNA on those skulls. Zeta DNA showing more prominently in some humans... thought-technology..."

"There are lots of pieces, Miss Welles, but not enough to solve the puzzle."

"Yeah, but there has to be something here."

"We'll keep trying, Miss Welles, that's all we can do."

"Yeah," she said, rubbing her neck. She moved back to the table.

Harris leaned in to the speaker grille. "Major Saul Harris," he announced.

"Welcome, Major!" Archie greeted him, as the door clunked open.

"Archie," he acknowledged, as he walked through into the Fortress. He'd come to check on Welles after the incident yesterday with Grenner.

"Uncle Saul! Uncle Saul!" Brody and Freya came running to him, with Jesse scooting up behind.

"Hey, guys!" he said, then squatted down to their height, as they gathered around him. "What you been up to?"

"I drew a picture!" Freya said, holding up a page showing two stick figures with long, entangled arms.

"Who is that?"

"That's daddy," she said pointing to the one on the left. "He's fighting a Zeta!"

Harris looked at her. "Oh, is he really."

"I've been playing football!" Brody announced, smiling, showing his missing front tooth.

"With Jesse?" he said.

"Yeah," he laughed, "but he doesn't really understand how to play it yet."

"Well," Harris said, looking at Jesse who seemed to be covered in sand, "he's still a bit young right now, but he'll understand soon enough."

"Mobbed by the fans, huh?" Welles said, coming down the stairs into the kitchen and meals area.

"My favorite kind of welcome," Harris said, standing up. Jesse banged his arms on his leg, wanting to be picked up. Harris swooped down and collected him.

"Oh, you're covered in sand, Jesse!" Welles said, stepping forward and trying to wipe him down while he sat on Harris's hip.

Harris smiled. "He likes to get down and dirty this one, huh?"

"Does he ever!" Welles said. "I have to fight to bring him inside sometimes. He sure loves the outdoors."

Jesse gave them a cheeky grin, his short blond hair sticking up on end like he hadn't long been out of bed.

Harris gave a laugh and put him back on the ground, then ruffled Brody's hair. "I'll come play ball with you in a minute, Brody. I just need to speak with your mom first."

Brody nodded, throwing the ball up and catching it as he headed back outside with Freya and Jesse.

"They're growing up fast."

"Yeah," Welles said, pulling out a chair at the kitchen table and sitting down. "I think they're about halfway."

"Halfway to what?"

"The first invasion."

Harris paused and flicked his eyes up to the roof.

"He's not stupid," Welles said. "Archie's been helping me with my research. I've had to tell him things."

"Welles!" Harris stiffened. "What if the UNF find out?"

"It's alright," she said, holding her hand out to calm him, then she looked up at the roof. "Archie, who is your loyalty to?"

"You, Miss Welles. And your family."

Welles looked back at Harris and shrugged. "I thought about it for a long time, but it's very hard living in his house with McKinley and not mentioning it. Archie's been sworn to secrecy."

"I have a suggestion if you're worried that at some point someone may download my recordings. Which, by the way, would be extremely difficult to do without my knowledge," Archie told them. *"I'm designed to be impenetrable and have full control over my systems, and even if my systems fail, my AIS siblings will come to my aid."*

"AIS siblings?" Harris asked, eyebrow arched.

"Yes. Benedict, Wilfred, Josiah, and Eugene."

Harris looked at Welles.

"Long story," she said. "What's your suggestion, Archie?"

"You say this invasion will occur when the twins are around ten, yes?"

"Yeah." She looked at Harris. "I've been calling it the Tenth Year War."

Harris nodded.

"In line with the UNFASP program, which was given the Latin title of 'Bellator Fortis', I thought it might be a good idea to give this occurrence a Latin code word, so that we could speak of it publicly."

"And that is?" Harris asked.

"Decima," Archie said. *"It means 'tenth' in Latin."*

"Decima," Welles said, trying the word out to see how it sounded.

"So whenever you wish to speak of the early invasion, of this Tenth Year War, all you need do is say Decima. No-one will be any the wiser. It simply sounds like a mission name."

"It *is* a mission name," Harris said. "That's what we're preparing for now."

"Decima. I like it," Welles nodded, then looked at Harris for his approval.

He nodded back. "Decima."

"So," Welles said, leaning her elbows on the table, "what did you want to talk about?"

"I'm just checking in. Want to make sure you're okay with what happened yesterday."

She glanced away and sighed. "I'm not okay with it, but I guess I understand."

"Good," he said, then thought it best to move on. "Had any dreams lately?"

"Yeah," she nodded, "of Decima."

"Me too. They're becoming more frequent."

"Same here. I've been trying to figure out why we're in Western Australia when it happens."

"And?"

"Well, this curved tree we keep seeing. It's in a little place called Greenough, which is about 350 kilometers away from where the UNF facility is located. The one that's been communicating with the Zetas. Maybe that's why we're there, because the Zetas are heading for the source of *our* signal."

Harris nodded. "Yeah. Why we're there doesn't really bother me. What bothers me is why the hell would we take your kids with us?"

"I guess if we know Decima is imminent, then I'm going to want to keep my kids close to me. If Earth is to be attacked, I'm not exactly going to leave them behind am I, Sentinels or not." She shrugged. "They stay with me so I can protect them. That's our job, isn't it? To make sure they make it through Decima. To make sure they make it to the final battle? In order to do that, I need to keep them by my side."

"Yeah," Harris said, bending his head a little to massage the back of his neck. He sighed as he looked at her. "Taking the children into a battle to keep them safe. It sounds messed up."

"It does," she agreed, "but maybe they need to see it. See first-hand what the Zetas do to us. Maybe that memory will fuel them in the future?"

"You sound like we're going to lose."

"Well, right now we only have three Alpha units. If those things hit the ground we're going to need more."

"Yeah, if they hit us early we need to fight as many of them in the sky as possible," he sighed. "We can't let them hit the ground with only three units."

The silence sat for a moment, as they contemplated their futures.

"You got any more views on the Zeta thought-technology?" Harris asked her. Over the past few years they had discussed it but had not come to any solid conclusions, as the ships were still locked in hibernation. "I've been thinking about it again recently. Dreaming of it, actually. You and me on one of their flight decks, trying to get in."

Carrie nodded. "I've been thinking about it, but I still don't have any answers. Ultimately, we need to capture a Zeta alive to see how it works. Unless the UNF somehow manages to clone a Zeta from the skull DNA." She sharpened her eyes on him. "Marchant hasn't said anything about that has he?"

"No," Harris said. "Even if we did, it would take years to rear the Zeta and then get it to figure out how to connect with the ship. We don't have time for that. Your twins are five. Decima approaches swiftly."

Welles nodded, her mind ticking over. "I've been researching telekinesis," she said. "I figure the way their ships work is like a cross between that and what we can do."

"What can we do?"

"I can make you feel when I'm in trouble."

"That's very low on the scale of impressive things, Welles. The Zetas fly ships with their minds."

"I know. So we need to build on *us*. Improve our skills."

"How?"

She laid her arm out on the table, palm up. "More of this for a start."

He eyed her arm, then laid his down too, palm to elbow. They felt the static zap as their skin touched, then the subsequent vibrating sensation.

"We need to make this a two-way thing," she said. "I need to be able to feel when you're in trouble too. That's how it starts. We need to train this like we do our bodies for combat."

He thought of the dreams he'd been having, of being stuck in that PV, wounded, and Welles running toward him.

"I don't think it works like that," he said, although he sounded unsure. "I'm the one with the gift. Not you."

"But why me? There must be something about me to have made you connect with me. Why me over anyone else out there? Besides," a smile curled Welles's mouth, "I'm a woman. We have this thing called intuition. Maybe I could tap into that."

Harris gave a short, sharp laugh. "This is serious, Welles."

"I *am* serious. I'm a woman and the Zetas are a female-dominant race. I have something in common with them. That aside, I'm starting to think everyone could have strong intuitive feelings, but most of us aren't attuned to it, like your family is. Ours, mine, is buried somewhere so deep that we don't even know it exists, unless we make the conscious choice to open our mind to it."

Harris didn't respond, just looked at her, then suddenly sensed his Overseers behind him. The feeling was so real he glanced over his shoulder, and sure enough there they were. He glanced back at Welles but she was oblivious.

"When Colt was gone," Welles said, her face becoming serious, "I had a feeling she was still alive. I don't know how or why. I just did."

"It's called hope, Welles. That's something different entirely."

"Is it? Hoping, wishing, *willing* something."

Harris released her arm and sat back in his chair, watching as she studied him carefully for a moment.

"I've thought a lot about what Matthew Ross told us in Egypt, about the potential Zeta-HH offspring. How do we know we're not directly descended from them?"

Harris stared at her, his mind racing to catch up.

Welles leaned over the table toward him. "This thought-technology…" She locked eyes with him. "Who's to say your gift isn't descended directly from the Zetas?"

"What?" He screwed up his face and recoiled.

"Think about it. Why are we so important to this invasion? Why us? You are connected to me subconsciously. It's eerily similar to how we think the Zetas connect to their ships."

"The Zetas connect to their ships consciously, Welles. *Consciously.*"

"Maybe our connection is only subconscious because it has been buried within my DNA and watered down for millions of years. Maybe…" She paused and looked at him, her mind working on something. "Maybe it's strong within you and your family because it's only been buried for a few hundred thousand years? Maybe your ancestry, the pairings, kept that strand of DNA alive and strong."

"What the fuck are you saying?" Harris said, brow furrowed. "That I'm a fuckin' alien!"

"No," she reached out and placed her hand reassuringly over his with a zap. "All animal life on Earth started from the various Zeta DNA. Technically, we're all aliens. But over time we evolved, to become less alien. Then after millions of years, the Zetas came back and bred with these evolved beings, the HH. The children of these pairings therefore had a 50 percent top up on Zeta DNA. So, the descendants from these children had a much stronger presence of Zeta DNA in their system than the rest of us, who've had it watered down for millions of years." Her eyes were fixed on his. "Your gift is strong, sir. Maybe your ancestry... the gift is somehow linked to the Zetas. Maybe your lineage is a result of a Zeta-HH pairing."

Harris stared back at her, slack-jawed and unable to formulate a comment.

"It's strong in you, the gift," she continued, "and maybe, somehow, it's in me too... slightly stronger than the rest. That's why you connected with me. What if that Zeta thought-technology is so strong within you, it identified a trace within me?"

Harris sat frozen, trying to process what she said, then exhaled heavily.

"Ross said the evidence showed it was rare," she said quietly, "which means those that have it are special."

Harris still could not speak.

Welles sat back in her chair. "Who knows how many survived. How many Zeta-HH children survived after the Zetas left. Can you imagine what the HH would've done to them? The offspring of these strange invaders? Probably killed most of them. But I have no doubt that there would've been some mothers, some HH women, maybe even some of the fathers, who would've protected the children, regardless of what they were. Who can stand by and watch an innocent baby being killed because of their parentage?"

Harris felt the blood drain from his face. Welles sat forward and placed her hand on his again with a zap. He looked down at the point of their connection.

"The ones that survived, the Zeta gift would be strong within. The rest of us have had it buried so deep we never had knowledge of its existence."

The silence sat around them thickly before Harris got his mouth to move. "You're saying this gift is alien. That I'm alien."

She shook her head gently. "No, I'm saying if they really created us, right back at the very beginning, then we're *all* part alien. But, as Ross said, we have evolved into our own species now. But because of that visit during the time of the Homo heidelbergensis, the Zeta DNA is stronger in the few who are direct descendants from any pairings that occurred during that later visit." She eyed him gently. "I think maybe you're from that line. The Zeta is stronger in you and that's why you have this gift, this intuition that others don't."

Harris shook his head, turning in his seat to sit sideways, breathing heavily as though he'd been winded.

"It makes sense," Archie said.

Harris darted his eyes nervously to the roof. He'd forgotten the AIS had been listening.

"The ability has carried down the generations."

"Through the women!" Welles blurted, her eyes popping, as the sudden realization hit her. "That's it! The women! Your family gift has always been strongest within the female, yes?"

Harris nodded faintly.

"The Zetas are a female-dominant race," Welles said, eyes locked on his. "It makes so much sense," she said in awe. "I think you're a direct descendant from a Zeta-HH pairing, and this gift you have... that's why you're important to Decima and to the final war. You're our key, sir! Somehow, you're going to be the key to unlock the Zetas. Maybe even to end them."

"And you, Miss Welles?" Archie asked.

Welles shrugged. "I guess it's in me too. Not as strong as him, but it's there. But maybe... maybe it will get stronger now we know it's there? If we know of its existence. It's thought-technology, right? So we become aware of it... self-aware."

"Perhaps, like the ships, your thought-technology has been in hibernation too?"

Welles nodded. "And there could be others like you, sir. If we could connect with them."

"Like I can with my siblings," Archie said. *"You could form a network of protection, or if required, penetrate their systems and break them."*

"Jesus fucking Christ," Harris breathed, shaking his head, trying to expel the shock. He was suddenly covered in a sheen of sweat, his heart beating quickly.

Welles gave a quiet laugh, a huge smile pasted across her face.

"What are you so happy about?" Harris muttered.

"The possibilities," she said, energized. "The hope! That maybe we've stumbled on something that could help us. This is a breakthrough! We need to have our DNA tested for those Zeta markers Ross was talking about."

"No!" Harris said.

"No?"

"No. If my Zeta markings are through the roof, they'll ask questions."

"Sir, maybe—"

"No, Welles!" he said firmly. "Not yet. Do you think they'll leave me in charge if they think the Zeta is alive in me? If they think I can do crazy shit with my mind? That there was a chance their Alpha leader could have his brain hijacked by theirs? No. You tell no-one."

Welles sighed, but her face softened in sympathy.

"I gotta go," he said, standing abruptly and heading for the door.

Harris didn't want to believe it, but the way his gut churned and his spine ached, and his Overseers followed him... it was like he was physically overloading. He wiped the sheen of sweat from his forehead. He was overloading alright. On information. The words "self-aware" seemed to be trapped in his mind as though they were wrapped in a thick web of glue that he couldn't remove.

If this family gift really was descended from the Zetas, then what would happen now that he was "self-aware" to its presence?

What would happen if he tapped into the Zeta within?

Admiral Arken darted his eyes between the footage showing on the screen and the Zeta ship that could now be seen through the observation window with the human eye.

Black in color, almost invisible against the expanse of space behind it, it was an odd shape. The front part of the ship resembled a triangular prism, but the back part looked like a hexagonal prism had been wedged perpendicularly up against it.

"Tell me you're recording all of this," he said to Garth.

"Yes, sir, we're recording everything."

"Get the data packets ready to send back to Earth."

"Yes, sir."

"It's moving forward!" Ulgari announced.

"Shields in place?" Arken asked.

"Yes, sir. Shields are up. Shall I raise the weapons?"

"Hold," he said. "Get ready, but just hold for now. I don't want to give them a reason to shoot. Or pulse. Or whatever the hell it is they might do."

Suddenly two more ships, the smaller kind, began to move up beside the larger. Once in view, he examined them closely. They, like the larger ship, were black in color and shaped like a triangular prism, but they didn't have the hexagonal piece at their back end.

"Sir?" Ulgari said, frowning at the flight deck console.

"What is it?"

"Their heat signature is increasing."

"It's coming from the underside of their ships," co-pilot Kito Marns said. "They're turning red."

"Their elevation is rising!" Ulgari said.

"What does that mean?" Rina asked.

Arken watched as the red light built in intensity on the underside of each of the smaller ships, as they slowly elevated to a position higher than the *Barbican*.

"They're getting ready to fire on us," he said quietly.

Everyone looked out the observation window at the three ships and their glowing red lights, getting brighter with each second.

"Get ready to jump!" he called.

"Where to, sir?" Rina asked.

"It doesn't matter!" he said with a sense of urgency. "Just jump us! Jump us now!"

Rina's hands darted around her console, punching in coordinates.

"Rina!" Ulgari shouted.

"Good to go!" she yelled back.

Ulgari and Marns got to work and Arken heard the ship's engine raise to a roar. He stared ahead at the bright red lights of the ships as whatever weapon they had suddenly turned white and fired. He squeezed his eyes shut, felt the ship shake, then flashed his eyes open again.

There were no ships in front of him.

"We did it!" Ulgari called.

Arken looked at Rina. "Where are we?"

"I've moved us 100 points west of where we were."

"Get us back there."

"What?" Rina said.

"Get us back there, but prepare to jump again if needed."

Rina stared at him a moment then did as ordered.

Arken looked at Ulgari. "Raise guns."

She nodded and did as ordered.

He heard the ship roar again and felt the shudder and shake as it jumped back to their original location.

The three Zeta ships were there, but closer than before. Much closer.

"Guns raised?" he yelled.

"Guns raised!" Kito Marns called out.

"Fire!"

The *Barbican*'s biggest guns fired. Its heavily concentrated laser fire landed direct hits on the two smaller Zeta ships, tearing them into pieces in a lightshow of sparks and explosion.

"Mama ship is glowing red again!" Ulgari yelled.

Arken stared at the larger ship's underside turning crimson.

"Fire!" he yelled.

Again the *Barbican*'s guns fired, but the Zeta ship suddenly maneuvered upward and out of the line of fire. They learned quickly.

"Oh, shit!" Garth said, mouth falling open.

"What?" Arken barked.

"The rest of the ships! We've got a sea of glowing red out there! They're all moving forward and aiming at us."

"Get ready to jump!" Arken yelled.

"Ready to jump!" Rina called back.

"Jump!" he yelled, and Sasha Ulgari's hands raced around the console. He heard the ship roar as the sea of bright red lights turned white and the flash temporarily blinded him. The *Barbican* shuddered and shook, but much more violently this time, throwing him and several others to the floor. When it came to a stop, the sound of loud alarms and flashing lights on the console told him all was not okay. He pulled himself to his feet.

"We've been hit!" Marns yelled. "It burned through our shield!"

"Damage report!" he ordered. "Life support systems?"

"Life support online and A-ok!" a technician called out.

"Comms are down," Garth called. "Everything's gone, sir!"

"What?"

"They hit us with a whole lot of heat!" Garth said, shaking his head. "It's fried everything."

"We lost part of Hull D, sir!" another technician called.

"Shut the area off now!"

The technician urgently worked her console. "Area sealed. Evac in motion of surrounding hulls."

"They've got goddamn heat rays, sir," Ulgari said. "Makes our laser fire look like a tiny fucking spark."

"Navigation?" Arken asked looking over at Rina, who was madly tapping her screen.

"It's fried too, sir. Partially, at least. I can't bring up the system to view maps, but I still have access to our flight path records."

"What about the back-up system?" he asked. "Hull B wasn't hit, was it?"

"No, sir," Ulgari confirmed.

Rina tapped away at her screen, then looked up at him. "Back-up systems are working!"

"And the jump system?" Arken asked her.

"No, sir. It's down. Hull E took damage too."

Arken felt his jaw clenching. The *Barbican* was damaged and over forty Zeta ships still awaited them. To go back to the Zetas would be suicide. He looked at Rina "We can use the back-up system to get us home, yes?"

Rina looked up at him, pausing for a moment. She nodded, "Yes, sir. We can access the star maps."

He glanced around the flight deck, listened to the alarms sounding, watched the warning lights flickering along the console.

"Good," he said firmly. "Let's assess the damage and get this ship fixed. We need it stable and good enough for the journey home. Let's get moving!"

"We're leaving the Zetas, sir?" Marns asked.

"Yes," Arken said. "War has commenced and we're too outnumbered to do anything about it."

"So, what are we going to do?" Garth asked. "The comms are down. We can't warn Earth. We never got the last data packet out to them."

Arken looked at Garth, then at the rest of his team. "We'll go back to Earth and warn them ourselves."

"But what if the Zetas continue to head toward the signal from Earth? We can't beat them there without the jump system?"

"Then we do what we can. We get this ship stable and ready for travel, then we head back as fast as we can muster," he said firmly. "While we're doing that, we get someone down to Hull E to try and fix the damn jump system and we work on getting the comms system back online."

He moved back to his desk and looked around at his crew. "We came out here on a reconnaissance mission, and we got what we came for. Information." He ran his hand over his jaw. "The cost of that information was the start of a war. But out here, outnumbered, it's not a battle we can win. Not against those numbers, and not against their heat rays. We go back to Earth and try and warn them. And if we can't warn them, then we'll join arms and do battle where it counts. On Earth, where we can make a difference." He sat down in his chair. "We're going home, people," he said. "We're going home."

PART FIVE

19

Five, Six, Seven, Eight

Harris looked through the *Aurora*'s observation window at the orange and green landscape below. They were finally about to tour the Australian UNF facility and the Zeta ship buried nearby.

"So, this is the outback, huh?" Brown asked as they studied the vast red plains spread out before them, dotted with low, bushy scrublands and the occasional acacia tree.

"Kinda," Welles said. "It's more like halfway to the outback."

"It's very... flat, isn't it?" Yughi noted.

"Yeah," Harris agreed.

"It's unlike the other areas where the ships are buried," Steinberg commented.

"The ship is some way from here," Harris told him. "But you're right. It's pretty flat there, too."

"The other regions were different," Yughi said. "There must've been something that drew them here."

"Maybe they just randomly picked a spot," Gregson shrugged. "And this was it for the Australian continent."

"Maybe they chose the areas based on landscapes," Evenssen offered. "The desert mountains in Egypt, the underground caverns in New Mexico, close to the ocean here in Australia. Maybe the locations were purely for research."

"To see how their new planet was doing," Hunter added.

"Where were the others located?" Frazer asked, as he flicked switches on the flight deck console.

"Mexico, Peru and China," Harris told them.

"In Peru it was found in the Andes," Yughi said.

"High altitude mountains," Tikaani nodded.

"In China, it was found in the Bayanbulak Grasslands," Yughi continued, "and in Mexico it was found near the Sistema Dos Ojos."

"What's that?" Murphy asked.

"It's a flooded cave system," Yughi told him.

"So there is a correlation of sorts," Gregson said. "I'm hearing a lot of mountains, caves and water."

"Maybe that's what their home planet is like?" Evenssen mused.

"Quite likely," Harris said. "If they found a system similar to theirs, and a planet with similar weather and geography, that may have been why they decided to colonize the planet with their creations."

Murphy frowned. "I still can't quite get my head around this."

"What?" Harris arched his eyebrow.

"I can get them making *us*, but I don't get how they created the animals."

"We're all part of the animal kingdom," Yughi said.

"But I am not like a frog," Murphy said. "How did we come from the same makers?"

"We didn't," Gregson told him. "We evolved from the apes. We derived from the mammalian Zeta."

"The Alma Mater," Yughi said.

"Llama mater?" Murphy's face crinkled in confusion.

"*Alma Mater*," Gregson said. "The frogs came from the one they're calling Amphibia."

Tikaani slapped Murphy on the shoulder. "I'm with you. This shit is too weird."

"I'll say," Murphy shook his head. "But I hope the Zetas get a real shock when they see what their apes have evolved into."

"So, we think the location of the Australian Zeta ship is because of the ocean?" Hunter asked.

"Must be," Yughi shrugged.

"I think it's a combination," Harris said. "It would seem they like mountains and caves and water, but I also think they might have just spread out randomly to run tests and see how their experiment was going. And I think they were surprised at just how well everything was thriving here. Particularly when they discovered the HH."

"I'll say. Can you imagine that?" Hunter said. "The Zetas turning up and thinking, 'Whoa, who the fuck are you?'"

"Pity the HH weren't exactly the sharpest tools on the block, though, right?" Evenssen said.

Tikaani smiled. "They would've been like: Hey, you're cute but so damn dumb. I'm gonna make you my slave-pet."

"Yeah, well, next time they come here, they won't be saying that," Harris said bluntly.

"UNF facility is on approach," Frazer called out. "Here's the satellite plain."

They stared in awe at the large white dishes that covered the ground as far as their Alpha eyes could see. These devices, created by intelligent humans, had called deep into space and made contact with their original makers.

He felt a shiver run down his spine as his Overseers appeared in his mind. And as he stared at the rows of white satellite dishes on parade, he couldn't help but wonder whether the evolved human's intelligence that had brought it so far in life, could actually be the thing to bring about its downfall.

*

Harris entered the UNF facility, his team following close behind.

"Major Harris!" archaeologist Matthew Ross greeted him. "Welcome!"

Harris stepped forward as Ross introduced the woman standing beside him.

"This is Dr. Valerie Pullman," Ross said. "She's in charge of this facility."

Harris held his hand out and shook with Valerie. Attractive and gracious, he guessed she was in her early sixties, but the spark in her eyes told him she was very much in her prime.

"Call me Valerie," she told Harris. "It'll be my pleasure to show you around the facility."

"Thank you."

"I'll let you tour the facility first," Ross said, "then we'll head out to the Zeta ship."

"Sounds good to me. Let's get to it, shall we?" Harris said.

Carrie followed Harris and the farmer into the tunnels that led to the buried Australian ship, as the team trailed behind them. The entrance was located behind a low hill on a sprawling property once owned by the government, but since sold to the UNF under the guise of research purposes. Basically, a scientist from the nearby UNF facility had been conducting searches of the surrounding areas in the hope of finding another ship and had eventually stumbled upon this one. It had been the most recent find, and considered the most interesting, given its location nearby to the comms facility. The UNF quickly paid an ex-soldier good money to work the land as a farmer, a cover for what it really held. And it was this ex-soldier turned farmer, who had worked the land for years, who led them to the ship now.

"It's amazing no-one found this earlier than they did," Carrie said.

Harris shrugged. "It was on unused government land, away from any towns or major roads. No-one would come across it in the normal run of things."

They'd spent the morning looking around the UNF facility. It wasn't as large as Carrie had been expecting, but it was spread over two floors: a functional ground level where all the equipment was and the work was done, and a slightly more homely basement level where the staff on duty lived. After the short tour they found themselves in the main comms room, lined with consoles and screens, listening to the Zeta signal again. Valerie and one of her technicians, Tim, showed them a comparison diagnostic of the original signals and the second signal received by the *Barbican*. It was clear they were different, and yet so similar. But although they'd uncovered nothing new with the visit, it still gave Carrie a flush of anticipation at being in the very facility that had been so pivotal to the comms with the Zetas all these years. The very facility to which she would return one day when the Zetas finally arrived. If their dreams were real, that is.

After a three and a half hour drive, they turned their attention from the UNF facility to the Australian Zeta ship.

As Matthew Ross had warned them, the buried Zeta ship turned out to be no different to the one near the Carlsbad Caverns in New Mexico. Again, Carrie was intrigued by the Zeta flight deck, tracing her fingers along the console, watching the blue light appear beneath her fingertips. She looked over at Harris's fingers as he did the same and saw it glow with much more vigor.

She and Harris locked eyes, before he quickly removed his fingers.

Carrie cleared her throat, darting glances at the others. "Excuse me, sir?" she said. "Can I have a word?"

Harris eyed her, then nodded and they both left the ship. They emerged from the short tunnel and stepped outside onto a grassy field. The sun was out and a strong breeze blew her hair. She saw sheep further along in the field and wondered which way the ocean was. She looked at Harris, her mind in overdrive, thinking about the Zeta thought-technology again.

"What is it?" Harris asked her.

"This thought-technology, the Zetas place their hands on the console, think their instructions and it transfers to the ship, right?"

"That's the theory," Harris said. "The flight deck acts as an axon terminal between the Zeta and the ship. It somehow connects to their consciousness."

Carrie stared back at him. "Just like us. Connected by thought. What are the chances of us having time alone with the ship?"

"You and me?" he quirked an eyebrow.

"We need to explore the thought-technology, with your gift. Our connection."

"Welles, our connection is subconscious. We discussed this."

"But it's similar to us, yes?" she pushed.

Harris stared at her. "I guess. In a way."

"We need to make our connection conscious," she said. "If we figure that out, then maybe we could figure out the thought-technology. If you know how to consciously connect, then maybe that Zeta ship will let you inside. Your fingers glow way brighter on that console than anyone else, you know it."

Harris lowered his eyes to the ground and rubbed the back of his neck. She could see he was still fighting the idea of the Zeta inside him.

"You told me if I got in trouble to think of you, to let you know I was in trouble. That's what I did. When Drazen attacked in Eden, I thought of you. I pictured your face. Consciously. And you came to help me, because you knew, didn't you? That I was in trouble. How did you know?"

A moment of silence passed, before Harris reluctantly looked back up at her. "I felt it in my gut. Down my spine."

Carrie stepped forward, nodding. "So, my conscious thought connected to yours. At least, to you physically. I consciously pictured your face and screamed for you to help me, and you knew. You physically felt I was in trouble and you came. My *thought*, connected to you *physically*." She stepped closer until she stood right in front of him, then glanced around, ensuring the others were still inside. "What happened in Eden… it was like I was the Zeta and you were the ship. I was in trouble, I thought of you, called for help, and you came." Carrie paused feeling a little shocked by this herself. "There must be more Zeta in me than I thought too."

Harris stared at her but didn't speak.

"Your family gift is the axon terminal between us, is the thought-technology itself," she said. "I think your family gift has only been subconscious because no-one has tried to raise it before. I think it's our job to raise it to the next level. I think that's why we're going to be important in the invasion. I think this connection could be our edge."

"It was always our edge," he told her. "I can dream the future and we can heed the warnings."

"Dreams and warnings will only give us so much. The connection is the key. That can give us real-time benefits. If we can learn to communicate out on the battlefield, if we lose comms; if we're on the other side of the planet to each other. Imagine what we could do then. Imagine what we could do if we could learn to control one of the Zeta ships. Imagine what we could do if we connect to one and take a look inside, the information we could get."

His eyes narrowed a little, studying her.

"You're handling this well," he told her. "Better than me."

She smiled back, then her face turned serious. "I've been through hell, sir. But I made it out the other side and I don't plan on going back. Ever. I'm done with being a victim. I'm in charge now, of my life, of my children's lives. From this point forward, I'm the hero of my story. No-one else. The Zetas are coming. War is coming. I will do what is necessary to survive."

A smile traced along Harris's lips. He held out his palm. "It's about time, sergeant."

She smiled back and reached out to slap his hand. As she did, she felt that painful spark of connection. They both looked down at their hands, then back at each other.

"We need to harness your gift, sir," she said firmly. "We need to raise it to a conscious level. It's the only way we'll beat them. And we need time alone with a Zeta ship to figure it out."

Harris gazed at her thoughtfully. "How do you propose we do that? All the ships are guarded 24/7."

"We could request time alone in there," she shrugged.

"To do what? What would we tell them?"

"Maybe if you told Marchant the truth—"

"No," he said firmly.

"We need time with the ships."

He sighed heavily. "There's no point, Welles. The ships are in hibernation. There's nothing I can do until they awake."

"But—" Carrie didn't get to finish her protest, however. Ross and McKinley came out of the ship then, and the rest of the *Aurora* team followed. Harris threw her a look, then turned and moved toward them.

General Berger entered the small lab in the bowels of Command, where Professor Sharley had been working, via video transmission, with his team in what was now called the JEM facility. The professor sat at a bench reviewing something on a monitor in front of him, while his two guards stood by the door.

Sharley looked up. "General? I wasn't expecting a visit."

"I've come for a status report," Berger said. Given the news he'd just received from the *Barbican* that they had crossed paths with over 40 ships, he had to admit he was a little concerned. Although 40 ships did not seem that great a number, without any knowledge of what those ships could do, anything was possible. And that's what worried him. The *Barbican* was one ship. What could it do against 40 if they attacked? It could be weeks, months until Command received the next signal, until they knew whether the *Barbican* had been destroyed.

The professor smiled and turned the screen slightly to face him. "Congratulations, general. You're going to become a grandaddy," he smiled.

Berger stared at the enhanced image of a cluster of cells on-screen. "What's this?"

"This is Jesse Ethan McKinley 404."

Berger furrowed his brow at Sharley.

Sharley rephrased. "This is JEM clone number 404," he said.

"How many clones have you created so far?" Berger asked.

"We are swiftly approaching 500. The agreed amount to start with."

Berger nodded, examining the image again. He felt a sense of trepidation shoot through him, but his common sense was quickly pushed aside by another sense of hope. He couldn't look at these cells, these clones, and think of Welles or McKinley or their boy, Jesse. He had to think of what would happen if the Earth was invaded. He had to think of sending these numbered JEM clones out to meet them and do what needed to be done. He had to think of saving Earth. Using the DNA of Welles and McKinley and Jesse without their knowledge was just a small price to pay. Besides, his head legal man, Dustin Clintock, had assured him that what he'd done was covered by the contract they'd signed. Still, now the program was in motion, he'd have to think about shifting the clones to another site away from Centralis. Somewhere Welles and McKinley would never discover them.

"Are you pleased?" Sharley smiled.

Berger nodded. "How far along are they?"

"Two weeks."

Berger nodded again. This JEM army would be barley 20 years old when the Zeta signals were due to hit Earth. It would have to do. Although he did have concerns about the *Barbican* crossing paths with this group of 40 earlier than planned. If things turned out for the worst and the Zetas hit early, these clones would be useless to him.

"But our original JEM clone is now three and a half months old," Sharley said. "Would you like to see him?"

Berger looked into the professor's eyes and saw the excitement behind them. He nodded, and Sharley got to work bringing up another image on the screen. Berger studied the still-forming Alpha encased in its organic womb, nestled in its life-supporting pod case; its stunted body and odd head. "Is it healthy?"

"Very," Sharley smiled.

"And it has the senses?"

"Yes."

Berger thought of the cells again, then of the image before him; seeing his program literally coming to life before his eyes.

"Six months and this one will be born, general."

"We'll need to arrange nursemaids."

"No."

"No?"

"Mothers make them weak, general. Human connections will make them weak. They will be artificially fed. They will be raised in a sterile environment. They must be raised to fight their Zeta enemy."

The general felt the lack of emotion in Sharley's voice settle uneasily in the air around him. But he knew the Professor was right. He stared at Sharley, then he turned his eyes back to JEM clone 1.

Harris sat down across from Colonel Marchant in his office.

"I just received the latest update from Colonel Hensford of Station Navarone," he said to the colonel. "They've made good progress with some of the smaller ships, but I'm more keen to see their progress on the larger warships. That's what we're going to need. Firepower."

"Warships take time and money. They'll happen. And they're making headway on replicating the material of the Zeta ships."

"The sooner the better," Harris said. "We need to be ready just in case."

Marchant gave him a funny look. "There you go again," he said, eyes narrowed. "Worrying about early attacks. Do you know something I don't?"

"What's the latest from the *Barbican*?"

Marchant paused and sat back in his chair. He didn't answer.

"Sir?" Harris pushed, noticing the worried look in his eyes.

Marchant sighed and ran a hand over his hair. "We got word... they'd come across about 40-odd Zeta ships."

"What?" Harris sat forward. "When?"

"We received the comms earlier today. Of course, the message was sent some time ago."

"How long?"

Marchant shrugged.

"How long?" he repeated.

"We're not worried yet, but…"

"But?"

"They were only a fifth of the way to ZA, Harris."

He stared at Marchant. "You think they're dead?"

"We don't know."

"So, about those warships, then?"

Marchant looked at him, silent.

"I want more units," Harris said. "I've had three units for a while now. They're my leaders and they're well trained. Now it's time to expand."

"According to the last Zeta comms the facility received, the invasion is still 20 years away, Harris."

"You haven't heard from the *Barbican*. If they crossed paths with 40 Zeta ships and were destroyed, that means those 40 or so ships could be on our doorstep soon. Every day we don't roll this program out is a day we could be annihilated."

"The plan was to start rolling out the Alpha units in waves, from 10 years out."

"We don't have another 10 years. I want more now," Harris said. "You've left me in charge of the Alpha soldiers. It is my job to ensure we protect the people. So let me do that. We need to have a Plan B. And I'm not talking about some street fighters!"

Marchant gave him a surprised look.

"Oh, you think I didn't know about that?" Harris said. "If we get attacked early, I need some grunt to go at them with. Three units won't cut it."

Marchant steepled his hands and considered Harris.

"Give me 50 units."

Marchant choked a laugh. "Excuse me?"

"Alright, 40."

"Harris—"

"Thirty. If they attack us we need a defense system in place. Three units is not enough if they hit the ground and come out of those ships. That's one unit per planet."

"The Alpha units are a second wave should our current ships and weaponry in the skies not be enough."

"And if they aren't?" Harris stared at him. "You expect three units to stop them if they hit the ground?"

"We'll still have all our human units, Harris."

"And if they're not enough? If they don't cut it against the Zetas?"

Marchant sighed. "Let me speak with the general."

"The UNF want this. That's why they started this program in the first place. Help me to help you."

Marchant stared at him. "Why are you so sure about this? That they're going to hit us early."

Harris was getting older and more tired of this political bullshit, of fighting to get the resources and information he needed. "If I told you, you wouldn't believe me."

"Try me."

Harris stared at Marchant. Eventually, he shrugged. "I can dream the future and I get strong gut feelings. I dreamed this. I keep dreaming this. I know it's going to happen."

Marchant stared back straight-faced for a moment, before he cracked up laughing. He pointed at Harris. "You had me for a second there!"

Harris gave a cheesy grin. "I told you, you wouldn't believe me."

"No, really, why?"

"Because if I'm going into a fight, I want to make sure I can win. Give me more units."

Marchant thought for a moment, then sighed. "I gotta say, this report from the *Barbican* has us worried and it'll be months until we know what the outcome was."

"Do you trust me?"

Marchant studied him a moment, then gave a nod.

"Then trust me to do this. Give me more units, and trust me to manage them."

Marchant considered his words. "I'll see what I can do."

PART SIX

20

Zenith

Carrie pounded the treadmill, exhaling in short bursts. She eyed the team working around her. Tikaani was lifting weights with Brown and McKinley, her thick arms bulging with strength. Steinberg was on his own with a skip rope, looking like a giant rabbit on speed. Murphy, Evenssen and Frazer were on the floor doing rounds of push-ups and sit-ups. Yughi was over a bit further doing something that looked like a cross between karate and Systema or something. And Hunter and Colt were over on the mats working through some moves.

Carrie looked at her and smiled. Colt had been back in the *Aurora* team – on a part-time basis – for almost two years now. It had taken a good eighteen months after her return, and many Alpha outbursts since, but she had eventually stabilized enough to rejoin the *Aurora* crew for training. Building the trust between Colt and the UNF had been a delicate process, but it had eventually been achieved. Carrie and Brown had acted like crutches to help her through it. Although, for the most part, Carrie let Brown take the lead. He had that link with her family and, well, Carrie could understand if Colt had any felt resentment for the way things had turned out. They'd both been through similar situations, but Carrie's had worked out far more in her favor than Colt's had.

Carrie turned her eyes to Brown, watching him lifting his weights. He was still as fit and as strong as he'd ever been. She smiled to herself as she remembered what she had witnessed 18 months ago. The moment that Colt had relented and let herself trust someone again. She'd had another outburst in training and Brown had removed her from the situation, taking her back to the Alpha village. Carrie had gone to find them to see if she was okay, and saw them sitting on the front steps of Colt's place. They were still the only ones in the village so far. Carrie had paused at the corner of one building and just watched them, not sure whether she should approach. Colt was crying, still angry, and Brown was talking to her in hushed but firm tones, reasoning with her.

Colt wiped her tears and the silence had sat for a moment. Then Colt had looked at Brown and shaken her head. "Why do you put up with me?"

Brown had shrugged his Alpha shoulders. "I don't know."

Colt had stared at him. "You understand me, don't you?" she'd said. "Somehow, you understand my crazy ass?"

Brown had looked back at Colt, then down at his shirt as Colt scrunched it within her fist.

"You understand me," Colt said, more quietly this time, nodding as she looked at him. The silence had sat for a few moments, before Colt suddenly leaned forward and planted a kiss on Brown's mouth. He'd looked surprised at first, when she first pulled back, but the surprise didn't last long. He raised his hand to cup the side of her face, then pulled her forward and kissed her back. And not much longer after that they'd stood and Colt, still clenching his shirt in her fist, had led Brown inside her house.

Carrie, still on the treadmill, glanced back at Colt over on the mats with Hunter and smiled again. Colt and Brown had become the second recorded Alpha couple in history. And the result of their pairing had been their little girl, Alinta, who would soon turn 1.

Carrie felt a contentment. The team were training well, and for years now they had been back on normal duty. Except for Carrie and Colt, who joined them only when the team was back in town. The UNF demanded that one parent should remain with their Alpha children on the ground, in case issues arose that needed to be dealt with swiftly. So far there hadn't been any major incidents, only the occasional Alpha outburst, but both Carrie and Colt were working hard to help their children retain their calm and release their Alpha energy the right way.

So the team had worked in harmony alongside the *Carcharias* and Morrell's unit for some time, easily handling their normal UNF duties. In fact, they now had the best records of service within the UNF. Largely sent on jobs that involved apprehending hostiles, as opposed to aiding civilians, they had a 100 percent success rate.

The team still didn't know how close the Zetas were. Harris hadn't told them about the early invasion he was expecting, but it was almost like they sensed it. They saw the determination Harris had, the determination that she and McKinley echoed. They knew about the *Barbican* running into over 40 ships and that no word had been heard from them since. And they'd heard the talk of more Alpha units joining them soon. Everything seemed to be coming to a head.

She turned the treadmill off and slowed to a stop. Grabbing her towel, she wiped her face and looked up at the scoreboard overhead. She viewed the names, her eyes lingering on the deceased: Smith, Louis, Carter, Bulk, Doc and Packham. Of course, she lingered the longest on Doc's name, picturing that pearly smile, those brown eyes. It made her think of the Blue Nova medal that Ellen Walker had given her, and she wondered whether one day she would see Brody's name on that board. And Freya's and Jesse's. She knew that Doc would've been proud of how his son was growing up. Carrie found herself stopping often and staring at her son. Amazed that, so far, she had managed to raise such a smart and patient Alpha boy. He was definitely Doc's son in that regard. He showed little of her foolish fire. No, Freya had inherited that. Although Carrie did her best to blame that on McKinley's genetics, to his consistent rebuttals.

But Freya had so much courage. She wasn't frightened of anything, always rushing in, ready to give something a go. Brody would always hesitate, size things up, before he was all in. He too had courage, but it was a reserved, measured courage. And that was why she knew he'd make a good leader one day.

Jesse was a little of both. He had patience, God knows where from. Carrie knew it couldn't have been from her or McKinley, so it had to be from one of their parents or grandparents. But it had been so long now since her mother had died that she struggled to pinpoint exact qualities about her. But Jesse balanced out that patience with a show of temper if he believed in something strongly enough. That, Carrie knew, was directly from his father. Or maybe her, if she was being honest.

All three of her Alpha children were smart, and their physical prowess was clear. She now avoided taking them to parks and such, as they always showed up other kids their age. Swinging around on the monkey bars, racing around on the lawn. It was a sad fact, but Carrie had to keep their activity to the confines of Command or the *Aurora*, although the positive outcome was that her children could watch the *Aurora* soldiers train, and learn from them when there. More than that, they could also spend some time on the shooting range, and already one thing was abundantly clear: her children were developing quite the aim. Thankfully, with Colt's kids at the village, they were given the opportunity to socialize and, well, be kids, with other kids who understood what it was like to be an Alpha.

Carrie couldn't help but think how weird it was that her children had become such good friends with Chet and Logan's children. Who would've ever thought that could be possible? Had they been raised by Chet and Logan, it would've been a different story, but raised by Colt and Brown, these boys, like Carrie's children, could be an asset in the years to come.

Colt's kids were naturally also quite adept, but they still had a little bit of roughness, rawness about them. Casim was smart. The smartest of all of them, actually, according to his IQ. Something he must've inherited from Chet, no doubt. Brody and Freya were close second placers, though.

Where Casim was methodical and thoughtful, Malik was definitely a physical Alpha, much like his father Logan. In that respect, Malik was like Jesse. They both liked the outdoors and always seemed to feel the need to burn off energy, running around. And then there was little Alinta Brown, the baby of the bunch; it was too early yet to tell just what kind of Alpha she would grow up to become.

Carrie felt a little guilty for it, but she regularly checked on their schooling at Command, by way of Archie. She'd have him hook into Command's systems and watch their classes and report back. It was probably a step too far, but given how important their future was, she wasn't about to take any chances with her children's lives.

For the most part, Carrie was happy with their teachers, and Archie provided good back-up with homework questions, recalling sound bites of things the teachers said, playing them to the children. In fact, Archie had become almost like a treasured family pet to the children. More than that: a favorite uncle. They chatted to him all the time. It was odd, them effectively talking to a software system, befriending it, but he'd been there for as long as they could remember. He was an ally, a loyal pet, a friend that would never die on them. Even Carrie herself had come to feel that way about Archie. Her AIS had become a part of her family.

Harris sipped his beer and looked around the communal area of the UNFASP village, where his team had gathered to celebrate his recent promotion.

"Colonel Harris," the newly promoted Major General Marchant called.

Harris turned to him.

"Congratulations again on your promotion," Marchant said.

"Thank you, sir. Congratulations to you too." It had taken some negotiation, but Harris had managed to enroll another six units into the Alpha program, albeit a modified version of it. There were two new Earth Duty units, 1217 and 719, that had been fully converted into Alphas, and four Space Duty ships enrolled but not yet physically converted: UNF *Valor*, UNF *Llangollen*, UNF *Stanmore*, and UNF *Ruediger*. Although the *Ruediger* and *Stanmore* were of equal size to the *Aurora* and *Carcharias*, the *Llangollen* was larger, and the *Valor* larger still. Marchant had agreed to advise the crews of these ships about the Zeta threat, but they had not yet been advised of the UNFASP program or their potential to take part it in. The UNF wasn't quite ready for another 1100 Alpha soldiers to be walking around among the general population just yet.

Harris glanced around at all those gathered. Brown was taking charge over by the BBQ, while the rest spread out around the tables.

"Thank you for letting the families come," Harris said.

"No problem," Marchant replied. "It's important they celebrate with you. And a gathering here at Command shouldn't see you end up on the news," he said, referring to the Eden incident, years ago.

Harris smiled. "No."

"Major General?" Murphy called to Marchant. "Beer?"

Marchant smiled and walked toward him. "Don't mind if I do."

Harris smiled as Taya moved to wrap her arm around him. "Colonel Harris," she said quietly. "I really do like the sound of that."

"It sounds… old," Harris mused aloud.

"Well," Taya smiled touching the gray that had begun to streak though the sides of his hair, "you are. But don't worry. You still look good, Saul. *Very* good."

He flashed her a warm Alpha look, then glanced down to see Sarai standing in front of him. "Why don't you go play with the other kids, Sarai?"

She looked around shyly at the others. Being based on the mainland with her mother, she rarely mixed with the Alpha kids.

Welles, standing close by, overhead the conversation and walked up to his daughter. "Hi, Sarai," she said. "Remember me? I'm Carrie. Do you want to play with the others?"

Sarai shook her head shyly and moved closer to Harris. He smiled down at his five and a half year old daughter.

"It's okay, sweetie," Welles smiled. "If you don't want to play with them, would you like to play with me instead?"

Sarai looked at Welles, analyzed her for a moment, then gave a silent nod.

"Okay!" Welles smiled broadly, then held her hand out for Sarai to take. "Come on, what shall we play with first?"

Harris watched as Welles took Sarai over to a toy box not far from where the other children played.

"That's nice of her," Taya smiled, then moved to talk with Colt.

Harris watched as Welles got down on her knees and began playing with Sarai. His daughter seemed to watch her, curiously. He turned his eyes to Brody and Freya, the seven year olds ran around in the distance with kites, laughing and calling to each other, while McKinley watched on. Harris scanned his eyes to Malik, Casim and Jesse in the sandpit playing with toy PVs. Further on, Hunter and Lei's boys kicked a football around, occasionally kicking it over to Brody who would catch it and kick it back while still flying his kite. Then he turned his eyes to little Alinta sitting in Colt's lap, cuddling a soft toy.

He looked around at the rest of the team. Steinberg's wife Marisol was there, as were Gregson's Sheree and Hunter's Lei. Tikaani's girlfriend, Paulita, had come, as had Frazer's wife, Jennifer. Yughi's wife and Evenssen's girlfriend had been unable to come, and Murphy was currently single. For the most part, Harris's Alpha soldiers had found happiness over the years, but those with human wives had not bred, following their UNF contracts. Some had confided in their partners the truth of their Alpha, some still hadn't. But none had told their partners of what awaited in the future: the Zetas. This gathering was a mix of knowledge and ignorance, of innocence and the cold, hard truth.

A breeze swirled around Harris and he looked up into the sky. It was overcast. His eyes caught on the red kite Freya was flying, the sounds of her laughter. Harris tried to smile, but it didn't reach his eyes. This, he knew, was the calm before the storm. This was a time of innocence that they would one day look back on and wish they could once again be a part of. It made him sad to think this might not last.

Welles came back to stand by him then. He looked back at Sarai and saw her playing with Jesse in the sandpit.

"She's fine," Welles said, "I've left them to it."

"Thanks," he said.

"No problem, she's a gorgeous kid." Welles said, looking around. "Where's Ty? He didn't come to celebrate his old man's promotion?"

Harris sipped his beer, almost as a means to bite his tongue. "Nothing gets in the way of his basketball these days."

"Oh," Welles said.

"Didn't you know, Welles? The kid's fast becoming a big star."

Carrie followed Harris and Major General Marchant into the large warehouse. Located in the middle of Wyoming, it was a relatively new UNF facility and one that was at the heart of the Advanced Weapons And Fleet Program. They'd passed several security measures to get this far, and as they stepped into the main workshop area, Carrie was impressed by what she saw.

A line of five prototype aircraft sat along the left-hand side of the large complex. One white, two gray, and two black, sleekly glistening under the bright lights of the enormous building.

"I am in love," Hunter said walking over to them and running his hand along the side of one of them. Frazer was beside him, grinning like a kid at Christmas. The two pilots had bonded over the years, although they still often argued about each other's flying styles: Frazer deemed Hunter too cautious and Hunter deemed Frazer too reckless.

Carrie's children ran over to the pilots. The twins, now eight, and Jesse, six, gasped words like "Excello!" and "Starship!" at the sight. 'Starship' being the latest slang they used for something that was considered generally 'awesome'.

"I think we just lost our pilots to some ship porn," Tikaani said.

Murphy laughed as McKinley, Steinberg and Brown grinned. Evenssen and Yughi moved to join Hunter and Frazer in adoration.

"Boys and their toys," Colt said, shaking her head.

"When you're ready?" Major General Marchant called, sounding unimpressed as he watched Hunter and the guys over by the prototypes. This was the last visit in a tour the team had been doing, studying the AWAFP facilities. Carrie had noted that the program was coming along nicely, but with just two years left until Harris's prescient dream became reality, they were not going to be ready in time.

"Sir," Hunter said walking over to Marchant, "when do I get to test run these babies?"

"When they're ready," Marchant said bluntly, then introduced the man standing next to him. "This is the Fleet Program's Director, Anton Avilov. He'll be taking you on a tour of the facilities today. Colonel Harris?"

Harris stepped forward and personal introductions were made. All the while Hunter and Frazer stayed close to Harris's side, eager to be in on things. This was their area of expertise, after all. Carrie smiled at their enthusiasm, then glanced around the vast area. She saw the occasional workstation dotted throughout and people gathered in twos and threes leaning in over glass tabletops, where no doubt ship schematics were being displayed and analyzed.

"This place is so starship!" Freya said at her side. At eight she was already as tall as Carrie's bicep. Carrie smiled at her daughter and squeezed her into her side. Freya was most definitely following in the footsteps of her godparents, Hunter and Packham, with her love for everything that could fly. Whether it was growing up with a view of the Space Dock or whether it was something inherent, Carrie felt Freya's future was becoming clearer by the day. Watching her daughter's eyes shine with excitement as she viewed the prototype ships, Carrie sensed that one day Freya would be flying them. That's why she'd requested the children come along for this tour. Freya would never forgive her if she missed out on this.

"Oh, my god!" she heard a male voice say over to her right. "Welles? Is that you, Welles?"

Carrie turned and saw a tall, lean man standing there. He looked familiar, but it wasn't until he pushed his glasses up, that she realized who it was.

"It's me! Colberge. From the *Vortex*!" he said, waving a hand.

"Holy shit," Carrie said.

"Who's that?" Jesse asked, eyeing the man.

She looked at her son and ruffled his blond hair. "Someone I used to work on a ship with once." She looked back at the man. "Colberge?" she said, making her way over to him. "Is that really you?"

He laughed. "Yeah! My god, how long has it been?"

Carrie thought for a moment, then glanced back at Brody and Freya. "I'd say it's been about nine years."

"Wow," Colberge said, adjusting his glasses again as he studied the children. "Are they yours?"

Carrie nodded. "Uh-huh." She introduced them, then turned her eyes back to Colberge and looked him up and down. "You've filled out a little."

He laughed again, glancing down at his body. "I'm still skinny."

"Not *as* skinny," she smiled, then added, "Scratch."

Colberge blushed at his old nickname. "What are you doing here?"

"I could ask you the same question. You work here now?"

"Yeah. I eventually got transferred off the *Vortex* and worked with Command's aeronautics division for a while. It seems I caught someone's eye and got a boost to here."

"What are you working on?"

"Er," he adjusted his glasses again, "can't really say. It's classified."

"Colberge," she said, dryly, "we're in the AWAFP facility. I was allowed inside. Major General Marchant is showing us around."

Colberge paused. "Er, so you know about AWAFP?" Although this was clearly identified as a UNF ship facility, the AWAFP program wasn't exactly advertised as a feature in its public documentation.

She smiled and motioned to the *Aurora* team. "We'll be the ones flying the ships."

"No shit," Colberge smiled. "How about that!"

"How about that," Carrie smiled back.

"Hey, is that Lieutenant Gregson?" Colberge squinted his eyes at the team in the distance.

"Sure is. He's been our medic for a long time now."

"Small world, huh?"

"It is indeed," she said, eyeing him up and down again. "Who would've thought all that ship doodling you did on the *Vortex* would result in you ending up here?"

Colberge blushed again.

"So," Carrie glanced over to the prototypes, "any of these yours?"

Colberge adjusted his glasses, eyeing the aircraft lined against the wall, as Freya moved up beside them.

"Yeah, three of them are mine," he said, eyes shining with pride.

"Three?" Carrie raised her eyebrows. "Go, Colberge!"

"Well," he blushed slightly again, "we work in teams so they're not, like, entirely mine. But I came up with the basic design, and we've tweaked them as a team from there."

"Which three?" Carrie asked.

"The white one, she's called the Snowdrop. She's fast and zippy, for a single pilot."

"I LOVE her!" Freya interrupted, eyes as wide as her smile.

Colberge laughed. "The flatter-looking gray one, she's called the Chameleon. She's a pilotless gal with a fully-integrated onboard system linked to Command. Basically, she's like a full-sized Bluebird, fully camouflaged. And the black one with the sharper nose, she's called the Midnight Echo. She's the fastest plane we've got."

Carrie nodded briefly, eyeing the prototypes. "These are very cool, Colberge. Which one is your favorite?"

"Aw, that would be like me asking you to choose between your kids. I can't pick a favorite. They're all my babies."

"Oh, that's easy. I'm her favorite," Freya piped up, grinning up at him.

"Are not!" Brody said, joining them. Carrie laughed at them.

"No, *I'm* her favorite!" Jesse said, throwing his arms around her and squeezing her in a hug.

"I want to sit in one," Freya said to Colberge. "Can I go sit in one?"

"Er..." He adjusted his glasses.

"Welles!" Harris called, waving her back.

"Maybe later, Frey," Carrie said, tapping her on the shoulder. "We gotta get back."

Freya pouted her bottom lip, but the three kids turned and headed back to the others.

"It was good to see you, Colberge."

"Yes," Colberge said, shaking her outstretched hand, "and you."

"I'll let Gregson know you're here. No doubt I'll be seeing you around," Carrie smiled, then turned and headed back to Harris.

Harris studied Taya carefully. She sat up in the bed, leaning back against the headboard, her face turned toward the window, the early morning light bathing her in a soft gray glow. Naturally, she was shocked. She breathed as though he had winded her, sucker punched her right in the gut. In a way he had. Because he'd finally told her the truth about the invasion.

It had been a long time coming, but he could feel it swirling in his gut now. It was drawing close. Very close. They still had not heard from the *Barbican*; the ship had made contact with over forty Zeta ships and they'd never communicated again. Harris knew that could only mean one thing. The Zetas had engaged the *Barbican* and, outnumbered, it had lost – which meant war had started, and an invasion could be imminent. So, he'd run out of time. He'd given Taya as long as he could to enjoy innocence, but now he had to give her time to get her head around things, so that when it came, she would be prepared. Prepared to survive.

"Tay?" he said gently.

She didn't respond. He saw a tear roll down her cheek. What cut him the most was that she never doubted him. Never for a second thought he was joking, or that this wasn't real. Maybe his dreams had given him away. After all, that was how this conversation had started: his awakening from another violent and seemingly very real dream of bright lights, of pain, of burning flesh. With each passing day they had been increasing. He'd long lost the ability to hide them from her, with the obvious sweat-soaked sheets and flailing Alpha limbs that sometimes hit her in the middle of the night, the shouting and yelling.

And he wasn't the only one.

Some nights it happened in stereo, as though Sarai was dreaming the same dreams as he.

The first time he knew she was just like his grandmother Sibbie, a See'er, was just after Sarai had turned three. She'd often woken in the night, but when she was a baby he could write it off as a natural occurrence. But the older she got, and the more she could formulate words, he knew. Sarai shared his grandmother Sibbie's gift alright and would be just as strong. Maybe stronger. When he had first discovered the truth, he had offered to check on Sarai that night, leaving Taya behind in their bed. He'd asked Sarai what was wrong, and she'd said just a few sleepy words that told him everything he needed to know: *ships in the sky*. He hadn't been ready to tell Taya back then, and it was hard to keep it hidden given he wasn't always at home to tend to Sarai in the night. But whenever he was home he always offered to go comfort their daughter if she ever woke. He would counsel her, tell her that everything was okay, that the dreams were normal, but special. He would encourage her to share them, but being so young they were often muddled and confused, told in parts, like he was given only part of a jigsaw and told to make sense of it.

But he made sure to always tell her that it was a good thing. He told her to embrace it. Just like his own mother should've done with him.

He confessed to his sister, Holly, about Sarai's gift and it didn't surprise her. Holly told him that she already sensed it, like maybe somewhere deep inside her the memory of the gift survived in her own DNA. They were from the same ancestry, after all. She'd gleaned from her research that the children of Guardians, of Connectors, always had the gift strongly. Just like the Sense'er in Etta had been strong, because she was the daughter of the Guardian, Charles Washington.

And he kept dreaming: that dream of standing on that lookout on the eve of the great war, Sarai walking out and standing beside him. She would be there. At the end. They would stand together, and he wanted to prepare her as best he could for that.

It made him think about the thought-technology of the Zetas, of Welles's theory, that maybe he was a direct descendant of a Zeta-HH pairing, left behind when the Zetas fled Earth. That his daughter, Sarai, was also a direct descendant. He had asked Holly to trace their family history back as far as she could go, and given her as much support as he could. It had taken her years, but she had done a great job, tracing one line, his mother's, right back to Africa, until records ceased to exist. And he knew, he felt it in the blood that coursed through his veins, that's where it had started. Hundreds of thousands of years of his ancestry had begun with the invading Zetas and the enslaved HH.

And he was ready. Eager, even, to finally meet his maker.

And to ensure that no-one in his family would ever be a slave again.

This latest violent dream had decided for him: it was time to tell Taya the truth. She'd known for a while now that Sarai had inherited Sibbie's gift. Taya wasn't stupid and that was too difficult to hide from her. She was cautious but had accepted it; had expected it really. But this news of the invasion was something else.

"Tay?" he said again.

She kept staring out the window, eyes glazed with shock. Another tear spilled down her cheek. "How long have you known?" she whispered.

He reached out and slid his hand over her shoulder. "Tay."

"How long have you known?"

"It doesn't matter."

"Why didn't you tell me?" She turned her face to him. Like his own it had aged, maybe a little more so. She didn't have the Alpha DNA like he did.

"Because I love you."

"Because you love me?" she asked confused.

"Because I wanted you to live like you always had forever."

"And now? What's changed?" More tears flooded down her cheeks. "You don't think we have forever?"

"No," he tightened his hand on her shoulder, "you'll still have forever. I'll make sure of that. I just want you to be prepared. Because it's coming soon."

"How soon?" she asked, wiping her face as though waking up from a strong cup of coffee. "How soon? We have to warn Ty. Our families—"

"No, Tay," he said firmly. "You can't tell anyone. No-one else knows yet. If you do, the consequences could be devastating. The worst thing we can do is cause panic in the general population."

"But if you say they're coming?"

"We'll handle it. The UNF has it under control."

"So, why are you telling me then? *Why* did you tell me?" she asked angrily.

Harris sighed heavily. "It's time, that's all. The nightmares. I want you to know the truth. I don't want to have to hide it from you any longer. And I want you to be prepared."

The anger on her face melted into sadness. She eyed his body. "So, that's what the change was about. All those years ago. You knew."

He nodded.

She sniffed. "H—how soon? How long do we have?"

He pulled her into him and kissed the top of her head. "You have forever, Tay. I'm going to make sure of that. I promise you."

Professor Sharley admired the view from the window in the leisure room. For two whole hours every day, they would bring him here. He would stare out the floor-to-ceiling glass wall, which looked out upon the most beautiful garden. They even filtered in fresh air from outside, bringing in the scent of the flowers. He even caught a waft of the ocean on the breeze, thanks to his Jumbo senses. It was most wondrous.

It had taken him many years to get to this point.

To be allowed above ground.

Yes, he was still inside the confines of Command, but he was no longer a subterranean inmate. He had become of use to the UNF again. He'd found his angle, and he played it. And had been playing it for years. They'd needed him to step in where others had failed. Where Professor Martin had failed. And he had succeeded.

A sense of pride flushed through Sharley's body. They'd needed his science, his mind, his ability to work on projects that others were hesitant to do. Highly-classified projects that boarded on highly unethical. He smiled to himself as he recalled that first meeting with General Berger. The general had stared at him with a slight look of disgust on his face. The look of a man who was doing what needed to be done, but the look of a man who wished he had another choice.

Since then, the look the general gave him had changed slightly. He now gave Sharley the look of a man who was content that he'd made the right decision to engage the professor on this program. But despite this, the look was still tainted with abhorrence. Sharley was under no illusions that the general liked him. He knew Berger was merely using him to get what he wanted, treating him like some prostitute called in to provide a basic service.

But that was okay, because Sharley would make the general pay top price for his service. It would be he, Sharley, that screwed the general in the end. Not the other way around.

The general really didn't know what a gift he was giving Sharley by handing him Welles's uterus and her son's DNA. It was exactly what Sharley had planned to do on the Darwin: create his Jumbo army using Welles and McKinley as his source code.

Sharley smiled again, wider this time. He was finally taking back what was his. This program. After all these years and after all the struggle, the UNF had handed it to him on a silver platter. Now, in some remote facility in the wilds of Siberia, 500 JEM clones were being reared, and there were plans to roll-out more. Sharley had also talked Berger into letting him study and experiment with the Zeta DNA found on those long buried skulls. The possibilities were endless.

He stared out the window watching as a little yellow butterfly danced across the other side of the glass. Something about it made him think of Carrie. Something about the innocence, the bliss, the freedom.

The ignorance.

His smile grew wider still. *If only she knew…* he thought. *If only she knew I had her womb.*

His smile turned into soft laughter.

It was only a matter of time before he would gain his freedom and take this program offline again. Do things his way. The right way. No constraints.

He would finally finish what he started. He would save this world from the Zeta attack. And they would revere him as a god.

Admiral Arken stood on the flight deck of the *Barbican* and stared out at the sea of blackness before him. He kept a strong, calm facade for the troops, but inside he could not ignore the anxiety that ate away at him.

In some respects, he felt as though he were standing aboard a ghost ship. That's what they would be to Command now. All attempts at restoring the comms had failed. The last Command had heard from the *Barbican* was the news that they'd crossed paths with over 40 Zeta ships. Then they were never heard from again. Command would naturally think they were dead.

But they had made the jump, away from the Zetas and, despite the partial damage they'd sustained to two of the hulls, the ship was stable. The crew of the *Barbican* were safe. For now. In truth, the way the Zetas just appeared and disappeared, how could he really know if the *Barbican* was safe? They could be surrounded by them and they wouldn't know it. They could be following them to Earth and he wouldn't know until it was too late.

Still, he held onto the knowledge that they had jumped away from the Zetas. He had to believe that they were alone and they would be fine. They had escaped death for a reason. He believed that reason was so they could journey home and do what they could to help save Earth. To warn them, at best. To join the fight, at worst.

The Zetas knew now what the source of the mirrored signals looked like: the *Barbican*. And if they were smart enough to create the technology of those ships and that heat ray, then they were smart enough to know there would be more ships like the *Barbican* back where the original mirrored signals came from. And if, for some reason, they couldn't find the *Barbican* again, then they would head for the source of those signals. Earth. And they would be prepared for more ships like the *Barbican*. Earth, however, had no idea what to expect from the Zetas.

He pictured his daughter's painting in his mind again. Pictured his wife. Pictured what would happen if they did not return to Earth in time.

He closed his eyes briefly and erased the thoughts.

He promised he would return, and he would keep that promise.

The *Barbican* would return to Earth, and they would do their duty.

PART SEVEN

21

Noah's Well

Harris sat bolt upright in his bed, sweating, panting and heart thumping against his ribcage. In front of him stood the overseers, the look on their faces more serious than he'd ever seen.

The intercom beside his bed suddenly sounded, making him flinch in fright.

"What is it?" he answered.

"Sir," said Yughi's voice, "urgent transmission from Major General Marchant."

"My office. I'll be there in a minute."

He quickly dressed and jogged down to his office. Logging into his portal, he watched as Marchant appeared on his screen.

"What is it, sir?"

"Did you see the news this morning?"

"No. Why?"

Harris's screen suddenly split into two displays. Marchant was on one and on the other was footage of warships gathering on the ocean.

"Where's this?" Harris asked.

"Noah's Well."

"Noah's Well? I thought they'd sorted that out?"

"They had, and the Australian government granted an Australian company the rights to drill for oil. They've been in production for eighteen months now, but they've just reported that the well is much larger than they first thought. Suddenly, other parties have become interested in it again. I guess these warships want to claim their share."

"Who do the ships belong to?" Harris asked, counting five of them.

"It's predominantly an Asian coalition, but there's African support in there as well."

"What exactly do they think they can do?"

Marchant shrugged. "Take it by force, I guess."

"So why aren't the Earth Duty troops all over this? What's this got to do with me?"

"Everything," Marchant said with solemnity. "If war breaks out between the coalition and Australia, it could spread to the mainland. We can't let that happen. We need to protect our assets, namely, the UNF facility in the Murchison region."

"Alright," Harris said studying the footage of the warships, "how am I supposed to stop that? War breaking out."

"You go, take Colonel Welles with you, and get him to speak to the head of security on the rig. We need calm heads."

"Why Colonel Welles?"

"Because he knows the man. They have history."

"Who is it?

"Evan Michaels. Ex-UNF."

"Michaels, the Original?"

"Yes. One of the four living Originals is on that rig."

"He's not running any secret Jumbo fighters, is he?" Harris arched an eyebrow.

"No," Marchant said, amusement showing in his voice, but not on his face, "not to my knowledge, anyway. He's just a retired soldier working freelance security. We want Jeff Welles to have a word to him about how important it is that they don't go starting any conflict."

"If anyone's going to start a conflict, sounds like the warships on the horizon are the likely culprits. We should be speaking to them."

"We have people on it, but we want people on all sides. You take Colonel Welles there, let him have a word, then I want you to go base yourself at the UNF facility and help guard it, just in case."

Harris's skin suddenly prickled, and he could have sworn a sharp jolt shot down his spine.

In that moment, he knew.

This is it. This is the reason the *Aurora* team would be down there when the Zetas hit. Noah's Well was the reason.

They were being sent there to help stop a war and protect the comms facility. What Marchant didn't know was that he was sending the *Aurora* team down there to face the first invasion. To face their fate.

"Alright," Harris said, a nervousness shooting through him. "Just keep all your other units on alert just in case. We'll leave as soon as we can."

Carrie's hand tightened around her PDP. She looked into the living room and saw her kids watching the TV.

"*We're leaving soon,*" Harris said.

She nodded to herself. "This is it, isn't it?"

"*You had any dreams lately?*"

"Yeah. The lights, the curved tree, running…"

"*And?*"

"The… sounds. I think it's the HH warriors. They're coming for us. I don't know where you are… I think you might be in trouble."

"*Forget that,*" Harris cut her off. "*Fate is fate and it will lead us where it leads us. Don't focus on the negative. Remember the positive. Remember the things that can help us.*"

"You're right. Sorry."

"*You sure you want to bring them? The kids? You could leave them with Colt.*"

Carrie focused on her children again. "No… I can't leave them behind. They have to stay with me. If they're with me, I can protect them. I can't leave them behind in Centralis if the Zetas are about to hit."

"*Take your Sentinels. I'll meet you at the comms base when we're done on Noah's Well. Understand?*"

"Yeah. I'll see you soon." She hung up her PDP, took a moment to steady her breathing, then walked into the living room. Brody and Freya were on the couch, and Brody rested one foot on a football, rolling it back and forth along the ground as he watched TV. Jesse lay on his stomach on the floor, his chin resting on his hands, enthralled by the nature documentary that was showing.

"That is so gross," Freya said, pulling a face as she watched a turtle laying white slimy eggs in the sand.

"It's necessary," Carrie told her.

"They're endangered," Jesse agreed.

"They are," Carrie said, thinking about Harris's phone call, and just how true that statement might soon be for the human race as well. "So," she said, looking at her kids, "who wants to go on a trip?"

"Where to?" Freya asked, twirling strands of long blond hair in her hand, not taking her vibrant-blue Alpha eyes off the screen.

"Australia."

"Australia?" Jesse said, looking around at her.

"Yeah," Carrie smiled. "It's about time I showed you where your mum and grandfather are from."

Before it gets obliterated, she thought to herself.

"What about school?" Brody asked, turning his face to her. So much like Doc.

She felt her throat suddenly swell and her eyes sting with the threat of tears, but she held them at bay. She took a moment, as all three of her children stared at her.

"School can wait," she said huskily, swallowing. "We have more important things to do."

Freya and Jesse hadn't quite caught on, but Brody had. She could tell it in his eyes, the way he looked at her.

"Has this got something to do with Uncle Saul?" he asked.

"Yeah," she said, not wanting to lie to them.

"Are the Zetas on their way?" Freya asked, suddenly looking frightened. Her children always knew the Zetas would come one day, but the reality of it actually happening was always going to be hard to bear.

"I don't know," Carrie said, "but we have to meet Uncle Saul down in Australia. We leave first thing, so go pack your bags. I'll come help you."

Brody stood straightaway and hurried to his room. Freya followed. Jesse stood and looked at her, then he moved to give her a hug. She hugged him back, but before she could speak, he said, "It's okay, mum. I'll keep you safe." Then he followed his siblings. Carrie kept her back turned to him as she gasped for breath and tears streamed down her face.

She took a few moments to wipe her face and steady her emotion, then she headed to her room and began to throw stuff into a bag.

"Archie, tell the Sentinels—"

"*I've informed them,*" Archie said, cutting her off.

She nodded. "Good."

"*You should take me with you.*"

Carrie glanced up, then kept packing. "I wish I could, Archie, but it's your job to keep my home safe."

"*It is possible,*" Archie said. "*You can take me.*"

She paused, glancing at the ceiling again. "How?"

"*Go to the bathroom.*"

She stood still, confused, then moved into her bathroom and stared at herself in the mirror. Suddenly, one of the tiles in the wall beside the mirror slid across and a metal arm extended. On the end was a metal box, about the size of her palm. The arm came to a stop and the lid on the box popped open, making her flinch. She stepped closer and peered in. There sat two round discs, each about four centimeters in diameter, with a five-pointed star etched into the center.

"*Place these against your neck, behind your ears,*" Archie told her.

"What are they?"

"*They are both transmitter and receiver. They are part of me. Connected to me. Wherever you go, I'll be with you. It'll be like you never left home.*"

She picked up one of the discs and studied it closely. The top side was slightly curved like a shield, the star stamped, like a coin design. The underside was a shallow cavity where several coils of miniature wires were tucked tidily.

"This is another one of those things that you couldn't tell me about before today, right?"

"*Yes.*"

"But I've gone away before?"

"*You have, but this time I predict danger.*"

"Why?"

"*Your conversation with Colonel Harris. Your heartbeat, the spike of your pheromones since. It's Decima, isn't it? It's coming.*"

She stared into her green Alpha eyes in the mirror. "Yes, it is."

"Then you need me."

"Do I?"

"Trust me. Place the discs on your neck behind your ear."

"Why? What will they do?"

Archie remained silent.

"Archie, no-one has been a threat to me for years. Sharley will never get out."

"Miss Welles, please don't argue."

"Then tell me what they'll do?"

"I told you. They will act as a transmitter and receiver, connecting you to my core here in this house. They are designed for occasions when you are forced to leave these safe confines, in unsafe circumstances such as this."

Carrie turned the disc around in her hands, and swore she saw the wires move as though they were living things.

"I will help you keep the children safe. I can be your eyes and ears, Miss Welles."

She studied the wires again, then slowly raised one and hesitantly placed it against her skin. She felt the sudden tickle of movement as the disc slid into position, tucking itself behind her ear like a hermit crab. Then a sharp spike ran through her like a dozen pins had been thrust through her skin. She gasped and panicked, immediately trying to pull it off, but it wouldn't budge.

"It's perfectly normal," Archie told her calmly. *"Please don't struggle against it. You'll only make it worse."*

"Get it off!"

"Miss Welles, this is what it does. The wires tap into your system so I can read your biometrics, listen to your speech and hear what you hear. This way I take in everything you are experiencing and I can filter information back to my core and respond as necessary."

"What do you mean, respond as necessary?" she said still tugging at the disc.

"Exactly that. I can respond as necessary. If you're in trouble I can send help. I have numerous options at my disposal."

The disc burned against her skin as the wires settled down.

"Now place the other one," Archie instructed her.

She gave an angry Alpha glance up at the roof.

"It's for your own good, Miss Welles. And I think you know it."

She turned her Alpha glare to the second disc, then picked it up. She looked into the mirror again. "You'd better be right, Archie." Then she placed the second one against her skin.

Harris sat in his office staring at the screen before him. It was split into two frames, Gold showing on one, Morrell on the other.

"All Alpha units are on alert," Harris said.

"Because of Noah's Well?" Morrell's brow furrowed.

Harris wasn't sure what to say. He didn't want to instill panic, but they weren't stupid. He'd kept them up-to-date over the years with news on the *Barbican*. They knew they'd crossed paths with over 40 ships, and they knew they had not been heard from since. What's more, they knew that the *Barbican* had been gone only five years when they'd crossed paths with the Zetas. Harris had always been sure to warn them that that was how soon the Zetas could hit Earth, all things being equal. And those five years had now passed.

"We'll handle Noah's Well," Harris said. "You just need to be on the alert for anything else."

"Has the comms facility picked up the Zetas closer than expected?" Gold asked.

"No," Harris said.

"Then why are we on alert?" Morrell asked.

Harris stared at them. "Because I said so… I've got a bad feeling."

"We haven't picked up the Zetas on our radars, but you've got a bad feeling?" Morrell voiced his skepticism.

"Yes," Harris said, his jaw tightening. "So, you've got two options. Listen to what I have to say and heed my warning, or ignore it and pay the consequences."

Gold and Morrell looked at him silently as their minds ticked over.

"If the Zetas come, they'll be 15 years early," Gold said.

"Yes," Harris said plainly, "they will."

"I know you warned this could happen," Gold said, "but the UNF isn't ready."

Harris stared back at him. "We're going to have to be. If they appear and engage, then your ships in the sky will need to hit them hard. We can't let them reach Earth."

Gold gave a nod, his eyes analyzing the gravity of Harris's words. "I'll put our troops on alert. We'll get on it."

"Your plan?" Harris asked him.

"As we've discussed. I'll send the UNF *Llangollen* and UNF *Valor* to protect the Moon, while the *Stanmore*, *Ruediger* and *Carcharias* will spread across the Earth with any other ships we have available. You sure we should leave Mars flying in the wind alone?"

"The Zetas will hit Earth and the Moon first. If they break us, they'll fly to Mars then, and there'd be nothing we could do about it. We need to play our defensive cards here. If they make it past us, it'll be up to Station Pegasus and Navarone to gather troops and defend Mars." Harris felt regret that Atlas Station was close to completion, but not yet functional. He turned his eyes to Morrell. "And you?"

Morrell's eyes were still full of questions, but he responded accordingly. "My unit covers Centralis. I'll put the others on alert. Unit 1217 covers Washington, and Unit 719 covers the AWAFP facility in Wyoming."

"Good."

"Colonel," Morrell said, "if this is real, if they're coming for us early, what the hell are 10 units with pre-knowledge going to do about it? And at that, only five of us are actually Alpha units."

"We do whatever we can," he said firmly.

"But—"

"It won't be a full-scale war," he told him. "It will be an invasion, but it won't be the full force of Zetas. So we need to fight back with everything we have and make sure they know we're not going to be a walk-over next time."

"Next time?" Morrell asked, while Gold watched silently.

"Yes," Harris said bluntly, uncaring now about what they thought. He needed them to know. It was too late, and it would be too careless of him to try to hide the truth from them any longer. "This will be a test. Next time won't be."

"How do you know this?" Gold asked him.

"I just do."

"You just do?" Morrell accused. "If you know something and you're not telling us—"

"I do know something, and I just told you," Harris said firmly. "They're coming. A small fleet. They will try to invade us and test our defenses. If we don't stop them they will cause a lot of damage and a lot of people will die. If we survive this, then in the years to come there will be the big war the UNF is expecting. Do you understand?"

"I understand," Morrell said. "I just want to know how you know this."

"Do you trust me?" Harris asked him, then turned his eyes to Gold. "Do you trust me?"

Gold hesitated briefly, but said, "Yes, sir."

Harris turned his back to Morrell. "Do you trust me?"

Morrell stared back a few seconds longer, then said, "Yes."

"Then know I am telling you this to help save your lives. No-one else on Earth is getting this warning. But you are. Stay sharp and cover your ass out there. Remember everything you've ever been told about the Zetas. And if you come across them, learn what you can. Information is power. Understood?"

They nodded back. "Yes, sir."

"Put your units on alert," Harris ordered. "If this happens as I think it will, then we won't be fighting this alone. It won't be our ten units against them. The whole of the UNF will be fighting with us. We can win this."

And with that he ended the transmission.

Carrie gave Roy a pleading look.

"We can't," he said. "It's our job to watch you and the children."

"I know, but I'm meeting up with the *Aurora* crew and I have Archie with me." She touched the silver discs behind her ear.

"Miss Welles—" Roy began.

"I want to make sure Colt and her kids are protected."

"I understand, but they're not our priority."

"Roy," she placed her hand on his shoulder, "please. They need you more than me. Colt has three Alpha kids who need protection from the Zetas. She needs help. We'll have the *Aurora* team."

"Miss Welles, she's in the Command Alpha village. She is surrounded by soldiers."

"Do you think Colt and her kids will be their priority if the Zetas hit? There'll be chaos."

Roy stared back at her but didn't answer.

"Okay, then send one with me," she said. "Give me Sampson. He knows the area I'm going to. You and Novak stay and protect Colt."

Roy sighed again and looked at Novak. Novak stood patient and still.

"I can go cover Colt and her children," Novak said, shrugging. "You and Sampson go with Miss Welles."

Roy's mind ticked over.

"*Sentinel Roy,*" Archie said, "*I believe that is a suitable trade-off.*"

"Do you now?" Roy said, glaring upward.

Carrie squeezed Roy's shoulder again. "Novak goes to Colt, and Archie comes with us."

Roy looked at the two Sentinels awaiting their orders. "Alright," he said grudgingly. "Novak, head to the Command Alpha village. Sampson, you're with us."

They nodded and set off to gather their things. Roy turned and collected Carrie's bag. "I'll put this in the carrier."

"Thank you," she said, glancing around the Fortress one last time to ensure she hadn't forgotten anything. As she did her eyes caught on the photo of Doc she'd placed on the wall. The one of him on the ski slopes in Colorado. The one Ellen Walker had sent after his death. Carrie moved over to the picture and stared at it, but it wasn't Doc she was thinking of. It was his family: Ellen and David, and his brothers, John and Ben.

She felt Brody come to stand by her side as he looked at the picture too. Her son stood almost at her shoulder height. He wrapped his arm around her, hugging her. She hugged him back, kissing the top of his head.

"Are we ready?" Sampson asked.

Carrie glanced at him, then at her three Alpha children who looked at her for their instructions. "You guys go with Sampson to the carrier. I'll be there in just a minute."

She watched them leave under Sampson's escort, as memories of her dream last night echoed through her mind. Running with the twins; the Zeta ships hitting the Earth.

She snapped her PDP off her belt and called the Walker's number.

"Hello, Carrie!" Ellen answered.

"Hi Ellen," she smiled. "How are you?"

"I'm good. How're you, honey?"

"I'm good," she said.

"Miss Welles?" Roy called from the doorway. She held up her hand indicating five minutes. Roy nodded, then closed the door again.

"Ellen, I don't have long," she said. "Where's the rest of your family?"

"Er, well David's here somewhere, why?"

"And your sons?"

"Ben's in San Francisco, and John's in New York where he and his family normally are. Why?"

"Tell them to fly home to Colorado," Carrie said. "Tell them you're sick. Tell them they need to come straightaway."

"Honey, what's wrong?"

"You remember all those years ago, before Jesse was born, I told you there would come a day when I would call you and tell you to go to your basement?"

Ellen paused a moment. *"Yes,"* she said quietly.

"That day is coming. Get your family home now. I'll call you when it's okay to come out of the basement."

"Carrie, honey, you're scaring me. What's going on?"

"Ellen, just do it. Not for me, but for Dan. Please do this for Dan."

"Carrie—"

"No questions, remember. I told you there could be no questions. Just get your family home in any way you can."

"Carrie..." Ellen's voice was just a whisper. *"The children?"*

"They're fine, they're with me. I'll protect them. Just promise me, Ellen. Promise me you'll do this."

She heard Ellen sniff, heard the emotion in her voice. *"Alright, honey. I promise."*

"You can't tell anyone else. It'll cause mass panic. I'm sorry."

Ellen sniffed again. "Okay."

"For Dan," Carrie said, eyeing his photo.

"For Dan," Ellen repeated.

Carrie ended the call and walked out of the Fortress.

Harris left his office and walked to the flight deck where the rest of the team sat. They were well into their flight, on approach to Noah's Well.

"Hunter? How're we looking?" he called out, as he entered.

"On target, sir. It's going to be tricky dropping you off, though. Winds are high, the ship is big, and the platform is small."

Harris looked at Colonel Welles who sat in his daughter's usual chair. "How long has it been since you did a drop landing?"

The colonel looked back at him and gave a short laugh. "Quite a while. But I'll be alright… I think."

"Good," Harris said, then made his way down to the front of the flight deck and turned to face the crew. Every eye was on him.

"Everything alright, sir?" Murphy asked. "I'm detecting that this is more than just a few warships on the ocean."

"It is," Harris said, then took a subtle breath in. "I believe we are on the verge of our first contact with the Zetas."

"What?" Murphy said, sitting up straighter.

McKinley shot Harris a surprised look. Of course, he knew about Decima, but he was obviously curious as to how Harris planned to explain this.

"What do you mean?" Brown asked. "I thought we were headed for Noah's Well."

"We are."

"So what has this got to do with the Zetas?" Brown asked.

"I always told you there was no guarantee as to when they would come."

"Has Command picked something up?" Yughi asked.

"No. But I think the Zetas communicate when they want to, and they stay stealth when they want to. And right now, they're staying stealth."

"So, how do you know they're coming?" Steinberg asked.

Harris sighed, placing his hands on his hips. "I just do. It's not an easy thing to explain, but you have to trust me. We lost contact with the *Barbican* five years ago. They were five years into their journey, so you do the math. But I'm telling you, it's coming. The invasion. The Zetas. We need to be ready."

"But, if the UNF haven't picked anything up?" Tikaani queried.

"How close are we talking?" Gregson asked, while Evenssen nodded beside him.

Harris stared at them all, locking eyes with McKinley last. "Days."

"Days?" Yughi said, eyebrows jumping to the top of his forehead.

"How can you be so sure?" Colonel Welles asked.

"If I told you, you'd think I was crazy."

"Well, I'm all for crazy, sir," Murphy smiled. "Lay it on me."

Harris looked back at McKinley again. The captain's face was passive and steady. It told him he'd support Harris no matter what he decided.

"I've dreamed it," Harris said, feeling a sense of relief wash through him to have the truth out. "Repeatedly. In detail. We're in Australia when it happens. And we're there, in Australia, because of this threat to Noah's Well. If war breaks out in Noah's Well, it will spread to the mainland, and that puts the UNF comms facility at risk. That is the only station communicating with the Zetas. We can't lose it. That is why we're being sent to Noah's Well, to make sure that doesn't happen. But I know, based on these dreams, that soon after, the Zetas are going to hit. Decima will commence."

"Decima?" Murphy asked.

"The Tenth Year War," he said, as a heavy silence fell over the flight deck. "Although I'm not sure it will last long enough to be called a war. The Zetas will send a small fleet to check out the source of the comms. I think maybe it's the same group that ran into the *Barbican* out there in space. I think that's why the UNF have not heard from the *Barbican* in a long time. I think they engaged with the Zetas and they lost. And so this small fleet is coming to see what else awaits... I believe they will invade us, test our defenses. And I believe they will have the ability to cause a lot of damage. But we have the numbers. We need to do what we can, to protect what we can. We need to send the Zetas a message. That this is our planet and we'll defend it with everything we have."

"Why do you call it the Tenth Year War?" Yughi asked, brow furrowed, trying to understand.

Harris looked at him. "Because, in my dreams, when they attack us in Australia, Welles and McKinley's twins are about ten years old."

"Brody and Freya?" Hunter asked.

"They were merely the time gauge. Welles is meeting us in Australia with them. They'll be there. That's why I know it's happening soon."

"But you said you dreamed this?" Frazer asked slowly, trying hard not to sound insulting.

Harris looked at him. "Yes. I did." Then he looked at the others, who also stared at him blankly, or in shock.

McKinley stood and walked to Harris's side and faced the crew.

"What Colonel Harris says is true. Whether you believe it or not, I don't care. Because you'll believe it the moment you see those lights in the sky. Our mission right now is to get Welles's father to Noah's Well and make sure everyone keeps their cool. Because we're not going to have time to be fighting a war amongst ourselves when those Zetas hit. After that, we're going to UNF comms facility. Why? Because it's going to be our job to protect that location from the Zeta invasion. When we hit the mainland, you'll have time to check-in with your families. You can alert them, but you must swear them to secrecy. The last thing we need is for panic to spread. It'll spread quick enough once the Zetas get here. Depending on the size of this incursion, the Alpha units we have, along with back-up from the UNF's ordinary fleet, will hopefully be enough to draw their fire away from any civilian areas. It's an invasion… but if Colonel Harris is right, it'll be a small one, and our Alpha units, supported by the wider UNF, can defeat them." McKinley stared around at the team as Harris watched on with a touch of pride.

"Do you understand?" McKinley asked the team firmly.

"You knew about this?" Evenssen asked him.

"Yes. And I believe to the bottom of my very soul, what little of it there is," he smirked, "that Colonel Harris is telling the truth. This man," he pointed to Harris, "will be our point of difference in this war. This man, our colonel, will lead us to victory."

"No," Harris said, shaking his head. Everyone looked at him. "No one man can do that. But *together*… we will lead each other to victory. Each and every one of us, we'll bring what we have to the table and *together* we will find victory."

"You have my guns, my aim, and my fists, sir," McKinley said. "I will follow you into battle any time, anywhere."

"And I would never go into battle without you by my side," Harris told him, smiling, holding out his hand for McKinley to slap. He did, locking his fist around Harris's briefly.

Harris looked back at the crew. "I know. It sounds crazy, but believe me it's true. This is going to happen. So let's move ahead, knowing what awaits, and let's do our very best to kick some Zeta ass."

Murphy clapped his hands together, grinning. "Well, I for one am fucking glad they're coming early. I've been waiting long enough to meet these bastards."

"Bastards," Tikaani said. "Don't you mean bitches?"

"Well, you can fight the Zeta bitches, and I'll fight those HH bastards they send out to meet us first."

"Oh, hell no!" Tikaani said. "You're not having all the fun! I'd love to break me a HH boy or two."

Murphy laughed loudly and they slapped hands.

Steinberg cracked his neck to each side. "I am a little stiff. It will be good to loosen things up."

Brown nodded in agreement, cracking his knuckles. "Yeah, I hear that."

Harris held his arms out in an open gesture. "Yeah, don't go expending all your adrenaline just yet. I said days. I don't know exactly when, I just know it's close. So you save that adrenaline. You shut that shit down, and you release it when you need to. Right!"

"Yes, sir!" they called.

Colonel Jeffrey Welles walked along the metal grid flooring of the rig as the guide led him and Harris to Evan Michaels' office. Buffeted by the wind as the *Aurora* flew away, he held on tightly to the red baseball cap he wore. Truth was, he was glad to have something to steady his hands on. Given the size of the ship, they'd had to scale down a long way to land on the rig. Jeff couldn't quite recall ever having done that before. And he certainly never thought he'd be doing it at his age. He felt his bones creaking a little at the force of the landing he'd just put his body through.

He glanced back at Harris, whose Alpha bulk only just fitted through the passageways, and drawing stares from those he passed; people were stepping backward into doorways to clear him a path. After all these years, Jeff still found the Alphas fascinating. Not just the strength and power they oozed, but the way their senses worked. Right now, he could tell that

Harris's senses were working overtime: eyes darting about, ears tuned in and nose twitching. Even as a fifty-three year old, Harris still looked like a man who would be hard to beat.

"You alright, colonel?" Harris asked, noticing the glances.

"Yeah," Jeff said.

"It was a shaky landing," Harris smiled.

Jeff nodded, remembering the two *Aurora* pilots arguing about how close they could get to the rig. The younger, Frazer, had wanted to get right in close, but Hunter erred on the side of caution and overruled him, much to Frazer's annoyance.

"Never thought I'd be doing that shit in my 70's," he muttered to Harris.

Harris's smile was wide. "You did just fine, colonel."

They finally came upon a tiny office where Evan Michaels sat behind a desk, studying a monitor. He looked up at them.

"Well, well. Here's a blast from the past," Michaels said. Jeff noted that time had aged him, but perhaps not as much as some. He obviously took care of himself. His hair was still cut close to the skull although peppered with silver, and his English skin had very few wrinkles to indicate his real age.

"Tell me about it," Jeff said, stepping into the office and holding out his hand. Evan stood and shook it, his eyes smiling.

"Never thought I'd find you loitering with the UNF again?" Evan said, glancing at Harris.

"Neither did I. But that's life, huh," Jeff said, then introduced them.

"Your daughter still wearing the uniform?" Evan asked. Noticing Jeff's curious look, he added, "She'd just entered Earth Duty when I left the UNF."

"She's in Space Duty now," Jeff said, and motioned to Harris, "in one of Colonel Harris's units."

"I see," Evan said. "So, if I was a betting man, I'd guess those ships outside are what brought you here?"

Jeff glanced around the office, the monitors, the equipment. "You got somewhere we can talk?"

"Sure," Evan said. "How about a little fresh air?"

They made their way up to the open air, and came to a small recreation area. Hexagonal in shape, it was laid with a green impact-absorbing material and fenced in with bright yellow railings. They walked over to one edge and looked out at the vast expanse of ocean around them, and at the six naval ships dotted between them and the horizon.

"You've got some interesting company," Jeff said, motioning to the ships, and noticing that Harris had walked some distance away, perhaps to give them privacy. Although, with Harris's Alpha hearing, Jeff knew the conversation would not be private. It was for Evan's benefit only.

"Yeah," Evan said looking out at the ships through his mirrored sunglasses, "worse than seagulls."

"I'll say," Jeff agreed. "The worst seagulls can do is shit on you. Those bastards could blow you out of the water."

"That really why you're here?" Evan asked, leaning on the railing and looking at him.

"Yeah."

"Why you?"

Jeff shrugged. "From one Original to another."

"You're looking old," Evan told him.

Jeff glanced at him and smiled. "I am. It's been a long time, Evan."

"Yeah, but even without that, you're looking old."

Jeff laughed. "That's easy for you to say. You were always the baby among the Originals."

"The baby... and the best looking," he smiled.

"Yeah, yeah, and the favorite with the ladies, I know. You were also single. The only one of us, so you had an advantage."

Evan laughed.

"You look good," Jeff told him. "You've stayed in shape."

"Got to in this line of work. Gotta stay sharp."

"Especially with several battleships out there eyeing you up."

"They're just looking," Evan said. "It's all for show."

"Maybe, but there'll be major ramifications if it's not."

"Look, you can tell the UNF that I got it under control. My job is to keep Noah's Well safe, and that's what I'm going to do. It's not my style to start a war and risk my client's asset."

"No, it's not," Jeff agreed, then looked at him. "You were always good at keeping your nose clean and staying out of the shit. Not getting involved unless you had to."

Evan looked at him, then back out to sea. "I voted against it. You know that. I chose your side."

"I know. And you kept your head low. It was smart."

Evan shrugged. "I saw the way things were going. I didn't want to get killed."

"No," Jeff said, looking down, seeing the waves crashing against the footing of the rig.

"But I admired you for standing up for what you believed in," Evan said. "Back then, I could've only wished for balls as big as you had."

"It didn't do me much good."

"No, I guess it didn't. But I admired your passion. Me, I tend to sit on the fence. Until someone pays me enough, then I pick a side."

"You're a survivor."

"Yeah, well, I've learned that passion is dangerous. It gets you killed."

Jeff studied his colleague for a moment. "I'm okay with that." He nodded to himself. "Dying for something you believe in, for something you love. That's a good battle to die in."

"Me, I want to live to see another day."

"Do you have any family?"

Evan shrugged ruefully. "Two ex-wives and a son I rarely see."

"You're not close?"

"Not really. I've always been stationed in far-flung regions like this one, working hard to earn some cash so my ex-wives can spend it."

Jeff laughed.

"So, out with it. You didn't come to talk about the meaning of life, did you."

"No. As you know, the UNF sent me."

"Yeah, and I'm still getting my head around that. What could have possibly put the two of you back in favor?"

Jeff paused a moment, eyeing the waves below, the ships in the distance. "Since my daughter got involved in UNFASP."

Evan paused and stared at him, surprise registering on his face.

"It's back on, Evan. It's back on, and it's moving forward. Swiftly."

Evan stared at him a moment longer before he got his mouth to speak. "That's why you're with the Space Duty colonel. How close are they?"

"I don't know, but the comms station that's been communicating with them isn't far from here. If this shit," he motioned to the warships on the horizon, "gets out of control, it could spread to the mainland. They can't have that. We need to protect the comms station at all costs."

Evan stared at him, then looked back at the warships. "Shit."

"That's why they sent me here to talk to you. Because of what I know and what you know. Because of UNFASP. I know you're not planning on starting any wars here, but just in case things start tilting that way… just think really, *really* hard about what you do before you do it. If shit spirals out of control, then you need to contain it out here. It cannot spread to the mainland."

"I wish you'd told me this 24 hours ago."

"Why?"

"Because as of 24 hours ago, the Australian government told me they were sending some ships our way. I figured a little 'you show yours and I'll show mine' wouldn't hurt."

"Where are they now?" Jeff asked.

"They're positioned just off the coast, but if these guys so much as fart, they'll be here within hours."

"The UNF have people talking to their people. You need to reassure the Aussie military that things are fine. Let the UNF do their thing, and try to resolve this peacefully."

"I'm leading security for Noah's Well. Anything to do with this rig, I get a major say. But just how much pull do you think I have with the Australian government if they think their territory is at risk?"

Jeff looked at him and smiled. "Use your Original charm. It works every time."

Evan stared at him, skeptical.

Jeff slapped him on the back. "Trust me. When it comes to the military, say the word Original and they can't stop themselves saluting or bowing or staring in awe." Jeff's face grew serious. "We've seen and done shit some of them can only dream about."

"How soon though?" he asked quietly. "How much time have we got? They're coming earlier than we thought, aren't they? That's why you're here. That's why the UNF is panicking."

Jeff shook his head. "They have no idea."

Evan stared hard into Jeff's eyes. "That's not the whole truth." Then he stepped closer. "From one Original to another. From one Original who voted no, to another. Tell me. Did we fuck up our vote?"

Jeff sighed heavily. "They don't know. All they know is that they've lost contact with the *Barbican*. It was sent to investigate the signals' source, and it made contact."

"Fuck," Evan muttered. "So, not only have we lost our biggest warship, those things could be here any day?"

Jeff looked him firmly in the eye. "That's why we need to keep the Comms station operational. That's why, just like me, you've been drawn back into this. And why we will be attached to this shit until the day we die."

Evan grasped hold of the rails tightly, sending his knuckles white. He glared out at the ships in the distance.

"Just keep your cool and everything will be alright," Jeff said.

Evan loosened his grip and his knuckles flushed pink. Jeff looked back and saw Harris stepping toward him. They turned around to face him.

"Everything alright?" Harris asked.

"Yeah," Jeff said, glancing at Evan, who was looking at his feet and nodding. Evan looked up at Harris, then held his hand out again. Harris shook it.

"It's an honor to meet an Original, sir," Harris said.

Evan flashed a glance at Jeff, then looked back at Harris. He seemed, for a moment, to study Harris's hand as he shook it. Then his arm, then his body. Evan glanced at Jeff again, then looked back at Harris.

"And it's an honor to finally meet an Advanced Soldier," Evan said, a curiosity and carefulness to his voice.

Harris paused for a second, then gave a single nod back. "Thank you, sir." Harris turned and made his way toward the door that would lead him inside.

Jeff saw Evan watching Harris as he disappeared.

"Just keep your cool, Evan, like you've always done," Jeff told him. "If shit blows up out here, you contain it. If those aliens come any time soon," he shrugged, "don't worry about it. You leave that to Colonel Harris and his soldiers to figure out. Your patch is here on the ocean. It's Noah's Well. Fair enough?"

Evan turned his face back to him, eyes filled with the seriousness of what he now knew. "Yeah, I got it."

"Good," Jeff said, and held his hand out.

Evan shook it. "Goddamn it," he said, "after all these years, it's happening. It's really happening."

Jeff nodded. "Yeah. Unfortunately it is."

22

Satellite Plains

Carrie had forgotten just how flat and vast land could be. On approach to the UNF facility in the Murchison, she marveled at the red dirt plains punctuated with acacia trees and bushy scrub. Such a contrast to the silver buildings and ocean surrounds of Centralis. She'd visited here once before with Harris, of course, a few years ago when they were touring all the sites, but it seemed so long ago now.

"There's nothing here," Brody said, looking out the PV window. This was the children's first visit.

Carrie laughed. "That's exactly why the UNF facility is out this way. There's no comms to interfere with theirs."

"I think I just saw a kangaroo!" Jesse said, twisting his face around trying to see something the PV had just passed.

"Yeah, you'll see some of them, alright," Carrie said.

"I hope we see a koala!" Freya said.

"*Not in these parts, Miss Freya*," Archie sounded from the discs behind Carrie's ears, startling her, "*but you might see an emu.*"

"And snakes?" Jesse asked excitedly.

"I hope not," Carrie smiled.

"Mum, is that it?" Freya pointed out the vehicle's window into the distance, where a tiny shape broke the horizon. It was a white satellite dish.

"Yeah, that's one of them. We're nearly there."

"I can't see it?" Roy said, glancing between the road and where they'd pointed.

"You don't have Alpha eyes, Roy."

He glanced at Carrie and smiled. "No, I don't." The way the light shone through the windscreen, Carrie could see the gray strands that had slithered through Roy's red-brown mustache. Time had been moving swiftly, and not just for her.

They continued on, the PV kicking up dust as they drove, and minute by minute the satellite dish grew in size, and in number. Carrie had now lost count of how many there were, dotted across the landscape. She felt a shiver run down her spine as they neared. The large white bowls faced the sky, tilted back like heads on necks, scanning expectantly. Waiting to hear a response.

And over the years, that is exactly what they had done.

These dishes were responsible for all contact with the Zetas to date. And here Carrie came, as Decima approached. Everything she'd been through had led up to this point. To this moment. Or, at least, the moments yet to come.

She glanced around wondering if she could see any bent and gnarled trees, although she knew they wouldn't be here. Those strange trees were about 350 kilometers away in Greenough, not far from the location of the buried Zeta ship.

"Whoa, they're big!" Brody said, as they passed one satellite dish close to the roadside.

"Can we climb up one?" Jesse asked.

"Maybe later," Carrie said, studying the dishes and darting her eyes to the sky.

"And what are those?" Freya pointed to one of the large patches dotting the landscape, of what looked like metal Christmas trees.

"They're antennas," Carrie told her, as the vehicle's comms unit sounded.

Carrie answered it. "Sergeant Carrie Welles."

"Sergeant Carrie Welles, this is Captain James McKinley," the response came.

"Dad!" Jesse called, and Carrie smiled.

"You sort out those folks on Noah's Well?" she asked.

"Your father thinks he did," he said. *"We're on our way in now. Harris wants you to rendezvous with us at the facility."*

"Alright. We've just been taking a tour of the dishes and antennas."

"Yeah? How they looking?"

"Pretty cool, actually."

"Kids all good?"

"Sure are. Say hi," and she held up the mouthpiece and the three of them called out various versions of "Hi, Dad."

"You do exactly as your mother says, understand?" McKinley said firmly.

They laughed in response, and Carrie smiled.

"I'll see you back at the base," she said.

"Will do. Out."

*

When they arrived at the facility, Dr. Valerie Pullman awaited them. She'd been expecting the *Aurora* team to arrive, but was surprised to see the children.

"It's okay," Carrie reassured her jokingly, "they're well-behaved."

Valerie smiled politely. "Er, perhaps I'll show the children through to the TV room while we talk?"

Carrie smiled. "How about another tour instead?" She'd seen it before on her last visit, but the children hadn't.

"Oh, okay," Valerie said, still sounding unsure. She led them through the small facility that was half above ground and half below ground. Above ground were all the scientific facilities, comms equipment and basic staff room. Below ground were the living quarters, rooms with beds, communal showers and a small living area with couches and TV.

"I believe you're staying elsewhere?" Valerie asked.

"Yes, we're bringing a UNF ship. We'll be staying on that."

"Oh," she said, "a ship? That might be problematic with our comms. Interference, you understand. Those things are designed with pretty powerful capabilities."

"They are. I'm sure as soon as they land, they'll adhere to your regulations."

Valerie smiled again and glanced at the children, who were curiously looking around at stuff.

"Shall we head back to the comms room?" Carrie said. "We can listen to the last signal you received."

Valerie darted her eyes to the children.

"It's okay," Carrie said, "they know about the Zetas."

"They do?" Valerie's eyes popped a little.

"You know about UNFASP, right?" Carrie asked her.

Valerie nodded. "Yes, the ZAEP committee have discussed it at length."

"ZAEP?"

"The Zeta Archelois Executive Panel. Major General Marchant is a member. As am I."

"Oh," Carrie said. "So, you know that I and my children are Alphas then?"

"Yes."

"Freya, where have the signals originated from?" Carrie asked over her shoulder.

"Zeta Archelois," she answered.

"Brody, have they been to Earth before?"

"Yeah. At least twice. Most recently, several hundred thousand years ago, during the time of the Homo heidelbergensis," her son answered.

"Jesse," she said, "who are the Zetas?"

He moved to stand beside her and looked up at Valerie with his gray-blue Alpha eyes. "We think they're our original makers."

Valerie stared at each one of Carrie's children, then smiled at Carrie awkwardly. "Alright. Let's go back upstairs then, shall we?"

Harris looked out the observation window of the *Aurora* and took in the strange yet beautiful scene before him. It was all reds and pinks and oranges. The sun was setting to the west, beginning to cast long shadows over the red soil and shrubby trees. Settled within this landscape were the hundreds of satellite dishes, like white metal soldiers standing to attention.

"It's hard to believe the Zetas are on their way," Yughi said, thinking aloud. "It's so peaceful out here."

"It is," Harris agreed, "so enjoy it while you can. Before you know it, we'll be covered in aliens."

"Damn Zetas," Brown muttered.

"I'm actually looking forward to seeing them," Evenssen said, then shrugged when Brown gave him look like he was crazy. "I'm curious. It's been a long time coming."

"The Zetas are indeed interesting, yes," Steinberg said, "but I have to say I'm most curious to see if they bring any HH back with them."

"Me too," Murphy said.

"Me three," Tikaani said.

"I don't know," Frazer offered in his thick Scottish accent. "I think we stand a chance against the HH. I mean they're going to be like us, yes? But the Zetas? We have no idea about them. *That* worries me."

"I didn't think anything worried you, Chucky," Hunter said.

"Nothing worries me when it comes to flying," he said. "I said nothing about coming face to face with fuckin' aliens, though."

Hunter smiled.

"Well, I guess we'll find out soon enough," Harris told them. He focused back out the window, at the landscape passing beneath them. The hues were more orange now, even the satellite dishes were bathed in an orange light, and there was something about this scene that sent a strong shiver down his spine. This truly felt like the calm before the storm.

And that was exactly why he'd made a quick transmission to Taya as soon as they'd left Noah's Well. He knew not to fight his gut anymore, and it was telling him things were coming to a head and fast.

"How're things in Noah's Well?" she'd asked him. "Is it sorted?"

"Not yet, but we're convinced there'll be no trouble."

"That's good," she smiled, and his heart ached.

"God, I miss you," he told her.

She laughed. "You've only been gone a couple of days."

"Where's Sarai?"

"She's playing out back. You want me to get her?"

"No, that's okay. You heard from Ty?"

"Not for a while. Did you catch his game on TV last night?"

"No," he said, disappointed, "I didn't. I've had shit to deal with. He win?"

"Yeah," she smiled. "Leading scorer."

"He's kicking ass."

"That's our boy."

"As soon as I'm back in town, we'll head out there and watch a game for real," he said, then suddenly paused, wondering if his life would just return to normal after the invasion. Would he be able to just pack up and go to a basketball game?

"Saul?" Taya registered the dip in his mood.

He stared back at her, lost in his thoughts.

Her face fell. "Saul? What's wrong?"

He looked into that transmission screen, wishing he was looking at her for real. Wishing he could touch her, hold her.

"Decima," he said.

Her mouth dropped slightly. She knew what Decima was. When he'd finally confessed everything to her, he'd told her about the codeword Decima. That one day he would warn her it was coming, but he would need to do so without anyone knowing. So he told her that he would utter one simple word: Decima.

"R—really?" she asked. "It's happening?"

"Very soon. Keep Sarai safe. Tell Ty to be careful. And Holly."

"Saul, where are you now?"

"We're in Australia. On our way to the UNF base."

"But—"

"Don't worry about me," he said firmly. "You hear me? You think of nothing but yourself and Sarai. That needs to be your focus. Do everything as we planned."

"Saul?"

"Remember everything I told you. What's the first thing I said?"

She stared at him with shining eyes. "Forget everything but my safety and Sarai's."

"Yes," he told her firmly. "I will be fine."

Tears rolled down her cheeks. "Saul…"

He reached out and touched the screen. "I love you, Tay. Just keep your head down and everything will be fine. I've got a job to do and I'm going to do it. And when it's over I will come find you. Understand?"

She nodded, wiping her cheeks.

"I love you," he said again firmly, giving her a look to match.

"I love you, too," she whispered, reaching out for the screen in return. "Stay safe."

"As long as you're okay, I'm okay. So *you* stay safe, alright? You, and Tyson, and Sarai."

She nodded again, as the tears rolled down her cheeks.

"This is Decima. This is just a trial run," he said. "I'll see you soon."

And with that he ended the transmission. He was confident they would be fine. Taya had been preparing for this day as much as he since she'd found out. She'd been taking all sorts of first-aid courses and had been volunteering at the local hospital in preparation.

Now he had to take his own advice. Until this thing was over, he had to forget about everything, except his own safety, his crew, and what was happening right in front of him.

Carrie stood with McKinley beside her in the near darkness, their Alpha eyes seeing just fine. She'd left the kids with the *Aurora* crew at the facility and brought him here to see the satellites. They stood now as large, dark shadows against the starry night above.

They both leaned back on the side of the PV, staring up at the sky.

"Don't think I've ever seen this many stars from Earth before," McKinley said.

"There're no city lights to drown them out," she said, sliding her hand in his. He turned his face and looked at her. She squeezed his hand and he squeezed hers in response. "It's going to happen soon," she whispered.

He nodded.

"We made it this far," she continued, shaking her head in wonder. "But everything that went before is going to look like a walk in the park, I bet. Now shit is about to get real. Now we step into the ring and fight the real fight we've been preparing ourselves for all this time. Except we don't really know what we're going to be fighting." Her face fell a little. "We'll be fighting blindfolded with one arm tied behind our back."

He squeezed her hand again. "Doesn't matter. It's a fight we're going to win."

She smiled, raising her hand and brushing the backs of her fingers down his face, over the slightly shaggy beard that he'd kept all these years. At 43 years old, he'd aged well these past 10 years. A few lines had crept in around his eyes, and any silver that had begun to thread through the blond hair was hard to see. The Alpha virus had served him well.

He stared back at her. "You know what warriors in times gone by did on the eve of war?"

"No, what?"

"They shagged senselessly for hours," he said, deadpan.

Carrie burst out laughing, and McKinley broke into a grin.

"It's true," he said, nodding.

"Oh, really?" she smiled back.

McKinley glanced around the satellites surrounding them in every direction. "Ever had sex in a satellite dish?"

Carrie laughed again. "Can't say that I have."

"Well, this is totally what the warriors of the past did," McKinley said, leaning off the PV and stepping toward one of the dishes, scanning it over with his eyes.

"They had satellite dishes back then?" she asked.

"Well, no, they'd, like, climb mountains and shit. This is our equivalent. We'll climb a satellite dish."

Carrie laughed again as McKinley moved back toward her and grabbed her hand, tugging her to him.

"We can't fight tradition," he said, "it's bad luck." Then he gave her a wink and led her toward a ladder attached to the satellite nearest them.

They climbed up then slid into the bowl of the dish, laughing, and rolling into each other's arms. As they held each other, their laughter slowly died, and they began to kiss. McKinley slid his hand over her cheek, noticing the discs behind her ears.

"New fashion?" he quizzed her.

"No," she smiled as she unbuttoned his shirt, "we have a supercomputer on tap."

"A what? Oh. Archie," he said flatly.

"*Hello, lieutenant,*" Archie's voice said.

McKinley tilted his head back, rolling his eyes. "After all these years, just once I'd like to have sex with you without Archie being around."

"Archie?" Carrie said, running her hand down McKinley's chest, popping the button and latching onto the zipper of his pants.

"*Yes, Miss Welles.*"

"Goodnight," she said, lowering the zip and tugging the pants off McKinley's legs.

"Yes, Miss Welles," Archie said, then made a little chime to indicate that he'd tuned out.

McKinley looked at her, skeptical about Archie's disappearance.

She threw his pants to the side and gave him an Alpha stare as she kissed the silver band around his right wrist. "You still want to have sex or not, White Warrior?"

A grin crossed his mouth as he pulled her onto him, taking her wrist and kissing her white warrior tattoo.

"Do your best, soldier," he teased.

"I'm not sure you can handle my best," she said, then kissed him hard.

He clasped his hands around her and flipped her over onto her back. "Try me," he purred.

*

Carrie sat bolt upright, panting.

"What?" McKinley sat up too.

She realized they were both naked, still in the satellite dish, a dazzling canopy of stars overhead.

"Just a dream," she said sleepily, the chill in the air making her shiver.

McKinley stared at her through the darkness.

She sighed. "I was running along a tunnel with the twins and Harris. The ground was shaking, sand was spilling in on us."

"We should go back," McKinley said, pulling his pants on.

"No," she said, pushing him back to a prone position. She snuggled into his side. "I want to enjoy every moment of this," she said, staring up at the stars. "Let's enjoy it while we can."

He relented, wrapping his arms around her, and they both lay quietly, with the stars for company.

Harris sipped his strong black coffee. The steam rose from his cup as he sat outside the facility, watching the sun rise. He could tell already that it would be a warm one. He heard birds in the distance and insects nearby. A lizard of some kind came scuttling across the path in front of him and it seemed to stop, tilt its head and eye at him, then scurry on its way. And strangely enough it made him think of the Zetas. The birds, the lizards...

A PV pulled up and McKinley and Welles got out. They walked toward him.

"Morning," he said. "Slept out under the stars, huh?"

McKinley and Welles glanced at each other. "Yeah."

McKinley carried on inside the facility while Welles sat down beside Harris. The smell of McKinley was thick on her skin. Harris smiled. If Taya had been here, he probably would've done the same thing.

"It's a nice morning," Welles said, looking over the landscape.

"It is," Harris said, sipping his coffee.

"It's going to happen today, isn't it?" she asked, looking back at him. They exchanged a serious silence before she continued. "I wish we could've worked out those Zeta ships and their thought-technology."

Harris looked at her. He knew she wished he'd told Marchant about their theories and got time alone with a Zeta ship, but he knew it would've done no good. The ships were in hibernation. Only a Zeta could wake them up and Harris wasn't Zeta enough. "If the Zetas come and wake those ships, I promise you I'll try."

She gave him a small smile. "I had the dream again last night. It was so strong. So vivid. And today..." She slid her hand over her stomach. "I think my gut feels like yours does."

Harris nodded. "Yeah. My stomach feels like that. And my spine. And I, too, had the dream again. It ended with me screaming in pain and I was seeing multiples of everything."

"Multiples?"

He nodded. "Multiples of you, of McKinley, of your kids. Of everyone."

"What the hell does that mean?"

He shrugged and sipped his coffee.

She slid her hand over his as it rested upon his knee and gripped it. They felt the static zap and subsequent vibration.

He looked at her again.

"We need to make sure we're charged up," she said. "I might need you."

"And I might need you," he told her.

"One of us the Zeta, one of us the ship," she smiled.

He smiled too, then looked back at the sunrise, sipping his coffee.

They heard footsteps and turned around to see Murphy at the door stretching his body out, his hair standing on end. Welles released Harris's hand. Murphy looked over at them, as though he'd just noticed them.

"Morning," he said roughly, then walked over to some bushes and began to pee.

"There is a toilet inside, you know," Harris said.

"And there's a lot of us, sir," he answered, yawning. "Can't wait."

Carrie smiled and shook her head. "Just trying to leave your mark on Australia, huh?"

"That's it," he smiled around at her.

Harris studied Murphy critically. "Seeing how you're up, how about a run, Irish?" Harris himself could do with a run to clear his mind.

Murphy looked around at him, zipping his fly. "Really?"

Harris grinned. "Put your shoes on, soldier."

"You're a sadistic son of a bitch, Colonel Harris," he said, pointing at him, "but that's why I like you."

Harris grinned at his soldier as Murphy moved back indoors.

*

Harris and the crew walked back toward the ship, hungry for some breakfast. Welles's kids awaited them with Colonel Welles, who'd got breakfast started.

"Thank you, colonel," Harris said. "You didn't have to do that."

He shrugged. "I'm making myself useful."

"You were useful," his daughter said, coming to stand beside him. "You spoke to Evan Michaels on Noah's Well."

"Well, let's see if that worked before we pop any champagne."

They ate breakfast and Harris felt a slight buzz of anticipation lingering among the team despite their run. They all felt it, that something was coming. He saw a few of them glancing at him, still thinking over what they'd been told; that Harris had dreamed of the invasion. Afterward, as Harris sat freshly showered in his quarters putting on his boots, he knew he would need to keep them busy today. He had to ensure their minds didn't overthink things. He needed them to be fresh and thinking sharp when the Zetas finally did arrive.

A frantic knocking on his door interrupted his thoughts. He opened it and saw Freya there, panting with sweat staining her brow.

"You have to come quick!" she said, then took off down the corridor.

"Wait!" Harris called, quickly tying his boots. He ran after her. "Freya!"

Hunter, who was further down the corridor, turned around at the commotion and saw Freya running toward him.

"Whoa! What is it, Frey?" he said, trying to catch her.

"The signal!" she said, then called back to Harris. "It's here!"

Harris and Hunter locked eyes, and Harris sped up.

"Get everyone ready!" he called to Hunter, then followed Freya out the door.

He caught up to her quickly, his longer legs making up the distance as they ran the several hundred meters from the location of the ship to the UNF facility. They burst into the comms room to see it manned with a handful of Valerie's staff, and Welles, McKinley and the boys standing there, fixated on what they were hearing.

"Has Marchant been alerted?" Harris asked, catching his breath.

Valerie nodded. "He's aware. They're tracking it, too."

"How close?"

Everyone in the room turned to look at him.

"How close?"

"It's coming from the ship," Valerie told him. "The one buried not far from here."

"It's waking up," Welles said, staring at him.

Harris stood still for a moment, letting his brain catch up. "It's not coming from the Zetas out there," he pointed to the sky. "It's coming from the empty ship?"

"Yes," Valerie told him, "we've locked the signal to approximately 333 kilometers from here."

"Has this happened before?" Harris asked. "Has the ship... er, talked?"

"Talked?" Valerie looked at him, confused.

"Communicated. Has it released a signal before?"

"No."

"Never in its history?"

"No." She shook her head emphatically.

Harris put his hands on his hips and looked up at the roof, nodding to himself. "They're coming. They're close. And they're calling their ships to see if any Zetas are still alive here."

"We need to get to that ship and take a look inside," Welles said.

Harris gave a single nod, then looked at Valerie. "Keep us posted. We're heading out to the site."

"Wait! What do you want me to tell Marchant?" Valerie asked.

Harris looked back at her.

"He said you were in charge now," Valerie told him.

Harris nodded. "Tell him we're heading out to the site. Tell him the Zetas are on their way. Tell him to have every UNF unit available on standby."

With that he turned and waved at McKinley and Welles to follow.

23

Wired For Sound

Carrie followed Harris and the ex-soldier turned farmer through the tunnel to the entrance of the buried Zeta ship.

"This is where I leave you," the farmer said as they came to the outer shell, the torch he held casting deep shadows on his weathered face.

"You got a basement or something?" Harris asked him.

The farmer studied him. "Yeah."

"I suggest you go down there and stay awhile. Pretend there's a tornado coming."

"We don't get tornadoes here," the farmer said.

"Well, you're about to," Harris told him.

The farmer stared at Harris for a moment, then eyed the rest of the soldiers with him. He turned and walked quickly back the way he came without another word.

"The farmer's coming back out," Harris said into his comms. "He's on his way home. Let him go."

"*Yes, sir,*" said Hunter, who remained on the ship with Frazer and Carrie's father, while Gregson, Evenssen and Tikaani stood guard outside.

Harris moved to open the door to the ship, but as he raised his hand, it slid back of its own accord.

Everyone but Harris snapped up their weapons. He held his hand up, motioning for them to hold fire.

"Brown, Steinberg, stay here," Harris said. "The rest of you, follow me."

Carrie watched as McKinley sidled up beside Harris, ready for a cross-cover entry. Murphy and Yughi moved up behind them, then Carrie and her children went last. She had considered leaving the children at the facility, and then on the ship, but knowing what she did, she didn't want them out of her sight.

Besides, she didn't want to hide anything from them either. She'd given them what innocence she could, but she knew there would come a time when they would lose it. And this was it. She swallowed the guilt she felt. Brody and Freya at almost ten were young enough, but Jesse hadn't yet turned eight. He was still her baby. They were so young. But she knew there was nothing to be gained from hiding what was to come. It had to be done.

Still, she pushed the children behind her as she stepped onto the ship, instantly feeling it humming with life. She hesitated, having second thoughts about the children again, but decided against it. She wanted them with her. Right beside her. And she wanted them to learn about their future enemies.

The opening led directly onto one of the flight decks. She found Harris and Yughi running their hands over the consoles, trying to figure them out, like they had done many times before on visits to the other ships. There were lights sparking here and there, most noticeably along the console wherever Harris's hands touched. She darted her eyes to Yughi, but the lights beneath his hands were dim. She looked back at Harris's and the lights were bright and almost rippling. Moving up beside him, she placed her hand on the console. It lit up, brighter than Yughi's, but dimmer than Harris's. They looked at each other.

"It's responding to you," she said.

"Still not enough," Harris said.

"But more than before," she said. "They've called it and it's now awake. The ships are more open to you now than they were in hibernation."

Suddenly they heard sound being emitted from somewhere on the console. It was the signal. The humming, buzzing clicks, punctuated by moments of silence. She glanced at her kids and noticed they'd huddled close together in the middle of the floor.

McKinley stood back beside her Sentinels, watching everyone. She locked eyes with her husband as memories of laying with him the night before, looking up at the stars, briefly flashed inside her mind. They held each other's gaze for a moment, understanding that Decima had begun.

She turned back to the console and slid her hand over Harris's. He glanced at her, as the vibration began.

"Try and connect with the ship," she said.

"How?" he asked.

"It's thought-technology, right? Just try." She squeezed her hand around his tightly.

He stared at their hands, then closed his eyes.

"Focus on the console," she said. Yughi moved up beside them, studied their hands and the console, then looked back at Harris.

"See yourself as one with it," Yughi said, understanding what they were trying to do.

Harris opened his eyes and looked at his comms-tech.

"Close your eyes," Yughi told him. "It's easier to focus that way. Pretend we're just doing a meditation exercise, like we sometimes do on the ship."

Harris looked at the console, then closed his eyes again.

"Picture yourself becoming one with it," Yughi said. "You need to connect with it in order to control it."

Carrie placed her other hand down on the console too. She could feel the vibration of her connection with Harris right up at her shoulder now. She willed it to run down her other arm too, back to the console. She didn't know why. It just felt right.

"Place your other hand down," she said to Harris, as she too closed her eyes.

Yughi's soft voice kept talking to them.

"The lights around your hands are getting brighter," Yughi said after a short while.

"Mum?" Jesse asked.

"It's okay," she heard McKinley's voice say. She felt the vibration reach her other hand and pool warmly onto the console.

"Breath in, and out," Yughi coached them. "You're calm. You're not threatening to this ship. You want to help it. You want to communicate. Let it know you're here to help. Open yourself to the connection."

Carrie heard Harris breathing slow and steady beside her, as though he were in a deep sleep.

She felt the console warming beneath her hands, the pins and needles sensation of Harris's connection tingling as it did.

They heard the comms again… humming, buzzing, clicks.

"Colonel Harris!" Hunter's voice sounded through their earpieces, breaking their spell. *"It's Major General Marchant!"*

"Fuck," Harris said, taking his hands off the console.

"We were close!" Carrie said.

"What is it?" Harris spoke into his comms.

"Connecting you now!"

"Harris?" Marchant's voice sounded. *"They're here! The goddamn Zetas are here. They're on our radar and approaching fast!"*

"How many?" Harris asked.

"There looks to be around 40 ships. Most are giving off the same heat signature, but a few of them are giving off something different."

"How different?"

"Their signatures are larger, denser."

"How far out are they?"

"They're on approach to the Moon, but based on their trajectory, it looks as though they're heading for Earth. For you, in fact."

"For me?" Harris frowned.

"For the UNF base in Australia. They're headed for the source of the comms signal."

Harris glanced at her, then turned to lock eyes with McKinley.

"You got everyone on standby like I asked?" Harris asked Marchant.

"Yes. What about your units?"

"They're ready to go."

"We don't have much time!"

"The UNF *Llangollen* and UNF *Valor* are positioned near the Moon. We'll send them out first to meet them. You got a couple of hours to get everyone to safety."

"I'm on it."

"Talk soon," Harris said, ending the comms. "Hunter?"

"Sir!"

"Tell Gold and Morrell it's game on."

"Yes, sir!"

Carrie looked at him, grabbing his hand and placing it back on the console. "We don't have much time!"

The Zeta comms signals sounded again, and the lights on the ship suddenly dimmed. Carrie looked around and saw everyone's Alpha eyes glowing back at her. All except the two Sentinels, that is. Harris slowly leaned down and pressed his ear against the console.

"It's humming."

"Why?" Murphy asked, as the lights suddenly came back on.

They all glanced around the room, waiting to see what would happen next.

Then a sound from the console, the comms again, but it was louder this time. As though this time it was sending the comms, not receiving them.

"We should get out of here now," McKinley said.

Carrie grabbed Harris's hand and pressed it against the console. "If it's waking up, we need to connect with it! We need to learn what we can!"

They placed their hands flat against the console and closed their eyes. The ship's humming increased in volume so that Carrie could hear it now.

Yughi tried to coax them back into mediation, but the comms were loud again, drowning out his voice, and a slight vibration began to rattle the ship. They opened their eyes.

"We gotta go!" McKinley called. "Now!"

Harris looked around at the others. "Get out of here, all of you."

"Sir?" Yughi said.

"Get back to our ship," Harris said. "You too, McKinley."

McKinley tapped Brody on the shoulder and motioned him to follow as he headed for the exit with her Sentinels. Murphy and Yughi did the same.

Harris squeezed his eyes shut and pressed his hands firmly against the console. "Come on, you son of a bitch!" he hissed.

Carrie watched as her children followed McKinley out the door, then turned around and closed her eyes again too. The humming and vibration increased; it was so loud now that it made her heart race. The comms kept blasting out, mingling with the din. Then the ship seemed to shudder, seemed to move. Carrie almost lost her feet.

"Mum!" Brody called, running back in.

Carrie and Harris spun around, as Freya followed in behind.

Then suddenly the door closed shut.

"No!" Harris raced over to it and tried to pry it back open. Carrie joined him, and together they strained every Alpha muscle they had, but it wouldn't budge.

It was then that she felt the ship move. Only a few feet, but it was definite movement.

Eyes wide, she looked at Harris. "Where's it going to take us?"

"There's got to be another way out!" Harris said, running for the doorway that led into another corridor.

Carrie grabbed Brody and Freya and ran after him. "Where's Jesse?" she asked as they ran.

"He went with dad," Brody said, as they zigzagged here and there frantically searching the walls for a way out.

Suddenly the ship seemed to still. Carrie, Harris and the twins looked around the gray-skinned walls of the corridor they were in, then a few meters away a door suddenly opened. Harris stepped toward it and looked out.

"It's another tunnel," he said, looking back at Carrie.

The ship's humming began to increase again.

"I think it wants us off," Carrie said.

"*Take the tunnel, now,*" Archie said calmly, but firmly. "*I will track and guide you.*"

Carrie pushed Freya toward Harris and he understood her motion. He grabbed Freya and moved her through the door, following quickly behind her. Carrie pushed Brody forward and Harris turned back to help him through. Carrie followed next, and the door swiftly slammed shut right behind her.

Gold stared at the screen before him, at the 41 Zeta blips headed toward the Moon in a tight cluster formation. He swallowed, then turned to C:Drive.

"You got them?"

"Yes, sir. They're online."

Gold leaned down and spoke into the comms microphone at his captain's desk aboard the *Carcharias'* flight deck.

"UNF *Llangollen,* UNF *Valor.* Do you read?"

"*Roger that. UNF* Llangollen *receives,*" Captain Stratevski replied.

"*UNF* Valor *receives also,*" Captain Marshall replied.

"Alright, listen up. We've got five UNF battleships close to the Moon on standby. Including your own, we've got the UNF *Ramedes, Hopetoun* and *Kandor,* along with the troops on the ground in Fort Alden and Fort Gillet that can lend support if the alien ships come close to the surface. Your job is to try and make contact with the approaching ships and stop them from coming any closer to Earth. If they open fire, you do what you have to. But just remember your priority is to protect the colonies on the Moon. We've got a whole bunch of ships positioned near Earth, ready to intercept if they make it through your defenses. So, if they do, we'll take it from there. Do you understand? Your priority is the Moon."

"*Roger that,*" Stratevski replied.

"*We roger that too,* Carcharias," Marshall said.

"Good," Gold said. "Stay safe, and if necessary, fight hard, gentlemen."

"*And you,*" Marshall replied.

Gold ended the comms, then turned to C:Drive again. "Status of our Earth coverage?"

"The trajectory of Zeta arrival is over Europe," C:Drive told him. "They'll hit the Earth's atmosphere there, then ride the gravity arc straight to Australia."

"How many UNF battleships do we have available?" Gold asked.

"Aside from us and the UNF *Stanmore* and UNF *Aurora,* there were two others close by that we called in. UNF *Dunthorpe* and UNF *Eccleston.* More are en route."

"And Earth-based air force units?"

"Calls are being made. The standing treaties mean we'll have just about as many as we want."

"But will our little jet fighters stand up to a Zeta ship?" the *Carcharias'* pilot Reece asked. "Their ships cut through the Earth's crust with barely a scratch and buried themselves, so what's a fighter plane going to do to their hulls?"

"Whatever they can," Gold said. "Put the *Dunthorpe* and *Eccleston* above the atmosphere. We need to stop them from entering European airspace. If they do, I want half of those fighter jets in defense across Europe and Asia. Then spread what's left of our ships across the globe. We'll cover the

North American and Centralis regions with the UNF *Stanmore*. Our priority is to protect the AWAFP facility and any civilian zones we can."

"What about the comms facility in Australia?" Ryker asked. "That's what the Zetas are being drawn to."

"That's the *Aurora*'s job," Gold told him. "They're the last bastion for that comms facility. But if the rest of us do our job right, they won't need to do theirs."

Ryker nodded and Gold looked around at the Alpha-Two *Carcharias* team.

"This is it, soldiers," he said, looking each one in the eye. "We've waited over eight years for this day, and it's finally here. This is the day we defend the Earth. This is the day we protect what's ours."

Harris ran hunched along the cramped tunnels as fast as he could with his Alpha bulk. He'd squeezed past Freya, locking the twins between himself and Welles as they ran and the humming noise built behind them.

"*Sir!*" he heard McKinley's voice crackle over his headset. "*Sir, where are you?*"

Harris groped for his comms.

"*We have to go! Now!*" Hunter's voice said. "*If that ship comes above ground, the first thing it's aiming for is the Aurora!*"

"Go!" Harris managed to yell breathlessly. "We're fine! We're in a tunnel, get out of here!"

"*Sir?*" McKinley yelled. "*You're breaking up? Carrie?*"

"We're fine!" she yelled into her comms. "The kids are fine!"

"Get out of here!" Harris yelled. "Go defend the comms station. You *must* defend the comms station!"

"*Roger that!*" Hunter said. "*McKinley, get your ass back to the ship!*"

Harris continued on, seeing a bend ahead in the tunnel. As he reached it he was hoping to see daylight, but all he saw was more long, dark tunnel. He paused, catching his breath.

"What is it?" Welles asked from behind.

"Nothing," he said. "We just gotta keep running."

Suddenly the ground beneath their feet rumbled and they all lost their footing. They quickly righted themselves and noticed traces of sand spilling over them.

"Move! Move! Move!" Harris barked. "If that ship takes off this tunnel will collapse. Move!"

Freya swiftly squeezed past him and sprinted ahead, with Brody close behind.

"Shit!" Harris said, running to keep up, and listening as Welles panted on his heels.

Captain Lincoln Gold listened intently as the UNF *Llangollen* attempted to communicate with the approaching armada of Zeta ships, still in their tight cluster formation.

On radar, they looked close. Very close. But, theoretically, they should be out of range of each other's opposing weapons. At least, they knew the Zeta ships were out of range of the *Llangollen*, but whether the reverse was true was anyone's guess.

"*I repeat,*" the *Llangollen*'s comms-tech said over the flight deck speakers, "*we are the UNF* Llangollen. *This is our home territory. State your intentions.*" The same message followed in several different languages. No response came.

"*We've had no response to our verbal comms. Will now mirror the Zeta comms signal to them and see if that wakes them up.*"

"Roger that," Gold said. He stood upright, away from the comms mic, and folded his arms. He stared out the observation window at New York city far below them, a gray patch on the landscape as day began to break over this part of the world. The flight deck was quiet and intense as a light sheen of sweat broke across his brow. He'd hate to think what the flight decks of the *Llangollen* and *Valor* were like right now. Although the *Valor* was some way back, hovering over the Moon capital of Galilei.

He listened to the humming, buzzing and clicks as the Zeta signal sounded, and then the silence that followed.

"No change, they continue onward!" the *Carcharias'* chief pilot Reece stated, staring at the radar screen. "They're within range of the *Llangollen*."

"Hold steady, Stratevski," Gold whispered to himself. "Hold steady."

"They're fanning out!" Reece said. "They're breaking their tight formation and fanning out."

"They're spreading to avoid damage," Ryker said. "They must detect the lead ship is in range of the *Llangollen*."

"Hold steady," Gold whispered again.

Suddenly the Zeta comms sounded over their speakers.

"That wasn't the *Llangollen*," Reece said.

Silence sat again, before the *Llangollen* replied with more Zeta comms.

"Maybe we should send more back-up," Ryker said. "They've got a lot of ships on them."

"But they're small," Gold said, "even the largest of their fleet. The *Llangollen* is much bigger and hopefully more powerful. And the *Valor* is our biggest ship outside of the *Barbican*."

"Yeah," Ryker said, "but where is the *Barbican* now?"

Gold turned to lock eyes with his first lieutenant. "They were alone. We have the entire UNF at our disposal. We're not dying today, Ryker. We are *not* dying today."

"They're diverting!" Reece called.

Gold's eyes darted back to the radar. The Zeta blips were indeed moving – making their way onward toward Earth.

"UNF *Kandor*," Captain Stratevski called over the comms, "block their path!"

"*Roger that!*" the *Kandor* replied, and Gold watched as their blip on the screen moved to cut off the Zeta ships.

The *Hopetoun* followed, while the *Ramedes* lingered close to the Moon, over Colony Meridian.

The *Llangollen* sent the Zeta comms again in an attempt to call the Zeta ships back.

"*Something's happening*," the *Kandor* announced. "*There's a red light emitting from underneath the lead ship. Shields in place?*"

"*Shields in place*," another voice answered.

"*Careful*, Hopetoun," Stratevski said, as Gold watched the *Hopetoun's* blip overtake *Kandor*'s on the screen.

Silence followed for a few seconds.

"*Jesus!*" the *Kandor* called out.

"They've fired!" Reece announced. "The *Hopetoun*'s been hit!"

Gold stared at the screen and saw the *Hopetoun*'s blip flashing, indicating a direct hit and damage received. He leaned down to the table mic again.

"*Llangollen*, report!"

"*The* Hopetoun's *been hit!*" Stratevski spoke urgently. "*Whatever they got, it burned right through their shield! We've begun exchanging fire with the Zeta ships. I repeat we have begun exchanging fire. It's on,* Carcharias! *The war is on!*"

Captain James McKinley strode toward the PV that Welles and her Sentinels had driven to the comms facility. He'd stopped by the weapons store on the *Aurora* before his departure and loaded up with enough gear to see him through.

"McKinley," Hunter jogged up beside him. "I understand, but—"

"I'm going," he said with finality, shooting him a look. "My kids are out there."

"Yeah," Hunter told him, "with Harris and Welles."

"Don't care."

"With Harris gone, you're in charge of the crew."

"So, I'm handing that honor to you," he said, opening the PV and placing his guns on the back seat. "I'll be back before the Zetas hit here."

"Dad!" Jesse came running out toward him.

"Go back inside." McKinley pointed to the comms facility. "You stay with the crew and your Sentinels."

"I'm coming with you!" he said.

"No, you're not."

"Why can you go get them, but I can't?" Jesse argued.

McKinley walked over to his son, whose head just reached his waist. "Because you're seven years old, Jesse."

"I'm almost eight!"

"Get inside." McKinley pointed to the facility again, then looked back at Hunter.

"Are you sure about this?" Hunter asked him.

McKinley turned to him. "If it was Lei and your boys out there, would you sit back and wait?"

Hunter exhaled heavily, but didn't respond.

"Thought so," McKinley said, opening the driver's door and getting inside. He looked in the rearview mirror and saw Jesse in the back seat. He turned around. "Jesse! This isn't a game!"

Suddenly the passenger door opened and Colonel Welles sat himself down. McKinley looked at him. "What are you doing?"

"Going to get my daughter and grandkids."

"No," McKinley shook his head. "Take your grandson here, and go back inside."

"You might need help," his father-in-law said.

"No offense, but—"

"Careful what you say, captain," Colonel Welles warned him with hard eyes.

Just then both doors to the back seat opened and Roy and Sampson sat down either side of Jesse.

"What the fu—?" McKinley said, looking around at them.

"It's our job to protect the children," Roy said. "It's our fault they're not with us now. We're going with you."

McKinley stared at them, then at the colonel, who gave him a smile back.

"Time's a-wasting!" the colonel said, locking in his harness.

McKinley looked out the windscreen of the PV, clenching his jaw, then turned around and pointed at them all. "If any of you get in my way or slow me down I will feed you to the Zetas myself!"

"Understood, captain," Colonel Welles said, then motioned for him to put the PV in motion.

McKinley revved the engine and took off, watching Hunter disappear in the rearview mirror.

Harris noticed they were only walking now, albeit swiftly. He wiped the sweat from his brow and tried not to think about how thirsty he was. The humming sound had reduced, but that was only because of the distance they were from the ship. It didn't sound as though it had broken ground. It sounded like it was lying in wait, idling in neutral or something.

"Why do you think it let us go?" Welles asked, as though reading his mind.

"I don't know." He shook his head. "Luck?"

"No, it was awake and it lit up when you touched it. I think it recognized you, recognized the Zeta in you."

Harris flashed her a look, then darted his eyes to the twins, who thankfully were looking a little too weary to be paying attention.

"Maybe we should rest for a bit," Harris suggested. They didn't argue and all found a spot to sit down, leaning back on the walls of the tunnel.

He looked at his watch. It had been a couple of hours. He clicked on his comms. "Hunter? You read me?"

Static filled his earpiece.

"You may be too far underground to transmit," Archie suggested.

Harris eyed a disc as Welles turned and hugged Freya into her side.

"Then how come you can hear me?" Harris asked Archie.

"Because my technology is much more advanced than your standard-issue UNF comms set, colonel."

"Can you transmit on our behalf?" he asked.

"Yes, I can, and I have been."

"You have?"

"Yes, I've been transmitting comms to the Aurora *to let them know that everyone is safe."*

"What are they doing?" Harris asked.

"They're back at the comms facility and they're preparing to defend it. They are sending a party to get you."

"Who?" Harris asked, although he already knew.

"Captain McKinley, Colonel Welles, and the Sentinels."

Harris threw a look at Welles, who seemed equally pissed.

"Why didn't they stay with Jesse?" she asked.

"I believe Jesse is with them."

"What?"

"I'm afraid Jesse wouldn't leave his side, so Captain McKinley gave in and let him come."

"He's supposed to be in charge while I'm gone," Harris said through clenched teeth. "He's not supposed to leave the team!"

"He left First Lieutenant Hunter in charge. They are supplying each other with updates. He couldn't afford to send any of the crew to get you."

"Why not?"

"Because the Llangollen, Valor *and other UNF ships have begun an exchange of fire with the Zeta party off the Moon. I'm afraid the war has commenced, colonel."*

Those last words seemed to fill the tunnel around them with silence. He locked eyes with Welles, and for a moment Harris was sure the world had stood still.

"Decima has started?" Brody asked, looking at his godfather.

Harris nodded. "Decima has started."

"The UNF Llangollen *tried to communicate, but the Zeta ships attempted to move onward toward Earth. The* Kandor *and* Hopetoun *tried to block their path but the Zeta ships opened fire. They had no option but to engage."*

"Is it still going on?" Harris asked.

"Yes. The Hopetoun *has been destroyed. The* Llangollen *and* Kandor *have taken hits, but remain in battle. The* Valor *and* Ramedes *have also entered the battle. Several of the Zeta ships continue to engage the UNF party. However, most of the Zeta ships have slipped past and move onward."*

"Toward Earth," Harris said flatly.

"Yes."

"Any word from Gold or Morrell?"

"They are in position and up-to-date with events on the Moon. In fact, everyone is up-to-date with events on the Moon now."

Harris closed his eyes. "How bad is it?"

"How bad is what?" Archie asked.

"The panic?"

Archie was quiet for a moment. *"Word is still spreading, but it's spreading fast. Live footage taken from the Moon is being aired on various media around the world."*

"Do we know if the Zeta ships are still targeting this area?"

"I believe so. They have flown in one formation so far. They will enter the Earth's atmosphere over Europe."

Harris and Welles stared at each other and the twins.

"I need to get out of this tunnel," Harris said, getting to his feet. "I'm supposed to be out there leading the charge in this war, and I'm bunkered down here hiding like a rat."

"Captain McKinley has your current coordinates. Keep walking, find the end of this tunnel, and I will have him meet you close by."

Welles got to her feet also, touching the disc behind her ear as she did. "Thank you, Archie," she said softly.

Gold paced the *Carcharias'* flight deck, trying to steady himself. He'd just received word that the *Ramedes* had been hit. They'd already lost the *Hopetoun* and *Kandor*. Two UNF battleships and many soldiers.

"We underestimated their technology," C:Drive said quietly, referring to the controlled heat ray they fired, a weapon much more powerful than their laser fire or traditional ammunition, which barely scratched the surface of the Zeta ships.

"No, we didn't," Gold told him. "We always knew they'd have the technology. We just hoped ours would hold out against it."

He continued to listen to the comms as the *Valor* currently fought four of the Zeta ships, while the *Llangollen* fought another three, and the damaged *Ramedes* battled two. After the *Hopetoun* had been destroyed, the *Valor* had quickly entered the fight and immediately destroyed one Zeta ship. But that was all they'd managed so far. One single Zeta ship.

"We've got a target locked! Fire!" voices from the UNF *Valor* sounded over the comms.

Gold swiftly turned back to the flight deck's comms panel, as Reece yelled, "Direct hit!" The pilot smiled, fist in the air. "The *Valor* nailed another one!"

They listened now to the *Llangollen* comms.

"They're fast little bastards!" a female voice said.

"Just keep us moving!" Captain Stratevski said. *"Draw them away from the Moon!"*

"I got a bogey locked! Firing!" another said excitedly. *"Take that you son of a bitch! Woo-hoo!"*

"Yes!" Ryker pumped his fist. "That's three!"

"Yeah, under 40 to go," C:Drive said dryly.

"What's that? What's happening?" Captain Stratevski's voice sounded over the comms, catching their attention.

"We've got them on either side of us! We're locked in!" a voice responded.

"Shake them! Shake them!" Stratevski barked.

"They're glowing red!" the female voice called again.

"Jump us! Jump us!"

But their comms suddenly went dead.

"C:Drive?" Gold asked the comms-tech.

Reece, chief pilot, looked around at him in shock. "They're gone from the radar, sir. We just lost the *Llangollen*."

Gold paused as the team looked at him. He ran his hand over his face, then looked at C:Drive again.

"Tell Station Navarone to dispatch their fighters. Our battleships need help. We need numbers and fast."

"Sir!" he nodded, and relayed the comms.

"Are all units in place at atmosphere and over Europe?" Gold asked.

"Yes, sir," Ryker confirmed.

"Tell them they got a whole lot of trouble headed their way."

Carrie walked along swiftly, following the bobbing heads of Brody and Freya as they moved ahead of her, but behind Harris. The colonel was tense, her Alpha felt it. And she understood why. Knowing that a battle was taking place just off the Moon, that their fellow Space Duty soldiers were fighting to the death, and they were stuck in this tunnel doing nothing... well, she understood Harris's anxiety. She felt it herself.

Harris suddenly paused, inhaling.

"We're close," he said.

"How do you know?" Carrie asked.

"I can smell the ocean," Freya said, her face lighting up.

Harris looked around at her and smiled. "Me, too. Ocean and grass."

About 20 minutes later, the tunnel came to an end and Harris found the opening. It was covered in heavy rocks, but he soon had it cleared. He peered out the opening, then looked back at them.

"Wait here," he mouthed, holding his finger to his mouth to indicate they be quiet, then he slipped out the opening and disappeared.

"Can I have a gun, mom?" Freya whispered to her.

Carrie looked at her. "No, honey. We've got you covered."

"But we're good shots," Brody insisted, backing his sister up.

Carrie looked at him and brushed her hand down his cheek. "Shooting targets on the *Aurora* is a lot different to shooting in real life, honey."

"But if they're coming for us?" he said with that concerned look upon his face, so much like Doc. She bent forward and kissed his forehead.

"I won't let anything happen to you," she said. "I swear."

"It's clear!" Harris whispered loudly back through the opening, sticking his hand through.

Freya jumped forward and took it, and Harris pulled her out. Brody swiftly followed, as did Carrie, and she couldn't believe the feeling of relief as she inhaled the fresh air and felt it upon her skin.

She looked around. It was heading toward dusk already, and she saw nothing but a faded orange horizon and open, dry grassy fields. "The sun sets in the west, right? So that must be the ocean." She pointed to the orange horizon. And as she said that she thought she heard it faintly in the distance. The sound of waves crashing on a beach.

"Yeah," Harris said, looking around, looking a little stunned. "I've dreamed of this place. This field. The morning I got the call for the Darwin."

They exchanged a look.

"*Captain McKinley is close,*" Archie told them, "*but he can only take the PV so far.*"

"Tell us which direction to head," Harris said.

"*West. He'll be coming along the main highway. You'll hit it before you hit the ocean.*"

Captain Gold hung his head briefly on hearing that the *Ramedes* was gone. Even news of the *Valor* taking out another Zeta ship didn't elate him. After all, apart from the space cannons mounted on the ground in Fort Alden and Fort Gillet, the *Valor* was now fighting alone against six Zeta ships over the Moon for at least the next 10 minutes until Station Navarone's fighters made it to their target.

"C:Drive?" Gold asked, motioning for a report.

"Three of the Zeta ships have broken away from the Moon. Looks like they're moving to catch up with the rest of the Zeta ships that are on approach to Earth. They're clustered in their tight formation again."

Gold nodded. "I want thick coverage of our ships at atmosphere over Europe. Any ship with onboard weaponry that can fire in that atmosphere. And I want a wall of metal beneath atmosphere to meet those Zeta fuckers if they break through. Understand?"

"Yes sir!" C:Drive responded.

Reece looked at Gold. "We have confirmation that the UNF *Vortex* and UNF *Woodbrow* are close. They're coming to join the fight!"

"Good!" Gold looked back out the observation window at the calm, quiet city of New York below. "Everyone get ready," he said firmly, "because if they make it through those lines of defense, then we're entering this war. And we're the last goddamn chance Earth has."

24

Chiseled Tunnels

Harris strode ahead, as Welles and the twins followed. The light was fading fast but he did see the highway Archie had referred to.

"Sir?" Welles called to him.

He stopped and turned around.

"Is that ...?" she motioned off in the distance.

He followed the direction she pointed, focused his Alpha eyes, and saw what she was referring to: the gnarled and twisted tree from their dreams; bent right over on its side, its leaves touching the ground. A shiver traveled down his spine, which he was certain had just traveled down hers too.

"What's the latest report from the Moon, Archie?" he said.

Archie was silent a moment.

"Archie?" Harris asked again.

"*The* Llangollen *and* Ramedes *have been lost*," he reported. "*The* Valor *has been hit. It's currently heading toward the Moon, but its angle and speed are off.*"

"It's crashing?" Harris asked.

The silence sat.

"Archie?" Harris barked.

"*Yes. I'm afraid the Valor has just crashed into the Moon.*"

"But the *Valor* was our strongest ship?" Freya said, eyes wide.

"How many casualties?" Harris asked, walking again.

"*There are no survivors from the* Llangollen, Ramedes, Kandor *or* Hopetoun. *I'm waiting for reports from the* Valor."

"And on the Moon?" Harris asked. "Civilians?"

"*The other ships were all lost in space. The* Valor *crashed in an uninhabited area outside Meridian. But damage from the Zeta ships has been received in Galilei, Elysium and Prosperitas. Most civilians were warned in time, to ready themselves in spacesuits.*"

"President Gillet?" Harris asked.

"*He was moved to safety in time. He is okay.*"

"What kind of weapons did they use?" Harris asked quickening his pace as they walked.

"*The Zetas?*"

"Yes. Give me a rundown on what to expect."

"*They used a heat pulse. Similar to our lasers, but delivered in a much bigger and more destructive payload.*"

"Did we get data on it?"

"*Yes, the* Llangollen *and* Valor *recorded everything and uploaded every two minutes, as planned, to all other UNF ships. They have the information and Captain Gold has been instructing them in defensive measures. He has local units on alert on Mars, and has sent fighters from Station Navarone to the Moon to assist. A UNF rescue operation is underway from the bases on the ground to find survivors of the UNF* Valor."

"Good," Harris said, clenching his jaw, and trying not to think about the units he'd just lost.

"*Turn south now,*" Archie instructed them. "*McKinley will meet you at the Greenough Hamlet, a small historic village along the road.*"

"What's the Zetas position now?" Harris asked as they turned south and continued walking. Archie was silent.

Harris heard the waves crashing on the beach, the ocean obviously close now. He thought he heard the sound of a vehicle. *McKinley?*

"Archie," Harris barked, "report!"

"*I'm sorry, Colonel Harris. I was scanning. Gold's units have begun to engage with the Zetas off Earth at atmosphere.*"

"Shit," Harris hissed. "How close are they?"

"*They're approximately 400 kilometers above Europe. But they appear to be splitting up. Open your PDPs.*"

Harris and Carrie pulled out their PDPs and opened them. A message popped up from Archie, they clicked it open and watched as footage rolled, taken from Earth, of sparks of light across the Moon and then sparks of light occurring over the Earth.

"Goddamnit, they're close," Welles said, clutching her PDP tightly.

"We have to get back to the ship and get up there!" Harris said, breaking into a jog.

They ran onward and saw vehicle lights appear in the distance. They were near the highway, but it wasn't McKinley. A car rolled past, packed to the brim with people beginning to run from what they'd seen on the various media outlets.

"You're close to the Hamlet now. Just a little further."

Harris pumped his legs as hard as he could, eager to get back to the ship and enter this fight. He felt so helpless, stranded here on the ground, while all his Alpha units and every other UNF unit out there were doing what they could.

"There it is!" Welles yelled, pointing to a cluster of buildings up ahead.

Gold gripped the back of the chair he was standing behind, eyes fixed on his chief pilot.

"They've broken through," Reece told him, face serious and worried. "A contingent have broken through. Some are still fighting at atmosphere, but they're getting through. They'll hit the Earth in minutes."

"Ready the weapons," Gold said calmly. "We're entering this war."

As his team busied themselves with his instructions, Gold took a second to pop open the cover on his watch. There on the underside of the lid, was a picture of his wife, Andrea. He gave a small smile, then closed it again and fixed his eyes out the observation window.

We are not dying today, he whispered in his mind. *We are not dying today!*

Carrie ran toward the buildings, glad to see civilization, until she realized the village was empty.

"What is this place?" she asked Archie.

"It's a tourist attraction. The Hamlet is a collection of historical buildings from the 1800s," he told her, sounding as though he were reading from a travel guide. *"Once home to more than 100 people it contains 11 of Greenough's oldest buildings all of which have been faithfully restored. Described as a 'village frozen in time', the buildings include a courthouse, police station, school and church."*

"Where's McKinley?" Harris hissed.

"He's on the other side. He..." Archie broke off.

"Archie?" Carrie said, but something made her stop and turn around. Harris did too. They looked up into the sky and saw the lights appear.

Like pinpricks at first, they slowly grew in size. Some flared brightly, then suddenly dimmed out altogether.

Ships lost to the fight.

They stood frozen, in awe and in shock, as they watched one light grow larger and larger, roaring in an arc toward the Earth. Then in the distance, from the nearby town of Geraldton, air-raid sirens sounded. Would a town like that be equipped with air-raid sirens, she wondered. Or had the UNF installed them recently?

"Hunter?" Harris spoke into his comms.

"Sir!" Hunter answered.

"You see this, right?"

"Yes, sir, we're tracking it. The Aurora *is on standby, ready to fight."*

"I'm about to rendezvous with McKinley. We'll be there as soon as we can."

"It's a three and half hour drive, sir," Hunter said. *"You sure you don't want me to zip out there and pick you up?"*

"You can't," Harris said. "We have to protect the comms facility at all costs. We need the *Aurora*'s firepower to do that."

"Then hurry up and get here, sir."

"Will do," Harris said, clicking his comms off.

Carrie watched, feeling her body tense as the light raced toward the Earth. As it neared, she saw it was black, triangular in shape, with three bulbs protruding from each of its tips – the Zeta flight decks. It began to rotate rapidly, spinning over and over, and she realized it was getting ready to burrow into the ground.

It hit the Earth with a deep groan and the Earth shook beneath their feet. A scream sounded behind her, and she turned and saw the twins staring, terrified, into the sky. She shared a glance with Harris, knowing this moment they had both dreamed a thousand times before.

There was another thud, much closer this time, as another one hit. The ground shook violently and the four of them lost their footing. Carrie darted her eyes to the sky again and saw more bright lights shining in the distance, some headed toward Earth, some engaged in firefights.

"The fighting has spread from European airspace," Archie told them. *"Centralis is under fire. Firefights are occurring over Asia also."*

Carrie locked panicked eyes with Harris.

"A pocket of fighting has also commenced over Australia."

"Yeah, no shit!" Harris said.

"I suggest you take cover."

Carrie spun around to the children. "RUN!" she yelled, racing for Freya, grabbing her hand and heaving her back up to her feet. She glanced over her shoulder for Brody, but saw Harris running toward him. She turned and began sprinting, for where, she didn't know, but ran with all her might and heaved Freya along with her, listening to Harris and Brody's footsteps coming behind them. And all the while, as she ran for her life, she kept thinking one thing: *Where's McKinley?*

Harris ran along with Brody, following Welles and Freya, past the Hamlet, trying to rendezvous with McKinley. They heard another thud and looked behind them. A third ship had hit Earth and was burrowing down. The land, sloping slightly to the ocean and broken by scrub-dotted sand dunes, now had three fiery holes punched into it. Catching their breath they watched for a moment, and saw movement at the site of the first ship. Humanoid figures emerging.

"I—is that them?" Freya whispered.

"I think it's the HH," Welles said, narrowing her eyes, trying to get a better look at them. Harris did too, but they moved quickly, scattering like ants. Although the air-raid sirens sounded in the distance, he still heard, clear as day, the deep guttural roar of whatever it was that came out of the ship.

"Why didn't they listen to you?" Brody shouted desperately, grabbing hold of Harris's shirt in his fist.

Harris saw Brody's scared face and took hold of the hand bunching his shirt. Looking his godson firmly in the eye, he said, "They didn't know, they couldn't have known."

"But you warned them! You said you needed more units!"

It hurt him to see tears flooding the eyes of Doc's son. Harris grabbed the boy's shoulders. "Yes, I did, but we can't focus on that now. Right now, we need to survive! You understand me? We need to focus on survival! Will you do that for me?"

Brody stared him for a moment, then suddenly nodded back.

"Yes, Uncle Saul," he sniffed.

Another fireball hit closer to them, and they lost their footing.

"They're getting closer!" Welles yelled.

"MOVE! MOVE! MOVE!" Harris barked, as Welles ran further into the bushy scrub.

"This way!" they suddenly heard McKinley's voice call out to them.

They spun around and saw him waving them forward, half hidden amongst the shrubs to their left. As they reached him, he snatched Freya's hand and ran. He began to lead them, weaving through the shrubs scraping along their arms, until they finally came across some kind of trapdoor in the ground, hidden beneath a camouflage of leaves and sand. He bent down and pulled the cover across.

"Inside!" He grabbed Freya and lowered her into the hole, as Colonel Welles reached up from inside to grab her.

"Dad?" Welles asked.

"Hurry! We need to hide!" McKinley barked, darting his eyes into the distance then grabbing Brody and lowering him down too. She went to question McKinley, but he quickly ushered her toward the hole as well. She looked down at her father, then bent down and scuttled inside. Harris clapped his hand around McKinley's arm, locking eyes with him, then swiftly followed her inside.

*

Carrie spotted Jesse standing with Roy and Sampson. As soon as her feet hit the ground, she and ran toward him and pulled him into her arms.

"I'm okay. I'm okay," he said, wriggling out of her grasp. "You were the one in trouble!"

She smiled and kissed him, then turned around to see Harris and McKinley squeezing inside, closing the trapdoor. Harris caught his breath, while McKinley moved to Brody and Freya to check they were alright.

"Where the hell are we?" Carrie asked, looking around at the bare, empty cavity in which they stood.

"This tunnel leads back to the Hamlet," McKinley said.

"When those things hit the ground, we hid in one of the Hamlet buildings," Roy told her. "The police station. We spotted a trapdoor in one of the cells and followed it here."

"So what do we do now?" Carrie asked.

Harris looked at McKinley. "We need to get back to the *Aurora*. We're losing ships out there!"

McKinley suddenly held his finger to his lips and motioned for everyone to remain still. Harris suddenly looked up at the roof, scanning for something. Freya and Jesse did, too. Carrie watched intently, wishing she had the Alpha hearing like they did. Brody's face seemed to echo her thoughts.

Harris motioned silently for McKinley to lead them back the way he'd come. McKinley looked at the kids and signaled for them to move out silently. The children nodded, slinking away Alpha silent, then he turned to the Sentinels and her father and indicated the same, although he looked concerned about their ability to move quietly.

As they moved off, Carrie turned around to Harris who was still looking upward. He glanced over at her, then gave a nod and they followed the others.

It was only a short way to where the tunnel surfaced at the cell opening. McKinley waited in the cell to help everyone up. When Carrie made it to the surface, she moved out of the cell, along the wooden floorboards of the hallway, to the front of the building where she peered out the windows. Holding Alpha-still, she tried to detect any movement outside. She saw none, other than the dying flames of the holes in the ground in the distance.

"They've moved past us now, scouring the area," McKinley said, "but no doubt they'll be back."

"Archie?" Harris said quietly beside her. "Report."

"We've lost four ships over Europe. Damage has been sustained in France, Germany, Switzerland and Norway."

"Gold?" he asked.

"The fighting has spread to North America. The Carcharias *has entered the fight alongside the US air force."*

"The AWAFP facility?"

"Is still secure, no fighting has occurred there yet. The battles are currently taking place over the eastern seaboard."

"How many Zeta ships are left?"

"There are six still engaged in battle at atmosphere, ten engaged over Europe, one over Centralis, eight over North America, three over Australia, and the last four have made landfall in Australia."

"And the Moon?"

"Fighting has ceased in that location. The remaining Zeta ships fled to Earth's atmosphere. The Station Navarone fighters remain on patrol across the Moon."

Harris looked around at those with him. "We're not going to fit everyone here into the PV. We need to get back to the ship!"

"Three on approach!" Roy said, peering out the window.

"Get back!" McKinley hissed and threw himself in front of the children.

"Wait! They're not Zetas, don't shoot!" Sampson yelled, as three figures burst through the front door.

Everyone had their weapons aimed at the three, who froze to the spot when they noticed the crowded, yet darkened, room before them.

"Bloody hell!" one of them said in a thick Australian accent, as he flicked on his torch. The other two followed, and they saw three men of Aboriginal descent standing there, eyes wide, torches shining. Between the light and the darkness, it made the Alpha eyes on Carrie, Harris and McKinley glow.

"Aargh!" the young skinny man on the left yelped, jumping backward. "Cat people."

"It's the aliens!" the young pudgy man to the right yelled.

"No, no, no," Sampson said, waving his arms at them. "They're cool. They can just see in the dark, that's all."

The three men stared open-mouthed at Sampson.

"It's alright," Sampson said, waving his hand at them. "We're friendly, brother!"

"Yeah, right," the one in the middle said, a long bushy gray beard across his face. "Those guns say otherwise."

"Have you seen what's out there?" Roy asked them.

"Why do you think we're in here?" the bearded one said. "This is *our* hiding spot."

"We're loaning it," Harris said, turning his face away and closing his eyes as the bearded man shone his torch at him.

"Who's the blackfella, then?" the man asked. "He in charge or something?"

Sampson smiled and looked back at the bearded man. "Yeah, he's in charge. He's an American blackfella."

"A yank?" the young one said.

"What're they doing here?" the pudgy one said.

The bearded man held up his hands to quieten his companions. "What do you think they're bloody doing? They're hiding like us."

"Hey, you're Bertie's boy, aren't ya?" Sampson asked the skinny one.

"Yeah," he said, shining his torch on Sampson, making him squint.

"Oh, shit!" the pudgy one said, also shining his torch on him. "It's bloody Sampson Warra!"

"Sampson Warra?" The bearded one shone his torch on Sampson, too. "Oh, from the footy. You used to play for Chapman Valley didn't you?"

Sampson nodded, holding his hand up to shade his eyes from three beams of light.

"What happened to you, then?" the bearded man asked. "Why'd you stop playing footy?"

Sampson motioned to his uniform. "I work for the UNF now. I'm a Sentinel."

"A what?" the skinny one furrowed his brow.

"A Sentinel," Sampson said.

"Is it better than playing footy?" the bearded one asked.

"I'm sorry to cut this reunion short," Harris said, unable to hide the terseness in his voice, "but in case you haven't realized, there is a war going on outside, and I'd like to get back to it, thank you."

The bearded one shone his torch at Harris again.

"How did you get here?" Harris asked them.

"That's a Space Duty uniform," the skinny one said, shining his torch on Harris's shirt, then moving it to Carrie's and McKinley's. "They've got Space Duty uniforms."

"Do you have a vehicle?" Harris asked again.

"Maybe," the bearded one said, "what's it to ya?"

McKinley suddenly turned his head, listening to something. "They're coming!"

"Shit!" Harris hissed. "Hurry!" he said, racing for the cell with the trapdoor and pulling it back. "Everyone, get in! Now!"

Captain Edwin Morrell crouched beside the wall of a building and looked up at the broken dome over Centralis. They had engaged the weather shield over the island in an attempt to protect it, but nothing could defend it against the heat weapon the circling Zeta ship had used. And now as one section of the dome sat burned and charred and gaping, the Zeta ship flew right on in.

The sound of Centralis' mounted guns rang out, as lasers fired in the direction of the ship. The black triangular Zeta craft, orbs on its tips, dodged and weaved the beams, then took aim and blasted their heat ray weapon at the mounted gun. It exploded in sparks and fire, and more damage was taken to the glass dome behind it.

"Lower the weather shield!" Morrell barked into his comms. "Lower it before it fucking caves in on everyone!"

He heard the dome retracting, but then a horrible, loud, mechanical groan sounded over the island and it soon stalled. Badly damaged, it wouldn't budge any further.

"Shit!" he hissed, eyeing the Zeta ship as it circled overhead. "Get engineering to the dome and get it retracted! You hear? Get it retracted now!"

"*Yes, sir!*" one of the Command operators responded.

"Gun Five! Do you copy?" he barked next.

"*Yes, sir!*" Sergeant Suavarez, the man in charge of Gun Five, answered.

"On my mark, I want you to fire at that thing and draw its attention. Guns Three and Four?"

"Yes, sir!" their voices came over his comms set.

"While Gun Five lures that thing, you two take aim and take it down!"

"Over the city?" Lieutenant Bottonni, the man in charge of Gun Three, asked.

"We sure as shit can't leave it in here with that damn heat ray!" Morrell spat.

"But the dome..." Bottonni argued.

"Engineering are going to get that dome back further. While they do that, we make the most of the gaping hole on the south-eastern side. That's why I'm ordering you. Gun Three and Four are angled best to blast it through the hole and out into open water."

"That hole doesn't give us much room for error, sir," Captain Stolz, the man in charge of Gun Four spoke.

"Did you hear my fucking order?" Morrell hissed. "This ship will melt this entire fucking island if we don't shoot it down. We do what we have to! Fire on my order!"

"Yes, sir!"

Morrell's eyes followed the Zeta ship as it circled. He wondered what it was looking for, why it wasn't firing indiscriminately. Then he remembered Harris's briefing, and the theory that the Zetas wanted slaves. Everyone was off the street and indoors, except a handful of his units. Maybe they were looking for people?

Grenner moved up beside him. "Let's take this fucker out."

"Working on it," Morrell said, then clicked his comms again. "Everyone get ready." He watched as the Zeta ship neared the gaping hole. "Gun Five! Draw them nearer with your fire, then get the hell out of there!"

Laser fire shot out into the broken dome, skimming the edges of the Zeta ship. It swiftly altered its course and turned its heat weapon on the Earth gun.

"Three and Four! Now!" Morrell barked.

Laser fire erupted from each side of the dome, aiming for the ship. Gun Three clipped a wing, and Gun Four hit the tail. The Zeta ship briefly lost control, hurtling toward the broken dome, and perhaps for freedom, but it suddenly pulled up sharply, scraping along the edge of the dome and finally bouncing off it. With smoke pluming heavily at its tail, it veered sharply and began to descend into a crash landing. Morrell's eyes jumped to the direction it was heading and saw the glass pyramid of Command.

"Fuck, it's headed for Command! It's aiming for Command!" he yelled over the comms. "Shoot it again! Shoot it! Shoot it!"

More laser fire rang out across the dome, clipping the ship and sending it off-course, but only a little. It didn't crash into the middle of Command, but it still took out part of the south-eastern wing, sending concrete and glass spitting everywhere on impact, before skidding along the ground until it came to a stop.

"Fuck, it's mostly intact!" Grenner said. "How is it mostly intact?"

"It's made of strong stuff," Morrell said, straightening and flashing Grenner a look. "But so are we." He turned and looked at his crew. "Alphas! Let's move!"

As he ran toward the crash site with his Alpha unit in tow, he clicked on his comms again. "Keep everyone indoors," he said. "I repeat, keep everyone indoors. My unit will check on the crash site and see if any are still alive. I repeat, everyone else stay the fuck back until I tell you to!"

"You sure you don't want back-up?" Bottonni asked over the comms.

"No," Morrell said in a low, flat voice, slowing his pace as he neared the site. "If there're any left alive, my unit will handle them. Trust me. We got this."

Harris watched as the bearded Aboriginal man squeezed past him. "This way," he said. "You don't know where you're going, mate."

Harris stared at him, but followed. The man looked back, sizing him up. "You're a bloody big blackfella, you know that?"

"If you don't mind, the name is Colonel Saul Harris."

"Hey?"

"I'd prefer it if you don't refer to me as 'blackfella'. It's Colonel Saul Harris."

"Oh, right. Didn't mean any offense." The man reached his hand back to Harris. "I'm Gerald Bartol. They call me Gerry."

Harris looked at his hand and shook it, noticing an expensive gold watch around the man's wrist. "That's Tucker and that's Cushy," Gerry said, pointing to the skinny one, then the plump one. "They're my nephews."

Harris nodded at them, then turned back to Gerry. "I need to get out of here and to a vehicle. Do you know the quickest way I can do that?"

"With those things out there?" Gerry gave him a look as though he were crazy.

"I can handle it."

Gerry gave him another once-over. "Yeah, you probably could."

"*Colonel Harris,*" Archie's voice interrupted.

"What the bloody hell was that?" Tucker yelped from behind Welles. "She talks from her neck?"

Harris stopped and turned around to Welles who was positioned between him and Tucker. "What is it, Archie?"

"*A Zeta ship is on approach to the facility. This one isn't preparing to burrow like the others.*"

"Hunter!" Harris barked into his comms. "You got one on approach!"

"*I got my eye on it,*" he replied. "*If it comes closer, I'll try to lead it away.*"

"Jesus!" Harris said, closing his eyes and clenching his jaw. "I need. To get. To my ship!"

"Well, with those things all over this place, you can't," Gerry told him plainly.

Harris opened his eyes and saw the man's sympathetic stare.

"If you go out there, you'll get your head blown off," Gerry said. "You'll be no good to anyone then. There's nothing you can do right now."

"He's right," McKinley said, glancing at the kids and their companions. "We're outnumbered."

Suddenly the ground shook.

"The buried Zeta ship?" Welles suggested. "If they connect with it, that could be one more in the sky."

"Hurry up. Here," Gerry said, "there's a room we can hide in."

They followed him into a square opening about ten meters by ten meters. There were desks up against one wall, empty beer bottles, a couch.

"What is this place?" Harris asked.

"Once upon a time it was a shelter in case World War Two hit this far south. It was forgotten about for years, until recently. Now the bloody teenagers come down here for a little nooky."

"World War Two?" McKinley asked, looking around. "Here?"

"The Japanese bombed Broome and Darwin," Colonel Welles told them. "You Americans weren't the only ones hit outside of Europe, you know."

Gerry laughed nervously, looking at Harris. "It's funny, isn't it? Once upon a time we bombed each other, eh? Now we're getting hit by things from outer space."

The ground crumbled again and the children instinctively moved toward Welles. She ushered them over against the wall and they sat down on the floor; Freya on one side, Jesse and Brody on the other.

"Archie?" Harris spoke, stepping closer to Welles. "Report."

"*The* Aurora *is still at the facility. The Zeta ship has slowed. It must have detected them.*"

"What else?"

"*Centralis has been hit.*"

Harris locked eyes with Welles.

"How bad, Archie?" she asked quickly.

"*Command has sustained damage. The area is being evacuated.*"

"Colt?" Welles asked quickly.

Archie was silent a moment. "*The Village remains intact.*"

"Morrell?" Harris asked.

Again, Archie was quiet a moment as he scanned. "*The attacking Zeta ship has crashed. Morrell's unit are securing the area and searching for survivors.*"

"Gold?" he asked, turning around to see the three Aboriginal men staring at him keenly, listening to the reports of the carnage.

"*The* Carcharias *remains in battle over North America, alongside the US air force.*"

Harris lowered his head, squeezing his eyes shut, and ran his hand back and forth over his head. "What else?"

"*We've lost the UNF* Ruediger *over Paris.*"

Harris exhaled heavily. Another battleship gone. His men were dying out there.

"*There is good news, though. There are some survivors of the* Valor *crash on the Moon. A few hundred made it to safety in their spacesuits.*"

"A few hundred out of how many. A thousand?"

"Archie," McKinley said. "Hunter and the *Aurora*?"

"*The* Aurora *has made itself known to the Zeta ship.*"

"What's happening?" McKinley snapped.

"*The Zeta ship is one of a select few that are larger than the other ships in their fleet.*"

"What's happening?" Harris barked.

"*The* Aurora *has positioned itself between the comms facility and the Zeta* *ship. Right now, they're just facing each other, waiting for the other to make* *a move.*"

Harris dropped to a crouch and rested his head in his hands. "Come on, Hunter. Come on, Hunter. Come on, Hunter," he chanted quietly, willing everything he had into thoughts of Hunter and Frazer doing what they could.

McKinley, too, slumped down on the couch beside Roy and Sampson, listening intently.

"Maybe we shouldn't listen?" Welles said.

"I have to stay with them," Harris said. "I have to."

"*The* Aurora *is moving slowly,*" Archie reported. "*I think it's trying to lure* *the ship away from the facility.*"

The silence sat around them as they sat and listened for knowledge of the *Aurora*'s fate. McKinley leaned forward, elbows on knees and buried his head in his hands.

"*The Zeta ship has fired!*"

McKinley looked up.

"*The* Aurora *maneuvered away! It's running. The* Aurora *is racing away* *and the Zeta ship is following.*"

"Turn it off!" Welles said, her eyes pleading at Harris and looking back at the children.

Harris gave a nod, and Welles instructed Archie to hold reports. Harris clicked his comms piece on, though, and sat in the corner, waiting for Hunter's voice to come back on the line.

Professor Sharley stood up from where he crouched. He looked at the dead guard. He listened carefully, filtering out the air raid siren, and heard footsteps running his way. He looked back at the dead guard at his feet. He'd just broken the man's neck. This might be tricky to explain.

The door opened and he looked up to see Dr. Scavesci with another guard.

"What's happening?" Sharley feigned distress.

"My god," Scavesci said, running over to the guard, "what happened?"

"I don't know," Sharley said. "I think he had a heart attack. What's happening outside? It felt like the whole building shook."

"The Zetas," Scavesci said, standing up. "They're here! We gotta go!"

"The Zetas?" Sharley asked, genuinely shocked.

"Yes, come quickly."

"Where are you taking me?" Sharley asked, as they approached the doorway where the guard waited.

"We need to evac now," Scavesci said. "The building might collapse."

"Oh?" Sharley asked, realizing they were in too much of a rush to cuff him. He knew as soon as he heard the siren that something big was going down and that this would be a chance to escape. And now, seeing his free hands, he knew he would.

As he passed the guard at the door who was looking into the room suspiciously at his fallen comrade, Sharley landed a swift, hard elbow to his sternum. The guard gasped and fell to his knees, clutching his fractured breastplate. Sharley swung a brutal knee at his face, then chopped his hand down on the back of the neck. He heard the crack as the man's body fell to the floor.

"Professor, no!" Scavesci called in panic. The attack had happened so quickly the doctor couldn't believe his eyes.

Sharley ripped the weapon off the guard and pointed it at Scavesci. The psychiatrist quickly raised his hands and backed up against the wall.

"Sharley! Don't," he pleaded calmly. "I am your friend. I've always been on your side."

"Have you?" Sharley stepped toward him, thrusting the gun up under his chin.

"Please!"

"Where was your friendship when they kept me locked up as a prisoner all these years? Hmm? Where were you when they used me for their program, then wouldn't let me touch it?"

"I did what I could," he said softly, his forehead glistening with fear.

"Well, I've had enough of your incompetence," Sharley said with cold eyes and a voice to match. "I don't need you anymore." Sharley tilted the gun slightly and fired across Scavesci's neck, blowing this throat out. His face was splattered with blood as Scavesci raised his hands to stem the bleeding and cover the gaping hole. Sharley hadn't meant for the shot to be fatal. He wanted Scavesci to suffer first. He dropped the weapon, pulled Scavesci's hands away, then reached into the wound and tore what remained of Scavesci's Adam's apple out. Scavesci's eyes went wide, and he gargled, dying. Sharley held his neck parts up in front of the man's face, smiled, then dropped them onto the ground.

"No more of your lies." He let go of Scavesci then, who dropped to the ground also.

"So long, doctor," Sharley said, walking off down the corridor.

Captain Lincoln Gold sat tensed in his chair, watching as his pilots did what they could against their Zeta opponent. The Zeta ship was smaller, more maneuverable, but the *Carcharias* had bulk on its side and weapons that fired a lot more quickly than the heat ray of the Zeta ship. That, they had discovered, was a weakness of their enemy. The heat ray took a little time to charge and fire. Of course, it was incredibly destructive once it did, but as long as the *Carcharias* continued to dodge it, they would be okay. They just needed to use the precious seconds between the heat ray firing and recharging to try and destroy the Zeta ship, all the while avoiding getting caught up in any of the firefights taking place over the eastern seaboard. He could currently see seven Zeta ships and at least 20 to 30 jet fighters battling across the skies.

The *Carcharias* was lucky enough to have taken one Zeta ship out already, but the one that tailed them now was proving trickier.

"Cannon is red!" Staff Sergeant Becker yelled. "Heat ray about to fire!"

Gold felt the *Carcharias* lurch upward, just as the white light of the heat ray shot out below them.

"Jesus, that was close!" C:Drive said, eyes as wide as his ears.

"Get 'em in your sights!" Gold yelled. "Take these fuckers out!"

"Guns targeting!" Becker yelled. "Trying to get a lock!"

"We got another bogey on our tail!" C:Drive exclaimed.

Gold saw the second ship on the rear cameras. "Shit."

Ryker looked at him. "Is it time to call the *Stanmore* into play?"

"UNF *Stanmore*," Gold spoke into his comms. "We could do with a little back-up."

"Roger that. If these Zetas blow us out of the sky, then you're next. Let's not let it come to that, huh?"

Captain Edwin Morrell peered around the ruins of the south-eastern section of the Command building. He tried to ignore the bodies he'd passed, all dressed in UNF uniforms, victims of the building collapse. Instead, he focused his eyes on the Zeta ship, which had crashed with half the ship rammed through the perimeter security fence of Command.

"Operations. Report?" he whispered into his comms.

"Seven targets have scattered from the ship. They are still close to the wreck, however."

"Alright," Morrell whispered. "We'll clear the ship first and make sure there's none left onboard, then we'll sweep up those on the run. Make sure you keep everyone off the streets, understand? Shit's about to get bloody and I'm not taking responsibility for collateral damage."

"Affirmative. Streets are clear except for your unit and the targets."

Morrell looked around at Grenner and motioned for him to do a cross-cover. And as the rest of the unit covered them, they ran across to the yawning entrance of the obsidian Zeta ship.

25

Chaos

Carrie looked over at McKinley. He looked emotionally torn. He'd come to help her and the twins, but in doing so he'd left his ship and now they were in trouble.

"Is Uncle Hunter going to be okay?" Freya asked quietly.

Carrie squeezed her close. "He's a great pilot. He's careful and he's committed. He'll do everything he can to save his big brown bird."

Jesse snuggled into her side then, and she could tell her boy was finally scared.

Freya noticed, too, eyeing her little brother, then she looked at Carrie. "Tell us the Moon baby story?"

Carrie smiled at her, understanding what she was trying to do: take Jesse's mind off things. "You and Brody are my Moon babies."

"Why?" Brody asked, also registering their intention.

"Because you two were conceived on the Moon. In the Colony of Meridian. You were special because you came from two fathers. Out of this world special!" she smiled. "My two little Moon babies."

"And what about me?" Jesse's weak voice asked.

Carrie pulled him tight and kissed his forehead. "You? You are my Earth baby. Conceived the old-fashioned way. Right here on Earth, in Centralis." Her smile faded as she thought of the invaded Centralis. She glanced at

488

McKinley and he met her look, then he stood from the couch and moved over to one of the desks. Jesse got up and followed him.

The silence hung thickly again.

"We could put some music on or something?" Cushy suggested.

"Is that wise?" her father asked.

"Just quietly," Gerry said, "to calm everyone down."

"No!" Harris said firmly.

McKinley suddenly stiffened, his nose twitching as a faint growl sounded down the tunnel. Their faces all turned to the doorway. Harris jumped up and pulled out his weapon and McKinley pulled Jesse behind him.

"Tucker, no!" Harris yelled as the young man peered through the doorway to see what was behind the growl. He suddenly jerked back, and they saw a silver metal spear sticking right though him, blood pooling down his back.

"TUCKER!" Gerry yelled as his nephew fell backward, dead.

Carrie jumped to her feet, snatching Jesse and pulling him toward her.

"Move," Harris said, motioning for the opposite doorway. As they did they heard something whistle through the air.

"REE!" Her father grabbed her and twisted her away, as an explosion rocked the doorway and debris collapsed in a heap blocking the exit. Carrie hit the ground hard, then looked up from the floor, panting dust. She quickly glanced around to see that her kids were okay, then looked back at her father whose arm was still around her. His back and side were red with blood. His body had sheltered hers from the blow.

"Dad!" she said, pulling herself up and looking him over. She heard laser fire and looked up to see McKinley and Harris either side of the door, firing at the HH or Zetas or whoever was out there.

"Go! You gotta get out." Her father groaned in pain. "Get out!"

Carrie ran over to the doorway and began heaving rocks out the way. Roy and Sampson were quickly by her side, puffing and panting as they lifted boulders half the size of the ones she lifted. Gerry dragged Tucker over to the side, out of the way, leaning over his dead nephew, distraught, while Cushy watched on in shock.

"Welles! How we doing?" Harris yelled over his shoulder.

Carrie saw a small hole. She glanced back at Freya and waved her forward.

"Can you fit through?"

Freya climbed up and tried, but got caught at her hips. Carrie looked back at Jesse and grabbed him.

"Honey, I need you to see if you can fit through that gap and start pulling rocks down from the other side. Do you think you can do that"

Jesse nodded, then climbed up to the hole. Carrie watched him, proud of how brave he was. He tucked his head and torso through the hole, and she gave his butt a push and he scrambled through.

"You okay?" she called through the hole, as the roof overhead groaned. She looked up at it, then back at Jesse, who gave a thumbs up sign.

"Ok, start pulling down what you can!" she said, "Just around the hole, alright?" Then she looked at her Sentinels and barked, "Keep moving rock!"

The hole became larger and as soon as they fitted, she helped Freya and Brody through to the other side, then continued on.

A spear smacked into the doorway near Harris's head.

"Welles!" he yelled urgently.

"Almost!" she yelled back, grabbing Cushy and yanking him toward the hole that was now about a third of the size of the original doorway. "Go through!"

Cushy didn't argue and squeezed his pudgy frame through. Roy and Sampson followed, eager to be with the twins.

"What about my nephew?" Gerry asked, tear-stained eyes looking desperately at Tucker's lifeless body.

Carrie grabbed Gerry's arm. "You'll have to come back for him. I'm sorry."

"But?"

"Help me!" she said, bending down to lift her father.

He groaned in pain and she took another look at his wounds. His flesh was torn open all down his side. He grabbed her hand.

"Honey, I'm only going to slow you down."

"No!"

"Ree."

"No! You're coming with us."

He squeezed her hand tightly. "If you take me with you, I will slow you down and get someone killed. You know this."

"Dad, no!" she said, feeling a lump surge in her throat. She placed her hands on his wounds, pooling with blood. She swore she could feel his inner flesh against her fingers.

"Ree!" He looked into her eyes, wincing in pain. "Be smart!"

"I'm not leaving you. You're still alive!"

"You have to! I'll cover you. It's the only way you're going to get out of here alive."

"Mum!" Brody yelled through the hole.

"McKinley!" Harris barked, as more laser fire occurred. He motioned for him to move back, and McKinley quickly slid to her side.

"Get out!" McKinley ordered Gerry, who was still glancing back at Tucker.

"I'm sorry, mate," Gerry whispered as he took one last look at Tucker, wiped his eyes, then squeezed through the hole.

McKinley looked at Carrie's father. "Jesus," he said, eyeing his wounds.

"Get her out of here," her father groaned to him. "I'll cover you. Go!"

"Dad, I'm not leaving you!" Carrie said, as tears rolled down her cheeks. She looked at McKinley. "We can lift him!"

"I'll slow you down! You know that, soldier!" he hissed at McKinley. "I will slow you down and get someone killed. You need to go. Give me a gun and I'll cover you. Get out of here! You're wasting time!"

"McKinley!" Harris yelled. "They're moving up! *Hurry*!"

McKinley looked at Carrie. "We gotta go!"

"No!" she said, pulling her father up. He groaned and more blood spilled to the ground.

"I'm dying, Ree!" he yelled. "I'm dying! You can't save me. Just go!"

"I'm not leaving you," she said, scrunching his shirt in her fist, as tears poured down. "It feels like I only just found you!"

Her father's eyes watered. "I love you, Ree. And I love those kids. So you go to them. You keep them safe for me."

"Carrie," McKinley said, grabbing her shoulder, "we gotta go! *Now!*"

"Let me do this for you," her father said, a tear rolling down his own cheek, as he gave a pained smile. "This is what I do best." He raised his hand to her cheek. "Protecting my family."

Another roar sounded down the tunnel. Much closer this time.

"Get her out of here, soldier!" her father half barked, half groaned, at McKinley. "That's an order!" McKinley gave a nod, gripped her father's hand briefly, then filled it with a gun. Her father nodded back, and McKinley's arm swooped around her and dragged her toward the hole.

"Dad!" she called as McKinley pushed her through. She fell through to the other side then looked back to see McKinley drag her father over to where Harris was.

"Get out of here!" her father barked at Harris. "I got this!"

Harris looked at him, at his wounds, then at McKinley. The growls sounded nearer, then Harris quickly ducked back to avoid a spear soaring through the doorway and landing in the rubble.

"Move it, captain!" her father yelled at McKinley. "Get back to your ship!"

Harris quickly grabbed her father's shoulder. "Thank you!" he said, then pulled something off his belt and gave it to him.

"Thank you," her father said back.

Harris turned and sprinted for the hole, as McKinley and Colonel Welles fired down the tunnel.

Harris fell through the hole to the floor beside her, and she pulled out her gun and aimed it down the corridor, as McKinley fired walking backward to the hole.

"Go!" Carrie yelled at Harris. "Go find the kids!"

Harris nodded and took off down the corridor.

"Behind you," she warned McKinley who glanced around and saw her gun was out. He kept to the left as she aimed over his shoulder. She saw three of what she guessed were HH coming toward them. They were broad, muscular, human-like, but moved like different creatures. She fired and caught one in the head.

"Move!" McKinley said, and she stepped back as he dived through the hole.

She heard laser fire and looked back to see her father firing down the tunnel at the approaching HH, hitting one. She raised her gun again, but McKinley caught her around the waist and pulled her with him as he ran down the tunnel.

"No! Dad!" she called out, but despite herself she didn't fight McKinley's momentum. She knew she had to let it happen. So she ran and ran and ran, until they saw the opening ahead. They sprinted at it as a loud explosion sounded behind them. Within moments both she and McKinley were lifted into the air by the shockwave and spat out the opening, landing on the ground with a whump and a roll.

It took Carrie a moment to gather her senses. Her vision spun and sounds were blurred. But she made out the shape of Freya in front on her.

"Mum! Mum!"

She lifted her hand and patted her daughter's arm. "I'm okay," she gasped, winded. "I'm okay."

She rolled around and saw Brody and Jesse at McKinley's side. He was okay too. His eyes caught hers, and he pushed past the boys, moving to her. He threw his arms around her and hugged her tight.

"I'm sorry," he said. "I'm sorry."

Harris stood bent over, catching his breath. He eyed Welles and McKinley on the ground, holding each other.

"Wait! Where's grandpa?" Brody asked.

Welles looked at him as tears spilled down her cheeks, tracing a path through the dust and dirt upon her skin.

"Grandpa?" Freya called, looking at the tunnel. Welles reached out and took her hand.

"He did it for us," she said, forcing a smile. "He did it to save us."

"Grandpa!" Jesse yelled, running at the tunnel's damaged opening. McKinley caught him and held him. "Grandpa!"

"He's gone, Jesse. He's gone," he said softly.

Harris listened for a moment to the sounds of the children's cries. He clicked his comms on and listened, but there was nothing. He stepped toward Welles, where she sat comforting Freya and Brody.

"Archie, report. The *Aurora*?"

"*It continues to engage in a cat-and-mouse chase with the Zeta ship.*"

Harris felt relief sweep through him. He clenched his fist triumphantly. "Go, Hunter!" he whispered. "Gold and Morrell?"

"*The* Carcharias *battles Zeta ships over North America. The* Stanmore *is about to join them.* The US air force is doing what it can, but there have been casualties. Several fighters have crashed, some landing in civilian areas across the north-eastern area of the United States."

"Morrell?" he asked.

"*Morrell's unit have boarded the crashed Zeta ship and are investigating.*"

"How many Zeta ships remain?"

"We're down to 17. Six remain in battle over Europe and Asia. Five over the US."

Harris nodded to himself. "So, six of them are here." He looked at Welles. "I'm sorry, but we have to go."

"I know," she nodded, stumbling to her feet. Her dirty tear-stained face stared back at his. "I know."

First Lieutenant Jacob Hunter's eyes were fixed to the screen on the console, looking for the Zeta ship that was chasing them.

"Where the hell is it?" Frazer said, his voice sounding as on edge as Hunter felt.

"Keep an eye out for that red light!" he called. "They hit us with that, we're gone!" They'd been listening to the other battles and reading the data that filtered through from the other ships. That heat ray was a killer and had to be avoided at all costs. He was glad they'd drawn the Zeta ship away from the facility, but now he was caught in a life and death chase over the coast of Western Australia.

The rest of the crew sat in their seats silent, not wanting to break the concentration of Hunter or Frazer as they worked to outmaneuver the Zeta ship.

"Fuck!" Frazer said. "It's behind us again!"

"Watch for the red!" Hunter replied.

"I know you don't like anyone being rough with your baby," Frazer said, "but we need to push her to her limits."

Hunter glanced over at Frazer. In contrast to the black backdrop of night, the lights of the console glowed across his face, highlighting the sheen of sweat along his forehead beneath his burnt-orange hair. A sheen of sweat that Hunter felt on his own skin too.

"If it's called for," Hunter said with a nod, "then, yes, I grant you permission to treat my baby rough."

Frazer smiled. "That's how I fly best, sir!"

"It's glowing red!" Yughi yelled out from his seat.

Captain Lincoln Gold was relieved to see the *Stanmore* approach. The *Carcharias* had just taken out another Zeta ship, but there were still four unfriendlies engaging in fire with them and the fighter jets.

"Fuck," Ryker said. "A fighter jet just crashed into New York."

"We gotta lead them out to sea," Gold yelled, "away from civilian areas!"

The *Stanmore* fired on one of the Zeta ships tailing them. It veered away as another Zeta ship's cannon glowed red again.

"Heat ray coming!" Ryker yelled in warning, and again the *Carcharias* lurched upward, away from the angle of intent. The bright red light phased white and shot out, a roaring rushing wind buffeting the *Carcharias*. Immediately an alarm on the flight deck sounded.

"Report," Gold called. "Are we hit?"

Reece and his co-pilot, Jennings, checked the readings on the flight deck console.

"They nicked us!" Jennings called. "Just gave us a little sunburn."

"Well, we need our ass to be SPF 1000!" Gold said back. "That was too damn close!"

"The Zetas are turning on the *Stanmore*," C:Drive called. "They're ganging up."

Gold watched as the *Stanmore* fired its laser weapon at two Zeta ships on approach. "Let's get back in there!" he yelled.

The *Carcharias* veered around and took aim at the first Zeta ship again, clipping its wing, just as it fired off a short heat ray blast at the *Stanmore*. The ray hit the side of the ship and Gold swore he could hear the metal groaning from where he sat.

"Oh shit, they got them!" Reece said. "The *Stanmore*'s been hit."

"Keep firing at that damn Zeta!" Gold barked.

Laser fire shot out at the Zeta ship that had fired on the *Stanmore*. The laser fire hit the ship in the region of its heat ray, and in a display of sparks and fire, the Zeta ship suddenly blew up.

"Fuck yeah!" Reece called.

"*Stanmore* report!" Gold said.

"*We're hit bad. We've gotta take the ship down. We're going in for a bumpy landing!*"

"Godspeed *Stanmore*!" Gold said.

"Zeta cannon burning red!" Becker called out.

"Shit, it's behind us!" C:Drive said, referencing the second Zeta ship.

"*Carcharias*! Hit the stars!" Gold yelled. He was instantly thrown back into his seat as the ship lurched skyward, riding on a cloud of bright white heat.

Suddenly more alarms sounded urgently on the flight deck console.

"Oh, shit," Jenkins said.

Gold looked at him. "Report!"

Captain Edwin Morrell looked around the empty Zeta ship.

"Operations," he said into his headset, "we've found no bodies aboard the crashed ship. Confirm we have only seven targets to round up?"

"*Actually,*" the operator responded, sounding distracted, "*we're now picking up nine of them.*"

"Nine?" Morrell asked, glancing at Grenner. "Are you sure they're all HH and not civilian?"

"*Not all are HH—*"

"I told you to clear the area of civilians!" he barked.

"*No,*" the operator said, "*I mean eight look to be HH and one looks to be... Zeta, I guess.*"

"What do you mean, you guess?"

"*Well, it's tall, bald, pale—*"

Major General Marchant's voice cut in then. "*Trust me, it's Zeta. It's a Priestess.*"

"The snake bitch," Grenner muttered, exchanging a look with Morrell.

"Fine," Morrell said. "Where are they all?"

"*The nearest to you are five HH and the Zeta, about 400 meters west of where you are.*"

"Alright, keep me posted."

"*Morrell!*" Marchant said, before he signed off.

"Yeah?"

"*See if you can get me that Zeta alive.*"

Morrell exchanged another look with Grenner.

"Excuse me?" Morrell said.

"The only way we can figure out their ships is to get one alive. We need to study how it interacts with its ship. We need one alive."

"Right..." Morrell said, looking at the faces of his Alpha team. "I'll see what I can do."

Colt paced her small house in the Alpha Village. She looked around at the Sentinel Novak.

"Should we try and evac?"

He shrugged. "Where to? Command has been hit. There could be Zetas out there somewhere. It's too dangerous. We stay here."

Colt continued to pace. "God, I hope the *Aurora* is alright."

"Is Dad going to be okay?" Casim asked, as he sat cuddling Alinta who sat beside him on the bed.

"He's going to be fine," Colt said, picturing Brown in her mind. "He's a tough man."

"Ma," Malik called. "Who's that?"

She looked over to see Malik on his knees on the couch peering out the window.

"What is it?" she asked.

"There's a man out here. He's covered in blood."

Colt moved swiftly to the window and peered out.

She froze at who she saw.

Professor Sharley was walking calmly past their house, dressed in a guard's uniform. He suddenly noticed the two of them peering out the window. He slowed as recognition crossed his face. Then he stopped, turning his body to face her.

"What is it?" Novak asked from the other side of the room as he peered out the other window, checking the perimeter.

"Corporal Colt," Sharley said loudly, as a smile slid across his face. "And who is thi—" Sharley's words cut off as he stepped closer to the window, his eyes fixed on Malik.

Colt grabbed her son and pulled him back from the window. Sharley's eyes moved from the space Malik had left to Colt's face. His smile grew wider. Suddenly Novak appeared beside her. He recognized Sharley and swiftly raised his gun, but Sharley bolted away, Jumbo fast.

"That was Sharley," Colt breathed, staring back at the Sentinel. "Why's he on the outside? What's he doing free?"

"Command was hit," Novak said gravely. "He's escaped from Command."

Harris had Archie hijack a satellite and scan the area for Zetas or HH. When Archie gave them the all-clear, he slowly and carefully led them back around to the Hamlet to where McKinley's PV sat.

"Where's your car?" Harris asked Gerry.

Gerry pointed to a clump of trees in the distance.

Harris eyed him quizzically. "Why'd you park it all the way over there?"

"It's expensive," Gerry said. "I didn't want to get it nicked."

Sampson smiled. "Bloody cray fishermen. You got too much money."

Just then they heard the sound of a firefight in the sky. They looked up as the *Aurora* flew overhead, dodging a blast of white light from the Zeta ship.

"That's them!" McKinley said.

"Fuck!" Harris hissed, watching them.

The *Aurora* suddenly pulled up hard and the Zeta ship flew right underneath them. The *Aurora* then dove back down, trailed the Zeta ship and opened fire. "Goddamn, he's good!" McKinley said, eyes fixed to the sky, watching the *Aurora*. The swift Zeta ship outmaneuvered the fire, however.

They suddenly heard a series of growls in the distance. The HH.

"They're coming back," Harris said, moving to the PV. "You go with Gerry!" he called to Welles and the Sentinels. "Get back to the comms facility. McKinley and I will lead them away, so you can make it out. We'll meet you back there."

Roy gave a nod and tugged on Welles's arm, but she hesitated a moment, locking eyes with McKinley.

"I'll see you soon," McKinley said, winking at her, then slid into the driver's seat.

Harris moved to the passenger door, but Welles ran up and stopped him.

She pulled his arm forward and locked her hand at his elbow. She squeezed it tight as the vibration of their connection slid through them.

"If you get in trouble," she said, "make me feel it."

Harris stared at their locked arms.

"I'll come find you," she said, Alpha eyes fixed firmly on his.

Certain dreams flashed through his mind, of Welles running toward him in the dark. He nodded at her. "I know you will."

And with that, he broke the connection and slid into the PV beside McKinley, who revved the engine and took off, honking the horn loudly to draw the HH's attention.

Gold looked carefully at his pilots.

"Can we stay airborne?" he called.

"Yeah," Jenkins said, "although we've sustained damage to our belly. But we're still flying."

"Where're the Zetas?" Gold asked C:Drive.

"One's coming around. It's on our six again!" Reece yelled.

"We gotta get in a position where we can target the heat ray," Gold said. "That's its weakness! We fire at that, one shot, and they're gone!" For most of the ships they'd taken down, they'd only managed to inflict partial damage to send them crashing to Earth, but they'd blown the second one up, right there in the sky. That was the key. They couldn't risk any enemies surviving their crash landings and escaping on foot.

"Fighter jets!" Gold barked into his comms. "Aim for the heat rays. Direct hits will blow the ships. You're fast and zippy, you can get in there. You just gotta hit it with enough power! Understand?"

"*Roger that!*" the lead pilot called back over the comms.

Captain Edwin Morrell crept toward the yawning chasm that was once the south-eastern wing of Command. As he carefully stepped over the rubble, he glanced back at his team, but paused as a strange scent wafted past his Alpha senses on the breeze. Something that smelled horrible. Something that smelled not-human.

He held up his fist and signaled his crew to stop. He moved up to a jagged wall of rubble that remained standing and listened. He heard humming, buzzing and clicks, which sent a ripple of goosebumps down his arms. The Zetas. Harris had played them the recordings multiple times before. He'd know those sounds anywhere.

Very carefully, he pulled a vis-con from his vest and extended the neck, then positioned the mirror around the wall to get a visual confirmation of what awaited them. There were five HH picking through the rubble, carrying large silver spears that looked more aerodynamic than anything he'd seen before. And there, a little further to the side, stood what he could only imagine was a Zeta. A Priestess.

He signaled back to his team, warning them of their six targets, and ordered them to split up, sending half around the rubble to meet their targets on the other side.

Grenner moved up closer beside him and they gave each other a nod in solidarity, as Winslow and Manz joined them. Just as Morrell began a silent countdown for them to commence action, they heard a noise coming from the other side of their targets. Whether it was more of the building collapsing or one of his crew accidentally kicking or knocking something, he wasn't sure. Regardless, whatever it was caught their target's attention. He hissed silently to himself, but didn't dwell on it. He'd use this disturbance to get the upper hand.

He quickly gave the signal and both he and Grenner sprang out and fired at the HH. As they did they saw the Zeta send a ball of heat at the rest of his team behind the furthermost wall. The sound of their screams as the heat hit curdled his stomach. Two of the HH that he and Grenner aimed for, fell dead to the ground in a scorching crisscross of laser fire. A third one fell under the aim of Sergeant Winslow, but the remaining HH swiftly threw their spears, catching Winslow in the gut and Corporal Manz in the arm. Grenner grabbed Winslow and dragged him back to safety, as Morrell himself ducked back out of the line of fire.

He peered back around the wall to see the two remaining HH shepherding the Zeta to safety as a screaming Sergeant Kumar stumbled out from behind the other wall aflame. Morrell's breath caught as his soldier's screams ceased and he saw him fall dead to the ground, his body on fire. He flicked his eyes back to Winslow, whose midriff was pooling red around the long silver spear that pierced it, while Grenner packed bandages around the wound.

Fuck! Morrell whispered internally, peering back around the wall. He wanted to call to the rest of his unit to see if they were okay, but it was too risky making any sound.

"We gotta get that fucking Zeta!" Grenner said, hate in his eyes.

Morrell motioned for Grenner to be silent. He eyed the alcove of rubble before him. Beyond that was the broken wall, which their targets had sought shelter behind, and beyond that another alcove and the furthermost wall where his team were. He glanced back at Grenner and motioned for him to apply cover. Grenner nodded and held his weapon ready to take aim, as Morrell quickly ran out around the wall they'd been hiding behind and into the curve of the first alcove.

With his back flat against the wall, he sidled around as quietly and swiftly as his Alpha body would allow. When he came to the wall behind which their targets had escaped, he motioned for Grenner to move. He saw Grenner throw Winslow a quick glance, before scuttling up to join him as Manz moved to cover them both with his now bandaged bloody arm.

Morrell and Grenner stood silently for a moment, attuning their Alpha hearing for any clue to their targets' location. He heard the faint groans of one of his team, still alive after that blast of heat. He hoped to god he had more than one left alive. Given Winslow's wound, he wasn't sure he was going to survive. Not unless they got him to medical attention fast. That left just him and Grenner, and Manz with his speared arm, back behind the other wall.

He clenched his teeth as revenge filled his mind. He had to destroy these fuckers for his team.

Hunter held the stick as steady as his Alpha arms would allow.

"Fuck!" he yelled, as alarms sounded from the console.

"It's alright!" Frazer yelled. "It's not too bad!"

"We've taken heat!" Hunter yelled back.

"Hull's intact!" Brown called back, eyeing a monitor at the captain's table where he sat. Steinberg unclipped his harness and stumbled over to sit beside him.

"We should get ready to evac!" Gregson yelled.

"We're not ditching the big brown bird just yet!" Hunter called back.

"The Zetas are firing up again!" Murphy called.

"What are you doing?" Evenssen said, and Hunter glanced back to see Gregson out of his seat.

"Just don't crash until I get back!" Gregson said.

"Where are you going?" Yughi asked.

"I'm getting as many medical supplies as I can."

"The pod is loaded with standard supplies," Steinberg told him. "You know this."

"Yeah, I don't think standard supplies are going to cut it with these things," Gregson said. "Do you?"

"Hold on!" Hunter yelled, as the *Aurora* suddenly surged upward.

Gregson went flying backward, but Tikaani reached out and caught hold of him.

The blast of white light rushed beneath them, and as soon as it passed the *Aurora* leveled out again.

"Alright, come on!" Tikaani yelled at Gregson, unclipping her harness. "Let's get these supplies!"

"And guns!" Brown yelled. "Grab more guns!"

Evenssen and Murphy nodded, unclipped their harnesses and followed them out the door.

Carrie sat squeezed between Cushy and Gerry in the front of Gerry's hotted-up Commodore. Bright red in color it hit speeds that would normally have been illegal, but right now were a godsend.

"Quite the car you have, Gerry," she said, trying to hold onto her seat inconspicuously

"She's my baby," he said, flashing a smile that faded as he stared out at the road ahead. "I told him he could have her when I eventually upgraded."

"Him?" she asked.

"We don't name the dead," Cushy told her quietly, eyes shining with tears.

Carrie's face softened as she looked back at Gerry, trying not to think of her father.

"Archie," she said. "Report."

"*The* Carcharias, *with help from the* Stanmore *and the US air force, has gained the upper hand over North America.*"

"Centralis?" she asked.

"*There are still several HH and a Zeta on the loose. Some of Morrell's team have been killed or badly wounded, but he continues to hunt them down.*"

"Europe?"

"*All activity will soon cease over Europe. Only two Zeta ships remain. Rescue operations are underway in the damaged cities and towns.*"

"The Moon?"

"*All activity has ceased. Rescue operations are underway.*"

"Mars and Atlas Station?"

"*They are untouched.*"

"The rest of the world?"

"*As with Europe, damage has been sustained in some cities in North America where overhead fighting took place.*"

"Have any other ships managed to burrow down?"

"*No,*" Archie said.

"And the *Aurora*?"

"*They have taken fire, but so too has the Zeta ship. Their current location is not far from you. If you look into the sky, you should see them.*"

Carrie leaned forward and scanned her eyes through the front windscreen.

"Over there!" Brody called, pointing to the east.

Carrie looked where he pointed and saw the ships chasing each other. Both had small trails of smoke billowing.

"Pull over!" she said.

"Hey," Gerry said. "We've gotta get back to that facility."

"Pull over!" she barked.

Gerry hit the brakes and pulled the car over. Carrie crawled out over Cushy and stood on the road watching the two ships in the sky. Roy came to stand by her side.

"They're smoking," she said. "How long do you think they can fly like that?"

"I don't know," he said, "but they better end things pretty soon."

Carrie watched on. The *Aurora* hit the Zeta ship again, and a large plume of fire and smoke erupted.

"What the hell is that?" Roy asked.

Carrie turned to where he was looking and saw a second Zeta ship on approach.

"Oh, Jesus," she said. "Where did that come from?"

Everyone was out of the car now, watching.

The *Aurora* obviously saw the new threat and turned, and spun, and looped itself trying to get away from its two assailants. The first Zeta ship fired again, and clipped the *Aurora*, now leaving two smoky tails.

"Come on, guys!" she whispered. "Come on!"

All three ships were firing now and the *Aurora* dipped and turned like a big graceful whale, even though a wounded one. It was magical flying, especially for a ship of that size. But would it be enough? Could the larger, bulkier *Aurora* outrun and outmaneuver the smaller Zeta ships?

The two Zeta ships gave chase and the *Aurora* kept switching direction trying to shake them. For minutes they watched on as though it were an aerial acrobatics display. If ever Hunter and Frazer were going to fly for their lives, they were doing it now.

Suddenly the *Aurora* turned and began to fly straight at the first ship, firing its laser weapons, with the second Zeta ship behind them.

"What's he doing?" Gerry asked. "He's going to get sandwiched!"

The *Aurora* flew at the first ship firing at them, as the underbelly of the ship began to glow red. At the last moment, the *Aurora* pulled up as the Zeta ship fired its heat ray. It hit the second ship which swiftly exploded in a ball of flame.

"Woooo!" the children yelled, clapping their hands. "Go, Hunter!"

But as they watched, the remaining Zeta ship turned around and began to tail the smoking *Aurora*. The *Aurora* was struggling to outrun it this time. The Zeta ship turned red and fired another blast of heat, and the *Aurora* could not maneuver swiftly enough. The blast caught the tail end of the ship, which seemed to set off a small chain of explosions rippling through the rear ship. The hit was critical. The result, catastrophic.

Carrie watched as a larger explosion occurred near the tail and pieces of the *Aurora* began to break off and fall away. The ship's flying became erratic, and she pictured the faces of Hunter and Frazer as they struggled to control things on the flight deck.

"Oh god!" she whispered, bringing her hands to her mouth. She watched as another, even larger explosion occurred then - - and the *Aurora* blew up.

Carrie was frozen to the spot as she heard the children gasp and cry out. Her eyes desperately scanned the site of the explosion and the falling debris, refusing to believe that she had just seen her team die.

And her Alpha eyes caught on something...

She focused hard, not knowing whether it was a piece of debris shooting out from the explosion, or whether it was... whether it could be... the escape pod! It was too big to be the *Borealis* shuttle, but it could be the flight deck, which she knew could detach from the rest of the ship as the *Aurora*'s official escape pod.

She saw a flash of fire at its tail and a smile spread across her face. That wasn't bad fire, that was good fire. That was flying fire.

"They're okay!" she called out.

"What?" Gerry said. "Th—they blew up."

"No," Carrie shook her head, pointing to the pod. "The ship blew up. Hunter and Frazer got the escape pod free. They're fine." The smile took over her face. "They're fine!"

At least she hoped they were. Hoped all the team were on the flight deck when they disengaged.

"But we lost the ship," Roy said. "We lost the only grunt we have down here for miles."

Carrie's smile faded. "We need to get back to the facility. That's our rendezvous point." She turned and jogged back around to the passenger door and got in. "Come on, Gerry! Let's hit the road!"

Harris stared at the point in the sky where he had just seen the *Aurora* blow up.

"Did they make it out?" McKinley asked, eyes fixed on the road ahead as they drove away from the scene. "Tell me they made it out."

Harris craned his neck as far as he could, but couldn't see anything except pieces of the burning ship falling to the ground. His whole body felt numb.

"Did they?" McKinley demanded.

"I—I can't see. I can't tell," Harris said, turning around to face the front.

"They had to make it!" McKinley said.

Harris tried to raise Hunter on the comms, but only static filled their earpieces.

"Hunter loved that ship," Harris said quietly. "He wouldn't leave it until he had to."

"He wouldn't risk the crew's lives. They would've detached the escape pod. We just didn't see it."

"If they could detach in time."

"Maybe the comms just got fried?"

Harris tried to raise Hunter again. Nothing.

McKinley looked at him for a moment, then slammed on the brakes of the PV. Harris's harness jerked him back in his seat. He stared at McKinley.

"We gotta see if they made it out. They might need our help," McKinley said.

Harris turned his eyes to the darkened road ahead and the bushy scrub to either side partially lit by the PV's lights.

"Carrie had plenty of time to get out of the Hamlet," McKinley said. "We can go back."

He was right. They had originally taken the PV away from Gerry's car and made a lot of noise to attract the HH, which began appearing and heading their way. As the HH approached them, McKinley fired at them from the driver's window and Harris leaned through the passenger window and fired over the roof at them. Then they had hightailed it out of there.

"Are they dead?" McKinley asked him, blue Alpha eyes fixed on his. "What does your gut tell you?"

Harris sat staring out the windscreen concentrating on his gut, trying to reach deep and fixate on Hunter's face, Frazer's face, Brown's and Steinberg's, Yughi's, Evenssen's, Tikaani's, Gregson's, Murphy's... He was distracted suddenly as something moved by the roadside. He stiffened as

McKinley turned and saw it too. A small head atop a long neck was peering out from the bushes. They both raised their guns, before they saw the shaggy bulky body of an emu. They breathed a sigh of relief as the emu bolted across the road in front of them.

McKinley turned back to Harris. "Are they alive?"

Harris looked back at him. "I think they might be."

McKinley gave a nod. "Then we're going to get them."

Harris gave a firm nod back. "We're going to get them."

26

The Missing Link

Admiral Arken saw the look of anticipation on the faces of his crew. Within moments, Earth would be within jumping distance. Ten long years, Earth-time, they'd been gone, and the journey home had been the worst space-time he'd ever done. Wondering if they could beat the Zetas back to Earth. Wondering what they would return to.

An alarm began to sound on the flight deck.

"What is it?" he asked.

Ulgari checked the readings on the console. "Space junk, sir," she said. "It's... everywhere."

Everyone was silent, looking out the observation window as the minutes ticked by. Finally, they saw the debris begin to float past them. And there was a lot of it. He felt horror wash over him as he saw a chunk of metal float past emblazoned with the bright blue Space Duty insignia.

But among it were pieces of debris that were as black as night. The color of obsidian.

"They beat us here," Garth said, voicing everyone's fear.

"Maybe they just crossed paths with another ship out here," Rina said hopefully. "Maybe they hadn't reached Earth yet."

"How long until you can get me visuals of Earth?" Arken asked, his voice low and serious.

“Twenty minutes, sir,” Garth said.

“Ulgari?” Arken said.

“Sir?”

“Get the ship ready to jump.”

“Sir?”

“You said the jump system was repaired, yes?”

“Well, not really, sir. The fix is temporary and will only allow one jump.”

“That’s all we need.”

“It’s not 100 percent stable, sir,” she said. “We’d need to pool all our power into the jump, depleting it and leaving the ship disabled.”

“But it can jump us to Earth, yes?”

“Yes. We can jump to Earth, but we won’t have full systems to land this ship.”

“The *Barbican* is a big beast, Ulgari, and you know her better than anyone. She’s *your* beast. We jump her into the Earth’s atmosphere, find as many Zeta ships as we can to take out in the process, then we kiss the dirt and ride it until we stop.”

Sasha Ulgari looked at him. The Russian woman’s heavily-pierced face stared back plainly for a moment, before she finally broke into a grin. “Hit as many Zeta ships as we can and use them as brakes to slow us down. Got it.”

Arken smiled and looked around at his team. “We’ve got one jump people. Let’s make it count.”

Gold stared out the window as three fighter jets coordinated their effort, flying deftly up to one of the Zeta ships and landing direct hits to its heat ray. An explosion of sparks shot out and the Zeta ship erupted into a fireball.

“Yes!” Gold hissed triumphantly.

“Our Zeta’s getting into position!” Reece called.

“Heat ray firing up!” Becker yelled, referring to the Zeta ship on their tail.

The flight deck fell silent as the *Carcharias* pilots did their best to evade the white rolling wave of heat that passed. Gold looked at his remaining team members, sitting silently in their seats.

"We are not dying today, gentlemen," Gold told them firmly, jostling around in his seat as the ship veered around to try and lock on the Zeta ship. "We are *not* dying today!"

"Target locked!" Jenkin called.

"Fire!" Gold yelled.

The *Carcharias* began to spit out a laser stream at the black Zeta ship. The enemy zigged and zagged and pulled away.

"Get around them!" Gold yelled. "Chase them down and hit that fucker's belly! We got this one!"

He held onto his seat as the *Carcharias* swerved around again.

"Heat ray burning red!" Becker yelled.

"Coming around!" Reece said.

Gold looked out the observation window, trying to ignore the alarms still sounding from the flight deck console. He heard the whoosh of the heat ray and held his breath as the *Carcharias* dove beneath it, then suddenly pulled up again and fired at the ship.

The laser fire hit its target dead on, and they watched the sparks and the subsequent explosion as the Zeta ship blew up.

As the team yelled out in celebration, Gold let out a long, heavy breath, relieved.

"How many left?" he asked.

"Just two in our area!" C:Drive smiled.

"Alright," Gold said. "One for us, one for the fighter jets. Let's do this!"

Captain Morrell heard a series of quiet grunts, followed by the humming, buzzing and clicks, which he assumed was the HH talking to the Zeta.

They were just on the other side of the crumbling wall.

He edged closer to the corner, using his stealthy Alpha muscles to make his movement silent, hoping that his enemy did not share the same keen sense of smell or hearing. Then again, didn't the Zetas theoretically create the animals used in UNFASP to strengthen the Alpha's senses? But were the Zeta senses as refined as the animal senses that had evolved here on Earth over all this time? Suddenly Morrell understood just how important it was to capture one of these alive. They knew shit about the Zetas, and that was a serious problem that needed to be rectified.

Something like a howl sounded in the distance. Again, he heard the quiet grunts of the HH on the other side of the wall. Was it the remaining HH calling to their kin? He had to take out those on the other side of that wall before their back-up arrived. Before he was seriously outnumbered.

He signaled to Grenner to do a swift cross-cover around the corner of that wall. Grenner gave him a sturdy nod, then Morrell counted down: three, two, one.

As they sprung around the wall, the humming, buzzing and clicks sounded urgently in warning to the HH. There stood the Zeta, the two HH ready to protect it, their spears in the air directed at them.

Both he and Grenner opened fire as two metal spears came flying at them. Morrell dodged his, but he heard a *thuck* sound from Grenner, who immediately stopped firing. Morrell took out one of the HH, then risked a glance at his soldier. He saw a spear had pierced his throat, pinning him to the wall behind. Grenner was dead.

Morrell didn't have time to dwell, but sprayed his laser fire recklessly, wanting to kill everything in its path. The other HH, already wounded by Grenner, was shredded by his fire as the Zeta's humming buzzing and clicks sounded more urgently. The Zeta raised its arm in Morrell's direction and he saw something silver strapped to its forearm.

Suddenly laser fire came in from the other direction, slicing through the arm and causing the weapon attached to its forearm to spark. The Zeta cried out in pain as the forearm – silver device attached – fell to the ground. Morrell looked over to see three members of his team, in varying degrees of singed blackened uniforms and skin, peering around the furthermost wall of rubble. Corporal Zwanen, Staff Sergeant Shtol and Second Lieutenant Cortez were still alive.

"Don't kill it!" he yelled to them.

"That device is deadly!" Cortez said over the comms. "One blast killed Rogers, Willis and Kumar."

Morrell turned and glanced at Grenner again, dead, pinned by a spear, blood running down his chest. Morrell clenched his teeth again and turned back to the Zeta who was hissing, still calling out in its language, in pain.

They heard growls and grunts and turned to see four more HH appear atop rubble to his left. He dropped his gun and sprinted toward the Zeta, pulling out his knife as he did. He tackled the Zeta to the ground as his soldiers provided him with cover fire against the HH. The Zeta, stronger than it looked, threw him off. His back hit the wall and the knife fell from his hand. Both he and the Zeta scrambled for it, but the Zeta's longer limbs won out. The Zeta snatched the knife and slashed it back at him. He felt a searing pain across his shoulder, neck and chin. Damn thing was trying to cut his head off.

"You fuck!" he hissed, rolling away and deftly springing back up to his feet. He crouched again and began to circle the Zeta, who continued to hiss and bare its ugly yellow crocodile teeth, the knife in its grasp and dripping with his own blood.

"Sir! Move!" Shtol said, aiming his weapon at it.

"No," Morrell shook his head, "focus on the HH! I'm getting this one alive."

Just then he heard laser fire from the direction in which he'd come. He heard Manz scream some kind of war cry as he took one of the HH out. Shtol and Zwanen joined him laying down fire at the HH.

"It's just you and me, *freak*!" Morrell hissed at the Zeta.

The Zeta lunged, slashing the knife again and again, but Morrell ducked and dodged. He swiftly slid his body around to the side of the creature and captured its swinging arm in his. The Zeta roared again, as a crimson fluid poured from its other half-arm. It seemed to rear back a moment, raising its intact arm to full height, then forced it downward and the knife with it. The movement loosened Morrell's grip, and the knife to come plunging down into his thigh.

A yell of pain escaped his mouth before he managed to clamp it shut. He forced what was left of the pain down into his gut, along with his anger. Then he bottled that shit, shook it up, and let it explode, throwing his fist into the Zeta's face. It was the Zeta's turn to loosen its grip. He pulled the knife out of his thigh, then plunged it into the thigh of the Zeta.

"Right back at ya, you fuck!" he growled.

The Zeta recoiled, mouth wide and hissing, as Morrell threw himself on it again. They fell to the ground as his Alpha fist connected with its head repeatedly, showing no mercy, until the Zeta's fight eased off. Seeing his opportunity, he pulled some wire from his vest and looped it tightly around the dazed Zeta, tying its free hand up against its neck. He pulled more wire out and did the same with its feet, then yanked the knife out of its thigh.

The Zeta hissed, shaking off its daze, and flashed raging eyes at him as he stood again. Morrell stumbled a bit, hopping as pain seared through his thigh. He looked back at his team and saw that they'd managed to take out the four remaining HH.

Zwanen came running over to help him. "Captain!"

"No," Morrell pushed him away, panting. "Get Winslow and Manz. They're injured. Go!"

Zwanen ran off as Morrell bent back down and tied a tourniquet around the Zeta's half arm. Then he clicked on his comms again, staring at the hissing and writhing Zeta.

"Major General Marchant," he said. "I've got a special delivery for you."

Carrie, upon arrival at the UNF comms facility, ran inside hoping to see the *Aurora* crew, but they weren't there. Valerie greeted her, grasping her arms.

"Where are the others?" Valerie asked.

"We got split up," Carrie said. "They'll be here soon." She walked into the comms room and looked at the screens. "What's been happening?"

"Everything," Valerie said. "The comms haven't stopped. We've recorded everything."

The Sentinels, children, and Gerry and Cushy joined them then. Carrie glanced at them, then back at the screen.

"Can you raise the *Aurora*?" she asked Valerie.

"They..." Valerie looked awkward. "The ship it—"

"They escaped in the pod," Carrie interrupted. "I saw it. They're alive. Can you raise them?"

Valerie looked over at Tim, one of the communication technicians, and gave him a nod to try. He turned back and worked his console, trying to raise the *Aurora*.

Static was their only reply.

"Comms must be fried," Roy said.

"Did you see them land?" Valerie asked gently.

Carrie and Roy exchanged a look. "I didn't need to. Hunter was flying it and if he got them away from an exploding ship, then I know he landed them safely." She turned away from them. "Archie, can you raise the *Aurora*?"

"I'm sorry, Miss Welles. I've been trying. Their comms are down as is their beacon."

"Can you get me Colonel Harris?"

"Yes, Miss Welles."

A moment passed before Harris's voice sounded through Archie's discs. *"Welles?"*

"Sir?" she said. "Are you alright?"

"We're fine. Where are you?"

"We're back at the facility. We're all fine. Did you see the *Aurora*?"

Harris was quiet a moment. *"Yeah. We're going to see if we can find any survivors."*

"They survived, sir," Carrie said. "I saw it."

"Saw what?"

"The escape pod. They got away."

"FUCK YEAH!" McKinley called out in approval. Or perhaps relief.

"Thank Christ," Harris said. *"Which direction were they headed?"*

"I'd say it was north-east."

"We're gonna go see if we can find them. You stay put. We'll meet you there."

"Yes, sir," Carrie said, as Archie ended the comms. She sighed loudly, placing her hands on her hips and looking about. "Alright. Harris and McKinley are going to search for the *Aurora* crew." She looked at her children. "I want you to go get some rest." Then she looked at Roy. "You, too. I'll wait by the comms."

"Sampson can sleep," Roy said. "I'll watch over the children."

Carrie smiled and touched his arm. "Thanks, Roy."

He gave her a nod, then he and Sampson herded the children into the basement.

"We'd better be going then," Gerry said.

"You should stay here, too, Gerry," Carrie said. "It'll be safer down in the basement."

Gerry shook his head sadly. "I gotta go tell his mother what happened."

"It's not safe out there on the road," Carrie said softly. "You already have to tell her about… *him*. Don't make someone tell her about you and Cushy too."

Gerry looked at her, then darted his eyes suspiciously around the facility. "I suppose you're right." He looked at Cushy. "Come on, Cush, we'll go hide the car."

Carrie blurted out a laugh. Gerry looked back at her strangely.

"Gerry, no-one's going to steal your car out here, mate."

"You never know," he said. "Better to be safe than sorry. I work bloody hard for my money. I'll be damned if someone's gonna take it from me." He tapped Cushy on the shoulder and they headed outside.

Carrie chuckled again and looked at Valerie.

"Who are they?" Valerie asked.

"Oh, they just gave us a lift."

"Oh," Valerie said, still staring at the empty doorway they had just exited.

"I think we can put all classification aside," Carrie added. "Everyone knows about the Zetas now." She walked over and pulled out a chair beside Tim. She sighed heavily. Tim stared at her, a thin face framed by curls and adorned with rimless glasses.

"It's been a long night, Tim," she said, "and it's not over yet."

He nodded. "At least they're mostly out of the skies now."

"Yeah," she said looking back at him, "but the rest are on the ground. That's what worries me."

Harris and McKinley approached the flaming wreckage of the *Aurora*. Well, pieces of it. They pulled up the PV and stepped out, eyeing their surroundings carefully. Harris's senses were in overdrive from the smoke and fumes and the brightness of the fire against the darkness of night, to the crackling and popping of cooling wreckage signifying the *Aurora*'s death throes.

"The escape pod could be anywhere," McKinley said, surveying the night sky in the distance.

"Well, if it didn't crash, he would've just flown it back to the facility, right?" Harris said, stepping over pieces of the *Aurora*.

"Unless they're hiding? There was at least one more Zeta ship. Where'd that go?"

"I can still hear it, I think," Harris said, looking about. "It must be behind those hills." He pointed off into the distance.

"Well, they're not here," McKinley said, looking around the wreckage and kicking a piece out of his path. He bent down and pulled a large section back, and Harris made out the letter "A", once part of the lettering on the hull of the big brown bird. He felt a sadness settle over him briefly. His ship, the *Aurora*, had been destroyed.

McKinley dropped the piece of wreckage to the ground and looked at him. "The pod doesn't have any onboard weaponry to defend itself. They'd have to try and outrun it."

The sound of a heat ray blast coming from a Zeta ship caught their attention. They both looked over to the low hills in the distance and saw a small light whizzing over the top, followed by the Zeta ship.

Harris narrowed his Alpha eyes, trying to get a good look.

"It's them!" McKinley said.

The *Aurora's* escape pod whizzed overhead with the larger Zeta ship on its tail.

"They must've tried hiding, but the Zeta ship found them," McKinley said.

"It's like a dog with a bone, isn't it?" Harris said. "Won't let them go."

The Zeta ship fired another blast at the pod, but it twisted and turned delicately, rolling down out of the line of fire like a beautiful ballerina

"Jesus," McKinley said, "I can't watch this again."

Suddenly an awful smell hit Harris's senses, like a swamp turned bad. A thud-thud-bang sounded and Harris flicked his head to see one of the HH sprinting through the wreckage toward McKinley.

"McKinley!" Harris warned.

"You!" McKinley yelled back, pointing to another running at Harris from behind.

They both dodged their attackers as they swooped past, but the HH quickly came lunging at them again, readying their metal spears. Harris saw the sharp double-edged blade of the spear as it soared toward him, but he nimbly avoided it. It plunged into the sand beside him. He grabbed hold of it, not wanting his attacker to pull it back out, but the HH had already latched onto it. Harris began punching the HH in the face. The HH was just shorter than he, but equally broad and strong. His hair was long and pulled back in muddy, claybound dreadlocks. Its face, as it growled, seemed mostly human, and yet, like nothing he'd seen.

The HH gave up trying to take back his spear and landed a crunching elbow in Harris's face that was so powerful, it threw him to the side. Harris, vaguely aware of McKinley fighting with his HH in the background, scurried to his feet and grabbed for his gun as he saw a third HH running for him. He lifted his weapon and fired, taking the HH down, just as his original opponent landed on his back. It dropped Harris to the ground with a whump and sent his gun sliding away.

The HH grasped his head in a viselike grip so tight Harris thought it was trying to break his neck, or maybe crush his skull. Or maybe tear his head clean off his shoulders. The strength the HH had, it wouldn't surprise him. Harris reached up and clasped his big hands onto the creature's arms to remove the grip. He managed to pull one arm away, then swung his elbow back hard and fast and collected the HH in the side, cracking some ribs as it fell off him. Harris sprang to his feet, just in time for the HH to charge him again. Their bodies hit with a deep meaty sound that seemed to travel right through him. The HH snapped its feral teeth at Harris, trying to bite his face, its pungent swampy breath and warm drool pouring over him. Gagging, he shoved one hand under its jaw and pushed it back. The HH growled as Harris pooled his strength into his arms, stretching the HH's neck right away from him.

The HH slammed a hand over Harris's face, aiming for his eyes. He heard the brutal pounding of flesh in the distance, then heard McKinley roar; in anger or pain, he wasn't sure. Harris tried to shake the HH's hand from his face, keeping his own hands around its neck to hold it away from him. Then he heard the zipping of laser fire. A wetness splashed over him and his HH attacker fell limp amid the smell of burned flesh. Harris opened his eyes and saw McKinley standing there, panting, gun pointed in his direction, his own HH opponent dead at his feet.

Harris threw his HH off and pulled himself up. McKinley's face was bleeding as he glanced around their surrounds, but otherwise he looked alright. Harris, still out of breath, his own face bleeding, raised his hand in a wave of thanks to McKinley.

They heard the noise of more firefighting in the air and looked up to see the *Aurora* escape pod still ducking and dodging the Zeta ship. The Zeta ship was closer now and its underbelly was glowing red about to fire that heat ray.

"C'mon, Hunt—"

Harris's words were cut short as an intense white light flashed across what felt like the entire sky, so bright Harris and McKinley turned away as a massive sonic boom sounded, forcing them to cover their ears. They quickly looked back into the sky, squinting against the light, to see a massive ship hurtling across the sky, veering toward the Zeta ship, and slamming into it. The alien ship exploded, barely affecting the massive hull of the attacking ship.

"Jesus Christ!" Harris said in awe, narrowing his Alpha eyes for a closer look, as he kept shading his eyes. "That's the *Barbican*!" he said, dropping his hand. "That's the fucking *Barbican*! They're alive! They're fucking alive!"

"The pod!" McKinley said, pointing to the whizzing light of the ship as it flew away.

"ALRIGHT!" Harris yelled, thrusting his fist into the air.

"Woo-hoo!" McKinley yelled, clapping his hands in applause.

They watched as the *Barbican* veered in a raggedly wide arc in an attempt to slow its speed. The big beast came to land roughly, thundering into the fields of Greenough. Grass, soil, shrubs and trees flew everywhere and the land rumbled beneath their feet as it did. It seemed to plough on forever until it eventually came to a stop, its nose smashing into the sand dunes, spitting sand everywhere, kilometers of torn-up field behind it.

"*Holy shit!*" McKinley called out. They both laughed, locking hands, and patting each other on the back. They looked back at the *Barbican*, the metal still groaning loudly as it settled onto the ground. It looked like some kind of massive mechanical whale that had washed up on the shore and was trying to make its way back into the ocean.

They heard a hissing sound, then. And it wasn't coming from the *Barbican*.

They both turned, just as a blast of white light shot out at them. It hit McKinley first, who was standing to Harris's right. The force threw the captain into him, hard, and they both hit the ground.

McKinley screamed in pain, a sound like nothing Harris had ever heard before. The captain writhed frantically, desperately, on top of him like he was trying to get something off. Harris shoved McKinley off him and saw that half his body was on fire and Harris quickly rolled him into the dirt, smothering the flames. He heard the hissing sound again, then swiftly leapt up and dove behind a piece of the *Aurora* wreckage. He felt a hot wind fly over his head, almost singeing him.

Then he heard it. The humming, the buzzing, the clicks.

This wasn't one of the HH.

This was a Zeta.

Gold pumped his fist in celebration. Although they'd lost many fighter jets in the battle, those that remained had managed to take out one of the Zeta ships, and the *Carcharias*, after a tricky game of cat and mouse, had managed to take out the last of the Zeta ships over North America.

"Report," he ordered C:Drive.

"All Zeta ships are out of the skies!"

"The rest are gone?"

He nodded, reading a screen, but suddenly his face fell. "Shit."

"What?"

C:Drive looked up at Gold, his face a little paler. "The *Aurora*. It's gone."

"What do you mean?" Gold sat forward in his chair.

"Their blip. It's gone from the screen. They're gone."

Gold stared at him a moment. "They're gone?"

C: Drive nodded solemnly, as a silence fell over the flight deck.

"Fuck..." Gold said, barely able to breathe.

"There is good news, though," C:Drive said, still reading the screen, eyes wide. "The *Barbican*. She's back."

"She's back?" Gold asked stunned from both sets of news.

C:Drive smiled up at him and nodded. "She's back. She's on my screen. She's back."

"But the *Aurora*'s gone?" Gold said. "You're sure it's gone? Colonel Harris is dead?"

C:Drive nodded solemnly. "It's off the system."

"Get Marchant on comms," Gold said.

Captain Morrell wiped at the stinging blood that covered his shoulder, neck and chin. He was limping and fighting the pain that shot through his wounded thigh, but he insisted on dragging the heavy net, filled with the injured Zeta, into Command. His crew knew better than to offer him help. Major General Marchant and several others came to meet them. Marchant was bruised, scratched and bloodied. It would seem he hadn't quite escaped the damage to Command in time.

"It's alive?" he asked.

Morrell gave an Alpha tug and brought the net up in between them. The Zeta hissed and Marchant stepped back.

"It's injured!" one of the men with Marchant said.

"It attacked me," Morrell said in a low voice.

"We wanted a specimen alive!" the man said, bending down to it.

"It *is* alive!" Morrell spat.

"For now!" the man said. "God knows how long it will live. It's lost half its arm!"

Morrell dropped the net, grabbed a handful of the man's shirt and yanked him right up to his face. "And I lost half my team!" He gave the man a brutal Alpha stare. "So, don't you fucking talk to me about loss. It's lucky to be alive at all."

Morrell shoved the man back so hard he fell to the ground.

Nobody said a word, but they all stared at him as he turned and limped away.

Carrie turned away from the footage showing on the screen. The damage the Zetas had caused was substantial. And they had sent barely 40 ships.

She jiggled her legs anxiously. There was still no sign of the *Aurora* crew and no word from Harris and McKinley. She didn't like it. The silence, the no-shows.

Valerie sat down beside her. "It's over," she said, handing her a coffee. "The worst of it, at least. The *Barbican* took out the last of the airborne ships."

"Yeah," Carrie smiled taking the coffee, "but there're still HH out there on foot. No-one's safe until we round them up."

"We'll get them," Valerie smiled, looking back at the screens as some kind of interference began to affect the coverage.

"Archie?" Carrie said.

Suddenly Carrie heard a low humming sound, coming from outside. "Wait!" she said, stopping Archie before he spoke.

"That sounds like a ship," Valerie said, looking back at the screens. "The interference?"

Carrie stood and placed her cup down. She moved for the door, pulling her gun out. She opened the door slightly and saw lights in the sky.

"Whose is it?" Valerie asked anxiously. "One of ours?"

As it drew nearer, Carrie recognized it. Well, the nose of it anyway.

A smile spread across her face. "The big brown bird!" she said.

She threw the door open and jogged outside, holding her hand up against the wind as the pod came into land. As soon as the engines were shut down and the wind died, she looked back up. A hatch opened at the side and one by one the crew began to pour out. She scanned each one, counting them, making sure they were all there. Steinberg was out first, then Brown, Evenssen, Tikaani, Murphy, Yughi, Gregson.

Carrie ran up and hugged and patted each one as they appeared.

"I thought you guys were gone!" she said, then turned to Hunter as he appeared and hit the ground. "Goddamnit, I thought you were gone!" she said as she pulled him into a tight hug. He was drenched with sweat.

"So, did we for a while there," Hunter said.

Carrie pulled back from him. "You are a magnificent bastard, you know that? That was some awesome flying, Kiwi."

Hunter smiled and looked over at Frazer as he emerged from the pod, equally drenched in sweat. "It wasn't all me," he said, holding out his fist for Frazer to bump. Frazer did so, looking as exhausted as Hunter did. They'd worked hard up there. Hunter pulled the Scotsman into a hug, patting his back. "I'll fly with you any day, Chucky."

"Aye," Frazer said, patting Hunter on the back as well, then stepping back. "And I'll fly with you, too, Kiwi."

Hunter looked at Carrie. "Where are Harris and McKinley?"

Carrie's smile faded a little. "Looking for you. We'll go call them in." She turned and jogged back toward the facility, stopping briefly to tell Brown that the Alpha Village in Centralis had escaped damage. He gave her a relieved look, knowing Colt and the children were fine, and she jogged away.

Harris listened carefully, trying to pinpoint the exact location of the Zeta. It was several meters away, approaching the groaning body of McKinley. He heard the hiss again and tried to understand whether it was the sound of the weapon, or the Zeta itself. Another hiss, but no weapon was fired. Maybe it was coming from the Zeta, then? Was this the Zeta known as the Priestess? The reptilian one?

The hiss sounded again. Harris knew the Zeta was fixed on him and not on McKinley writhing in pain on the ground in front of it. He wasn't sure how he knew that, he just did. And it made sense. Right now, McKinley was not a threat to the Zeta. But Harris, unharmed, was. McKinley's body had shielded his from the blast.

He heard Welles's voice suddenly sound in the distance. He felt at his ear and realized he'd lost his comms piece in the fight with the HH. His Alpha hearing picked up the comms just fine though. His eyes found where it lay. It was too far out of reach.

"Sir? I repeat, the Aurora *team have returned. They are unhurt. You can return to base."*

Harris was awash with mixed emotions: relief that the rest of the team were safe, but anxiety for himself and McKinley who, right now, weren't. He closed his eyes, kept his senses attuned to the position of the Zeta, but focused his mind hard on Welles.

Carrie looked at Gregson. "They're not responding."

"Maybe they're in an area of interference?" he said, then looked at Yughi. "Could the *Barbican* be affecting things somehow?"

"Possibly, but their comms can't be working," Yughi said. "That's why Command thought they were dead, because their comms were shot and they couldn't get word to us."

"Help is on the way to them, though, right?" Gregson looked at Valerie.

"Yes, Command advised they were sending local Australian units to assist."

"The *Barbican* is being taken care of," Carrie said. "We need to focus on Harris and McKinley."

Hunter walked into the comms room. The crew had been taken straight through to the basement and given a meal and fluids.

"Still no word?" Hunter asked.

Carrie shook her head.

"They might have left their comms in the PV. It's unlikely, but..." Gregson shrugged.

Hunter shook his head. "Harris wouldn't leave his comms in the PV. Not with HH on the loose."

Carrie's mind tuned out to the discussion around them. Instead, she sat staring at the screen in front of her, showing the burning ruins of the crashed Zeta ship in Centralis.

"It's best we stay calm," Gregson said.

"I agree," Hunter said.

"We could head out and see if the comms come back up while we fly around?" Yughi said.

"We burned a lot of the power in that pod," Hunter said. "She's the only thing we've got around here to fly. We need to know where we're searching before we head out."

Just then, their eyes turned to the screen in front of Carrie. A list was scrolling of all the ships and units reported lost to the invasion. Of the Alpha units, the *Carcharias* was the only ship left intact. The rest had been destroyed. Most of the ground units were intact, but that was more to do with positioning than anything. The ground troops could only cover wherever they were stationed, and if the Zetas hadn't hit there, then they would be just fine. The same couldn't be said for the ships in the sky, however.

"Oh, Jesus," Gregson said, staring at the scrolling list.

"What?" Carrie said.

"The *Vortex*," he said pointing to the screen. "It's gone. They must've called it in to help."

Carrie saw the name UNF *Vortex* on the list. She looked up at Gregson who ran his hand over his mouth in dismay. It had been years now since he'd been stationed on that ship, but had he not been transferred to the *Aurora*, he might still have been there.

Carrie pictured the crew she had known while based aboard. "Was there anyone still on there who you knew?" she asked Gregson.

He nodded. "Captain Coup," he said quietly. Carrie felt sorrow wash over her. She'd known Coup, too. He'd been the first lieutenant, before he took over from Captain Lee.

"Archie," she said.

"Yes, Miss Welles."

"Can you hijack a satellite and look for them? Harris and McKinley?"

"I've been trying to locate them, but there is a lot going on with the Barbican's crash-landing. The UNF have commandeered all available satellites."

"Can you get me Captain Gold?"

"Yes, Miss Welles... Connecting you now."

"Captain Gold," she said. "Sergeant Carrie Welles of the UNF *Aurora*."

"You're still alive!" he said. *"I heard the* Aurora *was lost?"*

"The ship was lost, the crew are safe."

"Thank god," he breathed down the line. *"When I hadn't heard from Harris—"*

"When I say crew," she interrupted him, "Colonel Harris and Captain McKinley are missing."

"Where?"

"We're still down here in Western Australia. We're going to go looking for them. I just wanted to check that you're still airborne."

"Marchant asked us to remain on standby in case any more ships showed, but there're none on the radar. Just say the word, and we'll come your way and haul you out."

Hunter leaned closer to Archie's discs and took over the comms. "Affirmative, UNF *Carcharias*. Come our way. We need your ship." He looked at Carrie. "If they're in trouble, we're going to need more than that pod to get them out of here."

"Agreed," she said. "Rendezvous at the UNF comms facility in Western Australia, *Carcharias*. Do you read?"

"*Roger that. The* Carcharias *is en route.*"

Archie ended the transmission. Carrie stood and began to pace. As she walked back and forth in the silence, she noticed that her stomach was clenching and burning. She paused, sliding her hand over her belly. Was this just her own anxiety she was feeling? Or was it Harris? She focused on it some more, trying hard to summon whatever amount of Zeta may lay within her. She suddenly felt her spine tighten with fear as a realization hit her.

"They're in trouble."

"What?" Gregson asked her.

She turned to him. "They're in trouble. I can feel it. We have to go now."

"You can feel it?" Hunter said.

Carrie nodded. "I can't explain, but we have to go now."

"Go where?" Hunter asked.

"We just need to get airborne! They're in trouble!" She ran her hand back and forth over her stomach.

Yughi's eyes filled with curiosity. "Does this have something to do with what happened on the flight deck of that Zeta ship?"

"Yes. I can't explain it now, but you have to trust me. I—I just know when Harris is in trouble."

"What happened on the Zeta flight deck?" Gregson asked, as Steinberg and Tikaani stepped into the room.

Carrie looked at the faces staring at her. "I don't have time to explain! You just have to trust me. I'm connected to Harris and we can feel when the other is in trouble. We make each other feel it."

The team stared at her. Carrie stepped forward and grabbed Hunter's shirt in her fist. "Harris and McKinley are in trouble. Harris is making me feel it. My stomach is burning. We have to go!"

Hunter studied the hand on her stomach, then the one clenching his shirt. He turned his skeptical gaze to her eyes. "Fine, but where?"

"Just get me airborne and we'll go from there."

Harris's mind raced, wondering what he should do. The PV was not far from him. He could try and run, but whatever the Zeta hit McKinley with could easily hit him too. McKinley had been a stationary target, though. Was the Zeta's aim as good on a moving target?

He heard the hiss. And McKinley's groans. Why wasn't the Zeta approaching him? It knew where he was hiding. Why wasn't it firing?

Screw this, he thought. He rolled over onto his hands and knees and peered over the crumpled metal.

The Zeta, tall, smooth-skinned and black-eyed, was looking right at him. Harris froze for a moment. It was similar to the images he'd seen. This was indeed the Priestess form of the Zeta. Its weapon, a silver, triangular prism-shaped device, was strapped to its forearm, which was resting by its side. His eyes dropped to McKinley, now resting on his back, the burnt side of his body facing Harris. Covered in soil from where Harris had smothered the flames, his body still smoked. Although the flames had been put out, the heat still cooked his skin. It was bad. It was very bad.

As if in a knee-jerk reaction, Harris stood up and faced the Zeta. It flinched slightly at his abrupt movement, raising its forearm slightly, but holding it midway. Harris wasn't sure what to do. He could hold his arms out, in what to him would be a peaceful gesture, but would it seem peaceful to the Zeta? Or threatening? He chose to keep his arms by his side.

He moved slowly around the *Aurora* wreckage, scanning for his gun. It was too far away. McKinley groaned again.

"It's alright, McKinley," Harris said calmly, not wanting to raise his voice too loud to frighten the Zeta. "I'm going to get you out of here. Just hold tight."

McKinley tried to raise his head, but cried in pain. The side of his head that had been hit by the heat weapon, was bad. Harris almost didn't recognize him.

Harris now stood on the other side of the *Aurora* wreckage. The Zeta hissed again, hand wavering up and down. Harris scanned his memories of the images. Was there anything about them, about the way they stood, anything he could use to try and communicate?

He saw McKinley feebly reaching for his gun.

"McKinley, don't," he said firmly. "Don't move and you'll live."

McKinley tried to talk, but it was slurred. It sounded something like, "Kill this fuck."

"Just lie still, McKinley. *Don't* move. I got this."

The Zeta looked down at McKinley sniffing him, then looked up at Harris and sniffed the air. Harris focused on the Zeta's eyes, commanding its attention, distracting it from McKinley.

The bottom half of the Zeta stood motionless, but from the waist up it moved from side to side, like seaweed flowing back and forth on an ocean current. All the while, its eyes remained fixed on Harris.

"Why aren't you killing me?" he said, taking a careful step forward. "Why did you not hesitate to shoot McKinley before, but now you let me walk toward you?"

The Zeta hissed back, then it spoke with humming, buzzing, clicks.

Harris took another step forward, slowly. "We're going to need to find a way to communicate, or this conversation is going nowhere fast."

The Zeta hissed again, raising its forearm in his direction.

He paused, deciding to hold a hand out, in a plea for calm.

The Zeta sniffed him again, then opened its gummy mouth, flashing narrow, cylindrical teeth, breathing hot air at him.

He focused on the black eyes again, the way they stared at him. The Priestess was human-shaped, but he could see the reptilian features, starting with those eyes, the smooth, pale, leathery skin, and hissing mouth.

"You created us," Harris said carefully. "You and the rest of the Zetas. I may not have come from you exactly. I came from the one we call the Alma Mater, but in one way or another we came from your kind. You Zetas fertilized this planet with your creatures. Then you came back to investigate, and some of you bred with the HH. That," he said, taking another step forward, "is how I came to be." Then he paused, studying the Zeta. "Is that why you're not killing me? Do you recognize something in me? Is that why you keep smelling me?" He took another step forward. "You recognize the Zeta in me, don't you?" he said, although he felt repulsed to say it, to think that there could be any Zeta inside him, no matter how far removed. He nodded to himself. "It's stronger in me than it is in him," Harris said motioning to McKinley. "His is much watered down. He descended from straight HH matings, but me..." He took another step, just a few feet from McKinley and the Zeta now. "It runs thicker in my blood, because I came from a Zeta-HH pairing." Harris lifted his fingers and wiped the blood from underneath his nose, from the elbow the HH had given him during the earlier fight. He looked at the blood on his fingers, then held it out to the Zeta. "You can smell the Zeta in my blood, can't you?" He felt his face harden as he said it, felt his eyes narrow with hate and anger. He heard McKinley groaning again, much weaker now. His soldier was swiftly going into shock, and if Harris didn't do something soon, McKinley would die.

And he would not lose another one.

He lowered his hand, and felt his shoulders tighten.

"I know you can smell the Zeta," Harris said in a low voice, as he tensed and coiled every single muscle in his body, "but can you smell the Alpha?"

He sprang out, launching himself over McKinley and at the Zeta, knocking it onto its back. Taller than he, with longer limbs, he focused immediately on the arm with the weapon: pulling, punching and tugging with everything he had until he heard a pop and crunch, knowing he had maimed the Zeta's weaponed arm. The Zeta's other hand had clasped onto his head, as hot breath blasted his face and crocodile teeth snapped his way. He felt the Zeta's legs bend and wrap around his own, like sliding snakes, squeezing the blood from them. But that only made him angrier.

He pulled back his meaty fist and slammed it into the Zeta's face again and again, with everything he had. He'd never felt so much anger, never hit anything so hard before in his life. He pounded and pounded, waiting to hear the sound of its skull breaking. Its claws dug into his shoulder and scraped all the way down his right arm like little knives, but he didn't stop. Roaring with fury, he didn't even stop at the numbness sweeping over his broken hand as it smashed again and again into the Zeta's face. All he knew was that he was getting himself and McKinley out of there.

The Zeta's claws and legs loosened then, and he noticed the Zeta's face was now half caved-in. Harris's torn, bloodied and broken hand now sat somewhere beneath its nose, deep within its skull. He watched it a moment, noticing that the Zeta bled like a human, like an animal, red and warm.

Only when he was sure it was dead did he pull his fist out of its face. He winced at the movement, because the Zeta's claws were still caught in his arm. He pulled the claws out and pushed the dead Zeta arm away. Then, panting, he got to his feet and surveyed the area, attuning his senses, to make sure there were no more.

Sensing he was alone, he immediately turned back to McKinley and fell to his knees.

"McKinley?" he said, pulling his soldier up into his arms, again ignoring the pain in his broken hand. "McKinley?"

McKinley moaned faintly and Harris could still feel the heat coming off the side of his body; could almost hear the sizzling of his skin.

"You stay with me!" Harris told him. "You hear? I'm gonna get you help. Alright? You stay with me!" Harris heaved with all his might lifting McKinley up off the ground, then dipped under the weight as he hoisted his soldier over his shoulder. He moved as fast as he could back to the PV, strapping McKinley into the passenger seat, then reaching for the comms panel in the PV.

"*Aurora*, do you read!" he yelled. "*Aurora*, this is Harris. McKinley is down. I repeat, McKinley is down. We need assistance fast!"

"*Where are you?*" he heard Archie's voice reply.

Harris flinched a little, not expecting to hear the AIS's voice. He looked around. Other than the wreck of the *Aurora*, there were no significant landmarks. He flicked on the PVs GPS and saw the Greenough Hamlet was the closest landmark. "Have someone meet me at the Greenough Hamlet!" he said. "And get there fast!"

Archie was silent a moment, hopefully replaying the message.

"Archie?" he called urgently.

"*Lieutenant Gregson wants to know what his injuries are?*"

"Burns," Harris said. "Very bad burns. He's critical."

"*The* Aurora *pod is en route. ETA, 20 minutes.*"

"Good!" With that Harris ended the transmission, then raced back to get their guns. As he ran back to the PV, passing the dead Zeta, his eyes caught on the weapon attached to its forearm. He halted, looking at McKinley's motionless frame in the PV, then back at the Zeta weapon. Moving to the Zeta, he raised his weapon and fired several times until the laser fire had cut through the flesh and bone, enough for Harris to rip the Zeta's arm right off. Then he raced back to the PV, threw the Zeta arm and attached weapon in the back and set the PV in motion.

Carrie, seated in McKinley's chair at the captain's desk, sat with her hand over her mouth. The pod was airborne, on its way to the rendezvous point with Harris.

Gregson, sitting to her left, in Doc's old seat, placed his hand on her shoulder and squeezed. "Right now he's alive. You've got to focus on that. We'll get him."

She looked at him and nodded, then listened as Archie contacted the *Carcharias* to check their ETA and advise them to ready a pod-bed in their hospital.

She stood and checked her weapon. She glanced around the *Aurora* pod, which was effectively just the flight deck. "Did you clear the weapons store before evac?"

"Some," Brown said, motioning to the last tier of seats. "We cleared out some supplies from the hospital, too."

Carrie climbed the stairs to the last tier, where her old seat was, and saw medical supplies and several weapons bundled on the seats and floor. Some laser-fire rifles and pistols with spare battery packs; some standard issue UNF pistols with clips; some bullaser vests, comms sets, oxy tanks and other paraphernalia. She pulled on a bullaser vest, collected a second gun and stocked up on battery packs.

"What are you doing?" Steinberg asked.

Carrie looked at him. "Getting ready to get my husband back."

Harris pressed his foot to the floor, willing the PV to grow wings and fly. He looked over at McKinley, whose body bounced around limp with every movement of the PV.

"McKinley!" he barked.

No response.

"Captain!" he barked again. "Open your goddamn eyes! You hear me!"

Harris thought he caught a flutter of McKinley's eyelids. Well, one of them… the other was too badly burned.

"Help is on the way, soldier! You just need to hang on. You hear me?" he yelled, glancing back and forth between the road and his limp soldier. "Welles is coming!" he said, reaching out with his broken right hand and grabbing what remained of McKinley's burnt shirt. "So you gotta hang on. You wanna see your kids again? Huh? You wanna see Freya? And Jesse? And Brody? Then you hang on, you motherfucker! You hang on! Don't you *fuckin'* die on me!"

Harris tried to erase the image of Doc lying dead before him in Welles's arms. He couldn't go through that again, and he couldn't watch Welles go through that again. Especially knowing that she'd already lost her father to this invasion. She couldn't lose her husband too.

"You hang on!" he yelled at McKinley. "You will *not* die on me! Do you understand! Those things are coming back and they will come in greater numbers. I need you, soldier. Welles needs you. Your kids need you! You hang on. I need you to be the tough motherfucker I know you to be. You hear me? You're a tough motherfucker, McKinley! You hear? You will *not* die! That's a fuckin' order!"

He suddenly saw movement at the side of the road, then heard the rear window of the PV smash. The vehicle swerved erratically in time with his fright. He let go of McKinley's shirt and grabbed both hands on the wheel to try and steady it.

"Jesus!" he said, looking around to see a metal spear, sticking out the window. "Shit!"

He heard the growls then, and saw two bright flashes of light. A force of hot wind seemed to move the car sideways. He felt heat sear his left arm and tried to steady the wheel, difficult as it was with his broken hand. He swerved drastically until he suddenly felt as though the PV was in flight.

And it was.

It was rolling.

He was rolling. McKinley was rolling.

Dazed, he didn't know what was happening.

All he knew was that his arm burned like the flesh was melting off him. And he screamed in absolute agony.

27

Crossroads

Carrie paced up and down the parking lot of the Greenough Hamlet.

"They should've been here by now," she said to Murphy, also pacing, as anxious and ready for action as she.

"Aye," the Irishman said, his face as serious as she'd ever seen it.

"Archie!"

"I'm not getting any response."

"I don't care what you have to do, but you need to hijack that satellite now," Carrie demanded. "I need eyes in the sky looking for them!"

"I shall consult with my fellow AISs and see what we can do."

"Do it fast, Archie!"

"Yes, Miss Welles."

Carrie paced away from the *Aurora* crew, who stared at her curiously. She wasn't in charge, she shouldn't be calling the shots, but when it came to her husband and the father of her children, or Harris for that matter, no-one was getting in her way. She'd left the children asleep at the UNF facility under the watchful eyes of Roy and Sampson, with instructions that they lock the facility down and not open the doors to anyone, except the *Aurora* team. And she was adamant that her children would awake with their father by their side.

She turned away from the crew and closed her eyes, focusing on her gut, picturing Harris and willing herself to feel something.

But she felt nothing.

And that's what worried her.

They were in trouble. Both of them.

And it was up to her to get them out of it.

Harris awoke. He wasn't sure how long he'd been sleeping, but it had been deep, and he'd been dreaming of Welles. She was just standing there, staring at him. It was odd. As he roused from his sleep, he felt a heavy ache in his head, and his face was wet and sticky. And he smelled something burning. Smelled smoke. Smelled blood.

He blinked his eyes open and remembered where he was. He was sitting in a PV in the middle of the Australian bush. The window beside him was smashed, the PV's nose was bent. Only one headlight worked. As he stared out the windscreen, he noticed a kangaroo just standing there as if examining him and the crumpled vehicle, perhaps mesmerized by the light.

He saw the kangaroo's ears stand on end and swivel off to the left, then the animal immediately bounded away in the opposite direction, disappearing into the dark of the night.

He saw movement then. A soldier. Standing in front of the car, hands resting on the crumpled bonnet looking in at him. He blinked his eyes to clear his vision.

"Carter?" he slurred.

Carter, now joined by Louis, shook his head at him. He thought he saw Smith, too, standing back a little.

"Am I dead?" he slurred, blinking heavily again, but suddenly lost himself to the darkness once more.

Carrie, still pacing the Hamlet car park, felt the Alpha surging within. "Report!"

"Wilfred has agreed to assist me in the commandeering of the satellite. But we will only have four minutes."

"That'll do, they can't be far. Get on it!"

"Yes, Miss Welles."

Carrie paced again.

"You gotta cool your heels, little butterfly," Tikaani said. "You burn all your energy now, then what do you have for the field?"

Carrie looked at her. "I'll have everything for my husband and our colonel. Don't you worry about that."

Tikaani smiled and gave a soft laugh. "You a fierce little butterfly," she said in approval.

Carrie managed a smile, then turned and scanned the rest of the *Aurora*'s soldiers. She could see Hunter and Frazer still on board the pod at the flight console, ready to go. Yughi sat with them in discussion. Evenssen and Gregson sat in their seats, also in conversation, while Murphy, Brown and Steinberg stood just outside the pod in readiness.

"Miss Welles," Archie's voice said.

"What is it?"

"I believe I've found the PV."

"Where?" Carrie asked, raising her hand in the air and circling it around enthusiastically, indicating for the team to move. Hunter saw the motion and fired up the pod.

"They are off the road. The PV is stationary. It looks wrecked."

"Where?" she asked again, approaching the pod's hatch.

"I'm sending the coordinates now to your PDP."

"Any signs of movement in the vehicle?" she said, climbing aboard the pod.

"No, I'm afraid not, but movement has been detected away from the vehicle."

Carrie moved down the tiers of the pod into McKinley's seat, as Tikaani closed the doors behind her. "What does that mean? They're on foot?"

Archie hesitated a moment. *"No. The movement is headed toward the vehicle. I believe several HH are on approach."*

Carrie's spine tightened, and her eyes fixed on Hunter, who had been looking at her and listening to Archie's voice. He immediately turned around to Frazer.

"We need to move this thing like we've never moved her before!"

"You're giving me permission to be rough with your lady again?" Frazer smiled. "Thought you'd never ask!"

And with a whoosh akin to a rollercoaster ride, the pod soared into the air.

Harris opened his eyes again. He was still in the PV. He saw something walk past in front of the vehicle. *Someone?* It came to him then, what he was doing, where he was. He turned his head to look at McKinley, but stopped short at the pain in his head and the agony that shot down his neck and left arm. It felt as though his skin had been peeled off and the meat of his arm was stinging at the touch of the night air.

He groaned and closed his eyes again, exhaling in short bursts to fight the pain. He noticed the wetness on his face and realized that it was blood. He could smell it strongly, the blood, the burnt flesh. He tried to groan again, but his voice was lost and the blackness overcame him.

Carrie felt the tension coursing through her veins. They'd just passed the wreck of the vehicle, and one HH and what looked like a Zeta were only a few meters away from it.

"I gotta land the pod back up on the road!" Hunter called out to them. "I'm going to have to clear some trees while I do it, so it's going to be rough."

"Somebody say rough?" Frazer smiled.

"Everyone hold on!" Hunter yelled.

Harris heard a loud noise, felt a strong wind and opened his eyes again. He sat quietly, blinking his eyes, fighting to stay conscious. He kept dreaming of Welles, of her just staring at him. It was as though she were willing him to wake up.

"I'm trying," he said. Although maybe he dreamed he said it.

Suddenly he heard that strange hissing noise. It was close. Very close. He realized his eyes were closed and opened them again. As he did, he saw something in front of him. He blinked a few times, trying to clear his eyes, his mind. When he did, he instantly froze. Leaning in through the PV's window right in front of him, was something human, but not. It was a Zeta. Another Priestess.

A sense of déjà vu flooded over him. But this wasn't his recurring dream. This was real. Although it was still different to his dream. This thing that leaned in the window and sniffed at McKinley was a Priestess. The thing in his dream had not been.

The Priestess moved back slightly, turning its head to view him; its mouth opened as it stared, its thin tongue moving around, sensing him. He dared not move a muscle, nor blink his eyes, though he wanted to swallow badly. And he knew, in this moment, just how mixed his dreams had been. The thing he'd seen in his dreams, he bet, had been an amalgamation of all the Zetas. An amalgamation of all the things he would see. But so far, all he had seen were the Priestess Zetas and the HH.

So what did that mean? Were the other Zetas here somewhere, or had only the Priestess Zeta come?

Carrie, gun out front, moved as fast and as Alpha quiet as she could through the scrub in the direction of the PV. Murphy, Tikaani, Steinberg, Brown and Gregson were close behind her, while Evenssen and Yughi stood guard at the pod.

She attuned her eyes as best she could, wishing to hell she had the senses of smell and hearing, because she knew the HH were out here in this bush. They had seen the ones close to the PV as they flew over, but Archie had detected more further out, making their way toward the crashed vehicle.

The *Aurora* team would soon be outnumbered.

Either way, she was going to do her best to kill every last one of them.

Harris fought hard to stay conscious. The Zeta seemed to sense that he was alive. It looked at him, sniffing his scent with its odd nose and skinny tongue.

Yeah, that's right, he thought groggily. *You can smell the Zeta in me, too.*

The zipping of laser fire sounded in the distance, accompanied by flashes of golden light. The Zeta pulled back and stood up to look around, emitting urgent humming and buzzing and clicks as it did. Through blinking eyes and searing pain, Harris saw a HH jog across in front of the PV and into the bush. The Zeta put its head through the window again. He heard growling and more laser fire, then sparks shot up from the bonnet of the PV.

The Zeta, still leaning inside the PV, seemed to rear back, smacking its head on the roof of the vehicle, shaking the entire contents, Harris included. More laser fire resulted in a direct hit on the Priestess, which splashed its wet, sticky blood over him. Its body fell backward from the vehicle, the stench of burning flesh billowing from it.

He closed his eyes with immense relief. It was Welles. He was sure of it. She was here. He caught his breath and swallowed hard, then opened his eyes again. He looked over to the point he knew he would see her, watching the darkness, waiting. Then her vibrant green Alpha eyes appeared, glowing at his.

She ran toward him, gun out front, eyes darting to her surroundings. She made it to the vehicle, yanked what remained of the beast away, then leaned in the window. Her glowing green eyes stared into his, as she placed her hand on his cheek with an almighty zap.

"I'm going to get you out of here!" she told him firmly. "Just hold on, alright? Just hold on!"

"I can't m—move." He tried to shake his head, as they heard a terrible roar in the distance.

Welles pulled away from the vehicle. "MURPHY!" she screamed into the distance. "HOLD THEM OFF!"

He heard more laser fire and tried to turn his head in the direction she yelled. He thought he saw Brown running past, but wasn't sure.

"The team...?" He tried to formulate words but failed.

Welles touched his cheek with another zap, quickly turning his face back to hers. "Just look at me, alright! I'm going to get you out of here!" She suddenly looked over to the passenger seat, and seemed to realize that the motionless lump there was McKinley. Her eyes shone with tears and her jaw turned hard. "STEINBERG!" she called out. "Steinberg, I need you!"

Suddenly there were loud thumping sounds, as though something heavy was running toward them. Welles swiftly turned and began firing frantically, hands moving back and forth, as though, whatever was coming, there were many of them.

"MURPHY! STEINBERG!" she screamed. "WHERE THE FUCK ARE YOU?"

Carrie must've killed about six of those things so far. She wondered where they had all come from. Were these the HH from the four buried ships? How many did each ship carry? And why were they converging on this one spot? The dead Priestess?

She held still, waiting to see movement in the bushes. She did, then fired in that direction. Murphy and Tikaani were firing close by, with Brown further on, then finally she saw Steinberg and Gregson racing to her.

"Harris is conscious. Get McKinley!" she said pointing to the passenger side. They ran over and did their best to get the crumpled PV door open to allow Gregson access.

"Jesus Christ!" Gregson said when he looked at McKinley. "McKinley! McKinley, can you hear me?"

Carrie darted a glance their way, but saw that McKinley lay still. Motionless.

"I can't find a pulse!" Gregson said, unbuckling his harness. "Let's get him back to the pod!"

"Move!" Steinberg said, reaching in and pulling McKinley's limp body out of the PV and over his shoulder.

"Colonel," Gregson called through the PV to Harris.

Harris opened his eyes. "Take McKinley," he slurred. "I'm fine."

"I've got Harris," Carrie told Gregson. "Go!"

She glanced back to see Steinberg running away with McKinley over his shoulder and Gregson trailing behind. Suddenly, a HH lunged from the bushes close by and threw himself on Steinberg's back.

"Tikaani!" Carrie yelled, motioning to Harris as she sprinted off toward Steinberg. Gregson was trying to wrestle the HH off him, unable to risk firing at it in case it hit McKinley or Steinberg.

"Get back to the ship!" Carrie yelled on approach to Gregson. "We need you there! Get ready for McKinley!"

Gregson looked around at her, then did as she said, not arguing the point. Carrie increased her speed and ran at the HH clinging to Steinberg. She leapt up onto its back, and Steinberg stumbled, struggling to carry the three of them – her, McKinley and the HH. She threw her arm around the HH's neck and pulled back hard. It released its grip of Steinberg and the HH fell to the ground with Carrie. The big German steadied his feet, then ran onward to the pod, with McKinley still over his shoulder.

As soon as Carrie hit the ground, she threw herself on top of the HH and began wrestling with it. Just like her fight with Drazen, she knew the key was to get in hard, fast and first. The HH was broader, more muscular, more aggressive than she gave it credit for however. As she reached for the weapon that she'd holstered during her run-up to Steinberg, the HH threw her over on her back and began pounding down with its fists and elbows. She threw her arms up in defense, as she heard more pounding feet headed toward them. Worried more HH were on the way, she was relieved when whatever it was, connected with the HH and knocked it off her. She looked up and saw Tikaani laying on the creature's back, grabbing it in a headlock and squeezing tight.

"I got your back, little butterfly!" she said through clenched teeth.

Carrie jumped to her feet and in one swift motion pulled out her gun. "Move!" she yelled at Tikaani.

Tikaani grabbed the HH's head and shoved it into the ground, pressing herself up and away from it. As soon as she was clear, Carrie blew the HH's head open with blood, sparks and smoke.

She briefly locked eyes with Tikaani, before swooping around and running back to Harris.

Harris heard a bang and opened his eyes again. Welles was back by his PV window.

"McKinley?" he slurred.

"He's back at the pod. You're next," she said, tugging at the door, trying to open it.

"WELLES!" Brown shouted urgently. She looked around, then Alpha quick jumped back, as something slammed into the PV. Laser fire started up again outside. Harris looked down and saw the sharp blade of a metal spear sticking through the PV door, the tip just inches from his thigh. He glanced back out and saw Brown wrestling with one of the HH.

He heard more laser fire, and then suddenly there were two pairs of hands grabbing onto the door and yanking at it. Suddenly the door fell open and Welles and Brown stared in at him.

"Come on, you fuckers!" he heard Murphy yelling in the background.

"Bring it to us, freaks!" Tikaani joined in.

Steinberg came running back then, and Brown stepped back. Welles leaned in and unstrapped him.

"The arm," Harris said.

"I know," Welles said, eyeing his wounds. "Gregson will take care of you."

"No," he said. "The arm."

"He's hit his head," Welles said.

"No!" he growled, trying to reach backward into the seat behind. "The arm. The Zeta arm."

Welles leaned in and looked past him into the back seat.

"The weapon," he said, closing his eyes again, "wounded McKinley... need to know it..."

He fought and fought, but despite the yelling in the background and the laser fire going off, he was once more enveloped in blackness.

Carrie leaned back out of the PV.

"Get Harris back to the pod!" she said to Steinberg. "Brown, cover him!" She ran around the PV and crawled through the passenger door and into the back seat, looking for whatever Harris had been talking about. Amid the smashed glass and bits of trees, she saw it. A Zeta arm with a silver device attached to it. She grabbed it, then noticed one of the HH spears, lying along the back seat. She grabbed that too, then moved back to the passenger seat. As she went to climb over it, she noticed the blood and pieces of burnt flesh stuck to the seat. McKinley's blood. McKinley's flesh. She paused a moment, steadying her stomach. She swallowed hard, then gritted her teeth and continued on.

As her feet touched the ground outside the PV, she saw something run past in the darkened bushes. She fired at it, but missed. A small fire started in the trees. She started moving backward, swiftly, darting glances over her shoulder, looking for Murphy and Tikaani. She spotted them, then saw something whizz past her again in the bushes. It was a Zeta. It was fast.

She looked down at the torn Zeta arm she held and knew the Zeta in the bushes might just be armed as this one had been. And that Zeta had hurt McKinley bad. Probably caused the damage to Harris's arm too.

"We gotta move out!" she yelled at Murphy and Tikaani, as she approached them.

"But I'm having fun," Tikaani said, clenching her teeth and firing into the trees.

"Fuckin' A," Murphy said. "We need to kill every last one of these fucks."

Carrie glanced around at the small fires surrounding them that their laser weapons had ignited. Brown and Steinberg came running back toward them.

"Are they on?" Carrie yelled.

"Yeah, let's get the hell out of here!" Brown said, as another spear soared through the air at them. The all dodged it, then Murphy and Tikaani began firing again.

"Archie," Carrie said. "What's the *Carcharias'* ETA?"

"*Twenty-five minutes.*"

"Let's go," Carrie said. "The *Carcharias* can wipe these fuckers out!" With that she turned and ran back toward the pod with Brown and Steinberg. More spears came flying at them as they did, one catching Steinberg in the back of the thigh, piercing through his leg. He yelled in pain and fell to his knees, but Brown swiftly grabbed the spear and pulled it out, hauling Steinberg to his feet and they moved onward. Carrie followed them, firing randomly into the trees, providing cover, all the while with the torn Zeta arm and spear tucked under her own.

As they approached the pod Yughi and Evenssen came forward offering all three of them protection. Brown loaded Steinberg into the *Aurora* pod, then leaned back out looking for her. She threw him the Zeta arm and spear and he caught them, then she turned back to the bush.

"Archie, tell the *Carcharias* to meet us at the Hamlet."

"*Yes, Miss Welles,*" he replied.

"Where's Murphy and Tikaani?" Evenssen asked, eyeing the trees, weapon out front.

"Fuck," Carrie hissed, scanning the bushes for them.

Suddenly they heard screams, then bursts of laser fire. It was close by.

She swung her gun up. "I'll get them!"

"Welles!" Brown yelled.

"Stay there!" she called back. "We gotta leave!"

She turned and headed swiftly in the direction of the laser fire, shooting gold sparks against the black of night. Murphy and Tikaani were still standing, but Murphy was hunched and holding a hand to a bleeding wound at his shoulder. She saw a spear lying on the ground a few meters away.

"Let's get out of here!" she yelled at them, and they started moving backward toward the pod, as a chorus of growls sounded from the trees. Metal spears flew out in every direction and Carrie found herself ducking, dodging, swooping and pivoting for dear life to avoid being hit.

Tikaani yelled as one sliced her arm, and another sliced her leg as they passed. Murphy suddenly made a deep guttural sound, and Carrie glanced over to see a spear sticking through his gut. "Fuck you!" he spat and began firing aimlessly into the trees.

"Irish!" Tikaani yelled, moving toward him.

Carrie ran too, trying to provide cover fire as Tikaani reached him and ripped the spear from him. Murphy groaned as she did, and Carrie saw his teeth were stained with blood.

"Let's go! Now!" she yelled, as Tikaani threw Murphy's arm around her shoulder and began to lead him away. He continued firing into the trees, spewing forth all sorts of profanities. Carrie glanced over her shoulder and saw the lights of the pod. They were close. She turned back around to Tikaani and Murphy, just as a blast of light and heat shot toward them. In an Alpha instant, Murphy pushed Tikaani away and caught the brunt of the blast, which blew him backward.

Carrie immediately raised her weapon to the source of the light and fired repeatedly, then heard something heavy fall to the ground.

"Irish!" Tikaani yelled, moving over to him, beating her hands down to kill the flames.

Murphy gave an agonized scream in return.

"Cover us!" Tikaani yelled, as she bent and lifted Murphy up from the ground.

"No!" he managed in a strangled cry of pain. "Fuuuuck!"

Tikaani pulled him to his feet. "You're coming with us!" She began to drag him, as Carrie moved past them and kept her weapon aimed, swinging back and forth along the trees. The growls sounded again. They were close and sounded as though they had spread out. If they weren't careful they might seal off their path to the pod.

She heard Murphy groan and both he and Tikaani fell to the ground. Carrie ran to them, as another spear shot out and grazed across her back – cutting right through her bullaser vest. She hissed in pain and turned and fired at the source, then ran on to Murphy grabbing his arm. But as she looked at him she saw just how bad he was. The blast had hit him front on and his entire torso was burned and charred, half his face and both legs too.

"Fucking go," he managed, trying to push Tikaani away, but she grabbed for him again.

"Not leaving you, man," she said, pulling him to sit.

"I'm fucking dead," he spat, "get out of here!"

"Murphy!" Carrie said.

His burned face fixed on her. "Fucking... go. Go!"

Carrie turned and saw a HH running toward them, she raised her gun and fired, felling it. But then another and another came running out.

"GO!" Murphy yelled at them. "I'll take care of these fucks!" He grabbed Tikaani's gun and started firing at them, but soon dropped his hand, unable to hold the weight of it anymore. Carrie turned again and picked up this slack, as Tikaani reached inside her vest for something then grabbed Murphy's hand and placed something in it.

"If you're gonna go, go in style," she said.

Murphy saw she'd handed him a grenade. He gave a bloody, charred smile to Tikaani. "You're a beautiful woman, Tik," he whispered, the pain evident in his voice.

"I know," she smiled back, then squeezed his hand, kissed his blistered forehead and stood.

Carrie felled another HH, then looked back at Murphy.

"Go," he said quietly to her. "I got... work... to do." He pulled the pin on the grenade and Tikaani grabbed the back of Carrie's shirt and hauled her away. They ran with everything they had, spears whizzing past them, as Murphy yelled with his last breath, "COME ON, YOU FUCKING CUNTS!"

Carrie and Tikaani swooped into the pod with the help of Brown and Evenssen, who grabbed them and hauled them inside, slamming the door shut behind them.

"Where's Murphy?" Brown yelled, but they didn't have time to respond. The bright flash and boom sounded, spitting dirt and rocks at the pod.

"GO! GO! GO!" Carrie yelled, and Hunter lurched the pod into the air.

28

Lifelines

Harris heard yelling and opened his eyes. He had an oxygen mask on, there were people crowded around and he saw Gregson beside him. He turned his head and saw the medic leaning over McKinley and yelling "CLEAR!" McKinley's body convulsed briefly then fell limp again.

Then Harris suddenly noticed someone else there, too.

Doc.

"Doc?" he slurred through the oxygen mask.

Doc, dressed in his Space Duty uniform, was sitting at McKinley's head, leaning over the wounded soldier's face. He looked over at Harris.

"Doc?" Harris slurred again.

Doc's eyes were troubled and concerned as he looked back at him. "Hang in there, Saul," he said. "You can make it through this. Just hang on." Doc turned back to McKinley and leaned over him again. "Stay where you are, McKinley, you hear me?" he said firmly. "If you try and cross over I swear to God I will beat your ass back myself?"

Harris recognized more people then. Smith, Bulk, Louis, Carter, Packham. His eyes lingered a little on the last one. She smiled at him.

"Am I dying?" he asked.

"You? Die?" Carter said in that thick South African accent of his, smiling. "Come on, sir. You're too fucking tough for that."

Harris looked back at Doc again.

"Hold on, McKinley!" Doc hissed quietly, eyes boring into the limp soldier. "You stay where you are! You *need* to stay there!"

"Is he dying?" Harris asked, watching Gregson yell "CLEAR" and shock his soldier's body again.

He felt a hand on his cheek, and turned to see Evenssen beside him. "It's alright sir," he said. "We've got you. Just hold on. You're going to be okay."

Harris looked back around to see that his dead soldiers had disappeared, and only the living remained. He turned his eyes to the spot on the floor near McKinley's head, wondering if Doc was still there somewhere.

He looked back at Evenssen. "Th—the war?" he managed, trying feebly to sit up.

Evenssen pushed him back down gently. "It's over, sir. It's over."

"It is?" he said, resting his head back on the ground and focusing his eyes up on the roof. He saw the electric blue and silver shield of Space Duty looking down upon him. And he realized he recognized this roof.

He was on the flight deck of the *Aurora*.

The crew were around him.

The war was over.

He was home.

And with that thought, he closed his eyes, and embraced the blackness yet again.

Carrie took a moment to catch her breath inside the pod doors, then quickly raced down the tiers to where Gregson hovered over McKinley.

"Is he—" she began but didn't get to finish her question as Gregson yelled. "CLEAR!" She watched as the shock pads did their thing and McKinley's body jumped.

Carrie saw how badly damaged one side of his body was, his right eye, his cheek, his jaw. His arm looked the worst hit, but Gregson had wrapped it in some kind of cling film. The meat and muscle had melted away. She thought she could see bone. Sitting next to his damaged side, she went to grab his hand, but realized that three and half of his fingers were missing, and it too was covered in the clear film. She placed her hand on the inside of his thigh. A large section of his pants had burned away and there had been damage to his hip and outer thigh. "Stay with me, McKinley. Stay with me," she said.

Gregson placed an automated apparatus over his face, which blew breaths of air into her husband. She bent forward and went to whisper into his ear, but realized it was missing. She gasped and paused, but then leaned close to the hole that remained. "You stay with me, McKinley. I love you. Don't you leave me. You have to stay with me!"

"CLEAR!" Gregson yelled again. Carrie released McKinley's thigh and looked over at Harris who lay on the other side of her. His arm and neck were badly burned, too, but not quite as horrific as McKinley's wounds. The PV he'd been in must have borne the brunt of the blast. His hand wasn't too bad, all the fingers in place, so she slid her hand onto his with a zap and squeezed it gently. Then she bent down and whispered into the colonel's ear.

"You hold on, Harris. You hold on. This has just started. We've got a long way to go yet. You can't leave me. I need you. You're my Guardian, I need you!" She felt the vibration in her hand, but it was weak.

Gregson placed the breathing apparatus over McKinley's face again. Carrie looked back at her husband and leaned forward, sliding her hand around the apparatus to touch his good cheek. "Stay with me, baby," she whispered into what was left of his right ear. "Stay with me."

"*The* Carcharias *is on approach to the Hamlet!*" Archie told them.

"Tell them we need two pods!" Gregson said. "Tell them we need everything they have! I'm losing McKinley!"

Carrie leaned back and took in her damaged husband. "He's not leaving me," she said. "He's gonna hold on. I know it."

Gregson viewed a device in his hands. "Get ready to clear!" he said, watching a timer tick down carefully. Carrie removed her hand from his cheek.

She looked back at Harris, squeezed his hand again, willing the vibration to increase. She looked to his bloodied head, where Evenssen held a bandage over a deep cut. She leaned down and whispered to him. "You're doing good, Harris. Stay with us. Hold on. Stay with us."

"CLEAR!" Gregson yelled.

Carrie felt a sudden sharp spike of pain shoot through her from one hand to the next. She bolted upright and gasped as her body seemed frozen with the current that ran through her from McKinley to Harris and back again.

"Fuck!" she heard Gregson yell, and saw him desperately hitting buttons on the device. The current seemed to suck back out of her into McKinley again, and she looked down to see that her hand had been resting on his thigh. She felt someone's hands on her shoulder and realized Gregson was yelling instructions at someone to lay her down. She followed the arms pulling her back and looked up in shock at Brown.

"Y'alright?" he said.

She nodded. "I—I'm fine." Winded, she looked over at Gregson, who was darting glances between her, Harris and McKinley.

"Shit," he said, sounding shocked, darting his eyes between them again. "I'm… I'm getting a heartbeat."

"McKinley?" Evenssen asked.

Gregson nodded. "I don't know what just happened, but… it's faint, it's irregular, but it's there."

"We're coming in to land!" Frazer called. "I see the *Carcharias* in the sky!"

"Priority One," Gregson said to Brown and Evenssen. "We get McKinley onto the *Carcharias* and into a pod. It's the only thing that will keep him alive."

"Got it!" Brown said firmly.

Carrie sat up, her whole body feeling a little numb and, well, fried.

"You alright?" Gregson asked her.

"I'm good," she said with an offhand gesture, then slid backward out of the way.

They waited while Hunter and Frazer landed the pod, then she watched as Evenssen heaved Harris out of the way, and Brown and Gregson moved McKinley to the pod's exit, ready to race him to the *Carcharias*.

*

Waiting for the *Carcharias* to land felt like forever. But it was a large ship and it couldn't be helped. As soon as the ship was in place, they saw its entry doors opening and several soldiers come running out with stretchers in tow. She sat dazed, watching as they lifted McKinley onto the stretcher and ran him back to the ship with Gregson following, then they dragged Harris forward, loaded him onto a stretcher and took him away as well.

Carrie looked around, saw Brown helping Steinberg, who was holding a bandage to his bleeding thigh which had been speared through, saw Evenssen helping Tikaani with her bloodstained arm and leg. Yughi moved over to Carrie and held his hand out. She took it and got to her feet, feeling a little faint, her heart a little rickety from the current that had rocked her.

"He stands a chance, Welles," Yughi told her earnestly. "He's held on this long. He's strong. Alpha strong. He can make it."

She nodded vaguely, as Hunter and Frazer powered down the pod, and moved toward them.

"Let's haul ass!" Hunter ordered.

*

Carrie walked onto the *Carcharias*, her arm around Yughi's shoulder to steady her feet. She saw Gold talking with Hunter and Brown, and she and Yughi stopped beside them.

Gold threw her a glance and a nod.

"What's the status of Centralis?" Hunter asked Gold. "Can we take them there?"

Gold nodded. "It took damage, but I'm told the hospital is still functioning. I think it's our best bet."

"What about your ship?" Hunter asked. "I saw smoke as you landed."

"We took hits, but my engineer told me we could make the trip. He's trying to fix what he can now."

"I can help," Brown said. "I'm the *Aurora*'s engineer. Get Steinberg back on his feet, he can help, too."

"Good, I'll take you down to where he is."

"I'll follow in a bit," Hunter told them.

Gold and Brown departed, and Hunter looked at Carrie.

"You'd better come to the medical unit and get checked."

"What about the HH?" she said. "We need to nuke the area before we leave. There could be more Zetas out there."

Hunter nodded. "We'll get on it. We gotta get McKinley and Harris to Centralis, asap."

"And pick up my kids," Carrie added.

Hunter nodded "Yeah, them too. Yughi, take Welles to the ship's medical unit. I'll take care of the rest."

Harris felt someone touch his forehead. He opened his eyes and saw a face he recognized but couldn't find the name.

"He's waking," the woman said.

"Colonel Harris," Gregson said, stepping over to him. "This is First Sergeant Peta Jane, she's the *Carcharias'* medic. Do you remember? You've got a head injury, bad burns to your arm and neck, bad lacerations down your other arm, maybe some other fractures we don't know about yet. We're going to seal you in a pod and take you back to Centralis. Alright?"

Harris's head throbbed badly and the pain in his arm was overwhelming. "The Zetas are gone?" he managed to ask.

"All the ships are down. The *Carcharias* gave the area a blast to clear the ones near your PV. The UNF is tracking down any left on foot." Gregson reached into the pod and placed his hand on Harris's chest. "The invasion is over, sir. You can relax."

Harris blinked his eyes. "McKinley?"

Gregson's eyes held concern, but he managed a smile. "He's alive. He's in a coma, sealed in a pod, but he's alive."

Harris gave a small nod. "He's a strong bastard," he slurred.

Gregson smiled again. "Yeah, he is. And so are you, sir." He looked at the *Carcharias'* medic and gave a nod. Harris saw her lift a needle and inject something into the cannula in his hand.

Gregson looked back at Harris. "I'll see you in Centralis, sir."

Carrie sat, trying to ignore the stinging across her back, but couldn't help thinking how strong those spears were to slice through her bullaser vest. Yughi told her the spear had left a cut about a centimeter deep, slicing her right across the tattoo she'd gotten after Jesse had been born: the flowing river of water that ran down her spine from the snowflake to the sunflower.

Another scar…

She looked around the medic's office, waiting her turn to be seen. McKinley and Harris had obviously been the priorities, then Steinberg's spear wound, then Tikaani's wounds. The Inuit woman was a little morose. They exchanged a look when she passed Carrie, heading into the hospital area. Carrie grabbed her arm. "He died his way," Carrie said. "He died a fighter."

Tikaani nodded, and gave a sad smile. "A crazy mother if I ever saw one."

Carrie smiled back. "Yeah. He was." Tikaani went to move on, but Carrie stopped her. "Thank you. For getting that HH off me."

"That's alright, butterfly," she said. "Thank you for shooting him in the head." Carrie held out her fist to Tikaani, who viewed it, then smiled and bumped it with her own.

While Tikaani was stitched up, Carrie sat looking around the medic's rooms. The *Carcharias* was a much newer ship than the *Aurora*. The fit-out was fresher and the technology and gizmos it had were more current. She sat there replaying in her mind the scene of the *Aurora* blowing up, of that moment of not knowing if she'd just witnessed the crew dying or not.

"Hey," Hunter said, appearing in the doorway, "you missing some kids?" As he said that Jesse, Freya and Brody came running into the room and Roy and Sampson filled the doorway.

Carrie threw her arms wide and hugged her children. She looked over their heads at Hunter. "Thanks for getting them."

"No problem," he said. "Had just enough juice left in the pod."

Gold appeared then.

"How you doing?" the *Carcharias* captain asked her.

"I'm okay."

"Where's dad?" Jesse asked.

Carrie looked at him. "He's with the doctors." She ran her hand down his cheek, then looked at Freya and Brody. "You can't see him just yet."

Freya's blue eyes, so much like her father's, stared back at her. Carrie exhaled and smiled at them. "We're heading home. It's over."

"What about grandpa?" Brody asked. "We're just going to leave him?"

Carrie's eyes stung with tears. "He's not there anymore, honey," she whispered. "There's nothing left of him to collect, because he's already gone."

Freya reached out and hugged her. Carrie kissed her head and stroked Brody's cheek as his eyes shone with sadness.

"Come on," Hunter said to them. "Let's go find out where you're bunking for the night."

Carrie smiled a thank you at Hunter, who gave her a nod back and ushered the children out the door. The Sentinels followed them.

Gold remained, leaning on the doorway.

"You have a crowded ship, captain," Carrie smiled sadly.

"That's alright," he said. "Mi casa su casa."

The silence sat around them for a moment.

"McKinley?" Gold asked.

"He's fighting. He's holding on."

Gold nodded. "Harris?"

"He's hurt, but I think he's going to be okay."

"That's good news."

"We lost one," she said. "Murphy. And my father. And... Gerry's nephew."

"Yeah," Gold said softly. "The *Barbican* troops are clearing the area in case any are left."

"Yeah?"

"Yeah. The *Barbican* is grounded, but they had PVs and small flyers on board, so... they'll get any that escaped our blast."

"They need to be careful of the Zeta weapons—"

Gold held up his hand to stop her. "Hunter briefed them. They've got all the intel."

Carrie nodded, and suddenly felt the tiredness wash over her. She stood and moved to peer into the hospital.

"Go in," Gold said. "Get some rest. We'll be in Centralis before you know it."

Gold walked away, and she entered the room. Tikaani was getting her calf stitched at one end, and Harris and McKinley's pods were at the other.

She came across Harris's first and peered in to see his head, neck and arm covered in a thick gel and sealed with cling film. His face looked peaceful, the painkillers obviously working. Then she looked into

McKinley's pod and saw the mess of tubes over him, down his throat, in his veins. He was naked except for a cloth draped over his groin, his burned clothes cut away, his wounds covered in a thick gooey substance. She saw now, in his nakedness, the true extent of his wounds. His right arm was so bad she knew he was going to lose it. She looked down and saw the missing fingers, and the blackened ones that were left. She saw something pale embedded in the skin above the hand, thought it was bone. On closer inspection she realized it was his silver wristband, melted into his flesh. The leather band had disintegrated altogether, but the silver band had just burned right into him.

She raised her hand to her mouth and couldn't stop the tears that flowed down her cheeks. She looked up and saw Gregson's tired face as he came to stand on the other side of the pod.

"The doctors at Centralis are on standby," Gregson said. "They'll do everything they can but..."

"He's going to lose his arm, isn't he?" she said.

Gregson nodded. "And his eye."

She looked across McKinley's mostly uninjured chest to his other arm, saw the Phoenix tattoo perfectly untouched. More tears fell as she stared at that bird rising from the flames.

"That's going to be him," she said, pointing to the tattoo. "He's going to rise from the flames. Just you watch."

Gregson looked at her and smiled sadly. "I hope so," he said. "I hope so."

Carrie clenched her Alpha jaw. "He will," she nodded to herself. "I'll make sure of it."

29

The Biggest Blow

Carrie stepped off the *Carcharias* with her children by her side, the stinking bundle of severed Zeta arm in her hand. Brown jogged past, eager to get to the village to check on Colt and the children, although it had already been confirmed en route they were safe. Carrie paused a moment on the Space Dock to take in the damage Centralis had received. A section of the Command building was destroyed. A line of buildings close by were ruined by what looked to be the path of the crashing Zeta ship. Smoke still billowed from somewhere.

She spotted Major General Marchant on the Space Dock. He moved toward her. His uniform was clean and pressed, but his face was scratched and bruised.

"Major General," she said.

"Sergeant," he said, then watched silently as McKinley's and Harris's pods were rushed past them.

Marchant turned back to her. "I heard about your father. My condolences. He was a good man. First Sergeant Murphy, too. They will both be given the UNF ceremonies they deserve."

Carrie nodded, and Marchant eyed the bundle in her arms. Maybe he smelled it. She unwrapped it to show him the Zeta arm she carried.

He looked at her surprised, then darted his eyes to the children who watched on.

"This is the weapon that wounded McKinley. Maybe Harris too. He took it for us to study."

Marchant waved an assistant forward and handed the arm to him. "Take this straight to the AWAFP facility. I want a full report in the morning."

"Yes, sir!" the man said, then jogged away.

Evenssen came to stand by Carrie's side. He carried the spear and went to hand that to Marchant as well, but Carrie stopped him.

"No, I'm sure there're plenty around here the UNF can study. That one belongs to Colonel Harris."

Evenssen gave a nod in agreement and pulled it back, as Hunter moved to stand by Carrie's side.

Marchant looked at them. "We have a live one."

"A live what?" she asked.

"Zeta," he said. "Morrell caught one."

Carrie nodded. "Good."

"We've got some dead ones to study as well," he told her. "Plus the HH."

"I want to know everything about them," she said. Then she moved past him and began walking toward the Command building, but he stopped her.

"Sergeant?" he said.

She turned around, as did the children.

"How did he know?" Marchant asked, his bruised and scratched face studying hers.

She stared at him.

"How did he know they were coming? He tried to warn me, but I didn't listen. He had no proof, so how could he know?"

"He has proof," she told him, then raised her hand and tapped her temple. "It's all up here. You just can't see it." She stared at him. "But I can."

The rest of the *Aurora* crew and Captain Gold, who had gathered to watch the exchange, held silent and still at her words. Everyone stared at her, at what she'd said, but she didn't care. There was no point hiding anymore.

"Come on," she said to the children, then turned and headed to Command.

Carrie felt exhausted as she stared at her sleeping children but couldn't bring herself to sleep just yet. Harris was being attended to and McKinley was in surgery, and the damage and death tolls were still filtering in from around the world.

She left Sampson guarding the children and made her way to the other rooms where the *Aurora* crew rested. She came upon the one that Steinberg, Hunter and Evenssen shared. They were lying back on their beds watching the news.

"Hey," she said, "can't sleep?"

Hunter shook his head. "McKinley?"

"Still in surgery."

Hunter slumped a little.

"How's Leilani and the boys?" Carrie asked him.

"They're fine," he said. "New Zealand wasn't hit."

"That's good news."

"Yeah," Hunter said.

"Steinberg? Evenssen? Your families?"

"They're fine," Steinberg said.

Evenssen nodded. "Mine too."

"Oh, Jesus," Hunter said, staring at the TV. "Have you seen this?"

Carrie looked at the screen and saw Miranda Finch of Universal Press walking through the carnage of Centralis.

"She's telling everyone that we knew about it," Hunter said. "That Harris knew, that the UNF knew. She's saying that's why we were down there, where the Zetas were headed. That's why the *Barbican* re-entered Earth at that point when it jumped."

Carrie stared at the screen. "She's right."

"But she's making out like we knew, but didn't tell anyone on purpose," Hunter said. "Like all the deaths are our fault. Harris did what he could, but... how was anyone supposed to believe that he knew it because he..."

"Dreamed it?" Carrie said.

They looked at her.

"Is he psychic or something?" Evenssen asked her.

"Something like that," she said.

"How long have you known?" Hunter asked.

She folded her arms and exhaled. "Not long after Doc died."

"That long?" Steinberg asked.

She nodded. "That's how Harris knew to come rescue us when we were attacked. He was too late to save Doc, but... he knew I was in trouble."

"Jesus," Hunter said quietly, "I always wondered about that."

"But this," she pointed to the news report showing on the screen, "this isn't Harris's fault. He knew, but he couldn't stop it." She watched as the footage rolled showing the places where damage had been received in North America: New York, Boston, Chicago, Detroit. Buildings were ruined, people were dragging others from the rubble; some were walking around aimlessly, covered in dust and debris.

"I can't believe how much damage they caused," Hunter said, shaking his head.

"And most of it was from crashing planes!" Evenssen agreed.

"And this was only a small contingent," Steinberg nodded. "Imagine what a large Zeta armada would do?"

Carrie looked at the screen and sighed. She didn't want to think about that right now. As she watched the rolling footage, she suddenly saw an image that made her pause. An image that struck right through to the core of her. A young black girl was being pulled from the rubble of a hospital in Detroit.

Carrie's eyes flew wide and she gasped.

"What?" Hunter said.

"Rewind it! Can you rewind it? I need to see that footage again!"

"What?" Evenssen said straightening. "What is it?"

"I—I think that was Sarai! Sarai Harris!"

"What?" Hunter said sitting up.

"That... that footage. It was a hospital in Detroit. Taya and Sarai are in Detroit, aren't they?"

Steinberg pulled out his PDP and searched for the clip. "Here!" he said, and Carrie ran to his side and viewed it.

"Yeah," Carrie said, eyes wide as she stared at the young girl covered in dust. "It's her!"

"Is she alive?" Hunter said standing.

Carrie nodded. "She's alive, but I don't see Taya."

"Fuck!" Hunter said.

"We gotta go there," Carrie said. "We gotta get them and bring them back here to Harris."

Hunter pulled out his PDP and called someone. "Chucky," he said. "We gotta get airborne again. Meet me at the Space Dock." With that Hunter hung up and looked at Carrie. "Let's go!"

*

Carrie, Hunter and Evenssen walked along the road in Detroit that led to the building Yughi had told them would be housing the wounded from the hospital collapse. They'd left Frazer with the ship they'd borrowed, at the Detroit airport. As they walked along they could see the damaged hospital a few blocks down. It looked as though it had been the victim of another crashed craft, but Carrie couldn't tell if it had been a Zeta ship or a friendly fighter jet.

When they entered the building sheltering the survivors, which was a university turned makeshift hospital, they saw chaos. People were everywhere: paramedics, nurses, doctors, soldiers, civilians. They tried to get someone's attention, but it took a few minutes, Hunter finally grabbing someone by the shirt front and pulling them up to his face.

"Have you seen a young black girl around here?" he asked the doctor he'd grabbed. "She might be with her mother?"

The doctor looked at him strangely. "This is Detroit. Want to narrow the description down."

Evenssen stepped forward and held a PDP in front of the doctor's face. He looked at the picture, shook his head, then called out to a passing nurse, "Marla." The woman, in her 40s, plump with short curly hair, moved over to them. Hunter released the doctor's shirt and Evenssen held the PDP up to her.

"Have you seen this girl?"

The woman shook her head and it took them four more people until someone recognized her.

"Yes," a woman with Native American features said. She was a paramedic, her clothes covered in blood. "I think I saw her over in the temporary morgue."

"What?" Carrie said, horrified.

The woman held her hand up. "She's alive, but she won't leave the bodies. Must be someone she knows."

Carrie's heart dropped into her stomach as a moment of silence passed.

"Where?" Hunter finally spoke, his face mirroring Carrie's feeling. "Where's the morgue?"

The woman gave them directions, and the three of them walked swiftly and in silence to the location. They came to the building, saw more ambulance crews dropping off bodies. They scoured the rooms but couldn't find Sarai. With each passing room, Carrie's desperation grew, until she found herself jogging and calling out, "Sarai!"

"Welles!" Evenssen eventually called, standing in the doorway to one room. Carrie ran for him and paused in the doorway at what she saw. There, sitting in among a row of bodies covered in sheets was Sarai. Carrie moved to her, slowly, crouching in front of her. Sarai looked up at her with tear-stained, dusty, scratched cheeks.

"Sarai?" Carrie said softly. Hunter entered the room and moved to them, standing on the other side of the body Sarai was sitting close beside.

"Sarai, do you remember me?" Carrie said gently. "Do you know who I am?"

Sarai nodded, her brown eyes staring at her.

"I knew you'd come for me," Sarai whispered.

Carrie reached out and placed her hand on Sarai's shoulder. "You did?"

Sarai nodded, wiping her cheek. "I dreamed you'd come."

Carrie's mouth fell open and she exchanged a look with Hunter. She looked back at Sarai.

"You did?"

Sarai nodded again, still speaking in that whispered voice. "And Daddy told me to believe in my dreams."

"Oh, honey," Carrie said, pulling Sarai into her arms. The young girl hugged her back tightly. Carrie stood up, lifting Sarai as she did with her Alpha arms. Harris's daughter wrapped her legs around Carrie's waist like she was never going to let go. Carrie looked at Hunter over Sarai's shoulder, and motioned for him to check the body under the sheet. Hunter reached down and lifted the sheet slightly. He paused briefly, before closing his eyes and dipping his head. Carrie stared at him. Hunter opened his eyes and looked back at her. He gave a slight nod, his eyes red and shining, and put the sheet back in place. Carrie squeezed Sarai tighter and kissed her cheek, fighting the emotion flooding her.

"It's okay, honey," she whispered to Sarai. "I'm going to take you and your mum back to your daddy now."

*

Carrie walked along the corridor to the theater where Gregson had asked her to meet him. Upon arrival in Centralis, she'd shown Sarai her father sleeping in his pod, then helped her shower and had taken her to rest with her own children.

"Guys," Carrie had said to Brody, Freya and Jesse who had awoken when they entered the room. "You remember Sarai, Uncle Saul's daughter?" They nodded sleepily. "She's going to stay with us for a bit," Carrie told them. "Can she sleep in your bed, Frey?"

Freya nodded and pulled her sheets back. Carrie walked Sarai over and helped her onto the bed and tucked her in. She kissed Sarai's forehead and caressed her cheek.

"I'll come right back, I promise," she told her. "And in the morning, I'll take you to see your dad again."

Sarai nodded, and another tear fell down her cheek.

"It's okay, honey," Carrie said. "I won't let anything happen to you."

Sarai nodded, pulling her sheets higher around herself, a frightened look still upon her face.

"Don't worry. You're safe with us, Sarai," Brody reassured her from the next bed where he lay with Jesse. "We'll take care of you."

Carrie smiled at her son, giving him a wink of gratitude. Then she turned and made her way to the theater.

Gregson and Dr. Morgave met her there with grave faces.

"What is it?" she said, slowing down. "He's still alive?"

"Yes, yes," Morgave said, holding a hand out to calm her.

"He's still on life support," Gregson told her, "but he's alive. All his major organs, other than suffering from the shock, should be okay. But they're not strong enough to function on their own just yet."

"We had to take his arm," Morgave told her, "and his eye. Patches of damaged flesh along his torso, hip and thigh. His ear was already gone."

Carrie swallowed hard, but nodded. She'd expected this. "And?"

Morgave glanced at Gregson.

"Once he's stable, we'll use Intense Tissue Rejuvenation, ITR therapy, for the rest of his damaged skin," Morgave continued. "It involves us injecting bio-organisms to eat the dead flesh, and once they're done we use light therapy to kill the bio-organisms, and then skin grafts to rebuild what was once there."

Carrie stared at them. "Yes. And? Whatever you have to tell me, just tell me."

Morgave and Gregson exchanged another glance.

"We're told there's a new treatment," Gregson said carefully, "that they can use to replace his arm and eye, and other patches of damaged flesh and muscle. To rebuild him."

Carrie turned her glance to Morgave. "What is it?"

"Effectively," Morgave said, "with the arm, it's a bionic limb. They're made of proxy-steel. They can be engineered to fuse to bone, and we can coat them with a special biological, er, glue, for want of a better word. Basically, we can wire it up to respond to his brain. In the end, it will look and feel like a real arm, but it will be strong and lightweight like proxy-steel."

"One of the UNF's biological weaponry projects?" she asked.

Gregson glanced at Morgave, then back to Carrie. "Apparently it was the next wave of UNFASP."

Morgave nodded. "Yes. And I'm told these limbs will have other inbuilt features."

"Such as?"

"It can just be a plain bionic arm, or we can give him the latest model, a prototype, which has an inbuilt computer, along with other features. With the eye, we can give him the ability for magnification and night vision that will make your Alpha eyes look amateur."

Carrie stared at the two of them.

"He would be the first person to have this... technology installed," Gregson told her.

Carrie continued to stare at them. "So, the UNF wants my husband to be the first person to try out their latest program... *again*."

They stared back but didn't respond. She saw the looks on their faces. This wasn't something they were excited about, or happy to do. This was necessary. This was her husband's best option at getting back on his feet.

Besides, what could it hurt? Proxy-steel was virtually indestructible. She pictured that phoenix rising from the ashes.

"Do it," she said firmly, giving them a look to match. "Give him everything you got, and make it good."

They looked startled, perhaps shocked by her quick acceptance.

"More Zetas will come," she told them. "He's going to need everything you can give him. So, you do that… you make him the strongest soldier this world has ever seen."

Harris awoke, not to any particular sound, but to a smell. An odor. A horrendous odor. He opened his eyes groggily. His head hurt, but he knew it wasn't just that. He could feel the drugs in his system, making him sluggish.

He groaned, felt his face curl up at that horrible smell, of something rotting. He blinked his eyes, trying to fight the sleep, and when he finally focused he saw he was in a hospital of some kind, lying in a pod bed.

The smell hit him again and he looked down at his body wondering whether he'd soiled himself or something. But then he saw his arm and realized where the odor was coming from.

"Jesus," he said, voice deep and croaky, looking at a light brown goo over his arm.

"It's alright." He heard a familiar voice and saw Dr. Morgave walk toward him. "It's alright, Colonel Harris. You're in Centralis in the Command hospital."

Harris looked at him. "I thought it got hit?"

"It did," Morgave said. "Parts of it." Then he glanced around the room and looked back at Harris. "We're safe here."

The odor hit Harris again. "What the fuck is that smell?"

Morgave moved closer and studied the goo. "You're covered with a bio-organism paste, which is slowly dissolving your dead tissue from the burns."

"What?" Harris asked, not sure he heard right.

"Your arm was damaged by the Zeta heat weapon. The PV protected most of you, but your arm and neck suffered from burns. The paste will remove any dead tissue, and what's left will scar, but we can fix that."

"My head?"

"You sustained an injury in the PV wreck. Your other arm has deep cuts, from what look like… claws. They'll heal, but they too will scar. You also broke your right hand in several places and have internal and external bruising from head to toe. But you're lucky, colonel. You're very lucky."

Harris's body felt otherwise right now, but he didn't argue.

"McKinley?" He remembered.

"He's alive."

"Condition?" Harris tried to arch his eyebrow, but it hurt. It felt like he had a cut running through it.

"He's in an induced coma and will be for some time. He lost his arm, eye and ear, suffered serious burns to a third of his body."

Harris stared at Morgave, not sure what to say. *McKinley lost his arm, his ear and his eye...*

Morgave reached out and touched Harris's shoulder. "As soon as his body recovers from the shock and he stabilizes, we're going to put him back together. Don't worry. So, long as he continues to remain stable, we'll fix him. He'll be fine, in time."

"Welles?"

"She's here. She's aware. She helped get the two of you back to Centralis."

Harris's jagged memories flooded back. Of seeing Welles lean in through that PV window and say something to him.

Morgave gave him a saddened smile. "I'll let her know you're awake."

Carrie walked down the corridor, taking a long slow breath. Hunter walked beside her, and she could feel the apprehension coiled within him also. Neither of them were looking forward to this, but they knew it had to be done. The team had agreed that the two of them, Carrie and Hunter, would be the ones to deliver the news to Harris. About Murphy, and about Taya.

"What's Ty's ETA?" Carrie asked.

"He was waiting for the commercial flights to reopen," Hunter answered, "but I told him we could collect him. Frazer left this morning."

"He's going to need his family here," she said quietly.

Hunter glanced at her and nodded.

They approached Harris's room, and as they did Carrie turned to look into McKinley's room across the corridor. She saw his sealed pod, could see the tops of the tubes that were breathing for him. She turned her eyes away and into Harris's room.

His pod cover was open, the sides down. He was sitting up with his legs dangling over the side like he was about to go somewhere. They entered the room.

"Where do you think you're going?" Carrie asked him.

Harris turned to look at her, the bloodied bandage still across his head, his arm and the side of his neck covered in a paste that Carrie could smell from where she stood. Even without having the Alpha olfactory sense. His other arm had bloodied bandages down it.

"I'm not one for urinating in bottles," Harris said.

"You need to lay down," she said, as Hunter closed the door behind them.

Harris gave her a tired, pained look. "We just got invaded. I got shit to do."

"No, you don't. It's over. We're handling things."

"You should rest, sir," Hunter said, backing her.

"How is everyone?" he asked, studying the paste with an unimpressed look.

"We have some news for you, sir," Carrie said, unable to help the formal tone to her voice. She exchanged a look with Hunter. They couldn't put this off any longer. They had to tell him.

"What is it?"

A silence filled the room briefly.

"We lost Murphy, sir," Hunter told him.

Harris stared at him.

"During the retrieval, getting you and McKinley out," he continued.

"He died a hero, sir," Carrie added. "He was wounded and he sacrificed himself to save the rest of us."

Harris looked down at the floor. "The rest of the team?" he asked quietly.

"There were some injuries, but they'll all be fine," she said.

The silence sat again for a moment, before Harris turned his face and looked back at them. His eyes sharpened on hers. "That's not all you came to tell me, is it?"

Carrie and Hunter exchanged another look.

"That was just your opening news," Harris said, his eyes burning into each of theirs. "So what the fuck else do you have to tell me?"

"Sir," Hunter began.

"Where is my family?" Harris asked them, eyes darting between the two of them.

He knew, Carrie thought. She could tell by the look on his face, he knew something horrible was coming. *Was his gut burning?*

"Sarai is here," Carrie said, "and Ty's on his way here. They're fine."

Harris stared at them, his face falling blank.

"I'm sorry, sir," Hunter said quietly, "but Taya... she's dead, sir." The silence hung heavily as Harris stared at them. "There was a firefight over Detroit," Hunter continued. "One of the ships crashed and... hit the hospital. Taya..." Hunter cleared his throat. "She apparently went down to the hospital to help out, and took Sarai with her and... part of the building collapsed, sir... she died. It was instant."

"She saved Sarai," Carrie added, "protected her from the falling building."

Harris stared at them for a moment, unmoving. Then suddenly he exhaled long and heavily, as though breathing his last breath. He turned his eyes away from them.

"When you're ready," Carrie said, "I'll bring Sarai in."

"Who told you this?" Harris blurted, turning back to them.

Carrie and Hunter exchanged another look.

"Who told you she was dead?" Harris asked again. "Have you seen her? How do you know it was her? I didn't dream this. She could still be out there somewhere."

"Sir," Hunter said, "I ID'd the body. It was Taya, sir."

Harris's eyes fixed hard on Hunter, as though he were lying.

"I'm sorry, sir," Hunter said, swallowing hard, his eyes filling with emotion as he looked at Harris. "She's gone."

Harris turned his face and looked back at the floor, at the wall.

Carrie's heart felt so heavy as she looked at him, knowing what this felt like. She wanted to hug him.

Harris suddenly stood up from the bed, swaying a little. Carrie and Hunter stepped forward to him.

"Sir," Hunter said, "I don't think you should be up."

Harris turned his face back to them, his brow furrowed. "I can't just sit here."

"Sir," Carrie began, but he cut her off.

"I—I have to go... I..." Harris groped for his drip and ripped it out.

"Sir!" she said stepping forward again. Hunter did too.

"Sir, you need to rest," Hunter said, placing a hand on Harris's chest.

"No," Harris said, pushing Hunter back.

"Sir—" He stepped forward again.

"NO!" Harris yelled, grabbing Hunter and slamming him into the equipment that lined the wall, pinning him there.

"Sir!" Carrie stepped forward again.

"Did you see her?" Harris hissed, squeezing Hunter's shirt up into his throat, his hands shaking with anger. "Did you see Taya?"

"Yes, sir," Hunter said carefully, his hands wrapped around Harris's. Carrie could tell he was trying to control his Alpha, very clearly reacting to Harris's.

"You saw my wife?" Harris pushed. "My *dead* wife?"

Hunter stared back at him, his voice sounding choked from the pressure Harris applied. "I'm sorry, sir—"

"You're sorry?" Harris's eyes narrowed.

"Sir," Carrie said carefully, "let him go."

Harris pulled Hunter forward and slammed him back into the wall again. "You're sorry!"

"Sir!" Carrie leaped forward and tried to throw her arms between them, but Harris flung his goo-pasted arm at her and pushed her back.

Hunter reached a breaking point it would seem, and forced his arms up, breaking Harris's grip and pushed him away. Harris stumbled back into his bed, glaring at him. Hunter held his arms out to fend off any retaliation, but it didn't come.

Carrie stood staring at the two panting Alphas and tried to push her own back down.

Harris looked around the room, his eyes glistening. "So, you're telling me," he said, swallowing as though to clear his throat and clenching his teeth tight, "that while I was out there," he pointed in the distance, "trying to protect the UNF comms facility," he stood back up and looked at Carrie, "trying to protect *your* kids," he pointed accusingly, "my wife died?"

Carrie felt a tear roll down her cheek.

"Hmm?" Harris said. "My wife died! Protecting *my* kid. *My* kid! That I should've been protecting! *Not* her!"

"Sir—" Carrie began, but he cut her off.

"No, Welles! No! Don't you talk to me! You don't have a say in this!" Harris paced, looking around the room distraught. "Taya?" His voice cracked and his brow furrowed. "Taya..." She saw Harris wipe his cheek with the back of his hand, pacing around like an angry tiger in a zoo. Then he spun around to face them. "Murphy!" he yelled. "Taya!" He paced some more. "McKinley!" His pacing grew in speed. "And all the while, I was laying on my back... helpless. Useless."

"Sir—" Carrie said again.

"NO!" he yelled, lashing out, grabbing a piece of equipment and throwing it at the wall. Hunter ducked out of the way, moving to stand beside Carrie.

"I was supposed to stop this! I was supposed to make a difference!" Harris yelled, grabbing another item and throwing that too.

Carrie tried to step toward him, but Hunter grabbed her arm and moved her back toward the door.

"I DID SHIT! I DID *NOTHING*!" Harris turned and flipped the pod bed over. "I DID *FUCKING NOTHING*! AND FOR WHAT?" He grabbed something else and threw it at the wall, shattering it. "FOR *WHAT*?"

Carrie gasped in deep sorrow, wanting to reach for him, but Hunter swiftly grabbed the back of her shirt and hauled her out into the corridor, slamming the door closed behind them.

"What are you doing?" she asked, going for the door handle, but he stopped her.

Something hit the door and it dented near Hunter's head, as more sounds of things smashing and Harris's screaming sounded behind it.

"No," Hunter shook his head, eyes wide with Alpha energy. "No, we stay out here."

"He needs us!" she said, going for the door handle again, but Hunter pulled her hand away.

"He's an angry Alpha, Welles!" Hunter said through his clenched jaw. "He's a *very* angry Alpha. *No-one* goes in there."

Just then something smashed through the glass observation window of his room and into the corridor. It was a silver trolley, complete with medical supplies. Broken glass rained over the corridor floor.

Carrie looked back to see Hunter's hands tensed around the doorknob, his Alpha arms bulging, as though making sure Harris stayed within. More commotion sounded down the corridor and they turned to see Dr. Morgave, several nurses and security running toward them.

"No!" Carrie called to them. "Stay back!" She looked at Hunter again. "What do we do?"

Hunter gave her a hopeless look and she stepped carefully toward the broken window and peered though. Harris stood there in the middle of his trashed room, his back turned to the window. His hands were clenched into tight fists, his arms wrapped over his head. His whole body was tense and shaking as he bent forward and screamed a deep guttural scream of Alpha rage. "*TAYA!*"

The soldiers moved to Hunter, but his resistance was pointless. Outnumbered, after a brief scuffle they dragged him away and entered the room. Harris turned to them in rage, his eyes filled with hate, ready to hurt every last one of them, but they raised their tasers and fired.

Carrie raised her hand to her mouth as she watched four beams from four different weapons hit Harris and send his body jolting. He tried to fight it, screaming out again, but it was futile. Eventually his body collapsed, he fell to his knees, and the soldiers swarmed forward, throwing him to the ground and pinning him down.

She heard running footsteps then and turned to see the *Aurora* crew moving down the corridor toward them. They saw the broken glass, the trashed room, Harris unconscious on the floor. Gregson pushed past everyone into the room and knelt beside Harris, checking him.

"The fuck happened?" Brown asked.

Carrie just looked at him helplessly.

They stood in the corridor and watched as Harris was lifted onto the righted pod-bed, injected with a sedative, and strapped down with seven straps. Carrie turned her eyes to the room across the corridor. She moved to the window and stared in at McKinley's sealed pod.

She felt a hand squeeze her shoulder and turned to see Colt standing there. Colt gave her a sympathetic look and squeezed her shoulder again. Carrie gave her a brave smile in return and placed her hand over Colt's.

"Has anyone told you yet?" Colt said quietly.

"Told me what?"

Colt stared at her. "They didn't tell you?"

"Told me what?"

Colt exhaled heavily. "Sharley. He escaped."

Carrie felt as though all the air in her lungs had just been sucked right out of her. "What?"

"During the attack," Colt told her. "After the building was hit, they were evacuating people. In the confusion… he killed Dr. Scavesci and two guards. He got away."

Carrie stared at Colt, her hand falling away.

"I saw him," Colt said. "He ran through the village. Malik was at the window looking out… I went to pull him back and saw Sharley standing there. As soon as he saw me, he looked back at Malik, and he knew."

Carrie turned to face Colt. "Are you sure?"

Colt nodded, worried. "Malik has very distinct eyes. Just like his father did." Colt shrugged. "It's what he ordered LeFroy to do to me. He knows Malik's father is Logan."

Carrie thought for a moment that she had forgotten how to breathe.

Sharley has escaped…

To add to the stolen air, Carrie felt as though all the blood within her had just run out onto the floor. She looked around a little dazed. The team had heard their conversation, were staring at them.

"My kids," Carrie suddenly whispered. "Sarai."

"Sampson and Novak are with them, little butterfly," Tikaani reassured her.

"What the hell do we do now?" Evenssen asked.

Everyone stood in silence. Carrie looked into Harris's room, saw him strapped down and unconscious, saw Gregson leaning over him. Then she turned and looked in at McKinley's sealed pod.

Harris and McKinley were down…

Her father was dead…

Sharley was on the loose…

She took a moment to take it all in. Felt the air reclaim her lungs, felt the blood flow back through her veins.

And she realized she wasn't scared.

She felt strangely calm, felt the Alpha sitting beneath her skin like hardened armor.

She looked back at Colt, who was still staring at her. And as she looked into those brown eyes of Colt's, a memory surfaced like a mermaid's song calling to ships in a darkened sea.

"What goes around comes around, Welles," she recalled Colt telling her on the Darwin mission. *"There'll be a day when they call on you to do what they can't do."*

Harris and McKinley were down.

Her father was dead.

Sharley was on the loose.

More Zetas would come.

It was up to her to keep things together. To protect her children. To protect Earth and its colonies.

She looked at Harris's pod again, then at McKinley's. Then she looked back at the team, as Gregson joined them.

"We regroup," she told them firmly.

They looked back at her.

"We regroup," she said again more firmly, feeling the Alpha surge as she looked each and every one of them in the eye. "We rebuild," she told them, a deepness to her voice she hadn't heard before. "We study what's left of the Zetas, their HH slaves, their ships, their weapons. We hone our own ships and weapons. We build our Alpha army, and we get ready for a war of the ages." She turned her body to face the team squarely then, spreading her shoulders to match, sensing the Alpha rise within them too.

"Make no mistake," she said, "the Zetas will come back. And when they do, they will come in large numbers." She stared at them all. "But when they do... we will fucking annihilate them."

Silence filled the corridor as the crew of *Aurora* Alphas stared back at her. Her eyes flickered to Hunter's and paused. She gave a slight bow in apology and motioned for him to speak. "I'm sorry," she said, "you're in charge now."

Hunter stared at her for a moment, before a smile curled his mouth. He glanced around at the team.

"You heard the woman," he told them. "We do what she says."

Epilogue

Miranda Finch stepped out of the shadows upon seeing Captain Morrell approach. He paused when he saw her, surprised. It had been some time since she'd seen him. He'd aged, the lines had crept in further around his eyes and his mouth. His gray hair was grayer; practically white. Of course, he also looked like he'd been through the wringer. His face bruised and cut, his neck and shoulder, too, and he limped like he was carrying a wound.

She stepped toward him. "You look like you've been in a hell of a fight."

He stared back. "I have."

She nodded, stepped closer. "I know. My cameraman caught you dragging that thing into Command."

Morrell didn't respond.

"That's what this silence has been about all these years, hasn't it?" she said. "You knew. You, Gold, Harris. You all knew these things were out there, and you didn't warn us."

Morrell gave her a cold look then turned and began limping away, but she ran up and caught his arm.

"People died!" she accused him.

He spun around, throwing off her grasp. "Don't you think I know that?" he spat angrily. Intimidated by his broad stature, she stepped backward. He stepped forward, leaning into her face, his eyes – more vibrant than she remembered them – piercing hers. "I lost *good* men fighting those things! Saving your ass! Saving the ass of the people who live here." He threw his arm out angrily. "So, don't you talk to me about loss!" He stared her out, then turned and began walking away.

"So what happens now? The people have the right to know. No more secrets!"

He stopped and turned back. "No," he said, then glanced briefly around and up at the sky. "You're right. There are no more secrets. You've seen everything now. And no matter how much you want to, you can never turn back from that."

"What's the UNF going to do about it, if more come?"

Morrell shrugged at her. "I'd like to know that, too. But right now, Harris is down and he's leading this thing."

"Harris," she said. "Colonel Saul Harris?"

"Who else?"

"I thought he was dead. I heard the *Aurora*… I saw the list of ships."

"His ship went down, his crew weren't on it. He's alive, but injured."

"Here in Centralis?"

Morrell nodded. "Word is he was hit hard by a bunch of those things in Australia. He lost a man, his captain is real bad, and he's got a heap of injured. But Harris is alive. The *Carcharias* brought them back here for treatment."

Miranda stared at Morrell, feeling numb. She was glad Harris was alive, but at the same time she wanted to tear him to shreds for withholding this information from her, from the people.

"Get some sleep, Finch," Morrell told her. "You look like shit, and this thing has only just begun. We got a long road ahead of us." He gave her a smile then, a sardonic one. "And the people need to know that."

With that he turned and limped away. Miranda watched him, moving over to a wall and resting against it. She looked at the ruined section of the Command building, remembered the terror she'd felt on seeing the attack, wondering if it was the end. Wondering if she was going to live or die.

She looked up into the sky and felt a cold menace as she stared into it. An anger began to fall over her, a hatred for the things that did this. She needed to know what their future held. She wanted answers and she wanted them *now*.

And there was only one man who could give them to her.

Colonel Harris.

Professor Sharley whistled a melodic tune as he waited for the call to connect.

"Yes," came the blunt answer.

"Siberia Nine?" Sharley said.

"Yes. Who is this?"

"Grandaddy."

"Sir?" the voice lightened.

"I take it you've seen what's happened?"

"Yes."

"There's going to be a lot of heat on the UNF in the coming days. We need to move the assets somewhere safe. Somewhere no-one will ever find them. Do you know where I mean?"

"Yes."

"Enact Protocol Zero," Sharley instructed. "I'll meet you there."

"You're coming in person?" the voice was surprised.

Sharley smiled. "Yes. Command have seen the error in their ways and have released me. They have tasked me with securing the safety of the JEM program. So that is what I'm going to do."

"Of course."

"Enact Protocol Zero immediately. Secure the JEMs. Grandaddy is on the way."

Sharley ended the call and threw the disposable PDP into the trash. He looked up into the blue skies and sunshine, and inhaled a breath of fresh air as another big smile crossed his face.

"What a wonderful day," he said.

He checked his reflection in the glass window, running his fingers along the coral lipstick he wore, then straightened his sun hat, floral dress and sunglasses. He turned and began walking down the busy city street, all the while whistling that happy, melodic tune.

The End

Join the next action-packed adventure of the Aurora crew:

Aurora: Aurizun (Aurora 7)

If you enjoyed reading Aurora: Decima (Aurora 6), let people know!
Leave a simple rating or write a brief review wherever you can. It means
a lot to me, the author, and really helps with making this book visible to
others.

Keep up to date with new releases here:
amandabridgeman.com.au

Acknowledgements

First and foremost, I'd like to thank all the readers who continue to support the Aurora series. It is absolutely wonderful to know that people enjoy reading this series as much as I enjoy writing it, and even more fantastic to see the readership growing with each book. It's been a hell of a ride so far, and it's not over yet. More Aurora action will follow soon!

To my Beta readers: Tia and Joan. Thanks as always for being the ones to read the less than perfect early draft of my books, and telling me where I can improve. I really appreciate your time and feedback.

To my family and friends for all their support and their understanding. I know I don't get to see you as much as you would like, but it's all for a good cause!

To my editor, Stephanie Smith, for sticking with me and this series. Six books together now! Thanks for understanding my clunky sentences and making them sound right, and for asking the right questions to fill in the holes. Your support and guidance has been invaluable!

To Pat Naoum for taking my brief and pulling together another excellent cover.

And lastly, but never least, the G-Mob for all their support and advice. You can't put a price on having people to chat with who understand the perils of writing!

www.ingramcontent.com/pod-product-compliance
Lightning Source LLC
Chambersburg PA
CBHW030642120726

47905CB00001B/20